WITCH'S MOON CALLING

THE BROKEN STONE CHRONICLE
BOOK IV

DAMIEN BLACK

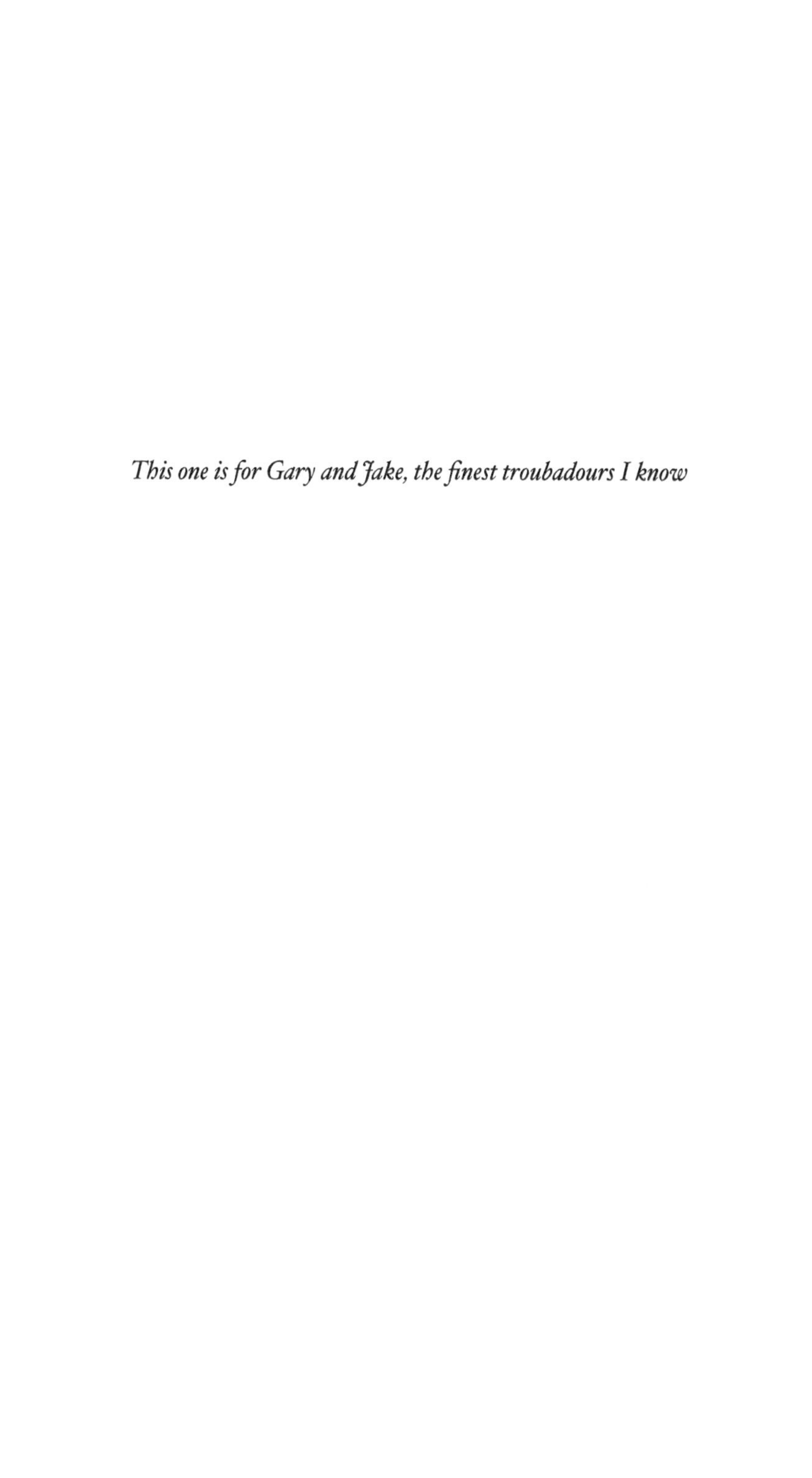

This one is for Gary and Jake, the finest troubadours I know

CONTENTS

ISBNS:

978-1-0682886-0-9 [print]
978-1-0682886-1-6 [ePub]

PART I

A LONG-DELAYED
HOMECOMING

The bloody gash where Vaskrian's left earlobe had been flared with pain as the cart bumped over another rut in the highway. The first time he'd tried to escape, they'd been camping for the night in the foothills of the With-Y-Passes on the Thraxian side of the mountains. Harnal Cutter had freed the bonds about his ankles so he could relieve himself, but warned him not to run off. Vaskrian being Vaskrian, he'd tried to escape at the first opportunity. That time Edric had caught up with him and given him a prize beating for his trouble, and Harnal had told him next time he tried that he'd lose half an ear. The bounty hunter hadn't been joking.

The second failed attempt had occurred during their journey along the disused trade road that led through the mountains to Northalde. This time Vaskrian had prepared more carefully, secreting a sharp flint stone in his tunic pocket and using it to saw through his bonds at night. He'd used another stone to clobber one of Cutter's men standing on watch over the back of the head, only wishing it had been Edric. He'd been so close on that occasion – but halfway up a storm-drenched ravine, he'd slipped on wet stones and near plummeted to his death. The outcropping he landed on had saved his life, but it hadn't done his ribs much good, nor his escape attempt. When Cutter caught up with Vaskrian and found him lying prone, he'd made good on his promise. Next time, he'd warned, it would be a finger – from his sword hand.

Vaskrian had seen the wisdom in compliance ever since.

Now here they were, descending the foothills on the eastern side of the mountains that his people called the Hyrkrainians, back in the province of Efrilund, the place he'd called home for seventeen winters.

Yes, he'd returned home to Northalde – a belted knight, a war hero, and a fugitive from justice.

'We'll stop here the night,' said Harnal, motioning for his henchmen to pull up the cart in the lee of a gorse-strewn hill. The four burly men whom Vaskrian had come to know all too well scurried to obey Harnal's orders, setting up camp and preparing a fire against the encroaching shadows of evening. Harnal plonked him down roughly on a rock; his hands and legs had been retied, and the bounty hunter had sworn that the next blacksmith they met would have paying work, putting shackles on the fugitive.

Edric sat across from Vaskrian on another rock, leering at him through broken teeth as he peeled an apple he'd managed to filch from a peasant farmer the previous day. Vaskrian did his best to kill him with a look of pure hatred, but Edric only grinned more broadly before flicking apple peel at him contemptuously.

He still couldn't believe this was happening to him. And he'd had more than two weeks to get used to the idea, for their journey home had been painfully slow. Harnal had taken him back up the pothole-scarred highway to Ongist before approaching the With-Y-Passes, keeping him bound and gagged beneath the tarpaulin in the wayn, steering them out of the city and north-east on the road to Daxtir Keep. The ruined castle, so recently a victim of the highland raiders Vaskrian had helped to defeat, had made for a fearful sight, but it had brought the young knight hope. His erstwhile guvnor and comrade-in-arms Braxus wasn't far off; the Thraxian would be suppressing the last of Slánga's followers in the Brekkens. But of the Lord of Gaellentir there had been no sign. Perhaps anticipating trouble, Harnal had in any case ordered Vaskrian gagged and covered again, only releasing him at night when they'd got clear of the castle and its desmesnes. He'd shown him a measure of trust then, and Vaskrian had shown the bounty hunter that he could not be trusted where his freedom was at stake.

When the fire was ready, a couple of Harnal's men dragged him over to sit by it. The other pair of stooges were busy roasting meat over a fire; they'd purchased what little could be had in the last market town so there'd be no need to hunt tonight. One of the men dragging him was the fellow he'd near brained with a rock in the passes, Aethelstang he thought his name was. Aethelstang hadn't forgotten the lump on his head, and demonstrated this with a sound thwack on Vaskrian's bloody ear that brought tears to his eyes.

He bit his lip to stop himself from crying out, but the physical pain was nothing compared to the sorrow of heart that stung him. A belted knight who'd taken on Sir Leathan the giant Thraxian knight and won, survived countless perils and supernatural horrors... reduced to this ignominy.

Once again he tried to reason with Harnal, though he knew by now it was futile.

'I'm a knight in service to Lady Rowena of Tul Aeren, by the Code of Chivalry that means I'm entitled to fair treatment even if I am a captive. Send word to her and she'll gladly pay my ransom –'

Harnal stood up and struck Vaskrian across the face in one fluid motion. 'I've told you already to stop with that nonsense,' he said firmly. Harnal never shouted or got angry. Vaskrian supposed that made the bounty hunter all the more chilling, but after all he'd been through he wasn't scared of a common hireling, however formidable he might be.

'As far as I'm concerned, you're a treacherous squire who betrayed your master Sir Branas to his death – guilty until proven innocent, that's the way of the law around here, in case you'd forgotten.'

'For the love of the Unseen, I DIDN'T KILL HIM!' protested Vaskrian for the umpteenth time. Edric had sidled over to warm himself at the fire and snickered nastily. Vaskrian swore silently he'd have the lout's head, whatever it took.

Harnal stood over him, shaking his head. 'Still banging that drum, are we?' he sneered. 'Oh, yes, let me remember... you lost him on a – what was it lads? – quest in Tintagael forest, which you don't actually remember anything about because the faeries who live there conveniently wiped your memory.' The bounty hunter's henchmen were openly laughing now. 'And of course this quest led to other quests, but you can't tell us anything about *those*, because it's top-secret Argolian business.' The henchmen were roaring with laughter now. *Ha ha, a fine jest,* thought Vaskrian bitterly, *passes the time of an evening.*

The bounty hunter leaned down towards the young knight menacingly. 'Know what I think, Vaskrian? I think you're a liar and a thief. I think those rumours we heard about you being a war hero were just that – rumours. I think that fancy suit of armour and sword we had off you were pinched, and maybe you even murdered for them. I mean, what's a low-born lad like you doing with a sword of the White Valravyn? Oh wait, I'm sorry, you already told us that as well – Sir Aronn of the Order gave it to you as a gift after you helped him defeat a – what was it, lads? – "gow-lum" in another creepy forest.' More guffaws, Edric joining in now with gusto. Harnal straightened up, turning to address his willing audience. 'And of course, we can't verify that either, because this Aronn's dead too! Killed by some warlock who was hell-bent on taking over the world.' He returned his piercing blue eyes to Vaskrian. 'You're just a sad little man who couldn't accept his place in life, aren't you? Had to piss higher than the wind – well, let me tell you, "sir knight", the wind's about to blow back, and hard!'

So long a false friend to him, the choler rose up inside Vaskrian again. Struggling to master his rage, the young knight forced his voice to sound even. 'Untie me and put a sword in my hand, fight me fairly like a man,' he said. 'Then you'll know what a hard wind feels like.'

He half expected Harnal to strike him again, but he didn't. 'Shut up, Vaskrian,' he sneered, turning away to warm his hands at the fire. More laughs from Edric and the henchmen.

As quick as it had come on, the choler subsided, bleeding out of him resentfully to leave just another depression of the spirits. Vaskrian felt invisible nuggets of lead dragging him down. So far he'd come, so far. And now this was his fate, to be humiliated all over again by his old rivals.

Not for the first time, he wondered if a swift death wouldn't be the best possible outcome for him now. Perhaps he should feel glad in that case: the way things were looking, it also seemed the most likely.

The next few days took them along the rutted road through the southern Brekawood. He'd hunted game here on more than one occasion with Sir Branas, though that seemed like a lifetime ago now. All the same, he couldn't help but feel a slight stirring of the spirits at the familiar scents and sounds. Spring was in full flourish now, and even his harsh northern homeland had begun to surrender to its verdant touch; birds trilled in the branches and squirrels and foxes scampered across their paths, hurrying to avoid the lumbering giants encroaching upon their land. It hardly seemed magical after the Earth Witch's bower, but it was home.

As the cart rumbled and juddered its way along the road and his ear continued to sting, Vaskrian found himself swearing he'd turn the tables on his antagonists, somehow. Fenrig would have to be made to see sense. Rutgar was a coward; he was a hero: surely Virtus and Stygnos would smile on his suit, if he pleaded it strongly enough.

But instead it was Invidia's acid tongue that found his inner ear: *those bluebloods won't listen to a word you say*, it told him. *One look at you and all they'll see is Vaskrian, common churl of Hroghar.*

The prayer he offered up to the Almighty that night was a half-hearted one.

Kaupstad hadn't changed much in his absence, but it could not have felt more different. The same quietly prosperous little town of three hundred families or so, enclosed by the same wooden stockade. Once it had thrilled Vaskrian, coming here on the way to tournaments in Harrang. It had been here where his great adventure had begun. But that same adventure had changed him forever; he'd looked on Strongholm and Rima, not to mention the ancient monstrous edifices built by Them.

Kaupstad. What a dump it was, what a dump it had always been.

But wait, one thing *had* changed. As they drew nearer Kaupstad's western gate, Vaskrian saw it was shut and barred.

They never do that during the day, he thought. *Except in times of... war.*

A sidelong glance at Harnal told him the bounty hunter had realised the same thing, though Edric remained oblivious. 'Why've they got the gates closed at this time of day?' the oaf wondered aloud.

'Shut it, Edric,' snarled Harnal. The tension in the bounty hunter's voice was palpable. But the Thraxians couldn't have stolen a march on the Northlendings, or they'd have seen their armies mustering on the other side of the mountains. Wouldn't they?

Suddenly tense and alert, Vaskrian waited for the guard to show his face on the wooden stockade. No, not guard – two guards, the faces of the yeomen volunteers looking worried and drawn.

This lot are on a war footing alright, you can practically smell the blood in the air. Vaskrian's stomach was a roil of emotions. He'd been in enough wars to know that they offered opportunity for all sorts of life changes, including death.

'Who goes there?' barked a timorous sentry.

'Name's Harnal Cutter, bounty hunter,' replied Vaskrian's captor. 'Returning with a captive in charge, on business commissioned by Jarl Fenrig of Hroghar.' He waved a hand casually Vaskrian's way. 'Fugitive returned alive, as stipulated. Stand aside and make way for us.'

The sentry abruptly found some form. 'Business of the Jarl's is it?' he barked down at Harnal. 'I'd say you'll find the Jarl's got bigger business than criminals. Haven't ye heard, bounty hunter? We've been invaded – his lordship's mustering for war as we speak.'

Harnal scratched his chest as his henchmen exchanged glances. 'We heard all about the rumours of war with the

Thraxians,' he said. 'But we've just come from that way and I can assure you they're too busy rebuilding their own kingdom to march on Northalde.'

'No, not the Thraxians,' said the sentry impatiently. 'There'll be no war with them now – we've been invaded from across the Valhalla, it's the Northlanders we're fighting. They've landed on our shores and invested Strongholm. Lot's happened while you lads were away.'

That caught them all on the back foot and no mistake. All except Vaskrian. *Well, Master Horskram, looks like that world war you predicted all along is finally coming to pass,* he thought, not without some satisfaction.

Harnal took a few moments to digest the sentry's news. Then he said: 'That's all well and good, but a job's a job and I've a bounty to collect. Are you going to let us in or not?'

The sentries swapped glances and the one speaking shrugged. 'Can't see a problem with that. But don't expect to get a room for the night – the *Crossroads* and the *Journeyman* both are crammed to the rafters with freeswords and craftsmen heading to the muster. If you want my advice, you'll head up to the castle now and offer your services. Could use some strong-looking fellows like you, from what we've been hearing the Northlanders have beached more than a hundred longships.'

That provoked a few whistles all right. Even Edric looked perturbed – he'd finally managed to get that thick head of his around the situation. And it did not look good for their homeland.

Northlanders – they nearly killed us on our own soil a year ago, now it looks as though they're coming back for more. A lot more.

The gates ground open, admitting them into the dirty street. It was quieter than usual, no bustle of merchants and traders and craftsmen. *Probably half of them are up at the castle offering their services as well,* thought Vaskrian. *All I need to do is figure out how I can do just the same.*

And as they drew level with the *Crossroads*, where he'd met Adelko and his irascible mentor all those moons ago, the idea came to him.

'My ear is killing me,' he said. 'Think it might be infected.'

Harnal grunted. 'So?'

'Infections can kill,' Vaskrian pointed out. 'I doubt Fenrig will pay out on the bounty if I arrive sick and die in custody before a trial can take place. You may not believe me about being a knight, but you can't deny I was a squire in this country for years – I know the Jarl of Hroghar, and trust me, he's a stickler for form. If he can use that as an excuse to diddle you out of money he owes you on the eve of an expensive war, he will.'

Harnal scowled, then called a halt. 'Do you know, Vaskrian, that might just be the first intelligent thing you've said during our association. All right, suppose a round of ale won't hurt – look lively lads, let's be having you! We'll get that wound treated and some hot food in our bellies, then be on our way.'

You'll soon find out just how clever I can be, thought Vaskrian triumphantly, as Edric bullied him down off the cart.

Vaskrian's eyes were scanning the crowded taproom as soon as they entered. He couldn't see any sign of Vagan – where was the innkeeper, dammit? An unpleasant thought crossed his mind then: perhaps he'd died while Vaskrian was away. There hadn't been a serious outbreak for a while, the region was due another round of disease... But no, here he was, coming in from the stables via the side door.

'Vagan!' he yelled, so loudly that several craftsmen sat at a table near him started. 'Vagan, it's me, Vaskrian!' The innkeeper turned and peered at him. 'Vaskrian,' he breathed. 'Well, well, so the wanderer returns.'

He had to keep talking, while he had everyone's attention; get the story out, before Harnal and Edric silenced him. 'I've been taken captive by these curs,' he said breathlessly. 'They think I murdered Sir Branas, but it's a damned lie! You know I'd never do that, right? I'm a belted knight now, got the spurs to prove it and everything, you have to send word to Fenrig, vouch for me...' His voice trailed off as he realised that Harnal had made no move to silence him, instead restraining Edric as he went to strike him. The bounty hunter was chuckling softly to himself. Vagan simply stood and stared, a nonplussed expression on his kindly face.

'Vaskrian, I'm sorry,' the innkeeper faltered. 'But we all heard... You're a wanted man. I don't know what else to say.'

'But you *know* me! You know I'm a hothead, but I'd never hurt Sir Branas! I'd...' His voice died on his lips again. A couple of the craftsmen were chuckling into their stoups and shaking their heads. Most of the others in the common room had gone back to their drinking and dicing. Harnal chose this moment to speak up.

'You still don't get it, do you?' he said. 'You're a wanted man, just like the innkeep says. Until you can clear your name at Hroghar, no one'll believe a word you say. Vagan — stoups of ale, a bowl of warm water and some clean linen if you please, and I promise we'll be on our way. We've a fugitive from the Jarl's justice to deliver.'

The innkeeper complied, calling loudly for the potboy Rudi, before shooting Vaskrian an awkward look and hurrying off to attend to another table. Over in the corner he caught the eye of Kyra, the winsome serving wench he'd flirted with ineptly last year. She looked a little sadder and older than he remembered, and noting her swollen belly realised she was with child. She favoured him with a dark-eyed stare, one that seemed to say: *I told you fighting types were no good, didn't I?*

The disgraced knight offered no resistance as Harnal pushed him down onto a bench.

~

Vaskrian tried not to blench when they passed the clearing where he'd killed Derrick. Not that he cared for the hapless squire – he'd deserved what he got, and the young knight had erased that bloody deed since with yet more blood. But that had been the whole point of knighthood – to shed it with impunity. Now his knighthood was in question, and the old demons were coming out to play. Come to think of it, real demons terrified him less than his own, and he of all people should know the difference.

For a few agonising moments he'd thought Harnal would order them to camp there, but no: now that they'd cleaned up his wound, the bounty hunter was devilish keen to get him delivered to Fenrig and wash his hands of him. On into the night they trundled, the henchmen lighting torches. Once or twice they passed messengers on horseback, but no one came to trouble them: with the jarldom on a war footing there would be far too many soldiers about for any highwaymen to try their luck.

Vaskrian fell into a woozy slumber as dusk deepened into night. He hadn't been lying completely about his wound: he did feel feverish. Kyra had said nothing to him while she tended it, though he could tell by her expression that she was appalled by the scars and injuries the past year had bequeathed him. *Fighting types, we're trouble all right,* he'd mused. *Kyra, you weren't wrong there.*

He awoke to Edric elbowing him painfully in the ribs. Dawn had broken on a gloomy spring day in Efrilund, and there it was, looming over them from its age-old perch on the high hill: Hroghar, the place where his dreams had been born, and where they might well end forever.

Knights and squires were drilling in the bailey as they entered. The same quintain he'd practised on during his last morning in Hroghar was there, having the stuffing knocked out of it by lancers keen to test their mettle in the field. He recognised more than a few, though no one paid him any heed as Harnal took him down off the cart and his men frog-marched him over to the keep: just another runaway criminal being returned to the Jarl's justice, scarcely worth taking an interest in now the country was at war again. Not that Vaskrian minded, the last thing he wanted was to be singled out now: he was grateful for the anonymity.

All his gratitude promptly evaporated as Harnal and his men escorted him into the keep. Its gloomy precinct – with its austere decorations of crossed swords and heater shields and the old whitestone statue of Ezekiel in the alcove at the far end – hadn't changed. Nor had the seneschal, Sir Branton, a hoary old greybeard of nigh on sixty winters, who now stepped forwards to receive them.

What had changed was the under-seneschal, the man who limped beside Sir Branton, a gloating expression on his face.

'Well, well, churl of Hroghar,' sneered Rutgar. 'How nice it is to see you after all these months.'

Sir Branton shot his understudy a piercing glance, and Rutgar held his tongue. But the broad grin didn't leave his face. At least the months had been no kinder to him than Vaskrian; he leaned on an ornate hardwood staff, his leg had clearly never healed properly after he was cast from the saddle fleeing the field at Linden. Beside that his injuries had evidently taken their toll on the rest of his body; never the strongest of knights, Rutgar's frail form testified to months of infirmity.

Thanks ye angels, thought Vaskrian sarcastically. *Nice to know the Unseen have some sense of justice, at least.*

'And who have we here?' Branton asked the bounty hunter.

As if you didn't know, thought Vaskrian sourly. Like most of Hroghar's noble inhabitants, Branton had scarce given him the time of day, but they'd shared the same roof for years.

'Vaskrian, renegade esquire of Hroghar, brought back to face the Jarl's justice,' declaimed Harnal. 'Bounty of a hundred marks to be paid out upon his safe return, by oath of Fenrig sworn here at his court.'

Branton arched a robust salt-and-pepper eyebrow. Vaskrian had always thought the steward looked more like a badger than a man, though right now he was the one who felt like burrowing down a deep hole.

'Fenrig rode south yesterday,' said Branton. 'To join the muster with Lord Aesgir and Lord Vymar. Efrilund is marching to war, the capital has been invested by Northland raiders. So I'm afraid your agreement with His Lordship will have to wait.'

Harnal made to protest, but Sir Branton silenced him with a raised hand. 'As an experienced bounty hunter, you will know the law is quite specific on this point. In time of war, all prior agreements are held temporarily null until the threat to the realm is deemed extinguished. You are free to enjoy the hospitality of the castle while you await Lord Fenrig's return.' He turned to Vaskrian's old nemesis. 'Sir Rutgar, see that our guests are properly victualled and quartered. As for this one,' – he cast a cold glance Vaskrian's way – 'have the duty guard take him down to the cells.'

'At once, sire,' replied Rutgar, his voice dripping with pleasure.

'Don't move too fast,' Vaskrian called after him. 'Wouldn't want you to trip over that walking stick of yours.'

The young knight smirked as Rutgar nearly lost his balance, but his retort soon wiped the smile off his face.

'Enjoy your little jest, churl,' he spat back. 'It's the last one you'll be making for a while – by my reckoning, you'll be amusing yourself in the dungeon for a good few months.'

Without another word, Rutgar hobbled out of the hall, leaving Vaskrian to chew over his words.

'This is all a mistake, you know,' he told Sir Branton, trying one last desperate effort. 'I was dubbed in Thraxia, by the Lady Rowena, First Woman of Clan McCulloch and ruler of Tul Aeren. I'm no criminal, I'm a bloody war hero! Send word to her and she can vouch for me.'

The alacrity of his claim surprised Branton. Even Harnal had given up on silencing him: now he'd delivered his charge, all that remained to him was to wait out his pay.

'That is quite a high tale and no mistake,' said the steward after a brief pause. 'Doubtless its veracity will be established – or not – at your trial. But that I'm afraid will have to wait until we've repulsed the Northlanders.'

'I've fought Northlanders,' said Vaskrian, trying not to sound desperate. 'Return to me the arms and armour this bounty hunter took from me, I'll be useful in the field – dammit, Sir Branton, you need every good man you can get! And didn't I prove my courage in the last Northlending war?'

For just a moment or two, Vaskrian thought the old steward would relent and see sense. At least send him south with an escort to Fenrig, to plead his case. But then the grey-beard shook his head. 'I'm sorry, Vaskrian, I've no idea if you're telling the truth or not. But a condemned man will say anything to save his skin, that much I do know. War or no war, proper procedure must be followed. I'll see you're wounds are treated and that you're fed properly at least – that way, Reus willing, you should be healthy enough to give your side of the story when this war is over.'

'But that could be months away!' protested Vaskrian.

Branton nodded, unsmiling. 'Indeed it could,' was all he said to that. Guards arrived to take the captive down, and the seneschal turned his back on him.

The dungeons were the one part of Hroghar that Vaskrian had never seen. Now he could see – and smell – them in all their noisome glory. A few doors up from the cell he was ushered into, another prisoner could be heard groaning piteously with the last of his strength. The room was barely big enough to lie down in and had nothing in it besides a rough wooden bench and a chamberpot.

The gaolers came and undid his ties, swapping the chafing rope for cold iron links that chained him to the wall. Without another word they left, slamming the door behind them and bolting it firmly in place. The air was dank and stifling, and the only light came from the torches burning in stanchions in the corridor outside.

As the darkness engulfed him, Vaskrian felt a tear slide down his ravaged cheek. That side of his face had been left scarred by Andragorix's sorcery; he'd risked his life to oppose the mad mage – and for what?

To return to a homeland on the brink of another invasion that regarded him as just another enemy.

CHAPTER 2
THE BLOODY BARON

The sound of women and children burning alive did not move him. As far as Lord Braxus was concerned, the highlanders were less than human: they had proved that with their own depredations, when they'd raped his homeland to within an inch of its life. He held the blazing torch aloft for all his surviving men to see, as he watched the log huts and their inhabitants burn. All about them lay the hewn and spattered corpses of the menfolk, bodies ruined by the misfortunes of war. Give them their due, they'd fought bravely to the last man – but by now Slánga's hounds knew better than to expect any mercy from their new master.

Slánga. The name burned a hole in Braxus's soul that made him feel more uncomfortable than the stench of roasting flesh that now permeated the rocky valley they'd just fought in. Nearby one of the younger soldiers was being sick. Conwyn, he thought his name was: at seventeen summers, the lad still hadn't developed the stomach for this kind of fighting.

Handing the torch to his squire, Braxus strode over to reprimand the youth.

'Don't turn away – look!' he cried, seizing the young man by his brigandine and forcing him to watch a cabin burn. 'Every last one of them in there – *every last one of them* – would have grown up to be a warrior who would slay your kin without mercy, or a woman who would bear more warriors.' He stabbed a finger towards the flaming building, from which the cries were dying off. 'This is a *good thing*, understand? A service to future generations of our people. In Palom's name, don't blench at the work that has to be done to secure our freedom and safety.'

The ragged youth nodded wordlessly, wiping incipient tears from his white face. Turning from him, Braxus surveyed his motley army. Of the seven hundred men who'd followed him into the Brekkens, just over half remained after a few weeks of fierce fighting.

But the toll they'd extracted was many times that: like a greedy merchant counting the contents of his strongbox, Braxus had assiduously kept track of severed heads and charred corpses, before finally losing count at over a thousand.

Many more would perish from the famine and disease that would follow in their wake: any stray animal they'd come upon had been slaughtered to feed the army. The highlanders barely subsisted in this choked craggy land as it was: it wouldn't take much more than a hungry and successful invading army to tip the balance fatally.

All of that pleased Lord Braxus. What did not was how evasive Slánga Mac Bryon was proving to be. He'd nearly caught up with him two weeks ago, at Maddon Hill; but the wily highlander had slipped away with a handful of men, leaving the rest to taste the sword. The erstwhile leader of the highlanders hadn't expected such a bold move: no one in recent memory had dared to beard the savages in their rocky lair.

But this had been the time to strike. The loss of lowland gains had been accompanied by the loss of many able fighting men: yes, now was the time to strike, once and for all. The northern hills would be harried into extinction.

'We'll set up camp on yonder ridge,' he told Sir Madogan, nodding up towards where a fractured lip of rock and scree overlooked the ruined village. His new second-in-command was an able man, cunning and ruthless, with little time for the antiquated Code of Chivalry. Perhaps that had something to do with his having been a freesword before earning an impromptu title at Braxus' sword: whatever the truth of it, Madogan was just the kind of man he needed to help him finish this business once and for all.

'Good spot,' replied Madogan curtly. 'Plenty of vantage, in case the rug rats try anything clever by night.'

'Oh, I hope they do,' said Braxus. 'The quicker we kill them, the better I shall like it. Once this is done, we can all go home, rest and rebuild.' He raised his voice so all the men could hear. 'Hearth and home, troubadours and wenches, and tales of our exploits to redound through the ages, eh lads!?'

But his rousing speech sounded hollow in his ears. Braxus knew full well many of the warriors who survived this campaign would be fighting it long after it was done. Such were the horrors of war.

Banishing his gloomy thoughts, the First Man of Clan Fitzrow busied himself leading his hardened veterans up to their chosen place of rest. Sentries were posted, tents pitched, campfires built.

Surveying the grim grey rocks of the lands he had come to conquer, Braxus inhaled the highland air deeply. It was like the terrain it swept; rough and bracing, savagely sensual. But it made little difference to his mood: Braxus rather fancied that was reflected instead by the sinking sun on the western horizon.

His gloom stayed with him like an ulcer throughout the rest of the evening, and into the night that followed. Contrary to his wishes, no attack came: clearly the remnants of Slánga's clansfolk were licking their fresh wounds, gearing themselves up for the final struggle.

How many more fighting men, I wonder? Can't be more than five hundred left in these broken hills, all of them half-starved and poorly equipped. By summer's end, the leaves will have fallen from the highland tree – then I can rest. By Reus, I need rest.

His reverie was interrupted by Madogan. The warrior's scarred face was crammed resentfully beneath his close-cropped dark hair: the newly dubbed knight might be successful, but he would never be comely.

Such a far cry from Regan, and my other old brothers in arms. Brothers, I'll avenge ye yet. See if I don't. But I'm tired, I'm so damned tired.

'My lord, one of the men has found something. You should come and see it.'

Madogan, talking to him. Blinking away his weariness, Braxus turned to stare at his lieutenant.

'What something?' he asked sourly. Right now, leaving the rock he was perched on didn't appeal. Perhaps being spared another fight tonight would be a blessing, after all.

Madogan's face betrayed no emotion as he repeated: 'Better if you just come and see it.'

At first glance, the little cairn of stones was unremarkable to the eye.

'One of the footsoldiers stumbled on it when he was off to

take a pi-relieve himself,' said Sir Madogan, awkwardly recalling he was supposed to be a knight now.

'I told everyone not to stray too far!' barked Braxus. 'Those highland wretches are deadly cunning at the best of times – all the more so on the brink of death.'

'I've reprimanded the soldier in question, sire,' said Madogan flatly. 'But you should take a closer look at what he found.'

Braxus bent to peer at the stones. Each was etched with some sort of sigil. He felt his hackles suddenly crawl into life as he recognised the eldritch sorcerer's script.

'Signs of witchery,' he mused aloud. *One thing I could go the rest of my blasted life without seeing ever again.*

'Elementalist witchcraft, most like,' suggested Madogan. 'Highlanders have longed prayed to the North Wind – and other darker spirits. Revere 'em as gods, they do.'

'I need no education on the heathen ways of highlanders,' Braxus reminded him. 'But no, you did the right thing bringing it to my attention. I'll think on this tonight before I turn in. In the meantime, double the watch.'

Madogan nodded bluffly and stalked off to obey.

Braxus remained a while, gazing at the hieratic markings where they appeared to writhe on rocks kissed sullenly by firelight. So out of place they seemed, but then they were – Braxus' adventures with Horskram and his allies had taught him that the script had been bequeathed by angels and demons to an ancient race of mortals, far across the earth from where he stood now. An earth they had changed forever by its power.

So, it would appear Slánga has a court wizard, Braxus thought wryly. *Perhaps this changes things, perhaps it doesn't... Well, in any case, I've fought sorcerers before.*

As he went to seek his tent, Braxus felt his weariness drop away somewhat. But then the prospect of fighting the supernatural tended to inject a man with feverish energy. He didn't know just then which he hated more: the mountain ranges, the highlanders who dwelled in them, or the warlocks who manipulated them. Now it looked as though he was up against all three at once.

~

The next day passed uneventfully enough, but the following one yielded more of interest. In a razed village they found a couple of old crones left behind by the highlanders, who'd clearly seen the wisdom in applying scorched-earth tactics of their own. Thankfully the white-haired women had crumbled at the first threat of torture: Slánga and his remaining men had passed through, taking every woman and child with him, arming those he could. About a thousand all told, half of them as Braxus had suspected lightly equipped clansmen who might give his rag-tag army some trouble. He'd rewarded the crones with a swift hanging for their pains.

Every execution took a piece of his soul, to a dark place on the Other Side where he expected to spend the rest of his existence after his mortal frame was done. But to Gehenna with Gehenna: he was a lord of men now, and that meant seeing clearly what needed to be done and doing it.

Father, I hope this makes you proud at least, he thought and not for the first time. *At long last, I'm doing what even you could not. Wayward and feckless, was I? Well, the eagle has come home to roost. When this is done all shall know the name of Clan Fitzrow and fear it.*

The elementalist still worried him though. A warlock with nature magick at his fingertips might even up the odds considerably – he'd seen enough of the Sea Wizard's antics at Linden to know that much. The Battle of Linden, how far away that seemed now. Hard to believe it had only been a year ago. He wondered what his erstwhile comrades were up to now, then quashed the thought. Dwelling on days of former glory was for weaklings. He was a lord of men now – and a lord had to be strong and present for those men.

'All right lads,' he said that night, addressing his four-hundred strong band of knights, footsoldiers and squires. 'We've fought hard and well this past month, and seen our share of losses. But know this – the endgame is in sight! According to yon crones, Slánga is mustering his forces for one last battle – he wants this thing over as badly as we do. Let's rally together a final time, and put the highlanders out of their misery once and for all!'

Some of the tougher knights and soldiers gave voice to throaty cheers at that, but on the fringes of their exuberance Braxus could detect many a sullen mien. He'd warned them what to expect – but no words could ever convey the true savagery of barbarian warfare. Well, let the survivors weigh their consciences in their own time – land and title came at a price, measured in blood and souls.

He was wondering whether to say any more or quit while he was marginally ahead, when a sound tore the darkling skies hunched menacingly above the rocky wilderness. Hands instinctively reached for weapons, but this was no hit-and-run strike: the unmistakeable sound of a warhorn repeated itself, a little closer this time.

'By all the archangels,' said one of the younger knights, Sir Casper. 'That's Slánga on the march – he's bringing the fight back to us!'

I'll give him his due, he's as unpredictable as he is brave and fool-hardy, thought Braxus. *He really does want this over with. All the burning and slaying, we've driven Slánga to breaking point. Brutali-ty's an ill tune to play, but by Reus it pays the wages.*

The valley they had camped in was steep, with precious

little in the way of footholds. That wouldn't prevent a small army of agile savages from hurling rocks and spears down on them though. Braxus had fought highlanders long enough to know what they were capable of – but even then the casualties were always grievous. The lord wondered how many of his four hundred veterans would live to weigh their consciences at all.

'Form up in four divisions!' he barked. 'One for each of the Four Winds, shield walls – you know the drill. Don't bother with the horses, we'll not find good use for them on such uneven ground.'

Braxus strained his eyes for a first sign of the enemy as his men scrambled to obey his orders. Disregarding them himself, he mounted up on the stallion he'd won at the Graufluss Bridge Tourney the previous year, so he could get a better view. And then he saw them coming, sketched darkly against the night skies. Not that the highlanders were interested in subterfuge: a burning halo seemed to crest the air above them, throwing the brightly painted savages into hideous relief. At its epicentre was its crafter: dressed in a mantlet of shrunken skulls sewn into a dirty robe, the warlock in service to Slánga. In his right hand was a staff topped with another skull, his left clutched a silver sickle. Beside the elementalist Braxus saw Slánga. He could sense rather than see the expression of hatred carved into his heathen face.

By the halo's light Braxus could see their antagonists numbered well over a thousand, arranged in several lines along the western lip of the valley. Many were smaller than man-sized: the doomed crones hadn't been lying about women and children being pressed into service. He felt his gut tighten instinctively: he knew this would be a shameful end to a shocking and brutal campaign. What would his old love rival Sir Torgun say if he could see him now?

But the Northlending was a second son, free of the cares of responsibility that came with more privileged birth.

'Hold fast!' he cried to his men. 'They're trying to intimidate us with hedge sorcery. We might be outnumbered, but we outclass them. This is Slánga's last stand, lads – let's make it a brief one!'

More cheers from the hardier veterans. More sullen glances from the less experienced.

Braxus drew his blade and pointed it up the valley slope towards where Slánga crouched, ready to descend like the jackal he was.

'Slánga Mac Bryon!' he yelled. 'Here we are – the men responsible for butchering your women, your children, your warriors. Come and wreak vengeance on us, if you dare! Or are you here to parlay, for your miserable lives?'

He hoped to provoke the highland chieftain into rash action. Even with shields to protect them, his army might still take a fatal amount of casualties if Slánga chose to hang back and use spears and rocks.

But it wasn't spears or rocks they had to worry about.

Without a word, Slánga turned to the warlock next to him and nodded curtly. Responding to the pre-arranged signal, the mage lifted his staff and incanted something in the fell tongue of magick.

Without warning, the heavens opened. Lightning stabbed the skies as rain showered down on his men with unnatural speed, turning the soil at their feet into a muddy bog within seconds.

At that moment Slánga gave vent to a ululating cry, and as one the last highlanders of the Brekkens surged down the valley slope towards them.

Impossible, thought Braxus, straining to peer through the thick sheets of water cascading about him. *They'll slip and fall in this mess.*

But as the highlanders drew nearer, he realised how wrong he was. They seemed to glide across the brown boggy morass, stepping as lightly over the fast-flowing mud as a man might a freshly cropped field at summer's end. His army on the other hand were already struggling to maintain formation, sinking knee-deep into the softened soil.

Clever bastard, thought Braxus grudgingly. *One single move, and he's recreated the conditions of the Battle for Rathlain Corridor.*

His side had won that day thanks to Lady Rowena's superior tactics, but Braxus had no such advance planning to draw upon. Cursing, he dismounted from his warhorse. Though a faithful and sturdy beast, it was clearly discomfited by the preternatural change in circumstances.

Better to fight, aye and die if need be, on foot with the rest of the troops anyway, thought Braxus, though he struggled to keep his footing in the raging swells.

His first opponent could not have been older than twelve summers. The scrawny youth mustered a half-decent war cry as he swiped at him with a stone axe. Without thinking about it, Braxus deflected the clumsy blow and riposted, spearing the lad through the gut. He wrenched the blade free and the boy slipped over, dying with a strange sigh. Somehow it felt worse, to kill a green lad like that in mockery of single combat rather than just bundling him into a cabin and putting it to the torch.

Killing. It came in so many different guises, just like the Angel of Death himself: sometimes it felt like sex, at others more akin to rape.

His next two foes came and went in a blur of blood. Hardened by years of war and quest as he was, Braxus found himself equal to the dreadful fighting conditions. Not all his men could say the same: the pitiful shrieks of his brothers-in-arms clogged his ears, as Azrael's tally piled up and up. How many eyes on the dark angel's wings would have to close before the killing was finally done, he wondered?

His fourth antagonist was a worthy opponent at least. A bull-necked highland screamer, wearing a trophy necklace of severed ears and wielding a giant two-handed mattock like a greatsword, he managed to knock Braxus into the mud.

High rose the mattock, as the savage made to club him into the dark muddy earth and oblivion. Wrenching his torso up with a strength and speed borne of desperate battle instinct, Braxus drove his sword in a two-handed thrust straight into the unarmoured highlander's groin. His war cry turned pitiful as he shrieked away the abrupt loss of his manhood. Not that he'd ever miss it anyway – Braxus's second thrust saw to that.

Dragging himself up out of the reddish-brown mire, he surveyed the frothing scene of carnage erupting all about him. Combatants on both sides, covered in mud and blood. A pigtailed woman armed with a heavy cooking pot was busy braining a fallen squire, smashing the iron repeatedly into his cracked skull, spilling brains into the bog.

Braxus lurched up to her. She turned, a wild feral look in eyes that were strangely beautiful. Beautiful for the last time. Braxus clove her skull in twain, barely noticing as blood spattered across his face, filling his mouth with its metallic tang.

On he roved, seeking more victims for his wettened blade. The fighting raged back and forth, and before long he was able to use bodies to prevent him from sinking into the deep mud. He searched for Slánga, but the heroic final confrontation he'd yearned for never came. Small surprise that: there was nothing heroic about this campaign.

When he did find him, it was in the peaceful repose of death. Whatever elan the elementalist had mustered was long spent; no hedge witch could hope to sustain such powerful Thaumaturgy for long. The night skies were clear again, tasselled wisps of cloud parting to reveal moon and stars that shone luridly on the horrible spectacle mortal folly had created.

Slánga's corpse had been butchered by spear and sword. Beside him lay half a dozen bodies of Thraxians; his life had been bought dearly. The highlanders were no more. The last few remnants were being slaughtered like oxen by his remaining troops. Of the seven hundred he'd taken with him into the hills, perhaps two hundred had survived the harrying of the Brekkens.

But one highlander remained alive. Gazing up to the top of the valley, Braxus could see him silhouetted beneath the dying halo of preternatural light.

Banishing his weary limbs from his mind, the lord left his men to finish their gruesome work and began the slippery climb.

It took him a long while to reach the top, but the nature priest was waiting for him. His elan spent, he stood staring at Braxus with eyes that were impassive and doomed at the same time. As the lord approached, sword in hand, the hedge witch sank to his knees and raised his arms aloft. No final incantation this; just the supplicant gesture of one who knows he is about to be sacrificed, and perhaps meet his gods.

Drawing level with the old man, Braxus stared at him. Lean and straggly-haired like most of his folk, he must have seen sixty winters at least. He wouldn't see another.

Reversing the grip on his sword, Braxus placed the point in the groove at the centre of the man's scrawny clavicle. He rested his left hand on the pommel, and met the savage's eyes. He did not avert his gaze as he pushed the blade down through the man's heart and bowels. The savage priest shuddered once, then his eyes flickered shut. Braxus felt the weight of the man's body lie heavy on his sword.

Above them, the halo of fire guttered and went out.

They counted the cost of victory beneath a drizzly dawn. Sir Madogan had survived without so much as a scratch on him, but somehow that did not surprise Braxus.

'There's some fifty of ours who may yet survive their wounds, but they're in no fit state to ride or walk,' said the lieutenant. 'If we search around for some trees, maybe we can build stretchers - '

Braxus cut him off. 'We're deep into highland territory, and supplies are running low. We've scourged the lands hereabout for miles, and Kaia knows they didn't have much to offer in the first place! By my reckoning, we've supplies enough left to make the journey back south to civilisation, but it'll take us a week at least. Anyone not fit enough to travel, put them out of their misery and bury them here. Their families will be compensated.'

Madogan blinked. He was a hard man, but even for him this was cruel.

'You of all people don't need reminding of the realities of war,' Braxus told him sternly. 'Each surviving man leaves here a vassal or a bachelor − land and title for service rendered, that was the bargain that was struck. Any man questions my terms or judgment, let him speak up or forever hold his peace.'

Several of the nearby knights heard the exchange. All averted their eyes, and held their peace.

'Very good, sire,' said Sir Madogan, before stalking off to see the thing done.

Slánga's corpse caught his eye again. Gripping his sword,

Braxus walked over to the body. Summoning his squire, he ordered him to lift the body out of the mud. He'd take the highland chieftain's head for a trophy, and mount it on the walls of the keep his yeomen were rebuilding. The sight of it would hopefully inspire them to work harder and faster.

Late that afternoon, they took their leave of the corpse-blanketed valley and began the tortuous journey home. Any remnants of highlanders he'd missed would perish from disease and famine with the onset of winter: the highland threat in the Brekkens was extinguished forever.

As they rode from the valley, Braxus felt thoughts of his defeated enemy already begin to slide from his mind. His gaze was fixed firmly on home now. He had a ward to rebuild, and people to rule.

HEROES FROM THE WILDERNESS

E reth went about his work with heavy heart. The armourer of Hroghar had managed to keep cheerful for most of his forty-odd winters. He had a respectable and essential craft, was beloved by all of the castle's inhabitants, high-born and low. Luviah had smiled on him, whispering in Kaia's ear to ensure his marriage was fruitful: three sons had lived to adulthood and would follow him into the family trade. He'd never had a reason to be downcast. Even when the Young Pretender Krulheim had risen out of the south last year, Ereth had known – just *known* – that King Freidheim would see him off, that everything would be all right in the end. And so it had proved.

How much could change in a year. Just a handful of weeks ago, Fenrig had ridden off in full panoply of war to try and lift the siege of Strongholm. Northland raiders from across the Valhalla had done what Krulheim the pretender could not, and overrun the capital. The news that came up from the King's Dominions was worse by the day. Fenrig and the other Efrilund jarls had been beaten back; now the remaining barons were flocking to Vandheim, where Lord Toros was mustering a desperate relief. Ereth didn't like to dwell on the ugly rumours he'd been hearing of late: that the Northlanders had put the entire Ingwin ruling royal family to the sword.

But even those were not the worst of the tales he'd heard.

Horrid aquatic sea monsters were said to be emerging from the waves, joining their queer coral spears to the axes and swords of the barbarian invaders, slaying all who resisted and carrying hapless captives back across the waves with them, to who knew what fate.

On top of all that, there'd been ugly news closer to home as well. Vaskrian had been tracked down and brought to justice. Ereth felt sick just thinking about it. He'd tried over the years to instil a bit of common sense into the lad, but that head of his had just grown hotter and hotter. Now he languished in the dungeons, awaiting the Jarl's justice upon Fenrig's return – assuming his liege returned at all.

The world's gone mad. No wonder the castle perfect keeps preaching it's the end of days.

Ereth finished hammering out the blade he'd spent the morning working on. A lump of molten metal now resembled the broad blade of a sword. He'd heard that the bladesmiths of the southern sultanates did something called *pattern forging*, where they mixed another softer metal into their mix to create a more nuanced blade. But Ereth swore by what he'd been taught by his father, and practised for more than twenty years himself.

Taking the blade in his tongs Ereth doused it. He normally loved that hissing sound, the acrid stench of cooling steel that marked the first stage of a job well done. But nowadays, little cheered him. How many more of these swords would he forge before the north was overrun and the Efrilunders shared the fate of the King's Dominions? Ereth was normally an optimist, but not even he could deny that Lord Toros' beleaguered rag-tag band of knights, soldiers, squires and archers would be hard pressed to keep the marauding Northlanders checked, never mind take back Strongholm.

His gloomy thoughts were interrupted by a shadow in the doorway. Looking up he blinked in surprise. For one ghastly moment he thought his worst fears had been realised on the spot, that here was a Northland champion come to beard him in his lair. The warrior who stood before him was certainly of Northland stock, but taking in his black tabard and travel-worn mail armour, he realised this was a Northlending, probably a noble errant of some sort judging by his mien and pure complexion. But unlike many of the younger Northlending knights his age, the stranger was bearded, and his eyes had the haunted cast of someone who knows too much. He towered over Ereth, himself not a small man, and had to stoop to enter his forge.

Scarcely five and twenty summers, but he seems so much older, thought Ereth, before politely clearing his throat and saying: 'How may I help ye, sirrah?'

'You are the armourer and bladesmith of Hroghar I take it?' asked the knight. The voice was soft yet strong, refined and aristocratic, yet with nothing of the dandy about it. Ereth had a curious feeling he'd seen this man before, though he could not recall having met him.

'That I am, sirrah,' he replied. 'And who might you be, begging your knightly pardon?'

'No pardon needed,' said the mysterious knight, before reaching into his undertunic and pulling something out. It caught the light with a scintillant radiance: Ereth had looked on all kinds of metals in his life, but he'd never seen anything quite like this. The shard looked to be made of silver, yet it had a lustre to it quite unlike any precious metal he'd set eyes on.

The towering knight placed the shard on the workbench next to Ereth. Then he slowly drew his sword and placed it next to the sliver. The bastard blade was honed and well-kept: the errant might not have many opportunities to keep his armour in good nick, but his sword was razor-sharp and bereft of notches.

He doesn't often miss with that thing, thought Ereth admiringly. *Unless it's for show, that's a sword that's found many in a chink in a man's armour.*

The knight went on, oblivious to Ereth's observations. 'Can you reforge my sword, with yon sliver of metal in it?' he asked. 'I have it on good authority that you're the best armourer and bladesmith in Efrilund.'

Ignoring the sudden swelling of pride at the compliment, Ereth replied: 'As to being the best, I know nothing about that. But I can certainly reforge your sword with yonder shard in it, if that's what you desire.'

Though a stranger job I was never asked to perform, he added mentally.

The knight nodded. 'Excellent. You'll be well paid for your work.' Reaching into his money pouch, he produced twenty silver marks. 'There'll be another twenty for you, when the job's done.'

'That's more than a fair price,' remarked Ereth. 'Excuse me, sirrah, but you never gave me your name...'

'That's right, I didn't,' replied the errant, more mildly than anything else. 'I'll be staying in Hroghar for a week, after that I ride south to the muster at Vandheim. I assume that's enough time for you to complete the job.'

Ereth had barely had time to murmur something in the affirmative before the tall knight turned and stalked from the lean-to. The burly armourer watched him go.

I've definitely seen him somewhere before... but where?

Heavy strides took Sir Torgun away from the armourer's forge. His homecoming had not been a happy one. That the Northlanders had invaded, he'd known: that they had overrun the capital and put the royal family to the sword, he could only have fathomed in his darkest imaginings.

The thought of it conjured up a darkling rage in him that not all his chivalrous sentiments could hope to quell. The royal family – murdered by barbarian savages. Hjala, his one-time lover, butchered in her palace home, her corpse strung up and used as a decoration along with all the others by the new conquerors.

Torgun could only hope the rumours were nothing more than that, but something told him otherwise. His night with the animal lords in the Valley of the Barrow Kings in the Island Realms recurred in his dreams with a frightening intensity. There the faceless servitor that had gifted him the shard had doomed him, revealing a brief but terrifying glimpse of his fate.

If that could happen to him, who knew what other horrors the Unseen might visit upon mortalkind. He was supposedly descended from the Northland demigod Søren – that thought alone was appalling enough – yet even he would not be spared the Angel of Death's touch.

No one is exempt, and none of us are special, he thought broodingly as he made his way into the main hall. *All that remains is to perform the tasks allotted to each one of us, before time has a stop.*

The under-seneschal was making great show of doing just that. Torgun took one look at the man and disliked him immediately. Another rumour he'd picked up on his journey across Efrilund was that this Rutgar had disgraced himself in the field at Linden – and apparently been rewarded for it with a position of high office. Something about helping to bring a fugitive to justice – the peasants he'd lodged with and questioned had been somewhat hazy on the details. Torgun had never questioned the social order, but things like this made him doubt it, once in a while.

Rutgar, dressed in ermine robes too meretricious for a steward never mind his assistant, looked up at him superciliously.

'And what have we here?' he demanded, leaning heavily on his staff. 'A knight errant, by the looks of things. Why aren't you down south at the muster, where you belong?'

I could ask you much the same, thought Torgun.

'My sword is at the armoury, being reforged. That done, I'll ride post-haste to the muster, where I can serve the realm.' He hadn't intended to emphasise the last few words, but he did: catching the inference, Rutgar glared at him. 'I can assure you I'd be doing likewise, were it not for this injury sustained in the last war – that and my pressing duties about Hroghar.'

Of course you would, thought Torgun. *Thank Virtus the churls in the lands hereabout are more honest than you are, else I might even have believed you.*

'I've come to plead sanctuary for the time it takes to have my blade made anew,' said Torgun, drawing on court protocol. He was determined no one would know his true identity, not until he'd learned more. Announce his name and the fawning would start. Sir Torgun the saviour, returned to us in our darkest hour! Sir Torgun, hero of Linden, come to avenge the House of Ingwin and drive the invaders back into the sea! The thought of it made him sick. Had he once connived at that kind of praise, soaking it up behind a patina of false modesty, and really considered himself a humble knight?

The follies of our youth sicken us more with every greying hair, he thought, recalling the words of the troubadour Maegellan.

'Succour you shall have,' replied Rutgar, who at least had the decency to stick to court protocol himself. 'You have the mien of a tidy warrior – we'll see you to arms and the field well fed and rested.'

'My horse shall also require victualling,' added Torgun. 'I took the liberty of entrusting him to the ostler.'

'Liberty granted in retrospect,' said Rutgar, affecting a bored tone. His eye was already straying towards a comely serving wench that was busy lighting torches in the darkening hall.

That was well, though. He needed this fool distracted. He'd even resorted to bribing the stable boy to keep quiet about Hilmir – a Farovian destrier in a poor lordless knight's possession would attract suspicion. Luckily there were few knights left in Hroghar, chances were Hilmir would go unremarked upon as long as the lad kept his word. He'd been paid five silvers, so the boy had better.

Supper that night was a cheerless affair. The castle was virtually empty; nearly every able-bodied man had been packed off south to join the muster. Ereth would be about his work, then he too would leave, with the last group of knights led by Sir Benedict, an ageing banneret in service to Fenrig.

Benedict was at table, presuming to hold court in his liege lord's absence. He steadfastly refused to believe the rumours about the Ingwin family being put to the sword. Torgun could hardly fault him for that – it was a horrible tale to put one's faith in. 'We'll see those Northlanders off our land, not to worry,' Benedict said, for the third time during the meal. 'Lord Toros is a canny leader of men, he'll have something up his sleeve, no doubt.'

My brother is an able ruler of men, thought Torgun as he chewed perfunctorily at his meat. *But that doesn't make him a miracle-worker.*

So far Benedict hadn't recognised Torgun – but then a knight was hard to recognise bereft his Order's insignia or ancestral coat of arms. The seneschal Sir Branton was another matter – once or twice Torgun had caught him peering sidelong at him, trying to fathom the face behind the beard.

You'll find out who I am soon enough. Then you'd better pray I can somehow live up to your vaunted expectations.

Rutgar for his part behaved as though nothing were amiss, taking time to grope the hapless wench as she moved about them, serving the last of the meat and wine. Most of the castle's supplies had been requisitioned by the army, but that was to be expected.

Pray Euphrosakritos we get to eat and drink for a little while longer. He didn't often invoke the avatar of merriment, but it seemed appropriate and Reus knew he needed to muster a little cheer in himself.

'You have the mien of a strong warrior,' said Benedict, turning suddenly to address Sir Torgun. 'You should join us when we ride south.'

What in Ezekiel's name do you think I'm doing here, sirrah?

'That I shall do gladly,' replied Sir Torgun politely. He meant it, too: doom or no doom, he was anxious to engage the foe.

'And where do you hail from, pray tell? You've a southern accent.'

Torgun nodded, trying to seem casual. 'I spent my youth squiring in Vandheim, for Sir Brethald of Maltheim.' He despised subterfuge, but still felt it necessary. Sir Brethald had been a loyal vassal of Torgun's father, and taught him hawking when he was a page boy. Half a lie was better than a complete one, Torgun reasoned.

'Ah, Sir Brethald,' said Benedict, tugging absently at his moustaches. 'Met him once, at Linden Tourney. Good knight, in his day. Sad to hear he passed of the pox a few summers ago – we could've used a man like him now.'

Branton wasn't about to be thrown so easily off the scent, however. 'So you squired for a respected vassal of one of the most powerful lords of our realm – and then chose a life of errantry. Unusual decision, I must say.' The seneschal peered at him over the rim of his wine cup.

Torgun shrugged. 'I wanted a life of adventure,' he said simply. 'Errantry has oft been viewed as an irregular, but never a dishonourable, calling.'

'Well said,' interjected Benedict, raising his own goblet. 'Perhaps when this wretched business is done, you can regale us with tales of your adventures.'

How little you would enjoy that, thought Torgun glumly. *Sir Aronn and the Chequered Twins could tell you all about my adventures, from the Heavenly Halls.*

Thought of his dead brothers-in-arms did little to lift his flagging spirits. Torgun was about to make his excuses and seek his pallet on the hall floor, when Rutgar said something that surprised him.

'This war has delayed more than mere tale-telling,' said the weaselly under-seneschal. 'Justice has had to take a pause as well – to that churl Vaskrian's benefit.'

It wasn't a particularly common name among Northlendings nowadays; based on the Old Norric word for courage, it had fallen into disuse in the past generation. And Vaskrian had grown up right here in Hroghar, squired to one of Fenrig's vassals...

Even still, surely it couldn't be him?

The seneschal was replying: 'Sir Rutgar, need I remind you that the lord's justice is hardly in your purview. Let Fenrig fight the war, then he'll see to the renegade squire – assuming he lives to administer said justice.' Only the crabby steward was allowed to give voice to the thing they all feared.

Torgun felt himself relax slightly. Vaskrian was no squire nowadays, but a belted knight. Yet still...

'I once had occasion to travel with a squire of that name,' hedged Torgun. 'A reckless youth, yet his heart seemed true. I hope I was not deceived in his character.'

'You weren't,' said Branton. 'Unless this squire companion of yours claimed to be a knight. This rascal tore off into the wilderness a year ago, with his knightly master Sir Branas. He's disappeared – Vaskrian claims he perished in Tintagael, of all places! More likely the squire murdered him on the road, along with another vassal of the Jarl and his squire – their bodies we found soon enough. He'll be tried and hanged when Fenrig returns. It happens from time to time, commoners forgetting their place and taking evil into their hearts. Still, a bad business all in all – as if we hadn't enough to worry about.'

Slowly but steadily, Sir Torgun rose. 'Sirrah, I regret to inform you that you have been most notoriously deceived,' he said, meeting the steward's eye.

Branton looked at him in surprise. 'I'm afraid I don't follow you, sir knight,' he responded coldly.

'Sir Vaskrian of Hroghar was a squire when I met him on the road from Tintagael. A squire he remained, 'tis true, for many a moon after that – though he did service that many a true knight would have envied. He was finally rewarded for his labours when Lady Rowena of Tul Aeren knighted him in Thraxia, after he slew Sir Leathan of that country in single combat defending her honour. I was witness to it myself.'

Torgun barely paid Rutgar any heed as his jaw dropped into his trencher. Branton folded his arms and peered inscrutably at Torgun.

'Oh really? And who might you be, exactly? I won't deny your story corroborates the one Vaskrian has been pleading from his dungeon cell these past few weeks. But you've been rather chary of revealing your identity, sir knight... for a nobleman's testimony to be believed, he has to declare his name and ancestry – as I'm sure you know full well.'

All eyes had turned to the looming knight. Torgun sighed inwardly. So much for subterfuge, but it had never been his strong suit anyway.

Once again the words of the spectral servitor he'd met in the Island Realms came floating back to him, across time and space.

No man outruns his Wyrd.

RUNNING THE GAUNTLET

'Are ye sure this is a good idea?' Gem-encrusted teeth scored an ugly grimace across Garhan's face; imminent fear of his life did little to improve the grizzled sea-dog's looks.

'Not entirely,' Wrackwulf had to admit. Clearly the rumours they'd heard about the blockade of Westerburg being broken hadn't been altogether accurate. Sure enough, Vorstlending galleys flying the flag of Eorl Eadgar of Drey-lund were making a good fist of harrying the Pangonian warships, but mastery of the Bay of Belfarling was hardly a decided matter: even now, this close to sunset, mariners on both sides could be seen exchanging lethal volleys of ballista quarrels and Arathenian fire. Vessels on either side burned, sending charring corridors of smoke into the blood-red heavens.

Nothing heavenly about such a sight, thought Wrackwulf glumly. *A land fight I know how to deal with. This makes me feel about as useful as teets on a warhorse.*

'Well now, seein' as said idea was yours, oi'd loike ter know what yer plans ter do with it,' pressed Garhan. The skiff that had carried them across the Tyrnian Straits and back had taken them many leagues south of Ongist to the shores of Vorstlund. At least Westerburg Point was still standing; those rumours had proved well founded. Wrackwulf could make it out now, silhouetted against the dying skies, a grim sentinel of war. Perched on a promontory of rock overlooking the cityport and guarded by its gargantuan triangular keep, it would be the last to fall should the Pangonians succeed in overrunning Westenlund.

Garhan was looking at him expectantly. Likewise the warrior-woman Ariadha, who had followed him back to the mainland from her home in the Island Realms, had quizzical eyes fixed on him.

How did you end up the leader of this expedition, Wrackwulf old boy? So much for bright ideas.

Returning his own gaze to the clashing ships, Wrackwulf sized up the situation as best he could.

'There,' he said presently, pointing towards where a gap in the flotilla was thrown into sharp relief by a burning warship. 'Betwixt yonder galleys. It's a narrow opening, but should be enough for the skiff to get through.' He glanced heavenwards. 'The sun will be gone soon, that should help us get through undetected.'

Two of Garhan's sailors exchanged doubtful looks. They had followed their scurrilous leader to the Island Realms and back, but that didn't make them foolhardy, which might be bad news for Wrackwulf's plan. The three new sailors Garhan had taken on at Ongist didn't look doubtful; they looked terrified.

'One of yonder ships is a blazing wreck,' Garhan reminded him. 'Oh, they'll see us alroight.'

'We're small fish,' countered the freelancer. 'In case you hadn't noticed, that lot are busy fighting a naval war for mastery of a principality. I doubt they'll spare us so much as a quarrel.'

Well, I hope not anyway.

Ariadha's savage tattooed face looked scarcely prettier than Garhan's, and just as unnerved. Wrackwulf struggled to explain the situation to her. The warrior wench had barely picked up the rudiments of Vorstlending during their two-week journey south; Wrackwulf only hoped she'd live to improve her language skills further.

Garhan was already steering the skiff towards the gap indicated by Wrackwulf. 'Dogra!' he yelled at one of the new recruits, a lad on the threshold of his sixteenth summer at most. 'Keep yer eyes abaft, we're heading into a squadron of warships, and I don't want any surprises! The rest of ye, eyes before the beam!'

Naval warfare was a messy affair, to say the least: ships flying the colours of Dreylund and the Occitanian barons of Pangonia scudded across the waves, great wooden giants meleeing one another with little or no thought of formation. Garhan's skiff took them past one pair, clinched tightly in the pitiless embrace of war: Wrackwulf could hear the screams of the dying and wounded from the Dreylending galley as a crew from Gorleon boarded, weapons flashing in the fires of war.

Stand fast my countrymen, thought Wrackwulf desperately. *Buy us enough time to make the docks at least.*

The nearest vessel to the burning ship was a many-oared galley flying the azure hippogriff displayed on a vert field that signified the margravate of Jura, but even that was far enough away to allow them a clean run through. It wouldn't be enough to keep them out of range of any missile attacks though. Towards the opening their skiff now sped, its single sail belling as Garhan's pirates turned her about through the eye of the wind.

The Juran war galley had just engaged another enemy

vessel; that should stand them in good stead. Wrackwulf clutched the inwale as Garhan's seacraft took them speeding past it.

Shouts from up on the deck of the galley. Wrackwulf stifled a curse as crew members on the starboard side scurried over to the taffrail to peer at them. The ballistas and catapults were directed towards the Dreylending galley, which was a good thing. The half dozen or so mariners that had spotted their skiff were cranking hand-held crossbows, which most definitely was not.

'Reus dammit, they've seen us!' cried Wrackwulf. 'Stand by to receive a volley!'

'Ready about!' Garhan yelled at his men. 'We need to get away from that Juran galley, we're sitting ducks at this range!'

'But that'll take us closer to the fireship, cap'n!' cried the mate.

'Avast yer whining and do as I say,' snarled Garhan, in no mood to argue.

Over on the deck of the war galley, the crew had finished reloading their crossbows.

'Prepare to receive!' yelled Wrackwulf, just as they loosed.

All the quarrels missed. All that is, save one, which buried itself in Dogra's throat, propelling him into the sea.

Guess you won't live to see that sixteenth summer after all lad, thought Wrackwulf sadly.

Stifling a curse, Garhan bellowed more orders. Wrackwulf clutched his axe for reassurance more than any practical use as he kept his eyes trained on the Juran galley. The Dreylunders had taken advantage of the unexpected distraction to press their foemen harder.

That's it, thought the freelancer. *You keep scratching our backs, my countrymen, and we'll keep scratching yours.*

With what seemed like agonising slowness their skiff

pulled clear of the warring flotillas. Up ahead through the twilight Wrackwulf could make out the lights of Westerburg's harbour, twinkling eyes that seemed to smile at them.

They weren't far from the docks when another hail of bolts fell about them. The nearest one embedded itself in the inwale right next to Wrackwulf.

'Dammit, those quarrels came from the waterfront!' yelled Garhan. 'They must 'ave mistaken us for an enemy vessel!'

'We need to show them a flag of parlay!' said Wrackwulf. 'Garhan, where's the spare sail?'

The pirate captain nodded curtly towards a locker just behind Wrackwulf. Throwing it open the freelancer pulled out a folded white sail, slashing off a piece with his dagger. Casting around for something to use as a flagpole, he saw... Ariadha's spear. It would just have to do.

The warrior-woman favoured him with a stare that was half threatening, half confused, as he gestured towards the heirloom weapon she carried across her back.

'We... need... to... tie... this... to... your... SPEAR!' he yelled, gesticulating like a madman in an effort to make himself understood. Palom's wounds, why had the Almighty seen fit to sunder the speech of mortalkind? Probably the heavenly guvnor's idea of a twisted joke.

It took a while to show Ariadha what he meant, and by the time they'd constructed a makeshift flag the cross-bowmen on the wharf had reloaded. Standing up and waving it manically, Wrackwulf silently prayed none of the shafts in the next volley would find him.

Reus was clearly in an ungenerous mood today, because one of them lodged painfully in his shoulder, while a second speared a crew member's thigh.

Thank Ezekiel for good mail, thought Wrackwulf, grimacing as he plucked the quarrel from his armoured shoulder.

Another flesh wound to add to a lifetime collection, it had caused him to drop the spear. Luckily Ariadha wasn't about to give up her prized possession so easily; the islander caught it just before it could fall into the sea, and began waving it herself.

Pulling himself upright again, Wrackwulf peered at the harbour. He could see a dozen-strong contingent of crossbowmen in the torchlight, suddenly looking unsure of themselves.

'We're VORSTLENDINGS!!!' he cried at the top of his lungs, while Ariadha continued to wave the makeshift flag frantically. Technically that was half a lie, but time enough to clarify things once they were safely on dry ground and not impersonating giant pin-cushions.

'Steady as she goes!' cried Garhan, as the skiff made its way doggedly towards where the docks extended from the wharf like the broken teeth of a giant. Wrackwulf had to hope said giant would quickly learn to make its guests feel a tad more welcome.

As the skiff drew nearer Wrackwulf could make out the duty serjeant, ordering his men to hold. Relief washed over him, a good salve for his fresh wound. The crossbows remained trained on them as Garhan's men steered the skiff into a berth and tied her up. The injured sailor groaned pitifully as Wrackwulf knelt beside him. 'Have no fear,' he told him. 'The worst is over. We'll have this quarrel out of your leg in no time.' He needn't have bothered. The sailor had passed out while he was speaking, though Stygnos willing he'd live to sail another day.

The serjeant looked over the new arrivals, eyes hard and suspicious in a face set grim. 'Vorstlendings, is it?' he challenged. 'Looks more like Cobian pirates and stranger yet to me.' His eyes lingered on Ariadha, and not in the way a man's eyes normally linger on a woman.

'Sir Wrackwulf of Bringenheim, at your service,' replied the knight, doing his best to smile through the stinging pain in his shoulder. 'Last time I checked, yon manor lay in Vorstlending territory.'

'It might not any more,' replied the serjeant, unsmiling.

Wrackwulf felt his reviving spirits stall. 'That bad, is it?' he asked.

The serjeant sighed. 'They've got our border castles pinned – all three of 'em, Howfaste, Vizvant and Altkass. To make matters worse, we've but now been hearing reports that Howfaste has fallen. That means more reinforcements for the Pangonians – we'll have an army thousands strong at our gatehouse before long. There's some good news – the Pangonian commander Sir Hugon has already paused his vanguard to give the other two battalions a chance to join him. Looks like he'll be waiting a few more days now, if the rumours are true – give the reserves from Howfaste a chance to join him as well. As for the other two castles, who knows what could happen with them in the meantime. Even as things stand, we don't have the numbers to meet them in the field – we're settling in for a long and bitter siege, sir knight. We've managed to get a few supply ships through since Lord Eadgar broke the blockade, but as you can see they come back for more every day.'

'Who's in charge of the Vorstlending alliance?' asked Wrackwulf. 'Crown Prince Franz?'

The serjeant smiled crookedly. 'Him, aye, and some might say his mother Princess Utha. The lords of all the western baronies of Vorstlund have mustered to our banner – but they're perilous hard pushed. As for the easterners, last we heard they're doing a fair job of holding off the Thalamians, got 'em penned up in Wulfric's Pass.'

In other words, we're hanging on by a thread. 'Well, we're here to help in any way we can,' said Wrackwulf, doing his best to sound cheerful.

The serjeant nodded. 'Ye're right few, but every swinging sword arm helps at a time like this,' he said. 'Even sworders as outlandish as these,' he added, glancing sidelong at Wrackwulf's companions.

'Well then, what are we waiting for?' demanded the freelancer, motioning for Garhan and his men to unload the skiff. 'I think it's time we were properly received at court.'

Princess Utha surveyed the newcomers distastefully. 'Impressed' was not the first word that sprang to mind, though she did recognise the freelancer Sir Wrackwulf from his coat of arms.

Won more than his fair share of battles and tourneys that one, she thought, taking in the argent bear rampant on purpure field emblazoned on his surcoat. The man inside it was what really got her attention: not the tallest of knights or the kemptest, with his greasy black plaits and broken teeth, but she fancied she could see his thews rippling beneath his rusted mail. *Could be useful, if expensive. Such low company he keeps, though.*

Perhaps 'low' wasn't quite the word she was looking for after all. *Barbarous* would be nearer the mark. The savage woman with the strange spear standing next to him was like no one Utha had ever laid eyes on, nor ever hoped to again. Where in the Known World did she come from?

Poor lass – her barber shaved one side of her head, is that a custom wherever she hails from? Or some sadistic jest? Trust Sir Wrackwulf to dig up such a peculiar paramour. Or is she a comrade-in-arms? I wouldn't put anything past him, come to think of it.

As for the rest, they looked like Cobian scallywags if she'd lived more than fifty winters. Utha sighed inwardly.

In such desperate times, anything would have to do.

'Sir Wrackwulf of Bringenheim, your presence at court is

a gift unlooked for in troublous times,' she said graciously, inclining her head politely.

The freelancer bowed low, his mail jingling. A spot of blood stained the flagstoned floor of the court as he did: if his fresh injury hurt him, the knight gave no sign of it.

'A pleasure to be of service!' he replied, drawing himself up. 'And if you still do a fine feast as of old, make that a pleasure twice over!' The courtiers frowned disdainfully as the poor knight favoured them with a rakish grin. A couple of months' hard training under Franz as acting marshal of Westenlund had seen them toughen up considerably: but Utha wouldn't be surprised if they were jealous of a jumped-up freesword who'd probably put most of them to shame in the lists more than once before.

'Well, we *are* on a war footing,' said Utha, just a hint of severity entering her tone. 'But I'll see to it that you and your... companions are victualled and quartered. As befits their station, naturally. More importantly, we'd better have the castle chirurgeon see to that wound.'

Just then the herald without announced another arrival. 'His royal highness, defender of the folk of Westenlund and heir to the High Hall of Kings – Crown Prince Franz, Third Scion of the House of Drüler!'

A few excited murmurings flittered about the court. Ladies suddenly made themselves a shade more presentable, whilst Utha was gratified to see the court knights draw themselves up a little higher.

All eyes were thus fixed on her son and heir as he marched into the chamber, several battle-weary knights in tow. Prince Franz was clad in the fine suit of armour he'd taken during a skirmish with the Pangonians near Altkass. The commanding knight he'd captured for ransom had been duly relieved of his equipage, which had included a swift strong charger from Mandolacia province in Mercadia, and the splendid new harness. *Plate armour,* the knights were calling it – something about it turning bodkin heads better than chain links, and protecting the limbs from melee weapons at close quarters... Utha tried to show an interest in the martial aspects of the realm, though she knew her son was best left to that side of things.

One thing she did know for certain: her son cut a fine dash in the newfangled armour, complemented as it was by his rich woollen cloak and surcoat bearing the gules carrack on yellow sunburst Drüler coat of arms. *Whatever it takes to inspire this lot to victory*, she thought hopefully.

'My dear boy,' she said, dropping all pretence at formality in her happiness at seeing her son alive and whole. 'Ushira's joy and Ezekiel's grace it is to see you safely returned home. Pray tell us what news you bring from the front.'

Franz took a knee briefly before rising, a little stiffly she thought. Perhaps the new armour was heavier than the old; it certainly looked more robust.

'I fear it isn't good, mother,' he said. 'We can confirm Howfaste fell three nights ago, and the besieging forces there have marched to join the main army at the River Raudaz. Lords Kaye and Aravin have brought their battalions to the muster there, and if Altkass and Vizvant should fall too, there'll be more reserves coming to join them.'

Utha hoped the sinking feeling in her gut didn't show on her face, as she replied: 'A besieging army, no matter how large, still has to reckon with the walls of Westerburg. And we all here know the history of this castle.'

What her son said next shocked her, though perhaps given his character perhaps it shouldn't have surprised her.

'There isn't going to be a siege – not if I can help it.'

Mouths dropped slightly as the significance of the Crown Prince's words began to sink in. 'We're going to gather what forces we have and meet them in the field – the Raudaz is but two days' march from here. Our outriders report that Lords Kaye and Aravin will meet Hugon there with the rear and main battles before we can intercept them, but if we hurry we can get to them before the reserves from Howfaste arrive. Now is the time to strike!'

Utha blinked. Out of the corner of her eye she caught the inscrutable expression on Sir Wrackwulf's face. She couldn't tell if the freelancer approved, or was thinking he'd just pledged allegiance to a madman. The looks on the faces of many of the courtiers told all too clearly what they thought.

'I won't cower behind these walls whilst foreign invaders dishonour and plunder my lands,' persisted Franz, striking a lobstered fist into his gauntleted palm. 'We're outnumbered, aye, but the terrain is ours and we know it better than they do! More importantly, we're fighting for our *homes*, Ezekiel dammit.'

Franz swept the assembled worthies with a much meaner look than Wrackwulf had done. 'This is the time I've been training you for these past weeks,' he said in an even voice. 'So you'd better all be ready.'

Utha's son wasn't given to rousing battle speeches. Instead he had a way of calmly stating things that cut through; men of arms and commoners alike listened to him.

'We won't have to fight alone either,' Franz went on, trying to rouse the timorous knights and lordlings Ezekiel had ironically gifted him with. 'Lords Bjornwulf and Aethelfrith are making their way back to Westerburg from Vizvant and Altkass, I've sent word to them to divert to the Raudaz. They couldn't lift the sieges, they'll be keen to fight in an open field.'

They don't stand to lose their homelands if they fail, or not straight away at least, thought Utha disparagingly. She couldn't approve of such a reckless move − though having agreed that military tactics were her son's prerogative, she could hardly gainsay him.

Some of the younger court knights had found some semblance of martial spirit and were banging on tables and chanting war cries; but Utha felt sadness and fear, not optimism and determination, lend extra venom to her burning bowels.

Oh Franz, you've drilled them well, she thought, suppressing a wince as her old condition flared up again, *but if half of what we hear about the Pangonians is true, most of these lads won't live to sire heirs. That banneret you captured isn't the only invader who's so well caparisoned. We're up against the best trained and equipped army in Western Urovia – and on top of that, they over-match us in numbers.*

Her reverie was broken by Franz pointedly clearing his throat. Apparently he'd just noticed Sir Wrackwulf and his strange rag-tag band.

'Sir Wrackwulf of Bringenheim,' he said, acknowledging the poor knight formally. 'A surprise to see you here.'

'I'm not sure what you mean by that,' replied the freelancer, grinning. 'I've heard Drüler is paying a comely coin for every sword it can get.'

A few paces from where she sat, Princess Utha could practically feel Wenfold, her treasurer, wincing. He still disapproved strongly of the use of treasury coffers – but it hadn't been in vain. The Pangonians continually renewing the blockade had made things difficult, but they'd managed to sign up five hundred freelancers.

'Is that all you fight for?' Franz queried after a few moments of awkward silence. 'Coin, and naught else?'

Something peculiar came over Wrackwulf then. A serious cast to the man's mien that she doubted many had seen in him before. His eyes momentarily became flints as he replied: 'I've fought for a hell of a lot more than that, I can tell you.

You think Pangonian knights and soldiers are cause for concern? Try fighting a horde of man-eating plants, or a ravening demon of fire.'

The arch perfect of Westerburg, Otho – an ineffectual but inevitable contribution to court life – chose that moment to speak up. A silent man in his wintering years, he was rarely roused from his stuporous contemplation. Which Utha was generally grateful for. 'What blaspheming devilry is this the knight speaks of?' he wheezed, watery eyes struggling to focus on who'd just said something that actually interested him.

'More than you've elan enough to contend with,' Wrack-wulf shot back. 'Oh yes, I've held covenant with men of the Creed – and if the Argolians couldn't deal with the things I've seen, I doubt a common priest like you ever could!'

Otho's eyes, which looked like they bulged on the ends of stalks at the best of times, looked fit to pop out of their rheumy sockets. The murmurings in the court had turned sinister now. Talk of war was one thing, but nobody had expected words of this sort from a mercenary knight errant.

Otho had collected himself and was about to reply, but Utha raised a hand to silence him. For some reason, she thought of Adhelina, the runaway heiress of Dulsinor whom she'd sent a hand-picked trio of knights to seek a fortnight ago.

'Sir Wrackwulf, clearly you have weathered some very real dangers to be here now,' she said diplomatically. 'But your injuries and exertions have overtaxed you, methinks. Retire now to quarters, and please accept the comforts our best chirurgury can provide. After you are rested and treated, I shall grant you a private audience. For now, I would do like-wise with my son.'

Franz inclined his head deferentially, though he didn't

spare Wrackwulf another reproachful glance as the freelancer and his vagabonds left the courtroom.

'All men of arms here present – the training grounds *now*,' said Franz in his soft but firm voice. 'I'll be with you directly.'

The court knights lost no time in complying, leaving the high-born ladies to their gossip and intrigue. There would be plenty more of both this summer. Utha knew that much.

CHAPTER 5

LAST TO THE MUSTER

As soon as he began to reforge the weapon, Ereth knew it would be like no other. The first part of the process had been straightforward enough: taking the old sword apart and melting down the blade and tang, crosspiece, hilt and pommel had been just another day's work. But when he'd added the strange silvery sliver to the molten metal in the wolf-furnace, something peculiar had begun to happen.

It normally took Ereth a week working all the hours he could muster to forge a decent sword. The stranger had paid well, and every bit helped on the eve of war, so he hadn't minded. When he'd learned the next day that the stranger was none other than Sir Torgun, knight commander in the White Valravyn and Northalde's greatest warrior returned to them in their hour of need, Ereth had redoubled his efforts.

As it turned out, he almost hadn't needed to. The newly constructed piece of steel rippled under his hammer as he began to belt out the tang. By mid-afternoon of the third day, Ereth was convinced the metal was actually *helping* him. He'd heard that some master armourers spoke of an almost mystical aspect to sword-making; how the craftsman became

57

Nurë's agent, the un-angel of fire's right hand against Aurgelmir's flesh in the age-old struggle of weapon-making. That kind of talk was all well and good down south in the big cities, and Ereth had rightly never paid it much credence.

Now he was beginning to rethink his position. Only, this didn't feel so much like a struggle as...

Well, a *dance*, for want of a better word.

The steel (if that's what it was any longer) seemed to guide his hammer blows, urging him on, yielding to his craft with a willingness that no ordinary stubborn piece of iron would ever care to offer up. By the morning of the fifth day, Ereth was chiselling a fuller down the length of the newly crafted blade. It shouldn't have been this quick, this easy: all his instincts as an armourer and bladesmith of thirty years told him a blade rushed through like this one must surely break or bend before long. And yet something in him, a deeper instinct, told him it wouldn't.

At sunset, by which time he was running a whetstone of oiled lime up and down the edges, he had to pause. Not from tiredness, but sheer disbelief. Half a day's work had yielded a razor-like keenness that should have taken three; more than that, the bastard weapon felt light in his hand. The regular arming sword he'd been working on before was probably a shade heavier. The shimmering blade caught the dying rays of golden sun, as Northalde's summer shyly hinted at her long-awaited appearance in the weeks to come.

A shadow fell across the armourer. With a start he registered Sir Torgun, the exceptional knight who would wield this exceptional sword he'd had the honour of crafting.

'I see you are speeding well,' said the knight, nodding curtly. Despite having been at court for nearly a week, he was still clad in his travel-soiled black tabard and stained armour. They looked painfully at odds with the marvellous weapon both of them now scrutinised in the fading light.

'I've sped better than I could ever have expected,' muttered Ereth, hardly daring to give voice to his thoughts. Though well pleased with his work (was it even really his, he wondered?), this was undoubtedly a queer turn of events, too much in keeping with the fell rumours coming out of the Valhalla and Wyvern seas lately.

As if sensing his disquiet, the knight laid an iron hand on Ereth's shoulder. 'Have no fear,' he told the bladesmith. 'Rest assured, this is the Unseen's work you are about.'

Something in the knight's messianic tone unsettled Ereth even more. 'That's precisely what I'm afraid of,' he found the courage to say.

'We're all afraid,' replied Torgun, turning to stare out bleakly into the encroaching dusk. 'It's what we do with that fear that will matter.'

Ereth found another fragment of courage. 'Something... happened to you, didn't it, sir knight? On your travels, I mean...' He faltered. He knew the famous warrior's reputation for modesty, but the Torgun he'd heard the criers and troubadours tell of had been a worldly man, steeped in the affairs of the realm, with little cares beyond whatever the given day brought.

This bearded brooding giant seemed like something altogether different than the perfect gentle knight.

'Well, it's almost done anyway,' said Ereth, keen to change the subject. 'Just need to polish the quillons and wind the binding on to the hilt – I hope you don't mind, I'm just going to use shagreen. Nothing fancy as a blade such as this deserves, but we're nothing fancy this far up north, tell ye the truth.'

Torgun smiled wanly and shook his head. 'Nothing of the sort required – in fact shagreen will be perfect, it should facilitate the grip.'

Ereth nodded, content. 'As ye can see, the grip's in two

sections, should help with all those two-handed techniques you young knights seem to prefer these days.'

He paused again. Though he knew Torgun couldn't be more than five and twenty summers, it felt wrong to call him young somehow. Those blue eyes looked as old as the firmament itself.

But Torgun's thoughts were clearly elsewhere. 'Yes, that will be fine,' he said, not taking his eyes away from the skies. 'I won't be needing a shield where I'm going.'

Something in the way he said that set Ereth's hackles rising, though he couldn't say why. The armourer suddenly felt right keen to get this job done. All he wanted now was to go home to his wife and sons.

'You've more than excelled yourself,' said Torgun, again perhaps sensing his discomfort. 'Go home to your family. You can finish this up tomorrow – we aren't marching until the day after, so there's time.'

Ereth nodded again. One other thing that had slipped his mind occurred to him. 'What of the squi- I mean knight, Sir Vaskrian?' he asked. 'I heard you had him freed from the dungeons. I hope he's bearing up all right.'

Torgun's face darkened. 'He was most notoriously calumniated,' said the knight. 'He fares well enough, for one who spent weeks in captivity. He rides with us to war, I'm away to check on him now. The thirst for vengeance on his kidnappers burns in him, but his knightly honour will just have to wait for now. Yes, his knightly honour.' The looming knight said the last two words absently, as if they described a strange foreign idea, rather than the code he had lived his life by.

Just what in the Known World happened to you out there? Ereth wondered to himself. As Torgun strode off into gloom, the armourer had the feeling he would never find out. Perhaps that was just as well.

Vaskrian's limbs ached as he forced himself through another series of manoeuvres. No, his whole body ached. His wrists still chafed from weeks of being trussed up like a package; the dungeon manacles he'd spent the last few weeks wearing hadn't helped either. His ear had become infected too: the chirurgeon had treated it with a horrid-smelling poultice and assured him that if he kept it bandaged the wound would heal, eventually. But it still hurt like hell – every time he moved he felt as though someone had just struck him with a mace.

His legs still carried the bite marks from where the rat had gnawed him in his sleep, before he'd awoken and crushed it with his bare hands. He'd eaten the scullery half-empty since Torgun had ordered him to be released and transferred to the guest wing of the castle, but he was still painfully thin. On top of all that, his eldritch witch-wound was playing up again: the burn scars throbbed in the night, and when he looked at his pitiful reflection in the polished brass mirror in the corner of the room he and Torgun shared, he could swear at times that half of his face took on a strange luminous caste.

Look at what the Unseen make us give, he thought sadly. *And I don't even get to be treated like a proper knight when I come home.*

The unquenched desire for revenge welled up in him like sewage. But Harnal Cutter and his gang were long gone, taking with them all the booty they'd plundered from their captive. At least they'd left the sword Sir Aronn had given him behind: the bounty hunter would have been too smart to try to fence property of the White Valravyn.

He twirled it a couple more times for good measure: the only outward sign of his knighthood left to him, it was more precious than ever. His gilded spurs, his decorated belt, the armour and horses Rowena had given him, all gone. He and

Torgun had visited the armoury together, but on the eve of war there was hardly anything left. In the end, he'd been forced to settle for...

A shabby brigandine. The same choice article he'd started out with, here in Hroghar all those moons ago. You had to laugh. He'd been for challenging Rutgar on the spot, winner take all in a duel of honour to the death, but both the seneschal Sir Branton and Sir Torgun had forbidden it. Now was hardly the time for settling personal matters, with the future of the entire realm in jeopardy.

The annoying thing was, Vaskrian had known they were right. His adventures had taught him that much at least.

Sighing wearily, the young knight re-sheathed his sword and hung it up on the wall. As he did a glinting glaucous light caught his eye from the shelf nearby. One other possession Harnal and his men had left to him: the strange talisman the Earth Witch had gifted him in the Argael forest last summer seemed to glow softly in the gloaming. None of Harnal's thugs had rightly wanted to touch it, and when the bounty hunter himself had tried he'd pulled his hand away as though it had been frostbitten. It was the only time during their brief and painful association that his captor had looked at all cowed.

Picking it up, Vaskrian strung it about his neck, tucking it into his undertunic. It felt cold on his skin, but there was no bite to it; rather it seemed to refresh his flagging spirits.

I hope it brings me better luck than I've had of late, he thought to himself. *Where we're headed, I'll be needing it.*

Just then the door opened and Sir Torgun entered.

Sir Vaskrian sized him up again. He wasn't the only one to have been changed by the past year's tumultuous events. It wasn't just the beard or the anonymous black apparel of the knight errant: the change wrought in his hero had been internal. At first he'd supposed naively it was something to do with

Adhelina, the lady love he'd ultimately failed to win and been forced to abandon. The troubadours often sang of knights who fell into a deep depression of the spirits when such things happened to them, and Torgun was a knight straight out of bard's song.

But now he could see it was more than that, much more. Together they had witnessed many horrors, but on those accursed islands Torgun had been privy to something else... something altogether more personal, Vaskrian suspected, though the older knight was chary of revealing details.

'Ah, Sir Vaskrian, you are up and about – that's good,' said Torgun, the old formality returning. 'I trust each day renews your strength and vigour for the coming fight.'

Not quite how I'd put it. 'I'm faring as well as can be expected, Sir Torgun,' he managed. 'Though it'll be a while before I'm back to my best.'

'You'll have time on the road to continue your regimen,' replied the blond knight. 'And Stygnos knows, even your second best is better than many knights – you've proven that much already.'

Vaskrian flushed at the compliment. He still lionised Sir Torgun. Once the thought of riding off to war at his side would have thrilled him. Now... nothing quite so euphoric, but it still pleased him nonetheless.

'I'll do my best to be worthy of your praise,' said the younger knight. Glancing down at his worn apparel, he couldn't help adding: 'Though I could well wish for better harness.'

Sir Torgun nodded sympathetically. 'In two days' time we march south to join the muster in my homeland. I'll put in a word with my brother, Lord Toros – see if we can get you outfitted in something that befits your station.'

Befits my station, and more likely to keep me alive in a war. Not that he minded fighting one in light armour – Stygnos knew, he'd done most of his adventuring and campaigning with the bare minimum of equipment. And lived to tell the tale, though only just.

They took a light supper in their room before turning in. Before seeking his cot, Sir Torgun took out the circifix the Argolians had given him at Rima, kneeling in prayer and facing south towards the Redeemer's birthplace. Another thing that was different about the knight – the Unseen knew, he'd always been an exemplar of chivalry, but piety?

What good did taking up with the Temple ever do us, Vaskrian wondered disconsolately as he undressed for bed. He wondered absently how his old friend Adelko was doing. Probably cloistered up in his monastery down south, living a quiet cosy life.

Hroghar's few remaining occupants gathered to bid them a gloomy farewell. The Rodmonath sun was out, but that only belied the grim conflict they now rode to, Torgun knew. Next to him Sir Vaskrian exchanged hate-filled stares with Rutgar. The recreant would remain at home of course, while real knights went off to do the hard work. At least they'd managed to find a stout courser for the lad, he reflected as Vaskrian nudged the stallion around to face south. Intended more for hunting and carrying messengers than battle, it was no charger but would have to do for now.

Their immediate route took them through the Ferren Marshes. They were said to be haunted, but if they stuck to the causeway leading to Sjórvard, Lord Aesgir's coastal seat, their journey should be trouble-free if a little uncomfortable. Once again, Sir Torgun stroked the relic he wore about his neck. In truth, he had no idea if there was much difference between the old gods and the new, but one way or another the Unseen had seen fit to spare him thus far.

Torgun scanned the tree-topped hills haloed by the firmament with sad eyes. He knew full well Their munificence wouldn't last.

The Unseen serve no purpose but their own. So a half-mad hermit had told him once, during his first period of errantry. He hadn't paid the old man's words much heed back then. But that had been back then.

Sir Benedict gave the signal to set off. Together with squires they were about twenty strong, the last of the muster heading to Vandheim. Word had reached them that even the recalcitrant Woldings had turned up at last, the highland clans not far behind them.

We're mustering everything we have for a desperate last struggle, thought Torgun. Ordinarily such a heroic stand would have pleased him, but he could not get the thought of his erstwhile lover Hjala out of his mind, her bloodied corpse hanging from the walls of Strongholm. Once again he touched the relic, a silver circifix containing the fingerbone of St Argo gifted to him by monks of the Order for his failed quest in the Island Realms. He prayed that particular rumour was untrue. He had a nasty feeling it wasn't.

The two-day journey through the fens was uneventful. Shades howled at night, clearly unsettling Benedict and the other knights in their party, but Torgun and Vaskrian just exchanged wry glances. After all their adventures with Horskram, a few marsh ghosts and faeries were nothing to get worked up about. The presence of a great relic gave some comfort, bolstering the party's spirits, though one or two of the older knights clearly wondered how their hero had come by such a thing. The misty reek of the boglands seemed an eerie precursor to the doom they rode to meet: tales of the horrible toad-like creatures ravaging the coastlands loomed large in everyone's minds.

On the morning of their third day, when they emerged from the Ferrens to follow the river east towards its mouth, they began to see the first signs that the terrible tales were true. Villages razed from existence; that was a common enough sight in war, but the stinking burning corpses in piles were what really set the men's teeth on edge. Lord Aesgir's forces had managed to re-secure the area; the dead yeomen and women had been buried. The charred bodies were clearly not human: their stink put Torgun in mind of a poisonous fish he'd once accidentally cooked as a boy, before his father sternly informed him of his mistake.

Many of the men made the sign as they marched past the stinking mounds towards Sjórvard, one or two even insisting on touching the Rood of St Argo about Sir Torgun's neck. By late afternoon they saw it: Sjórvard castle stood on a promontory of rock overlooking the cliffs lashed by the Wyvern Sea. Built of limestone, its concentric cream-coloured walls bore no blemishes; whatever the fell creatures were, at least they used no siegecraft. But taking in the miserable camp of refugees that huddled without the citadel, Torgun knew that the invaders had done their work all too well: the thousand-yard stares that greeted their retinue could only belong to those who had simultaneously witnessed the horrors of war and those of the Other Side.

The steward of Sjórvard, a hunchbacked greybeard of seventy winters named Ralphus, was there to greet them in the castle keep's empty hall. Aesgir's wife Lady Valha had taken ill several nights ago, he explained, shutting herself up in her bedchamber with her two small children and wailing of dark kingdoms to come. Ralphus himself looked as though he'd rather not see that seventy-first winter. The thousand-yard stare had got into him, too.

'Such times we live in,' he muttered, staring absently about him with eyes that blinked once or twice before returning to wild openness. 'Such times...'

Torgun and Benedict pressed the old man for details, obtaining them with some difficulty over a snatched supper. A single war galley had remained in anticipation of their arrival; it lay to in the harbour of the town, waiting to take them and a final clutch of men-at-arms to the muster at Vandheim. A skeleton guard would remain to garrison the walls, in case the toad things came back.

'The sea demons attacked Vandheim two weeks ago, the same time as they came at us,' said Ralphus, his beard quivering as he told the story through lips that trembled. 'They managed to repulse them as well, thank Stygnos. The last we heard, they were ravaging the coasts farther south in greater numbers − along with reavers, who still seem hell-bent on taking slaves.'

'Possibly their aim is to keep the Southern Dominions pinned,' volunteered Sir Benedict. 'Prevent them from converging with the northern muster on Strongholm. Though what black sorceries those Northland idolators have conjured to have such devils for allies, I can barely fathom.'

I can fathom them well enough, if that Sea Wizard fellow is still allied to the reavers' cause, thought Torgun grimly. *Ezekiel knows, we left our work unfinished last year. Our victory at Linden was too swift, too easy − it could never forge a lasting peace.*

But something else had caught Torgun's attention. 'Slave-taking is a strange activity in the midst of a full-scale war,' he observed. 'The reavers would have to transport them back to their homeland − that means fewer fighting men for their invasion.'

'Aye, it is a peculiar thing,' allowed the old steward. Three cups of wine seemed to have revived his spirits somewhat, though he still looked terrified. 'Who can say what their motive is? These are not ordinary times.'

Torgun exchanged another knowing glance with Vaskrian across the table. The disfigured young knight had sat in sullen silence throughout the meal, keeping his own counsel.

Barely nineteen summers, and already he knows more about fighting the Other Side than every man here besides myself. A heavy burden for the lad to carry.

But that was the least of his concerns. Morphonus spurned Torgun cruelly that night, refusing him even a good night's sleep. He dreamed of giant toads with pointed teeth in wide mouths that opened up to devour him whole, while in the background winged serpents wreathed in fire laid waste to the land. His sword shone in his hand, but for every one of the things he cut down, two more appeared in its place.

The sun was still low when they boarded the *Gilded Pegasus* the following morning. One of Aesgir's fast-moving warships, crewed by sixty rowers, it would take them to Vandheim in a day. The thought of visiting his ancestral home lifted Torgun's spirits somewhat, but it saddened him too.

The last sip of wine is always the saddest, he thought, surprised he could remember a line from one of Maegellin's lays. Poetry had never been his strong point, but he was living it now he supposed.

Best not to dwell on it. His Wyrd had been ordained, perhaps as long ago as Søren's time. He carried the descendent of his ancestor's blade on his back: Ereth had fashioned it to be a shade longer than his old one, muttering something about the steel stretching further with the shard melded into it. The silvery sword felt light yet strong, and hummed with a deadly force whenever he practised with it. Ereth, though good at his trade, fell short of the master armourers of Staerkvit – yet the weapon had perfect balance, the like of which Torgun had never felt. He itched to use it, yet the thought of wielding a weapon steeped in legend and witchcraft appalled him too. Was it his imagination, or did the sacred rood he wore register silent disapproval whenever he strapped the thing on?

His reverie was broken by the captain giving the order to weigh anchor and cast off. The surging seas embraced them, and Torgun inhaled deeply of the briny air. Though he'd been born and raised a man of the land, returning to sea felt right – it had always run thickly in the blood of his kinsfolk.

We share the same ancestors as those who've come to conquer us – now here we are set on killing each other. Torgun's rising spirits stalled at the thought. Once upon a time he'd lived for war and quest, but they seemed increasingly futile to him. They always led to the same place in the end.

Torgun's gloom intensified as he felt his Wyrd gaining on him, speeding through an infinite dark space, borne aloft on Azrael's wings.

CHAPTER 6

OF HEARTH AND HOME

Braxus surveyed the wooden hall with gloomy eyes. The servants and page boys had done their best to make it look noble: hangings of fox fur and bearskin, standards emblazoned with the Fitzrow coat of arms, crossed swords and shields, even a tapestry sent from Ongist as a gift from King Cadwy. But it was still a motte-and-bailey hall for all that.

A fine seat for a victorious lord of men, thought Braxus miserably. But his ancestral home would take many moons to restore; some of the master restorers and upholsterers were even talking about years.

The highland savages burnt it down in a day, he reflected. *Always so much easier to destroy than to build.*

That wasn't quite true. It had taken him two months of hard campaigning to wipe out the Brekken highlanders. Looking at his primitive surroundings, hastily erected during his absence, Braxus found himself wishing there were some more of them to kill.

If it wasn't against the law, I'd have taken a few slaves. The brutal thought wasn't out of place nowadays. He'd been home for a tenday, but the darkness of war remained on him like a shroud. His advisers had come and gone, newly appointed men to the offices of constable, treasurer and steward, plus half a dozen other lesser positions. In truth, he'd barely registered any of them. His sleep was troubled by dark dreams of his adventures: spectres and monsters that rose from the grave of suppressed memory to haunt him at night.

Braxus took another sip of the souring wine. Also a gift from Cadwy, the keg of Armandy red was near done: after that he'd be back to mead. He'd tried wenching a couple of times, but been unable to perform: thoughts of his long-lost lady love Adhelina had also returned to plague him.

If I could have won her heart, perhaps things could have been different. The thought, irrational as it was, tormented him. Where was she now? Probably still being held at Rima, a pawn for King Carolus in his games of high politicking. Once or twice he'd thought about despatching a messenger to the distant Pangonian court, but something had stayed his hand. He had a ward to run, after all, though his duties as a lord pleased him far less than he had hoped.

Truth to tell, for all the pain it had brought him, he yearned for the road again. His father had tried to instil in him a sense of responsibility as the firstborn son, but that was one of many things he and the old man had never seen eye to eye on. War and quest and romance might be hazardous things, but the thrills they brought were unsurpassed. Last year he'd been involved in a secret undertaking to save the Known World: now his part in that was done and here he was, relegated to shepherding this backwater towards some kind of civilised existence.

Braxus drained his cup and ran his fingers through his long auburn locks... before remembering they weren't there any more. He'd shaved them off, thinking a shorter cut more manly. At least he'd grown in his beard a bit, in an effort to look more regal. At the end of the year he would look upon his thirtieth winter, oft seen as the threshold of middle age. Siona knew he felt old enough, but none of the archangel's grace seemed to have come with that.

He called loudly for more wine. He was determined to finish off the keg this afternoon: might as well have some fun while he could. Next week he'd receive his first arranged marriage proposal. From what he'd heard, Lord Cael's daughter Elyn had a face like an ox and the wits to match, but the ruler of Varrogh had proved a stalwart ally, and he was a neighbour. Politically, the match made sense, and Elyn's dowry would go a long way towards paying the craftsmen restoring Gaellen castle.

He was rudely interrupted by the castle herald, Fanwyn, entering and banging his staff of office down on the wooden floorboards.

'I've told you before not to do that,' snapped Braxus.

'Apologies, sire, but it's protocol,' replied Fanwyn. 'Your father always emphasised the importance of - '

'Yes, yes, yes,' sighed Braxus impatiently. 'What is it? I presume we have a visitor. And who comes to see us this fine summer morning? One of Lord Cael's squires to check all is ready to receive him? Let them rest assured – we may be living like peasants trussed up in wood not stone, but we still know how to entertain noble guests.'

Fanwyn shifted uncomfortably. 'Actually no, my lord,' he said sheepishly. 'It's your brother, Drojan.'

Braxus paused at his stoup. His brother? He hadn't laid eyes on his younger sibling since he'd left to take holy orders more than a decade ago. Hadn't thought of him much either: they'd hardly been close.

'So the prodigal son returns,' deadpanned Braxus, struggling to hide his surprise behind his irony. 'Better show him in then.'

Drojan had grown into his five-and-twenty summers, but that was about all you could say for the man. Half a head shorter than Braxus, the only family trait he shared with him was the auburn hair. His face was flatter, his forehead higher, the shoulders narrower. In every way, dressed in the black scapular and robes of a mendicant friar of the Temple, he looked inferior.

The counterweight to that was that his little brother had a towering intellect. Some said he might have gone for an Argolian, if only his psychic intuition had been keener. But Drojan was a man of this world, not the next: the last Braxus heard, he'd set off for foreign lands to preach and panhandle for money wherever he might. That had hardly come as a surprise: by the time he left home at fourteen Drojan already spoke six languages fluently.

'Brother – or should I say Father – well met,' said Braxus, raising his goblet in mock salute. 'Pray join me in a stoup of wine, but you'll have to hurry, for there's not much left.'

Drojan bowed perfunctorily. 'My lord and kinsman Braxus,' he said in velvet tones. 'I see the years have only ripened your appetites. At least you don't have to steal mead from the castle kitchens any more.'

'You, if I recall, were invited to join us on those adventures, but roundly refused,' said Braxus. 'Hardly my fault if my little brother doesn't know how to enjoy life.'

Drojan smiled brittlely. 'Oh, I enjoy life well enough,' he said. 'In service to the Redeemer. Can you say the same?'

Braxus glared at him. 'If I told you half the things I've done in service to the Redeemer, that scapular of yours would turn white,' he said coldly.

'So I've been hearing,' said Drojan. 'Some gossip about a secret quest with the legendary Argolian monk Horskram. And then of course the wars here and in Northalde, followed by a campaign of extermination in the Brekkens. You've been busy haven't you, brother?'

Braxus felt his face souring along with his mood. 'What do you want, Drojan?' he snapped. 'Some of us have real work to do, rebuilding a realm – why aren't you abroad wheedling commoners out of money they can't spare to feed the fat priests of your precious Temple?'

'As a matter of fact, I was,' replied Drojan, apparently unfazed by the jibe. 'But the Northlendings are at war again – it was no longer safe for a perfect of the Creed, so I decided to return home across the mountains and pay my older brother a long-delayed visit.'

'Oh yes, I've been hearing about that,' said Braxus, ignoring the sarcasm. 'Something about the Northland thegns invading, they want to take their old colonies back. Good luck to them – I've seen what Northlending cavalry can do to berserker footmen.'

'Then perhaps it will surprise you to learn that the Northlanders have taken Strongholm.'

Braxus almost let go of his goblet. That *was* a surprise.

Drojan smiled wryly. 'You really have been preoccupied with your own back yard, haven't you? That news is winging its way across every pass in the Hyrkrainians. The Northlendings are trying to muster a fightback out of Efrilund and the southern Dominions, but they're really up against it. "The rock of ages shall be used to break the prideful in their complacency," as the Redeemer sayeth. And the Northlendings, it seems, grew very complacent after you fought with them last year. Something about the new king Wolfram going mad and planning to invade *us*, when he should have been looking east.'

'Well, if the Northlendings were foolish enough to consider breaking peace with us, perhaps they got what they deserved,' said Braxus coolly. His association with Northlendings, particularly his love rival Torgun, had done little to erase any of his prejudices.

'I think you're missing the point, brother,' said Drojan, pointedly dropping all pretence of calling him lord. 'The Northland army are led by a single ruler, the Shield Queen they call her. Rumour has it black sorceries ride in her wake, though I know nothing of such things. But either way, they look set to conquer Northalde. And once that's done, who's to say they'll stop there? Northalde used to be part of the old Westerling empire, before it was taken by the reavers of old. Some loremasters say the rulers of the time, Olav Ironhand among them, considered crossing the mountains to finish the job and take the entire peninsula.'

Braxus took a thoughtful sip of wine. Now his brother was saying things that interested him. 'You really think their descendants' ambitions might run so high? The Ice Thegns haven't conquered anything in centuries – surely one mainland kingdom would be enough for them.'

Drojan shrugged. 'You know more of military men than I do,' he said. 'I'm just saying it's a possibility, don't you think?'

Braxus took another sip. His brother had certainly given him something to ponder. 'All right, thank you for the information,' he said politely, before narrowing his eyes. 'I can only assume you want something in return for it.'

His brother grinned then. 'What more could a kinsman ask for than hearth and board, at his ancestral home?' He spread his arms emphatically, indicating the rude wooden motte with mock grandeur.

'I've no coin to spare for donations, so that's all you'll be getting,' said Braxus, not unsmiling. His younger brother was every bit as snide and irritating as he remembered, but all the same it was good to see a kinsman alive and well. Their only other sibling to survive childhood had perished in a riding accident some years before Drojan left home.

As if reading his thoughts, Drojan said: 'By your leave, brother, I'd pay a visit to the family plot. I presume those paganers didn't burn that down too. It has been many a summer since I looked upon Elowyn's grave.'

'You might also pay your respects to our father's while you're there,' said Braxus pointedly. Drojan nodded reluctantly, before turning to leave. His little brother hadn't seen eye to eye with the old man either, but for different reasons. Braun had raised both his sons in the Creed, but while Braxus hadn't taken the lessons much to heart his brother had done so rather too much for their father's liking. The final straw had been on the eve of Drojan's leaving, when he'd accused his father in front of the entire household of being a godless man for shedding blood.

War is the age-old duty of a knight and a lord, you sententious fool, had been Braun's scathing rebuke that night.

And peace is the duty of all who would know the Redeemer's embrace at the Final Hour, had been his brother's comeback.

Little Drojan. Always so clever; too clever by half. Though he approved of his younger son's decision to take orders, Lord Braun had never forgiven him such hurtful remarks, and forbidden the family from mentioning him under his roof ever again.

Braxus sighed at the recollection. All water under the bridge now, in any case. Better to dwell on the present than the past. And right now, the present was getting interesting again. The Northlendings at risk of being conquered – he'd never thought to see that in his lifetime, unless of course...

It had to be linked to the Sea Wizard, and Horskram's secret mission. The mission he was no longer part of.

Braxus spent the afternoon as planned, finishing off his wine. His brother did not return, leaving him time to himself to think. And think he did. He pondered, he weighed, he reflected.

And when he'd finished the last drop of Armandy red, he called for his squire.

'Saddle my courser, and yours,' he told the youth. 'And load a sumpter with the necessary supplies for a journey. Have Fanwyn send message to Lord Cael that I'm away on urgent business, I'll have to delay his visit until the next moon. He's also to summon every vassal within a country mile and tell them to be here by tomorrow morning, ready to travel as well.'

Erawyn was a stout lad of a good family, anxious to please but curious of spirit as well. 'That I'll do gladly, my lord,' he said. 'But may I ask where we're going?'

'You may,' said Braxus, smiling more to himself than Erawyn. 'We're going to Ongist, to pay the King a visit.'

CHAPTER 7

A SUNDERING OF HEROES

From up the darkened coastline, the winking lights of Shazra'am beckoned them. Adelko took a deep breath of cool night air. After weeks of adventuring in strange places, a mundane city would be welcome – albeit a foreign one he'd never visited.

Next to him, Abdel Sha'arza rested his hand gently on the glowing crystal that guided the *Chariot of the Skies*. In its pulsing febrile light, the sorcerer's long lacquered fingernails looked like talons. The young journeyman didn't care much for the effect.

'This is as close as I can bring you,' said Sha'arza. 'I'll set her down in a cove and you can make your way along the coastal road to Shazra'am. From there you should be able to take ship to Montrevellyn – though why your superior wants to return to a viper's nest is beyond me.'

Adelko sighed. He wasn't sure going back to the Most Reverend Priory of St Argo was such a good plan either. 'You know Master Horskram well enough by now,' said the journeyman. 'He still thinks we can expose Hannequin and stop him. We left the fourth fragment safe at Ortiz, so I suppose there's still time.'

'But you have no evidence,' protested the sorcerer, bringing the ship down towards the lashing seas. Adelko fancied he could smell the briny surf already. The wind whistled raw about his cowl.

'Our word against his,' Adelko acknowledged gloomily. 'At least the wider Temple will be happy to support our claims. I'm sure His Supreme Holiness Cyprian has been waiting for a chance like this for years.'

That was the worst part of Horskram's plan. Returning to the Pangonian capital Rima amid treachery, skulduggery, war and crusade was bad enough; seeking the Temple's support was even worse. Cyprian, the very same man who'd put his mentor in irons and tortured him during the Purge some twenty years ago; Cyprian, the man who would happily see the entire Argolian Order destroyed in the here and now given half a chance. And that was undoubtedly precisely what they were going to give Cyprian, if their new mission succeeded: Adelko had worked for years to become an accepted member of a fraternity that would soon no longer exist. He despised the thought, as vain and selfish and unbefitting a disciple of the Redeemer, but it plagued him nonetheless.

The warlock shook his head. 'Don't be surprised if this Cyprian doesn't put your heads on the block as well,' he said, clearly divining Adelko's thoughts. 'I say this plan is folly.'

'You're probably right,' Adelko allowed. 'But what else can we do?'

The black cliffs of the night-shrouded bay loomed up to embrace them with rocky arms, as Sha'arza flashed a pearly smile in the crystal's eldritch light. 'You could run like the North Wind, is what you could do,' he said, before muttering an incantation. A tortured creaking sound marked the retraction of the *Chariot's* side wings; for a short while, Sha'arza's enchanted vessel would become an ordinary seafaring ship.

'And just where would we run to?' Adelko asked pointedly, grasping the taffrail as the *Chariot* hit the seas with a crashing splash. Now they had left the starry embrace of the night skies, they were flanked on all sides by pitch darkness; Sha'arza had ordered his elemental Saraphi to wink out as they drew closer to land, for fear of terrifying the shepherds that grazed their flocks on the foothills overlooking the northern coastal lands of Murad.

'Anywhere but western Urovia,' replied the sorcerer, answering Adelko's question.

'It's where I'm from,' protested Adelko. 'I can hardly flee my home.'

Sha'arza fixed him with one of his sly looks, before giggling: 'Are you sure that isn't what you've spent the past few years doing?'

I suppose I shouldn't be surprised when a sorcerer turns out to be clever, Adelko thought wryly.

'You might have me there,' he allowed.

The sorcerer's face grew serious again. 'Listen to me, Adelko of Narvik,' he said, scrutinising the journeyman in the gloom. The crystal had gone dark, but by Sha'arza's command a handful of the fiery Saraphi had winked back into life, providing just enough light to see by. 'Your mentor – as I have said before – is far too set in his ways to be swayed from them. In time it will fall to the apprentice to lead where the master cannot.'

'But I'm not what you think I am. I'm just – '

'No, don't interrupt me,' he added, wagging a taloned finger in Adelko's face. 'Your modesty does you credit as always, but I don't have time for it now. My mother once told me "the fires weave a crooked path around the fates of mortalkind" – and I for one believe her words were correct.

Your journey may lie north again for now – but in time you will return south, and sooner time than you think! My own scrying has hinted at as much.'

Adelko made to respond, but again the wizard silenced him. 'When that time comes, I shall be ready to aid you in whatever way I can. The force you call Wyrd and others fate or destiny cannot be gainsaid or averted – we all must play our part in it, even an old demonolator like me.' The sorcerer gave one of his characteristic desultory giggles, which seemed to Adelko quite out of place with the gravity of his words.

Heedless of the monk's misgivings, he reached into the folds of his crimson cape and produced something. A fire-stone on a silver pendant, it caught the light of the nearby Elementi, seeming to amplify it. Before Adelko could protest, the wizard pressed it into his hand. It felt warm to the touch.

'With this you and I can communicate,' the sorcerer told him. 'No ordinary mortal unversed in the arts could use it, but you are no ordinary mortal. Your elan will enable you to attune yourself.'

'But that's blasphemy!' said Adelko, instinctively recoiling. Sha'arza fixed him with a curious look, and the journeyman suddenly remembered Arnulf of Balzac's treatise, the one he'd read in the great library at the Grand High Monastery in Rima.

Argolians and witches are but two halves of a whole.

Sha'arza, seeming to read his thoughts again, nodded. 'You understand far better than you let on, journeyman of the Order,' he said. His face became cunning again. 'Keep this talisman safe and hidden. Above all, make sure your mentor doesn't know you have it! You'll know when the right time comes to use it.'

Before Adelko could say anything more, the sorcerer bustled past him and began to descend to the main deck. 'Come along,' he said, sounding disconcertingly like

Horskram for a moment. 'We must rouse your mentor from his vigil – and of course there's the matter of that blackguard of a thief to deal with.'

Adelko frowned. What with everything, he'd almost forgotten about Hari Yassin. Trust the rogue to get himself into trouble.

~

'But it was just sitting there, asking to be pinched!' said Hari, no longer even bothering to struggle against the invisible force that held him pinned fast. 'You'd have done just the same, in my position!'

Anupe leaned back against the wall of the cabin, folding her arms insouciantly. 'Actually, no, I wouldn't,' she said. 'Stealing artefacts from a powerful wizard strikes me as – how do you put it? – idiotic.'

A faraway look entered the rogue's eyes. 'But the egg, you should have *seen* it, Anupe,' he breathed. 'So *beautiful*... not just for being fashioned of solid gold, you understand. Ah, those intricate carvings...!'

'Abdel Sha'arza did specifically warn you not to go poking around his things while we were in Ortiz with the Old Master of Time's Arrow,' sighed Anupe. 'You are lucky not to have triggered a worse trap.'

Hari became petulant again. 'A worse trap!? You try being frozen in place for several days,' he snapped.

'Well, you should have thought about that before your greed got the better of you,' smirked Anupe. 'And at least the sorcerer left you free to talk – and to breathe.'

In truth, the Harijan warrior wondered if it was just mere greed that had impelled the thief. Hari was no fool, and an experienced freebooter – surely he should have known better? Anupe suspected some kind of sorcery at work, though to what purpose she hadn't yet fathomed.

She would get no counsel on the matter from the others. The four holy men – Horskram, Tipu, the Zarumani, and Azelin – had taken to their private cabins. The revelation at Ortiz of Hannequin's betrayal had shocked them all, but none more than the Argolian. Ever since they had boarded the *Chariot* and left the Silver Shadow's stronghold in the Cerulean mountains behind, he had refused to emerge, insisting on taking meals alone in his room.

Hardly surprising, seeing as it's your leader who turned out to be the mastermind all this time, thought Anupe. *So much for the deductive power of the Argolians. Perhaps I should not have been so hasty to kill Andragorix – Hannequin's apprentice might have saved us all a very long journey.*

But no: the demonologist had killed her lover Kyra, he had deserved to die. Besides, what concern of hers was all of this? Her people had lived in the shadow of the Forbidden Isle for centuries – now that shadow was lengthening, let others feel the fear the Harijans felt.

The warrior-woman bit her lip. And yet, the priestesses of Hamazos had often spoken of a time like this, when the world would teeter on the brink and be forced to choose between life and death... And she had been given a part to play in the Godsgame, that much was clear.

What a part! To fight so many enemies and come all this way, only to fail.

Try as she might to pretend not to care, the thought of it galled her.

Her reverie was interrupted by Abdel Sha'arza and Adelko returning below decks.

'I take it we have, ahem, landed?' asked the Harijan. 'I think I felt something a minute ago.'

Abdel giggled, more nervously than usual Anupe thought.

'You are indeed correct,' he said. 'We are now berthed in a cove, a league or so from Shazra'am.'

'Ah, that is good,' said Anupe, trying to lighten her mood. 'I look forward to tasting some of this legendary Muradi wine I heard about in Ushalayim.'

'Wine?' barked Hari. 'I haven't had anything to *eat* for three days!'

Sha'arza squared up to the rogue. 'Be thankful I haven't turned you into a larder rat,' he snapped.

'Only Proteana mastered Transformation well enough to transmogrify someone against their will,' put in Adelko with a wry grin. 'I think you've punished him enough – why don't you just let him go?'

'For the love of Luviah, yes!' groaned Yassin. 'Bad enough I'm starving to death that I can barely move a muscle.'

'At least I left you able to move your mouth, you scurrilous poltroon,' said Sha'arza implacably.

'Yes, I did point this out to him myself,' offered Anupe helpfully. In truth she was rather enjoying the spectacle, but indulging her sardonic humour was fast becoming an old pasttime. 'Are you going to let him go, or not? As much as I've enjoyed your hospitality, I for one am anxious to get to Shazra'am and enjoy – how do you put it? – firm ground again.'

Sha'arza nodded, and fixed Hari with another stern look. 'Indeed, indeed,' said the wizard. 'But first I must decide what final punishment to mete out to this rascal.'

And now we come to it, thought Anupe. *The wizard's ploy.*

All of them instinctively flinched back as Sha'arza dropped without warning into the hateful sorcerer's speech: as long as she lived, Anupe felt she would never get used used to its jarring syllables and alien inflections. A queer look came over Hari Yassin, and before anyone realised quite what had happened he was free, rubbing his limbs awkwardly.

'By Ashanti, but that feels good!' he murmured, sighing gratefully. 'So you're letting me go, hey? I must say, your kind munificence does you credit - '

Sha'arza raised a hand to silence him. 'You will not speak until I tell you to.'

Hari obediently closed his mouth.

'You feel most abundantly regretful of your rash decision to try to rob me,' Abdel continued. 'In fact, you are most willing and eager to do penance. Having realised that the redoubtable Urovian monks may need someone of your guile and resourcefulness, you have decided to offer them your service until death or victory, in the dark days ahead. As the wronged party in this affair, I approve said penance and bind you by geas to fulfil it. That is all – you may speak now.'

Hari opened his mouth, then shut it again.

'I cannot help but observe,' said Anupe with some amusement. 'That of late, Hari Yassin's guile and resourcefulness – as you put it – have not served him so well.'

Sha'arza tipped a wink at the Harijan. 'He won't have me to contend with in future,' he said. 'I saw him coming from a league away, but others may not.'

I'm quite sure you did – was that egg treasure even real, I wonder, or just a conjured bait trap?

Anupe kept that question to herself as another door opened and Horskram entered the cabin.

'Ah, so you're back below decks, Sha'arza,' said the old monk, his nose wrinkling. 'I thought I detected the stench of sorcery.'

'Sorcery that has procured you a new companion for your latest fool's errand,' replied Sha'arza, unfazed. 'This knave has just volunteered to return with you to Pangonia and assist you in any way he can.'

Anupe and Adelko exchanged looks, but surprisingly the older monk did not demur. 'I won't ask the exact means by which you secured his pledge,' said Horskram. 'But I'm willing to bet it's a better-binding fetter than the word of a thief.' The adept turned a hollow glance Hari's way. 'I don't suppose there's much point in even trying to talk you out of this?'

The rogue shook his head emphatically. 'Til death or victory, by your side I am bound,' he said, with a sickly-sweet enthusiasm that made Anupe feel queasy.

'I do hope you aren't as persuasive when it comes to deciding where the rest of us should go,' said the Harijan, looking meaningfully at Sha'arza.

The mage giggled his customary giggle. 'Oh never fear,' he said. 'You are a free spirit – free as fate allows to wander where you will.'

Free as fate allows, yes – and since when have any who played the Godsgame been free of fate?

'I can't deny yon thief's skills have proved useful and may yet,' sighed Horskram. 'And frankly, now I've made common cause with a Left-Hand warlock, I can't go any lower for company.'

'A thousand thank-yous,' muttered Hari, still rubbing his cramping muscles, though if Sha'arza was offended by Horskram's remark he hid it well.

'And what of your other companions?' the sorcerer asked, giggling again. 'You have an apostate warrior-priest, a pagan fire-worshipper and a heathen Sassanian to choose from the rest of your unsavoury allies.'

Horskram shot the sorcerer a wry glance. 'As it happens, I've just been talking to said unsavoury allies,' he said. 'Tipu and the Zarumani intend to return south to Nazharya. Something about reconnoitring with General Zimri at Muqmurlish's army camp. As for Brother Sir Azelin... he's been even more reclusive than I have of late. Where he goes next is anyone's guess.'

'I'm coming with you.'

They all turned to see the disgraced warrior-monk standing in the doorway, looking even more gaunt and dishevelled than usual. 'I'll not spend a minute more in the Blessed Realm than I have to. And I'd sooner take my chances with the Order back in Pangonia than in the Pilgrim Kingdoms.'

Anupe chose that moment to speak up. 'Are you sure of this? You could stay here in Murad – they are Unorthodox, they won't mind a fugitive Bethler.'

Azelin sneered. 'No, and they won't mind killing a fugitive Bethler either, once Tobin puts a bounty on my head. I'm going to Pangonia – to petition the King for a pardon and try to get my lands back.'

Horskram looked at the fallen hero dubiously. 'You suddenly seem rather motivated to go on with life,' he observed dryly. 'When we plucked you from that fighting pit in Sha'iza'ar you didn't seem to care whether you lived or died.'

Azelin favoured Horskram with one of his nasty grins. 'Let's just say that learning you've failed to save the world from impending disaster has put some wind back in my sails – now everyone knows my pain, and we're all in it together!'

The old monk shook his head. 'Your self-pity disgusts me,' he said.

'Oh no – it's you I feel pity for, Horskram of Vilno,' said Azelin. 'You still labour under the delusion that you can somehow set things right. But there is no setting things right, if half of what I've heard is true.' The grin soured to an ugly grimace. 'Let's face the truth – mortalkind has been abed with the Fallen One since the First Clarion, now it's time to make the clinch official and wed him. If that means going down in a blaze of glory, then so be it! If I offer to fight for King Carolus, I might get my castle in Valacia back just in time for the war to end all wars – then I can die with a host of men behind me, as befits the true knight I once was. A decent ending, that's all I'm after – Abaddon can do what he likes with my soul after that.'

Stunned silence greeted the outburst.

'Well, that settles that then,' said Abdel Sha'arza after a pause, doing his best to sound genial.

Horskram sighed deeply and turned to Anupe. 'What about you?' he queried. 'We've asked more than enough of you – and besides that I've run out of coin to pay you any further for your services.'

Oh, how sad you seem at our impending parting.

But Anupe kept her sarcasm to herself too as she replied: 'I will venture south with the two Sassanians. By the sounds of it, there will be plenty of work for a freesword in Muqmurlish's army – and I for one aim to be on the winning side in this Fourth Pilgrim War! I haven't quite given up on the world just yet.'

Though I can't say Azelin doesn't have a point either.

She hesitated, then made up her mind to say something more. 'For what it is worth, Master Horskram, I am deeply sorry our venture did not end in success... It has been a strange honour to share the road with you.'

She favoured the monk with an awkward half-bow. Anupe rarely bowed before a man, yet somehow she felt the old monk deserved the courtesy. An irate patrician he might be, but all he had ever done was try to serve the best interests of mortalkind.

I can't think of many men – or women – I could say that about.

Horskram mirrored her awkward bow with one of his own. 'And though I would not normally sanction common cause with a pagan swordswoman, I cannot deny you have been a stalwart companion on what has been a dark and crooked path,' he said, drawing on protocol.

'This is all very touching,' said Azelin, 'but I for one am

famished. I've spent the past day and night fasting, and would fain get some food and drink inside me.'

'Fasting?' queried Abdel with a smirk. 'Have you rediscovered your faith as well as your warrior spirit on the eve of destruction, sir knight? Perhaps Grand Master Tobin might even be prepared to forgive your sins, if you ask him most cordially…'

'Don't try me,' growled Azelin. 'It's your tasty cooking I crave before we leave, not your saucy wit.'

'But of course!' smiled the sorcerer. 'It shall be arranged directly – a final repast to see my guests off on their merry way! Let us send for the fire priest and the mystic – we shall all break bread together one last time.'

Yes, one last time, thought Anupe uneasily. *One last time… before what?*

CHAPTER 8

A BRIEF RETURN TO THE HEARTH

Torgun gazed on the grey walls of his ancestral home. Vandheim was similar in design to Sjórvard, but for the third concentric wall that lay in a state of inchoacy about the second.

My older brother's grand project, thought Torgun wryly. *A pity the reavers didn't leave him a few more years to complete it.*

The masons and other craftsmen had long abandoned the essential work; now instead they were joined to the war camp that lay in the crook of the hill upon which Vandheim sat, nestling between the castle and the River Rymold. Hundreds of pennons ruffled in the high winds, the variegated coats of arms a sight to raise the spirits: enough men of arms had answered the muster to give some hope of recourse against the invaders.

Some, though not much.

The crew was already steering the ship upriver towards the camp. Sir Vaskrian came and joined Sir Torgun at the taff-rail. The young knight still looked a ghastly sight; half-starved gaunt features made only less wholesome by his mutilated ear and eldritch burn scars. Once more Torgun felt his own tingle uncomfortably across his chest; his own legacy of their deadly fight with Andragorix the previous year.

It wasn't the only thing that made him feel uncomfortable. Nothing Torgun had heard suggested the rumours were untrue: Princess Hjala, his erstwhile lover, and Queen Aeselif, his own sister germane, decorated the walls of Strongholm along with those of other high-ranking members of the royal family. The Shield Queen of the Frozen Principalities had showed no mercy to the rulers she had usurped, still less to those of her own sex.

Perhaps that's what our family deserves, for letting our sister marry a hothead like Wolfram. Torgun was well aware the thought was treasonous, and wouldn't have been capable of it more than a year ago. But everything had changed since then.

We married into a doomed house – now we get to share in their tragedy.

Sir Vaskrian was looking at him askance. 'Sir Torgun, are you well? You've got one of your faraway looks again.'

The older knight smiled wanly. 'Forgive me, Sir Vaskrian,' he said gently. 'Brooding times.'

'You're not wrong there,' muttered the erstwhile squire, plucking reproachfully at his tatty armour. 'I can't wait to be out of this wretched brigandine. Some decent harness might cheer a fellow up, you know?'

Torgun's smile broadened slightly. *If only that was all I had to be concerned about,* he thought. *Yet somehow the lad's humour cheers me.*

Torgun stifled his reverie. Gloomy self-pity might befit a romantic love-lorn knight, but he'd ceased to be such months ago. Now was the time for heroes to fight and die.

'Have no fear, Sir Vaskrian,' he said kindly. 'I'll speak with my brother and we'll have you outfitted in good mail as befits a valiant knight.'

Vaskrian smiled at that and drew himself up. 'You know, it

still thrills me to hear that. Valiant knight...' The youthful gallant took a deep breath of incipient summer, now perceptible in the slightly warmer air, and gazed upon the pennoned camp with a faraway look of his own.

Torgun's smile half froze on his lips. What did Wyrd have in store for the young Efrilunder? The apparition had only shown Torgun his own fate in that blasted wilderness in the Island Realms. Yet more thoughts he didn't care for.

The captain was barking a final round of orders at his crew, who were bringing their galley in to nestle among the forty-odd others that composed the Efrilund navy.

At least five ships fewer than we used to have, thought Torgun. *Actually, I'm pleasantly surprised. Without the King's brother Thorsvald to command them, I would have expected worse losses.*

But there would be no Thorsvald to lead them, because the Prince himself was lost; his body decorated the walls of the capital along with Hjala's and Walsa's and Aeselif's, if all the grim tales told it true.

The two knights disembarked with haste and made their way to the centre of the camp with Sir Benedict and his retinue. Torgun found his brother gathered around a table in the main pavilion, discussing the impending war with the other nobles of northern Northalde.

Lord Toric of Runstadt, High Commander of the White Valravyn, was there; along with the Efrilund barons Lord Aesgir of Sjórvard, Lord Vymar of Harrang, and Lord Fenrig of Hroghar. The Wolding lords and Highland chieftains were present as well; clustered about the nobles were bannerets and other high-ranking vassals and officers.

The great and good of the realm's northern chivalry – I only hope it's enough.

Perhaps word had reached Toros of his brother's long-delayed homecoming, or perhaps he just had his Jedrez face on: either way he didn't betray much surprise.

'Tis right good to see you in our hour of need, brother,' was all he said.

'The road has been a long one and a hard,' replied Torgun, returning protocol. 'But it has brought me back. What news? That I've heard of late has been little but foul.'

The assembled nobles exchanged uneasy glances. In the light of the braziers Torgun could see many were ashen-faced.

'If worst you've heard, then truest I fear,' said Toros, the words falling leaden from his lips.

Pain flared across Torgun's breast again, only this time it was pain of the heart that no sorcerer's spell could hope to conjure. 'All dead then?' was all he could manage.

Toros nodded sombrely. 'But for the King – whom they keep alive as... as a plaything of their barbarous court – 'twoud be regicide. The House of Ingwin is all but extinguished.'

'But what of Wolfram's babes? Young Freidhrim and Freidha, surely they were spared – even the Northlanders have a custom to spare the family of the vanquished!'

'Not these Northlanders,' growled Aesgir. A big burly man by nature, well used to the hearty life of a sea commander, he looked like a drawn wineskin now. 'Rumour has it the same foul wizardry that sped them to our shores and invoked demons of the deep in their wake has poisoned the mind of this Shield Queen. She is altogether without mercy.'

'What comes of putting a woman in charge,' muttered Vymar sullenly, though few had appetite for his misogyny.

Toros put a hand to his sword hilt. 'Rest assured, Sir Torgun, not one man here will rest until these invaders are put in their graves, or we in ours. No expense or effort shall be spared in this coming conflict, no quarter asked or given.'

The gathered nobles managed to voice some spirit at that, though it was obvious all were shaken badly.

'You have proof of this?' demanded Torgun, trying in vain

to keep his emotions in check. Tears limned his eyes for all to see, but not even the stoical Northlending nobility would chide him for unmanliness given the cause of his sorrow.

'As much proof as the eyes can tell,' sighed Toros. 'Outriders reported the bodies hanging from the walls a month ago. One of them was so grief-stricken that he died in sin on his own sword rather than endure such a spectacle. This is no false rumour, brother – our kinsfolk and most of the royal family are dead.'

Sir Vaskrian chose that moment to be his usual hothead self. 'Then we'll kill every last one of them,' he thundered. 'Northland scum – when we're done cleaning up here, we'll sail for the Frozen Wastes and serve them a taste of their own justice!'

Eyebrows rose. 'Sir Torgun, I think your squire speaks out of turn,' said Aesgir diplomatically.

Fenrig was staring at Vaskrian. He hadn't noticed him at first in his shabby attire, or maybe the scars and a month in a dungeon had rendered Torgun's companion unrecognisable.

'This is no regular squire,' exclaimed the Jarl of Hroghar, pointing an accusing finger at Vaskrian. 'And no squire at all, if I have my way – this man is a fugitive from justice! I recently had word he'd been apprehended and left to rot below my keep, what in Gehenna's name is he doing squiring for the realm's greatest knight!?'

'He isn't,' replied Torgun evenly, laying a restraining hand on Vaskrian's arm. 'Sir Vaskrian is a belted knight, as witnessed by myself and many other noble men born to arms. He has been calumniated and wrongly accused, the which his accusers shall answer for once this war is done. I explained this to your steward and had him freed immediately I realised he was being held without merit.'

Torgun met the proud lord's eye, silently daring him to gainsay him.

Fenrig's eyes found the tent floor. 'Such strange times of reversal,' he muttered, shaking his head. 'When princes are killed out of hand and common squires belted.'

'In times such as these, we ought to be grateful for every belted knight we have,' said Torgun, trying not to sound too pointed. Even now, he guarded his humility.

His brother had the sense and grace to acknowledge his statement. 'My brother has the right of it,' said the Jarl. 'If he vouches for this Sir Vaskrian then I say he is welcome at our table. Sir Torgun, do you need some time to assuage your grief, or will you stay and hear counsel?'

Truth to tell, neither of them had been close to their sister Aeselif, but they had both loved her after their own fashion. The sort of love that came from duty rather than passion, yet it had been genuine enough. And Aeselif had always been as sweet of temper as she was of countenance – perhaps more than Hjala, her death shocked Torgun.

But there was no time to indulge in grief.

'Say on, Lord Toros,' said Torgun formally. 'We are ready.'

Lord Toros nodded perfunctorily before returning his attention to the table. On it was a crude map of the King's Dominions: the city of Strongholm was flanked to north and south with two hosts of wooden figurines. Torgun guessed the smaller one was meant to represent the southern forces of the Dominions, making their own parallel muster. But what really caught his eye were the figurines representing the invaders; they clutched the sketched coastline of Northalde like so many limpets. Worst were the toad-like figures the craftsman had fashioned in queer mockery of the aquatic invaders from the sea. Naught but painted wood, yet they unnerved Torgun all the same.

'We are, as I was saying, gravely outnumbered,' said Toros. 'The Efrilunders have brought fourteen hundred fighting men to add to the fifteen hundred we've mustered from the northern reaches of the King's Dominions.' He nodded towards Lord Whaelin, chief spokesman for the Highland clan lords, and Olvar the representative of the Wolding barons. 'Besides that our friends from the north have brought another fourteen hundred betwixt them – that's four thousand three hundred in total.'

'Four thousand three hundred – if you count the squires, many of them green lads who've only just begun learning the arts of war,' grumbled Lord Vymar. 'That's half what we went to war against Thule with – hardly a formidable fighting force.'

A flicker of impatience crossed Toros's face before he suppressed it. But then Torgun's older sibling always did play things close. He'd need to more than ever now.

'We've heard word from the Southerly Dominions,' he went on. 'They've managed to muster nearly two thousand fighting men, last we heard they are camped just west of Lake Strom. And don't forget the White Valravyn – the best fighting force the realm has to offer.'

Several of the nobles looked about sourly at that, some muttering to themselves as the High Commander of the Order acknowledged the compliment with a curt but decisive nod. Even now, the old rivalries ran deep.

'I've managed to assemble twelve hundred men,' said Lord Toric, his bald pate shining in the brazier light. 'That's including footmen and archers – of knights you shall have but four hundred. We still haven't fully recovered from the last war.'

'So all told that's five and a half thousand,' said Toros. 'We have a slight numerical advantage at least – but that's assuming the Northland Thegns don't bring up reinforcements from the south. Our compatriots there have less than two thousand fighting men, I'm told – even with some of the Northlanders preoccupied with taking slaves, they're badly outnumbered and probably won't be able to hold them off forever. And of course, their ranks are stiffened every day by these accursed fiends from the sea.'

'And just how many *knights* do we have altogether?' asked Fenrig, returning the assembly's attention to the north. 'Mounted cavalry should be our best advantage against our barbarian cousins.'

Lord Toros nodded. 'I was coming to that. We can field just over fifteen hundred, counting out our southron kinsmen. But our squires can also fight on horseback.' He met Vymar's eye. 'Inexperienced many of them may be, but they are willing to do anything asked of them to save their homeland, and eager and hungry for a chance to prove themselves. I've already pruned them to take out the tenderest – those will be put to better use garrisoning castles should the worst happen.'

Grim silence greeted that last statement. Unperturbed, Toros went on. 'Now we come to the most frightful reckoning – the enemy's forces. Our outriders' best estimates run to some ten thousand men that the Shield Queen has brought to ravage our lands.' Cries of dismay went around the tent at that. Toros held up his hands patiently for silence. 'Not all of those are concentrated around the capital,' he said. 'We estimate around a fifth are preoccupied with raids and slave-taking up and down our coast.' He indicated the fish-like figures with a hand that seemed suddenly to tremble slightly. 'They are being aided in this black endeavour by at least a thousand creatures of the deep, and we hear their numbers increase daily.' The young lord took a deep breath. 'Though fortunately, it seems as though they are unable or unwilling to venture too far from the sea, so we shouldn't have to worry about them joining the battle for Strongholm.'

'Don't be too sure of that,' said Aesgir. 'Strongholm is by

the sea, after all. We need to find out more about these eldritch abominations.'

'We sent word to Prior Holfaste and his Argolian monks at Urling monastery,' said Toros. 'But they weren't much help, I'm afraid – they know little of these creatures beyond their ancient name Triton. Something about them being connected to a great serpent that sleeps beneath the sea...' The young lord shuddered. 'In any case, they said they are busy at Tintagael.'

'Tintagael?' Torgun's ears pricked up – he remembered all too well Horskram's frightful account of the haunted forest and the accursed tower of the same name built by Them.

His older brother shrugged his shoulders helplessly. 'Something about increased activity there – the messenger said his entire chapter's elan, whatever in the Known World that is, being needed to contain it. All Holfaste could tell us was that these Triton creatures can be killed by normal means, and that it's unusual for them to gather together in such numbers and leave the sea.'

'Fie, that's typical of the Argolians,' spat one grizzled banneret, 'for where were the Argolians when we needed them in the last war? The monks have ever fought but for their own interests.'

'That is an unjust remark to make,' interjected Sir Torgun. 'I know full well how recondite and difficult the friars of St Argo can be – but contrary to what you may have heard, they've always had the realm's best interests at heart.' He couldn't swear he fully believed his own words any more, but they seemed enough to gainsay the nobles for now. Everyone there – including his own brother – knew that Torgun had been party to some secret council of King Freidheim's on the eve of war last year; no one seemed prepared to doubt his word now.

His older brother flicked him a grateful glance as he

continued: 'Of course, we'll need to divert our own men to try and hold off the coastal raiders.' He began lightly moving pieces across the map. 'Some two thousand foot should be enough to stymie them – for now.' He swept the tent with a piercing gaze. 'Time is of the essence, noblemen. We must smash this Northland threat quickly and decisively. If the sea-demons continue to multiply, it's only a matter of time before their raiders divert to join the main army at Strongholm.'

'What makes you think the barbarians will be moved to meet us in the field anyway?' asked another noble. 'They've already taken the city – why not just settle in and prepare for a siege?'

Toros shook his head, a slight smile playing on his lips for the first time. 'From what I know of them, that is not the Northland way. Among the Shield Queen's troops are a thousand berserkers – fanatical worshippers of the archdemon Tyrnor. They welcome death on the battlefield, and are said to be influential – Magnhilda herself used to be one of them, before she rose to rule the Frozen Principalities. We believe we can provoke the Northlanders into open conflict. They'll be confident – after all, they outnumber us.'

'Grievously,' added Lord Vymar.

'I still say a few thousand peasant conscripts to even up those numbers wouldn't hurt,' said Olvar, stroking his braided beard with thick ugly fingers. The burly greasy lord looked as though he almost relished the thought of sending brutalised serfs into battle, but then the Woldings were notorious for their cruelty.

What a pity we can't sent them back across the Valhalla with the Northland thegns, thought Torgun disparagingly.

His brother was shaking his head. 'Nay, Lord Olvar – we've already lost far too many good men and women to the slave-takers. If we drain what's left of the realm, we'll die even if we win this war. Besides, yeomen levies will be useless against Northlanders – they may lack good horsemen but they are ferocious footsoldiers, even their ordinary shieldmen are doughty warriors.'

'Outnumbered and outclassed,' sighed Vymar gloomily. 'Thank Ezekiel for knights and squires.'

'The Northlanders will do everything they can to stop us deploying them advantageously,' Toros reminded him. 'I said they could be provoked into meeting us outwith the walls of Strongholm – but don't forget they have palisades criss-crossing the lands about the city, designed to disrupt any lance charges. They've prepared well for this.'

Silence fell about the tent again as the assembled worthies pondered the map and the forthcoming war it presaged.

'What about the sea?' asked Torgun. 'I saw more than forty stout galleys on the river when we arrived.'

Lord Aesgir nodded. 'Both ourselves and the North-landers will need to divert men towards the naval battle for the Strang Estuary,' he said, tugging at his flowing blond beard. The acting Sealord of Northalde seemed to have recovered something of his old spirit, and looked more like the jolly mariner. Even now his blue eyes sparkled at the thought of making war on his beloved water. 'I've already pressed what yeomanry could be spared to crew them, though, so I'll only be needing a few hundred good fighting men besides. Lads who aren't afraid of fighting on foot, with a heaving deck beneath their feet.'

The fat Jarl looked around the tent, as if daring anyone to volunteer on the spot.

Torgun's mind flashed back to the brief sea voyage from Sjórvard, the wind ruffling his hair and the tang of sea breeze on his lips. The sea, it had always run so thick in the veins of his ancestors. And if the apparition in the Valley of the Barrow Kings had told it true, one of his ancestors *was* the sea.

'I volunteer,' he said. 'If it please the assembly, I shall lead the contingent of troops assigned to Aesgir's flotilla.'

That surprised everybody, even his brother Lord Toros. 'But, Sir Torgun, you're our greatest knight,' flustered Fenrig. 'Surely your place is in the vanguard of the land assault.'

Lord Toric favoured his subordinate raven with a dark glance. 'In truth, it pleases me not,' he said. 'Lord Fenrig has the right of this, Sir Torgun – your place is by my side. Need I remind you that you are still a serving commander in the Order of the White Valravyn.'

No, I'm not – I ceased to be that the minute the King sent me away with Horskram and his mission. But the young knight kept his thoughts to himself.

Instead he raked the gathering with a piercing gaze of his own. 'Mark this,' he told the nobles, his voice gentle but even as always. 'What we are about to face will be the like of nothing the realm has ever had to contend with. Many of us will not return from this conflict – but most of you probably already realise that. What you may not yet understand is the magnitude of the forces ranged against us. Even now, the Sea Wizard conjures up worse horrors to plague our land, from his island fastness across the sea. As many of you know, I but lately returned from an Argolian mission I was assigned to by the late King. I've seen those horrors for myself, and they will not be overcome simply with sword and spear and valour in the field. A time of great reversals is fast upon us, and if knights should forsake horseback to fight by sea then that will be the smallest of them.' He let his gaze rest on Lord Toric. 'I have ever respected thee, Lord Toric – no better successor to Prince Freidhoff could the Order have asked for. But my Wyrd lies across the darkling seas – strip me of my cloak if you must, but I'm going with Lord Aesgir.'

Lord Toric blinked. If there was ever a time Sir Torgun had shown disobedience to duty, none there could recall it. As the nobles exchanged uncertain glances the realisation slowly dawned on them − their hero had changed, and nothing would be the same again.

The High Commander of the White Valravyn's face remained granite as he replied: 'Ordinarily, I'd expel you from the Order immediately. But on the eve of such calamitous conflict, I see no gain in demoralising our men even further. Stygnos knows, you've just chosen a course of action that will deflate their spirits enough as it is.'

Torgun nodded, keeping a civil tongue in his head. 'I understand your concerns, and feel deeply the pain this causes you. But howsoever be it, my mind is made up. I sail with Lord Aesgir, and yon knight Sir Vaskrian is coming with me as my lieutenant.'

Vaskrian blinked. He hadn't been expecting that, but then he hadn't been expecting anything said in the past minute or so.

Fenrig scowled. 'A green squire but lately knighted, by who knows what strange foreign lord,' he said. 'And now you want to call him your second. How many of these reversals must we endure to preserve the realm?'

'I did not say that we would preserve it,' said Torgun implacably. 'Only that we must strive to do so by doing the unthinkable. This young knight has shared in many of the dangers I just spoke of − he alone of any man here is best fitted to accompany me in this.'

Lord Toros sighed and nodded. 'I hope for all our sakes you know what you are doing, brother,' he said. 'But have it as you will − we shall not welcome our greatest warrior back in hour of need only to ignore his counsel.' He surveyed Vaskrian's motley apparel and harness. 'But if Sir Vaskrian is to be your second at sea, he isn't going dressed like that!'

Vaskrian could not suppress a triumphant smirk. Even Torgun found the heart to share his amusement. 'I trust you will get no argument there, Lord Toros,' he smiled, flicking the younger knight a sidelong glance.

'I still say this is a travesty,' said Fenrig stubbornly. 'But lately this man was a prisoner in my dungeon.'

'Ach, don't be so hard on the lad,' said Olvar jocosely. 'He's picked up a few scars since I last saw him, but I remember him now. He was squiring for Sir Branas when I raided your lands a few years ago – dealt my men a few tidy buffets, as I recall. One of them didn't come home.'

'You remember that?' asked Vaskrian, clearly astounded. 'That was my first kill.' He started to draw himself up proudly, but Torgun shot him an unusually fierce look.

'I remember a lot of things,' chuckled Olvar. 'Looks to me for all the world as though you've just let a good swordsman slip through your fingers, Lord Fenrig.'

Fenrig favoured Olvar with a brittle smile. 'And as I recall, you lost more than one man that day – we sent you back across the Warryn to where you bloody well belong!'

Toric called sternly for silence before the two lords could fall to bickering. 'Enough!' he cried. 'This is exactly the last thing we need while our realm is being dishonoured north and south! In case you've all forgotten, I'm High Marshal of the realm's forces – I've let Lord Toros hold this assembly so he could report on the findings of his outriders, now it's time for all of you to do your duty! On the double, noblemen – spread the news, we march at first light tomorrow!'

The pavilion emptied until only Torgun, his brother, the High Commander of the White Valravyn and Vaskrian remained.

Lord Toros leaned wearily on the table. He suddenly looked older than his twenty-nine summers. 'Brother, I hope you know what you are doing,' he said flatly. 'The men... they took such heart when they heard you'd returned.'

Lord Toric's gaze remained as hard as ever. 'I've no idea

what happened to you out there in the foreign wildernesses,'
he said. 'But I can't say I like the result, Sir Torgun. Since
when did you put a personal quest before duty to your
country and your standard?'

'Because both of those things – and far more – depend on
my personal quest, as you put it,' replied Torgun. He shook
his head. 'You'll just have to find it in your heart to forgive me
– and take my word on trust that everything I'm doing is for
the realm.'

Toric and Toros exchanged awkward glances. 'I did
wonder what Freidheim – Reus rest his soul! – was thinking
when he sent you off gallivanting with the monk Horskram,'
sighed Toric. 'You should ever have been here – the realm
might not be in such jeopardy had you remained.'

'Be that as it may, this is the pass we have come to,' said
Torgun with characteristic mildness. 'Now we must find a way
to traverse it, if we can.'

Toric still looked far from pleased, but held his peace.

Torgun's brother eyed Vaskrian sceptically. 'And you are
sure you vouch for this young knight?' he asked cautiously.

'With the faith of my body,' replied Sir Torgun.

'Very well,' said Lord Toros. 'Sir Vaskrian, you'd better
come with me. We still haven't replaced every knight we lost
in the war against Krulheim – I'm sure we can find a hauberk
and helm that fit you.'

Sir Vaskrian smiled again. He flashed Torgun a grateful
look before leaving with the Jarl of Vandheim. 'I can't ever
repay you for what you've done for me, Sir Torgun,' he said
earnestly.

Sir Torgun brushed off his thanks meekly, trying to ignore
Lord Toric's flinty stare.

'Think nothing of it,' he said gently. 'It's all your valour
merits.'

And you might not be thanking me by the time this is done.

CHAPTER 9

TO PETITION A KING

Lord Braxus arrived at the Palace of Bending Branches to find Cadwy's court in disarray. Had they really overcome Abrexta the Prescient last winter and returned the realm to its rightful ruler, he wondered.

Caratacus, now the King's chamberlain as well as his chief coin-counter, was doing his level best to keep order, but the gaggle of petitioners had clearly got out of hand; some had apparently been there all night. Sir Dantos, in charge of the newly appointed Royal Guard, had been instructed to let them in; but that had only had the result of transferring the pandaemonium from the antechamber to the throne room proper.

Braxus surveyed the tapestried precinct with uneasy eyes. He well remembered the scene of his last quest. As he stood beneath the antlered lintel of the throne room entrance, he recalled the screaming savages whose blood he'd shed there but six months ago; Joram's strange prayers and Morcant's unholy magicks.

He remembered Sir Dantos too: the enthralled knight's twin warhammers had nearly made an end of him and the freelancer Sir Wrackwulf. Now the gargantuan knight and his fellow champions were responsible for the King's protection at all times.

The very same champions who fought bewitched to defend the sorceress who put us in this mess, thought Braxus wryly. *There's an irony waiting to be put into a lay.*

But music was hardly the most pressing concern – in fact he found less time to enjoy playing it now he was a lord of men. Perhaps that should have saddened him, but it didn't – and that was saddest of all.

He finally managed to catch the burly bearded knight's eye. Sir Dantos looked a little abashed at seeing him: like the King himself, he had yet to fully overcome the chagrin of being enthralled by an enchantress.

'Lord Braxus, good to see you here,' he said courteously. 'I still recall the tidy buffets you dealt me last winter.'

Braxus forced a smile. 'As I recall, Sir Dantos, you gave as good as you got.'

An awkward grin cracked the huge warrior's grizzled black beard. 'Would that I had dealt them in service to the King – of the two of us, only you can say that.'

Braxus felt a stab of sympathy for the big man. Before his ensorcellment, Dantos had been the realm's greatest knight. Never the best of jousters, he'd distinguished himself in one tourney melee after another – and no few highlanders had been slammed into their graves by his twin hammers. Royal guard duties were all well and good by way of knightly penance – but like the six other bewitched myrmidons he'd fought with that night, Dantos would be eager to erase the smear on his honour with glorious deeds.

And that was exactly the kind of sentiment Braxus had come here to exploit.

'Be of better cheer, friend,' said Braxus, laying a hand on

the knight's mailed shoulder. 'You'll have fresh chances to add glory to your name, and in sooner time than you think.'

Dantos raised a bushy eyebrow, an old war scar that ran the length of his cheek creasing. 'So you say...' he muttered. 'Sounds like you have something of interest to broach with our King.'

Braxus smiled easily. 'You might say that... how fares His Majesty?'

Dantos poked a thumb over his shoulder. 'Why not go and see for yourself? I've given up trying to make order out of this chaos – the King is so anxious to please everyone, he tries to please everyone at once.'

Braxus gazed up the sloping throne room floor to where the throng of petitioners was being assembled by Caratacus into some kind of line. Sir Arianrod and Sir Diarmuid were there to help, their handsome faces stern and unyielding as they marshalled the petitioners.

Braxus chuckled. 'You'd think we'd ridden off to battle already,' he said. 'We'll need to be better organised than this for what I have in mind.'

Dantos cocked his head. 'Oh ho! You really *do* have something interesting to broach with His Majesty,' he said. 'But I should warn you, we've almost got another civil war on our hands thanks to the Crimson League.'

Braxus frowned. 'Rowena is still pressing her claims then?' he asked. He'd marched to war with the First Woman of Tul Aeren, and knew full well she was not to be trifled with. She was, however, perfect for what he had in mind.

'That and more,' sighed Dantos. 'The lords of Garro, Penllyn and Fythe are behind her – they've put aside their own squabbles to join her suit for greater autonomy. If the King isn't careful, we'll have a full-blown secession on our hands.'

'That didn't work out too well for the Northlendings

when I sojourned among them,' said Braxus. 'Did wonders for furnishing knights with warlike exploits though.'

Dantos shook his head. 'I love war as much as any knight, Sir Braxus, but a civil conflict is the last thing Thraxia needs. After all we've had to endure, it would surely break us.'

Braxus smiled again. 'I could not agree with you more, Sir Dantos. You and I shall speak again presently.' Without another word, he excused himself and began pushing his way through the petitioners towards the Seat of High Kings.

Cadwy's ensorcellment had aged him. Though of middling years, his hair was a snowy mane; creases and wrinkles lined his face. He scarcely recognised Braxus as Caratacus hastily announced him. The throng of commoners and minor nobles frowned at him: who was this northern lord barging in, they should like to know?

Wait until you hear my proposal, Braxus thought. They were a good mixture of types: tradesmen and craftsmen from the city, cottars and peddlers from out of town. Again, perfect for what he had in mind.

'Lord Braxus of Gaellen,' said Cadwy, drawing himself up and doing his best to look regal. 'How pleasant it is to receive you here at court.'

Was it his imagination, or did cobwebs cling to the King's fustian robes?

Doffing his elegant cap, the young lord favoured Cadwy with a florid bow. He'd dressed appropriately: the latest cut of doublet and hose, worn beneath a short cotte and cape trimmed with peacock feathers and lined with jewels and silver sequins, and supple leather shoes sporting winkle-picker points. He'd need to look his best.

'And a lively court it is,' he said, sweeping the courtiers

with his bright green eyes. There were far fewer of those since Abrexta had been slain: many had met the headsman's axe for treason, for not all of her thralls had been ensorcelled. Those that remained were for the most part loyal vassals who'd been imprisoned for long months in the dungeons by Abrexta. Many still looked emaciated, all of them aggrieved and resentful – and not just because the King wasn't paying them much attention right now.

Nursing grudges, and no outlet for their knightly passion – we'll soon sort that out if I have my way.

King Cadwy frowned, multiplying his creases. 'Lively is not quite how I'd put it,' he replied candidly. 'Break your words cleanly, Lord Braxus – you've come here because you want something, just the same as these.' He gestured towards the petitioners with a casual sweep of the arm.

And unlike these, I helped save your throne – dammit, Cadwy, you were a half-decent ruler ere Abrexta bewitched you.

Braxus drew himself up. 'You've shown me candour, now I'll do you the same turn,' he answered boldly. 'What I want is another war.'

Cadwy blinked furiously, dislodging a few cobwebs. A couple of nearby vassals stifled laughs. Most just looked surprised, or aghast.

Caratacus cleared his throat. 'War is perhaps rather what we are seeking to avoid right now, Lord Braxus,' he said diplomatically.

'War amongst ourselves, aye,' Braxus allowed. 'But I would not pit Thraxian against Thraxian – too much of one another's blood have we shed of late. I would send our armies to the east, across the With-Y-Passes into Northlending territory.'

Cadwy at least found presence of mind to laugh himself. 'You'd have us pick a fight with our age-old foes, when we're just recovering from our own travails?'

'No, not pick a fight *with* them,' said Braxus, pausing for dramatic effect. '... I'd have us fight *alongside* them. Doubtless you've heard of the invasion from the Frozen Wastes – the Northlanders have never been friends to us. I say we make common cause with our neighbours, and smash the barbarian threat before it comes looking for us. I know better than anyone here what Thraxia has suffered – but we can't just ignore this! We need to look to our defences, and I say attack is the best form of defence.'

Quite a few of the nobles were paying attention now. He'd piqued their interest, at the very least. Now was the time to press his advantage.

'Your Majesty, I implore you – trust me in this! Have I not proved myself in the field, aye and in this very hall? Have I not expunged the highland threat from my own lands, once and for all? I say a war beyond our borders is exactly what the realm needs right now – a chance to recoup lost honour as well as protect ourselves!'

Looks of intrigue among the nobles had turned to looks of approval. The commoners looked afraid, of course – commoners always had the most to lose in a war. But he'd bring them round soon enough.

'Sire, give me a fighting force to add to my own,' Braxus went on, facing the King again. 'Whatever Your Majesty thinks he can spare. The Northlendings are hard pressed – if we march to their aid, they will not be ungrateful. Help them repulse the Northlanders, and finally we'll have a chance to cement relations betwixt our two nations.' He looked Cadwy square in the eye. It was rheumy, but focused. 'Twas what your uncle, King Cullodyn, always wanted, when he sat the Seat of High Kings before you. Not just an uneasy peace – but a fruitful partnership, one to last for generations!'

Sir Gwydion, father of Arianrod and Diarmuid, stepped forwards. Twice as stern-looking as his sons, he was also

Thraxia's new High Constable. 'Your recent successes have obviously put your head too far above your shoulders, Lord Braxus,' he said unsmiling. 'We have not the resources to command such an expedition – and even if we did, there'd be no guarantee of victory.'

Braxus threw his hands up. 'Is there ever in war, or any other worthwhile undertaking? But I'll tell you what is guaranteed – if we sit here and do nothing, the realm will fragment again. Give Lady Rowena and the southern lords a foreign expedition to unite behind, and they might cease being a thorn in the side of the King's Fold.'

Gwydion shook his head. 'You'd invite the Crimson League up here for a muster? Sounds like putting one's head in the mouth of the lion to me.'

Braxus smiled. He'd been expecting this of course. 'Nay, Sir Gwydion,' he said. 'I wouldn't have them brought up here at all – as I've just said, I'll lead the expedition force to Northalde and it please the King. No, I'd send the Crimson League south and into Vorstlund. There's war there, too – and I'm sure the Prince of Westenlund would appreciate some help against the Pangonians.'

Cadwy interjected. 'You're proposing we embroil ourselves in some continental war, when we've barely recovered from our own,' he said. 'I cannot see the wisdom in this counsel, Lord Braxus.'

'Oh, can't you, Your Majesty? What if I were to tell you that this wider war and our own pains were linked? Do you really think Abrexta the Prescient came out of nowhere? She belonged to a secret alliance of wizards, one that's been pulling strings in the courts of western Urovia for years now. I spent the past year adventuring with the Argolian friar Horskram to try to prevent just such.'

That had them all on the back foot. What with the realm's problems, nobody had thought to question him much on his exploits abroad. Now he was going to tell them – everything. Horskram and his games be damned, the time for secrecy was over.

'You clearly have a tale to tell,' sighed Cadwy. 'Best if we hear it in private.'

'Nay, Your Majesty,' replied Braxus. 'And it please you, I'd have this said out in the open, before men of all castes. For too long I have carried this heavy burden alone – I'd lighten it now in the sharing.'

Cadwy sat back on his throne, exchanging bemused glances with Caratacus and Gwydion. Noble and commoner alike looked on tremulously as the King motioned for him to speak freely.

The tale was a long one, but Braxus was up to it. He'd lost his passion for music of late, but his flair for oratory had not left him. Courtiers and commoners stood agog as he told them of Wadwos and Gygants and Elementi, of undead warriors and demonic wizards. He left out anything that might put him in an unfavourable light of course – what profit to weaken his suit with cold honesty?

When he was done, a stunned silence filled the hall. Clearly many of those present had barely grasped it all – but they'd fathomed just enough.

'So if I have this correctly,' said the King slowly. 'My treacherous mistress was but servant to a darker master warlock, one you sought in vain, who would see the realms of mortalkind... what was your expression?'

'Covered in darkness, Your Majesty,' prompted Braxus. It was an old turn of phrase favoured by the troubadours, but an effective one.

'Horskram of Vilno is known to me,' said Cadwy thought-fully. 'He came to me several years ago, not long after I had ascended the throne, asking for help against this Andragorix. I sent Sir Belinos of Runcymede with him, deeming him as pious a knight as any who lived in Thraxia. I never did learn what became of them after they went to Roarkil.'

'And now you know,' said Braxus. 'And, I hope, understand the magnitude of the threat that faces us.'

And even if you don't, I've just as good as told the whole realm. You've no choice but to act now.

If the King hadn't realised that, his shrewd adviser certainly had. 'I think now would be a good time to empty the throne room,' said Caratacus, motioning for Sir Gwydion and his sons to usher the petitioners out. They were too busy contemplating what they'd just heard to complain.

'Your suit is not unfounded,' said Caratacus after they had gone. 'But you might have held off sharing it with all and sundry. A general panic about the end of the world is all we need.'

Braxus laughed at that. 'You remind me a lot of Master Horskram when you say that,' he replied. 'But in truth where did secrecy get him? As far as I know, he's still off gallivanting about in the wilderness somewhere, searching in vain for a secret sorcerer. I say we are better off using this spectre to our advantage – to inspire the multitude to support our war. Whoever he is, this wizard can't be powerful enough to take over the world without military aid – why intrigue for so long in the courts of mortal men otherwise? That means if we win on the battlefields of Urovia, we both put a check on his plans and cover ourselves in glory! Think on it – Thraxia could be a great nation again!'

The King frowned. 'From your own tale, Horskram certainly didn't seem to believe this mastermind could be defeated by military means alone,' he said. 'But I can't deny you make a compelling case. At the very least, warfare will play a vital part in this struggle you've so eloquently described. And I for one would fain take vengeance on those who've caused me and my people so much anguish. Very well

– if fighting alongside the Northlendings helps to hurt those who have hurt me, consider this my blessing and my sanction. Sir Gwydion, you will muster troops to support Lord Braxus in his venture immediately. Caratacus, see messengers speed southwards bearing letters to Lady Rowena and the other lords of the Crimson League. Try to make less of a meal of the story than Lord Braxus did.'

'I doubt I could spare the parchment and ink to tell it as he has done in any case,' said Caratacus dryly.

Gwydion remained unconvinced, though out of the corner of his eye Braxus caught Dantos grinning from ear to ear.

'I cannot say I support this venture, Your Majesty,' said the High Constable. 'We are committing ourselves to a taxing conflict on the second-hand testimony of an Argolian monk, brought to us by a former knight errant.' He looked Braxus in the eye defiantly.

'The same knight errant who freed you from sorcerous bondage and treason,' Braxus reminded him. 'The same knight errant who vouched for your head, knowing full well that good men compelled by witchcraft could not be held to iron and fire for their actions. The same knight errant now giving you the chance to clear your name once and for all.'

That silenced Sir Gwydion, though the look of hatred he shot Braxus told the young lord he had just made himself another powerful enemy. Let Gwydion sharpen his sword – the First Man of Clan Fitzrow had faced far worse in his time.

Lord Braxus indulged in a triumphant smile as he took his leave of the Thraxian King.

It was getting dark by the time he met his brother in the guest room they were sharing at the palace.

'Did you get your precious war?' asked Drojan with a thin smile.

'Two wars,' Braxus informed him. 'One to the east, and another to the south.'

'Naught will come of this, you know,' Drojan told him flatly. 'Fight all you will, but more blood won't wash off your sins. You may think yourself a high hero, Braxus, but you'll be judged just the same as the next soul when Azrael beckons.'

Braxus, only half listening, did not turn from the palace window he was gazing out of. A serving wench was scurrying across the courtyard; a typical Thraxian beauty, she had dark hair and narrow hips.

'Who said anything about cleansing sin,' the young lord replied absently. 'It's glory in this life I'm after, not forgiveness in the next.' He turned to face his younger sibling. 'You put too much faith in the Almighty, Drojan. Do you really think He'd put us to such trials just to keep us morally fit if He really cared a fig for us? You nurture a horse by training it, not flogging it half to death.'

Drojan opened his mouth to say something, but Braxus raised a hand to forestall him. His blood was up, and debating theology with his brother was the last place he wanted to expend his energies.

'You'll see to your own diversion this evening, won't you brother?' he asked, heading for the door. 'I have to go and see about a wench.'

CHAPTER 10
A RED SUN RISING

Wrackwulf watched as the last of the supply wagons were hauled into place at the rear of the third battle row. Princess Utha and her son Franz had done a good job of consolidating an alliance: with the lords of Dreylund, Hyrlund and the two Thulias they fielded a sizeable army, some seven thousand strong. But if the outriders were to be believed, the invaders had more than ten thousand assembled on their side of the Raudaz. What's more, every fighting man coming for them was highly trained and motivated. And from what Wrackwulf had been hearing, they'd already tasted blood and victory.

'Armies of mainland strong in number,' said Ariadha. The warrior-woman gazed at the mustering army with disbelieving eyes. But then she'd worn much the same expression ever since her arrival on the continent. Wrackwulf had spent the past couple of weeks trying to get some more Vorstlending into the outlander's skull: no use screaming orders at someone if they couldn't understand a word you were saying.

'I'm afraid that's almost twice as true of our enemy,' muttered Wrackwulf. The islander's naivetée troubled him, but at least he could now hold a rudimentary conversation with the Westerling, who was proving a quick study when it came to foreign languages. He hadn't had much else to do besides teach her: there'd be no roistering with the country on a war footing. A shame, because Wrackwulf wasn't sure he'd get another chance to drink and wench.

Prince Franz had assigned him to the mercenary cavalry contingent, with the rest of the freelancers; as for Ariadha, the only way he'd managed to get her involved was by claiming she was his squire. Everyone thought he'd lost his mind, of course, and he probably had. The warrior-woman might present a fierce exterior, but she lacked experience: the islanders hadn't had a full-scale war in centuries, as far as he could fathom.

At least it hadn't been hard to convince the outlander to ride into battle as his second: so far as Ariadha was concerned, there was little difference between knight and squire except that one wore heavier armour and rode a bigger horse. Perhaps she had a point there.

I'll do what I can to keep you alive, thought Wrackwulf. *But when we really get in the thick of it, you'll be on your own.*

'Why wooden horses?' she asked him, nodding towards the wagons.

'Carts, they're called *carts*,' said Wrackwulf. 'To carry supplies – food, weapons, that sort of thing.'

Ariadha scratched the shaven half of her head. 'But land give food,' she faltered. 'Take food in wooden – in *cart* – make slow.'

Wrackwulf grinned. 'You really do have a lot to learn, don't you? Nothing about war is quick, my dear.'

The islander just stared at him. Wrackwulf doubted she understood much of what he said. And a country's sense of humour was the last thing you ever picked up – months of campaigning in Thalamy when he was younger, and he still wasn't even sure they had one.

'Never mind,' he sighed, pointing to his sumpter. 'Check our horses. Make sure our own supplies are ready.'

Ariadha stared at him, before ambling over to where the sumpter stood next to the sturdy charger and sleek-looking courser Wrackwulf's coin had purchased them.

I'd be better off just pointing and shouting, he sighed inwardly. *Ezekiel knows how she'll fare when the fighting starts. So far as I can tell, she's never used that spear to kill more than an ice hound.*

Then again, if she was capable of besting a supernatural beast, the Westerling had a chance against the Pangonians, he supposed. And why did he care anyway? He hardly wanted to bed the wench.

But of all the people here, she was the only one who really understood what was at stake. Franz, Utha, lords Bjornwulf and Gunthor... they knew the real world, but not the dangers of the Other Side. That made the savage islander his only true companion, now all the others had gone.

Wrackwulf had never been the lonely type, and he didn't appreciate the feeling as it came over him.

Sir Marech of Salz strode over. The tall mercenary knight had close-cropped hair that seemed to accentuate the scars criss-crossing his blunt face. Wrackwulf had fought for him a couple of times before; he knew him for a stalwart captain, if a ruthless one.

'Sir Wrackwulf,' he nodded, 'I trust you're ready for more gold and glory.' Marech always said that on the eve of a campaign. He never said it joyously or with any real spirit: to him war and spoil were all in a day's work. Defeat too, if it came to that: the captain had survived so many scrapes over the years, his longest-serving men had come to believe he couldn't be killed in the field. Wrackwulf would like to have believed that was true.

'Ready as always, Sir Marech,' replied the freelancer, slapping his mailed gut by way of emphasis. 'Gold and glory... preferably in that order.'

Marech nodded humourlessly. He flicked a suspicious glance Ariadha's way. 'I've no idea where you picked her up, and I don't really want to know,' he said dourly. 'In truth, some of the lads have been kicking up quite a fuss about it... taking a woman into the field, it just isn't done, savage or no. If it wasn't for our longstanding association - '

Wrackwulf courteously raised a gauntleted hand. 'Rest assured, Sir Marech, she's been tried and tested. A savage she is, I'll grant. But where she's from, women do a lot more fighting. Besides, I lost my old squire on my last venture – she's the best I could get at short notice.'

The scarred captain looked at him askance. 'So far as I recall, Sir Wrackwulf, you always made do without a squire. Didn't you used to say they only slowed you down?'

Wrackwulf favoured him with a tidy grin. 'What can I say, Sir Marech? I'm getting old.'

The knight shook his head and stalked off. 'Be ready to saddle up in five minutes!' he barked over his shoulder. 'His Highness will be calling the sally-forth presently.'

'Nothing I'd sooner do, Sir Marech!' Wrackwulf called after him cheerfully.

Ariadha checked over the pack horse one last time. So far as she could tell, it was all there. But these mainlanders brought *so much* gear to war: rope, wine, tents, spare weapons (a real luxury that, and all of iron too), hard tack, empty sacks for plunder, spare bridles and those strange hoops the knights put their feet into when they rode a horse... the list went on, and it was bewildering to her.

But at least checking over their supplies brought a welcome distraction from their ultimate purpose. Ariadha was scarcely looking forward to her first proper battle. She had prided herself on avoiding death-duelling back on her lands: always when she could, she had tried to resolve disputes without violence. Her uncle Owyn had fought and killed a couple of men from a rival tribe living in the lands bordering Clan Nuallán's when she'd been a girl: she'd never forgotten the look in his eyes when he'd come back from that skirmish, covered in the blood of his foes.

She didn't want for all the Known World to end up with that on her conscience. True, the mainlanders were outsiders – that would make it easier, she supposed. But in her girlhood she had delighted in exploring the scree-covered slopes of the Farfahailan ranges in her homeland of Penhalain: she used to visit an old priestess who'd retired to the wilds to live out her twilight years in the wilderness. The old crone had never told Ariadha her name, but she'd told her a good many other things.

When mortals take the lives of animals, it is on sufferance from the land, to which we all belong. A gift from the Moon Goddess, Mother of All. An animal should only be killed out of need, never of want. That's why it is a great wickedness for mortals to kill one another – unless of course a sacrifice is demanded by the Goddess. Wars are not demanded by deities, but only by men: no good will come of them, nor ever has done.

Of course, criminals often found themselves put forward as candidates for sacrifice – Ariadha was wise enough to know the ways of her people were far from perfect. But men killing each other in wars over land that didn't belong to any of them in the first place? The thought of it disgusted her. Yet the mercenary Wrackwulf had assured her that here they did it all the time.

And here she was. An exile, with no other way of making

her way in the awful new world the Godsgame had flung her into.

'Everything good?' Wrackwulf had come over, and now laid a meaty hand on her hard bony shoulder. She didn't care for the gesture and ordinarily would have shrugged him off – but out here in this godsforsaken land, he was her only friend.

'Everything good,' she repeated, making sure she didn't forget the words. The sooner she learned this ugly tongue, the sooner she could begin to cut her own path.

'Good,' smiled the freelancer, then said something she didn't fully understand about the army moving.

Ariadha nodded perfunctorily. Best to get this started, so she could get used to her new condition as soon as possible. Unslinging her heirloom spear from her back, she examined the curious glyphs embossed along the length of its shaft. Made during the far-off Old Time, when druids and priest-esses had wielded power unknown to folk nowadays, it seemed to croon in her hands.

Ariadha suddenly had the uncomfortable feeling the spear had tasted human blood many times ere now. Another of the old crone's adages came back to her then.

It isn't the warrior who wields the sword, but the other way around.

Sir Hugon listened to the outriders give their reports before dismissing them. All was well. The enemy was marching to meet them, with a host inferior to their own. The boldness of the move had surprised him when he learned of it, but it hardly dismayed him. Let the Vorstlendings come and meet a true knight's end – on Pangonian swords.

Ahead of him, on the plains stretching from the banks of the Raudaz, the battalions commanded by Lords Kaye and

Aravin were drawing themselves up to either side of his own. Once the reinforcements from Howfaste joined them they would make up a fighting force of more than twelve thousand. Plenty of useful men to play with – Hugon was already tabling some interesting ideas for battle formations in his mind.

The Royal Marshal allowed himself a satisfied smile. The blades of grass that now glimmered green under summer's touch would soon be reddened – by blades of steel.

Sir Aremis, his fellow knight of the Purple Garter, cleared his throat politely.

'Royal Marshal, I think I see Lord Clovis approaching,' he said, bitterness marking every word.

Turning, Sir Hugon watched as Clovis and his retinue of knights crossed the arched bridge fording the Raudaz, and waited patiently as they drew near.

The young lord's face was set in its usual cruel grimace: the Margrave of Narbo had taken all too well to the grim realities of war, something Sir Aremis would never forgive him for.

'I've finished with the last captives back at Howfaste,' said Clovis, swinging from the stirrup and approaching them. Powerfully built with broad shoulders, his face flushed like a beetroot in the summer sun.

'I hope you didn't finish with them all permanently,' said Hugon sternly. 'Many of those knights and serjeants fought valiantly to protect their homeland, and they'll be worth good ransom money besides. Invasion or no, we're to obey the Code of Chivalry's dictates on warfare at all times.'

Hugon didn't like the fact he had to remind the Margrave of this constantly, nor the fact that the young lord seemed to enjoy the special favour of Kaye and Aravin. His conniving rivals unsettled him more daily – there was something about them that wasn't quite right, though he couldn't say what exactly.

'We only executed the ordinary footsoldiers and common levies,' Clovis assured him. 'And we questioned no one of noble blood with iron or fire. The womenfolk were left with their honour intact, as per your commands.'

If Clovis was disappointed by that, at least he was courteous enough to disguise it. Out of the corner of his eye, Hugon caught Sir Aremis looking at the Margrave of Narbo with barely concealed loathing. The young knight of the Purple Garter was honourable and brave – you could only say the latter for Lord Clovis, whose wanton savagery had appalled even the most hardened soldiers. All except Kaye and Aravin that is, who seemed privately to approve of his methods without endorsing them outright. They hadn't been quick to speak up in Hugon's favour when he'd put a stop to Clovis and his depraved antics.

Dishonouring a maiden with a dagger in front of her father – I've never seen its like before, and hope to Virtus I never do again.

And yet… every time his misgivings began to get the better of him, images of his paramour the Queen and her unwholesome ally Lord Ivon flashed through his mind, and something in him went quiet. Aravin and Kaye had been the Margrave of Vichy's chief cronies at court – but try as he might to follow through on that thought, something befuddled him whenever he did.

Best to keep his mind on what lay in front of him. And what lay in front of him was a full-scale battle that the Royal Marshal had every intention of winning.

'How speeds Lord Morvaine?' Hugon asked. 'Is he bringing fresh supplies from Howfaste? We march on the morrow to meet the defenders on the Wester Plains. If we can destroy their army a day's march from their precious capital, they'll be broken – too weak even to resist a siege. This reckless Crown Prince has gifted us a boon, and I'll not squander it for want of a single detail.'

Lord Clovis bowed again courteously. 'Lord Morvaine assures me that he is bringing ample supplies along with the rest of the besieging army from Howfaste – some of the churls we questioned were most talkative about concealed food caches.'

'Yes,' replied Hugon, lips curling in a sour smile. 'I'm sure they were. Thank you, Lord Margrave – you and your men should go and refresh yourselves. We'll wait for Morvaine, then we march to meet the enemy.'

Without another word Clovis turned on his heel and left.

'That man is a disgrace,' muttered Sir Aremis, his hare-lip looking all the uglier for curling. 'His behaviour scarcely warrants a knighthood, never mind a title.'

'I agree with you on the first point,' said Hugon, more sadly than anything else. 'But I'm afraid Clovis is just what is required of a lord of men – effective in the field and ruthless when needed. He leads from the front, even if his... eccentricities are shocking.'

The idealistic knight's eyes widened. 'Eccentricities? You were there when he – did what he did. Eccentricities doesn't begin to compass his depravity... Aaron the Wife Slayer wouldn't have stooped so low.'

'Don't be so sure of that,' said Hugon stoutly. As Captain of the Garter, he had to keep the elite knights of the Crescent in check when their ideals got the better of them – even though they were ideals he cherished himself. 'The King's great-uncle slew his own spouse, in full view of the entire court, not some low-ranking foreign noble's daughter. And he still managed to pass on the realm intact to Carolus the Elder... Depravity doesn't always detract from efficacy, Sir Aremis, much as it pains me to admit it.'

'Nevertheless, it's wrong for him to have such a position, and you know so,' persisted Aremis stubbornly.

Sir Hugon could only admire the young knight's chivalrous spirit, but he couldn't allow it to cloud his judgement either.

'This is about more than just the Code of Chivalry,' he reminded Aremis gently. 'This is your first serious campaign, you don't yet understand how fragile these coalitions of barons can be. Frankly, I'm a lot less worried about Clovis than I am about... others in our camp. The Margrave of Narbo is headstrong and hot-headed – a useful idiot I can control, though it's true he makes it difficult at times! I'm far more concerned about...' He paused, as his head seemed suddenly to cloud. Aremis gazed at him quizzically.

'... about Morvaine,' he continued quickly. 'He's got too much influence with the Occidental barons for my liking. We need to keep an eye on him – this is the King's campaign, prosecuted in his name, for the benefit of the entire realm. Those western margraves will break ranks to seek their own if we aren't careful! We can't allow personal distaste to distract us from our chief goal – making Greater Pangonia a reality.' He held the younger knight's eye. 'I trust I can count on you to help me in this, in the months to come, Sir Aremis.'

The young knight flushed, but held his gaze. 'Everything I do, by the faith of my body, is but in service to Pangonia,' he said, striking a gauntleted hand to his mailed breast.

Hugon nodded, favouring the young knight with a smile. 'Good,' he said. 'Keep that in mind from here on.'

The crescent knight excused himself and went to be about his duties. The smile dropped from Hugon's face as soon as his back was turned.

I'm far more concerned about Kaye and Aravin – that's what I wanted to say, Stygnos dammit. Morvaine's a schemer too, I've no doubt of that, but he isn't the one I keep worrying about. Why can't I just say their names?

No sooner had he asked himself the question than he saw Lord Ivon in his mind's eye, smiling urbanely in Queen Isolte's trysting chamber, telling him they were going to be the best of friends. Behind him the Queen smiled, that same seductive smile that had drawn him to her bower a hundred times. He felt his heart beat faster. How he missed her – already it had been too long since he'd enjoyed her favours.

And yet, it was Ivon who stayed uppermost in his mind.

Prince Franz's face looked as though it hadn't relaxed in days. Wan and drawn in the lantern light, it was the face of a man who has staked everything he has to lose after weighing the odds long and hard.

Wrackwulf didn't know if that was a good thing or not, but he edged his way further into the pavilion to try and hear better. Sir Marech had surprised the freelancer by nominating him as his second at the war council: perhaps word of Wrackwulf's outburst at court had reached the mercenary captain's ears.

Whatever the reason, here he was: privy to the Crown Prince's strategy.

'The Pangonians over-match us in numbers, so we're going to have to use terrain and tactics to our advantage,' said Franz, moving pieces across a map that Wrackwulf wasn't tall enough to see clearly. 'They'll do their best to outflank us, using their more manoeuvrable light cavalry, so we'll need to anticipate that. We're going to position ourselves between the woods here and the fens that stretch to meet the Raudaz – that'll give Sir Hugon's forces a narrow corridor of land on which to fight us.'

Corridors of land are good, thought Wrackwulf, recalling Lady Rowena of Tul Aeren's victory at Rathlain last year. *Except we had surprise reinforcements that day, and the weather on our side. It's high summer in southern Vorstlund, I don't see any muddy bogs coming to our rescue this time.*

What Franz said next did surprise him, however.

'We'll arrange our formation in concentric circles, like so. Footsoldier spearmen to the front, with a crossbowman positioned betwixt every pair. Our knights are to wait in the second circle behind, and not charge until I give the order.'

That provoked a rash of protest. Wrackwulf could hardly blame the young knights: Franz had spent the entire spring drilling the bannerets and their vassals, berating them for their lack of valour and discipline, now he planned on relegating them to the rear of the battle formation. And what a battle formation – Wrackwulf had never heard of its like before.

Lord Bjornwulf was clearly thinking much the same, for he said: 'Where in Ezekiel's name did you come up with such a strategy, Your Highness?' Gunthor and the other great barons voiced their assent to the sarcastic question.

'My uncle,' replied Franz. 'He fought in the Battle of Horaan Heights during the Third Pilgrim War, under King Guillemonde of Keraka. But Ezekiel is just about right too, Lord Bjornwulf – for the archangel of defensive war must have surely smiled on the King of Keraka. Fourfold the Sassanians outnumbered the crusading armies that day, but thanks to Guillemond's strategy the infidels lost. I believe tomorrow we can win too, if we do as he did.'

Mutterings and out-loud musings greeted that bold statement. 'All right then, go on,' said Bjornwulf. 'I'm sure nobody here doubts your uncle, a more stalwart man I for one never met.'

'Thank you,' replied the Crown Prince humbly, ignoring the implicit snub to his own competence.

Who'd be a young prince trying to prove his worth to a bunch of grizzled old warlords, by trying to save his homeland on his first outing as leader? Wrackwulf asked himself. But so far the Crown Prince at least seemed equal to the task.

'We should be able to keep their lightly armoured serjeants at bay with our crossbowmen,' Franz went on. 'Just behind every one shooting we'll have a second loading, ready to take his place – that should increase the rate of shots and force the enemy to deploy their heavier knights. As soon as they do that, I'll sound the sally-forth and our companies of knights can ride through and meet the enemy.'

'How does that stop the Pangonians flanking us?' asked Bjornwulf pointedly.

'Because by then we'll be fighting on a circular front,' Franz predicted confidently. 'Our knights against theirs, with soldiers and crossbowmen trading places with our horse and holding the inner circle. It's a numbers game, Lord Bjornwulf – as long as we hold formation, they can't send any more riders against us than we have. And our first couple of volleys should have softened them up too, at least whittled down the mounted serjeants somewhat.'

'It's a bold and unorthodox strategy, that I'll grant you,' said Lord Gunthor in his piping voice, tugging at his side whiskers. 'But what makes you so sure our line – no, our circle – will hold? If they break us with the first lance charge, we'll be trapped and crushed. It's too risky, Your Highness.'

'You're forgetting the terrain,' replied Franz. 'The ground I've picked is not far from the fens – it isn't marshland proper, but it's soft enough even at this time of year. They won't be able to muster a full tilt, so they'll be sending in their knights with swords not lances. That's a straight clash of blades – I may not have been in any real battles, Lord Gunthor, but I've fought enough tourneys to know that swordplay is never decided instantaneously, whether on horseback or foot. Don't forget the Pangonians are expecting to sweep us aside with sheer weight of numbers – the longer we hold them off, the more discomfited they'll become. And thanks to my unorthodox formation – as you put it – we won't have to deploy all our men at once. We can have a standard-formation battalion in reserve, ready to join when the fighting gets really thick.' Franz swept the tent with that oddly calm gaze of his. 'I mean to take away the Pangonians' tactics and their advantage in numbers – nothing more. When it comes down to the raw fighting, only Reus knows who will win.'

He does sound like he knows what he's doing, thought Wrackwulf. *Lady Rowena of Tul Aeren should marry this one when she's done swyving Vaskrian.*

Presently the Crown Prince dismissed the company, leaving Wrackwulf to seek the freelancers' camp with Sir Marech.

'Well, what do you think?' he asked the stoical mercenary captain as they picked their way through the darkling camp. 'Seems to know what he's about, the heir of Westerburg.'

Marech frowned and spat sidelong into a nearby cooking fire. Years of harsh campaigning had eroded the man's knightly manners somewhat. '*Seems* is about right,' he replied unsmiling. And as for being heir... I don't think he will be after tomorrow's fighting, not for very much longer.'

Wrackwulf arched a bushy eyebrow. 'You don't think his tactics will work?'

'Oh, they'll work – up to a point,' predicted Marech. 'We'll inflict casualties, probably more than we've a right to given the odds against us. But those odds are still against us, Sir Wrackwulf. Put your faith in Reus and legendary tales of crusading armies all you want – but more often than not it's superior numbers and better troops that win the day. You've seen enough campaigns yourself to know that, I shouldn't have to explain it to a knight of your seasons.'

'Then why fight at all?' Wrackwulf couldn't resist asking in exasperation. 'Nobody forced you to sign up to this campaign.'

Sir Marech stopped abruptly then, forcing Wrackwulf to pull up short as well. The scarred veteran met his eye in the flickering firelight.

'By my reckoning, Sir Wrackwulf, this year will be my fiftieth winter, should I live to see it,' he said flatly. 'I've cheated death more times than I deserve, but Reus has seen fit to extract a due toll for his kindness. Three sons I had, by different mistresses, and not one of them lived to see squiring age – despite my best attempts to keep them and their mothers well. Now, I've no one left to leave my monies to, and no lands to bequeath to any of my other relatives – even if I was on speaking terms with them.'

The mercenary captain suddenly looked weary, wearier than Wrackwulf had ever seen him. 'There comes a time when gold and gems lose their lustre, and all that's left to an old warrior is his legacy,' he continued soberly. 'But if he has no children to bear it, what's left to him then? To make a good end, and not much else besides.' The captain resumed walking as abruptly as he'd ceased. 'That's why I'm fighting, Sir Wrackwulf,' he said over his shoulder as the freelancer hurried after him. 'The question you should be asking your-self is – why are you?'

~

Sir Hugon surveyed the enemy with interest in the pre-dawn gloaming.

A novel formation, I'll give the Crown Prince that, he thought. *But I've a few tricks up my gauntlet too, Franz.*

He turned to the herald and motioned for him to relay his first commands of the day. Though it was still half-dark, he had insisted on using flags not trumpets to signal orders: the less idea the enemy had about his own movements, the better.

It took a while for the margraves to acknowledge receipt, but that just gave the sun more time to show itself. It promised to be a fair day, with little wind and few clouds. Perfect for his crossbowmen. A shame the ground wouldn't hold up to a lance charge; he'd had Clovis lead a contingent of outriders yesterday evening to size up the terrain.

You may know this soil better than I do, but you won't catch me out that easily, Your Highness.

Morvaine had grumbled about taking the far left battalion. Leading mounted serjeants in a flanking manoeuvre wasn't his idea of a glorious contribution to the campaign, but that only showed the man's lack of flair when it came to war.

Obey my orders, and you and Clovis on the far right flank will win us the day. I'm giving you glory not taking it away, you great bumptious fool.

Aravin and Kaye would lead the centre-left and centre-right, leaving Sir Hugon to command the middle: five battalions in a horseshoe pincer movement, that's how he'd described the manoeuvre in his pavilion the previous night.

But of course, the Crown Prince had anticipated his strategy with an unorthodox formation of his own. That and the reserve battalion the Vorstlendings were holding out of sight might have caused them problems, but Kaye's scouts had spied them out too.

Hugon felt uncomfortable thinking about that though. Once again, something about the margrave cronies of Lord Ivon made him uneasy. How had Kaye known where to send his outriders? By rights the Crown Prince's reserve battalion, concealed on the other side of the fens, should have caught them on the back foot. Perhaps Kaye's scouts had just got lucky, but still...

His reverie was interrupted by Sir Aremis riding up to him on a magnificently caparisoned piebald destrier, dressed head to toe in the newfangled plate armour. Tall and brawny and well-made, he was an impressive sight: if it hadn't been for his unfortunate facial deformity, the young knight would have been popular at court. As it was, he'd had to settle for triumphing in the field not the bedchamber, but again Sir Hugon could hardly fault him for that.

Court conquests are distinctly overrated, or so I've found, Hugon thought bitterly. And yet his loins still ached for Isolte. The thought of her idling in the Palace of White Towers with Lord Ivon made him feel even more uneasy: try as he might, he couldn't shake the nagging feeling that he might not be the Queen's only paramour. Though of course, he couldn't prove any-

'My lord?' Aremis was gazing at him, face anxious beneath his raised visor. 'What ails? The margraves have received your commands, we're ready to engage the foe at sunrise. Now is not the time to lose one's mettle, methinks.'

'I'm not losing anything, least of all today's battle!' snapped Hugon querulously. Barking an order to his squires, he nudged his own warhorse into line with Aremis's. He'd refused the new armour, reasoning that a hot summer campaign wouldn't be well served by an extra layer of metal. Besides, he was getting too old to adopt new ways. A good solid spear, a well-forged blade, and a stout well-kept hauberk were all he would need today.

That, and for his chosen tactics to pay off.

Ariadha shifted nervously in the saddle next to Wrackwulf as they watched the crossbowmen and footsoldiers draw up around them.

'This strange way to make fight,' observed the outlander haltingly.

'You aren't wrong there,' muttered the freelancer. Marech's gloomy prediction weighed heavy on his soul, though the stoical captain gave no indication of having spoken it as he inspected his freelancers one last time. The sun had broken free of the horizon's embrace: it promised to be a bright morning.

Though maybe not for us, if Sir Marech is right.

Clarion calls cut through the morning twilight as Bjornwulf and Aethelfrith ordered their spearmen and crossbowmen into position before them. There was no love lost between the ruling houses of the Two Thulias, but their old rivalries would have to wait till another day – assuming they survived this one. Turning in the saddle, Wrackwulf could just about make out the standards of Westerburg and Hyrlund, as Prince Franz and Lord Gunthor ordered their own footsoldiers into place, completing the outer circle.

The cavalry including Sir Marech's mercenary contingent were already drawn up in a concentric second circle within the first, ready to break formation at the Crown Prince's command.

A stranger formation I've never been in, thought Wrackwulf wonderingly. *I'd almost feel less out of place back adventuring in the Island Realms.*

Tensely they waited as the rising sun slowly painted the new day that lay before them. Wrackwulf suppressed a whistle as the size of Hugon's army became more readily apparent.

'He's got enough for five battalions by the looks of things,' he said to Marech. 'Though that won't make much difference now, thanks to Franz's tactics.' He cast a look sidelong at the dour captain. 'Ready to have a little more faith in His Highness?'

Marech shrugged, the links in his mail hauberk jingling. His face remained unsmiling beneath his open-faced helm.

'We'll see what the day brings,' was all he said.

In the first hour of battle, it looked as though Sir Wrackwulf's confidence might be well founded. Lightly armoured serjeants fell left and right as Franz's crossbowmen peppered them with one volley after another. Again and again, Hugon's horseshoe formation contracted and receded as the footsoldiers kept them at bay with long boar spears.

But as the morning grew older, it became clear that Marech was right: the Pangonians just had too many men to be dismayed by extra casualties. Hugon's formation reminded Wrackwulf more of a gauntlet, ever opening and closing about their tight little circle, gradually squeezing the life from them.

They received their first real piece of bad news towards the end of the second hour: a contingent of Pangonians had skirted the fens and smashed their reserves. Ezekiel knew how they'd spotted them, but they had: the clarion calls blaring down the line told of men routed and standards captured. There would be no relief if their central position became untenable.

'When are they going to let us break formation and charge, dammit?' growled Wrackwulf. 'Bad enough we're getting a pasting, we're not even in the thick of it!'

'You'll get your chance to make an ending worthy of bard's song, don't you worry,' replied Sir Marech in his monotone, as he surveyed the steady brutal attrition piling up corpses around them. Before long the signal came: the beleaguered footsoldiers drew back, offering gaps in the formation to allow the Vorstlending knights to sally forth.

'Now, company!' yelled Sir Marech. 'This is it, men! Ride forth and die with honour!'

Wrackwulf put spurs to flanks, hoping Ariadha would have the sense to follow suit. As poor as their chances seemed outside the breaking circle, he knew they would be better than if they remained within it to be crushed.

The more heavily armoured Pangonian knights had already joined the fray, mingling with the mounted serjeants. Wrackwulf rode hard into the thickening melee and began laying about him frenziedly with mace and axe: he hadn't fought two-handed since the Graufluss Bridge tourney, it felt good to cut loose.

I'll show you bard's song, Sir Marech.

A mounted serjeant screamed as Wrackwulf's mace drove his nose-guard sideways into his eye; a split second later a knight crumpled from the saddle as the freelancer's axe struck hard enough to split his collarbone beneath the armour. He'd always been uncommonly strong and tough, but now his cool fighting head was subsumed in a desperate battle rage that seemed to amplify his prowess. Next to him he was dimly aware of Ariadha, stabbing wildly about her with that enchanted spear she'd brought across the sea: had the battle choler really addled his wits, or was the thing *crooning* as she wielded it?

The spear her ancestors had bequeathed her seemed to pulse in Ariadha's hands as she used it to thrust past a serjeant's guard. The glyphs on the shaft flared briefly as the broad point sheared through the hauberk and ripped into his side; it trembled in her hands then and seemed to sigh in satisfaction. The look on the soldier's face was not just that of a dying man in pain, but of a man *horrified.* His face blanched and went white; with some effort Ariadha wrenched the eldritch weapon free.

It had certainly never behaved like that before. But then, she'd never used it to kill a man until now.

She had little time to reflect on that as a second serjeant took a swing at her with his blade. Reacting swiftly, the warrior woman knocked it aside, the spear seeming now to move with a life of its own that augmented her own movements. Before either combatant knew what had happened, the spear had torn a red rent through the soldier's throat.

This time the weapon shuddered the whole length of the shaft, and Ariadha felt that shudder pass into her. It wasn't just energy that was being conveyed, it was *desire* : the desire to kill and maim, a desire she had never known before.

Screaming a war cry, she reversed the spear and thrust it into the flanks of a warhorse ridden by an armoured knight menacing Wrackwulf. The spear almost seemed to howl resentfully at being relegated to ordinary beasts, but still it did its job: the destrier folded with a piteous scream as blood gushed from a steaming hole in the strange metal fish scales clothing it. The knight slipped from the saddle, but his foot held in the stirrup: struggling against the weight of his own armour, he tried desperately to haul himself upright.

The spear's howl turned triumphant as it yanked Ariadha's grip around and down. Before she even knew what she had done, the point had punched through the knight's visor, claiming another life. Wrackwulf spared her an amazed glance and quickly mouthed a word of thanks.

That brief communication was all they had before the storm of war engulfed them, tossing them on iron waves of bloody tumult.

The fighting dragged on as the sun crawled up the firmament towards its zenith. By the time it was shining directly above him, Wrackwulf was covered head to toe in the blood of his enemies: he'd lost track of the number of knights and soldiers he'd smitten down. He only had his axe left; the shaft of his mace had been cloven in twain by a knight, before Wrackwulf had done the same thing to his skull.

His last foe had struck him hard enough to crumple his helmet inwards. Wrackwulf wrenched the useless thing off, hoping his mail coif would be enough protection. The blow had drawn a deep gouge along the forehead; wiping the blood from his eyes, he took advantage of the brief respite to scour the battlefield.

The tidy battle formations that had begun the day had been steadily eroded during the morning, transmuted by bloodlust into the anarchic tides of true conflict. But, as far as Wrackwulf could see, their circle still held, just about: clustered units of horsemen continued to engage one another to either side, neither one seeming to gain the advantage.

A strange glaucous light seemed to suffuse Ariadha beside him, as though a portion of the sea had come inland with her, joining itself to her essence. Her face was a trance-like mask as she lay about her with the eldritch spear, felling another hapless serjeant. It was practically shrieking now; fighters on either side were giving the savage islander a wide berth, and Wrackwulf feared she might become separated from their unit.

'Ariadha, with me!' he called out. The warrior woman turned to look at him, blinking as if into wakefulness from a frightful dream, but seeming to recover her wits, she drew closer to him.

Off in the distance, trumpets blared.

Not ours, thought Wrackwulf. Scanning the corpse-blanketed field, he realised for the first time that he could see more than just a heaving shapeless mass of metal-clad bodies. Pangonian units were drawing back.

Wrackwulf felt his spirits rise.

They've sounded the retreat.

Sir Hugon wheeled his destrier around, falling in with his elite guard as they obeyed his order to withdraw. The losses on both sides had been grievous, but Franz's determined troops had held the line. Both sides were exhausted by hours of hard fighting in the rising heat; an afternoon of yet more conflict remained to decide the day.

But unlike his beleaguered enemies, Hugon had plenty of reserves to draw upon. The heralds were marshalling them now, ordering fresh units of knights and mounted serjeants forwards, to plug the gap created by their disengaging comrades.

Next to him Sir Aremis looked glum as they cantered in orderly fashion back to camp. 'We almost broke them a couple of times,' he muttered. 'Another push, and the glory would have been ours.'

Hugon smiled at the younger knight. 'The glory shall belong to all those on the victorious side,' he reassured his comrade. 'And we'll see victory before the sun is out, don't you worry.'

It took Wrackwulf a few minutes to realise what was happening.

'Ezekiel dammit, that's no retreat − it's a withdrawal,' he

cried. 'The Pangonians are just making room for their reserves.'

A few places up the line, Sir Marech cracked a gallows grin beneath his battle-scarred helm. 'I told you we'd be making an end worthy of bard's song today, didn't I?'

Just then trumpets blared again, only this time from their side. And they put the lie to Marech's words instantly.

Franz is ordering us to retreat, Wrackwulf realised. *He's conceding the field.*

From a high hill overlooking their camp, Sir Hugon watched his reserves muster into formation. Beyond them, he could see what he had half expected to: the Crown Prince's forces were breaking theirs, sounding a general retreat.

Next to him Sir Aremis looked nervous. 'Do you think it might be a feint?' he asked.

Hugon shook his head. 'I doubt it. Lord Clovis's forces smashed Franz's reserves hours ago.' He turned to smile at Aremis. 'He's lying in wait for their main army now – we'll harry them from both directions and smash the rest of them to pieces.'

Turning to the herald, Hugon ordered a general pursuit.

Wrackwulf knew they were well and truly swyved when the enemy lance charge took them in the side. Retreating had taken them back onto firmer ground beyond the marshes, rendering them sitting ducks for enemy cavalry. Above the surging mass of knights he could make out a standard waving in the breeze: a golden cockatrice *regardant* on a purpure and argent chequy, the coat of arms of Narbo. Shattered lances were swiftly replaced by sharp swords, as Lord Clovis's men hewed at their breaking column left and right.

'Fly!' cried Marech. 'Fly for Westerburg! It's every knight for himself now, lads! This is no retreat, it's a rout!'

As the column finally broke, no one could deny the truth of his words. The next half hour was pandaemonium, a whirling vortex of steel and blood that Wrackwulf would never rightly recall for the rest of his days. Somehow he and Ariadha managed to stay together; thundering past their army camp, they saw it was already being ransacked. He saw squires and camp washerwomen and prostitutes put pitilessly to the sword. The freelancer had no pity himself to spare for the poor wretches; all he could think of was to follow Marech's last order, and try and get to the safety of Wester-burg Point.

By mid-afternoon, the battle had become a hunt, with Pangonian knights seeking human prey across the Wester Plains. What became of the rest of his unit, Wrackwulf never learned: by sunset he and Ariadha were holed up in a copse, awaiting cover of darkness to make the last league across open country to the sanctuary of the castle. The freelancer could only pray the guards would hold the gate open a little longer.

He glanced sidelong at the warrior-woman in the gloaming, but she seemed not to realise where she was or what had happened. Instead she sat still and silent in the gathering gloom, cradling her spear like a long-lost lover. Her lips moved silently, as though she were carrying on a soundless conversation with the eldritch weapon.

Wrackwulf shook his head, and returned his gaze to the darkling fields.

CHAPTER 11

SWORDS AT DUSK

The silhouetted statuary of Montrevellyn seemed to peer at them meanly in the dusking light. Adelko's sixth sense buzzed uneasily as they stepped onto the wharf, a bustling morass of humanity the last time he'd seen it, now silent at evening's touch. After nearly two weeks at sea, he was grateful to be ashore again, but he would have picked a happier destination given the choice.

Of Shazra'am, he'd seen but little: the Muradi capital's twinkling domes and gilded spires had suggested a port city traded into easy prosperity over the centuries. Those of its eighty thousand souls he'd encountered had seem genial and urbane, mostly content with the rule of their Sultan, Hareem-Tek-Nazir. Unorthodoxers like Sha'arza's native Halepo to the east, the Muradis seemed content to stay out of the Pilgrim Wars, doing business with Palomedian and Sha'abatian alike.

Perhaps they've got the right idea, he reflected as the four of them waited patiently for their horses and supplies to be loaded off the merchantman that had brought them back across the Sundering Sea. *I'm beginning to wonder if neutrality wouldn't be the best side to pick in any conflict.*

If he was intimidated by being on Palomedian soil, Hari Yassin showed no signs of it. 'Impressive,' he said, scrutinising the statue of Rayonde the Scourge in the fading light. 'Though not half as impressive as my native city. A wonder it is, you Urovians conquered us.'

'As I recall,' interjected Horskram crisply. 'You trace half of your ancestry back here. Less talk of "we" and "you" might become you better, Hari.'

Yassin smirked at that, but said nothing more.

Presently the horses and saddlebags they'd purchased in Shazra'am arrived.

'I'm not sure about these Muradi breeds,' groused Azelin as he checked the sleek coursers. 'They're better suited to an arid climate, they might not serve us so well up north.'

'Well they better had,' snapped Horskram. 'After the comely coin we paid for them. I must be getting old – I should have driven a harder bargain with that scurrilous trader.'

'No,' smiled Hari, 'You should have let me steal them, as I suggested. Now we've paid for yon steeds and our passage across the sea, Sha'arza's money has barely left us enough to get to your precious Rima – and I had so looked forward to enjoying the finest Pangonian hospitality on our journey. Here in the great realm of my ancestors, as you put it.'

Horskram scowled. 'And I for one am looking forward to not being arrested, for a change. A pox on your thieving ways, Yassin – I'll thank you to employ them only at my say-so.'

Yassin's tart response faded into the background as Adelko's sixth sense suddenly jolted up several notches.

'We need to stop arguing and get out of here, fast,' the journeyman blurted.

The others eyed him quizzically.

'Men are coming for us,' said Adelko. 'And they don't mean us well.'

Hari arched an eyebrow, but Horskram nodded. 'We'd better do as the lad says,' he said. 'His sixth sense is keener than a *taziq*'s blade. Come! Let's tarry not!'

Without another word the four of them took to the saddle. The sun had disappeared altogether, but link-boys were already lighting the dockside lamps: they'd get no cover under darkness.

'Which way?' growled the adept.

'Anywhere but up the main thoroughfare,' replied Adelko. Even now, in his mind's eye, he could discern the shadowy images of several mounted men, armed and dangerous, approaching quickly.

'Follow me in that case,' said Horskram, nudging his steed over towards one of the meaner streets leading from the waterfront.

In the private suite of chambers in the Palace of White Towers where he ruled as Regent, Ivon smiled as he watched his prey flee the docks.

So you've fathomed my men, he thought, steering his attention towards the mercenary serjeants as they closed in on the waterfront. *You're every bit as resourceful as Hannequin led me to believe. I think I'm going to rather enjoy this little game of cat and mouse.*

Without taking his eye off the polished mirror he was using as a scrying tool, he motioned for Queen Isolte to pour him a goblet of Armandy red.

Tonight, he was going to enjoy himself.

Adelko felt his hackles rise as he sensed the men change direction to intercept them. He could also sense his three companions felt it too, though less keenly than him: even Yassin and Azelin had spent some time heightening their psychic intuition. But the journeyman had seen enough adventures by now to realise that their pursuers would not be bereft of preternatural guidance either.

'They're closing on us,' said Horskram, barging through the teeming crowds. The time when a city transitions from work to pleasure was upon Montrevellyn, and the crooked streets were thronged with people.

'Whoever they are, they won't risk open confrontation in the middle of the city,' said Azelin.

'Don't be so sure of that,' muttered Horskram.

The adept could not have been more right.

'Argolians! Demonolators all!'

The cry came from an ordinary citizen, and was soon taken up by others in the crowd.

'Somebody call the watch!' cried another.

All about them the surging mass of townsfolk became confused; those nearest now pushed back into the crowd, trying to put as much distance between themselves and the friars as they could. But on the fringes, some of the bolder citizens were arming themselves with whatever came to hand, and sizing them up.

In a flash, Azelin's blade was out. Its keen edge caught the nearby lantern light, glinting dangerously.

'Make way there!' he bellowed. 'Or by the archangels, you rug rats will taste my sword!'

The knight's sheer presence was enough to cow those thinking about taking matters into their own hands – but it also caused a general panic to break out.

'We need to get out while we can!' cried Horskram, spurring his horse forwards. The others followed suit. All thoughts of sparing the common folk their horses' hooves were gone; Adelko winced as his courser trampled a fallen milkwife.

Azelin showed no such compunction, lashing about him with the flat of his blade as he steered his horse expertly from the stirrups. Horskram and Adelko remained unarmed, but the older monk wasn't above getting in a few vicious kicks from the saddle: by the time the four of them had broken free of the bottleneck, a dozen men and women lay behind them, nursing bruises and broken limbs.

So much for the hero's return, thought Adelko, a sick feeling uncurling in his gut.

But at least they'd broken free. Spurring their coursers into a gallop, they pelted through the warren of side streets, following Horskram's lead as he took them towards the city's outskirts. All the while, Adelko's sixth sense continued to needle his psyche, reminding him that they weren't out of danger.

'They're going to head us off out of town!' he warned the others. 'There must be ten of them at least!'

'Fine odds for four wayfarers!' Azelin shot back, favouring him with one of his nasty grins.

Ivon sipped on his Armandy wine, and leaned back in his chair.

Just as I expected, they don't die that easily. You weren't exaggerating, Hannequin. This lot will be quite the prize.

Shifting his elan, he pushed out a suggestion to the mercenary commander he'd enthralled. Using Scrying and Enchantment together was always challenging, but he liked a challenge.

Behind him, he felt his sorcerous grip on Isolte relax

slightly. But that didn't trouble him: the Thalamian beauty was from an old people, who well understood the price of power. Ivon knew she'd stand with him, ensorcelled or no – having her under his control was just an extra layer of surety. It was also rather satisfying to enthral a queen.

Returning his focus to the night-time scene of skulduggery playing out before him, Ivon grinned wickedly as the mounted serjeants drew swords and prepared to engage the enemy.

Soon they hoved into view: the two monks had a pair of outlanders they'd brought back with them across the sea, but that didn't bother Ivon.

Let's see how your bodyguards cope with ten men.

The serjeants closed about the four of them. Swords flashed in the twilight. The two monks and one of the outlanders appeared just to be defending, trying to preserve their hides a bit longer. But the fourth... Something had to be wrong, nobody could fight that well. Two serjeants went down. Then another. The warrior moved so *quickly*. A fourth serjeant fell from the saddle. A fifth.

Mustering his elan, Ivon sharpened his focus, drawing in closer so he could get a better look. His serjeants were withdrawing, sheer terror getting the better of his sorcerous hold on them. Ivon let them go. Clearly ordinary mercenaries weren't going to be up to this job, and at least with them out of the way he could get a better look at –

The warlock allowed himself a sharp intake of breath as he recognised the man. The years had changed him. He was a lot more unkempt, and even through a scrying tool Ivon could see a sorrow written in his eyes that hadn't been there before.

But it was him.

'Well, well,' he said aloud, reaching for his goblet. 'So the great knight errant has returned, and he's not on our side. Now, isn't *that* an interesting development?'

They rode hard up the old Thalamian highway all night long, before taking refuge in the ruins of an ancient villa built by the same long-crumbled empire. Adelko thought the fractured obelisks a daunting place in which to hide, though his aching body thanked him for the respite.

Azelin showed no sign of being saddle-sore, or disconcerted by a lethal encounter that had seen him rob five hardened soldiers of their lives in less than a minute. Dismounting, he patted his lathered courser gently.

'Looks like I was wrong about these southern breeds,' he said. 'They seem to have taken to a coastal climate quite nicely.'

'How do you do it?' Adelko asked him.

'Do what?' returned the erstwhile warrior-monk, looking at the journeyman askance in the gloaming.

'Fight like that,' breathed Adelko. 'I've never seen anyone wield a blade the way you do – not even Sir Torgun, and he's the greatest knight Northalde has seen in decades.'

Azelin shrugged. 'You know my background well enough – I was always handy with sword and spear. Then the Order trained me to use my sixth sense to help me fight even better. Not to mention enough experience of conflict to fit into several busy lifetimes. Draw your own conclusions.'

Adelko thought about that as they broke out bedrolls and prepared to snatch a breakfast of oatcakes, dates and hard cheese before sleeping.

'I've heard it told you slew the last of the Wyrms,' he said. 'In the Orne ranges, before you went on crusade.'

Azelin smiled. It was the first time Adelko had ever seen

him do so without a hint of malice. 'Oh, that old bard's song is still doing the rounds, is it?' he asked gently. 'Baphomet died on my sword, yes – though in truth I feel he was lesser in stature than his sires of old. Yet still he was as long as a cavalcade of armoured knights, and just as well defended, for only by striking with the point of my lance could I penetrate between those leathern plates. If it wasn't for the magicked shield Aegis given to me by Darya the Rose Witch, I fear his spittle alone would have sloughed the flesh from my bones.'

'A crusader having truck with witches?' put in Hari, relishing the irony. 'No wonder you got into trouble with the Bethlers.'

'I wasn't a crusader back then,' replied Azelin sadly. 'Just another knight errant, enjoying the flower of his chivalry.' A dreamy, far-off look came into his eyes then. 'Those were better times,' he said, before falling silent.

Adelko didn't need his sixth sense to register the profound sadness in his companion. What must it be like, to rise so high and fall so low? He hoped he'd never have to find out.

'A man shall be judged by the sum of all his deeds, as the Redeemer sayeth,' he quoted. 'I know you don't hold truck with the scriptures nowadays, but surely you can find some comfort in those words?'

'Not really,' replied the disgraced crusader flatly.

'Why did Baphomet arise to trouble the realms of men in the first place?' asked Adelko, keen to change the subject back again. 'He was the last of his kind surely he knew it would be the end of his race.'

'It was vengeance that moved him,' interjected Horskram, breaking his silence. 'Baphomet's father Anglaurung was slain by Sir Lancelyn of the Pale Mountain, in the days of King Vasirius. After that Baphomet hid for many long years, knowing he could never hope to contend with the mighty paladins of that age. And so the legends tell he slept, lying in torpor until long after Vasirius perished at the Battle of Avalongne against the Traitor Prince Ancelet. When he awoke he found a kingdom weaker than before, the great knights long gone – or so he thought.'

The adept paused to glance meaningfully at Sir Azelin, before continuing the tale.

'And so Baphomet emerged to terrorise Azelin's lands in Valacia. He sought to be avenged on Sir Lancelyn's kin you see, for Azelin is a lineal descendant of that great knight by his illicit son Maglyn, whom he fathered on Queen Isoude in the Chivalrous King's heyday. After Azelin slew Baphomet, his account of the battle was written down by monks of our Order at Rima, for posterity. Yon knight's modesty becomes him – Baphomet was but a lesser Wyrm, scarcely more than a Wyvern himself, the last ebb of dwindled dragonkind.'

'A knight?' replied Azelin, the old bitterness creeping back into his voice. 'It's a while since I've thought of myself as such.'

'Yet a knight you remain,' replied the old monk implacably. 'Not even the Bethlers have the power to attaint a man – so in heaven's name, start acting like one! You just saved our lives back there. Redeemer's wounds, can't you see you aren't yet beyond redemption?'

Azelin stared at Horskram, an inscrutable expression on his harrowed face.

'No, I can't,' he said simply, before turning abruptly to seek his pallet.

Horskram sighed heavily, taking another sour bite of cheese and washing it down with some watered wine.

'He'll be his own death of a broken heart if he keeps tormenting himself so,' muttered the adept in between mouthfuls.

'But you've always counselled me yourself that knights are killers destined for perdition,' Adelko pointed out.

'If they don't repent and make up for it they are,' replied Horskram. 'The Almighty has gifted Sir Azelin with a rare opportunity to do just that – if only he can realise it.'

Not for the first time, Adelko had his doubts about his mentor. Horskram believed in doing the right thing, but even his morals seemed to walk crooked roads at times.

'Well, I don't know about you two,' said Hari, taking the wineskin from Horskram and pulling gratefully on it. 'But I for one am far less concerned with redemption than I am by what just happened to us in Montrevellyn. I knew your Order was controversial, Master Horskram – but back there we almost got lynched by a mob!'

'Yes, we did,' replied Horskram, his face set grim in the fading light. 'Unless I miss my guess, I'd say Cyprian has not been idle in our absence. If word of Hannequin's black betrayal has got out, that would be the perfect excuse for the Supreme Perfect to start persecuting us again.'

Which is why I thought coming back here was a really bad idea in the first place, thought Adelko. But he was too tired to argue with his mentor now.

Presently they sought their bedrolls and the sweet blessing of Morphonus. None of them had the energy to go on watch, but a couple of hours later Adelko awoke briefly to find Azelin already up. Sat on the stump of a shattered obelisk, he almost seemed to be a part of the ruined precinct they had taken shelter in. Slowly and methodically he sharpened his blade, staring up the highway with eyes that never seemed to blink.

Before drifting back to sleep, Adelko once again caught the inscription written in Decorlangue on the fuller of the blade.

Know Thyself.

CHAPTER 12

AN ILL TIDE RISING

Vaskrian gripped the taffrail tightly in mufflered hands as the surf lashed their vessel. The war galley was stout enough that he wasn't worried about being cast overboard this close to the coast – nor did the imminent prospect of a naval battle daunt him. What did concern him, however, was the sudden unwelcome bout of seasickness – he was a knight now, it wouldn't do to be seen vomiting over the side of the ship.

Torgun, also clad in helm and hauberk, drew level with him.

'How are your sea legs faring?' he asked, not unkindly.

'Not so well,' confessed the younger knight. 'You'd think after sailing to Rima and back I'd have got them by now. Why oh why are we in Lord Aesgir's fleet, and not fighting on land with Toros and Toric where we belong?'

'Because this war will be decided at sea,' Torgun reminded him. 'The Northland barbarians are too well dug in at the capital – but if we smash their navy, we can begin starving them out.'

'It'll go hard for our people,' Vaskrian sighed. 'The ones behind Strongholm's walls, I mean.'

'It will go harder for them if we do nothing,' replied Torgun unsmiling. 'Better to die of hunger than live as a slave.'

Vaskrian kept his next thought to himself. He could understand a high-born man of honour like Sir Torgun thinking that way – but an ordinary townsman might take a very different view of choosing death over bondage. Not for the first time, the difficulty of transitioning from commoner to noble was keenly apparent.

There's only one thing worse than not getting what you want, his father had once told him. *And that's getting what you want.* The old man's cryptic words seemed to make a lot more sense now.

Raising his eyes to the firmament, Sir Vaskrian offered up a silent prayer to his father's soul.

I hope I make you proud today at least.

Turning his gaze to the coastline, Sir Torgun lapsed back into brooding thoughts. His brother's strategy was sound, but he couldn't help but agree with Vaskrian privately. Sieges were a mean, brutal and ugly means to make war – but the Northland bastards had left them no choice. At least by joining the naval campaign they'd get a chance to see some real action.

And once again, the great knight Sir Torgun avoids doing the dirty work, he thought disparagingly before catching himself. By Virtus and Stygnos, but where had this latent cynicism come from? Once again Torgun thought of the apparition that had pronounced his doom far away across the sea – the encounter had changed him profoundly, and not in ways he liked.

Scouring the coastal seas for signs of the Northland flotilla, he sighed inwardly.

Perhaps no matter, if the visions it bequeathed me prove true – there'll be an end to things soon enough.

Gazing at the Northlending fleet as it hugged the coastline, Ragnar smiled his icy smile. The rippling pool he used for his scrying seemed to accentuate the heaving waves of the Strang Estuary; shifting his focus, he saw the Northland flotilla of longships ready in formation.

Ragnar would see to it that they didn't have to fight alone. The warlock some men called the Tamer of Oceans let the pool grow dark, before turning back towards the covered bridge that would take him into the Mouth of the Serpent. The shrine he had made his own was a welcoming presence; its spiny interior pleased him, as did the priests' corpses that hung from the walls.

Just punishment for men who had conspired against him over the winter, but his second in command Svinn had quickly rooted them out. Now his power had grown he no longer needed their paltry elan to perform the catechism to the Great World Serpent, but he'd been feeling merciful. Instead of feeding them to the Cauldron he'd decided to use them as ornaments – and a warning to any others who might take foolish ideas into their heads.

Inside the deathly cold precinct, Svinn was supervising the last of the day's feedings: a Northlending youth of no more than fourteen summers screamed horribly as two muscular berserkers gripped him tightly. Svinn only grinned: the past few months had seen him acquire a taste for blood and power. That was well: Ragnar would reward him with further knowledge, if he proved loyal.

The youth was begging now, tears streaking a once-handsome face as the berserkers lifted his half-starved frame over the whorled lip of the Cauldron. Ignoring his pathetic pleas, Ragnar reached out to stroke the boy's wet cheek.

'Ah, youth,' he breathed. 'Do you even realise the glory of your sacrifice? Your name will be celebrated along with all those others who made the Return possible. What is your name, boy?'

A glimmer of hope came to light in the boy's eyes as he stammered a reply.

Ragnar smiled darkly at him. 'Orvald, the gods thank you for your precious gift.' He motioned to the berserkers, who cast the boy screaming into the Cauldron. Ragnar watched as he disappeared from Middangeard forever, his scream dying off gradually as he fell to the heart of the world.

Dismissing Svinn and the berserkers, Ragnar raised his spidery arms and began to recite the Catechism in the language of magick:

> *Jürmengaard, thou that sleepeth*
> *In chthonian torpor at the heart of darkness!*
> *Through the shifting of thy coils,*
> *The world shall draw its final breath:*
> *Aurgelmir's bones shall break,*
> *And know the infinity of the celestial grave!*

> *Jürmengaard, stay thy cataclysm!*
> *Render up thy servants, spawn of the oceans,*
> *And quell mine enemies!*
> *True earth father that groaneth in slumber:*
> *No more thought, no more mind!*
> *Let Aurgelmir's sons share thy demise!*

> *Jürmengaard, eternal is thy hunger!*

Heed now this sacrifice of frail mortal flesh,
Those fragile vessels that creak in vain
Against the choppy foam of the seas of life!
Let men and giants tremble
As earth and water intertwine!

Thrice the White Eye spoke the name given by his ancestors to the Great World Serpent; the same name Søren had given to his enchanted longship in blasphemous defiance of the pre-deity. But Ragnar used it now for its intended purpose, with the utmost reverence.

Far beneath the waves, the Tritons heeded his prayer, and answered.

Vaskrian's pulse quickened as the lookout reported the first sighting of the Northland flotilla. Before long he could see them too: a multitude of warships clustered about the Strang. Next to him Sir Torgun unsheathed his weapon: the bastard blade caught the summer sun with a refulgent glow, rippling like quicksilver with blinding intensity.

Even the younger knight's own blade felt meagre by comparison as he pulled it free of its scabbard. The Valravyn sword gifted to him by Sir Aronn: at least it was better than the hauberk and kite shield Lord Toros had had his men dig up for him. Tainted with flecks of rust, they'd seen better days, but Sir Vaskrian was long used to making do with whatever came to hand.

Sir Torgun issued commands in his calm voice, never raising it. But all the knights and soldiers aboard the war galley heeded his words. A detachment of longships had broken off from the main flotilla and was coming towards them at haste; on the horizon, Vaskrian could make out the dour grey walls of Strongholm, the city they had come to save.

The fluttering of a golden anchor displayed on a blue-and-white lozengy field brought Vaskrian's attention back to the foreground. A squire was waving Lord Aesgir's pennon from the forecastle of his ship: the Sealord had issued the command to engage. Torgun and the other ship commanders repeated the command and a great cheer went up the line. Forty war galleys carrying a thousand men of arms hurtled towards a like number of longships. When they got within shooting range, Aesgir ordered half the Northlending fleet to turn to starboard, presenting the gunnels to the oncoming longships. Crossbowmen surged forwards, taking up positions at the inwales before loading.

But the Northland barbarians had anticipated this strategy, and rapidly turning their own ships to port, presented broad target shields: bristling porcupines of wood and iron were all the Northlending crossbowmen had to show for their first volley.

But the distraction had served its purpose. The other ten galleys, five on each side, continued forwards, fanning out in a double flanking manoeuvre. The agile longships were equal to this tactic as well, steering themselves around to meet the sidelong assault. Together with the others in the central line, Vaskrian's galley stood fast, waiting for the remaining longships to close with them.

The two knights and the cohort of footsoldiers they commanded swiftly replaced the crossbowmen as a barbarian ship closed in on them. Shieldmen equipped with stout axes and swords surged over the gunnels, led by two ferocious berserkers. Covered in naught but tattoos and bearskins, they cleaved a swathe through the defending line, hewing down soldiers left and right with great two-handed axes.

'With me, Sir Vaskrian!' cried Torgun, cutting down two

shieldmen in quick succession. 'We'll cut off both the serpent's heads!'

Vaskrian wrenched his blade free from the entrails of a barbarian he'd just skewered, and pushed his way through the melee towards the half-naked warriors. They were a fearsome sight, frothing at the mouth and giving vent to great ululating cries in the Norric tongue as they hacked and gouged their way across the deck.

Vaskrian's opponent towered a full head above him, but that didn't faze the young knight: he'd built a career on bringing down bigger, stronger fighters than himself. He crouched low, goading the berserker to attack. When he did, Vaskrian spun to the side, pivoting on one foot and whirling around, using the momentum to put extra force behind the strike. The berserker's axe cleaved air just as Vaskrian's sword point thrust deep into his leg, severing the artery.

It was just the kind of unorthodox move he'd cultivated in years of hard fighting, and it served him well now. But the berserker wasn't done: in his death throes he became twice as strong and fast, catching Vaskrian a crushing blow on the head. His helm saved his life, but Vaskrian saw stars as he crumpled into the mainmast, sword slipping from nerveless fingers. The berserker loomed over him. Ignorant of the fountain of red pumping from his thigh, he raised the axe to strike at Vaskrian's prone form. The young knight saw Azrael's vast wings loom across the firmament behind him...

The berserker's head shot off his shoulders, borne on another crimson tide as Torgun's magicked blade clove his neck in twain. Behind him the second berserker lay in pieces. Torgun extended a hand and helped Vaskrian to his feet. So far as the younger knight could tell, the big man had nary a scratch on him.

The tide began to turn as panicked shieldmen tried to flee back to the longship, their courage broken by the swift deaths of their champions. Northlending soldiers recovered their own as they harried them, sending more corpses tumbling into the wine-dark waves.

Groggily Vaskrian fumbled for his sword, though he didn't anticipate needing it again in this skirmish: his ship had decisively won its first encounter in the Battle of the Strang.

Less than a minute later, a queer bubbling from the waves lapping against the hull put the lie to that notion.

Vaskrian knew something was wrong when he heard the first soldier scream. It wasn't the throaty howl of a man in pain, but the high panicked cry of a man who is terrified. The spectre of his previous adventures ghosted across his mind as he saw them with his own eyes for the first time.

Toad-like hybrids of amphibian and human, they seemed to sport multiple joints that bent unnaturally at different angles; a thick spongy substance that looked like a cross between seaweed and coral sprouted from their slimy stinking bodies, which were hard and chitinous underneath. Three eyes bulged from each one's head, glinting malevolently like dungeon lanterns. A myriad of the spawn were crawling up all sides of the ship with a speed that could only be described as hideous: already several of the foremost had grasped a handful of soldiers, dragging them below the waves to a salty grave.

Desperately, Torgun tried to rally his unit. But Vaskrian knew the ordinary soldiers and mariners were already half beaten by fear: this was knight errants' work.

Engaging the new enemy, Sir Vaskrian felt a satisfaction as two of them went down to his singing blade – tough or not, their bodies were no match for good cold Northlending steel. The creatures were armed with sharp knives of flint and coral, poor weapons. But there were *so many* of them – a numberless horde, they kept coming over the gunnels, threatening to choke the ship with their briny stench.

Torgun's blade flashed as he destroyed one Triton after another, but the creatures seemed to know no fear, surging at them again and again.

Vaskrian was dimly aware of Aesgir's ship sounding the retreat, the high thin notes from its clarions suggesting that the rest of the fleet had been similarly assailed. On the left hand and the right he slew, until he was wading knee-deep in the stinking creatures' bodies and spattered with their inky gore. But still the Tritons came.

And ever so slightly, he began to tire. The sweat lashed off of him as his sword strokes began to falter. Torgun's near-superhuman strength had served him better, and his shimmering blade was starting to make an impression on the creatures, driving them back into the sea whence they'd come.

But it was too late for Vaskrian. Two of the creatures grappled him, bowling him over towards the gunnel while a third tried to find a chink in his armour with its coral dagger. The young knight's sword slipped from his fingers as a Triton bit hard on his gauntleted hand. Letting go of his shield, he mustered the last of his strength, putting out one of the stabbing Triton's eyes with his free hand. The creature screeched horribly as it leapt off of him, but just then the other two holding him leapt clear of the gunnel with an awful strength – taking the young knight with them.

Vaskrian gave vent to a scream of his own as he plunged into the frothing waters of the Strang. The two fiends had not let him go, but continued to pull at him, dragging him beneath the churning waves. Swimming in a heavy hauberk would have been a challenge at the best of times; grappled by two humanoid sea creatures, he didn't stand a chance.

The cold waters closed over his head, and Vaskrian sank like a stone.

AN ORDER BETRAYED

Horskram looked upon the burnt-out monastery with sad eyes. The walls of Chevraulaix still smouldered, their blackened forms at odds with the silvery sheen of the Lake Luac it overlooked. Worst of all were the corpses of the Argolian brethren, strung up on gibbets for all to see. A small preceptory, its thirty brothers had lived peacefully since the Purge, sustaining themselves with farming and fishing when not going about their Argolian duties.

'And so it's begun,' pronounced the adept grimly. 'Cyprian's New Purge is in full swing – we'll find no succour here. We can only assume Hannequin has either been exposed, or left with whatever followers he's garnered over the years. Either way, it's given the Supreme Perfect the opportunity he's been craving all these years to move against us.'

They'd ridden their horses hard up the Thalamian highway for another couple of days, before abandoning it to ride cross country towards the lake that marked the natural boundary between the margravates of Vania and Narbo. They hadn't encountered any soldiers in service to either of the ruling houses of Gormand or Oraunt – most of them would be out of the country on Cyprian's crusade in Vania's case or Carolus's invasion of Vorstlund in Narbo's. Horskram had dared to hope that had meant a change in their fortunes – or least that the Abbot of Chevraulaix could tell them what had transpired in their absence.

And now, this.

'I never really believed I'd live to see it,' said Adelko, shaking his head in disbelief. 'I thought men had learned from the Purge.'

But Horskram only sighed.

'Your adventures should have taught you this much, Adelko of Narvik – men never change and seldom learn anything.'

The journeyman fell silent at that. It was a bitterly cynical thing to tell his understudy, but right now Horskram was finding it hard to put much faith in mortalkind.

Instead it was Hari who spoke up. 'Well, I don't know about you, but I don't fancy spending the night in a burned-out monastery with dead monks for company – begging your pardon, Master Horskram.'

'He's right,' put in Azelin. 'Even if most of the army's out of the country, it won't be safe to linger here. Whoever did this to your brethren, chances are they had local help. Now is the perfect time for commoners to settle old scores and feed their grudges.'

Horskram nodded, barely listening.

And this is what we labour for, he thought. *Reus, you fashioned us so imperfectly, and yet you expect us to fight to save ourselves.*

By nightfall they'd put a few leagues' distance between themselves and Chevraulaix. A hamlet nestled in the hills nearby, but they dared not beg shelter for the night.

'I'm friendly with an old vassal of Lord Morvaine's,' mulled Horskram as they prepared for more snatched food and sleep under open skies. 'His manor lies half a day's ride north of here. I cured his daughter of possession years ago – I doubt he'll be caught up in this madness. He won't be away on campaign either, he's too long in years for active service.'

'Or we could strike out north-east to Valacia,' suggested Azelin. 'Men there may still be loyal to me, Bethlers be damned. And most of my erstwhile brethren will be away on the Fourth Pilgrim War.'

Horskram eyed the Pangonian keenly in the twilight.

At last, he's beginning to think like a knight and lord again. That's some progress, at least.

Now wasn't the time to put the fallen hero's mettle to the test, however. 'It's a bold suggestion, I'll grant you,' said Horskram, 'but too risky. And Valacia will take us out of our way. We need to get to the Grand High Monastery in Rima as quickly as possible.'

Azelin shrugged. 'I doubt we can take the most direct route there in any case,' he pointed out. 'The highway has become too dangerous for us to use.'

'If we make for Sir Regis's manor, we'll only have to cross it briefly,' said Horskram. 'Once we're there we can obtain disguises – much as it pains me to say this, Adelko and I will have to travel incognito. It won't do to have us sporting grey habits all the way to the capital.'

'But Master Horskram, we're up against another sorcerer,' Adelko reminded him. 'He'll be able to see what we're up to, won't he?'

'Yes, he will,' Horskram allowed. 'But he might not be able to communicate what he sees to all his henchmen. And honestly, right now I'm more worried about being lynched by a mob than facing off against another pack of hired thugs.'

'Your mentor has the right of it,' said Azelin. 'Not even I can keep killing everyone forever.' Again the gallows grin.

'I can help with the disguises,' put in Hari. 'It's — how do you say? — one of my strengths.'

'We'll have plenty of need for your skulduggerous ways, don't you worry,' Horskram said. 'If Hannequin has indeed absconded, I'm pinning my hopes on the loyal brethren he left behind acting swiftly and barricading themselves in. The Most Reverend Priory of St Argo is designed to withstand a siege for up to a year, perhaps more — it's no different from a castle in that respect. But that means getting in will be difficult — which is where you'll come in.'

Yassin shrugged. 'I still think it's folly to do it, but I'll help if I can.'

'If Hannequin's gone, we have to get in,' insisted Horskram. 'Hopefully he'll have left some clues behind in his chambers. And the brethren might know something.'

Adelko chewed his lip fretfully. 'But what if the Grand Master hasn't left and it's just Cyprian acting on his own initiative? Those traders we spoke to yesterday said the King left to oversee the campaign in Vorstlund weeks ago. And we know his regent Ivon is up to no good — Adhelina told us as much. Maybe he's let Cyprian have his Purge because it suits his own ends.'

Horskram nodded grimly, fidgeting absently with the silver rood he wore about his neck. A search of the ruins of Chevraulaix had turned up one piece of good luck: quarterstaves, circifixes, and other Argolian paraphernalia the depredators had managed to overlook. Those to replace the articles taken from the monks in Ushalayim, when yet another enemy of the Order had sought to visit the same fate upon them.

Night was on the land once more, and the silhouetted

images of his companions huddled around their fireless camp did little to reassure him.

'What you say may well be the case, Adelko,' he allowed. 'But that is something we will just have to find out for ourselves. We'll get Hari to reconnoitre the monastery once we arrive – if Hannequin is still there, we'll have to think up another plan. We obviously can't risk petitioning Ivon now the King is gone.'

'And what will this other plan consist of exactly?' quizzed Yassin.

Horskram sighed deeply. 'In all honesty, I don't know yet,' he replied.

Up on the plateau, the night air had taken on a chill that was almost autumnal, though it was high summer. Ivon inhaled deeply, and scanned the half dozen or so acolytes he'd brought with him. Below them the waters of the Athos washed their way through the trees of the Arbevere towards Rima. Turning his gaze from it, Ivon focused on the red rock at the plateau's centre that pulsed with eldritch power.

It was good to be back. He had not dared return to the scene of last year's conjuring of Molaach, and now he was Regent getting out of the palace unremarked upon was even more difficult. He'd only managed it by leaving in the dead of night, disguised: the guards on gate duty at the Palace of White Towers and the city walls he'd had to enthral. Bribery was out of the question, it was too risky. No matter, he'd use Enchantment to wipe their memories, that would save having to keep them ensorcelled.

Because he'd be needing all his spare elan for his next spell, and this one didn't belong to the Right Hand Path.

Curtly he motioned towards the blocked cave where they kept the chosen.

'Bring him,' he commanded the acolytes.

Wordlessly, they obeyed. A vagabond caught hunting deer in the Arbevere without royal privilege, no one would miss him. Ivon had stayed the usual execution, showing clemency: it was always useful to think ahead, to have an extra card up one's sleeve for situations such as this.

The young man tried to cry out through his gag as the acolytes brought him and pressed him down on the red shard.

Ivon felt tense. As much as he relished the prospect of buggering the lad senseless prior to tearing out his heart and sending his soul to the City of Burning Brass, he hadn't anticipated taking this risk. But Hannequin had been specific on this point: the two monks and their allies must be eliminated. The Master was always a stickler for tying up loose ends, even though the Argolians had failed to apprehend him.

In a pouch at his belt Ivon carried a phial of sleeping draft and enchanted silver dust, both products of his Alchemy.

Tearing the gag off the common huntsman, Ivon forced the philtre down his gullet. The youth soon went quiescent, his eyes glazing over, though Ivon knew he could still register what was about to happen to him. That was essential: the victim must know true terror, for such emotions demonkind savoured as a mortal might a fine draft of Armandy wine.

Ivon and his disciples began the preparations, drawing the pentangle about the shard using the artificed silver dust he'd fashioned for that purpose. When they were done they changed into more appropriate clothing, putting on black robes and donning goat's head masks, in honour of the Fallen One's first creations. The King of All would soon be on his rightful throne, and when he was, such ceremonies would no longer be clandestine ones. Ivon glanced back towards Rima, in the direction of the Argolian monastery. At least they'd be getting no trouble from the meddling monks tonight: they'd be too busy fending off the siege he and Cyprian had sanctioned.

Reaching into the folds of his robes, Ivon brought out the wavy kris knife and held it up to the moonlight. It caught the silvery beams, mingling these with the red haze coming off the ancient shard; Ivon could sense the Fifth-Tier demon he'd bound to the blade quivering in anticipation of the mortal blood it would soon taste.

But his demon-blade would just have to wait a little longer. Taking another deep breath, Ivon prepared to do something he'd never yet done. It was an ambitious undertaking, and one that lay close to his heart, but it was undoubtedly dangerous too.

'Now it's time for us to prepare the host,' he told his followers. 'Go and dig him up.'

Wordlessly his disciples complied, taking shovels from the cave and leaving the plateau. Walking over to his saddle bags, Ivon began preparing the tools he'd need for his Necromancy.

Night was nigh upon them by the time they reached Sir Regis's homestead. Unexpected rains had turned the road they were following into a muddy bog, delaying their journey. The manor was typical of those times and parts, being fashioned of stout wooden beams and stones: a chimney smoked, telling of a fire lit to keep the damp at bay. At least it wasn't really cold this far south: Adelko had seen much worse in his time.

Serfs tilling the lands gawped at the monks as they rode up the path towards the manor's front gate. A peasant on sentry duty tried to look stern, but soon backed down before

Azelin's thousand-yard stare. Hurriedly he went inside, to alert the master of the house.

Sir Regis was an elderly knight, of an age with Horskram but much less well preserved: the years hung off him like cobwebs. Peering at the travellers with rheumy eyes, it took him a while before he recognised the adept.

'Master Horskram, by all the archangels but it's really you!' he said in a hoarse, whispery voice. 'Reus knows, you've returned to these lands at an evil time.'

'Reus knows it, and so do we,' replied the old monk, unsmiling. 'Will you grant us succour for one night? We arrived in Montrevellyn some days ago – high time we learned exactly what has transpired in our absence.'

The elderly vassal nodded, waving them in. 'Thank Ushira my sons are all away at the wars,' he muttered, showing them into a spacious hall. 'They aren't as kindly disposed to the Order as I am.'

'Few are nowadays, it would seem,' replied Horskram glumly.

Ivon gazed down on Wolmar's rotting corpse. The soil of his unmarked grave hid the worst of the decay, but that didn't stop the stench. The warlock supposed he'd just have to get accustomed to such, if he was going to continue his studies of Necromancy. He'd spent years working on the Second School of the Left-Hand Way; months alone on the spell he was about to attempt. Demonology had always come more natu-rally to him: evil spirits *wanted* to be found, they were keen to be invited to the mortal plane, so they could have a chance to wreak havoc at will. But the shades of the departed... that was a different matter. It seemed that, whatever lay in wait for them on the Other Side, the souls of men were always reluctant to return.

Ivon could hardly fault them for that. To be sure, having a tortured fragment of your psyche trapped forever in the rotting carcass you once called home wasn't an attractive prospect.

Leaning down, he stroked his erstwhile lover's cadaverous lips.

'Alas, poor sweet, but this is really the best I can do for you, seeing as you refused to be a part of the Return,' he sighed softly.

He'd arranged the stones in a circle around the dead knight's body, painting each one with the necessary glyph of reanimation. Reaching into his medicine pouch again, he produced another phial, containing a night-black elixir. This he poured between Wolmar's ravaged lips.

'There now,' he simpered. 'At least once this is done, you'll no longer be food for the worms.'

'Ivon sanctioned the New Purge the week after Carolus left to join the campaign against the Vorstlendings up north,' said Regis. 'Some ill rumour coming out of Rima, that some of the brethren there had turned to darkness, sorcery... some even say your Grand Master is implicated.'

How very clever of you, Hannequin. You use your own betrayal as fuel for Cyprian's campaign, so he can do the dirty work and get rid of the true brothers for you. And of course your puppet Ivon is perfectly positioned to back him in this venture.

It told Horskram one thing at least – the rumours were probably true, and Hannequin almost certainly was no longer in the monastery. What black methods he'd used to vanish, it pained Horskram to think of – but he had to find out.

The old vassal shook his head, lost in his own thoughts. 'I can't believe such rumours would ever be true,' he sighed. 'Cyprian is a self-seeking fanatic if you ask me, and as for Ivon – I never did like the man, nor trust him,' he sighed. 'My lord Morvaine was ever right to doubt his true motives.'

If you only knew what those true motives really were, you'd have a few extra white hairs, thought Horskram grimly. *And what makes you so sure your lord hasn't been seduced by Ivon's wiles regardless, assuming he really is involved with Hannequin? You don't have to like a man to make common cause with him... sometimes you don't even have to trust him.*

'What else can you tell us?' the adept pressed, keeping those thoughts to himself. 'We saw for ourselves what happened to the brethren at Chevraulaix – but what of the other chapters? Our headquarters at Rima must surely be holding out, for now at least.'

Regis nodded, his face ashen in the light of the fire. Its warmth did little to comfort Horskram, though they were sat on stools nearby. The old vassal leaned back in his carved wooden chair, and sighed again.

'The last I heard, it is,' he confirmed. 'And you can thank Ezekiel that most of the knights and soldiers are out of the country, but from what I hear Ivon and Cyprian have managed to muster a few hundred troops to harry the Reverend Priory of St Argo.'

Horskram frowned, stroking his beard, once more unkempt from weeks of travel.

'We need to get in,' he said at last. 'Adelko and I will have to travel in disguise. My companions can pass for wandering freebooters.'

Regis glared blearily at Azelin and Hari. His rheumatic eyes hadn't recognised the erstwhile margrave of Valacia, which was probably just as well.

'Your choice of companions is somewhat unseemly, I must

say,' he said. 'But it's your decision to join your brothers at Rima that perturbs me the most. What in the Known World can you hope to achieve there?'

'I have to speak with the brethren – and Hannequin,' said Horskram, playing along with Regis's assumptions. It pained him to have to use dissimulation on an old friend, but now was not the time for perfect candour. 'At a time like this, it's vital that the Argolian brothers stand fast, in solidarity.'

Regis sighed again, but nodded. Horskram tried to ignore the bitter taste that had crept into his mouth.

Walking slowly widdershins, against the sundial around the ring of stones, Ivon began the necessary chant in the language of magick. As he did, he visualised the necessary abstract symbols: a tomb opening, a humanoid figure trapped within a ribcage, and Azrael, the Angel of Death, his wings clipped. From far beyond the interstices that joined the two worlds, Ivon felt his former lover resisting: but he was only trying to raise a single corpse, so he could muster plenty of elan for the fight.

Again and again Wolmar resisted. Again and again Ivon repeated the call, tugging gently on the dead knight's tormented soul.

Before long the body at his feet began to twitch. Ivon repeated the summons, mouthing words in the ancient language that Abaddon had altered forever when he took Ma'amun as his first disciple:

> *No grave on earth shall hold thy body down,*
> *No celestial gates shall keep thy soul at bay!*
> *No hellish bourne shall keep thy essence bound,*
> *From afterlife your spirit must away!*

Still flesh it quickens and arises from the ground,
Embrace the night eternal at the waning of the day!

Something gave, and abruptly Wolmar's corpse sat up. Ivon ceased chanting, and met his undead lover's blank stare. There was just about *something* in those decaying eyes, a flicker of recognition and − though it pained him to admit it − hatred, too.

Ivon smiled behind his mask.

'Oh Wolmar, how I've missed you,' he said.

Adelko tossed and turned on the cot Regis's servants had prepared for him in the main hall. The rain had stopped and the fire had banished the dampness, yet still he could not sleep.

His sixth sense blazed within him. Some evil was being done, right now, and not far off. And it was coming from the direction of Rima...

Glancing over at his mentor, he saw Horskram half asleep, in the grip of some ugly nightmare, his lips moving soundlessly.

Ivon stroked the five-pointed crystal pendant at his neck, and began to recite the preliminary incantation for his next summoning. This was Demonology: he was back on familiar ground now. His disciples had formed a circle about the pentagram and joined their susurrant voices to his.

Wolmar stood in the middle of the pentagram, his hulking corpse silent as he gazed upon the ruby red shard and its newest victim with half-dead eyes.

Tearing off the hapless poacher's loin cloth, Ivon raised his eyes to the crystalline skies and repeated the same invocation as he'd used the previous summer.

The same, but not quite. He wasn't trying to summon Molaach this time: he only had the power to manifest a Second-Tier demon for a short while.

A Third-Tier demon, on the other hand, would suit his purposes nicely.

The warlock felt his sex harden as he moved into the main incantation. Pulling his engorged member free of his robes, Ivon pushed himself slowly into the victim, not missing a syllable. He began to gyrate in time to the celestial music of the fallen ones, exulting in the dark magick of blood and sex. This was what he lived for; it was why he had signed his soul away long ago, on a moonless night when the Master had come to him with promises of power and darker kingdoms to come.

As he approached the climax, Ivon raised the kris knife high. The demon bound within it had joined its own cacophony to the chorus crescendo; it could smell blood, too.

Ivon roared out the last words of the incantation as he found sweet release: driving the kris knife down, he stabbed the young man to the left of the spine, penetrating his heart. The body convulsed spasmodically as Ivon wrenched the knife free, blood spurting over him. He pulled himself out of the youth's body, already growing limp.

Now for the tricky part.

He could feel the demon's essence coalescing within the pentagram. Prior to the Return, a Third-Tier demon couldn't manifest on the mortal plane in its true form: it had to have a host.

But to the best of Ivon's knowledge, no sorcerer in living memory had ever attempted to fuse the Two Schools; to bind a spirit to a reanimated host body.

Forcing that thought from his mind, he began the final ritual, declaiming in the darker modes of the language of magick as he visualised a demon, a corpse and two links of a chain in quick succession.

'Ha'arba'alon, a soul I have given thee, borne on a tide of blood and seed!' he cried. 'Now I bequeath thee also a host, a mortal frame to call thine own! A house from which to plot the suffering of men, a castle from which to scourge the hapless playthings of Reus! Be joined as one!'

He could sense rather than hear the disembodied voice that replied, and it dripped with scorn and malice.

You... call... this... a castle?

Wolmar's cadaver stared into the night with glazed eyes, unmoving. In the hellish light of the shard, his peeling bilious skin looked even more ghastly; his ribcage poked whitely through it in parts where decomposition was at its most advanced.

'A host that knows no fear, no pain, no fatigue or hunger,' Ivon persisted, continuing to visualise the abstract symbols over and over.

A demon knows nothing of these things anyway, hissed Ha'arba'alon. *You dare insult me with such a pitiful host?*

Beads of sweat sprang suddenly from Ivon's pores, as he felt Ha'arba'alon pushing back against his elan. His followers had fallen silent, passively awaiting the outcome of his efforts.

'The raised corpse of a great warrior,' persisted Ivon, continuing to visualise the vital symbols. 'Submit now to my will, as your King desires – play thy part in this great union of spectre and spirit, a more potent entity than the mortal vale hath seen in generations!'

In truth this was mere word-play: the matter would be decided by sorcery not debate. But Ivon was confident of one thing: the King of Gehenna was behind him. Like most of his unruly kind, Ha'arba'alon was stubborn, and would go his own way given half a chance. But no Third-Tier denizen of the City of Burning Brass could hope to gainsay his liege's will.

And so it proved. With a reluctant howl, Ha'arba'alon obeyed, merging with Wolmar's remains. The decaying patches in his rotten body seemed to fill with hellish light, as the demon's essence suffused it.

Ivon slumped to the ground, exhausted. His disciples moved to help him up, but he waved them away. Regaining his feet, he looked triumphantly upon the thing he had conjured into being.

The eldritch glow did not leave the demon-zombie as it stepped lightly out of the pentangle and took a knee before Ivon.

'Ivon, necromancer and demonologist, thy will be done,' it grated. The entity that addressed him was partly Wolmar, partly Ha'arba'alon: both might resent him, but neither would resist his commands.

Pulling off the goat's head mask, Ivon tasted the night air and exulted.

Let's see you outmatch that, Ragnar White Eye, he thought triumphantly.

CHAPTER 14

BENEATH THE WAVES

It took Vaskrian a few moments to realise he wasn't dying. The sea creatures continued to pull him down, their amphibian maws snapping at him, but he found he could breathe. He had no time to determine why that was. His sword he'd lost when he fell into the Strang; but his dirk was belted at his side. Pulling it free, he stabbed one of the creatures. The water didn't seem to obstruct his movement: he drove the blade inches deep into the Triton's midriff. Bubbles erupted from its maw as it shrieked, letting go of him.

The second Triton tried to close its mouth about Vaskrian's wrist; reacting quickly, he smashed the pommel of his dagger into one of its eyes, which burst like a ripe fruit. Reversing his grip, he stabbed it in the head, penetrating deep into whatever passed for the thing's brains.

His antagonists defeated, Vaskrian continued to sink. It was without a doubt one of the most surreal experiences of his adventurous life, descending fathoms deep into the inky waters without perishing.

His attention was drawn to the amulet the Earth Witch had gifted him last year, in her sorcerous bower: it was glowing with a refulgent glaucous light. To his shock, the sheen it emitted had extended to cover his entire body: something within the aura allowed him to breathe as though above water. And though he could sense the awful cold pressure of the waves building as he sank ever deeper, the pendant's magick kept that at bay too.

Perhaps I'll live to thank you yet, witch, thought Vaskrian, as he continued to sink down towards the sea bed.

He could not possibly say how long he continued to fall, but eventually his feet touched the sands. Looking around him, Vaskrian saw he was in the midst of a vast underwater landscape; the sediment was shaped like a deep valley, one side of which was crowned by a mighty plateau. High above it, he could make out schools of brightly coloured fish plying their routes beneath the waves: but down here at the sea bottom, there appeared to be few signs of life.

Vaskrian made his way up the valley floor, half walking, half swimming, as best he could. The Elementi the Earth Witch had trapped within his periapt seemed to help him move, air and water combining to aid him.

Even so, it took him the better part of an hour to reach the plateau crowning the seabed valley. This close, he could see it was made of some kind of basaltic substance he didn't recognise – but then why would he?

It took him a while longer to climb up to the top of the plateau, but when he did, he let out a torrent of bubbles as he took in the vista.

The valley peak dropped away again, but instead of rising up to form another, it stretched out for leagues about him, a vast aquatic plain. It was higher than the bottom of the sea valley he'd fallen into; many more basaltic structures dotted its surface, along with coral formations, strange underwater plants and more schools of fish.

Now he understood why some said Sjórkunan the unangel of the seas ruled his own kingdom; for here was a veritable landscape beneath the waves, one to rival those of his own realm in vastness and splendour.

He was so taken in by the spectacle that it took him a while to spot it: a glowing pinpoint, far away on the other side of the underwater plain. This far away he couldn't make out what was causing it, but he could sense the Elementi urging him towards it.

I've no better idea, he thought, still scarcely believing his new adventure. Launching himself off the plateau, he allowed himself to sink slowly down on to the plain, and began the long journey towards the source of light.

The coral formations and underwater plants were more densely packed than he'd realised, obscuring his vision of the light: forging ahead as best he could, Vaskrian hoped his sense of direction worked as well underwater. But he needn't have worried: the Elementi bound to his amulet seemed to steer him aright whenever he strayed, gently nudging him towards his destination.

After a while he spotted it again, glimmering and winking at him. Now he could see it was coming from the top of another basaltic tor, an underwater lighthouse beckoning him ever onwards. Vaskrian was so intent upon it that he almost didn't spot the danger until it was too late. From around a coral formation they came towards him, swimming with a deadly speed: three more of the humanoid sea creatures he'd fought above water.

Only this time they'd brought their cavalry with them. Vaskrian's heart froze over in horror as he saw each of the creatures clutched the fin of a giant silvery fish that propelled them along at ever greater speeds. Only these were like no fish Vaskrian had ever set eyes on: they had rows of sharp teeth, and a mean look in their beady black eyes. Their riders – if you could call them that – each clutched short stabbing spears in their free hands.

So this is how it ends, thought Vaskrian grimly, freeing his dirk. *I get to survive death by drowning only to end up as food for an oversized fish.*

He knew no troubadours would make songs out of this last stand.

At least he had the magicked periapt to augment his underwater reflexes: propelling himself to one side as his foremost antagonist came at him, Vaskrian lurched clear of the giant fish's snapping jaws and punched past its rider's guard in one fluid motion. His dirk found the creature's third eye, and it sloughed off its aquatic steed, a ribbon of inky blood trailing in its wake.

But quick as a fast-flowing river, the giant fish was on him, clamping its fearsome jaws about his left arm. Only his hauberk saved him from losing it, and were it not for his gambeson he'd have had a broken bone to add to his woes, for the fish's strength was terrible.

Reacting swiftly, Vaskrian drove his dagger frenziedly into the creature's snout, forcing it to let go. The fish appeared confused by the blow, blood erupting in slow-motion from the wound he'd inflicted as it began circling around frantically.

But by then the other two sea riders were upon him. Vaskrian was just mouthing a prayer and hoping he wouldn't end up as a sea spirit in the afterlife when he caught another flash of movement. He'd seen enough to amaze him already that day, but even still he could scarcely believe what was happening: six creatures – half man, half fish – suddenly descended upon his assailants wielding tridents.

Seakindred, thought Vaskrian incredulously. *By all the saints and archangels, now I've seen everything.*

The Tritons broke off from menacing Vaskrian to fight their new foe, but the mermen outnumbered them and soon outflanked their opponents. Their appetite for the fight gone, the horrid creatures spurred their steeds upwards, abruptly departing the scene of combat. Half the mermen pursued them, leaving the other three to surround Vaskrian.

Bubbles erupted from gills in the side of the leader's neck as he addressed the young knight, in halting Northlending.

'Strange to see an Earthwalker in our domains, alive and breathing,' he remarked. His skin was tinged a sea-green, and in place of human hair he had tiny fins running the length of his crown, but in all other respects his handsome features and muscular upper body were unmistakeably human. His eyes were a deep yellow, lacking pupils or irises, but Vaskrian had no doubt they saw him well enough.

It took the knight a while to gather himself together enough to speak.

'You... you speak our language?' he managed to gasp.

The merman favoured him with a crooked smile.

'Better than you speak ours, I am sure,' he replied. 'But come! These waters are teeming with Tritons, our mortal enemies, and are not safe. We will take you to our city and speak further there – our Farseer already knows of your coming.'

'You have a city?' said Vaskrian, still amazed.

'Of course,' replied the merman laughing. 'We are people, just as you are.'

His two fellows moved gracefully to either side of the young knight. Courteous though their leader was, Vaskrian knew it wasn't a request.

'Might I know your name?' he asked.

The merman leader only laughed again. 'You could try –

but our speech is unpronounceable to Earthwalkers. You may call me Logrim – it means "strong in the sea" in the tongue of your ancestors, no?' Turning to his two comrades, Logrim barked orders in a strange high fluting tongue, and Vaskrian could well believe their true names unpronounceable.

I'll bet even old Horskram would have trouble learning this language, he thought wryly.

'Pray forgive me,' said Logrim. 'My two warriors will escort you – you move better than most of your kind in the water, but no one moves through the sea like the Seakindred!'

Without waiting for his response, the two mermen took Vaskrian in a strong grip, propelling him forwards.

The young knight was too astonished to protest or resist as the Seakindred took him high above the underwater plain, propelling him like an arrow towards the glowing light atop the basalt tor. All the while Logrim swam ahead, his tail cutting an elegant pattern as he moved dextrously towards it.

As they drew nearer to the summit of the tor, Vaskrian could make out another merman – no, a *mermaid*. She was flitting to and fro in a manner that could only be described as anxious, directly above the light source – a spherical lump of luminescent coral.

Her beauty was breathtaking. Though she was bereft of clothing, Vaskrian didn't even register embarrassment as he took in the mermaid's ravishing form.

No wonder sailors get lost at sea.

Her hair – if you could call it that – appeared to be made of phosphorescent seaweed; it tumbled down her lithe upper torso, punctuated with shells and stones that only augmented its beauty. Her skin was a glaucous colour like those of the menfolk, her breasts full and ripe, her stomach flat and smooth, her face astonishingly winsome. Even Adhelina, the great beauty of Vorstlund, would have looked plain next to her. From the waist upwards at least.

Catching the young knight staring at her, the mermaid favoured him with a seductive smile. That smile was like the call of the sea in the Strang Estuary, when he'd first heard it on his arrival at Strongholm; even now he felt his willpower ebbing away.

The mermen only laughed at his plight.

'I see you transfix the Earthwalkers as always,' said Logrim, addressing the mermaid, before turning to Vaskrian. 'Please allow me to introduce Nereia, our Farseer.'

The mermaid favoured Vaskrian with a flick of her tail that he supposed passed for a curtsey down here.

'And a pleasure it is to make your acquaintance, sir Knight of the Waters,' she said. 'I've been watching you for some time now.'

'Knight of the Waters?' queried Vaskrian, briefly recovering from the spell – real or figurative – she'd put on him. 'Why do you call me that?'

'Because that is who you are,' replied Nereia. 'It's who you've always been, though you may not have realised it yet. She of the earth told me you'd be along, eventually.'

'She of the... You're talking about the Earth Witch, aren't you?'

'The very same,' replied Nereia, pointing at the glistering amulet around Vaskrian's neck. 'She whose Thaumaturgy has kept you alive today.'

Turning to address Logrim, she frowned. 'You almost missed him,' she chided. 'If you'd left it any later, our prophetic warrior would have ended up as food for sharks.'

'Don't scold me so,' replied Logrim tetchily. 'The Tritons mass in ever greater number by the day, as well you know. The Great Disturber stirs them up with yet more sacrifices to He Who Must Not Be Disturbed. The realms of water and earth stand on the brink of cataclysm.'

Nereia laughed at that, a high musical sound that seemed

to bend the waters about her, turning them into unearthly instruments. 'You certainly don't need to tell me that!' she exclaimed. 'But come, time is therefore rightly precious, and not abundant as are the minnows of the sea. Let us away now, to Kindredshome!'

The rest of the journey passed in an eddying blur for Vaskrian. Was it the sheer shock of being underwater, or the subtle effects of the sorcery that kept him alive in its watery clutches that dulled his senses so? He would never fathom the answer, but one way or another it seemed but little time before he found himself gazing upon a wide basin in the seabed cradling hundreds of buildings fashioned of coral and shell. The beauty of the merfolk city, or Kindredshome as they called it in Northlending, was undeniably breathtaking.

His aquatic escort sculled across the ornately baroque pinnacles of the cityscape; no meaner buildings seemed to exist here. Either the Seakindred did a better job of ruling equitably than his own folk, or here was a city only for noblekind.

The city buildings swirled inwards in concentric circles, resembling a vast conch shell from his aerial (or should that be underwater?) vantage point. At its heart lay a vast fluted coliseum of radiant colours that seemed to stretch his eyes beyond their natural compass. Down into the midst of this his escort brought him, where more than a hundred merfolk flitted to and fro. Most seemed anxious: the young knight couldn't shake the feeling that the mermaid had spoken truly, and his arrival was expected.

All the Seakindred were similarly beauteous to look upon; even their lower bodies rippled with a vigour and vitality that could not be dismissed with a casual glance. But their voices together in great numbers were an unbearable cacophony in Vaskrian's ears; not even the Earth Witch's periapt afforded him any protection from their jarring cadences.

'Enough!' cried Nereia, sensing the young knight's discomfort. 'Most among you speak the landwalker's tongue – oblige our most honoured guest now by using it! We have not waited so many tides to look upon the Knight of the Waters only to chastise him with our abstruse chattering.'

'So you say, Nereia,' shot back one of the other mermaids in her strangely accented Northlending. 'Knight of the Waters indeed! Your muddled prophecies predicted little of the Great Disturber's dark meddlings. Why should we believe a word you say about this landwalker – in any language you care to speak?'

'As to that,' replied Nereia, fixing lustrous eyes on her no-less beautiful critic, 'The waters themselves "spoke" clearly enough, to those that had ears to hearken unto their predictions.' Reaching out, she gripped Vaskrian in such a way as would have mesmerised him under other conditions. 'Behold, he is here with us! A sign that we must obey prophecy and give him the aid he will request.'

'What aid?' hissed Vaskrian, as a chorus of dissent literally drowned out his words.

'Just try to follow my lead,' replied Nereia in a bubbling whisper. 'Half the appointed council gathered here are already swayed by my arguments – the rest are too selfish or foolish to see the wisdom in uniting with your kind against the common enemy. You need to help me convince them that you really are a chosen one, spoken of in our ancient prophecies.'

Vaskrian had to laugh at that. 'I used to adventure with a certain fellow,' he told Nereia. 'He was as humble as the day is long, but a lot of important folk seemed to think him quite special. That's the closest I've ever got to a so-called "chosen one" outside of bard's song, and I think I'll not be getting any closer!'

Nereia fixed him with glowing eyes. 'The son of fireworkers,' she intoned solemnly, before repeating the Earth Witch's prophecy about Adelko word for word. The laughter died on Vaskrian's lips in a weak flurry of tiny bubbles.

'You may not believe what those wiser than you would have you know,' she said. 'But at least trust that others with more influence than you might.' She nodded meaningfully towards the circle of Seakindred, who had fallen to arguing amongst themselves, some in Northlending, others lapsing back into the strange fluting tongue of the merfolk.

'All right,' sighed the young knight. 'If it'll help you persuade your people to help mine, I suppose I'll believe anything you say.'

With some difficulty, Nereia called for silence and got it. Dozens of pairs of luminous eyes stared expectantly at Vaskrian, waiting for him to speak. Oratory had never been a strong point of his; brazen outbursts were the closest he usually got, but something told him that would avail him little now. A flurry of bubbles shot from his mouth as he cleared his throat nervously.

'Sir Vaskrian, Knight of the Waters, thanks you for your hospitality,' he began falteringly. The silence persisted. Out of the corner of his eye, he caught an elderly merman placing a conch shell to his pointy ear, in an apparent effort to hear better.

'And the valour of your warriors speaks for itself,' he stumbled on. It was hard to tell with an audience that didn't have pupils or irises, but Vaskrian was sure more than a few pairs of eyes were rolling.

'I think you can do better than this,' hissed Nereia beside him, still flitting anxiously to and fro in the water.

'I'm trying,' he hissed back, before saying more loudly: 'Those Tritons we met just now, we gave them a bloody good hiding!'

Now the merfolk simply looked baffled.

'I thought you said you speak our language!' said Vaskrian, looking reproachfully at Nereia.

'We do, but that doesn't mean we understand all your idioms,' she replied. 'What on earth does "hiding" mean, in such a context? Now they think you and Logrim and his men helped to conceal our mortal enemies.'

Vaskrian rolled his own eyes, then fumbled for an explanation. 'It's when you take the skin off someone, give them a good beating. Like flaying, you know, when you skin an animal!'

Nereia glared at him. 'And why in the seven seas would we know about that? Do you see any animals here?'

'Well, why don't *you* talk to them?' said Vaskrian, growing exasperated. 'Seeing as I obviously haven't the first clue how to speak to Seakindred.'

The mermaid shook her head stubbornly. 'They've already heard enough from me – I told you, this is for you now. You have to convince them that I'm right about you, that you're the one foretold in our legends.'

'But I'm not!'

'Don't tell *them* that – or do you want to go back above water with no allies and lose your war?'

The gathering was becoming unruly now, merfolk beginning to break off into schools and babble amongst themselves in their high fluting language. With some effort once again, Nereia returned their attention to Vaskrian.

'This is your last chance,' she told him quietly. 'I won't be able to hold their interest for much longer.'

I've never been in as strange a situation as this one, not even in Horskram's company, thought the young knight. *How am I supposed to know what these creatures want to hear?*

The answer came to him then, born on the wings of memory. Another of his father's soldiering maxims: *when you can't anticipate the other side's strategy, it's best just to follow your own as best you can.*

The old man had been right. Vaskrian knew nothing of these creatures or their customs, but if there was one thing he did know about, it was war. And it was obvious the Seakindred had been at war for a very long time.

'What's the only good Triton?' he asked suddenly. Now his audience managed to be both baffled and silent at the same time, but that didn't dissuade him.

'A DEAD ONE,' he cried. 'And how many dead Tritons are enough?'

The merfolk shifted, glancing uncertainly amongst themselves.

'There will never be enough,' continued the knight. 'We've only been fighting them a short time, and we already know that much. Again and again they come at us, in the war above water – we cut down one, two more appear. Two more we kill, another four came in their place.'

Vaskrian noted with satisfaction that their lambent eyes appeared to glow a shade brighter now. He had their attention.

'But we'll keep killing them if we have to, as many as we can. That's just what you've had to do, for so many centuries, am I right? Because these… things… they don't know mercy, or remorse, or decency! Reus' wounds, I don't even know if the damn things feel pain, though I'll keep doing my best to find out!'

A few bubbling chuckles told him he'd struck a chord.

Nice to know these creatures have a sense of humour, he thought as he went on: 'But we're over-matched – we're fighting our own kind too – '

'Why?' interrupted a burly fish-man near him. 'Always our land-cousins have made war on one another. The Seakindred have never done such – why should we help a race that only seeks to destroy itself?' Great flurries of bubbles spiralled upwards as the rest of the merfolk voiced their agreement.

'You're right,' said Vaskrian, raising his hands in acknowledgement. We... landwalkers, we're a bit cracked. All that sunlight we get up top, goes to our heads, you see?' He tapped his own by way of emphasis, to demonstrate his meaning.

More laughs. Several of the mermaids were looking at him coyly now; even the menfolk seemed to approve.

'But whatever you may think of us, this much is true – some maniac of a wizard has decided to take control of your mortal enemies, and send them against us. We need your help.'

'Why should we?' cried another merman. 'Let the Tritons get themselves killed fighting your lot. Less of them for us to worry about.'

More bubbles dotted the precinct. That opinion was very popular, and Vaskrian could easily see why.

This time he had a ready answer, however.

'Because at this rate, we won't be able to distract them for much longer. And when we fall, this sorcerer will release them – Tritons can't settle on land any more than you can, I'll bet, so what else would he do?'

The young knight paused for dramatic effect. 'Oh, no, wait,' he continued. 'I'll tell you what else he might do! He might just turn them right around when they're done with us and send them back against you. Only this time, they'll be armed with nice iron weapons they've stolen from our dead hands. Good luck fighting a Triton army that uses real swords and spears, not that flint and coral crap I've seen them wielding.'

Not all the merfolk were impressed. 'Iron rusts below water, or didn't you know that?' jeered one.

'Not immediately, it doesn't,' countered Vaskrian. 'Those swords and spears will last long enough to get used against your people, don't you worry! And besides, if this wizard is powerful enough to enthral an army's worth of Tritons, what other tricks might he have up his sleeve? Did you ever stop to think of that?'

Vaskrian folded his arms pointedly, meeting the last challenger's lucent gaze. The muscle-bound merman turned away, and a hubbub spread across the assembly. Several more sultry looks came his way from the females, but he didn't concern himself with that.

'So, how am I doing?' he asked Nereia instead.

The seer beamed at him. 'As well as I could have hoped,' she said, darting forwards and kissing him on the cheek. Vaskrian almost fancied he felt the water around him bubbling over as a hot flush surged through him.

The assembly debated for some time, but before long the verdict was reached: more was to be gained than lost by taking the fight to the age-old enemy.

'When will we march... er, I mean, um, swim?' asked Vaskrian, once Nereia had told him the good news.

'Right now,' she said. 'As you've probably fathomed by now, the Seakindred move swiftly when they need to.'

Looking around at the mermen and mermaids forming up into underwater battalions, the young knight could only concede the truth of her words.

'Not like you lot need pack horses and carts I suppose,' he said. One thing did occur to him though.

'But how will you fight on land? I mean, you can't…'

Nereia smiled her devilish smile again, and Vaskrian found himself wishing she weren't only half-humanoid.

'Oh, don't worry,' she told him. 'We won't be fighting them on land – you'll have to take care of that part yourselves. But that enemy fleet menacing your shores that I've seen in my scrying coral? It won't be a fleet for much longer.'

Nereia barked an order to the two mermen who had escorted Vaskrian to Kindredshome. Taking him in their strong hands again, they propelled him upwards, the hundreds of Seakindred he'd won over to the cause following in orderly formation.

As he sped up towards the surface, the young knight felt his heart pounding in time to the perennial heaving of the ocean deeps.

CHAPTER 15

THE DEATH KNIGHT

By the dusking light they could see the sun's dying rays glinting off the soldiers' helms as they moved to and fro. The Most Reverend Priory of St Argo stood defiantly against the investing camp clustered about the high ridge on which it perched, although Adelko could make out the skeletal frames of trebuchets, craftsmen still hard at work on them in the fading hours.

'They won't be much longer about their work,' said Azelin, giving voice to the journeyman's fears. 'Once they get those siege engines going, your brethren will be hard put to keep yon soldiers out, hill or no hill.'

'That's why we don't have any time to spare,' put in Horskram. 'Hari, I count at least two hundred men-at-arms, plus auxiliaries. Can you get us in?'

The outland rogue rubbed his chin. 'I can get myself in, I know that much,' he said. 'But the rest of you as well... you said there'd be fewer soldiers. Sneaking past a small host of men and getting you up the walls before anyone notices, it's a lot to ask.'

On the morning of their second day out from Regis's

holding they'd taken a detour into the wooded hills of the Arbevere, to get a good vantage point from undercover. From where they perched Adelko could see the panoramic landscape of north-central Pangonia, painted in the hushed tones of twilight: the Athos river as it flowed steadily through the trees from the hills towards Rima, now just a sketchy silhouette against the fading skies.

But that wasn't what occupied the journeyman's attention. His sixth sense, so long an unwelcome friend, was jangling again. He knew what was causing it this time too: deeper in the hills were the red ruins of buildings left by Them, the other novices had spoken of them furtively in the cloisters at night. Of course, everyone had talked about going there but no one had: the journeymen and adepts of Rima had been pretty clear that was out of bounds.

Peering towards that part of the hills, Adelko fancied he could make out one of the ruins glowing blood-red, as if mocking the setting sun and daring it to do better.

He tugged his mentor's sleeve. It wasn't his usual grey habit; that was packed away along with Adelko's own in their horses' saddle bags. Instead both were now dressed in old spare clothing Regis had kindly given them. Somewhat threadbare, it fitted their assumed disguise of wandering adventurers well enough, though Adelko felt awkward to be wearing secular garb again after so many years.

'Horskram...' he began.

'I know,' groused the adept. 'I can sense it too. Patience, we'll be on our way soon enough.'

Horskram resumed his conversation with Hari. 'I know it's a lot to ask,' he said testily. 'I wouldn't be asking you of all people if it wasn't. The point is – can it be done?'

'You say there's only one way into the fortress?' asked Hari.

'One and one only – and it's a monastery, not a fortress.'

Yassin quashed his smirk after flicking a wry glance Adelko's way. 'In that case, we should be able to get in if we go around to the other side,' he said. 'Two hundred is not so many for a main investing force – I doubt they'll have much more than skeleton guards posted on the other side of the hill.'

'I shouldn't think so,' Horskram agreed. 'On that side the ridge is almost sheer – it would be a challenge for an ordinary man to climb, though not impossible, and presumably child's' play for a fellow of your talents.'

Hari nodded, now openly smirking at the rare compliment. 'I'll have to take the lead on my own though – once I'm at the top of the ridge, I can lower a rope for the rest of you, then do likewise once I've climbed the wall.'

Horskram frowned. 'From the top of the walls you could tie your rope around a merlon – but from their base there won't be anything.'

'I'll deal with the skeleton guard and go with him as far as the base of the walls,' said Azelin.

Horskram paused to mull that over, then nodded.

'So long as you deal with the soldiers quickly and quietly, I don't see a problem.'

Azelin tapped his scabbarded great sword and flashed a vulpine grin.

'There won't be.'

If Horskram felt anguished by once more condoning the premeditated slaughter of men only doing their duty, he had no chance to voice it, for just then Hari interjected: 'But how to alert the monks that we're friend not foe? I can easily climb up to the battlements without them noticing, but if I'm spotted while I'm getting the rest of you up that might alert the enemy while you're still on the ground. It would seem we have two sets of guards to worry about.'

'That's the part I'm working on,' said Horskram. He paused in thought a while, then said: 'Just how religious are you?'

Hari blinked, surprised at the question. 'That depends on the circumstances,' replied the rogue coyly.

'About the answer I was hoping for,' said the adept. 'When you confront my brethren, you're to repeat a catechism I'm going to teach you. It's in Decorlangue, but you don't have to know what it means – it's important that you remember how to pronounce it correctly though. In times of war, the Argolians sometimes use it, as a kind of password if you will, to distinguish friend from foe.'

Hari tapped his head knowingly. 'I may not be the best educated man, Horskram,' he grinned, 'but a rascal always knows how to commit important knowledge to memory!'

'Let me guess,' interjected Azelin. 'It's one of St Alysius' proverbs, the one that roughly translates as "Ye shall know thy friend by the words of his heart, not the clothes on his back."'

'Ever the diligent student of scripture,' remarked Horskram dryly.

'All the better to spot peddling cant when I hear it,' snarked the disgraced warrior-monk, falling to his old cynicism again.

Ignoring him, Horskram pronounced the words in his crisp Decorlangue, slowly and clearly so Hari could memorise them phonetically. Azelin cast a dark look at Adelko, but the journeyman was too busy fielding his jarring sixth sense to pay him any heed. While the others were talking it had jilted up a notch.

This was no generic warning of evil now: something was coming their way.

'Master Horskram,' he repeated with renewed urgency.

'Redeemer's wounds, what is it now?' barked the adept.

Adelko simply pointed back towards the glowing ruin.

'Something's coming our way. I'll warrant it doesn't mean us well.'

Horskram's expression softened instantly; he knew the value of Adelko's sixth sense, which had become even more acute than his own. As he felt it pulsing behind his temples and quickening his heart painfully, Adelko took little pride in that.

'Alright, we'd best move then,' said the adept. 'Hari, the catechism, do you have it?'

Yassin tapped the side of his head again and winked. 'It's here, as firm as the teets of Luviah.'

'Not quite the simile I was looking for, but it will do,' sighed Horskram. 'Come, let's take the saddle again. We need to ride around the monastery to the sheer side of the hill – and try to outdistance whatever it is young Adelko senses is coming for us. Come, let's tarry not!'

The deathly apparition that had once been Wolmar felt a quickening across the darkling landscape. It could sense its prey. Ha'arba'alon's dark essence burned keenly within its ghastly frame. The composite entity could sense its quarry was mounted, but that bothered it little: it glided across the hilly scrublands that tumbled from the summit of the red rock upon which it had been born with a preternatural ease; blades of grass shrivelled at its passing, twigs and leaves ignited with a strange fire that consumed them without spreading to others nearby.

Yet that wasn't enough for the demonic entity that occupied the ruins of the undead knight's animated corpse: voicelessly it urged him on, the hellish being's impatience for the slaughter conveyed in sentiments no human could utter or ever know.

Be silent! Wolmar's tortured shade found some of the old stubbornness and defiance it had known in life. *You may have possessed my remains, but they're still my remains! We're gaining on them, you'll get your slaughter don't you worry.*

Too slow, hissed Ha'arba'alon, *too slow! Even with my power to spur thee on, thou movest like a slug of cold flesh. Ah, but the day draweth near when my kind shall not need yours to wreak havoc upon the world that so justly deserveth it!*

If your day is so damned near, why don't you leave me in peace and do your own dirty work? The thing that was now Wolmar snapped back mentally.

Peace!? He could sense rather than hear the demon mocking him, which was a thousand times worse. *Tell me, what peace hast thou known since my cousin Azrael took thee? Dost thou even recallest where thou wast?*

Wolmar felt his already twisted soul tighten another notch as the apparition he was now an integral part of glided through the hills towards the monastery he had visited in life as a messenger from a king. The demoniacal creature was right: he couldn't remember a thing about the afterlife. Try as he might, all he could conjure up of the intervening time – who could even say how much of it had passed since his forced suicide? – was inky blackness. A darkness more terrible perhaps even than the one he was now forced to endure. Sheer, unadulterated nothingness.

Just as I thought! cackled Ha'arba'alon, reading his discomfort like a heraldic device under open skies. *The Angel of Death bore thee to Purgatory, the Second Torment for unshriven souls... and those who take their own lives in defiance of the so-called Almighty's great gift of life!*

I had no choice! Wolmar baulked telepathically. *It was that or become bound to hellish fiends like you!*

Which thou now art in any case, less the eternal reward the Master would have conferred upon thee for thy willing service, mocked Ha'arba'alon triumphantly. *But come, enjoy this last reprieve with me, before thou returnest forever to thy grey bourne on the Other Side! Or perhaps, if thou servest well enough, a place awaits thee in the sewers of the City of Burning Brass...*

I'd sooner rot in Purgatory for all the ages than join your wicked brood, Wolmar's tortured spirit snapped back.

Have it as thou shalt, replied Ha'arba'alon, sounding almost mild now. Then another quickening, a pulse across the night-shrouded countryside that only the apparition could sense.

But hark! said the demon. *They're near, so very near! Our prey draweth nigh, and soon there will be blood and souls to feast upon!*

Returning his otherworldly senses to his mundane surroundings, Wolmar realised it was true. Four shadowy figures: horsemen making their way circuitously towards the other side of a building on a high ridge he recognised... Of course, the Argolian headquarters. It stood etched against the purpling skies, silhouetted against the stark backdrop of the darkened firmament.

And then he felt it. A terrible bloodlust, eclipsing any that he'd known in his mortal years as a knight – an ineluctable urge to violence unlike anything he'd experienced. Not even when he had slain Krulheim on the fields before Linden, forcing the poltroon to eat his blade and transfixing him to the reddened earth beneath, had he felt such hunger to kill.

Without slowing down, he whipped the greatsword Ivon had given him off his back. Soundlessly singing with a maniacal glee, Ha'arba'alon imbued the blade with a bilious green fire.

Now, hissed the demon. *Now, we feast on blood and souls!*

～

Adelko was the first to spot the apparition he could already sense. Horskram noticed it too, but Azelin and Hari remained oblivious, as they scaled the ridge towards the monastery. As they'd fathomed, there had been no more than a couple of sentries camped on this side of the hill, away from the main road where the investing force was camped. Azelin had made light work of them, cutting the two footsoldiers down before they even had time to react: Horskram had beseeched the erstwhile Bethler to avoid using lethal force, but that didn't appear to be part of Azelin's mental furniture.

Not that any of them had time to mourn the hapless guards now. Fighting his rising terror as the flaming apparition shot towards them, Adelko quickly grasped the futility of any further subterfuge: whatever the ghastly thing was, it was clearly visible from far away.

The two monks exchanged glances and nodded; their long months of adventuring together and conjoined sixth senses meant they acted in concert without thinking.

Horskram whistled a low note, alerting Hari and Azelin to the approaching danger. The pair turned around, looking back and down to see what their companions were preoccupied with: when they saw, both men let out startled oaths.

The thing that stalked towards them appeared not even to be running: yet it navigated the terrain with a swiftness that could only be described as unnatural, gliding across the tangled scrubland towards them effortlessly. As it drew nearer they realised it was an armoured knight, but one whose frame and harness were suffused with an ethereal flame that bore the unmistakeable hallmarks of hellfire.

Together the two monks began reciting the Psalm of Abjuration, Adelko holding out his circifix while Horskram brandished the phial containing the Redeemer's blood as they channelled His power.

But something wasn't right. The entity that drew nigh was

obviously possessed of some kind of demonic force, yet the sacred words seemed to give it no pause.

Adelko did not need to glance sidelong at his mentor to realise his confusion. Whatever this was, it was something Horskram had never encountered.

~

Ah, poor pitiful monks! cackled Ha'arba'alon. *So accustomed to fighting demonkind and undead, yet never before have they foughtest both combined! Even the Redeemer would have been confounded by such!*

The disguise the monks had assumed had neither Wolmar nor Ha'arba'alon fooled – they could sense the sacred aura that permeated the Argolians and the sacred relic they carried, as a mortal man smells a blocked latrine.

Just shut up and let me wet my sword, groused Wolmar as the apparition gobbled up the remaining distance between it and its prey.

Closing with the older monk – Wolmar dimly thought he recognised him from somewhere – the apparition slashed sideways at him, nearly severing his legs in one fell stroke. The greybeard leapt high to avoid it, but landed awkwardly in bushes clustered at the base of the hill, losing his balance and falling into them.

Good, let his fall be broken, so his death can be mine! thought Wolmar.

Mine, you mean, hissed Ha'arba'alon, as the apparition loomed over the stricken monk, flaming sword held high.

~

Looking up from where he'd fallen, Horskram stared aghast as his doom towered over him, a decayed knight consumed with flames that only seemed to amplify it. Terror paralysed him for a fatal second, which would have been his last had Adelko not interposed himself between them, lashing out at the death knight with his quarterstaff.

Almost casually, the apparition turned and flicked the downwards blow aside, its fiery blade shearing Adelko's staff in two. A lunge riposte nearly buried itself in the journeyman's heart, but he was saved by his sixth sense, which augmented his reflexes.

Augmented, but not perfected. Stepping back out of range of the strike, he stumbled over Horskram, who was trying to disentangle himself from the bush. Adelko was less fortunate in his fall than the older monk, catching his head on a rock with an ugly *crump* as he keeled over, before lying still in the long grass.

But the precious seconds had purchased Horskram his life, for now at least. Surging to his feet, he channelled his elan as he had not done since his showdown with Andragorix the previous year. Seizing his own quarterstaff, he began again to recite from the Psalm of Abjuration.

'Unclean devil, know thou own weakness and cower in shame before it! Thy true power thou relinquishest aeons ago, when in folly thou didst choose a darker master! Never shall the light of the Almighty shine upon thee, never shall the quickening of true life run its course through thy cankered frame!'

The demonic knight paused... and then swung again at Horskram. A mighty blow he knew better than to try and parry, it whistled past him as the monk darted to one side. He moved with a speed and agility that belied his ageing body; his elan, obedient to his summons, flowed through him like a clear spring river swollen by the last snows of dying winter.

But as the death knight struck at him again and again, the adept knew his power would avail him little. The ghastly warrior fought and moved with a strength and savagery he had never before seen; getting in a riposte was out of the question. And what could a quarterstaff do against such a thing in any case?

Movement at the edge of his vision. And as sudden as a gust from the swift-blowing North Wind, Azelin was there, sliding down the ridge, his sword catching the hellish light from the apparition and seeming to purify it somehow. With a desperate ferocity, the fallen knight propelled himself from the sloping hill on spring-like legs, landing clear of the bushes on the hilly ground beside. Launching himself at their ghastly new foe, he drove it back with fell strokes. Sparks flew resentfully between the two blades as both knights strived for an opening – but the erstwhile Bethler's sword, Horskram knew, had been consecrated for seven days and nights in honour of the Acolytes. Not so easily would it be cloven in two.

Still incanting the Redeemer's words, Horskram joined Azelin in pressing the attack, flanking the demonic knight and raining a frenzy of blows down upon it. He knew he could do little harm to the thing, whatever it was, but at least he could try to distract it.

Perhaps not his finest idea. A tendril of flame snaked outwards from the apparition's body, catching his sleeve and igniting it. Lurching backwards with a cry, Horskram struggled to beat the flames out, but still they burned. And it was his *soul* they burned, not his body: the adept felt his elan waning as the eerie green fire ran up the length of his arm.

Hurriedly, he forced himself to focus, muttering the Psalm of Cleansing as he strove to extinguish the preternatural flames that threatened to consume his very essence. Through that struggle he was dimly aware of the combat between Azelin and the death knight raging on: heaven and hell themselves appeared to shudder with each and every blow they exchanged.

Forcing himself to return concentration to his own problem, Horskram redoubled his efforts, reciting the mantra again and again.

A shield to my soul,
Let hell's sword sleep in darkness,
My faith is armour

A ward against evil,
To temptation I succumb not,
Fear shall not overwhelm me

Pain but illusion,
Main force be my salvation,
Lightly I go forth

Again and again, the words. The ethereal flames began to recede just as they approached his shoulder, flickering back down the length of his arm resentfully. Horskram invoked the mantra again, in a voice that grew stronger as he felt his elan returning.

Again and again, the words: the hellish fire ran back down towards his wrist, more quickly now. Sweat streamed from the adept's brow as he felt it fight him one last time... then, as suddenly as it had come on, it was gone, winking out in the darkness.

Horskram's legs gave way beneath him, and he collapsed to the hard ground, gratefully letting the sedge shroud him as he slipped into unconsciousness.

Azelin felt the sweat lash off of him as he and the hellish apparition traded blows. It wasn't just from the preternatural flames that suffused his opponent; in all his years, he'd never fought one anywhere near as deadly as this.

But then, he wasn't in the habit of facing down cadaverous knights imbued with demonic power.

The apparition's fiery greatsword twirled figures of eight as it regained the offensive, launching a salvo of deadly strikes that Azelin struggled to fend off. Footwork came naturally to him, it always had, but this wasn't a foe you wanted to give ground to.

They'd been fighting for several minutes, and he had yet to land a blow that came close. Most of his fights against mortal opponents seldom lasted more than a few brief exchanges.

But somewhere deep within him, Azelin felt something stir into life: the Bethlers attuned themselves to a variant of the Argolians' sixth sense, but unlike their more peaceable brethren they deployed it mainly for earthly combat.

He hadn't been the most spiritual of men, not for a long time, but he'd need every advantage he could get. Ducking out of range of the death knight's last strike and circling smartly around, Azelin regained the initiative, launching a punishing offensive of his own. As he did, he tried with all his darkened soul to do something he had not for many a year now.

He tried to believe.

At first it seemed futile. The animated corpse that sought to make his own had a hideous rictus etched across its rotted face: Azelin fancied he could almost hear it laughing at his puny and cynical efforts to tap the Creed. The thing regained the offensive, and this time was rewarded with first blood: Azelin yelped as its sword point caught his forehead a glancing blow.

It was just a flesh wound, but a terrible burning ran the length of it, causing the warrior-monk to flinch back. Worse, the ethereal flames didn't cauterise the wound: blood ran into his eyes, obscuring his vision. Desperately Azelin retreated, relying on instinct and years of swordcraft to keep his antagonist at bay.

Too powerful, he thought to himself dimly. *It's far more wicked than I am good. A true believer indeed.*

That wry thought should have been his last, but somehow he conjured up the will to keep fighting. Purely on the defensive now, he gave yet more ground, fending off the apparition's bloodlusting sword strokes. The sound of clashing blades rang into the night, savagely spearing the silence.

And then that something within him flickered... and caught a fire of its own. Unbidden, words of St Alysius he had once cherished came flooding back to him.

Do you struggle to believe? Then believe in spite of your disbelief. Make a play of believing, for oft times things said and done in play become reality.

Utter cant, the cynic in him responded. *Weasel words of priests, designed to confound the gullible and ignorant.*

Perhaps his inner cynic was right. But, as he struggled to fend off the fiery apparition and regain some ground, Azelin realised one thing with cold crystal clarity: being right this time would surely get him killed.

His opponent clearly knew nothing of fatigue, and would go on like this until the sun rose again. Caught up in a diabolical battle lust, it hungered incessantly for his death.

But... wasn't death something he had yearned after for years now?

Another attack by his assailant lent deadly urgency to that question, as the death knight brought him to his knees with a pulverising overhead strike that he'd only just managed to parry.

Staring up into the thing's glazed eyes, he saw its own hellish flames reflected in them: burning now yellow, now red, now green. The death knight raised its blade again, bringing it down with renewed vigour.

And Azelin had his answer.

It's one thing to wish for death when it's not so damnably close. Quite another when it's just a stroke away!

A primal scream erupted from his throat as he sprang up from the turf, sword held crosswise to meet the death knight's blow. The clashing of blades was immense; his iron sinews were tested to the limit as the force of their collision shook his body head to toe, but somehow he remained in a crouching position.

And then he felt it, hard on the heels of his earthly cry: his long-suppressed elan, kindling into a fire of its own, suffusing his limbs with unearthly strength. Pushing back the hellish warrior, he stood straight and proud. He could sense the thing's astonishment as it backed off, its flames flickering uncertainly as it gave ground.

Yes, you hell-spawned wretch, Azelin thought with satisfaction. *You didn't expect that, did you?*

That was the last conscious thought he permitted himself. Abandoning his thinking mind, he gave himself up entirely to the power of the Redeemer that now quickened him body and soul, unleashing a series of punishing strokes. His sword was a sword no longer; it was an extension of his being, spiritual and temporal.

And his being was a weapon, one the servants of the Fallen One should know well to fear.

~

Hari Yassin wasn't much of one for fighting ghostly

apparitions, but he had to say one thing for them: they made for a wonderful distraction.

He'd reached the monastery wall and begun to climb it, knowing that any monks guarding the parapets would have their eyes firmly fixed elsewhere than where he was.

Unfortunately, it was a gift that took too: by the time he was making his ascent, half a dozen guards were already making their way from the main army camp, doubtless to investigate the commotion.

Hari flicked a glance backwards and downwards. He could make out two imposing figures duelling: it must be Azelin and whatever monstrosity it was that had launched itself out of the gloom to terrorise them. The arriving soldiers had halted directly after rounding the hill, clutching swords and spears fretfully as they made fearful exchanges in Panglian.

You'll be a lot more scared when you get a closer look, Yassin thought wryly to himself, as he continued his climb.

Panicked cries from behind him told him he wasn't wrong; another backwards glance indicated silhouetted forms of the foremost soldiers, stumbling backwards as the true horror of the intruder revealed itself.

Smart move, my friends. Fighting something like that, whatever the hell it is, far exceeds the coin you're paid, I'll wager.

The panicked soldiers were yelling frantically at one another now, completely oblivious to Hari as he sloped up the wall. He'd had no time for his crampons, but fortunately the big stones offered plenty of handholds for his strong clever fingers.

Halfway up, he risked another backwards glance. The guards hadn't budged, and appeared to be gesticulating towards the combat taking place. Squinting in the darkness, Hari could make out his comrade by the hellish light of his assailant: Azelin appeared to be hard pressed, but he couldn't worry about that now.

Returning his attention to the climb, he was roughly two-thirds of the way up when he saw them: two monks peering nervously over the parapet. He paused, ignoring the aching in his muscles as they kept him suspended like a spider.

The Argolians were engaged in a fretful conversation of their own, quickly amplified as two more brothers came to join them. But clearly their attention was focused on the fight down below, as he'd hoped.

Some of your fancy Argolian prayers might go down well right now, thought Yassin, then felt his heart freeze over as he suddenly realised Adelko and Horskram had been nowhere to be seen when last he'd looked downwards.

Pushing that thought from his mind, he continued the climb, more slowly and stealthily now. As ill fortune would have it, the monks were directly above him, but if he could just get close enough to call out the catechism Horskram had taught him...

A sharp exclamation directly above. He'd been spotted.

Curse the Argolians and their damned sixth sense. Lantern light washed over him.

'Redeemer's wounds, who goes there?'

'Tis a sapper, I'll warrant. Brother Odus, yon pan of boiling water!'

A face full of scalding water was the last thing Hari needed now.

'No, don't!' he cried up at them, in his accented Panglian. 'I'm a friend, sent by Brother Horskram of your Order!' Hastily he recited the catechism.

One of the brothers had returned to the parapet and now clutched a wooden bucket. His old hands trembled with its weight, and some of the sloshing contents spilled over the brim, landing on Hari's shoulder with a splash.

'Ayee!' cried the rogue, clutching feverishly at the wall as he felt the boiling liquid seep through his jerkin. 'Please, don't pour that! You'll regret it if you do – not as much as I will, but you'll regret it!'

He repeated the catechism, praying they could understand it even if he didn't.

The lead monk narrowed his eyes at Yassin. 'And how do we know you aren't an agent, sent by the Regent to infiltrate us?'

'How else could I know the catechism if I hadn't been sent by an Argolian?'

The monk barked a cynical laugh that Hari did not like at all. 'Argolians aren't as trustworthy as they used to be – as recent events bear witness to!'

The ageing monk called Odus had at least settled the bucket on the parapet for now. 'Shh, Brother Tremulus,' he hissed at the leader. 'If he's a spy, we don't want to...' He let his voice trail off meaningfully.

To Gehenna with this, thought Hari, and abandoned caution to the wind.

'If it's Hannequin's betrayal you're referring to, I know all about that,' he said, taking some satisfaction at the four startled expressions that greeted the statement. 'But then, you tend to learn a lot when you spend time on the road with one of your Order's best investigators!'

The four monks exchanged uncertain looks. Clearly they hadn't expected this.

'You may recall Master Horskram left you, some moons ago, on a voyage to the Pilgrim Kingdoms,' pressed Hari. 'He contracted me there to help him on his mission – little did we realise your bloody own Grand Master was the source of our troubles all along!'

Brother Tremulus gasped. 'Horskram, he – he's here? He knows of Hannequin's...' Even now, the old coot clearly couldn't bring himself to utter the word 'betrayal'.

'Yes, yes,' snapped Hari impatiently. 'He's here – though I

can't make him out in this light – and he knows everything. Everything except what yon fiend is, and who sent it after us! Look, I don't have all night, and this is a passing uncomfortable position from which to parlay – so please let me up! You can disarm me if you like, just let me get off this damned wall!'

More uncertain glances were exchanged. After an agonising few seconds, Tremulus nodded. 'Come up then,' he said. 'But know that if you seek to beguile us with subterfuge, Brother Sancre here will be giving you a hot bath!'

A younger, sturdier monk had picked up the bucket, and hefted it menacingly.

Ashanti knows how these fools survived for five hundred years, Yassin thought wryly. But he kept that to himself as he finished the climb, hopping lightly over the parapet to stand on the walkway, arms raised high to show he meant no harm.

The four monks surrounded him on the planks, two of them brandishing quarterstaves while the monk called Sancre continued to clutch the steaming bucket and glare at him suspiciously.

'He's a heathen,' said the young monk. 'We must needs be careful.'

'Our Sha'abatian counterparts are not all so bad,' sighed Odus. But then, narrowing his eyes, he added: 'However, you're right, brother. We've yet to determine whether or not *this* one is.'

'Right now, I'm not the one you should be worrying about,' said Hari, flicking his eyes meaningfully in the direction of the ghastly duel raging on below. 'I've no idea what that thing is, and more worryingly, I don't know what has happened to Horskram or his apprentice Adelko. For all I know, they might have been injured, or worse.'

Yassin let his last words hang meaningfully in the evening air.

Turning to the parapet, Brother Odus squinted hard and focused.

'It's no Saraphus,' he said at last. 'Some kind of demonic entity... and yet something else as well, one of the... walking dead.'

'How can such a thing exist?' asked Tremulus sharply. 'It must surely be one or the other.'

Odus turned and glared at Tremulus. 'You've always been more forward in matters temporal than I, brother,' he said. 'But if you think you have a better idea what this apparition is, I'd like to hear it.'

'We've no time for this,' interjected Hari. 'Whatever it is, it's threatening the very life of my companion. And by the looks of it, it may have already done for Horskram and Adelko! We need to help them, right now!'

'There's half a dozen of the Regent's soldiers down there, or hadn't you noticed?' asked the fourth monk. A slight spare man with a pallid complexion, Hari liked him not at all.

'As a matter of fact, I probably did before you,' he replied coolly. 'But if we're to rescue my friends, we'll need to deal with them.'

'What do you suggest?' demanded Sancre sneeringly. He still hadn't let go of the bucket.

Hari favoured him with a sardonic smile. 'I'd suggest we do what they least expect,' he said. 'Take the fight to them...'

Wolmar could feel Ha'arba'alon's frustrated bloodlust. The strange holy knight had proved to be a far more formidable foe than either of them could have fathomed. But beyond that, he also sensed a kind of fear: the demon couldn't be truly harmed or killed, not on this plane at least, but it could certainly be defeated, banished, humiliated, sent back whence it came in failure.

And Wolmar was quite certain Ha'arba'alon's master did not take kindly to failure.

The conjoined apparition they both composed aimed a treacherous cut at the knight's leg, but he anticipated perfectly, leaping high over the blade and lashing out with his foot.

His boot caught Wolmar's animated body square in the chest, sending the apparition stumbling back. Flame immediately coiled around the knight's leg, but he ignored it, choosing instead to follow up his attack with a lethal two-handed thrust. Wolmar and Ha'arba'alon tried to block, but the demoniacal corpse was off balance and the knight moved with superhuman speed.

Azelin's sword found its way past their wavering guard, puncturing through the rusted mail and entering the chest of Wolmar's corpse...

Azelin felt the ethereal fire spiralling up his leg towards his groin, leaching his elan as it went. But the risk he'd taken had paid off, and he'd found his mark: driving his sword point into the death knight's chest, he put his whole body weight behind it, driving his antagonist to the ground.

As he did so, he muttered a prayer with the last of his fading elan. It was the Psalm of Righteous Wrath, and the sacred words imbued his blade with a keen energy. The ghastly apparition began to writhe horribly: a blessed blade through the heart was bad enough without holy words added to it.

As he slumped over the stricken death knight, Azelin felt the flames that threatened to engulf him begin to recede.

Staggering upright without letting go of his sword, he twisted the hilt while pushing downwards, forcing the hellish thing to taste more of its keen edge.

Still no sound escaped the apparition's mangled vocal cords, but already Azelin could see the flames that had sustained its animated corpse begin to fade, the variegated hues settling into a dull grey, followed by a tarnished black. The body seemed to shrivel and diminish before his very eyes... and then, in a great eruption, a tendril of smoke poured from the grinning rictus, leaving behind it a stench of brimstone to taint the dusking air. The corpse itself shuddered to a halt, its limbs suddenly freezing over as the natural stiffness of true death reasserted itself.

But Azelin was taking no chances. Pulling his blade free, he stepped to one side and lopped the head off in one fluid motion, as the last of the flames on his leg and the undead knight expired together. Then, with a methodical calmness, he dissected the rest, hewing off its limbs one by one.

And as the smoky essence of whatever fell demon had possessed the corpse spiralled up into the dark skies, before vanishing altogether, it bequeathed him a parting vision.

Azelin saw a thousandfold torments visited upon the earth that had borne him; manifold devils of indescribable shape and form crawling across its surface, poisoning and destroying all in their path. Tears sprang from his eyes as he realised that all his crimes multiplied a hundredfold could not ever match such iniquity.

And yet his crimes *were* monstrous, and that was the revelation that hurt most: however wicked he had been, his wickedness could not compass the tiniest fraction of what these beings were capable of, if left unchecked.

Letting go of the hilt, Azelin slumped to the soil, weeping like a newborn.

And in that bittersweet moment, he knew he still believed.

Wiping blood and tears from his eyes, he gazed upon his greatsword, where it lay buried in his fallen opponent's breast. The inscription in Decorlangue on the fuller of the blade seemed to have retained some of the ghastly light, and its two words blazoned themselves across his line of sight.

Know Thyself.

CHAPTER 16

BLOOD ON THE WATER

Lord Aesgir exchanged grim looks with the assembled knights and officers. Crammed onto the cramped forecastle of his war galley the *Sea Stallion*, they were gathered about the burly lord to hear his final words of encouragement before re-engaging the enemy.

Encouragement, thought Sir Torgun, *that is something the men need badly.*

They'd lost half a dozen of the forty-odd ships that had set out under the Sealord's command; of the thousand fighting men crewing them, scarcely more than half remained – even among ships not sunk, casualties had been high. At least they'd managed to take down a handful of Northland longships, slaughtering their crews and setting fire to them.

But that had been before the Tritons had intervened.

Gazing at the waters that lapped agitatedly against the *Stallion*'s hull in the gloaming, Sir Torgun knew sorrow. What was worse, he wondered – that he felt responsible for Vaskrian's demise, or that he mourned the passing of the young knight more than all his other brave comrades put together?

'Sir Torgun,' said Aesgir, abruptly snapping him out of his

melancholy rumination. 'We've agreed on tactics, have you anything to add?'

A surprise attack by night was about the best they could hope for. The Northland ships outnumbered them more than two to one, and that was without reckoning on the sea creatures that would undoubtedly come to their aid.

Slowly unsheathing his greatsword, Sir Torgun let the ship's lanterns play across its silvery blade as he prepared to give the speech he'd spent the afternoon rehearsing.

'Be in no doubt,' he told the men. 'The odds do not favour us. Victory is always possible when knights and soldiers fight with valour and discipline, but only a fool would call this a likely one.'

He paused to survey the lengthening faces in the lengthening shadows cast by the ship's shrouds and sails.

'So I would say this to all of thee,' he went on carefully. 'We may be remembered as the men who helped to save Strongholm, or the men who failed to reclaim her. But either way, we shall be remembered. Every foe you bring down this night will bring you one step closer to the Heavenly Halls – whether it is your destiny to travel there now or another day.'

Raising up the marvellous blade Erith had crafted for him from the fragment of Søren's sword, he exulted inwardly as it caught the light from the first star of evening as it blinked into watchfulness.

'Aye, comrades,' he said, his low even voice raising just a notch. 'For the very heavens themselves watch us tonight. And I do swear, here and now, that I shall return from this fight on the side of the victors, or not at all. And if the latter be my fate, let a hundred foes and more perish on this blade before I meet it!'

He'd raised his voice to a shout as he uttered the last sentence, and Torgun was never a man to shout. That alone had more of an impact on the assembled knights than any of his words themselves. As one, they drew weapons, holding swords and axes and warhammers and maces to the skies, as if in defiant acknowledgement of the heavenly spectators Torgun had just invoked. The war cries that escaped throats were muted, but lacked no conviction for all that. Down on the main deck the regular soldiers stirred, and began thumping weapons against shields rhythmically. The ordinary seamen joined in too, breaking into war shanties. Oddly contagious, the subdued clamour spread from the *Stallion* to the other ships next to it, and before long the entire line of vessels resounded to the clumping of metal against oak, punctuated by chanting and singing.

So I've managed to inspire them, Torgun thought. *Let's hope it makes a difference.*

Flitting skittishly about her scrying tool, Nereia forced herself to concentrate. The Great Disturber would be quick to spot armed schools of Seakindred approaching the coastline... but not if she blocked him first. Once again she murmured the words in the language of magick, focusing her counter-scrying spell on Logrim and the hundreds-strong host of merfolk he led.

As for the Great Disturber himself, she only knew her arch-enemy's approximate location, but that was all she needed. As she visualised the abstract symbols – an eyepatch, a broken mirror, and a veil – and repeated the sorcerous litany, she felt her elan begin to quicken. Though she was an accomplished diviner, it was quite a feat to cloak a small army. Her tail thrashed frenetically as her spell gathered power, then grew suddenly still as it took effect.

Drifting up and away from the orb, she let her entire body

relax, drifting calmly on the current as she allowed herself a triumphant smile.

There'll be no warning of your coming now, my friends. Let the Great Disturber send his Tritons.

~

They spotted the lights of the enemy's longships an hour after setting sail. During that time the evening had deepened into night.

'Dim the lights!' barked Aesgir. 'Relay the order down the line – the rest of you avast your mutterings, we'll have silence in His Majesty's fleet!'

As one the *Sea Gallant*'s soldiers and crew obeyed; only the mimicking of ravens remained to puncture the dead quiet that suddenly descended, as hand-picked sailors obeyed the Sealord's command to pass the signal.

Torgun tightened his grip on his sword as the fleet edged towards the foe, sailors rowing as quietly as they could. Up ahead a myriad lantern lights marked their target; already sounds of carousing could be heard aboard the Northland ships.

Their victories have left them overconfident, thought the knight. *That's another thing in our favour.*

He could only pray it would help tip the odds.

Closer still, and closer. It was impossible to tell in the darkness how many longships were berthed in the Strang Estuary, but estimates put it at anywhere between four score and a hundred: the rest of the Shield Queen's fleet would be ravaging the southerly coasts of Northalde.

Closer still. Aesgir gave his officer the nod, and again a signal relayed down the line; as part of the pre-arranged strategy, half the fleet unfurled sails, luffing to the wind so as to flank the enemy fleet. Torgun knew little of seamanship, but enough to realise the difficulty of accomplishing such a manoeuvre by night. As the other half of the fleet detached from his, he prayed once again that Stygnos and Ezekiel would favour them.

Then he paused for thought. Perhaps it was Sjórkunan, the un-angel of the waters, he should be praying to.

He clutched his sword hilt more tightly.

If you really are my ancestor, then by all that's good hear me now, he found himself thinking. Ordinarily such a prayer would be considered blasphemy, but to hell with blasphemy: his country's fate would be determined tonight.

Old Northalde forever. He silently mouthed the words, taking some comfort from them.

Closer still, and closer. Torgun's keen eyes could now just about make out the shapes of the carousing shieldmen, lantern light glinting off their iron-studded jerkins as they passed drinking horns around. A sideways glance to the larboard bow gave him but the barest sketch of the other half of the Sealord's fleet, foresails flapping in the wind as they disappeared into the night.

'Crossbows.' The steely order came from Aesgir. Half a dozen men crammed up on to the forecastle had theirs ready and primed; now they levelled them at the target.

More raven calls, as the order was relayed down the line.

Closer still, and closer... Torgun could now make out flaxen beards and glinting eyes, hear the Northlanders bellowing at one another in the coarse Norric tongue.

'Loose!'

Quarrels zinged from twenty ships. Not all found their mark, but several dozen cries told a different story. Bodies splashed into the water as shieldmen fell; drinking horns were swiftly abandoned for swords and axes as the survivors scrambled.

'Full ahead and turn her about!' yelled Aesgir. 'Weapons at the ready and prepare to board!'

Sir Torgun placed a booted foot on the taffrail at his position near the stern, sword held high. By the time the oarsmen had brought the *Stallion* level with a Northland longship, the shieldmen were armed and ready for the fight. The crew had brought her up a little shy, but a man's length posed no difficulties for a man like Torgun. His powerful thighs propelled him like a catapult as he leapt across the waves to land just inside the longship's prow.

Two warriors went down before his flashing blade. A couple of seconds more, and another two shared their fate. The longship was one of the largest of its kind, but even so no more than two big men could face him at once. That suited the Northlending knight perfectly.

I'll save the rest of you having to worry about this ship, he thought grimly as his blade traced arcs of crimson through the night air. He fought as never before, like a man possessed. All notions of chivalry were abandoned: these butchers had slaughtered his sister, his former lover, his King's kin.

The screams accompanying severed limbs and hewn skulls were music to his ears as he cut a bloody swathe the length of the longship. By the time he was done, Torgun found himself standing ankle-deep in blood at the stern, the pitiful moaning of the dying and maimed lying in his wake. Behind him Northlending soldiers were using the corpses he'd made to bridge the longship and close on the next in line.

Taking advantage of the respite he'd literally carved out for himself, Torgun quickly scanned the turgid waves. The second half of Aesgir's fleet had engaged the Northland blockade at a near perfect right angle to their own: the Sealord's manoeuvre had been successful. But the element of surprise was all but exhausted; the enemy's superior numbers would soon begin to tell.

And Torgun knew worse was probably to come. Again he scoured the darkling seas, but of the Tritons there was as yet no sign. The clamour of war raged behind him; he was about to turn and seek another foe when a gentle bumping against the ship's keel alerted him.

Glancing downwards, his heart leapt into his mouth as he caught the horrid form of a Triton, its lambent tripartite eyes catching the lantern light with a hideous luminosity.

But... this one appeared to be dead.

Reaching down, Torgun wrenched the limp thing up into the light. Three puncture marks to what passed for its chest, inky blood still oozing from the fatal wound.

And then he saw others, their chitinous corpses bobbing up above the surface of the waves. The lantern light only revealed a dozen or so, but beyond the circle who knew how many more there were?

Releasing the dead creature, he made a grab for another as it floated closer to him. Again the same triple wound: this one had found the Triton's three eyes, putting them out.

These are no Northlending weapons, thought the knight as he released the body and turned to survey the naval battle. All about, sea galleys and longships were clinched together in the bloody embrace of war, Northlendings and Northlanders slaying on the left hand and the right.

But no Tritons had surfaced to join the conflict, not besides these dead ones at any rate.

Despite his elation, Sir Torgun felt a chill ghost the length of his spine. It looked for all the world as though his fell ancestor had answered his prayer.

Vaskrian watched with satisfaction as the corpses of Tritons floated up towards the surface. Logrim had concealed the

Seakindred behind a vast underwater coral reef, anticipating their arrival. The foul creatures had come, many riding the great white man-eating fish; but a school of other giant fish had come to their aid, heeding Logrim's summons and bludgeoning their sharp-toothed counterparts with bone-hard beaks that struck with the force of a mace swung above water.

It was, without a doubt, the strangest battle Vaskrian had ever been in.

Taken by surprise, the Tritons had soon turned tail. Logrim had ordered a quarter of his surviving force to chase and harry them.

'We've cut off their reinforcements,' the merman told Vaskrian in his high fluting voice, which also bubbled as he spoke. 'Now we need to see about the main force, up there above water where you come from.'

'What do you have in mind?' the young knight asked him. 'Erm, meaning no disrespect, but I can't see how you lot will be much use boarding ships.'

Logrim favoured him with a grin that almost seemed to turn the waters about him icy.

'Who said anything about boarding?'

Torgun had just separated a berserker's head from his shoulders when the first Northland longship capsized. It was quickly followed by another, and another, shieldmen crying out in surprise and fear as they suddenly found themselves fighting to stay afloat in the chilly night-time waters.

A few seconds later, and they were fighting to stay alive: humanoid figures could be seen erupting from the waves, wielding tridents to deadly effect. Most Northlanders could swim well, but fighting *and* swimming was another thing altogether. Their assailants, on the other hand, moved with the speed and grace of court dancers, effortlessly flanking the barbarians before despatching them and disappearing again abruptly beneath the frothing seas.

Torgun glanced rapidly about him, but the Northlending galleys were unaffected – whatever these aquatic apparitions were, they were clearly on their side. More and more long-ships were tipping over now, and fixing his gaze on one of the nearer ones, his astounded suspicions were confirmed: the sea-humans, or whatever they were, were responsible, having swum up beneath the Northland vessels in groups of fifteen or twenty to upend their keels.

Merfolk, Torgun realised. *The fabled Seakindred have come to our aid.* Despite all his adventures, he could scarcely credit such a thing.

Panic was spreading among the Northlanders now, many of whom were thrashing about in the waters, trying in vain to fend off the Seakindred. Already some of the unaffected long-ships were trying to disengage, sensing the battle lost; but Aesgir was pitiless, ordering the Northlending galleys to pursue them.

Torgun was distracted by a desperate shieldman swim-ming over to the longship he'd boarded; with a feverish hand he clutched at its side. Without a second thought, Torgun took it off at the wrist. The hapless warrior sank back into the waves with a screaming splash; seconds later a merman erupted from the waves behind him, spearing him in the back with its trident.

The strange hybrid creature favoured him with a pearly grin, its teeth at odds with its glaucous skin, before diving back underwater again, giant fishtail flicking him a last goodbye.

Making his way back across the corpse-strewn flotilla, Torgun rejoined the *Stallion*. Aesgir was bellowing orders nine to the dozen; the Northlending galleys not busy chasing the fleeing longships were harassing those that had chosen to make a brave last stand. The seas were a scene of carnage, waters made thick with the bleeding bodies of dead and dying Northlanders. A few of the foremost fleeing longships were just about to pull out of range of their pursuers... But these too suddenly capsized, tumbled over by Seakindred, who picked them off mercilessly as they thrashed about in the waters.

Seeing that, the rest of the longships hurriedly turned about, hoping in desperation to board Aesgir's sea galleys and so escape a watery grave. But no: the Northlendings antici-pated, holding them off with bow and blade.

Soon it was all over. Of the four-score longships and more that had sought to strangle Strongholm, not one remained crewed. Aesgir gave the order to burn them, and before long the Strang Estuary was lit up by myriad blazing bonfires. Those Northlendings who had fallen into the sea found themselves swept up by the Seakindred and helped back to their galleys: even the dead were returned for burial.

With some satisfaction, Torgun surveyed the latter and saw that they were, on this occasion at least, small in number: scarcely more than two dozen had perished. How many Northland barbarians had died that night, he could not begin to count.

Their work done, the Seakindred disappeared below water as suddenly as they had come. At Aesgir's behest the Northlending war galleys pulled back together in formation; one of the more optimistic younger officers had thought to bring along a cask of strong Armandy wine, in case of victory. This was now broached, cups passed around.

As Sir Torgun waited patiently for his turn at the brim, he caught a lithe figure making its way across the flotilla towards the *Stallion*. But only when it finally boarded, moving into the light of the ship's lanterns, did he recognise him.

Sir Vaskrian still held a gore-spattered axe over one shoulder, and a broad grin was etched across his rakish scarred face.

'Did you like my new friends?' he asked cheerily, as he approached his stunned comrade. 'Pretty handy to have around in a naval engagement, wouldn't you agree?' The young gallant glanced sidelong at the dripping axe and frowned. 'It's really too bad I lost another sword – but killing Northlanders with their own weapons is quite satisfying, I must sa-'

Vaskrian never got to finish his last sentence, as Torgun took him in a giant, crushing bear hug.

INTERLUDE: HANNEQUIN'S LOG

Our days have been fraught. Finally, our defences are secure; upon arriving at the Forbidden City, we were assailed by a host of horrors, denizens of the Lower Tiers hungry for blood and souls. One of the brothers lost his mind immediately; the alien architecture here alone is enough to drive a man insane. But such losses were anticipated, desirable even: we fed poor Gothrik to the demons, as part of the binding pact. Now our pentagrams are drawn and consecrated: yes, the Redeemer's water helped us there.

Oh, this has been vindication of a lifelong pursuit! Our very survival here but bears out my theory as true: that the powers of an Argolian and that of a Demonologist can be married, to greater potentiation. And so it goes, the broken summit of Ma'amun's palatial tower is ours. Now our work can begin in earnest.

Two more of our cabal lost their minds recently: even with the protection our craft affords, Varya and her ancient eldritch occupants conspire to uproot the tree we have so painstakingly planted. Let them try! Adso and

Brehan shall furnish the sacrifice needed for our next summoning. The Great Old One-Eye shall rise up again, and by all the forces of our Necromancy he shall do our bidding for us.

But we must move swiftly, for the Appointed Hour draws ever nearer, and there is much yet to be done. Our Scrying is halted, for not easily is the sorcerous shroud that hangs over the Forbidden City penetrated; even if our conjoined elan were not focused on channelling the Abjuration needed to repel the things that dwell without, and the Necromancy required for the host we must now raise, nigh impossible would it be to access the cosmic interstices needed to commune with our allies without. So be it: long have I shepherded my flock, now it is time for them to fend for themselves.

As for our Eastern ally: I fear him not, though his powers be considerable. From lands never ruled over by the Elder Wizards does he hail, his sorceries can be but a tepid dilution of the power in my hand. Yet useful he shall prove, him and the emperor-warlord whose ear he has... Ah, sleeping Illyrium, thou shalt soon be awoken from thy carefree slumber: think not that the might of the Urovian New Empire shall remain standing to oppose my plans!

But I digress. I must retain my own composure, and remain bent to the task at hand. For even now, the forces of Varya would unhinge my mind, by ways more subtle if other methods should fail.

It is imperative that they do not succeed, for there can be no diversion – no, not for one second – from this mission.

The very fate of the world depends upon it.

PART II

AN OFFER OF MARRIAGE

Adhelina struggled to contain her laughter. In truth it was laugh or cry: weeks she and Hettie had spent, holed up in a modest suite of chambers in an obscure district of Ushalayim. Weeks of waiting for the recondite mystic Tipu's prophecy to come true: for friendly strangers from the Palomedian northlands to come and set the damosels on their next quest, one that would bring them back home. Weeks of eking out a living as a leech: the erstwhile heiress of Dulsinor's skills at herbalism had served them well enough, and Hettie continued to play well at cards, but the frustration of waiting it out in the high heat of Al'Nurë, the longest, hottest season in Sassania, keeping close company and out of sight as often as possible, had been almost unbearable.

But at last, the emissaries from their homeland had tracked them down: as it turned out, keeping a low profile while giving out just enough information to be identified hadn't been so difficult. The 'leech from Vorstlund' had proved popular with visiting Urovian pilgrims and merchants who had sickened in the festering climate of the Far South, but were too bigoted or ignorant to seek treatment from a native healer.

Far more difficult to swallow was what the young knight, crammed with his two companions onto a silk divan in her small atrium, was telling her now.

'So, Sir Ulfstan, please let me see if I have understood this correctly,' Adhelina said, deliberately and slowly, while trying not to look at where Hettie sat giggling impertinently on a giant cushion stuffed with ostrich feathers. 'You are in fact covert emissaries, travelling on behalf of Princess Consort Utha of Westenlund, and you are here to propose a union between myself and her son and heir apparent, the Crown Prince. This in order to facilitate an unprecedented bid for his kingship of Vorstlund, with a view to uniting the Nine Great Lords under a single banner, so as to repulse the invasion of our homeland by Pangonia – and its new ally Thalamy?'

Sir Ulfstan cleared his throat. A well-made knight in his twenties with close-cropped hair that matched his regimented manners, he appeared unfazed by her scepticism; he was, she had to suppose, a decent enough envoy. 'Not unprecedented, my lady,' he sought to correct. 'In fact His Highness's ancestor King Aelle - '

Adhelina raised a hand to cut him off, while Hettie continued to snigger into her brightly coloured fan. A sharp glance flicked sidelong told Hettie her silence was required too.

'Please, spare me the history lesson,' she told the envoy. 'I daresay I know it better than you.'

Sir Ulfstan inclined his head deferentially as she continued: 'But I find it rather difficult to believe that I am to be due such an honour. Given that I have been forced into exile, a virtual renegade, by the treachery of the Lanraks – above whom you would place me, by putting me on a throne next to

Prince Franz – it stretches the bounds of credibility to believe that I am now intended as the future Queen of the Realm. You do see my point, don't you?'

Once again, Ulfstan proffered the scroll he had brought with him. It bore the seal of Westenlund, imprinted on the wax: the carrack on sunburst insignia certainly looked authentic. And Tipu had been characteristically sure of his prophecy, maddeningly unspecific though it was...

Adhelina sighed. 'Hettie, please take these good knights to the parlour and provide them with refreshments as befits their station,' she commanded. 'And when you've done that, bring me a cup of that herbal tea I brewed this morning – I'd like to be alone with this missive, if you please.'

Sir Ulfstan and the two other knights rose and bowed, before following Hettie from the atrium.

Sighing, Adhelina broke the seal and unfurled the scroll. The scrawled handwriting was somewhat untidy, but legible:

My dearest Adhelina, Rightful Heiress of Dulsinor and all her Chattels,

I realise only too well that this message reaches you in dark times, not just for you and your house, but for all the folk of Vorstlund. For we are invaded! King Carolus has mustered an army fifteen thousands strong to assay us in Westenlund, whilst to the east another five thousands from Thalamy, his newfound ally, attack Ostvelt and Aslund.

My son the Crown Prince Franz and I

have managed to broker an alliance of the Great Lords, but without further unity I fear it will fracture, for ever our barons have been a fractious lot, as you can only know too well from your own personal tragedy.

Therefore, I implore thee to take on trust the words of my emissary, Sir Ulfstan of Braknost, and likewise these I write to you now. My daughter Lana is to be married to Lord Hengist, a man, if he can even be called that, you are so very right to despise. But alas, a considerable dowry from our coffers was the price paid to secure a cessation of hostilities against Dulsinor, your homeland.

Now it requires one union more to cement our nation: you and Franz must wed, and in doing so put forth a suit for kingship of Vorstlund. Only under a unified monarchy can our divided nation hope to regroup and repel these barbarous invaders.

As such, I implore thee to return with my emissary and his retinue: they are sworn to protect you, with their lives if necessary. Take up your rightful residence at Westerburg Point, marry my son the Crown Prince Franz, and become Queen of Vorstlund.

In doing so, see the Lanraks and their ill kind brought to heel once and for all, and these accursed foreign invaders off our treasured land!

Yours, etc,

Utha, Princess Consort & Acting Regent of Westenlund

Adhelina read and re-read the letter, chewing her lip fretfully. When Hettie arrived with her tea, she refused to meet the questioning look in her friend's eyes.

'Later, Hettie, please,' she said in a low voice. 'I have some thinking to do – in the meantime, please keep our guests diverted.'

'That I shall do gladly,' replied her lady-in-waiting with a lascivious smirk. 'The blond one is particularly handsome, I find.'

Adhelina tried not to smile back. The torrid heat and confinement had done something to her friend, without doubt – if she wasn't careful, she'd get herself dishonoured, albeit willingly.

Perhaps it is about bloody time the pair of us were married after all, she thought as Hettie bustled off again. *And anyone is better than Hengist.*

She mulled it over. Her adventures, or perhaps one should say misadventures, with her two swains Torgun and Braxus had taught her that courtly love must largely be a fiction. As for Franz... by all accounts he wasn't the best-looking of men, but he was said to be honourable. And, of course, powerful.

In fact, it was a match even her ambitious father would never have dared hope for. Glancing at the dappled rays of sunlight that filtered through the ornately latticed windows, Adhelina shook her head before taking a grateful sip of her tea. Life had brought her to a strange pass.

Glancing again at the scroll, she couldn't help but wonder if Utha had some kind of farseer or mystic of her own, or even her own powers of Second Sight: for surely without Tipu's prophecy, such a proposal must have seemed too implausible to be believed. Why in the Known World had Utha believed she would take it seriously? As it was she scarcely could, even with the mysterious Sha'abatian's words to prepare her for it.

And yet the realm was clearly in desperate straits – all the grand conflicts the monk Horskram had hinted at seemed to be coming about. These were not ordinary times.

And what was the other thing Tipu had told her? *At first these men will seek to use you, but in time the serpent shall turn in their hands...* something like that anyway. Not that she appreciated being likened to a snake, even in prophecy.

Another knock at her door, the one leading to the gallery that overlooked the stairs connecting her rooms to the vestibule facing the bustling street outside.

'Enter,' she commanded.

Jehan poked his head around the door. An *al'Hajin*, of mixed Urovian and Sassanian blood, he'd been an obvious choice of bodyguard. A former soldier in King Rexus of Usha-layim's standing army, he'd been pensioned off after losing half a hand in the last war. His other could still wield a stout cudgel when called for – which fortunately hadn't been too often.

'Just wanted to check you're well,' he said gruffly, tugging his cap. A stout tanned man, he was deferential and trust-worthy – an ideal minder, in other words.

Adhelina smiled reassuringly. 'I'm quite well, thank you Jehan. Our guests will be leaving shortly.' She glanced meaningfully towards the parlour, where Hettie could be heard laughing merrily. After a summer of self-imposed exile, any company was welcome – that of virile young knights even more so.

Jehan nodded before disappearing back downstairs to his post outside the front gate. Adhelina had decided against employing more than one bodyguard – too many would attract just the kind of attention they were supposed to protect against, she'd reasoned.

Presently, Hettie returned with the three knights. They were dressed in brightly coloured silks, having 'gone native' as soon as they arrived – Adhelina supposed that had been part of their orders, to blend in as quickly as possible while they searched for her. As Ulfstan had it, it had taken them more than a week to learn of her probable whereabouts. The men weren't armed but for the daggers they carried – straight broad blades, their only giveaway as non-native Urovians. Their faces had tanned in the long sea journey here, and Ulfstan even spoke Sassanic passably well. Adhelina wondered how he did and where Utha had dug him up from – she knew him vaguely for a wealthy banneret's son, but couldn't recall if any of his relatives had ever joined the Pilgrim Wars.

'My lady,' he said, bowing stiffly once again. 'You've had some time to ponder His Highness's suit – perhaps you might have an answer for it?'

Though polite, the young knight had been firmly instructed not to take no for an answer: Adhelina was well versed enough in politicking by now to sense that much.

But then, she reflected, was 'no' really an option? Even without Tipu's prognostication to guide her, what would her alternatives have been? Remain here, an outcast? Eventually perhaps she would marry a local burgher's son, or even a native nobleman – it wasn't unheard of, by any means. And then there would always be the threat of Grand Master Tobin and his Knights Bethler, the fanatical warrior-monks who had caused her companions so much trouble. Hettie would likely eventually lie with someone too, out of sheer boredom and frustration if nothing else, and have to be married off in haste...

Sir Ulfstan remained standing stock still, gazing keenly at her. His knights had the decency not to follow suit – out of the corner of her eye she caught the handsome blond fellow and Hettie exchanging flirtatious glances.

Adhelina sighed inwardly. There was really only one sensible option – she couldn't run and hide forever. Not if her recurring dreams about leading armies to victory in her homeland were to come true.

'We will come with you to Westenlund,' she said, rising and meeting Ulfstan's eye. 'But know this – his Royal Highness will have to press his suit himself, in person. I haven't toiled and travailed through fire and flood this past year to give myself away lightly.'

Ulfstan was about to say something, but Adhelina cut him off with another imperious wave of the hand.

'This letter calls me heiress of Dulsinor – but with my father gone I am in fact the Orla. You told me the Lanraks failed to take my seat at Graukolos, and this letter confirms that peace between the two baronies has been brokered by Princess Utha. Your house has my cordial thanks for that – but by the laws of our land, as well you know, it is for me, as the sole surviving heir of the Eorl, to determine whom I marry and when. So by all means, let us make speed from this sultry heat and return north to where we belong – but the final decision on any marriage will be mine. I hope that is understood from the outset.'

'By the laws of the land, she hasn't legally been invested as Orla yet,' the third knight, by far the most ill-favoured of the three, had the courage to mutter.

Adhelina fixed him with a withering stare. 'Since when did mere household knights presume to gainsay blue-blooded scions of high houses?' she asked pointedly, taking satisfaction as the weaselly knight shrank before her steely glare. 'As someone apparently so well versed in the law, you should know your basic protocol.'

Turning back to look at the envoy, she continued implacably: 'Sir Ulfstan, I trust you will have words with your unruly bachelor – the journey home will be one of many weeks, and I should not wish for such unwholesome companionship.'

Was that a smile playing about Ulfstan's lips as he replied? 'Never fear, My Lady, Sir Aescwine is but lately belted and can be somewhat impetuous of speech. Rest assured he shall not trouble you, nor even address you unless I specifically command it.'

The knight called Aescwine shrank a little further into his silken robes. Adhelina favoured Ulfstan with just the slightest inclination of the head by way of thanks. Hettie and the blond knight continued to flirt.

'So, is my position clear?' repeated Adhelina, her voice tinged with hardness once again.

Ulfstan favoured her with a bow more florid than the last, yet somehow she did not doubt his sincerity.

'As clear as the diamonds my liege will doubtless gift you personally when he presses his suit,' he replied suavely.

'Excellent,' replied Adhelina, returning the bow with a curtsey. 'Hettie! It's time for us to pack, we're for road and sail again. Please ensure our rents are paid up in full, and pension off Jehan with a full month's pay – and for Ushira's sake, give no notice to the crier that we're no longer in business! I want our departure to go as unremarked upon as possible.'

'Of course, milady,' said Hettie, flashing her handsome swain one more hot glance before bustling off again.

'Sir Ulfstan, I presume you have a ship berthed in the docks,' said Adhelina. 'When can we be ready to sail?'

Ulfstan smiled. 'When can you be ready to leave?' he asked.

In the minaret across the street, the sacred flautist began playing, calling the Sha'abatian faithful to mid-afternoon prayers. A high plangent sound, she had loved it the first time she heard it. There were many things she would miss about this exotic land, she reflected, though the heat and crowds weren't among them.

'Tonight.'

CHAPTER 2

A SACRED MUSTER

The notes from the flautist swept across the sultry plain, as the early morning sun bathed the army encampment in a sweltering wash of golden light.

It was quite a sight to see. Anupe had not looked upon such a mighty muster since her days of service in the Urovian New Empire; more than fifty thousand men of arms stood to attention, before kneeling as one and bowing their heads to the earth in submission. Beyond them the bejewelled minarets of Imanabad shimmered in the heat, already so strong, though the blazing orb that the locals called the avatar Cyrius had barely freed itself from the horizon.

A little way apart, Tipu abased himself in similar fashion, joining the great host in dawn prayers. Though of the Sufieli sect, the mystic still shared basic rites in common with the Orthodox army commanded by the Sultan Muqmurlish tek Nazar.

Muqmurlish, the very man they had come to see and pledge service to. Anupe glanced sidelong at the enigmatic Zarumani priest beside her. He was on his knees praying too, but as a fire-worshipper bonded to the conjoined avatar Mithras, it would be the rising sun that inspired his devotion.

That I can at least relate to, Anupe thought. *The sun comes up every day. As for the gods, where are they to be seen?*

She kept that thought to herself as the mass devotion went on, the flautist guiding the prayers with music that was haunting yet beautiful at the same time.

When it was done, the army rose and broke off into its many divisions: heavily armoured *fariz* going to see to their warhorses; agile *sarakim* testing their bows and checking their swift coursers; muscle-bound *amluqs* sharpening their scimitars and spears; motley but well-equipped platoons of infantry, archers, and conscripts falling into formation once again.

A mighty muster indeed, from all four corners of the Sultanate of Nazharya that Muqmurlish ruled: a holy host, heaven-bent on reconquering Ushalayim and driving the infidel Urovians back into the Sundering Sea whence they had come more than a century ago.

Tipu sidled over to rejoin them as Anupe's sharp eyes searched for Zimri. A respected general despite his former indentured status as an outlander from the Arid Kingdoms far to the south, he had promised to use what influence he could with the Sultan to plead their case.

'I can't see him,' muttered Anupe. Behind them the horses they had purchased at Argon whickered and stamped nervously; they mimicked how she felt, though the Harijan was accustomed never to show fear.

'Patience,' smiled Tipu, his gentle voice as tranquil as ever. 'General Zimri is a good man, I'm sure our journey has not been in vain.'

That journey had taken them by schooner across the Muradi Straits from Shazra'am to Argon, the capital of the Pilgrim Kingdom of Ranishmend. More preoccupied with trade than crusade, the city of eighty thousand souls had paid them little heed, despite most of the population being of Urovian stock. It hadn't been too difficult to purchase fresh steeds and keep a low profile in the bustling cityport, which welcomed visitors from all over the Known World.

From there they'd taken the road once again, travelling through the Sultanate of Kallandhar. As they waited for Zimri to return in the stultifying heat, Anupe mentally counted off the cities they'd passed through: Urguz, Barat Numan, Vassa, Reyah. Though differing in outlook and appearance, all had shared one common theme. War. The Sultana of Kallandhar had pledged her allegiance to her rival in the name of their shared faith: an Orthodoxer like Muqmurlish, the ambitious Nesrine had made no secret of her desire to expel the crusaders from Sassanian shores once and for all.

Rumour had it the Sultana would be bringing some thirty thousand troops to bolster Muqmurlish's forces. Two mighty armies that would launch a two-pronged attack on the Pilgrim Kingdoms: to make matters worse for the Urovians, the foremost houses of Ranishmend were rumoured to have made a deal with the Sultana, staying out of the coming Pilgrim War in return for having their lands spared.

And yet... The crusaders had fought and triumphed over great odds before. The very conquest of the Pilgrim Kingdoms had been nothing short of a dark miracle, a military victory that the latter-day scions of the Blessed Realm still revelled in. It was said that the Knights Bethler lent divine inspiration to the armies of Palom, now said to be bolstered by boatloads of fresh crusaders arriving in the Holy City, inspired to take the Wheel and forsake their northern homelands to fight in the prophet's name.

I've no idea if we're to be on the winning side, but at least there'll be pay and plunder aplenty for a good freesword — if Muqmurlish takes us in.

Anupe bit her lip as she continued to scan the break-fasting army camp for signs of Zimri. Sassanian society was said to be even more male-dominated than Urovian, and her travels through these lands had done little to dispel that notion. Would even an enlightened ruler like Muqmurlish countenance hiring a warrior-woman?

Again she glanced sidelong at her two companions. And what would the Sultan make of a near-heretic and a pagan? Zimri had spoken highly of his liege, but Muqmurlish would have to be astonishingly broad-minded to accept them too.

'Here he comes,' said Tipu softly.

Anupe returned her attention to the army camp, annoyed at having been distracted by her own thoughts. She could see Zimri riding towards them now, flanked by his two fellow Southrons, unsmiling Kufa and cheerful Batu.

The three soldiers from the Arid Kingdoms drew level with them. Zimri had been somewhat surprised to see them when they had sought him out at the end of their weeks-long journey from Murad: clearly he had not expected them to survive their meeting with the archmage Abdel Sha'arza. A clandestine conference to bring him up to speed with their mission had almost turned him as pale as an Urovian, but the resourceful general had recovered quickly enough. A fearsome freesword, albeit a pagan one, and a learned savant of the Sufieli would doubtless be welcome in the fight against the common enemy, he had assured them. As for the Zarumani... perhaps even an idolator with useful skills might be permitted to serve in Ashanti's just war.

Zimri cracked a broad smile, his *ketel*-stained teeth seeming to reflect the sun's orange glow.

'Be at ease, friends,' he declaimed from the saddle. 'His Eminence has agreed to grant you audience before we march north. I for one am sure he will find a use for you, but come! You must convince him yourselves.'

Wordlessly, the trio remounted and followed Zimri at an amble back towards the camp. Though a vast one, its tumult was oddly subdued; as if every protagonist understood the gravity of the struggle they embarked upon.

A huge army yet so disciplined, Anupe reflected as they passed among the variegated platoons and their standards, each bearing the arms of the various satraps, desert chieftains and mercenary commanders who had answered the muster. *Perhaps we have picked the right side after all. Assuming Muqmurlish decides we are on his side.*

Her first sight of the Sultan surprised her. He was not what she had expected: short of stature, though stockily built, he dressed simply, in the manner of a lightly armoured *sarakim* rather than a great warlord. Reports of his lost eye were accurate, though the patch he wore was plain and unadorned like the rest of his garb. His turban was a simple beige colour, and graced by no jewels – just a simple serpent brooch fashioned of silver set dead centre.

A man in early middling years, he appeared well kept for his age. His black beard and moustache betrayed a few grey strands but his tawny skin glowed with the vigour of youth. His one good eye shone with a keen intelligence, scrutinising the new arrivals as they were ushered into his pavilion. That too was plain enough: Anupe had seen errant knights encamped on the plains of Vorstlund who might have contented themselves with something similar.

In fact his only concession to finery was the ornate scimitar he wore belted at his side: its filigreed gold-chased hilt caught the brazier light, which suffused the single rich red ruby set in its pommel, imbuing it with a crimson lustre that would have set Hari's mouth watering. Anupe had no doubt that the beautiful damascened scabbard concealed a keen blade.

Muqmurlish tek Nazar, Sultan of Nazharya, Unifier of the Faith, Scourge of Infidels, waited impassively for his guests to join him. Squatting on a broad flat cushion, he appeared not to be discomfited in the slightest by that position, his back perfectly upright, every limb in its place. The Harijan would not have been surprised had she been told that the Sultan had sat in just the same position all night.

He's a king all right, she thought as they were escorted by *amluqs* and motioned to sit on cushions of their own. *More subtle by far than any Urovian monarch, but no less powerful for all that. If anything, more so.*

Anupe crouched down tensely on her cushion. Usually so lithe and athletic, she suddenly and inexplicably felt awkward in the Sultan's presence. It wasn't his royal status that discomfited her; of that she was sure.

No, there was something beyond his temporal authority, a kind of spiritual aplomb she couldn't explain: a faculty that seemed to burrow itself into her soul with an insistence that not Horskram, Tipu, Azelin or the Zarumani could ever have commanded.

What are you, ruler or mystic? Surely a man cannot be both.

Muqmurlish remained sitting, still and serene as a clear pond on a windless day: his one good eye appeared to take all three of his visitors in, head to toe, without so much as budging a fraction in its socket. The effect was peculiarly unnerving.

A long low table of teak was between them. Ceramic bowls and dishes of simple food were laid upon it: freshly steamed rice that bore not a hint of seasoning, plain viands and plainer vegetables.

Is this really how the would-be conqueror of Near Sassania breaks his fast? He knows how to set an example, I'll give him that.

Still the Sultan had not spoken. The *amluq* captain of the guard had curtly informed them that to address the Sultan before being bidden by him to do so was an offence punishable by beheading. Taking in his placid countenance, Anupe somehow did not believe Muqmurlish would do such a thing. Yet she kept her peace nonetheless.

At last, Muqmurlish broke the still silence. Languidly, he raised an arm.

'Please, eat. Be welcome as my honoured guests.'

The voice was soft as silk and only seemed to amplify the silence prevailing in the tent. Anupe fancied it crashed about them, as loudly as the high tides of the Sundering Sea in a gale, as she wordlessly obeyed. A gentle request, yet it had somehow felt like a command.

As one, the three guests ate, chewing silently. After the rich repasts of Sassania, the food tasted bland yet wholesome; washing down her few mouthfuls with water, Anupe felt strangely refreshed. The long dusty days on the road to Imanabad seemed to slough off her, a cleanliness she could not explain washing over her travel-weary spirit.

When they had finished, servants, unbidden, came to clear the table, leaving only the cups and plain silver ewer of water. Muqmurlish himself had not touched so much as a morsel; not a sip had passed his lips.

Anupe almost started when the Sultan broke the silence again.

'You wish to join my army.' It was a statement, not a question.

It was Tipu who summoned the wherewithal to speak first.

'Sufielis have ever shunned conflict,' said the mystic. 'But when the cause is just, we can lend spiritual guidance and fortitude if it is required.'

The Sultan's next words were undeniably a question.

'And is it required?' He met Tipu's gentle gaze with one of his own, yet this was the first time Anupe had seen the mystic discomfited since the ghoul mine.

Tipu inclined his head deferentially. 'In any undertaking done at Ashanti's will.'

'And is that not enough?' asked the Sultan. 'Surely His will alone will suffice for guidance.'

Tipu hesitated a moment. He knew he was being tested. 'Your Eminence will doubtless know what my sect believes – only through regular and sincere action of the body can the will of Ashanti be truly comprehended.'

Was that just the faintest of smiles to grace the Sultan's lips? 'That is correct,' he said. 'Tipu Sulia, you are known to me, as is your sect. Orthodox, Unorthodox... and those who walk a path between, the time for such distinctions is drawing to a close. The time for Sha'abatians to put aside their differences and unite against the common enemy is here. I welcome you to my camp, my army's victuals are your victuals. Repay my generosity by providing whatever wisdom you may on the road to war. I shall not ask you to do anything out of keeping with your vows.'

Tipu's thanks died on his lips as the Sultan abruptly turned from him to look at Anupe.

'You are strange to me,' he said simply. 'Whence came you?'

Anupe could not resist a slight smile of her own.

'Do you want the long story or the short story?'

The Harijan was relieved when the Sultan returned her smile. 'The short one will suffice.'

Anupe made as clean a breast of it as she could, keeping back most of the details of her questing with Horskram. Even truncated, the tale of her travels took some time to tell.

'You have wandered far and wide,' said Muqmurlish when she had finished. 'And seen many a wondrous thing – and just

as many awful things too, judging by the parts you leave out.'
He raised a hand again to forestall her feigned protestations.
'No one in wisdom tells his entire tale at the first sitting, as
our Prophet sayeth. I do not begrudge you your reticence. All
I ask of you is one thing – if I am to take a pagan outlander
into my army, I must have complete confidence that you will
obey orders given to you without hesitation or question.
Anything less, and I cannot countenance taking you into
service.' He indicated the stony-eyed *amluqs* with a sweep of
the arm that was curt yet graceful. 'My followers would not
tolerate it, and their opinions are precious to me. Making
common cause with other Sha'abatians is one thing, but you
are not of the Faith, nor of any faith that I recognise.'

Serene or not, when it comes down it he's just another warlord,
Anupe thought cynically. But she had expected no less.

'It shall be as you say,' she replied diplomatically. 'This is
not an unfair request, and I agree to abide by it.'

A hint of steel entered the Sultan's voice. 'Agree is not
enough. You must swear to do so, here in sight of all my
trusted bodyguards.'

For slave warriors, they certainly command a lot of status. But
then Anupe had yet to truly fathom the nature of Sassanian
society.

She permitted herself a soft sigh. 'Very well, for the duration of my contract with you, I swear to abide by your
commands, without hesitation or question.'

Though the Sultan smiled and even inclined his head,
Anupe had no doubt it would be her head if she was found
wanting. Judging by some of the looks from the *amluqs*, quite
a few were already hoping she would be.

Slave or no, a man is still a man, she reminded herself grimly.

'Then my first command is this,' said the Sultan. 'You will
at all times keep your head covered and face concealed. I do
not doubt your martial talents, for I have heard the legends

of your fabled people, but I cannot have a woman openly wielding steel in my army. I trust this is not the first time you have been asked to keep a low profile.'

You aren't asking, you're commanding, Anupe thought bitterly. But the Sultan was right about one thing – this too she had expected. And it was no less than she had been obliged to do in Vorstlund.

'It shall be as you say, even when the sun sleeps beneath the earth,' she replied, taking a stab at protocol and drawing her hood up by way of emphasis.

The steel did not leave the Sultan's voice as he turned to the priest of Zaruman and addressed him next.

'You of all the three I am most at a loss as to what to do with,' he declared. 'Ordinarily I should have you executed for even trespassing on my domains without a lightfinder's permit.'

The Zarumani seemed to be the only person in the tent not in awe of Muqmurlish. Meeting the Sultan's gaze, he said: 'I can assure you, Your Eminence, the business I have been about in your domains has been of far greater import than guiding greedy merchants through the desert.'

For the first time, the still waters rippled. Muqmurlish flushed, ever so slightly, but quickly mastered his anger. An *amluq* stepped forward, scimitar drawn, but the Sultan stayed him with a single fierce glance.

The chastened swordsman stepped back as Muqmurlish returned his gaze to the defiant Zarumani.

'The three of you have been on no ordinary journey, that much is obvious,' said the Sultan, measuring his words. 'And something tells me it is connected to my own endeavours, though I cannot fathom how.'

'You fathom enough as it is,' Anupe could not resist putting in. 'How do you know so much?'

Another *amluq* stepped forward to chastise her; again a

ferocious glance stopped him in his tracks. Muqmurlish barked something in the Sassanic tongue; up until then they had conversed only in Decorlangue.

Whatever he said, it clearly applied to his entire host of bodyguards: as one, they stepped back, bowing deferentially as they sheathed their swords.

'Pray forgive them,' said Muqmurlish. 'My sworn sword brothers are zealous, as befits their exalted station, but that alas can make them quick to anger sometimes.'

'I have a feeling anger is something you often seek to control.' Anupe was finding her courage now, and with that came freer speech.

Again the Sultan nodded.

'You are more than perceptive yourself,' he said. 'I am on my mother's side a lineal descendant of the last of the Seven Enlightened Sultans, who made a virtue of tempering all their emotions. And my ancestry is also perhaps why I can see much that is not obvious to other men.'

'You descend from the last of the Wisely Guided Ones, Abu Tek Jahib,' confirmed Tipu. 'And yet you cleave not to the Unorthodox Faith.' The mystic's last statement sounded dangerously pointed. Anupe was only too glad the Sultan had cowed his fanatical *amluqs*.

'That is correct,' replied the Sultan. 'For as you well know, on my father's side I also trace my ancestry back to the Nazhar dynasty that founded this very realm. The son must ever follow the father in matters of the Faith – as well you know, Tipu Sulia.'

'Forgive me, Your Eminence,' answered the mystic. 'I sought never to bait you, but simply to point out that you yourself, by your very provenance, embody the virtues we Sufielis have sought to espouse.'

Again the slightest hint of steel, enough to suggest that the passive guru could become a fierce potentate if provoked.

'Did I not say just now that the time for such distinctions was past?' the Sultan said. 'Yes, the Sufielis have spoken many more true words on matters of the Faith than they have been given credit for. That is why I take you into my army – I trust that you will repay my trust as I have asked.'

Tipu did not demur. 'It shall be as you wish, Your Eminence. But may I impose upon your patience one last time, and ask that you place the same trust in my companion here? 'Tis true we have not told you our entire story, but by Sha'abat's hallowed ascension, I swear it would have had a dark ending ere now were it not for this scion of light and fire.'

For a while the Sultan did not speak, and the still silence returned. Muqmurlish appeared to stare ahead into the middle distance, his one good eye taking on a faraway look that somehow did nothing to diminish its keenness.

At last the Sultan spoke, though his silky voice sounded more detached.

'So, this is how the Almighty tests me. I declare commonality across the Faith, to repulse a common foe – and He asks me if I am prepared to take such lenity one step further to realise that goal.'

The Sultan paused again, apparently lost in his reverie, before finally returning his attention to his guests.

'So be it – whether I have just failed or passed the test, Ashanti shall reveal in due course. Tipu Sulia, you have vouched for the infidel priest, by the faith of your soul and body. I shall accept this, but knowest thou that both shall suffer if you are proved unwisely guided in this matter.'

Tipu showed no signs of fearing for either his body or soul as he inclined his head in accordance. As for the priest of Zaruman, he remained the same as ever, stoical and unflinching to the last.

Those blasted flames of his really have claimed his soul, Anupe found herself thinking.

Another cursory nod from the Sultan, and the *amluqs* stepped forwards. The audience was over.

The three wayfarers who had just pledged themselves to the Sha'abatian cause rose and allowed themselves to be escorted back outside the tent, to where Zimri and his lieutenants awaited them.

The *amluq* captain advanced and addressed him formally in Sassanic. Zimri listened attentively, before turning to the trio. The broad smile was back on his lips.

'You are to be assigned to my host,' he said, flashing them an orange grin. 'A wise choice, methinks – outsiders like us should ever share blood and salt together.'

In the present circumstances, Anupe could not disagree. But as they followed Zimri towards his portion of the army camp, she also could not help wondering whether they had, after all, chosen wisely.

CHAPTER 3

IN THE PIPER'S WAKE

Adelko winced and tried not to touch the bloodied bandage Horskram had wound for him. Another head injury: just when they needed all their wits about them.

Bertram's face looked wan and pallid in the moonlight shining down through the oculus of the main auditorium. In the absence of the High Circle of the Seven, a handful of trusted adepts had agreed to Horskram's request for a private audience: as well as the master librarian, the two friars were joined by Jonas the apothecary and Elias from the infirmary.

The rest of the adepthood were too busy supervising the defence of the monastery; in the tumult of conflict, few senior monks had much appetite to hear of Horskram's findings.

The Order doesn't seem so keen on secret missions any more, and no wonder. Even if this one does relate to the mess we're in.

They were lucky to be alive, Adelko supposed. He'd come to with a bleeding head, to the sound of yet more combat. Picking himself up groggily, he'd seen them fighting: Hari's scimitar and steel-shod quarterstaves flashing in the night as the rogue and four monks squared off against the foot-soldiers.

At a glance he'd taken in the rope, tied to one of the merlons crowning the wall. A surprise attack had given the defenders some advantage – who in their right mind would have expected the beleaguered monks to sally forth?

He'd seen Azelin charging in, his two-handed greatsword lopping off a couple of heads... It hadn't taken long for the advantage to translate into a rout. But where was the deathly apparition that had menaced them? Adelko's sixth sense had guided him to the answer to that question: a rotted corpse in mail lay not far away. His sense had told him something else too... thought badly decayed, the corpse was familiar, some-how. He hadn't had time to reflect upon that, as his ordinary senses alerted him to another figure, crumpled in the grass at the foot of the ridge. Master Horskram!

Dashing over, he'd felt relief wash over him: his mentor was unconscious but still breathing. A quick touch of circifix to the forehead, followed by a sip of holy water and a hastily muttered Psalm of Fortitude, and the old monk had revived.

He had seemed every bit as confused as Adelko. By the time they had rejoined their companions the soldiers were fleeing: off to alert their comrades on the other side of the monastery.

Yassin had had his wits about him even if they didn't, hurrying them all up the rope and pulling it up after making the climb himself. And not a moment too soon: the soldiers had returned, with reinforcements in tow.

In charge of the night watch, Adelko's old combat tutor Edemus had recognised the two friars quickly enough when Brother Tremulus and the other monks on sentry duty brought them before him.

'So our worst fears are confirmed.' Bertram's voice could

have been made of lead as it resonated dully about the auditorium.

'I'm afraid so,' sighed Horskram, looking every day of his sixty-odd winters and more. 'The viper has bitten us and slunk off into the long grass – Hannequin has piped an ill tune and led us a merry dance.'

'There's nothing merry about it,' said the librarian, sitting down on one of the stone benches. He and Elias exchanged stupefied glances, unable to find words. Jonas simply stared ahead, his face set grim.

'So if I have this correctly,' said Horskram. 'Hannequin and half of the High Circle – Adamantus, Edelmir, and Gabrien – have disappeared, along with a third of the adept-hood including Johann.

'Not all of the missing monks are adepts,' corrected Bertram wearily. 'A handful of journeymen too, including my under-librarian, and one novice – Arik of Ulfang, who arrived here from the north last year.'

Adelko's ears pricked up at the same time as his sixth sense. Arik? What with everything that had occurred, he'd completely forgotten about his erstwhile cohorts.

'What about Hargus?' the young journeyman asked. 'Before I left, I set him and Arik...' Adelko faltered as he felt the sudden scrutiny of his superiors. 'I... I asked them both to keep an eye on things here, while I was gone. What with everything that transpired with Master Johann, it seemed like the right thing to do at the time.'

Jonas sighed. 'Your young friend passed, I'm afraid,' said the ageing adept. The smell of various herbs and compounds clung to him. 'His heart failed, a few weeks ago. It happens from time to time, there was naught we could do for him, he simply died in the night.'

Jonas glanced sadly at Elias, who nodded gloomily.

Adelko's sixth sense flared up a notch at the same time as the tears welled up in his eyes.

'But Hargus was healthy! I can't believe he died of natural causes... Oh Reus forgive me, I've gone and got him killed!'

After everything he'd been through, it was too much. Adelko sank into a bench, the cold flat stone offering scant comfort as he buried his face in his hands.

'Adelko, we don't know that,' said Horskram. 'The mortal thread is lightly tied, as the Redeemer sayeth, but one tug - '

But Adelko was in no mood for scripture. 'I'm telling you, he was murdered,' he said with a vehemence that shocked everyone present. 'You really think this is a coincidence? Somebody found out we were onto their... inner cabal or whatever it is Hannequin has put together, and had him assassinated! What else could it be?' He was staring back at the older monks now, his place completely forgotten in his grief.

Horskram sighed deeply, taking a seat himself. 'It must be owned, there is plausibility in what Brother Adelko is saying. According to both our stories, it would seem Hannequin has seduced forty Argolians, including half the High Circle and Brothers Joram and Johann, into going along with his madcap scheme to reunite the Headstone, and used Thaumaturgy to spirit them all away with him.'

'To where?' asked Bertram.

Horskram fixed him with a withering look. 'Did your concentration lapse while we spent half the evening reporting our findings? He's taken them to the Forbidden City – where else would he want to go, with three-quarters of the Headstone and the Grimoire that controls it in his possession?'

'To Ortiz perhaps,' suggested Elias. 'Whence you came. Hannequin – by all the saints but I still can't believe it's him we're talking about! – still needs the final fragment, remember.'

Horskram shook his head. 'Nay, the Old Master of Time's Arrow and his Shadowmen are too potent a force for Hannequin and a few dozen accomplices to take on directly – even now, there are limits to his power,' the adept mused out loud. 'But if what we suspect is true, that he has been studying grammarye in secret for years and training fellow conspirators to do likewise... Then his powers might be just enough to carve out a base of operations in Varya. Ortiz isn't so far... he means to mount an assault on it from the Forbidden Isle, unless I miss my guess.'

'But how?' protested Bertram. 'Without the Headstone's power...'

'There is still too much we don't know,' said Horskram by way of answer. 'We need to inspect Hannequin's private quarters, try to trace his spoor – only then will we be able to divine the full extent of his powers and fathom what he's up to.'

The librarian shuffled his feet and looked around awkwardly. 'None of us has been up there since we conducted the divining in the Grand Master's quarters. Normally we wouldn't even enter without his leave, but when he and the others failed to attend dawn prayers...'

'Yes, yes, spare me monastic protocol,' said Horskram irritably. 'I think it's safe to say what's happened renders half the Order's rules null and void for the foreseeable.'

'Nevertheless, no one dared to probe any further into the upper levels,' clarified Jonas. 'A few days after the divining, which only confirmed powerful sorceries had been practised on our grounds and for quite some time, the Regent's soldiers came...'

'We've been rather distracted since then,' finished Elias somewhat lamely. He'd had his share of casualties to treat, evinced by the dark speckles that dotted the sleeves of his grey habit.

Even without that, Adelko knew the physician wasn't

wrong. Passing from the outer circle into the monastery's inner ward had felt more like walking through a fortress than a place of study and contemplation. Which was exactly what the Reverend Priory had become in his absence: adepts barking orders at novices, who scurried to and fro bearing pails of boiling water, heavy stones taken from the less important buildings, and victuals for the journeymen guarding the perimeter.

We learned fighting and siegecraft ages ago, so we could be prepared for a time like this, he thought. *But it doesn't make it any less appalling now it's come.*

'Well, we'll need to muster as much elan as we can for this investigation,' said Horskram. 'Without the High Circle... ah, Gabrien I always suspected, but Adamantus and Edelmir!' The adept's drawn face looked unusually sorrowful in the sickly moonlight. 'By all the saints and archangels, this is the blackest day our Order has ever known.'

'What about Bartho?' asked Adelko. 'He's the last Archmaster we've got, what with Wolaf being killed in the binding and Cathbad sent into exile. Surely he could help us?'

Elias shook his head. 'Brother Bartho can barely even breathe, much less rise from his cot. He will not live to see the next new moon, I'm afraid – I've kept everything from him, if he found out what had happened it would probably kill him on the spot.'

Everyone lapsed into morbid gloom at that thought.

'Ah, Cathbad, 'tis a pity you were exiled!' exclaimed Horskram suddenly, breaking the silence. 'What an irony! The one Archmaster most likely to be suspect, and he was blameless all along – for surely Hannequin would have seduced him long ago with sorcerous promises if he could and taken him with him. Hedge witch though he was, we could have used him right now.'

Jonas glanced quizzically at the adept. 'What do you mean?'

Horskram cleared his throat and rose from the bench. 'Well, if what we suspect is true, Hannequin has almost certainly been hiding a laboratory and workshop up there' – he glanced meaningfully upwards to where the Grand Master's private chambers sat waiting for them – 'meaning anyone with previous knowledge of wizardry would have been useful to our investigation.'

Adelko's sixth sense nudged him, stirring him from his sorrowful reverie. The other monks were exchanging nervous glances. Horskram had noticed it too.

'Well, what is it?' he said brusquely.

Bertram cleared his throat nervously. 'Ordinarily, this is the last thing I would encourage, but as you said, these are exceptional times...'

'Well?' Horskram was glaring at him suspiciously now.

'If it's a sorcerer's services you require,' said the librarian, 'we do have someone in the holding chamber who might interest you...'

The mage was in an appalling state. Despite his inherent dislike of all sorcerers, Horskram could not help but grimace at the sight of him: shackled to the wall of the dungeon, he looked stricken and half-starved. Besides that, several of his front teeth were missing and his right eye was barely visible under the bloody bruise that covered half his face. His plaited silvery hair was streaked with red.

'I'm afraid some of the brothers took matters into their own hands after we learned of Hannequin's betrayal,' said Elias. 'I tried to enforce discipline, but there was naught I could do to stop some of the more zealous brethren paying him a visit.'

He glanced sorrowfully at the floor. 'They wouldn't even let me treat his wounds – if they find out we're here, we could have a... what do our lay brothers in the army call it? A mutiny, yes, a mutiny.'

'Feelings are running high,' confirmed Jonas. 'Very high indeed. The Order's tranquillity was ever a fragile thing. Now, with all this...' The old herbalist's voice trailed off dismally.

'Did the adepthood at least manage to conduct a proper interrogation when they weren't busy beating him to within an inch of his life?' asked Horskram, his lip curling in disgust.

Bertram spoke up. 'It was mostly the journeymen who insisted on chastising yon sorcerer, but we were at least allowed to question him in a more orthodox fashion. In any case he volunteered his story freely – and as far as we were able to divine, every word he says is true. He was a captive of Brother Joram's and went with him and your knightly friends on the mission to the Westerling Isles. He's half mad though, keeps babbling something about giant plants that eat men, a great conflagration, and... being bonded to Joram.'

Horskram arched an eyebrow. That he clearly hadn't expected.

The wizard, who called himself Morcant, was trying to slink into the corner of the cell, the iron links rattling as they prevented him. He whimpered as Horskram knelt before him.

'Have no fear,' said the adept calmly. 'Your torment is at an end. All we require is information – and possibly your help. I can have you freed – but if you try so much as a cantrip on us, I'll quash it like a candle and order our more pugnacious brethren to finish what they started. Is that understood?'

The hierophant's voice had suddenly become steely, and lacked for nothing in conviction.

The mage gasped words between teeth that bubbled with blood. 'Oh, y-yes! Muh-Morcant will be good, he'll be vuh-very very good!'

'Very well.' Horskram nodded to Bertram, who reached for a key ring hanging on the wall.

Adelko winced inwardly. He remembered his mentor's false promises to Ulla, the hedge witch they had captured in Northalde when their quest was young.

I wouldn't put too much trust in what Master Horskram says, he thought grimly as he looked upon the beaten warlock with pitying eyes.

Yet Morcant seemed grateful enough as Bertram unlocked his manacles and Jonas proffered him a cup of physic.

'This will soothe the pain of your wounds as well as quench your thirst,' he told the pitiful mage, not unkindly.

'I'll see to those wounds as well, zealots be damned,' said Elias. 'He's in no fit state to talk as he is – we'd best get him to the infirmary, the rest of the brotherhood will hopefully be too busy praying and guarding the walls to notice.'

Adelko's mind was spinning. *Journeymen disobeying adepts and even forbidding them from treating a suspect witch. After Hannequin's betrayal, I don't suppose authority carries much weight around here any more. It's a wonder they're taking orders at all – if it weren't for the Regent's soldiers attacking us, we'd probably all be fighting each other by now.*

That thought did little to cheer the journeyman as they bundled Morcant off to the infirmary. But it was as Elias had predicted: monks not sleeping were busy with the siege – even now flaming arrows strafed the night skies, in search of targets. The Regent's soldiers didn't have siege engines yet – but that didn't stop them harrying the defenders where they could.

Azelin and Hari would be with Edemus and the other sentries on the outer walls; the pair had decided to try and make themselves useful, not that there was much they could do under siege.

Though Sir Azelin looks as if he could take on a whole army single-handedly right now – at least we have a champion among us.

He'd only seen him briefly since the fight with the mysterious hellish apparition, but Adelko had intuited a sudden but profound change in the disgraced warrior-monk. Getting good news from his sixth sense was a rarity, and one he could only cherish in the circumstances.

The fallen shall rise up and know grace only when the high and mighty grovel in the soil. One of the Redeemer's more militant aphorisms, but perhaps it was more appropriate now than ever... He could only hope so.

Adelko gazed about the room he had been welcomed into by the Grand Master earlier that year; everything looked much the same as then, the low table and chairs, the shelves crammed with books. Hannequin's study, just as he'd last seen it. Following Horskram and the other adepts, he entered the sleeping quarters via an adjoining door. Those put him in mind of the old Abbot Sacristen's private chamber, a lifetime ago in Ulfang monastery: a simple cot with a private chapel adjoining, crowned by a life-sized stone effigy of the Redeemer being broken on the wheel.

Adelko had half expected to find it desecrated or even destroyed, but not a hint of damage besides that of time's ceaseless and gradual ruin could be discerned. Likewise none of the holy tomes they had inspected in Hannequin's study appeared to have been misused in any way. Whatever he had fallen to, the erstwhile Grand Master of the Order of St Argo did not appear outwardly motivated by any kind of fanaticism.

Just what kind of man are we really up against? Who are you really, Hannequin? And more to the point, what exactly are your plans for the world?

From the chapel another small door opened onto a tiny chamber. Taking in the levers next to it, Adelko realised this was the strange contraption that led directly down to the holding chamber in the dungeon. Built by the Ancient Thalamians, it was eerily reminiscent of the device built by Them which they'd used to enter the Warlock's Crown for their showdown with Andragorix.

Andragorix, the mad warlock whom they had believed to be their mastermind; all along merely an apprentice to the very man they had trusted to lead their mission. Even now, weeks later, the revelation still appalled Adelko.

For all we know, these monks aren't to be trusted either. But where Elias, Jonas, and Bertram were concerned, the journeyman's sixth sense remained cool; likewise the rest of the synod of adepts they had petitioned, though bordering on a state of hysterical fractiousness, had not alerted him. Whatever blanketing spell Hannequin had used to confound his chapter's sixth sense, it had lifted with his departure: presumably the Grand Master had anticipated this and left none of his cabal behind.

Or not here at the Reverend Priory at any rate – who knows how many allies and accomplices you've squirrelled away across the Free Kingdoms and beyond?

Horskram scrutinised the lifting contraption. 'It goes up too,' he said, indicating a second lever. 'To the observatory, no doubt. I expect that's where we'll find our evidence.'

'Are you sure this is wise?' asked Bertram. 'I want to get to the bottom of this as much as any monk, but the adepthood... We had to fight tooth and claw to get this investigation sanctioned. And the journeymen are growing ever more restive.'

'The journeymen can put their restiveness to use keeping the Pangonian soldiers at bay,' replied Horskram acidly. 'Or had you forgotten the reinforcements that arrived to bolster their numbers but yesterday?'

That day had seen a shouting match in the auditorium brought to an abrupt halt with the announcement that another thousand soldiers had arrived, ladders in tow, along with five hundred crossbowmen and a like number of mounted sergeants led by a contingent of knights; with the catapults nearing completion, the Regent's sortie was nearly ready to mount to begin the siege in earnest.

At least that had cut short the adepthood's internecine wrangling: Horskram had taken full advantage of it, declaring by the Redeemer's will and His sacred blood he bore to conduct a thorough inspection of the Inner Sanctum's summit, protocol be damned. The urgency of the situation without the monastery walls had silenced the last of his critics.

Silenced, but for how long? Strange to think that the Regent's assault might have actually bought us some time.

Bertram acceded reluctantly, though Adelko could sense the timorous librarian also longed to see what Hannequin had concealed up in the tower's summit. Always thirsty for knowledge, the mousy-haired adept had worked his way up to his position as master librarian diligently – he had to be curious as well as fearful.

I wonder if that's why Hannequin never tried to corrupt you – he knew you were curious, but didn't think you were curious enough to break the rules of the Order.

But Arik on the other hand, had a thirst for knowledge that consumed him all too much... It pained him deeply to think of his former friend, led so badly astray. But since their clash on the courtyard clay that rainy afternoon months ago, Adelko had known all too well that his ambitious rival could be corrupted.

And, so apparently, had Hannequin.

'It's time,' said Horskram. 'Bring the warlock.'

Adelko and Bertram entered the lifting room, pulling the sliding door to behind them. The librarian pulled the lever and the thing juddered into life, conveying them down to the dungeon. It certainly didn't move as smoothly as the ebonite machine they had used at the Warlock's Crown: impressive as the Thalamians' craft had been, it still fell far short of the Varyans that had come before them.

Age-old knowledge the Grand Master wants for himself, Adelko thought. *But what could he possibly expect to do with it? He can't seriously intend to bring the Fallen One back to this plane – can he?*

His reverie was interrupted by the lift jolting to a halt. Exiting, he and Bertram found Morcant where they had left him. After treating his injuries at the infirmary, Elias had felt obliged to return the warlock to his cell and put the chains back on him. He'd ordered Gustaff to send food from the kitchens, and made sure the warlock was well fed. That had nearly caused another furore; but once again the presence of a besieging army on the doorstep had worked in their favour.

Some favour. Even with a thousand battle-ready journeymen, we're seriously outnumbered. And the Regent's soldiers are armed to the teeth, if what Azelin and Hari say is true.

Morcant rose eagerly as they entered, the chains pulling him back down remorselessly. Taking the key ring from the wall again, Bertram unlocked the manacles. Rubbing his wrists gratefully, Morcant rose gingerly.

At least he didn't look half as bad as the previous day. Elias and Jonas had treated his wounds and got him cleaned up; but his missing teeth still showed painfully as the warlock mustered a half-hearted grin.

'Found it, have you?' he asked, in his lilting Thrax. 'Ready to be of service, is old Morcant. Oh yes, very good he'll be, you shall see!'

Bertram glared at the mage, trying to sound fierce as he replied: 'Yes, your services are required. But Brother Horskram's injunction stands – try anything untoward, and you'll be given over to the rest of the brethren.'

Morcant did at least look crestfallen at the prospect, though Adelko sensed the Islander had been chastised before on more than one occasion.

We force such a hard life on them, yet one of our own luminaries believed Right-Handers were little different to Argolians, he thought, once again recalling Arnulf of Balzac's controversial treatise.

And then another thought chilled him to the marrow. *It looks like Arnulf inspired other Grand Masters to think much the same. The Right drifts towards the Left... Master Horskram, perhaps you weren't wrong about there being no such thing as good magic. But then what does that say about us?*

That question plagued him all the way back up to Hannequin's chambers.

The lifting contraption was too small to take all of them up at once, so Elias and Horskram went first with Morcant, training the blood of the Redeemer on the hapless sorcerer. As they waited for the lifting chamber to reappear, something else occurred to Adelko.

'What if someone had access to the holding chamber and used the lifting room to come up here?' he asked Bertram. 'That would have enabled them to go up another level and discover... whatever it is Hannequin has been keeping up there.'

Bertram allowed himself a rare smile. 'First off, using the lifting chamber without the Grand Master's say-so would have been unthinkable to any monk, until now. Secondly, it was a matter of strict protocol always to leave the dungeon by the same way as you entered it. Therefore, Hannequin would always have kept the lifting room up here – the only time it wasn't would have been when he was present in the holding chamber.'

Adelko nodded absently, suddenly distracted. His sixth sense was yowling again, turning his thoughts elsewhere. He gazed up at the ceiling. Perhaps Hannequin's blanketing spell hadn't quite worn off, because how he could have failed to sense before what he now did was otherwise inexplicable... The Inner Sanctum back at Ulfang had been bad enough, the Warlock's Crown had been overwhelming, but this... this was a concentrated evil, the like of which he'd rarely if ever felt before.

The journeyman shivered. Glancing over at the two older monks, he could see they felt it too. The minutes slid on, with painful slowness...

Presently the lifting chamber sank back down, carrying only Elias. His face looked ashen.

'You'd better come next, Brothers Jonas and Bertram,' he said in a voice that was faint. 'Though I should warn you to prepare... It's quite a sight.'

'My sixth sense has been telling me as much,' muttered Jonas grimly.

'Adelko, I'll come back for you shortly,' said Bertram as the two adepts joined him.

The journeyman's sixth sense continued to jangle unpleasantly as the lifting room disappeared with the three adepts. He realised it wasn't just being triggered by what lay above a second before the first explosion rocked the outer wall of the monastery.

CHAPTER 4

DEADLOCKED AT DAWN

Magnhilda clenched the handles of the Twin Furies sheathed in her girdle as Canute confirmed what her Scrying had intimated. The magicked war axes were aptly named, for nothing could conceal her rising rage; it was as if the sail road heaved and churned within her breast.

'Dark weather of weapons came upon our fleet in the night,' said Mountainside, his booming voice filling the throne-room of Strongholm palace so all the gathered seacarls and berserkers could hear. 'A bloody furrow they ploughed, and our sea horses are well and truly lamed. Not one remains afloat.'

Gasps went up at that. The devastation wreaked was clearly bad; it had even inspired some eloquence in Canute, typically clumsy of speech.

The Shield Queen rose from the Pine Throne and held her hands aloft imperiously.

'SILENCE!' she shrieked. 'I'll not have this calamity met with faint-hearted hysteria! We are Northland warriors, not beardless children.'

From her place by the throne, Valkyria nodded approvingly, but it was obvious the berserker high priestess was shaken by the news.

'And of the made men and shieldmen aboard, what of them?' asked Magnhilda, returning her attention to Canute.

Mountainside shook his head gloomily, gesturing with a huge arm towards the sash windows, through which burnt-out husks of longships could be seen smudging the lapping waves of the Strang Estuary.

'What you see yonder tells the sum of all, my queen,' he said, in a voice suddenly flat and lifeless. 'Our men guarding the palisades sent outriders up and down the coasts of the Strang – naught is to be found but washed-up corpses and broken timbers. More than two thousand of our warriors have been given the sleep of the sword.'

This time not even Magnhilda could restrain the gasps of dismay, though she noted with satisfaction that these were mingled with many cries of outrage and talk of bloody revenge.

Her remaining *leidangs* would have it right soon, Tyrnor willing, though the god of war did not appear kindly disposed towards them at present.

'Do we have any idea how the Northlendings triumphed?' she asked. 'The last we knew, our fleet outnumbered theirs more than two-to-one, with no prospect of reinforcements.' Her Scrying wasn't nearly as keen as her half-brother Ragnar's, and had hardly served her better in the dark. Woken from her bed, she'd hastily cast the spell with Valkyria looking on timorously from the four-poster they shared. She'd been able to make out Northlendings fighting, and there had been creatures from the sea... Only this time, they had not been on her side.

Ragnar, if you've betrayed me, I will feed you to your serpent god, she thought bitterly. But she couldn't let on what she'd seen – if her seacarls and shieldmen suspected what she did, there would be a mutiny for sure. They had been reluctant enough to accept her brother's blasphemous help as it was.

Canute licked his lips. He actually looked nervous. 'My queen, other bodies we found... Those of the Triton folk your brother Ragnar sent to aid us, in like numbers to our slain comrades.'

'Slain comrades who sold their lives dearly!' yelled one seacarl. 'Your black-hearted brother has betrayed us – those dark witcheries he courts have corrupted his mind!'

'I said no good would come of aligning with Logi's spawn!' cried another, an opinion that was quickly taken up by many others.

Whirling on a huge heel, Mountainside unsheathed his battleaxes and lopped off the two dissenting heads in quick succession.

'THE SHIELD QUEEN CALLED FOR SILENCE!' he thundered. It was as if Toros the god of storms himself had spoken. In an instant Canute had the silence he craved, with only the strangely soothing sound of spurting blood to break it. One of the severed heads blinked as the dying seacarl struggled with his last seconds of life to comprehend what had just happened to him.

Dissent quashed for now, thought Magnhilda. *But you've just sent our leidang's morale to the Seakindred's Locker, Canute.*

A split second later, she realised what she'd just thought.

No, impossible. Merfolk never fight above the waves...

But she had to be sure.

'We don't know for certain that the Tritons did this – it could be a new foe, sent against us by the Northlendings,' she told the throng of warriors.

With Mountainside's axes still dripping, no one in the hall had the courage to speak up, not even to agree with her.

'At any rate, we have to expect a landing before long, the Northlendings will doubtless take advantage of this to establish a foothold,' she said. 'So I want eyes sharp on those palisades, and messengers sent to our forces down south – we still have fifty longships scouring the southern dominions.'

Or at least, I hope we do – if the Tritons really are compromised, Ravek and his men will have had to contend with the lords of the southern Dominions alone. But at least now we can free them up from their slave-taking to come and join us here – brother, your sea crea-tures have clearly outlived their usefulness.

'Canute, enforce discipline and have all shieldmen ready to sally forth when needed – try to enforce it without killing anyone else, we'll need every fighting hand we can muster.'

Then she beckoned to Valkyria. 'Come, sword sister,' she said in a low voice. 'I have to speak with my brother.'

Without another word, she descended from her dais and walked the horsehair carpet towards the double doors exiting the throne-room. Catching one of the tapestries lining the wall as she did, she saw a golden-haired knight on horseback, triumphantly beating back sea raiders. Probably commissioned to celebrate the Northlending victory at Ryøskil, decades ago. She'd never noticed it until now: mainland art was weak in her eyes, thread and paint poor substitutes for wood carving.

She made a mental note to order the thing burned, before exiting the chamber.

Ragnar's face was icy and stolid as ever as she gave him the news. A polished silver mirror on the dressing table of the king's bedchamber had sufficed as a scrying tool. In the corner, the former king himself grovelled and slobbered in jester's motley: his illness had made him easy fodder for her Enchantment, and now the erstwhile ruler of the kingdom she had come to conquer served adequately as a plaything.

Not that Magnhilda was in the mood for play just now.

'Well, brother?' she barked. 'I give you calamitous news, and you have little to say... Or did you already know?' She could not help asking.

Ragnar's gelid features remained as inscrutable as ever. His blind eye had its old nacreous lustre to it, an effect his sister cared for less and less. At her shoulder, she could positively feel Valkyria glowering at the blasphemous elementalist.

'In point of fact, no...' he responded at last. 'My elan has been focused elsewhere, and I had not given over much time to Scrying of late. You can rest assured, this comes as much a surprise to me as it does to you. Clearly, our enemies have... unexpected allies.'

'Seakindred? It's the only thing that makes sense. But our farseers and priests have always told us the merfolk take no part in the wars above water.'

'Indeed, that has always been true,' Ragnar confirmed. 'Until now, it would seem...'

Ragnar's demeanour did not change, but his sister could tell the development had him perturbed.

At least that means you probably weren't behind this, though my leidangs will take some convincing of that.

'Well, one good thing has come of it,' continued Magnhilda. 'I've given the order to have message sent to Ravek, this slave raid will be his last – your Tritons are defeated, Ragnar, no more appeasement of the Great World Serpent!'

Valkyria grunted in approval, as rare anger frosted her brother's hideous face.

'You shall do no such thing!' he snarled. 'My Tritons have served their purpose, it is true – which was but to smooth the sail road for a far more potent adversary.'

This time Magnhilda could not help but exchange

bemused looks with Valkyria. The berserker chieftain was similarly nonplussed.

'What are you talking about, brother?'

Again the icicle smile. 'Oh, have no fear, you shall soon see... But I must have more slaves, for He Who Must Not Be Disturbed must be appeased.'

'To appease him is to disturb him, you blasphemous idiot!' Valkyria could no longer restrain herself. Magnhilda was secretly thankful hundreds of miles separated the two − for her lover's sake.

'Rescind the order,' continued Ragnar calmly, completely ignoring Valkyria. 'Have Ravek go on with the slave-taking as planned. You shall soon see its benefit, I promise.'

'That might be a little more difficult for him now,' pointed out Magnhilda. 'He doesn't have Tritons coming to his aid and there are hundreds of knights and soldiers in the southern Dominions to reckon with.'

'But two thousand fighting men he has,' Ragnar reminded her in turn. 'So, here is how we shall proceed. Have Ravek divide his forces − half to fight the Northlendings in the southlands, half to bring me my slaves. Does this compromise satisfy you, sister?'

Magnhilda could practically feel Valkyria's agony as she reluctantly assented.

'Very well, brother,' she told him. 'But this secret weapon of yours had better be good − very, *very* good!'

Ragnar's sightless eye seemed to smoke with cold fire as he replied.

'Very, very good, yes... But not for our Northlending friends.'

❧

Braxus heaved an inward sigh of relief as his army emerged from the Brekawood into open countryside before calling a halt to rest. The With-Y-Passes had been the part of the journey from Daxor he disliked most – even with the highlanders expunged, his old irrational hatred of the mountains had not left him – but the disused road through the woodlands had remained potholed and unforgiving, slowing up the fifteen-hundred-strong force he led and its auxiliaries more than once.

If my plan comes to fruition, that's a road that'll be soon repaired – Thraxia and Northalde will trade again, but before that can happen we must fight alongside one another.

Scouring the rugged green fields, he frowned at the thought. He'd sent outriders ahead, bearing the white flag of truce and terms of parlay, but couldn't be sure they'd succeeded. Anyone glancing at his knights, footsoldiers and archers would immediately assume rumours of a Thraxian invasion had been proven true. Just to be sure, he'd ordered white banners to flutter alongside his own and those of the Kingsfold lords Cadwy had persuaded to join the expedition muster, but even so...

'Well, we've arrived in Northalde,' said Sir Gwydion, face unsmiling beneath his glinting helm as he surveyed the barren wilderness. 'Quite the hero's welcome, I must say.'

'At least we weren't ambushed in the Brekawood,' replied Braxus, ignoring the High Constable's sarcasm. 'Chances are, the messengers I sent have been heeded.'

'Really?' sneered Gwydion. 'Then where's the welcoming party?'

'I seriously doubt they have the resources for that,' snapped Braxus, losing patience with the haughty knight. 'Sir Gwydion, if you're so cold on this expedition, why did you insist on coming along?'

'To keep an eye on you,' replied the royal marshal bluntly.

'And if I'd had my way, it would have been solely under *my* command, as befits my office – oh, you might have curried favour with our King for your service, but make no mistake, Lord Braxus, I for one do not trust you.'

And you can't forgive me for being the one who rescued you from shame, execution, and perdition, thought the First Man of Clan Fitzrow. But he kept that to himself as he replied: 'Sir Gwydion, I for one care not a tinker's pot for the regard you hold me in – but His Majesty saw fit to put us jointly in command, so I'd say it behoves us to act in unison.'

Braxus tried one of his winning smiles, but the result was barely worth the effort.

Gwydion clearly thought much the same. Ignoring Braxus completely, he turned in the saddle and barked a command to his sons. 'Arianrod! Diarmuid! What's with all the delay? I gave the order to resume marching five minutes ago!'

Arianrod rode up, his gilded harness gleaming but his demeanour anything but bright. 'Problem with the hangers-on, sire,' he said. 'One of them has a twisted ankle from a pothole in the road.'

'And what purpose does said hanger-on fulfil?' demanded Gwydion, barely concealing his impatience.

'Washerwoman, sire,' replied his son. '... and I think she also sells her honour, too.'

'Tell them to leave her behind and get moving,' snarled Gwydion. 'We've plenty of women besides her to swyve the soldiery and clean their bedrolls when they're done – I'll not have this expedition delayed for mere trifles!'

Braxus held his peace. Gwydion was an unpleasant man and a hard, but he had the right of this: camp followers were essential to any marching army, but they could also become a liability.

'I'll see it done at once, sire,' said Arianrod, wheeling his warhorse around and riding off towards the back of the column.

'Your sons never refer to you by kinship,' Braxus couldn't help but observe, after a herald had given the order to resume marching. Beside them rode big, burly Sir Dantos; the other Kingsguarder had prudently kept his peace during the exchange, but nonetheless Braxus was grateful to have him along. As well as his obvious battle prowess, he was a far easier man to get along with.

Gwydion did not leave off staring sternly straight ahead as he answered Braxus. 'That's because I've instilled discipline into them,' he said. 'While they serve in my army, my sons will refer to me as their commanding officer – no special treatment.'

Dantos nodded in silent approval, but Braxus couldn't resist a smile. 'How very formal of you, Sir Gwydion,' he deadpanned. 'Almost like – dare I observe? – a Northlending.'

'Don't push your luck,' muttered Gwydion, nudging his charger ahead of Braxus's.

Dantos glanced sidelong at Braxus with a slight frown of disapproval. 'Maybe it wouldn't be wise to provoke him, sire,' he said quietly.

Braxus felt his returning high spirits ebb again as he silently cursed his big mouth. This internecine sniping between commanders served no purpose but the enemy's.

If we don't find a way to bridge this rift between us, the North-landers will carve one through our forces first chance they get.

Vaskrian gazed on the assembled host with hopeful eyes. The crushing defeat at the Strang had paid further dividends: Aesgir had beached the victorious fleet some ten miles up the coast and disembarked his army. A forced march after a night spent fighting had pushed them all to breaking point, but it had been worth it: joining up with Lord Toros and High Commander Toric gave them an army more than five thousand strong to take the fight to the Northlanders occupying Strongholm.

Strongholm. The young knight gazed on his beleaguered capital city with eyes that were more pitying than hopeful. Already its walls bore marks of being besieged: the Northland palisades were too cunningly arranged to permit belfries or escalades, so the Northlendings had had to settle for bombarding the walls with trebuchets.

'You should get some sleep,' Torgun told him. Both knights sat astride their chargers, saddle-sore and weary. At this time of the year the sun had hours to go before setting, but it had been a long day. Already squires and footsoldiers were setting up pavilions and tents, joining Aesgir's cohort to the investing camp.

'Won't we be needed?' asked Vaskrian. 'Aesgir said to stand by... I imagine Lord Toros and High Commander Toric will want to hear from us. I doubt they'll even believe our report. Ezekiel's wings, I scarcely believe it myself!'

Torgun managed a wan smile. 'That is why I'd counsel a few hours of rest,' he said. 'Convincing my brother that we haven't succumbed to delusion will be a task in itself. And yours will be the hardest of all.'

Vaskrian couldn't help smiling back. 'They might be bold in the field and great at tournaments,' he was bold enough to say, 'but these stay-at-home knights and lords certainly don't know much of adventuring, do they?'

Torgun's face darkened then, and not because he found the younger knight's remark insolent. 'And the happier they must be for it,' was all he said, before swinging down from Hilmir's back and beckoning to a passing squire.

Suppressing a sigh, Vaskrian dismounted likewise and

handed the reins to another squire. The weight of the past few days suddenly descended on him, and he almost staggered beneath the weight of his armour.

Torgun of course showed no signs of fatigue, or not physical fatigue at any rate.

Both belted knights, yet still he looks out for me, thought Sir Vaskrian. *He knew how exhausted I was before I did. I might have won my spurs and saved the day, but I'll never be as great a hero as you, Sir Torgun.*

Did that realisation gall him? Vaskrian was too tired to grapple with the thought, as he unstrapped his bedroll and blanket from the saddle and went in search of a space to lie down on.

CHAPTER 5

PARTISANS AT WORK

The glint of metal and sound of horses' hooves through the densely packed trees told of the approach of the supply convoy. Wrackwulf tightened his grip on his mace and nodded back towards Ariadha, who raised her fist – the prearranged signal that would tell Marech and the others their prey was fast drawing near. The jingling of mail and cranking of crossbows behind them was a reassuring sound – as the convoy rounded the corner, Wrackwulf counted them at a glance. Six heavily armoured knights and twice that number of mounted serjeants: turning back to look at the Westerling, he whispered the words clearly so she would understand.

'Eighteen horse: six heavy, twelve light.'

Ariadha nodded to indicate she had understood, but Wrackwulf checked closely to be sure she got the signalling right. Another clenched fist, a splayed hand, and a thumbs-up for six heavy horse; palm flat followed by two splayed hands and a double thumbs-up for the rest.

She takes to hand signals better than our language, the free-lancer thought. Ariadha's early swift progress with

Vorstlending had proved something of a false dawn: several weeks holed up in Westerburg while the Pangonians invested the city and began constructing siege engines hadn't left them much else to do, but teaching the outlander more than the rudiments of his language was proving difficult.

What struck Wrackwulf most was that words like 'maim', 'kill', 'bloodshed' and 'crush' seemed to come more naturally to her than ordinary words like 'cart' or 'privy' or 'feasting'.

That damned enchanted spear of hers will prove the death of her, he thought and not for the first time. At nights when they'd been posted on sentry duty, he'd caught her talking to the thing more than once in the Westerling tongue; it seemed to croon back at her in a language all of its own. No one wanted to walk the walls with them after the first couple of nights, so Marech had moved them on to other things.

Fortunately, 'other things' had entailed running a sortie from one of the recently reopened secret tunnel-ways leading out of the cliff on which Westerburg Point perched. Reopening the secret passage that his ancient predecessor Castanmere had closed centuries ago had been another of Prince Franz's daring ideas; his mother Utha had openly disapproved, but eventually he'd talked her round: the last thing the Pangonians would expect, he'd argued, were attacks erupting out of the wooded countryside that surrounded their camp. The Pangonian victory at the Battle of Wester Plains had seen the entire surviving allied army of Vorstlund forced back into the citadel. The castle proper was joined to the city by buttressed ramps that allowed soldiers to be swiftly deployed to defend it if the walls were breached, but those lay in plain view of the besieging army. On the other hand, a sudden wave of small-scale attacks by disparate units of knights and soldiers preying on their foraging and pillaging parties would catch the invaders by surprise.

At that point, the beleaguered alliance of Vorstlending

nobles had been desperate enough to try anything, Princess Utha and her caution be damned: several days ago, Wrackwulf and Ariadha had joined one of half a dozen companies sent out to harass the invading army.

Since then their unit had scoured the countryside, outriders on the lookout for vital convoys bringing supplies to the besieging army, or taking plunder seized from local manors and priories back to Vizvant, Howfaste, and Altkass, the three border castles that the Pangonians now held.

Finally, they'd spotted one. And now Marech's mercenary knights and a contingent of castle crossbowmen were ready to make the invaders pay with their lifeblood for presuming to enter sovereign Vorstlending territory.

Franz, it won't turn the tide of the war, but I'll give you this much – it'll be bloody good for morale if we pull it off.

Reaching up and around his back, Wrackwulf jerked free an axe to complement his mace. The need for subterfuge meant they'd had to forgo their horses, leaving them with their squires in a clearing farther back in the copse. Marech's instructions were clear and to the point: bring down the Pangonian horses first, despatch the riders second.

A pity, thought Wrackwulf, as he caught his first proper glimpse of the fine piebald destrier ridden by the lead knight. Pangonian horses were counted by some to be the finest in the world: but there was more at stake than mere plunder and booty now.

Ariadha slipped down through the undergrowth to crouch next to him, moving like a snake as she eased her rune-embossed spear from its holster and clutched it with feverish hands.

I bloody well hope the blasted thing has enough sense to keep quiet for a bit longer.

But the freelancer needn't have feared: the spear was deadly quiescent, as if sensing that silence would bring it closer to the bloodshed it craved. Judging by the way its owner peered ahead with shining, staring eyes, she shared its sentiments.

I almost feel sorry for you wretches, thought Wrackwulf, returning his own gaze to the approaching quarry.

~

'This had better work, Franz.' Utha paced her bedchamber frenetically. It wasn't just nerves; her bowels were flaring up again, hardly good timing for the old ailment to resurface.

Her son turned from the sash window he had been leaning against as he surveyed the city walls far below. The first Pangonian sortie of ladder-men they'd repulsed the previous night; casualties on the attackers' side had far outnumbered theirs, but Utha knew better than to be optimistic on that count. Sieges, she well knew, were a game of time that saw the odds against the defenders lengthen steadily and ineluctably, like the early evening shadows that presaged the coming of night. A gradual erosion of morale, as rations were whittled down, foundations tunnelled, fortifications damaged; disease, starvation and panic following in their wake, and before long the likelihood of a betrayal... A postern gate left inexplicably unguarded, sentries mysteriously absent at the crucial hour. Time. Always so precious, ever deadly: it would see deaths within the walls steadily rise, and those without diminish, a process that would not stop until the besieging army stood victorious and swathed in blood amidst streets filled with pain and terror.

In light of that consideration, perhaps she should have applauded her son's impetuous plan. But she did not.

'If so much as one of ours gets captured and interrogated...' she added meaningfully when her son did not reply immediately.

'They will die before they reveal the secret of the tunnels,' said her son with a faith Utha could only call idealistic. 'Besides,' he added more prosaically, 'we blocked it up again as soon as our sorties left. And you forget we have knights and soldiers from the Two Thulias and Hyrlund harassing them too – not to mention Eadgar and his Dreylending navy keeping theirs at bay. Ezekiel dammit mother, where there's war, there's hope!'

Courage and steadfastness, married to a sound grasp of military tactics: qualities she had always admired in her son and heir. Yet she could not help but feel he had overstepped the mark this time.

'I forget none of these things,' she told him in a voice more sorrowful than anything else. 'But you seem to be forgetting the last outriders' report – forces led by Lords Aravin and Kaye anticipated Bjornwulf and Gunthor yesterday. That means they either have a traitor in their midst – and it would hardly surprise me if that vindictive cripple Aethelfrith wasn't behind it, for he's hated Bjornwulf for years – or else...' She let her voice trail off again, the room suddenly becoming uncomfortably quiet.

'Or what, mother?' Franz was peering at her keenly now.

'... or I don't know,' she finished lamely. 'But there's something afoot, something I can't rightly place my finger on. Last night, I had the most vivid dreams of Adhelina of Dulsinor, and it wasn't the first time.'

Franz scoffed. 'I'm hardly surprised, given your madcap schemes for her – and me. Really, mother, you think *my* plans bold? At least I'm not intending to try to broker a marriage alliance that will reconstitute the kingdom after more than a century! A little ambitious in the midst of a full-scale invasion, don't you think?'

'It's far from the stupid plan you seem to think it is,' Utha replied, somewhat too pettishly for her own liking. Her nerves were frayed, but Morphonus' kisses, she was right about this too: something peculiar *was* afoot. In her dreams she could almost swear the runaway heiress was *talking* to her, warning of some preternatural devilry that threatened the whole course of the war. And the freelancer Wrackwulf had said as much when he'd recounted his own tales of adventure in far-flung realms. As for her more prosaic theories about Aethelfrith being a traitor... the man certainly had his grudges against his Vorstlending rivals, but one thing was yet more certain: he hated Pangonians even more. So how then had Kaye and Aravin proved so oddly prescient, fighting on foreign soil? Worldly as he was, Franz himself had remarked on it when their reserves had been inexplicably rooted out and smashed by Lord Clovis at the Battle of Wester Plains...

At least she could derive one crumb of comfort from her recurring dream. In it, Adhelina addressed her from below the deck of a heaving ship, with blurred figures in the background who appeared to be another female and men of arms. Could it be a premonition: a warning, but one that also told her the diplomatic mission she'd sent Sir Ulfstan on had succeeded?

She could only hope so.

Wrackwulf knew something was wrong the second they launched themselves from the foliage. As a freelancer not overly given to the niceties of chivalry, he'd been in his fair share of ambushes: a surprised soldier or horseman's instinctive reaction was always to reach for a weapon, but instead the lead knight whirled his warhorse around and whistled a command.

Ezekiel's arse, they were expecting us.

Wrackwulf dodged the lashing iron-shod hooves, but as

the Pangonian knight swept his sword free of its scabbard, he knew it would be back-foot fighting all the way. Knocking askew the downwards arc of his assailant's blade with his axe, he tried a riposte with the mace, aiming to smash the horse's foreleg. But no: the Pangonian swerved his steed aside, catching Wrackwulf a glancing blow to the helm as he swung his sword again.

Should have brought a bloody shield after all, the freelancer found time to think as he stumbled back towards the undergrowth.

At least Ariadha didn't seem to be fazed by the sudden turning of the tables. Shrieking a chilling war cry, she launched herself at one of the serjeants: her spear point found her victim's thigh, puncturing through hauberk, flesh and bone to transfix the screaming steed. Wrenching it free effortlessly, she was attacking another soldier before her first had time to hit the ground. The weapon howled in her hands: its awful cadence appeared to spook the steeds, which their riders now struggled to control. Crossbow bolts had been met with shields for the most part, and only a few riderless mounts to show for their volley: the Pangonians had been alerted to their ambush, that much was certain. Regardless, Marech and his mercenaries were engaging, using the high ground that sloped down to meet the path to their advantage as best they could.

That was when things went from bad to worse.

A distant clamour in the trees behind them, from the copse they'd just vacated. Shouts of surprise and the clash of steel on steel.

Our squires and horses, thought Wrackwulf, fighting the rising panic in his gut as he ducked another deadly stroke from the looming knight above him. *They've sent other soldiers to assail them, that's our escape route cut off.*

But he had no time to worry about that now. Wedged

between two overhanging trees, he could face off the knight one-to-one, but that would be the only advantage he'd get: again and again, his foeman hewed at him, splintering the hafts of his mace and axe. He'd staked his fighting style on the element of surprise; now it had been torn from him he needed a defensive one badly, but try that against a mounted opponent bereft of shield.

Before long he had little choice but to do something he'd only done a few times in his battle-scarred life.

Dropping his mangled weapons, he dropped to his knees and raised his mufflered hands in a gesture of supplication.

'I yield, sir knight,' he said in his thickly accented Panglian. 'You have the advantage, and a freelancer's ransom if you accept my surrender.'

Whether it was the prospect of gain or some notion of mercy that stayed the Pangonian knight's hand, at least Ushira was with him that day, even if Ezekiel was not: doubtless smirking beneath his full helm, the knight nodded his acceptance.

All around him it was much the same story: several of Marech's men lay in the roadside bleeding their lives away, but the others had seen the wisdom in discretion over valour and yielded as well. The grizzled mercenary captain did so himself with the same stoical demeanour as he always did anything: he'd somehow managed to survive the Battle of Wester Plains, and by the looks of things he'd survive this skirmish too.

The unfortunate crossbowmen couldn't say the same. Wrackwulf's captor issued a curt command, and the serjeants put them to the sword. One tried to flee back into the woods... But a scream, abruptly cut off, told that the other Pangonian contingent had found him.

An ordinary soldier's ransom is barely worth the cost of keeping him as a prisoner, Wrackwulf reflected bitterly, as he and the surviving freelancers were herded onto a wagon like so much cattle. *And foreigners wonder why we hold knighthood in such high esteem.*

The other soldiers were entering the road now, bringing their captive squires and horses with them – at least knight's sons and steeds were worth keeping alive.

The Pangonians bundled the rest of the prisoners on to another wagon, before the leader ordered them to load up the bodies of their four slain comrades as well.

Four enemies killed, and not one a knight – that's a paltry return for the loss of an entire company. Franz, you won't be happy. At least the Westerling woman did us proud –

It was only then that Wrackwulf realised Ariadha had vanished. From his place on the wagon, he scoured the surrounding trees, but there was no sign of her.

Wait, yes – his keen hunting instincts, honed by years spent campaigning in the wildernesses of Urovia, brought it firmly into his line of sight. A trail of blood, leading from where a fallen Pangonian serjeant had just been a moment ago, up a tree-lined slope in the opposite direction from where they'd lain in wait.

Ushira's tits, she got away.

The freelancer risked a quick glance around at his captors. None of them seemed to have noticed – or perhaps those that had rightly didn't fancy chasing a berserk warrior-woman armed with a demonic weapon through enemy territory.

Berserk or no, she managed to control her bloodrage enough to escape.

As the leader gave the order for the convoy to recommence, Wrackwulf addressed him cordially.

'It's customary for a captured knight to be informed of his intended prison,' he hedged.

The haughty Pangonian didn't bother to turn around in the saddle, but his answer caught the freelancer's attention.

'A great honour is in store for you,' he said. 'His Royal Majesty, King Carolus III, ruler of Greater Pangonia, has arrived to inspect his new desmesnes. You will be presented to your liege, to pay just obeisance.'

'King Carolus is here... At the siege of Westerburg?'

This time the knight did turn in the saddle, even raising his visor to talk to him. Favouring Wrackwulf with a smirk he could see all too well this time, he replied: 'Oh yes, and he fully intends to have your fealty. As I said, a great honour. Finally, an end to Vorstlund's feckless and divisional rule, and a chance for you to be part of something truly great.'

Without another word, the knight turned back to face the road, slamming his visor shut.

That suited Wrackwulf, he had plenty to mull over.

CHAPTER 6

THE SORCERER'S SPOOR

A fragment of buttressed stone whistled past Hari Yassin's head as he ducked to avoid it. A split second longer, and he wouldn't have had a head any more – the shard he'd just dodged had to be twice the size of a big man's fist. Or about the size of the pulverising missiles the enemy trebuchets had been hurling at them for the past three days and nights.

Next to him, Sir Azelin barked orders at the monks, who scurried to obey his orders, dropping pots of boiling water on the soldiers who even now tried to mount escalades against the beleaguered walls. Evidently the Pangonian captain wasn't too fussed about sustaining casualties of his own; several levymen went down screaming as fragments from the bombarding catapults struck home.

But then levies were expendable, Hari reflected grimly as his scimitar found the guts of one scaling the battlements. The man fell to the ground below with a wail, his belly opened up by razor-keen steel, trailing guts in his wake.

'How many more days of this?' Hari found time to yell at his companion, as Azelin's greatsword nearly sheared another levyman clean in twain. The monk called Edemus had reluctantly agreed to appoint the erstwhile Bethler as *de facto* military commander; as the greatest warrior in the Free Kingdoms his credentials were impeccable, even if his monastic virtues left something to be desired.

'As many as it takes,' yelled back the knight, spitting out blood that wasn't his. 'This lot aren't going anywhere, not any time soon.'

A brief respite from the assault showed Hari how true that was. Peering over the fractured lip of the parapet, he could see knights and footsoldiers mustered on the slopes down below, while engineers and other auxiliaries at the foot of the steep approach prepared the trebuchets for another barrage. The siege had entered its third night: by torchlight it was still possible to see the Regent's invading force had mushroomed to number several thousands, with hundreds of raw serfs deployed over the past couple of days to soak up the worst of the casualties. The plan was working well enough for the besiegers: though the peasant levies were being whittled down fast, their deaths had already cost the defenders more than a hundred journeymen.

Horskram, whatever you and your secretive cabal of monks are up to, it had better be good.

He'd seen nothing and heard little more of the crabby old adept or his youthful sidekick; all he'd managed to glean during brief breaks in the refectory had been something about an investigation into Hannequin's sorcerous doings.

Fat lot of good that will do us against a besieging army, but if it can uncover proof that the Argolians weren't entirely guilty it might earn us a reprieve.

Hari winced inwardly at the desperate naivete of the thought, which ill became a rogue of his worldliness. Men of power, he knew, seldom granted reprieves unless there was something in it for them.

Once they've put money and materiel into investing a fortress, they have to see it through – otherwise they won't see a return on their investment.

That thought did little to cheer him as the Pangonians below gave the order to renew the offensive.

⁓

'Can you do it or not? Horskram's voice, usually brittle at the best of times, sounded like that of a man whose composure is stretched to breaking point.

Which, to be fair, it was, Adelko reflected – and the same could be said of all of them. Outwardly, Hannequin's erstwhile laboratory was no horror show, as Andragorix's had been: picked clean of its contents, the only thing to indicate its true purpose was a smashed alembic one of the treacherous cabal members had apparently dropped, strange markings on the floor, and the hieratic etchings that sketched an imagined doorway on one wall. But the concentrated sense of evil lingered nonetheless: there could be little doubt to any Argolian with an iota of sixth sense that here indeed had been the keeping-place for the Headstone fragments, pilfered from Ulfang and Graukolos and the Westerling Isles, and good deal of other sorcerous paraphernalia besides.

The hieratic etchings on the wall had become the focus of their investigation, after the wizard Morcant had pronounced it a thing of Alchemy and Thaumaturgy combined, presumably the focus of some kind of gateway spell Hannequin had used to spirit himself and his cohorts away.

The weaselly mage stepped back from his latest incantation, sweat beading on his pale face as he struggled to recover his elan.

'I don't know,' he conceded glumly. 'Such a conjuring, hard to master at best of times – but by all the gods, this is near impossible! It's as I thought, a locking spell he's placed upon it.'

Jonas's admonishment that there was only one god was waved to silence irritably by Horskram as he responded: 'Is there anything we can do to help?'

The other adepts quickly found the floor with their eyes. What Horskram, celebrated hierophant and adept, was suggesting was probably blasphemy and heresy rolled in to one: the kind of undertaking that would have played perfectly into Cyprian's hands and provided him with the perfect justification for expunging the Argolian Order once and for all.

But Cyprian was already hell-bent on expunging the Order, justifications be damned. And, if the shattering sounds outside were anything to go by, inching ever closer towards that goal. And what Horskram was suggesting might delay or even avert their inevitable demise, rather than bring it down upon them.

All the same, everyone present had pause. They'd skirted around the issue for days now; nobody really wanted to venture to its heart. Nobody perhaps except Morcant, who had revealed during Horskram's thorough questioning that he'd already done as much with the apostate monk Joram.

As his own eyes found the floor, Adelko's gaze fell on the only other indication of the ghastly purpose to which the chamber had been put by Hannequin for Reus knew how many years. Traces of silvery dust hinted at the remnants of a pentagram, while other coarser stains suggested that whatever he had conjured up had been appeased by sacrifice.

Were it not for their sixth senses, the monks would have had nothing else to show for their investigation: but the cankered presence of evil they could still feel told all the rest. Adjoining the chamber they were now holed up in, the observatory with its great brass telescope had offered a more wholesome spectacle – until they'd looked through it. It was trained on the Morning Star, the foremost in the constellation known in pagan folklore as the Wand: the favoured cluster of Left-Hand warlocks.

Thus the stars point our way, Adelko sighed inwardly. But gloomy reflection was getting them nowhere. Raising his eyes, he addressed his superiors, carefully keeping his tone firm but deferential.

'Well, we've already learned from Morcant how he and Joram managed to... join forces, and defeat Abrexta. I'd suggest it's time we did the same – with all due respect, I don't see how else we're going to tap Hannequin's magic and follow him. We can't even divine where he's gone to – unless you really want to try that again.'

A glance at the strained faces of the older monks told him that they didn't. Standing in a circle and chanting St Argo's sacred litany over and over again had been a draining experience. All the more so because it had accomplished nothing. That had in all probability meant one thing: Hannequin was truly insane, and had used his sorcerous powers to transport himself and his followers to Varya, the Forbidden City of age-old lore, which no Argolian could hope to penetrate with a mere divination.

'No need, Adelko – we've already deduced where he is.' Horskram sighed as he reminded him of what they all already knew in any case. 'Now it's just a question of following him there. But if Morcant cannot get this dimensional gateway to open, that knowledge avails us nothing.' Drawing himself up and poking his chest out with an air of finality, the hierophant turned to look at his adept brethren.

'Brother Adelko has the right of this,' he said. 'Our conjoined elan might not be enough to confirm Hannequin's presence in far-off Varya, but it might be enough to weaken whatever locking spell he's placed on yon portal, and allow Morcant to activate it.'

Bertram swallowed nervously. Normally skittish, he seemed even more so now. 'Are you quite sure this is the best course of action?' he asked in a small voice. 'To use our powers and that of a warlock, to venture into the Forbidden City...' His voice trailed off as his eyes found the floor again.

Adelko was sure the library master had been secretly hoping Morcant's endeavours would fail. The journeyman could hardly fault him for that: if they were right, what awaited them on the other side of that gate would be worse than ten armies. But what other choice did they really have? Certain death fighting Hannequin and his hellspawn seemed like a marginally better alternative for an Argolian than being captured and executed by vindictive Pangonians.

'I've already told you all, I cannot compel any man here to come with me,' said Horskram. 'But I for one am determined to see this thing through – to whatever conclusion it must arrive at.' His voice suddenly became hard and steely. 'Our erstwhile Grand Master has played us all for gulls, me more than anyone, and I'll be damned if I let him get away without fighting him to my last breath.'

'That smacks of pride, brother,' Jonas could not help pointing out. The old apothecary looked as dessicated as some of his ingredients; a weary resignation was in his tone.

'No, Brother Jonas, it smacks of still believing that somebody, somewhere, has to try to save the world from a madman determined to cover it with hellfire,' replied Horskram acidly. The adept's irascibility, so long a companion to Adelko, was strangely welcome now; as if his bleak sarcasm somehow released some of the terrible pressure that had been forced down upon them.

'I stand with Master Horskram,' said the young monk. 'Whatever it takes to stop Hannequin – and, who knows, maybe even Hari Yassin and Sir Azelin will help us too, once we tell them what we're up to. It's up to the rest of you to decide for yourselves... whether you want to die trying to help us, or die on the end of a Pangonian sword when they finally take the monastery. I know which I prefer.'

Adelko wasn't even that surprised by his own words; by now, he'd been surprising himself for quite some time. And besides, after everything they'd been through, having to stand here and massage the timorous psyches of three tired old men was frankly exasperating.

Horskram suppressed a knowing smile as he rejoined: 'The most junior monk here puts us all to shame with his clarity, courage, and determination – brothers, I suggest you ponder on this awhile. Come along, Adelko, we should find some food – and find Hari and Azelin, as you say they should prove useful if we can somehow convince them to join us. Morcant, you're coming with us too – we'll need you well fed and rested for our next gambit. As for you three – don't take too long to make your minds up.' He nodded towards the sound of a particularly devastating hit from a besieging trebuchet, and the shouts and cries that erupted in its wake. 'In case you haven't fathomed, time is not an abundant commodity. As Brother Adelko said, the decision lies with you – but be sure that if you do not elect to help us, I'll find other brothers who will.'

'My decision is already taken,' said Elias, stopping Horskram in his tracks as he made to leave. 'I've seen enough of disease and sickness in my life to know when a malady must be fought, and when it cannot. This one must be fought, though the chances of cure are slim.' He nodded in acknowledgement at Horskram. 'When the time comes, I'll stand with you, brother, and do what needs to be done.'

Horskram smiled gratefully at him. 'I of all people understand how much is being asked of us, and I thank you humbly and cordially, brother.' He tossed an expectant glance at the other two monks.

Jonas almost rolled his eyes as he said: 'Very well, if you cannot be dissuaded in this matter, I see no point in trying to reason with you. It would appear reason has long abandoned the human mind, in any case. When the time comes, I'll muster my elan and do what I can to help.'

That just left Bertram. The librarian threw up his arms in a near-hysterical gesture. 'If it's a choice between ending my days fighting the forces I was intended to fight, or grappling it out with those jumped-up Pangonian thugs without, I don't suppose it's much of a choice at all!' he exclaimed, every word underscored with sardonic laughter. 'So, an end to the world, but at least we get to end our part in it trying to save it. This is sheer folly, all of it, but why in Palom's name not? Now can we all go, and at least get one last decent meal out of this good green earth before we leave it forever? I don't know about the rest of you, but I'm heartily sick of this room.'

That somehow broke the ice, and all of them suddenly began to laugh. It wasn't quite the hysterical laughter of Bertram, and smacked more of relief: to know that they could still sense humour even at a time like this.

As one, they left the chamber. Five monks, and one mage: all things going to plan, they would soon stand shoulder to shoulder with a disgraced warrior-monk and an outland rogue and face down the very forces of Gehenna.

Adelko tried not to think about that as his stomach rumbled with nervous hunger.

Hari wiped blood from his face. Luckily it wasn't his own – not yet, anyway. Below him he could make out the corpses he'd just made, crowning the pile of bodies thickening about the foot of the walls. On either side of him stood Azelin and the monk Sancre. The latter had talked tough enough when he'd first challenged Hari on the same wall, but his face looked ashen in the guttering torchlight: Yassin guessed killing didn't sit well with the monk's vows. Of course he hadn't technically struck any lethal blows, but striking a man hard enough to knock him off a ladder and send him plummeting was as good as killing him.

'I'm sure your vows make some allowances for self-defence,' he offered, trying to placate his unlikely ally as the latest sortie of decimated levies withdrew.

'They do,' replied the journeyman falteringly, clutching his quarterstaff in white-knuckled hands. 'But that doesn't make it any better.'

'It does get easier over time though,' Hari persisted, trying to be helpful. 'Besides, not all religious sects view murder in the same light – my own used to make a virtue out of killing.'

Sancre barely had time to stare sidelong at him aghast before Azelin cut in.

'Quit your jabbering, the pair of you,' he barked, pointing with his blood-soaked blade to where three formations of armoured soldiers were advancing up the slope towards the gatehouse. 'Looks like we've just seen off a feint and naught else – they mean to break down our front door.'

Peering at the three companies in the uneven light, Hari saw it was true. The central one was carrying the barked trunk of what must once have been a mighty oak, tipped with a giant iron piton; on either side, men with long kite shields flanked them for protection. Already two more companies were moving in smartly to flank the flankers, providing a double layer of protection.

Hari would have cursed had he had time, but just then Edemus' voice rang out, clear but shrill across the night sky.

'Trebuchets releasing!'

'Duck!' yelled Azelin, as half a dozen rocks and giant crossbow bolts whistled towards them.

Hari needed no warnings on how to avoid a missile, but this time it was Sancre's turn to draw the short straw: just a fraction too slow to obey, he was caught by the rock, which pulverised his chest in an explosion of blood and bone and sent him flying off the walkway. A backwards glance told Hari the unfortunate young monk had been smashed to the floor of the monastery courtyard, his mangled form eliciting cries of alarm and horror from other brothers within the compound.

That wasn't all they had to cry about: the trebuchets had been aimed at the outer wall battlements, but the three catapult stones had been slung high over, and now plummeted towards the southern quarter their part of the wall overlooked: Hari winced as he saw monks scramble to avoid being hit.

'Standard tactic,' snarled Azelin, still clutching his greatsword as the pair of them hunched down beneath the parapet. 'Soften up the men inside, so they'll be too panicked to offer resistance when the men outside come for them. They mean to breach our defences tonight.'

Risking a glance at the gatehouse, Hari popped his head briefly above the parapet. Edemus was in charge of the monks defending the gatehouse tower; he could make out his silhouetted form gesturing frantically, ordering monks to ready more vats of boiling water.

'At least Edemus seems to know what he's doing,' said Hari, ducking back down again just as a volley of standard-sized crossbow bolts whistled over the battlements.

But Azelin shook his head. 'He's stalwart enough, I'll grant. But he won't be able to stop an army as determined as this. We don't have much time left – if we want to preserve our hides, we need to look at sallying forth when that gate comes down. Mounted and armed we might just be able to make a break for it – in the dark there's a chance we could slip away.'

The rogue flashed the knight a sardonic grin. 'I hate to point this out,' he said, 'but that sounds more like something I'd suggest, sir knight.'

Azelin shook his head again, more irritably this time. 'Being a knight doesn't mean being suicidal,' he corrected. 'Against odds like these, it's better to live to fight another day than sacrifice your life needlessly. Besides, I didn't say cutting our way out would be easy.' He pointed at his dripping blade. 'If I have my way, this will taste more blood ere dawn.'

'So you've rediscovered the will to live,' Hari couldn't resist putting in. 'Right glad I am to learn it too, and I say yes to your plan! But what about our friends?'

Azelin frowned as he mulled that over. 'All right, we'll tell them,' he said at last. 'I suppose we owe Horskram and Adelko that much at least. They're welcome to come with us, but any more than that and my plan goes awry – a larger sortie, and they'll just send a company of knights after us.'

Hari nodded. Azelin's plan was cynical, but it made sense. 'Well, we'd better go and find them – I hope they're not still holed up in that inner sanctum these monks guard so carefully!'

Now it was Azelin's turn to smile sardonically. 'Even if they are, I'm sure a man of your talents won't struggle to get us up there.'

Hari laughed, clapping him briefly on the shoulder, before the two turned and made for the stairs leading down into the courtyard at a crouching lope. Another volley, this time from crossbowmen and trebuchets all together, flew across the battlements in their wake as they did, sending dozens of monks scurrying for cover again.

Just as they reached the clay floor of the courtyard, the

first booming thud shook the gatehouse. Glancing back at it, Hari saw dozens more journeymen straining against the inside of the gate, as adepts screeched orders at them. Behind them, dozens more were drawing themselves up into some semblance of formation, quarterstaves at the ready, some mounted, some not. Judging by the cries echoing across the monastery precinct, he guessed the other quarters were doing much the same.

No thought of flight or surrender: these monks are ready to go down fighting and fall to a man with their precious monastery. It's like they've been preparing for this moment a long time.

Preparing mentally perhaps, he corrected himself, as he and Azelin made their way across the south quarter towards the fortified compound that marked the inner segment of the Reverend Priory of St Argo, but not militarily. That the monks knew how to ride and fight, he had no doubt, and even Azelin had cautiously praised their knowledge of basic siegecraft, but there was no time, no space, for illusions: in a straight fight against trained knights and soldiers, the monks of St Argo could not hope to prevail.

Passing through a cloistered gate leading into the inner courtyard they saw yet more monks, at least a hundred strong and all mounted, sweeping their quarterstaves from sheaths on their backs. A like number of timid novices served as squires, checking their horses to see they were properly harnessed. But the lack of armour made for a painful sight.

Not so much as a brigandine or gambeson to their name – one good blow and they're as good as dead.

'Quite the crowd,' said Yassin. 'That's good – if we circle past them we should be able - '

'Wait,' growled Azelin. 'Maybe there's no need – look at yonder refectory. The lights are on.'

Yassin glanced sidelong at the knight before following his pointing finger. Both of them had benefited from rudimentary psychic training, cultivating a kind of discipline that approximated the Argolians' sixth sense, though it wasn't as powerful. Still, they'd both shared the road and danger long enough with their two companions to be somewhat attuned to them at least...

'You might be right, it could be them,' said Hari, understanding the warrior-monk's meaning. 'No harm in checking, we can always say we're hungry after killing so many levymen.'

He winked to show the implacable Azelin he was joking, but he apparently didn't care. Making his mind up, he sheathed his still-bloodied sword and marched straight towards the refectory.

Following smartly behind, Yassin swiftly cleaned his own blade with a silk rag before sheathing it too as they both entered the long low building.

Adelko had scarcely wolfed down the last morsel of food when Sir Azelin strode into the refectory, Hari dogging his heels. His sixth sense should have told him they were approaching, but it was snarled up with other things. A lot of other things.

Horskram for his part seemed unsurprised to see them. 'Ah, Hari Yassin and Sir Azelin of Valacia,' said the adept, rising from his bench with his mouth still full. Swallowing and clearing his throat, he added: 'Just the folk I wanted to see. Pray take a pew and have some ale – I'd break words with you both.'

Adelko winced inwardly. Although what they were about to ask would be the most unthinkable request in human history, this was surely hardly the time or place for one of Horskram's charm offensives.

'Don't mind Master Horskram,' he said, trying to sound

casual. 'Our psychic efforts have left him a bit frayed about the edges is all.'

Horskram shot him a scalding look as Adelko raised his flagon in greeting before taking a slurp of the delicious honeyed mead. A thing of the north, it was something to be grateful for: Brother Arthas had brought the recipe with him from his homeland in Efrilund. Before, that is, he'd lost his life on the battlements two nights ago.

Adelko tried not to think about that as Azelin and Hari approached the trestle table the six of them occupied. Apart from them the refectory was empty: once so regimented, mealtimes at the monastery had become sporadic and disjointed. The storehouses and cellars were capacious enough and stuffed to the brim: Edemus had ordered a check weeks before their arrival and pronounced them fit to feed the monastery's fifteen hundred occupants for months.

Not that that would be relevant by the looks of it, Adelko realised with a sinking heart as Azelin grabbed up pitcher and flagon and began speaking.

'As it happens, we wanted to speak to you too – they've brought a battering ram to bear against yon gate,' he said. 'I doubt we'll hold out for much longer. And I doubt those bastards outside will show us any mercy once they do break in. If we mean to survive this thing, we need to think about escaping.'

He paused to take a slug of mead, then grimaced. 'What is this stuff? It tastes disgusting. It's like... liquid sugarcane. Not even in the Blessed Realm did I ever encounter such a thing.'

Adelko could not help smirking as he replied: 'Actually, liquid *honey* would be closer to the mark, Sir Azelin. You see, it's mead, what we do is – '

Another scalding look from Horskram, and even in his fey mood Adelko knew better than to keep talking.

'Sir Azelin, if escape is on your mind then you will want to hear what we have to say,' said the adept, glancing sidelong nervously at his fellow monks. 'We too have accepted the inevitable, but we may also have found a way to get out of here.' Horskram's gaze fell on Morcant, sat at a corner of the table, where he picked at his food nervously.

Azelin completely ignored the mage as he sat down on the bench next to Jonas, pushing the pitcher and flagon dismissively away from him. Fresh from battle, he still dripped blood; Jonas shifted uncomfortably up the bench, nudging Elias to make room for him.

'So you have, have you?' replied Azelin, fixing Horskram with his dark eyes. 'Why do I get the feeling said escape route involves him?' He jerked a thumb in Morcant's direction, still refusing to deign the sorcerer with so much as a glance. Even now, he still carried traces of the fanatic: Bethlers and other crusading types took no more kindly to warlocks than did Argolians.

Sitting back down opposite the warrior-monk, Horskram feigned an affable smile. 'You divine correctly,' was what he said to that.

'So let me guess,' continued Azelin. 'While we've been fighting for our lives – not to mention yours as well – you and yon spell-tosser have been poking around in Hannequin's secret lair and found some godawful sorcerous contraption or some such that he used to vanish from here, after he was done playing the rest of you for idiots. Now you think to get him' – again he jerked a thumb at Morcant – 'to use said contraption to get us out of here too. Am I on the right hunting trail, Master Horskram?'

Again the dark eyes, staring straight into Horskram's bright blue ones.

The smile on the adept's face weakened slightly as he responded: 'That is the adumbration of my intentions, yes, though I would add a few more details to your sketch.'

'I'm sure you would,' sneered Azelin, reaching across the table and plucking a glazed chicken leg from Bertram's trencher. Ignoring the monk's splutter of indignation, he began chewing on it methodically as he said: 'I think I've told you before not to bandy scripture with me, Horskram – well, the same goes for erudition.' Leaning back, the knight spat a glob of phlegm-coated gristle from his mouth, where it landed on a flagstone with an ugly splat.

'So don't think you can sugar-coat this with fancy words,' he continued, leaning back towards Horskram in a manner than could only be described as menacing. 'If you have another hare-brained scheme in mind, now is the time to say so. Break words cleanly, as you said you would.' Azelin tossed the stripped chicken bone back onto Bertram's trencher. The monk positively yelped as it landed on the pewter plate with a clatter.

Now Horskram's face was hard as he replied: 'Very well, if you'd have it thus. We have indeed discovered and identified the paraphernalia of a Transportation spell in Hannequin's laboratory. With our powers here combined, we mean to acti-vate it – tonight if possible – and use it to follow him and his devilish cabal to wherever they went.'

A still silence descended as Horskram finished speaking. Hari had not sat down, but stood with one foot up on the bench, leaning with his elbow on his elevated knee as he peered down at them curiously.

We managed to trick the trickster once back in Ushalayim, Adelko recalled. *I doubt we'll do it again. Tread carefully, Master Horskram.*

'I see,' said Azelin flatly. 'And where precisely do you believe they went?' His dark eyes had not left Horskram's.

The old monk held his gaze as he softly drew breath, before replying: 'To the Forbidden City of Varya, on the Island of the Priest-Kings that the Thalamians called Seneca, once the capital of the mightiest empire the world has ever seen, and now a haven to demonkind and other infernal monstrosities without number.'

A low whistle that almost sounded like a groan escaped Hari's lips, and he drew himself up, passing a hand across his brow, but Azelin remained completely still. Apparently, Horskram's words had moved him not a jot, though he remained staring at him fixedly.

When finally they broke the silence, Azelin's words came as something of a surprise.

'I had something a little more prosaic in mind. I was going to suggest we merely wait for the besieging army to break through the gate, then try to cut our way past it and ride for our lives.' The knight shrugged. 'Not the best of odds, perhaps, but somewhat better I'd say than transporting ourselves to the middle of Varya to take on an entire sect of demonolators and Reus knows all too well what else.'

Hari couldn't resist a snicker at the last remark. In an instant Horskram had locked eyes on the rogue.

'I don't know what you are laughing at,' he said grimly. 'From what I gather, you yourself are an apostate. Oh, your erstwhile sect may not share the precise beliefs of mine, but we both serve the same god. Call him Reus, call him Ashanti, they are but different paths to the same destination.'

Hari maintained his composure, merely asking: 'And your point being?'

Leaning back a shade, Horskram folded his arms, and looked from Hari to Azelin and back.

'Both of you have been tested in the eyes of the Almighty, and found wanting. He hasn't forgotten that, even if you both have. If you're thinking a horde of hellspawn in Varya is something to fear, it's as nothing – *nothing* – compared to what awaits if you do not endeavour to aid us in this. Picture a thousand Varyas in the City of Burning Brass, and no prospect of escape. Ever. That's what awaits you on the Other Side if you refuse the hour, *this hour*, right here and now. And yon Pangonians will be sure to speed you on your way there, probably tonight, if you choose to remain and do not come with us. Or, you can embrace your destiny, and take up the challenge that Reus, or Ashanti or however you choose to name Him, has placed before you. A chance, aye a slender one at that, but a chance to stop Gehenna turning this precious, fragile Known World of ours into a mere province of hell... And should we fail, as most likely we will, at least we die knowing we have a chance of being received in the Heavenly Halls for our travails. You came here to speak of escape, Sir Azelin of Valacia and Hari Yassin? Well, that is the escape I offer.'

Adelko inwardly breathed a sigh of relief. Now was certainly the time for his mentor to deliver the speech of his life, even if the latter was probably shortly to end.

Hari laughed again, but his tone was conciliatory as he raised his hands. 'I am in any case bound to you, thanks to the efforts of another bloody sorcerer, as you might recall,' he said. 'But thank you nonetheless, Master Horskram, your words are most... comforting.' Reaching for the pitcher and flagon, he poured himself a drink – then thought better of it and put them both back down.

But Horskram had no more eyes for Hari. Adelko realised that his words had really been aimed at Azelin. The warrior-monk remained sitting and staring, though the hatred in his eyes was now obvious.

'You seek to condemn us to a certain death, and use a twisted paraphrasis of scripture to justify doing so,' he said icily.

Now it was Horskram's turn to chuckle. 'I thought we weren't going to bandy fancy words about? But yes, if you like, so I do. And need I remind you, we are all condemned to death, one way or the other. All I am really doing is offering you the opportunity – nay, the privilege! – of choosing the time and manner and purpose of yours.'

Before Azelin could respond, Horskram reached inside his habit and drew forth the blood of the Redeemer. Still trapped in its tiny crystal pendant, the single drop caught the flickering light of the torches in their stanchions with a glorious radiance. All the other monks present including Adelko involuntarily made the sign, and even Hari instinctively bowed his head in reverence, but Azelin remained cold, his hard bloodstained face an awkward contrast to its pure glint.

'This I have borne many leagues,' continued Horskram, unfazed. 'It will preserve us, I believe, long enough at least to formulate some kind of plan of attack against Hannequin and his followers. They aren't all-powerful yet: remember, the fourth fragment remains in the keeping of the Old Master of Time's Arrow's at Ortiz.'

Hari blenched at the mention of his former mentor, but Azelin just sneered again. 'I don't seem to recall the Redeemer's blood helping us much against yon apparition we fought a few days ago,' he pointed out.

'No, but you certainly did,' Horskram countered. 'That thing, whatever it was, was something new that I haven't yet been able to decipher, that I'll grant you. But the forces we'll encounter in Varya are older, far older. That makes them all the more powerful of course, but I'm confident – no, I have *faith* – that this will give them pause.' He dangled the relic meaningfully in front of Azelin.

That reminded Adelko of something. While all eyes were focused on Horskram and Azelin, he reached surreptitiously into the folds of his own habit and felt the talisman Abdel Sha'arza had given him just outside Shazra'am. The words the arch sorcerer had spoken to him back then ghosted across his memory.

Keep yonder talisman safe and hidden. Above all, make sure your mentor doesn't know you have it! You'll know when the right time comes to use it.

Closing a pudgy fist around the periapt, Adelko shut his own eyes painfully. It would almost certainly amount to a breaking of his vows, and a heinous one at that, but if Horskram meant to see this through, what else could he do? That his mentor did not expect or even intend for them to escape from Varya alive, he had no doubt. But Sha'arza had offered him a lifeline. Take it, and he might just get them all out of this alive, if they could only find a way to overcome Hannequin.

Horskram could call what he was about to do blasphemy, sacrilege, heresy, or apostasy – but at sixty winters, his mentor had seen enough of the world to be justifiably weary of it.

At sixteen summers, Adelko wasn't quite ready to leave it just yet. Especially if he was about to save it.

Suppressing his thoughts, he returned his attention to Horskram, who was speaking again.

'Azelin, I know something shifted in you when we fought yon horror outside these walls,' the adept said. 'I've sensed as much – some way back to redemption you've espied. This,' – he brandished the relic – 'this is it.'

At last Azelin lowered his eyes. It wasn't Horskram's keen gaze he couldn't abide, Adelko realised, but rather the holy light that seemed to radiate from the pendant-phial in a myriad beams like the spokes of the very Wheel the Redeemer had bled on. Everyone else in the room, Hari included, had been silenced by it.

Azelin may have rediscovered the will to seek redemption, Adelko found himself thinking, *but he's a long way off from the end of that road. Horskram, beware – push too far, and you'll push him off it.*

The torturous emotions that now played across the disgraced knight's pallid face told the truth of that thought.

'Sir Azelin,' the journeyman interjected gently. 'I know you've done many terrible things - '

'You know nothing of what I've done!' the tormented warrior-monk spat, flashing Adelko a blazing look that burned with resentment and anger.

'Yes, I do,' replied Adelko, suddenly growing implacable. 'The women, the children, all of it – I've seen it in my dreams. Or should I say visions.'

Horskram and the others turned to look at Adelko, surprise written plainly across tired faces. Azelin just continued to stare at him hatefully.

'Oh, the Redeemer talks to me too,' continued Adelko with a coolness he could scarcely believe in himself. 'And at times like that, I truly wish he didn't. Your crimes are horrible, Azelin. I've tried, but I can't fathom how anyone, you least of all, could have come to believe that what... the things you did, were in the Almighty's service. I'm sorry, sir, but you deserve your place in Gehenna. The lowest dungeon beneath the City of Burning Brass would be too good a place for you after all the innocents you've maimed and killed and tortured. Not to mention all the poor sods serving under you, men who looked up to you that you forced to join you in your sordid crimes.'

'SHUT UP!' Azelin had risen to his feet, a hand on his sword, and was screaming now. 'Horskram, SILENCE YOUR UNDERSTUDY OR BY PALOM I'LL DO IT FOR EVER!'

Horskram rose to act but Adelko swiftly forestalled him.

'Palom!?' he let out a little laugh. 'Yes, you'd know all about doing things in Palom's name, wouldn't you? Go on then – add me to the list.' He nodded towards the greatsword at the knight's back. A large weapon, Adelko had seen him use it often enough to know he could have it out of its sheath and buried in his skull in a split-second. Not even Hari with all his agility would be quick enough to stop him, assuming he dared try.

He did not let his fear show as he continued in the same soft voice: 'After all, at sixteen summers, I'd be quite old in comparison to half your victims. Still, at least I'm a man – that's more than can be said for some of those poor souls you slaughtered, and certainly more than can be said for you.' Without taking his eyes off Azelin, he added: 'Horskram, I don't know why we're bothering with him. Look at him, he's a disgrace. Let him fight his way out of here if he can, and carve out the rest of his miserable life however he can. We've real work to do.'

Very slowly, Adelko stood up. It took all his training to ignore his racing heart, the choler that thumped through his veins. Right now, he knew he was probably facing down the deadliest enemy he'd ever encountered.

And in a flash like lightning, Azelin's sword was out. It swept down in a dazzling arc before burying itself the length of the table they'd been sitting at. The blade, driven by a force that could almost be described as supernatural, sheared clean through the wood, bisecting the table so that it collapsed inward, depositing the trenchers and flagons and pitchers and other utensils on the floor. The other monks lurched back with startled cries, knocking benches over.

Azelin let out a howl of frustrated anguish as his sword came to rest in a flagstone beneath the table, cracking it apart. Letting go of the hilt, the man once considered the greatest knight in all the Free Kingdoms grabbed one half of the table in both hands, picking it up like a stool and hurling it across the refectory, where it crashed into another table nearby in a shower of splinters. Another tortured howl escaped from Azelin as he raised his foot and brought it down on the other half of the table where it wobbled at an angle on two remaining legs, splitting the oak board down the middle as if it were balsa wood. Picking it up, he wrenched it in two before hurling both pieces at the statues lining the far wall. By chance – or was it Palom's will? – one of the pieces caught the painted statue of St Ionus, smashing it and erasing the smug grin from its chiselled face.

Not the best of omens, Adelko found time to think, but he kept his composure as Azelin sank to his knees and hunched over, sobbing like a child.

The others including Horskram had stepped well back, but Adelko approached the pathetic, huddled figure and look down on him impassively.

'Yes, it's quite a thing to live in fear and pain, isn't it, sir knight?' he asked. His voice was still gentle, but now it carried a hint of steel that no one could miss. 'Perhaps now you truly realise that's how people like me – small, poor, common, weak, defenceless – feel when people like you turn up at our villages and wreak havoc in the name of your kings and gods and causes. At least the Redeemer gave us the power to reflect on our sins, to contemplate the misery we wreak on others, so we can start to share in it too and actually understand what we've done to others. That's your path to redemption, Azelin: to spend the rest of your life in the agony of true repentance. I suggest you get on with it, while you still have time. Now, get out of my sight.'

Bending down, he picked up the blood-stained greatsword. It was slippery and awkward in his hands, but he proffered it to the knight, who was still heaving on the floor.

'Here, take this,' said Adelko, his voice hardening. 'I wish I could say you won't be needing it, but you and I both know that probably isn't true.'

The knight looked up at him with tear-limned eyes that

were suddenly small and afraid. He'd stopped sobbing, and now his mouth just hung slackly off his face as if his jaw had been dislocated.

Again Adelko proffered the sword, hilt first.

'I said take it. And go.' The words now were harder than the steel he held.

Stumbling upright, Azelin passed a hand across his face. He only succeeded in mingling the blood and tears he'd shed, but he scarcely noticed as he wordlessly took the weapon and sheathed it again. Then, turning, he stumbled out of the refectory and into the night.

It took a while for everyone else to recover themselves. Adelko just stood, rooted to the spot, staring sadly at the doorway where Azelin had exited. From across the precinct, the relentless crashing of the battering ram against the gates and the cries of men could be heard through the open doorway.

'Adelko, would you mind explaining to me what on earth just happened there?' Horskram's voice as he approached Adelko was more baffled than anything else.

'I just opened the door to his salvation,' replied the journeyman, still staring at the doorway. 'Now it's up to him whether he chooses to step through it. Morcant will need time to muster his elan for the spell, and we'll need time to muster ours to try to cancel Hannequin's protection. So he still has a chance to join us.'

'But... what you said about visions, how could you know..?' For the first time in their association, Horskram seemed genuinely nonplussed.

Adelko favoured him with a sidelong glance and a wan smile. 'Oh, I was making that part up,' he said, trying to sound light. 'After everything I've seen and read of war, it didn't take a master diviner to work out what he's done.' The journeyman shrugged. 'As for the stuff about being a village commoner, well I am – or I was, anyway. And just because all those awful things didn't happen to me and my kin, it doesn't mean they couldn't have at any time. Because it certainly has to an awful lot of common folk I've seen these past two years.'

Horskram shut his eyes tightly. He seemed in the grip of powerful emotions himself, and for a moment Adelko feared his mentor might break down too.

'Adelko, lad, I'm sorry,' he said, placing a hand upon his shoulder. 'It's true, the things you've seen, that I've caused you to see. Perhaps I should never have – '

Adelko turned towards Horskram, silencing him with a shake of the head as he broke the physical contact between them.

'No, Master Horskram, this is what I swore an oath for. This is what I wanted, what I always wanted. I meant what I said, I *am* a man now – and that means taking responsibility for my own decisions. It's what it means for all of us, I think.'

Horskram said nothing more to that, but nodded silently.

Adelko sighed wearily, then turned to survey the others, still standing stunned by the exchange they had just witnessed.

'Listen,' he said, 'we're running out of time, and there's a lot to do. We've rested and eaten – I'd suggest we get back to it, and start trying to break this holding spell of Hannequin's. Sir Azelin will realise in time where his true path lies – or he won't.'

Hari nodded, seeming to recover his composure. 'Yes, but before we do I have one question,' he said. 'What about all these other monks? They'd be handy to have along, those that are willing and able. And if we leave them here, they're dead anyway.'

'He's right about that,' put in Jonas. 'Where we're going, we'll need all the help we can get.'

Morcant chose that moment to speak up. 'If the gateway I can open, unsure how long I can keep it so – this kind of magick Morcant does not normally use. And the locking spell you might only be able to suppress temporarily.'

Horskram's face darkened as he studied the weaselly mage. 'You're saying you can't replicate the spell perfectly?'

Morcant shrugged, grinning through broken teeth. 'Who is to say? But only one person can go through at a time – and with every passing second our elan will be taxed. The difficulty you must see, I am sure...'

'But surely with more of us to suppress the locking spell...?' Elias put in.

'Helpful no doubt,' said Bertram. 'But I think what the sorcerer is trying to tell us is that even if we suppress the locking spell entirely, his own powers of command over the Thaumaturgy required to activate the gate will be limited.' The librarian fixed the mage with a gaze that was both inquiring and accusative.

Morcant smiled again, rather more sheepishly this time. 'Helpful it would have been, if grimoires I'd had to peruse...'

Horskram raised his hands. 'It is as much as we can expect in the circumstances. Besides, if we noise further word of this, we risk a panicked stampede, which will scarcely aid our efforts. No, it must be just us – and Azelin, if he elects to come.'

'Horskram, are you sure?' Something had shifted between them, and Adelko had dropped the honorific he usually used to address his mentor. 'We're condemning the heart of our Order to being purged if we do it this way.'

'And risking the entire world being ruined if we don't,' replied Horskram firmly, reasserting his authority. 'We should be sufficiently powerful between us to suppress the locking spell long enough for Morcant to activate the gate – warlock, are you certain you can then hold it open long enough so all seven, or eight if Azelin comes to his senses, of us can pass through?'

The mage paused, flicking his beady eyes up to the ceiling, as if the answer to Horskram's question was written there. Flicking them back down again, he nodded, his hair plaits wobbling.

'Good, then it's decided,' said Horskram with an air of finality. 'Now let's do as Adelko said, and get back to work.'

Adelko felt the sweat sluicing down his face as they reached the crescendo of the Psalm of Grammarye's Quenching for the umpteenth time.

'Let their foul sorceries die on their lips, let them choke on their blasphemous words and see their dark arts unframed! Though all the hosts of Gehenna stretch shadows across the mortal vale, thy LIGHT SHALL DISPEL THEM ALL!'

As one, the five monks hollered out the final passage of the psalm. Once again, Adelko could feel the locking spell Hannequin had placed on the gateway faltering, its power receding back through the cosmic interstices through which all magick was channelled. Once again, Morcant stepped up to the etched markings, incanting the activation spell in the unsettling language of magick. And once again, the words died on his lips as his spell, too, faltered.

'No use it is,' he said, his thin shoulders slumping. 'Your psalmody quenches all – the locking spell that guards the gate, and the magicks I must use to open it.'

All of them let out a collective groan – even Hari, who was but a spectator of the bizarre ritual being enacted in Hannequin's old laboratory. Wearily Jonas passed around a flask of holy water so the monks could reconstitute their elan; no such salve for Morcant, but then he wasn't even being given the chance to drain his powers in the first place. The mage had the right of it: the Psalm of Grammarye's Quenching, invoked by five accomplished Argolians, was enough to quash all but the most powerful conjurings within earshot.

'So what in the Redeemer's name do we do next?' asked Bertram glumly. Adelko's sixth sense told him the librarian was secretly relieved that their attempts were failing, but also professionally disappointed.

'Die with me, by the looks of things.'

All whirled to face the speaker. Sir Azelin had entered the chamber while they were busy with the ritual; not even Hari, engrossed as he was in it, had spotted the disgraced knight slinking in. He stood leaning against the door-jamb, arms folded, greatsword sheathed across his back. He appeared to have recovered his composure from his terrible outburst a couple of hours ago, but Adelko didn't need his sixth sense to tell him the man was still acutely pained. He suddenly felt guilty: his stratagem appeared to have worked, but all the same it had been a nasty trick to play.

But now he'd have to play it through to its conclusion, in order for it to work.

'I thought I'd told you to leave us,' said the journeyman, doing his best to sound stern.

Azelin failed to meet his eyes as he responded: 'And I seem to recall your superior Horskram being rather keen on my joining you.' The knight nodded towards the etched markings of the gateway where they seemed to glimmer mockingly in the torchlight. 'Although judging by the looks of it, that may all be irrelevant.'

'How speeds the siege?' asked Horskram, perhaps anxious to change the subject.

'We're still holding out,' replied Azelin, clearly grateful to get matters back on to a military footing. 'The Regent's men mounted more escalades while their soldiers harried the gate

– we managed to drive those off again, but the entrance won't hold out for much longer. The adepts have ordered the barracks and stables emptied – everyone who can fight is saddled and armed. That includes about half the novices, meaning you've got yourselves a resistance force some twelve or thirteen hundreds strong. That should buy us some more time at least once they do get in.'

'So you mean to come with us – assuming we succeed?' Horskram asked, gesturing towards the gateway.

Still the knight did not look at Adelko as he inclined his head curtly. 'Aye. If need be I'll stand guard here on yon stairs, and defend you to my last breath. If, that is, you can stand the prospect of further bloodshed in your hallowed presence.'

Adelko winced inwardly. The warrior-monk was addressing his mentor, but it was painfully obvious at whom his last statement was directed.

If Horskram picked up on that he gave no sign of it as he nodded back. 'Very good. The Order humbly thanks you for your service. Let us resume then – another attempt, we haven't any time to lose.'

But Morcant was shaking his head. 'Futile it is, to proceed as we have done. Some other way there must be.'

Elias shrugged expansively. 'But what? We need the psalm to overturn Hannequin's locking spell, and we need your sorcery to activate the gateway. We can't do one without the other.'

'And yet both cancel each other out,' Jonas finished for him. 'Ach, our erstwhile leader has set us a Tyrnian Knot to unravel.'

Azelin turned from where he'd been about to exit the chamber towards the stairs leading back down to Hannequin's study.

'My learning falls short of the brotherhood's,' he said. 'But as I recall, the problem of the Tyrnian Knot was solved when the warlord Adraticus cut through it instead of untying it. Perhaps you're trying to be too clever about this.'

With that cryptic remark, the knight turned on his heel and left.

'What did he mean by that?' mused Bertram.

Adelko rubbed his chin thoughtfully, ignoring the incipient stubble growing there which had begun to perplex him in the past few months.

'He means maybe we should be using a more direct method to access the gateway – something more akin to brute force, I suppose.'

Horskram rolled his eyes. 'Trust him of all people to suggest that – but you forget we're already using brute force, in a sense. We're trying to batter down Hannequin's defences, just as yon invaders are trying to batter down our gates without.'

Adelko ignored the nervous looks that simile provoked from the other monks as he replied: 'Well, then perhaps Azelin is wrong – maybe we aren't using enough finesse. Trying to brute force our way past Hannequin's defences clearly isn't working, he'll have anticipated that.'

Morcant was staring at him quizzically. 'So what do you suggest?'

Adelko favoured him with a sly smile. 'Morcant, you were telling us how Joram found a way to combine his psalmody with your wizardry... What if we tried to do the same?'

Morcant frowned. 'Aren't we already doing that?'

'Not quite,' said Adelko, more thinking out loud now. 'All we've been doing is one thing after the other – we chant the Psalm of Grammarye's Quenching, then you step in and cast whatever spell it is that's needed to open the gate. But in the Palace of Bending Branches, you told us how you and Joram *harmonised* to stop the fays from killing you... I think we need to do something more along those lines.'

What Adelko said was true enough, assuming Morcant himself had told it truly: they'd spent much of the first night of their investigation grilling the mage for details of his mission and his interactions with the apostate monk. That had elicited uncomfortable responses from the other brethren, which is precisely what Adelko's suggestion did now. Horskram simply looked troubled, but his fellow adepts scoffed openly.

'What you are proposing is not only blasphemous and in contravention of all our vows, but nigh on impossible,' spluttered Jonas.

Adelko gesticulated at the chamber. 'What we're doing is already in contravention of our vows,' he said. 'And if Joram and Morcant were able to do it, I don't see how you can say it's impossible.'

Jonas folded his arms stubbornly and looked away. 'It's simply not done,' he said peevishly.

Now it was Adelko's turn to roll his eyes, but before he could respond Bertram interjected.

'Brother Adelko, you seem to forget that when Morcant and Joram joined forces – blasphemous as that was – they were using the Psalm and his magicks to compel the fays to stop. That isn't quite our situation – we're trying to use the psalm to overturn one spell so he can activate another.'

'Yes, and it isn't working because our psalm is cancelling out his magick too – but Morcant said himself that should also have happened to him in the palace, yet it didn't. We need to work out why, and try to replicate that.'

Elias and Jonas were shaking their heads, but Morcant was tugging at his braids thoughtfully.

'No, just possible it might be,' he said. 'One of yours Brother Joram was, yet he found a way to use Argolian powers in conjunction with mine.'

'He did so presumably because he'd spent Reus knows

how many years studying grammarye at the feet of Hannequin,' Horskram pointed out. 'I hardly think we have the time or tools at our disposal for a crash course in sorcery, even if we did choose to do such a foul thing.'

Morcant ignored the slight to his craft as he pondered the riddle. Then he tapped his head triumphantly.

'But of course!' the eccentric wizard actually looked excited now. 'Simply to try is what we must do! No, listen, wise monks – your psalm it works not immediately, yes? Time it takes to quash my foul art, as you call it.' He shot a sly grin Horskram's way. 'So why don't we try both at the same time? Perhaps a sweet spot there is – when your psalm has weakened Hannequin's protection spell enough but mine not so much... that just get through it might.'

Horskram was rubbing his beard thoughtfully. 'That's a fine line to tread,' he observed. 'Presumably Hannequin's locking spell is at least as powerful as the spell you cast to open the gate. I agree, it's worth a try, but I struggle to see where this "sweet spot" as you put it might be found.'

'No, I think it can be done,' said Adelko, clicking his fingers as he grew animated in turn. 'Right now we're going all in, with five of us putting our elan into the psalm. But what if we, well, staggered it, so to speak? As soon as we sense Hannequin's spell weakening enough for Morcant's to get through, we relax our efforts, just a little. Drop out of the psalm one by one, to give Morcant a chance to channel his energies better.'

'But that will reconstitute the protection spell as well,' Horskram protested.

'It will,' Adelko allowed. 'But we don't know how long the protection spell takes to reconstitute itself – a few precious seconds, if Morcant redoubles his efforts, he might just activate the gate. And when and if he does... Morcant, do you know if the protection spell will still be an issue once you've opened the gate?'

The mage reflected for a second or two, then shook his head emphatically. 'Quite specific Thaumaturgy is,' he explained. 'Yon spell is designed to keep a gate already closed, locked. A door already open you cannot lock... closed again first it must be. So as long as I can keep it open long enough, the protection spell cannot reactivate.'

Now all of them were nodding their heads. Rooted metaphorically in the physical world as it was, Morcant's explanation made perfect sense.

'Let's do this,' said Adelko, momentarily forgetting his place in his excitement.

But if he'd spoken out of turn, none of the others seemed to care: even Bertram looked thrilled to be on the cusp of untying his Tyrnian Knot.

Their high spirits were dampened by the sound of Azelin's hoarse voice a moment later, as he called up from the stairwell.

'Whatever you're doing up there, I'd be quick about it – we have guests!'

As the first soldier rounded the narrow spiral stairs and into view, Azelin realised a two-handed sword nearly the length of a man wasn't the best choice of weapon. He had no others, so he'd just have to improvise. The fellow came bellowing up the last steps towards him, a great bull-necked man who kept his shield up and his sword pointed over the top: not a subtle fighter, clearly he meant to charge straight in.

At the last moment, Azelin dodged to the soldier's left. His short stabbing blade found thin air as the knight grabbed his kite in both hands and slammed it into his jaw, cracking his teeth and eliciting a bloody yowl from the soldier.

Azelin wasn't as big as his antagonist, but every stretch of muscle on his body was sinewed and rock-hard: men had oft said his wiry frame concealed the strength of a Wadwo, and they weren't far wrong.

The soldier barely had time to gasp as Azelin wrenched the shield free of his grasp, simultaneously landing a devastating kick on his chest that send him flying back into the next soldier right behind him. As the short sword tumbled from his fingers, Azelin caught it smartly, levelling it down towards his opponents as he dropped into a fighting crouch.

The two soldiers were busy disentangling themselves from one another, so Azelin used the time to hook the kite's strap about his neck and arm. Shifting his stance slightly to accommodate the shield, he waited impassively for the men to approach again.

The big boy was out. Clearly used to bullying his way through a fight, he didn't deal well with being disarmed and having teeth and ribs broken in a single brief exchange. The next fellow to come at him could not have been more different: lean and wiry like Azelin, he carried a murderous glint in his eyes that suggested a cunning swordsman.

Just not quite cunning enough. Azelin read his feint, then parried and countered with one of his own before opening the soldier's throat with a single elegant slice.

Curse my bloodthirsty ways all you like, Adelko of Narvik, but they're saving your pudgy arse right now, he found time to think as he clashed with a third soldier, trading a few fierce strokes before burying his sword point in his eye just below the rim of his helm.

It took some half a dozen bodies, piled up in the stairwell, before it began to dawn on the soldiers that they were dealing with no ordinary defender. As they struggled to clear the corpses away and favoured him with fearful glances, Azelin decided to hammer the point home.

'That's right, I'm no mere monk you fools!' he yelled in a cracking voice. 'Sir Azelin of Valacia, have you heard of me perchance? But lately returned from Palom's crusade, to send your sorry arses straight to hell!'

That gave them another pause all right. With wary looks, the soldiers backed down around the corner, dragging some of their dead comrades with them.

Azelin allowed a vulpine grin to cross his face. The impertinent young monk had got under his skin and no mistake, but killing men in arms would never stop feeling good.

On their third recital, Adelko felt the locking spell begin to give way and falter. That was just as it had been the previous times. What was different was the eerie cadence that Morcant was contributing throughout, gathering his own elan in the hope of mustering enough power behind his spell so it could break through and activate the gateway when the time was right.

But as for harmonising – a cacophony was more like it. The eldritch syllables of the language that angels – still he found that hard to believe – had taught to mortalkind in Varya more than five millennia ago jarred uncomfortably with the mellifluous Decorlangue of the psalm, and for a brief while Adelko had feared that the situation would be merely reversed and their psalm cancelled out.

But of course, the language of magick was precisely what the words of Grammarye's Quenching had been uttered to deal with, and if anything it had only caused the monks to redouble their efforts. As much as they could, they willed the psalm to nullify the protection spell and not

Morcant's incantation: but that kind of precision had presumably taken Joram and Hannequin years to master in secret.

This would be a haphazard and experimental effort by comparison.

Again they began to recite the litany from the beginning: 'Reus Almighty, thy humble servant bends to thy will...'

Adelko could sense Morcant straining now, fighting to push his spell through.

'Though the servants of Abaddon assail me I shall not be frighted...'

And then he felt it. They all did, of that he was sure: even Hari, skulking to one side at the periphery of his vision. A low hum, as something gave.

'... they shall carry me across fields of fire, through winds of want, above waters of despair...'

As prearranged, Adelko broke off from his chanting, dropping out of the litany. In truth his elan was probably far greater than anyone else's but Horskram's, but even now some semblance of the old monastic order had to be preserved.

He felt a wave of relief wash over him as his strained elan relaxed; sparing a cursory examination of the chamber, he took it all in. Hari, standing and fidgeting nervously with the hilt of his scimitar, Horskram and the other adepts still standing in a semi-circle, with Morcant in their midst, facing the gateway, his arms raised high as he continued with his incantation.

The gateway...

Adelko returned his gaze to the hieratic symbols where they sketched a door on the far wall.

They were glimmering, just faintly, but unmistakeably. Peering at the brick wall inside them he saw the stones were beginning to shimmer and lose their corporeal form.

'It's working!' he cried triumphantly. 'The portal is opening!'

Turning to the doorway that led to the stairs connecting to Hannequin's study, he yelled: 'Sir Azelin, get up here! It's working!'

It was only then that he noticed the familiar sounds of battle, the clash of steel on steel, followed by a scream of pain. He knew well enough not to fear their last line of defence had failed.

But he also knew Azelin had to come with them. How or why, he couldn't say, but he was sure of it.

'AZELIN!' he bellowed again, more loudly this time. The low hum he'd heard was beginning to rise in volume, and to be replaced by an insistent keening sound.

'All right, Reus dammit!' came the throaty response. 'I'm a bit busy killing men so you can live!'

Moving through the short narrow corridor that led to the top of the stairwell, Adelko had to allow himself a sardonic smile. He might be able to manipulate men into doing the Redeemer's will, but he would never truly be able to change their hearts. But Azelin would just have to weigh his own sins, in his own time.

Advancing towards the end of the corridor, he saw the warrior-monk backing up it towards him. A fully armoured knight was menacing him, covered head to toe in some strange carapaced armour Adelko hadn't seen before. Fighting with a shield and sword, Azelin was having some trouble getting past the knight's flanged mace to find a chink in the newfangled harness.

Some, but not too much. Not for nothing was Azelin accounted the greatest knight ever to wield a weapon since his ancestor Lancelyn took up arms; bringing up the kite to take another shattering mace blow, he pushed the knight's weapon aside. Clearly the new armour was heavier; the enemy knight tottered briefly, losing his balance for a crucial split second. That was all Azelin needed to drive his sword point up and under his armpit where the armour was weak.

The knight sank to his knees with a clattering gasp as Azelin wrenched the blade free, light-red blood pumping from a severed artery onto the flagstones.

A great groan erupted from the soldiers behind as they witnessed the demise of their champion. But they wouldn't stay put for long.

Swiftly turning, Azelin positively barged Adelko back up the corridor.

'Don't just stand there gawping,' he cried. 'Run, you idiot!'

Dashing back into the chamber they saw it was suffused by a refulgent glow. The bricks inside the etched glyphs had vanished entirely to be replaced by a preternatural shimmer, one that appeared to be many colours and none all at once. Jonas and Bertram too had dropped out of the recital; only Horskram and Elias remained chanting, but now they broke off chanting themselves as Morcant reached the end of the spell.

No, not quite the end of it. In the scintillant light Adelko could see the mage was still sweating profusely, as he struggled to master the grammarye required to keep the gate open. Clearly the sorcerer had never used magick like this before; he wouldn't be able to keep up the effort for ever.

As if reading his mind, Horskram yelled: 'Now! We go through NOW! We haven't a second to lose!'

Grabbing Jonas and Bertram by the shoulders, he propelled them both towards the gate.

'One at a time, and quickly about it!' yelled Horskram. Behind him Adelko could hear more soldiers approaching as they recovered their courage. Azelin had turned to face the entrance, blocking it as he took up a fighting stance again.

Jonas was the first to go. Briefly making the sign, he

hurled himself into the shimmering portal. It appeared to wobble comically in a flash of light before righting itself again. Of Jonas there was no sign.

Bertram was still muttering a prayer, eyes tightly shut, when Horskram shoved him through the portal. Again it buckled and flashed before righting itself. Only not quite. It was flickering now rather than shimmering. A sideways glance at Morcant told how much the effort was costing him. Not when he'd been chastised by the Order in a dungeon cell had he looked so tortured.

Adelko nodded at Elias and Horskram. 'You go next,' he said. 'You're both more important to the mission than me.'

Horskram found time to nod approvingly at his understudy's humility before motioning for Elias to go. Adelko was just grateful he hadn't mistaken it for cowardice. As Elias stepped through the gate, Hari unsheathed his scimitar and took up his place just behind Azelin, who was already trading blows with another soldier.

Horskram was next to go, then it was Adelko's turn.

'Hari, you're next after me!' the journeyman yelled. 'Don't be long about it!'

One more sideways glance, at Morcant's pale stretched face locking in a gap-toothed grimace, as his slender frame trembled from head to toe.

Reus Almighty, whatever you really think of sorcerers, grant this one the power to see this through.

Adelko stepped through the portal...

Time and space stopped. It was as if they had never been, and never would be. An infinity of universes somehow condensed into a single microcosmic fraction of an indefinable *something*, unbearable. An unacceptable reversal of all that was natural, ordained. A place that was not a place, where nothing existed, not even nothing...

Adelko's senses returned to him with a shocking gasp. Where was he? *What* was he? *He*... that's right, he *existed*. An awareness of something, surroundings. Yes, he had eyes, he remembered, looking around him. That was how he perceived the world, sometimes.

But where in the Known World was he?

As his scrambled mind realigned, he realised he was in a vast cave. There was light, daylight, but it wasn't direct: the cavern he was in appeared to follow a rough dogleg or L-shape, the other section must be open to the skies.

Horskram, Elias, Jonas, and Bertram were there, looking similarly bewildered. Suddenly, as if from nowhere, Hari appeared beside them, collapsing to the hard rock floor as Adelko only now just realised he himself had done shortly before. A few seconds later, and Azelin did the same, still clutching the kite shield and bloodied short sword.

It took a little longer, but Morcant appeared as well. When he collapsed on to the ground, he did not get up.

Checking on him, they rolled him over. His breathing came in faint gasps, but he was alive – for now, at least.

'He's clean worn out,' said Elias. 'After what he just did, no wonder.'

Getting up and pulling out his circifix, Horskram waved it gingerly through the air, roughly above the spot where they'd all appeared.

'I can detect only residual traces of sorcery,' said the adept. 'I think the gateway has closed, Morcant could not possibly have kept it open a moment longer. That is a good thing – we'll have no soldiers following us.'

'I seriously doubt they would have chosen to step through even if they could have,' said Hari, looking shaken as he picked himself up. 'I don't know about you, gentlemen, but that was without a doubt the single most bizarre experience of my - '

His words were cut short by a great booming roar and a thunderous shaking that threatened to upend them all on to the floor again.

Turning to look in its direction, Adelko saw a sight he had fervently hoped never to see again in all his days. A dark shadow fell on them as the cave's occupant made itself known.

The Gygant was similar in appearance to the one that had menaced them at the Warlock's Crown. The same gargantuan thews of liquid rock, the glaring eyes of molten lava, the lichen hair and beard. But this one was bigger, much bigger: its hand alone was larger than any one of them.

Its hand... the fingertips were great hollows through which magma bubbled as it stomped forward and stretched out towards poor Bertram. The hapless monk screamed as a spurt of liquid fire caught him, setting his body aflame like a torch. Grabbing him up pitilessly as he flailed the last of his life away, the Gygant popped the freshly cooked meat into its mouth and chewed it between teeth the size of millstones.

Only Horskram had recovered enough composure to address the thing in the language of giants. Swallowing Bertram, the Gygant leaned down and scrutinised Horskram with fiery eyes that sputtered.

Again the adept held his nerve, repeating what he'd said in the ugly language of Aurgelmir's first creations. The Gygant appeared to cock its huge head to one side, before abruptly scooping them all up in its hands and carrying them towards the back of the cave and depositing them in a niche high up in the cavern wall.

Too stunned to do anything, the companions could only stare aghast as the Gygant took up a giant grating fashioned from trees, wedging it firmly in place to block up the niche in which they were now imprisoned.

Morcant was just coming to as Horskram tried one last plea in the giant's tongue. What passed for a chuckle escaped the creature's cavernous mouth, shaking the walls and dislodging motes of dust from the ceiling.

Horskram shook his head. 'Too stubborn and too hungry, it won't let us go,' he said. 'We're to be kept here until it decides which one of us to eat next. A plague on the stupidity of Gygants!'

'But this can't be Varya,' said Adelko, peering through the criss-crossed tree trunks as the creature stomped back up the cave towards the light. 'The Gygants kept as slaves there all perished in the Breaking of the World! And this doesn't look like a city to me.'

They shortly had the answer to that riddle. Sitting up and taking in his surroundings, Morcant turned a shade paler than usual.

'I think I might have miscast the spell,' he said in a small voice.

CHAPTER 7

VISIONS AT SEA

A flame-haired girl stood beside her, pointing imperiously towards an advancing host... A straw-haired baron, of noble mien, outfitted for war, leading a caval-cade of brightly armoured knights... Dark clouds on the hori-zon, their ugly black forms echoed by the swarming masses moving steadily towards them... A far greater foe than the one they had just triumphed over, scattered blue and silver crescent pennons receding, the thump of horses hooves, felt rather than heard... Black-clad apparitions stalking towards them, clutching ancient blades and staring at them with merciless eyes... Dessicated jaws dropping open, a roiling tide of smoke engulfing them all...

Adhelina continued to toss and turn in her frightful dream, as the carrack bearing her home tossed and turned on stormy seas. She was choking now, struggling for breath as she fought to claw her way back into wakefulness. Succeeding at last, she wrenched herself up from her hammock, gasping aloud. Blinking away the vestiges of her latest incoherent vision, she gazed around the cramped cabin with fearful eyes. The lashing rains without seemed matched by the torrents of sweat drenching her body; the squalling winds a perfect reflection of her troubled spirit.

Gripping the hem of her rope hammock tightly, she craned her neck downwards to peer at Hettie, where she lay sleeping soundly just below.

Hettie, you have no idea how much I envy you right now, the heiress thought to herself, lying back on the ropes as she tried to breathe properly.

Yes, incoherent her visions were, but they did seem to point clearly to one thing: she was returning to a homeland wracked by war, and if it truly was her destiny to face down the Pangonian army, then something far worse would come at them in its wake.

And she had an unpleasant inkling she knew what it might consist of. She hadn't forgotten their frightful encounter with the Draug lords on the moors last year; she and Hettie had escaped the worst effects of their horrid black breath, but it had laid low some of the best fighters the Free Kingdoms had to offer. She didn't like to think what such ghastly fiends could do to an army with a weapon like that at their disposal.

But... surely not even the beastly Pangonians would ally themselves with such horrors?

Then she remembered her encounter with Ivon, the serpentine Margrave, at the Riman court, and the words of the wise woman and her child apprentice afterwards when they'd sought her out in her chamber.

Reaching up, she passed a hand across her soaking brow, trying to clear her thoughts and still her heart. They'd been at sea for two weeks when the summer storm had suddenly struck, erupting out of nowhere to engulf them in its rough salty embrace. That had been what, two, three nights ago?

At least she'd got her sea legs, there'd be no unseemly vomiting over the ship's side or into a bucket – but by Ushira, she'd have killed to bathe. As her hammock swayed frenetically in time to the pounding waves, Adhelina allowed herself a small, wry smile. It was one of the ironies of seafaring life, she supposed: to be surrounded by an abundance of water, but have so little of the kind you really needed. Inordinately cleanly, she tried to wash at least once a week, a habit she had insisted on passing down to Hettie years ago. Asclephos' *Treatise On The Salutary Benefits of Bathing and Grooming* had been quite specific on the point: an unclean body was an unhealthy one. She'd been pleased to find the habit taken to new heights in the Sassanian lands: even the crusader settlers there could be relied upon to wash daily. But try telling that to the rough-hewn northern nobility.

Thinking on that, Adhelina allowed herself what was a rare luxury these days: she mulled the mundane. If she really was to be reinstated as a noblewoman, and crowned a queen no less, she'd damn well institute some more wholesome habits at her court.

But before she could do that, she knew, she had an unwholesome war to fight – against the dead as well as the living, if her visions told it true.

She found herself thinking of Tipu, the recondite Sha'abatian mystic. Though his imperturbable demeanour and ascetic serenity had been maddening at times, she'd have given almost as much to hear his advice now as she would to bathe.

But she'd get neither for the foreseeable. Sighing, she rose again, shifting herself awkwardly out of the hammock and gingerly placing a bare foot on the rough wooden ladder next to it. The first night she'd caught a splinter and nearly turned the heavens blue with her cursing, but one of her poultices had quickly put that right.

Oh no, milady, Hettie had insisted when Sir Ulfstan had first shown them to the tiny cabin they'd be sharing for the next six weeks. *You're the ranking noblewoman, you have to take the top bunk. It's only right and proper — you're to be a queen soon.*

Adhelina gave another wry smile as she gingerly descended to the cabin floor. *Thanks a lot, Hettie.*

Clad in naught but her shift, she dressed hastily and quietly, so as not to wake her companion. Not that there was much danger of that: aside from the noise of the storm, her lifelong friend slept with a carefree abandon Adhelina simply could not remember enjoying.

Fully clothed, she gazed down affectionately on Hettie's face, so innocent-looking in the flashing light of the storm. Her slender bosom moved gently up and down to the rhythm of her quiet snoring, her mouth half open as she slept sweet sleep.

Oh Hettie, I should never have dragged you into all of this. But by Ushira's wings, I'll find a way to make it up to you once all this horror is done with. If they really mean to give me a crown, I'll see to it that you're never far from the centre of power.

Power. Now there was an odd thought, from a runaway heiress who had done everything in hers to spurn the intrigues of the high-born.

That's what it is to grow old, she thought ruefully, before turning to leave the cabin.

She pulled her woollen travelling cloak more tightly about her as she emerged from the forecastle onto the deck. Drawing her hood up against the lashing rain, she scoured the blazing heavens, as if daring them to furnish her with a waking vision. But none were forthcoming. Sir Ulfstan would not approve of her being above decks in such conditions: even most of the crew members were down below, just a skeleton contingent left to keep the carrack afloat. No need for a night watch in such weather; pirates or other undesirables would be scarce likely to engage. But of course, a storm could present just as much danger as a pirate vessel.

Carefully keeping herself flush to the forecastle, she moved up its length towards the rail, away from the stairs leading to the fo'c'sle deck. Gripping the rail tightly, she parted her legs, standing with feet out wide for better balance. Though now fully clad in heavy travelling clothes, she knew her stance was unladylike, and unbecoming of a damosel especially. She didn't care: tipping her head back slightly and shutting her eyes, she exulted in the feeling of the icy spray as it strafed her face, borne on keen bracing gusts. Lightning flashed again overhead, another peal of rumbling thunder following it two heartbeats later, but Adhelina did not flinch.

She'd faced far worse than this, and would face worse still before her time was done.

'Your Majesty! What in Sjórkunan's name are you doing above decks?'

Adhelina felt her irritation return. She had not heard Sir Ulfstan approaching for the noise of the storm he evidently thought he was now saving her from. The bedraggled knight was stood beside her, clutching the inwale feverishly.

'I might ask you just the same,' she replied, spitting briny water from her mouth and not adjusting her stance. 'And I really don't think you should call me that until I've decided whether or not I want this crown you keep talking of.'

Ulfstan wiped sea water from his face and did his best to seem affable under the circumstances. 'Perhaps we might discuss the niceties of protocol below decks, Your – my lady,' he hedged.

'Perhaps,' was all she said to that. Turning back to look at the surging waters, she brought her legs together. She hated feeling self-conscious around men, but the customs of the old country died hard. As absurd as they were: Vorstlending damosels were permitted to sit astride a horse, unlike their counterparts in the rest of the Free Kingdoms – but they were still expected to behave in so-called ladylike fashion in other situations.

She mulled that over some more as she continued to ignore Sir Ulfstan with a relish she found difficult to conceal. What else might the future Queen of Vorstlund be able to do with her power? Changes could be made, slow at first, but no less certain for all that... *The serpent shall turn in their hands*, so Tipu had intimated. Still aware of the annoying knight gazing insistently at her, Adhelina had to admit the thought of turning that power against those that sought to use it to control her appealed more and more.

'My lady,' Sir Ulfstan repeated. She didn't need the sight to know the knight was still struggling to get his sea legs.

Turning from the pounding surf, she smiled at him. Even in the darkling light of the ship's beleaguered lanterns, she could tell he was flushing. Adhelina hated to admit it, even to herself, but she had the looks to bewitch a man. What the menfolk never seemed to grasp was that she had the brains to outmatch them as well: most nobles didn't even know what a brain was, for Siona's sake.

Adhelina held Ulfstan's gaze, exulting in the look of confusion as it crept across his handsome face. The ship continued to lurch up and down as it fought the storm; the young knight looked positively queasy, but the would-be queen of Vorstlund felt as though she were resting in said storm's very eye.

'Let's away below,' she told him at last. 'I've had my fill of fresh air.'

The knight gratefully complied. It was obvious he was relieved Adhelina had conceded him the illusion of control. He extended a hand and the damosel took it. A couple of times he staggered but she steadied him and they reached the doorway in the forecastle. With some difficulty he opened it and ushered her in towards the stairs leading back below decks. Entering behind her, the young knight shut the door, hushing the storm's howling. Glancing back at him, she saw he looked even more relieved now he was back indoors.

Enjoy your illusion while it lasts, Sir Ulfstan, she thought to herself as they descended.

CHAPTER 8

A CITY ENCOMPASSED

Vaskrian's kite shield caught the first two crossbow bolts, one skittering off the iron rim with a whine as the other buried itself in the painted oak with a dull thunk. The third one found flesh, though it wasn't his own: his charger reared up with an agonised whinny as the quarrel penetrated the thick leathern trapper protecting its flanks. Swivelling hard in the saddle, the young knight dug his spurs in as his thigh muscles tensed; the horse turned a pirouette before he managed to calm it down – he remained mounted and his steed was still alive, but his charge had been killed in its tracks.

Fortunately Torgun had better luck: a Farovian destrier, Hilmir was big and strong enough to wear metal barding, which did a better job of turning aside quarrels. Thundering towards the Northland crossbowmen flanking the palisade, knight and rider leapt across the ditch lying just before the row of sharpened tree trunks, clearing the row of stakes that lay waiting beneath. No sooner had Hilmir's hooves touched the ground than Torgun was lopping off heads; two of them rolled into the ditch to be impaled on the stakes as his flashing sword opened up another reaver's face.

Pressing spurs to flanks again, Vaskrian rounded the ditch and palisade on the other side, closing with the Northlanders who'd nearly unhorsed him. They'd had time to draw close-quarters weapons; Vaskrian cut one down before he could do anything else, but two more menaced him, one finding his shield with an axe while the other thrust remorselessly at his horse with a sword.

Once more the blade found flesh beneath the trapper; it still wasn't enough to kill his steed, but it reared up again screaming: this time Vaskrian wasn't agile enough, and his feet left the stirrups as he fell to the ground with a crash – before rolling into the ditch.

His natural dexterity saved his life. Clutching the lip of the ditch, he clung on for dear life. The reaver who'd unhorsed him stepped up and loomed over him with a leering grin, sword raised to deal the death blow... before Hilmir's iron-shod hoof caught the back of his skull, dashing out his brains. A swift sword stroke from Torgun made an end of the last reaver, the blade shearing through axe handle and collar-bone to finish buried in his heart.

Wrenching the blade free with a spurt Torgun alighted from the saddle and whistled loudly: obeying his master, Hilmir reared and smashed two more approaching North-lendings with his mighty hooves. Glancing around quickly, Torgun sheathed his sword and shouldered his kite shield before helping Vaskrian up.

'Good job you decided to switch back to sword and shield,' Vaskrian noted, glancing at where a quarrel still quivered in the bigger knight's kite. They'd had a week to prepare for the assault on Strongholm, during which Torgun had been persuaded to sheathe his mighty new blade in favour of some-thing more defensive. He still carried the puissant weapon at his back: doubtless the Northlanders would taste its edge again before long.

That time had also bought them precious reinforcements from down south: some two hundred knights and a like number of footsoldiers, with guarded assurances that more would come once the coastal slave raiders had been dealt with. That had caused some consternation within Toros's army camp: with the Triton threat apparently expunged, why continue to waste valuable fighting men on raiding expeditions? No one had found the answer to that question, yet.

Gazing about the approach to Strongholm, scarred with a hotchpotch of palisades and ditches, both knights could see they were getting the worst of it. The Northlanders were digging in: Magnhilda had sent reinforcements of her own through the main gate, and hundreds of crossbowmen and warriors could be seen engaging across the field.

'We're still badly outnumbered,' muttered Torgun. 'We'd better get those extra reinforcements – soon.'

As if on cue, another sortie of warriors charged towards them. Half a dozen strong, they clearly thought two dismounted knights easy pickings.

They thought wrongly. Their whooping war cries quickly turned to ones of pain and dismay as Torgun thundered into them, Vaskrian hard on his heels. Nimbly sidestepping the first, the young knight smashed his kite into the second, knocking him off balance as he disembowelled the third with his sword. These were lightly armoured; Vaskrian guessed none of them were 'made men' or seacarls, the closest the Northlendings had to proper knights. Circling round so he could keep both his remaining antagonists in view, he lunged and feinted, ducked and parried, keeping them both at bay until his blade severed the fingers off another's sword hand.

Serves you right for going to war without proper harness, he thought, just before Torgun stepped up and cut down the last reaver with a single powerful stroke. Behind him the other three Northlanders lay dead or dying.

'You always steal my thunder,' Vaskrian could not help grinning at the older knight.

Torgun blinked in surprise at that remark. But then wit had never been his forte.

'Never mind,' said Vaskrian quickly, nodding towards their horses. 'We'd best get back in the saddle, before more of them come at us.'

Torgun nodded and they both remounted. Vaskrian's charger whined pitifully; it didn't like bearing an armoured man while carrying two injuries, but if it could have, the beast would have been thankful just to be still alive: many other good horses lay butchered along with their owners.

Torgun is right, thought Vaskrian as they sought the next palisade. *We're not getting the best of this. There are just too many of them.*

They didn't even get a chance at another skirmish before a herald's clarion confirmed his fears: Toros was sounding the retreat and calling it a day. Naturally their footsoldiers had taken the worst of it; but many a knight and squire was left dead or soon to be – merciless to the core, Northlanders didn't take prisoners for ransom.

Another hail of quarrels dogged them as they retreated, heading back towards the muster point in an orderly fashion, but crossbows took time to reload and by the time the second volley loosed it found few targets.

Rejoining their units as they reformed into three battalions, Torgun and Vaskrian waited to see if the Northlanders would dare to launch a counter attack. But none was forthcoming: the enemy knew better than to abandon their defensive positions to take on mounted knights in a straight fight.

'So much for Northland berserker rage,' muttered one knight. 'That Shield Queen bitch has this lot well disciplined.'

He wasn't a raven, just a regular vassal fighting in the King's Knights along with the rest of them. Though they were back fighting on land again, Sir Torgun had not rejoined the White Valravyn, choosing instead to lead a troupe of knights from his native Vandheim. Vaskrian guessed that since his decision to take to the sea, tensions were running high between his hero and High Commander Toric.

'They aren't berserkers in any case,' put in Torgun. 'Just ordinary shieldmen with the odd seacarl to stiffen their ranks. We've barely put a dent in their forces.'

Scouring the sorry landscape with his eyes, Vaskrian saw the truth of that: many Northland corpses joined those of their men, but most were lightly equipped like the men they'd faced. Much hard fighting awaited them if ever they were to retake Strongholm.

And then the awful but predictable happened. Cries of outrage and disgust went up and down the line as warriors emerged from behind their palisades to finish off the wounded among the Northlendings. Toros swiftly ordered a volley from the archers, and the cries turned to triumphant jeers as the surviving executioners scurried back behind their logged walls.

'That'll teach them,' said the knight. 'Killing belted knights and common footsoldiers side by side, it just isn't right.'

Vaskrian could not resist flicking a reproachful glance his way. *And I suppose if that had been my father, you'd have said just the same*, he thought resentfully. *He was a footsoldier too, and showed greater courage than most knights.*

That thought set him on a gloomy train of thought. He was a knight now himself, but he'd always feel different.

His unwelcome reverie was soon dispelled, however. The sharp-eyed outriders were the first to spot them, cresting the ridges encircling Strongholm from a southerly direction.

Their triumphant calls were soon taken up by the rest of line, rippling through the hundreds-strong host.

'That's Theodoric's standard! It's the southrons! The southrons have come!'

Screwing up his eyes Vaskrian saw it was true: a vert lion *rampant regardant* on a blue and white chequy field, the coat of arms of the newly instated Jarl of Thule. The King's appointed successor to the dead traitor Krulheim rode at the head of a thick column of men, at least a thousand strong. Giving the city a wide berth, they were approaching Toros's forces from a roughly south-westerly direction. Well out of range of the Northlanders' crossbows, they would join them imminently.

'The southrons have come!' Vaskrian took up the cry as he nudged Torgun enthusiastically. He probably sounded like a village idiot, but he didn't care: any respite from morbid self-contemplation would do him nicely.

Only Torgun wasn't smiling. Instead he was staring fixedly to the west up the road to Staerkvit, face set grim. When Vaskrian looked at him askance the big knight simply raised a gauntleted hand and pointed.

Turning to follow his finger, Vaskrian saw the source of his consternation. Cresting the hills directly to the west was *another* host, only this one bore no standards that anyone there recognised.

Until someone did.

'Those are Thraxian arms!' another knight called out. 'The Thraxians have come to lay waste our kingdom!'

Thraxians... surely not. We left their realm in a mess, there's no way they'd –

Jubilation returned to Vaskrian as he recognised the foremost standard's coat of arms. A coiled serpent in gules encircling an azure jewel on a vert background – he'd recognise that one anywhere.

'No, it's Sir – I mean Lord – Braxus!' he cried, tugging at Torgun's mailed sleeve. 'That's his family crest, and he's in charge now. He must have come to help us!'

Vaskrian caught Torgun's frown. Clearly he recognised it too – but then relations between the two men had hardly been cordial during their adventures together. Memories of their courtly love rivalry over Adhelina returned to the younger knight.

But this was a time for war, not romance. 'Don't worry, Sir Torgun, I'm sure he's become a bit wiser since we saw him,' said Vaskrian. 'After all, he's got a fiefdom to run now. And he knows more than most how much is at stake.'

'Perhaps,' Torgun allowed, his face still unsmiling beneath his helm. 'But we'll have to convince our compatriots of that.'

Sure enough, Toros's herald sounded out the order to change formation. Two battalions were to remain where they were to greet Theodoric's approaching forces from the south, while the third – theirs – was to turn about and prepare to meet a hostile army from the other direction.

'We can't do this!' hissed Vaskrian as Torgun repeated the order to his unit and they wheeled their horses around. 'Send out a herald to parlay first at least!'

'Orders are orders,' replied Torgun. It was his usual mild tone, but Vaskrian knew him well enough to realise it brooked no argument. 'Besides,' the blond knight added, 'we have no way of knowing Lord Braxus's intentions. If he's really here to aid us, why did we receive no word of his coming from his outriders?'

Vaskrian chewed his lip fretfully as he pondered that. Torgun had a point – but surely Braxus would never betray them like this...

～

Gwydion scowled as Braxus gave the order to halt. Peering down into the basin of land that stretched towards the city and the sea beyond it, he shook his head as he saw the right flank of the Northlending army turn to face them.

Their journey had been uneventful enough. They'd taken the south road, circumventing Harrang before briefly rejoining the highway when it turned east towards the capital; they'd bypassed the mighty castle headquarters of the White Valravyn without incident, but reasoned that its entire garrison would have long mustered and converged on Strongholm.

Too uneventful: the Thraxian host had mostly shunned the main road, simply using it to guide their way, but the silence that had greeted their progress had been eerie. No one to parlay with, no one to communicate their arrival in the kingdom or its purpose, and no sign of their damned messengers days after despatching them.

'I'm still waiting on our heroes' welcome, Lord Braxus,' Gwydion said as if reading his thoughts, his tone icy. 'First our scouts go missing, and now this – doesn't look like our old Northlending friends are so friendly after all. Next thing they'll be couching lances.'

As if on cue, another trumpet blare was followed by several hundred bristling spears pointing in their direction.

'See?' The elite knight's tone was almost triumphant now as he turned to glare at Braxus. 'Once a Northlending, always a Northlending. All they see us as is enemies and rivals.'

'To be fair, we *are* on their lands,' said Braxus, trying to keep his temper with the infuriating High Constable. 'As for our messengers... dammit, I don't know, Sir Gwydion! Something must have happened to them.'

Gwydion laughed shrilly. 'Oh, do ye think? Aye, Lord Braxus, I'd say something must have happened to them indeed! And something else is about to happen, right here.'

He stabbed an accusing finger down towards the Northlending host, where knights waited for them to descend from the hills and into the fields below.

More trumpets, this an exchange: to the south, another host of men and horse hoved into view. Squinting against the sun's glare, Braxus saw they were Northlending standards; abruptly the second army shifted direction and began approaching the bank of hills his own army straddled.

It was then that Gwydion took matters into his own hands. He signalled to a nearby herald, who ordered his trumpeter to blow a series of short, sharp notes: already in formation, the Thraxian host couched lances of its own.

'Sir Gwydion, what are you doing?' barked Braxus. 'I didn't give that order!'

'That's *Lord* Gwydion to you,' snarled the High Constable. 'In case you've forgotten my rank, I'm in charge of the King's forces.'

'Not on this expedition, you aren't,' blazed Braxus. 'Herald! Give the order to stand down. That's an order, Ezekiel dammit!'

The liveried sub-officer looked uncertainly from one commander to the next. Next to them Dantos and Gwydion's sons Arianrod and Diarmuid shifted awkwardly in their saddles. Clearly power-sharing on the campaign trail wasn't working, if indeed it ever did.

'Gwydion,' he continued, pointedly dropping all honorifics. 'His Majesty put us both in charge of this campaign, as well you know. That means we both have to agree on any decision to attack, unless it's in self-defence.'

Gwydion waved an arm wildly at the Northlendings down below. 'What does that look like to you? A welcoming tourney parade? This *is* self-defence, you up-jumped fool!'

That was too much for Braxus. Letting a hand fall to his sword hilt, he fixed Gwydion with eyes that were deadly cold.

'High Constable, you will rescind your last remark and apologise, or by Virtus and Stygnos, I'll have satisfaction.'

Both men remained deadlocked in a staring match, a coldly contemptuous smile suffusing Gwydion's aquiline features.

'So, a duel of honour is it to be?' the constable asked, his voice still dangerously calm. 'A host, nay two hosts, of Northlendings not good enough for you – instead you have to pick one of your own to fight.'

And it was then suddenly that it hit him: Gwydion *wanted* to fight the Northlendings.

Of course, he's been hoping for this all along – so he can have a quick war and some plunder to recover his lost reputation. Gwydion, you great prideful fool, didn't I tell all and sundry how much is at stake?

Choosing his words carefully, Braxus forced himself to calm down and replied: 'Lord Gwydion, you know well enough who the real enemy is. All the troubles that befell our realm – and you and your valiant sons and Sir Dantos here suffered more than most – are down to an enemy that threatens to enslave us all if we stand by and let it.' He jabbed a finger of his own at the second Northlending host, which had ceased marching to take up a flanking position covering the first. 'This is not it.'

But Gwydion remained unmoved. 'So you say,' he sneered. 'I can't say I was as gull- as ready to believe you as our King. It seems to me, Lord Braxus, that you've curried rather too much favour and influence at court since you so valiantly rescued us.' The last few words were underscored with sarcasm, and Braxus knew there was no reasoning with him.

It was then that he took his first real gamble of the campaign. 'Sir Arianrod, Sir Diarmuid!' He called out the names of Gwydion's heroic sons in a clear ringing voice, causing both knights to start. 'Your father the High

Constable has exceeded his rank and station, and thereby contravened the King's express orders. Please take him into custody, pending trial for low treason.' Not slow to note the appalled expressions on their young faces, he quickly added: 'Assuming Lord Gwydion complies immediately and without resistance, I am sure His Majesty will be compelled to grant him a full pardon once the campaign is over, a position of clemency I swear in sight of belted knights to endorse fully – if, and only if, he consents to be arrested and detained immediately.'

Gwydion's mouth appeared to have dropped half a spear's length. It only closely partly as he began laughing. 'Even for you, this is ludicrous,' he mocked. 'You stayed overmuch at the harp in your youth, methinks – think you that this is one of your lays, Braxus?'

Braxus remained cool as an autumn wind as he responded: 'Nay, Lord Gwydion, this is nothing like one of my lays. It's far, far worse – or will be, if proud men such as you are permitted to act in dereliction of their duty. Sir Arianrod, Sir Diarmuid! I shan't ask again – please take your father into custody, or I shall be forced to assume that you are both accomplices in his insubordination, and have Sir Dantos arrest all three of you.'

A deathly silence hung in the air in response to his ultimatum. Braxus didn't dare risk breaking his gaze again to read the expressions on the faces of the men nearest to them, but he didn't really need to. Opinions would be divided on his controversial gambit, but he knew he'd taken a calculated risk.

Of the four hundred knights he'd brought with him, half including his staunch right hand Sir Madogan were directly loyal to him: they'd pledged their sword and service to the First Man of Clan Fitzrow, come heaven or hell. The other half were Kingsfolders: that technically made them answerable to the High Constable in the King's absence, but they hadn't *sworn* to him – like any royal bachelor or vassal, the name they had pledged lifelong fealty to on receiving their spurs was Cadwy's, not Gwydion's. As for Sir Dantos, he was beholden enough to Braxus that he felt confident of swaying him – and even if not, his newly made captain Sir Madogan would certainly obey his orders.

That of course, just left Gwydion's sons – the very knights he was asking to carry out the arrest. Risky yes, but it had to be this way. He needed to demonstrate the strength of his command, and the urgency of their mission, by winning them over for all to see. If he had to get Dantos, or worse yet, a recently knighted mercenary like Madogan to do it, he'd be sowing the seeds of his future undoing.

Only, winning over Gwydion's proud and loving kin wasn't going to be easy: Arianrod was already shaking his head stubbornly, while Diarmuid simply looked shocked.

Gwydion, meanwhile, was taking matters into his own hands again. 'This order is illicit and unfounded and will be ignored!' he cried. ''Tis Lord Braxus, not I, who has outstripped the boundaries of rank! 'Tis Lord Braxus, not I, who must be detained! Sir Dantos, disarm the First Man of Clan Fitzrow and take him into custody! Serve me now loyally as you always have done!'

Poor Dantos looked torn. But Madogan's own hand had already slipped down to his sword hilt. Braxus knew he had to act fast to prevent his expedition force descending into a mutinous shambles.

'Sir Dantos, your loyalty is to the King, not Gwydion,' he said, keeping his voice calm. 'His Majesty expressly ordered that we mount an expedition force to aid, not fight, the Northlendings. He decreed that Gwydion and I would share command for its duration. By ordering an attack on Northalde without my concurrence he has violated his pledge to uphold the King's will on two counts. You will arrest him and take him into custody – and his sons, if they refuse to carry out my order.'

To the brothers, he added: 'I understand your father is a great knight, and you both love him well as befits leal sons. But your loyalty is to Cadwy, first and foremost, above all other ties that bind. I have given you both my word in sight of witnesses that he shall be leniently treated – but this prideful and reckless behaviour cannot be allowed to stand, not when the fate of the Free Kingdoms hinges upon our cooperation.'

The brothers exchanged tormented looks. Sir Dantos chose that moment to speak up, humbly but firmly: 'Lord Braxus has the right of this. Every knight here heard his tale at Cadwy's court, and many suffered thanks to this conspiracy of witches. I second the First Man of Clan Fitzrow, and adjoin my oath to his – Lord Gwydion, you will be treated fairly but you must relinquish command.'

The haughty knight's eyes bulged, before a dangerous glint entered them. 'You would dare?' he seethed.

But Dantos remained unmoved. 'If not for Lord Braxus, we would be languishing in perdition, forever thralls to an enchantress, our honour and lives forfeit, our kingdom lost. I will not turn aside from him for the sake of one man's pride.' The burly bearded knight nodded towards his sons. 'You heard Lord Braxus – take your father from the field and put him under guard. Or else, I'll have someone else do it, and you'll be joining him.'

Braxus kept his triumphant feelings to himself, but Madogan was smirking openly. As a recently belted commoner, he'd already had to endure Gwydion's scorn, and that of his sons.

'We'll go into custody with our father,' replied Arianrod sullenly, glancing at his brother Diarmuid who nodded firmly.

'Better that than betray him at the behest of a fledgling lord who thinks he's still a knight errant.'

Madogan nudged his horse forwards, his sword half out of its scabbard, but Braxus stayed him. 'Nay, let it pass, Sir Madogan,' he said. 'Sir Dantos, you and your unit will escort Lord Gwydion and his sons to their pavilion, and keep them under armed guard at all times. I don't want them going free to cause us any more problems.'

Sir Dantos nodded and motioned for his men to comply with the order.

'You haven't heard the last of this,' spat Gwydion as he and his sons were disarmed and led away. 'I swear by Ezekiel and Virtus there will be a reckoning for this.'

'As to that, you may have satisfaction whenever you please, Lord Gwydion,' replied Braxus coolly. 'After the campaign is concluded.'

'I'm not sure,' said Torgun, 'I can't make it out.'

'Looks like some kind of dispute to me,' ventured Vaskrian. His hero would always be the better knight, but he'd seen enough tavern brawls in his time to recognise the signs. This was no formal duel being enacted on the crest of the ridge – or not yet, anyway – tempers had flared and things were getting out of hand between Braxus and his commanders.

Sir Vaskrian couldn't help a wry smile. *Same old Braxus, lord of men or no, you can't resist getting yourself into trouble.*

Then again, it was precisely the job of a lord to get himself into trouble. Only preferably not with his commanding officers.

'I think they can't agree on what to do next,' he said. Nodding towards Theodoric's host, drawn up roughly at a right angle to theirs, he added: 'We've made it clear we don't trust them, and they obviously don't trust us – Sir Torgun, let me parlay. I served Braxus, he'll listen to me, I'm sure of it!'

Torgun reflected a moment, then nodded briskly. 'Very well, Sir Vaskrian,' he said. 'But mind you make it quick – I have a feeling my brother is about to issue more orders.'

That was all the encouragement Vaskrian needed. Pressing spurs to flanks, he drove his chestnut charger towards the rise leading up to Braxus's position.

He was careful not to draw any weapons, but Torgun had him covered: another command, and Vaskrian glanced back to see a squire riding in his wake, waving a white flag.

Of course – Braxus wouldn't recognise his new coat of arms, he'd only just decided on it a few days ago. A trident-wielding merman displayed in gold on an azure field, he felt it well reflected his recent adventures.

What it wouldn't do is tell his erstwhile guvnor who he was.

~

'Someone's approaching,' said Sir Madogan, returning everyone's attention to the Northlendings. Squinting down into the basin, Braxus saw a knight bearing a heraldic device he didn't recognise approaching them from the first host, a squire riding in his wake waving the flag of parlay.

'Stand down!' he called to his troops. 'They wish to break words, let us hear what they have to say.'

His hopes blossomed into a second feeling of triumph as the knight slowed his gallop to a trot and then an amble as he crested the rise, drawing close enough for Braxus to recognise him. His face was half-hidden beneath his helm, but those burns scars were hard to miss.

'Sir Vaskrian!' he cried.

The young knight smiled in greeting. Braxus was just about to nudge his horse towards him when they were both alerted to cries of alarm. They weren't coming from his army, nor the two hosts drawn up to face it.

Braxus' eyes were already scanning the horizon as Madogan gasped beside him and Vaskrian wheeled his horse around to look in the same direction. The cries were coming from Northlanders stationed on the walls of Strongholm: looking across the chiselled battlements of the city to the Strang Estuary beyond, Braxus felt a feeling he had not experienced since he and Vaskrian had faced down the horrors of the Warlock's Crown with Horskram.

The Wyvern Sea was foaming, but no enemy ships could be seen furrowing its waves. Instead a host of winged reptilian creatures broke the surface, torrents of water cascading in their wake as they erupted from the deeps below to fly towards the coast at breakneck speed, lizardine forms darkening the firmament.

As the cries of alarm were taken up by the hosts mustered on the plain below and his own army, Braxus realised with a sinking feeling that the ancients had spoken literally when they named this stretch of waters.

After who knew how many centuries, the dragons of the sea had arisen again.

CHAPTER 9

A ROYAL PROPOSITION

'Y ou will kneel before the King!' Sir Hare-Lip's voice was stern enough, his disfigured face unsmiling beneath his raised visor, but Wrackwulf knew sincerity when he saw it... and when he didn't. The elite knight of the Purple Garter who had taken command of the prisoners as soon as they arrived at the investing army camp was scarcely a pretty sight, but nicknames aside Wrackwulf knew Aremis for a model of chivalry: upright and honourable, loyal, honest, and brave.

That couldn't be said for the smirking, preening monarch Ushira's unkindness had obliged him to serve: dressed head to toe in gilded plate armour and crowned in gold, wearing an outsized vair cloak of ermine weighed down with precious gems and platinum thread, Carolus looked more like a court dandy than the warrior-king he was obviously trying to mimic.

Keeping the contempt in his eyes as subdued as possible, Sir Wrackwulf complied with the request at the third asking, slowly and deliberately lowering his bulk to the sod but refusing to lower his gaze. King Carolus affected a look of boredom as he half slouched upon the gold-chased portable

353

throne his palace servants had brought hundreds of miles across the Orne ranges to Westerburg, whose scarred walls offered a piteous and all-too-real backdrop to the absurd spectacle being played out before the freelancer.

The intricately crafted joints in his new armour clinked as Carolus leaned forwards and said: 'And who precisely is this?'

'Sir Wrackwulf of Bringenheim,' supplied Aremis, his hare-lip making a cruel mockery of his attempt to look serious. 'But lately contracted to the rebel forces of Westerburg, and a distinguished Vorstlending veteran of diverse campaigns and tournaments.'

Now it was the King's turn to show his contempt. 'Well, he doesn't look very distinguished to me.'

That drew sycophantic mocking laughs from the other knights and lords gathered about the King on the stretch of sward in the midst of the Pangonian army camp. Wrackwulf had quickly learned to despise them all: Kaye and Aravin especially, their dandyish ways made him sick, but cruel Clovis and scheming Hugon were also men who easily inspired hatred. As for Morvaine, he was even further up his own arse than the King he served, holding himself aloof and pretending this was all beneath his dignity.

Which, in a way, Wrackwulf had to admit, it probably was: this ridiculous charade of presenting high-born prisoners captured for ransom before their supposed new ruler was a farce.

Why can't they just take us to Altkass or Vizvant or Howfaste, throw us in a dungeon and have done with it, Wrackwulf wondered. *Even a prison cell would be better than having to put up with this nonsense.*

Even as he thought that, he wasn't entirely sure he meant it: at least the skies were blue and mostly cloudless, the air clear and refreshing when it wasn't being spoiled by smoke from the siege. And while he was kept here, above ground in the viper's nest, he had a chance to try to learn more about his captors.

'Appearances can be deceptive, Your Majesty,' he responded to the King's jibe. 'As I'm sure you realise all too well.' He dropped his gaze for the first time, letting his eyes fall meaningfully on Carolus' meretricious garb.

The King's face hardened as he perceived the slight; was it Wrackwulf's fancy, or did the margraves Kaye and Aravin have to stifle their mirth?

Oh I'm not the only one who sees through your facade, Carolus. Why, even that chivalrous dolt Hare-Lip sees you for what you truly are.

Clovis stepped forward. Not yet out of his teens, he nonetheless commanded a powerful, mature frame. If only he had the head to match: his brutish features did little to conceal his nature.

'Sire, please allow me to chastise this low-born freelancer,' he said. 'I'm sure he will learn the meaning of courtesy and respect right soon.'

'Low-born is it?' snarled Wrackwulf, really losing his patience now. 'I'm a belted knight and the son of a landed vassal, if only a younger one. If you're half the lord you seem to think you are, you should know better than to treat honoured captives in such a churlish fashion.'

Clovis advanced, gauntleted hand raised to backhand Wrackwulf, but Aremis stepped in.

'Lord Clovis, hold!' he said. 'He may only be gentry, but still the blue blood runs in his veins. You shall not treat him like a common footsoldier.'

Clovis favoured Aremis with a sour sneer, and Wrackwulf had confirmation then of something he'd already suspected: the two men clearly despised each other.

Good, good... just keep feeding old Wrackwulf the knowledge he needs.

'As to the blood status of the lesser nobility, that has ever been a matter for debate,' replied Clovis coldly. 'And while we speak of rank, I think it ill-fitting that a *knight* tells a lord his business.'

'As to that,' replied Aremis, no less coldly. 'As a *knight of the Purple Garter* charged with care of the King's captives, I believe I outrank you in this matter.'

Carolus seemed too amused by the exchange to call a halt to it, but Sir Hugon chose that moment to get involved.

'And as the ranking officer in said Order of the Purple Garter and High Commander of His Majesty's forces, I hereby order the pair of you to desist immediately,' he said sharply. 'I'll not have the great and good of Pangonia fall to squabbling in sight of our most beloved King.' He glanced dismissively Wrackwulf's way, adding: 'Or his captives.'

Both men stood back, contenting themselves with one last mutual glance of hatred. Wrackwulf quickly suppressed a smile; his captivity had placed him in close proximity to Aremis, and he'd play on that animosity for all it was worth first chance he got.

Hugon was addressing him now. 'Sir Wrackwulf of Brin-genheim, you know why you have been brought here,' he declaimed. 'A simple choice lies before you. Either you swear fealty to His Majesty King Carolus, First Scion of Greater Pangonia, Prime Defender of the Creed, Foremost...' – Wrackwulf instinctively stopped listening as Sir Hugon went on declaiming his liege's pompous litany of titles – '...to be his sworn sword and householder, or else it's the dungeons for you. Even if your kin do have some treasure stashed away with which to pay your ransom, we can't guarantee it will buy your freedom. Nor can you count on their remaining free themselves to pay it for much longer.' He gestured meaning-fully at the walls of Westerburg, which the catapults had resumed pounding in the last minute or so.

For the first time during the audience, Wrackwulf was wracked with doubt. He'd known it was coming to this, but hadn't yet made up his mind what to do. As a free lance, he wasn't technically sworn to anyone: he could sign up with the likely victors, with no prior oath broken. And the Pangonians *did* look likely to be victorious: the latest reports had their Thalamian allies pushing back the Vorstlending baronies to the east, and rumour even had it that the cowardly sot Hengist, the bibulous and useless Herzog of Stornelund, might sue for peace.

From a mercenary's perspective, allying himself to the Greater Pangonian cause made sense: a chance of a guaranteed living, prestige even, if he impressed the conquerors enough.

But then he thought of his adventures in the past year... Adhelina would never forgive him, for one thing. And there was far more to mull than an exiled noblewoman's scorn: everything they had fought for on the Westerling Isles, the dread quest Horskram had made them privy to, the possibility that Carolus might even be part of the secretive plot the monk had alluded to.

And yet, with all that said, what use would he be to anyone trapped in a dungeon cell?

Everyone was staring at him now, with eyes as hard as the rocks being hurled against the walls of Westerburg. Hugon's face darkened as he exclaimed: 'Has Morphonus stolen your wits, man? By Virtus and by Stygnos, what is your decision? Tell us swiftly!'

Wrackwulf gazed reproachfully at the assembled host of his captors, before allowing his eyes to settle back on the King, who was sitting upright on the throne now, an expectant look on his pallid face.

Wrackwulf sighed.

'Bring me a sword,' he said.

CHAPTER 10

THE GIANT'S REPAST

Morcant collapsed again, sweat lashing off of him. 'No use it is!' he wailed. 'Too soon after all my endeavours this is, I cannot muster the Thaumaturgy we need.'

'Keep your voice down!' hissed Hari, alarmed at the mage's sudden outburst.

But Hari needn't have feared: night had fallen on the vast cave shortly after their capture, and its owner had gone to sleep soon after, curling up in a corner right beside their prison. Even now its thunderous snores rocked the cavern, a slow and monotonous rumbling that counted off the seconds to morning, when the Gygant would feed again.

The awful creature had lost no time in gloating, telling Horskram it planned to devour them one at a time at each sunrise over the next seven days.

'Yon brute doesn't get much variety in its diet,' the adept had said sourly. 'Anything that departs from mountain goats is to be savoured, as it were a delicacy. At least that should buy us some time.'

But several hours had already passed, and availed them nothing: the trees were lashed together with strands from the

Gygant's beard, far too tough for a blade to cut and certainly too strong to pull asunder. Not even Hari was slight enough to squeeze through the latticed gaps; their only hope had been Morcant's wizardry. If he could use his Thaumaturgy to effect an unnatural change in the lawful material world, perhaps they could escape...

But it looked for all the world as though Reus did not look kindly on such endeavours.

'Let him rest a while longer,' said Elias, trying not to show his obvious terror. 'We have many more hours until sunrise.'

'You forget we don't know where we are,' Horskram reminded him. 'Day and night vary less depending upon where one is in the world – we left Pangonia in high summer, but for all we know, where we are now the hours of darkness may well be shorter.'

Elias looked crestfallen at that revelation. 'Your lore puts mine to shame brother,' he conceded. 'And brings me one step closer to despair.'

'Here, let me try again,' said Azelin, getting up from where he'd been sitting towards the back of the rocky recess they now shared. 'Perhaps Morcant's magicks have at least weakened the bindings.'

From his own place in the shadows, Adelko once again fingered the periapt Abdel Sha'arza had gifted him. Hopefully the archmage would have some advice to impart, he just had to wait until the others were distracted enough so he could use it... Even now, he didn't feel comfortable sharing his secret, least of all with Horskram.

'Wait, let me try and help you,' the adept was saying. 'My thews are yet strong, by the Almighty's grace.'

'It's by the Almighty's grace that we're stuck here,' Azelin could not resist quipping, but he motioned for the hardy old monk to join him.

Together they strained, but once again to no avail.

'It felt slightly weaker, but not by much,' said Azelin, gasping for breath as the pair of them lurched back and stretched and rubbed their limbs.

'We need to try when Morcant is ready to use his magick again,' said Horskram. 'Perhaps if the three of us work together we can loosen one of the bonds – then we should be able to part yon trees just enough so Hari can slip out.'

'Yes, but then what?' asked the rogue. 'Make no mistake, I'll be only too happy to make good my escape – but that won't keep the rest of you out of the giant's larder!'

'Then we'll just have to try to part it further so all of us can fit through,' said Horskram stubbornly.

'What about cutting through the trunks themselves?' suggested Jonas, who had appeared withdrawn and meditative throughout and only now broke his silence.

'It would take forever,' said Azelin, shaking his head. 'A serrated blade we'd need, and if I start hacking at one of these trunks there's every chance of waking yon fiend.'

Everyone was engaged; now was the time. Retreating back further into the cave, Adelko closed his hand about the periapt, shut his eyes and focused his elan.

You'll know what to do, the sorcerer had told him when he'd spoken about using the amulet.

And, bizarrely, he was right. No sooner had he begun to concentrate than Adelko felt his psychic powers attuning to the periapt, somehow bonding seamlessly with it. There was no struggle as there had been when they grappled with Hannequin's artifice; this was like slipping on a glove that had been tailored to fit him perfectly.

– Adelko of Narvik, how very delightful to hear from you.

The journeyman started, stopping himself at the last second from gasping aloud. The words were abstract, a presence in his mind, but the meaning was as clear as if Abdel were standing right next to him. He had little time to marvel at the wizard's craft, however.

- *Things are not good*, he thought, hoping that was all he needed to do to communicate back. *We've been captured by a Gygant, we tried to use Hannequin's own magick to follow him to Varya, but it appears to have not worked properly.*

Adelko couldn't hear the sorcerer's infuriating little giggle, but he knew the archmage was laughing.

- *Now that sounds like quite a tale for Abdel...! Best if you start at the beginning...*

Any fears of the time this might take were quickly allayed: Adelko find that by simply reflecting on the events of the past few days, he was able to communicate them. It was as if he was laying the contents of his mind bare, for the sorcerer to pore over as though they had been written down on a scroll. The effect was disconcerting to say the least, and Adelko didn't like to think what else the sorcerer might be reading while he was about it.

But Sha'arza kept firmly to the matter in hand.

- *That is an unfortunate predicament and no mistake. But not an insurmountable obstacle. Your mentor speaks the Gygant's tongue, so he'll already be aware of how intensely stupid the creatures are.*

- *Yes, but right now I don't think it's the creature's brain we need to be afraid of*, responded Adelko. *And for all its stupidity, it's managed to pen us in like chickens in a coop! If we don't work something out before dawn... Wait, I don't suppose you can tell where we are? Knowing that might help us determine how much time we have left...*

- *If you don't know where you are, there's no way I can tell from this talisman alone. I'd need to attune it to my Scrying tool, I can do this if you like?*

- *Never mind that for now. Our first priority is trying to get out of here. Morcant has the magick needed to weaken our bonds, but he's clean out of elan after using Hannequin's portal. If we can only loosen it enough to fit us through – Hari brought his climbing gear, we could escape while the thing's sleeping!*

- Yes, yes... but if Morcant has to wait until his powers return, that might mean sacrificing one more of you. And of course, should your amicable host choose the wizard to feast on next, you're all as good as dead.

Adelko's blood ran cold as he contemplated that prospect. If it came to it, one of them would have to volunteer to be eaten next, to ensure Morcant's survival and give the others a chance to escape. He didn't like to think what measures would be taken to decide who got to be the 'volunteer'.

- There has to be another way. Can't you help? You're a much mightier mage than Morcant, Reus, um, bless him...

- Flattery will get you everywhere, my young savant!

- No, it won't. But some help from you just might! I assume you gave me this blasphemous talisman for a reason...

- Patience, Adelko of Narvik! Let me think...

- All right, think! But don't be too long about it, time isn't exactly something we've a lot of...

Adelko sensed the periapt go dormant in his hand. Returning his attention to the cave, he saw the picture of despondency: Horskram and Morcant were muttering at one another reproachfully, while Azelin had shuffled back to his place in the corner. Hari examined the vast grill-work that imprisoned them fretfully, while Elias prayed softly. As for Jonas, he had sunk back into his meditative reverie.

Adelko did his best to follow suit, running the Psalm of Spirit's Comforting through his mind as he tried to achieve a transcendent state. But it was no use: the words sounded hollow and false to his inner ear. If Reus Almighty was to be trusted, and they were about His work, why did He insist on placing them in one unlooked-for danger after another?

Again, the questions; always, the questions.

Abdel Sha'arza's telepathic voice brought him abruptly out of his morbid musings.

- I think I have an idea that might work.

- That's good! I'm all ears – figuratively speaking.

- But you might not like it...

Adelko wondered if the sorcerer could sense his inward groan.

- This Morcant, he's no master warlock, but he must be competent if he managed to tap Hannequin's grammarye to get you into this pickle in the first place... I assume like most wizards among his people he is well versed in the school of Enchantment?

- From what he told us of his adventures in Thraxia and his own lands, I'd say that's likely. Wait, you don't seriously think he can charm a Gygant do you?

- Enthral a creature that was born when the very mountains were young? Of course not!

- Well then, what?

- You should know Enchantment comes in many forms... it can be used to play tricks on the subject's mind, make them perceive things that are not. Even invisibility can be accomplished in this way.

Adelko thought about that. It *did* sound like something the weaselly mage would be capable of.

- I see what you're getting at. Make us invisible to the giant? But how does that get us out of this cage?

- You'll just have to wait until dawn. When the Gygant awakes, he will eat one of you, as promised. So, instead of using Morcant's wizardry to break out, you simply wait for your gaoler to do it for you...

- All right, but what if he sees – or thinks he sees – his prison cell empty? He'll just assume we somehow got out... how do we know he'll even bother to open the grille?

- Morcant's illusion will have to be twofold. One to conceal you and make it appear you aren't where you are. A second to make it seem you are where you are not...

Adelko thought quickly, and soon grasped what the sorcerer was saying.

- So the Gygant opens the grille and reaches towards what it thinks is us, but it's just a mirage! Meanwhile, the 'real we' take advantage of the distraction to escape... Clever. But, um, how do we get down safely? We must be higher up than a castle turret, I doubt Hari will have time to use his climbing gear before the Gygant realises it's been tricked by an illusion...

Again he sensed rather than heard the infuriating giggle.

- I did warn you that you might not like this plan...

Morcant's eyes bulged. To save time Adelko had decided not to tell them the idea he'd just described was Sha'arza's. Horskram was glaring at him suspiciously – but Adelko's familiarity with wizards and their ways could be explained by his adventures and studies.

You've kept enough secrets in your time, Master Horskram, now it's someone else's turn.

The wizard was shaking his head. 'The illusions alone would tax poor Morcant heavily,' he said. 'But the Thaumaturgy you are asking for on top, it cannot be done. Not even after a whole night of rest.'

Sha'arza had anticipated this, and Adelko knew what to say next.

'Well, your third spell doesn't have to be perfect...' The journeyman grimaced awkwardly as he waited for the mage to grasp his full meaning.

Horskram chose that moment to cut in. 'If it isn't, we risk breaking every bone in our bodies. Reus Almighty willed it in the beginning that all things must be pulled to the earth – what the Thalamian loremaster Archimus called gravity and the Muradi sage Ibn Bruni called the heavenly pull of celestial bodies. What you're asking Morcant to do is more difficult than breaking yon binds on our cage – and on top of that you expect him to conjure up illusions! Not only is your plan blasphemous, it's sheer folly.'

'Well, you come up with something, Master Horskram,' said Adelko, losing patience with his crabby mentor.

Horskram was preparing his next acid retort when Hari cut in. 'Wait, it might just work,' he said. Reaching into his pack, he produced the slickly oiled rope and grapnel he carried. 'If we use natural means and unnatural in tandem...' A crafty light entered the rogue's dark eyes as they rested on a suitably gnarled hole in the niche wall. 'If I fix my grapnel to that and loop the rope around us... it isn't long enough to cover the whole distance, but it should cover most of it.' He squinted down through the grille at the cavern floor far below, lit only by spurts of magma that came from the Gygant's extremities and pooled around it, his brow furrowing as he swiftly calculated the distance.

Turning back to address Morcant, he asked: 'Do you think you could conjure enough magick to break our fall, say from a height of half a dozen men or so?'

Morcant was wincing, but Adelko sensed a glimmer of hope in the mage. 'Very difficult still it would be,' he said. 'But perhaps reverse the laws of the *gods* ' – he shot a pointed glance Horskram's way – 'I could, somewhat. I warn you though, a bumpy landing it would be! And my concentration broken too... The illusion will fail and the Gygant will know it's not us up here in the cave!'

'But by then we'll be out,' said Adelko triumphantly. 'Hari cuts the rope, Morcant cushions our landing as best he can, and then we run for all we're worth. Horskram and I encountered a Gygant at the Warlock's Crown – they're as slow of foot as they are of wit, we have a chance of getting out!'

His mentor was rubbing his beard. 'It's by far the maddest plan I've ever heard, but it might just work.'

'I don't see what other plans we have,' said Jonas flatly. 'Unless you want to let it eat one more of us and hope to break out of the cage the following night. And, just to be clear, I may be the oldest and frailest here, but I am certainly not volunteering to be the sacrifice!'

'Who says we'd ask you, monk?' asked Azelin darkly. It was the word 'ask' and not 'you' he'd chosen to emphasise.

'It probably won't want him anyway,' quipped Hari. 'Look at him, he's all skin and bone!'

But the joke fell flat, and Adelko knew he couldn't afford to let his companions countenance the alternative a moment longer.

'No,' he said firmly. 'It has to be this way – everyone has to at least have a chance of escaping alive. If that doesn't happen... well, then at least we tried to do it the right way.'

Everyone was looking at him now. Not as one looks upon a madman, but as one does a leader. Tugging at his cowl, he tried to hide the flush that came to his cheeks as he continued quickly: 'So let's be about it, gents. Morcant, you should retire and get as much rest as you can. Hari, you tie the rope and loop it around us – you'll be the man doing the cutting, so don't forget to make sure you're at the top! I presume the Silver Shadow taught you how to break falls anyway, so it's probably best if you fall furthest if you don't mind my saying. Elias, is it true what the loremasters say about bones becoming more brittle as one gets older?'

The adept and physician blinked in surprise at the alacrity of the question, but nodded his assent.

'Excellent. Then, Jonas, you should go at the bottom. I'll be tied next after Hari, seeing as how I'm the youngest. Besides, it's my plan so it seems only fair that I take the most risk. Horskram, you'll have to go down the bottom after

Jonas. That leaves Azelin, Elias and Morcant to arrange themselves as they like.' He raked the company with his eyes. 'Are we agreed?'

As one, they nodded.

'Good. Now, let's all of us try to get some rest too! Tomorrow is going to be a busy morning.'

Refracted rays of sunlight eased stalky fingers about the doglegged cavern many hours later. All had slept fitfully; except Morcant, who much to their collective relief had experienced no difficulty in dropping off, exhausted as he was by his psychic travails.

A gusty wind was blowing from outside, and once again Adelko wondered just where in the Known World they were. The Gygant's body gave off enough heat and light to render no fires necessary: but the journeyman could sense the chill in the air nonetheless.

Hari had lashed them all together the previous night, arranging the group as Adelko had instructed. The grapnel he'd wedged firmly in the niche, the expertly crafted prongs experiencing no difficulty biting into the gnarled rock. It wouldn't hold all of them for long... but long enough for Morcant to cast his spell and Hari to cut them free. There'd been no chance to resume contact with Abdel Sha'arza – he'd just have to hope his interpretation of the archmage's plan would work.

As the light gradually hardened, Adelko nudged Morcant awake. He was next in line to the journeyman, with Azelin and Elias in the middle and Horskram and Jonas at the far end of the rope as arranged. Hari clutched his long knife and crouched by the grille, his body tense.

Below them, the Gygant abruptly stopped snoring as

daylight awoke it. It sounded like the sound the last rockfall of an avalanche would make, and all the companions quailed at the prospect of the madcap undertaking before them.

'Now!' hissed Adelko, but Morcant was already focusing, his eyes rolling into the back of his head as he mouthed the syllables to his spell and focused on the abstract symbols that had to be visualised perfectly for it to work.

For one heart-stopping moment, Adelko thought it wouldn't; but as the giant rose he sensed a subtle shift. He could still see all his friends, but the glamour was conjured: for as long as Morcant could keep it going, the Gygant would look upon them and see naught but thin air.

That done, he began another incantation. It sounded to Adelko's untrained ear much like the first: the syllables were syrupy sweet and brought a sickly pleasure, as one might take from eating too many glazed cakes at a rich lord's feasting table.

But nothing happened. No mirage duplicating them appeared. As the Gygant stood and stretched and gave vent to a crashing yawn that brought motes of dust showering down from the cavern ceiling, Adelko looked at Morcant in panic. But no, the mage's face remained taut but calm, a mask of concentration.

And then he realised.

No of course, it's an Enchantment. He's targeting the Gygant into believing it sees something that isn't there, not us.

His hopes were confirmed as the monstrous creature turned its gargantuan head to peer through the makeshift grille that had caused them so much trouble. It's molten eyes burned brightly as they fixed on an empty spot in the middle of the cave, and a loathsome tongue ran across millstone teeth that still had shreds of poor Bertram's habit stuck in it. There was nothing sweet about the sickly feeling that spectacle conjured up in Adelko's gut, but he didn't have to endure it for long.

With a hungry roar, the Gygant tore the grille free with one hand, reaching towards the illusion spot with the other, gobbets of magma spurting from its fingers. With an awful leer, it closed them around what it imagined to be one of them, tilting its head back to drop the morsel down its gullet. But as stupid as the monster was, it wasn't *that* stupid – already it was raising the grille back up to jam it in place again...

'Now!' hissed Hari.

Jonas's quick prayer was cut shorter by Horskram, who shoved him off the lip of the cave recess before jumping off the ledge. Hard on their heels Elias went next, then Azelin, followed by Morcant.

Adelko forced every rational instinct from his mind as he stepped out into thin air, but he couldn't help the cry of terror that erupted from his lungs as he plummeted.

When falling try as much as you can to relax, Hari had told them all. *Imagine your body to be a feather, even as you know yourself to be jumping of your own free will! Silver Shadow savants have said Enlightenment can come to one who learns how to fall.*

Esoteric bloody nonsense, Adelko found just enough time to think as the rope suddenly pulled up taught, jerking them around like rag dolls. The choler was pumping through his body now, muting the agonised wrench he felt under his armpits, where Hari had tied the rope tightly enough to be secure but not to restrict his breathing. The rogue's genius probably saved their lives at that point, for somehow they were all still in one piece.

For now. Morcant's concentration broken, his illusions faded. It took the Gygant a few seconds to realise its mouth was empty, before it turned fiery eyes to the floor of the cavern, wondering dully if it had dropped its morning meal.

Still it had not noticed them, though they were fully visible now, swinging wildly from the rope.

Below him Adelko could hear Morcant's rasping voice as he gasped out the syllables to his last spell. This one carried an unbearable lightness to its cadence, as one gets from drinking far too much wine or mead, carried away in a spirit of intoxicating joy that must be paid for eventually.

Glancing up, he saw Hari directly above him, his legs entwined dexterously about the rope, knife poised to cut. Adelko flicked a glance back down to Morcant, but he was still mouthing the words in the language of magick.

The Gygant had returned its gaze to the cave recess. Finding it empty, it gave vent to another roar, this one of surprised frustration. A shower of rock dust struck Adelko, causing him to splutter and cough. He prayed he'd taken the worst of it and Morcant wouldn't be put off his spell.

The Gygant cast its eyes around the cavern, struggling to fathom what had just happened. But it was only a matter of time before it turned back around, and caught them dangling like trussed mice on the end of the rope...

Just then he felt a tap on his boot, the signal from Morcant. Reaching up, he tugged frantically on Hari's calf. The outlander had sharpened his knife blade to a keen razor edge: a single slice, and the rope holding them was cloven in twain.

Adelko's heart lurched back into his mouth as they fell again... but this time was different. They were still descending at a frightening pace, but it seemed to slow as they moved towards the floor of the cavern. It wasn't quite floating, but it wasn't a headlong plummet either. Morcant's spell was working!

Working up to a point. Another cry escaped him as he landed with a jolt on the hard rock floor. Picking himself up, he was relieved to find no bones broken, or none that he needed right now at least. Reaching down, he yanked Morcant upright too; Hari had landed on his feet like a cat, and Horskram and Azelin were helping Jonas and Elias to theirs.

A hideous wash of heat told him the Gygant had finally noticed them with its white-hot eyes.

It reached down towards them, magma sputtering from its fingertips. They were still bound together, and only then did the flaw in Adelko's plan reveal itself: it would save all of them, or none at all.

A piercing cry from Jonas. He'd broken a leg; unable to stand, he collapsed back to the floor. In a flash Hari stepped across, slashing the rope between Jonas and Horskram.

'Now!' he cried. 'All together, run!'

The six of them made a shambolic dash towards the bend in the dogleg of the cavern. Twice they tripped and fell, but luckily for them the great brute's base instincts had got the better of it.

Luckily for them, but not for Jonas. The old monk screamed as a gobbet of lava landed on him, his body convulsing as it sizzled to a crisp and the Gygant plucked him from the floor, popping him in its mouth and chewing pitilessly. Just as they rounded the bend, it began to lope towards them, its crashing feet sending tremors through the cavern floor as it tried to muster some speed.

The blizzard hit them full force as they emerged into the part of the cavern that opened out on to the skies.

The natural heat of the Gygant's volcanic body, and the dogleg shape of the cavern, had obscured what was now all too apparent: they were high up in some mountain range, where snows lay thick and the winds blew raw and white.

But they had no time to worry about that. Another roar told them the giant was just around the corner, intent on finishing its meal. They dashed towards the cave entrance, which fortunately narrowed somewhat: it was still vast to them, but the Gygant had to stoop to enter it, slowing the monstrosity down even more.

Exiting the cavern mouth, they emerged on to a vast shelf of rock. The flurried snows obscured their vision, the cold wind biting them to the quick. Panic rose in Adelko once more as he realised the snows were knee deep; enough to slow them down, but nothing more than a light frost for their pursuer.

Hari was casting around, and his keen eyes saw it just as Adelko's sixth sense registered the same: directly to their left, the shelf terminated abruptly in a sheer drop. Dragging them over towards it with a speed and strength borne of instinct, Yassin peered over the edge.

It was a long drop, but a thick blanket of snow covered the ledge directly below. It might just break their fall...

Another roar, as the Gygant dragged its loathsome carcass through the cavern mouth. It struggled to spot its prey in the blizzard, but it wouldn't be much longer before it did.

The six of them exchanged terrified glances.

'It's this, or we die,' said Hari.

As if to confirm his words, the Gygant gave another roar as it finally spotted them. A spurt of magma landed an arm's length away from Elias, turning the snows nearby into a hissing pile of slush as the monster took one giant step out on to the shelf.

Clutching each other tightly, the companions stepped up to the edge, and jumped.

CHAPTER 11

HOLDING THE FORT

The captured Bethler knights moaned piteously atop the spikes they had been impaled upon, their white kirtles turning red as their bodies slid slowly down the poles.

But there was no pity to be spared for men who had brought so much misery to ordinary Sassanians: or so Muqmurlish had decreed, while swearing that ordinary knights and footsoldiers taken alive would be spared and treated chivalrously.

So far, he'd kept his word: the regular men-at-arms who'd laid down their arms when it became clear a garrison force scarcely more than a hundred strong would not hold out long against the Sultan's vast host had been disarmed and detained but nothing else.

Not so the warrior-monks, who'd refused to surrender and cut down many more *amluqs* before finally being overwhelmed. The soldier who'd betrayed them – opening the gate that permitted access to the square four-turreted bailey protecting the keep in response to Muqmurlish's offer of surrender – had been bundled off.

Anupe did not know what fate held in store for such a

traitor, but gazing upon the Bethlers dying agonisingly in the courtyard as the sharpened stakes gradually pierced deeper into their vitals, she felt little kindness to spare for them herself. The Kerakans were notorious for their oppression of the native populace, and besides that, several of them had just tried to kill her.

Tried, but failed. Cleaning the gore from her falchion she ignored the blanket of corpses carpeting the fortress grounds and looked around for the others, but they were nowhere to be seen. Doubtless Tipu was somewhere far removed, his blessings given, now washing his hands of the slaughter that had followed. As for the recondite Zarumani, who knew? His fire magicks had served a useful purpose, terrifying the garrison with explosions that sent them fleeing from the gate-house battlements, but since their surrender he too had disappeared.

Muqmurlish's decision to forsake the main road to Sha'iza'ar, striking out west before crossing the Utna'aruf ranges just south of Keraka instead of neighbouring Usha-layim had taken the crusaders unawares.

The Sultan's outriders had returned not long after the fort's surrender, bringing their latest reports: the main crusader army of Keraka had finally got wind of Muqmurlish's manoeuvre thanks to its own scouts, and was now marching to meet them on the southern plains of the kingdom.

Muqmurlish and most of the army had descended from the ranges to engage them in a pitched battle, but it was one Anupe was not destined to fight in.

The Sultan had chosen to leave Zimri's cohort behind to hold the fortress, just in case the *jhufa'ar* tried a circling movement of their own.

Anupe felt sour about that. *We proved ourselves handy enough in battle, but still he doesn't seem to trust outlanders – or women.* Resentfully she tugged at the makeshift veil she was obliged to wear – she couldn't deny that that and the hood of her cloak lent her a more fearsome appearance in the field, but still Anupe despised the reasons that compelled her to adopt such garb.

But she probably shouldn't complain: garrison duty was an easy way to earn the thirty silver denarii a week she'd been hired at. Taking out a whetstone to sharpen her freshly cleaned blade, she sat down casually on a corpse to calculate how much an extended campaign might earn her.

Not a corpse quite yet: the soldier gave a bloody belch as he took her full weight. In a flash her dirk was out, and Anupe buried it in his ear, transfixing his brain and putting a final end to his suffering.

She picked up her dropped falchion and whetstone and resumed her sharpening.

Where was she? Oh yes, money: twenty silvers to a golden riyaad, if the campaign lasted a year that would see her bring in some eighty golds. Not bad considering her upkeep would be covered by the Sceptre for the duration of her contract.

Her thoughts began to drift towards early retirement. Together with the sum she'd saved from her adventures with Horskram and Adhelina, that might just give her enough to buy a farm: as an added inducement, Muqmurlish had promised all serving soldiers, including mercenaries, a good deal on any lands taken from the *jhufa'ar* crusaders. And the Sultan planned to take it all.

Her pleasant reverie was interrupted by Zimri, who came striding up to her. He was alone this time, bereft of his lieutenants Kufa and Batu.

'So where did everyone go?' Anupe deadpanned as the young general drew level with her. She made a point of loosening the cloth scarf she wore as she spoke – the Southron at least had no problem looking upon her face.

Zimri cracked a smile. 'They are building palisades on the

approach,' he said. 'His Eminence will take no chances! I spared you the labour, though our captive *jhufa'ar* friends have their work cut out for them – but we must needs keep a close eye on them.'

Anupe nodded. 'This makes sense.' Then she nodded towards the keep, left intact thanks to the garrison's surrender. 'It would be nice to get somewhere cooler though.' Despite it being late in the day, the cloudy skies made for a sweltering sultry heat. Many in the attacking force must have been secretly glad to see the fighting over quickly.

Zimri clapped her on the shoulder. At least he knew how to treat her like the warrior she was: some of the idiots in his company still seemed to view her as some kind of lady.

'Have no fear, Anupe of Hamazos! Not all my men are needed to guard our captive workforce – we come now to take up residence, there is no telling how long we'll be here so we may as well get comfortable. Not too comfortable though, lest the crusaders should mount a counter attack.'

Anupe felt her hopes rise. 'You really think they'll try that?'

Zimri frowned. 'Admittedly, this is unlikely. The Kerakans are fierce fighters, but they'll be outnumbered – most likely they will have mustered all available forces to engage His Eminence.'

Anupe stroked the edge of her blade with her oilstone with a pointed flourish. 'Meaning, we sit here and do nothing while others take the glory.'

Zimri looked at her searchingly. Already she could see several dozen of his *taziqs* entering the courtyard, directing auxiliaries to start cleaning up the corpses.

'And why would that bother a freesword who gets paid by the day regardless?' he queried.

Anupe shrugged as she continued her sharpening.

'A girl gets bored is all,' she said non-committally. 'It seems a shame to be invited on the campaign of the century, only to miss most of the fun.'

Zimri's face darkened. 'You call this fun?' he gestured towards the dead bodies. 'I told you my story when first we met. I do what I must to secure my own future and, one day I hope, that of my people. But tell me what is glorious about this slaughter? Would you rather not live out your days in peace if you could?'

Another non-committal shrug. 'Peace has never run so quickly in the veins of my people,' replied Anupe. 'And besides, I don't have a kingdom to return to, unlike you. I have to make my own way in this world – and battles mean plunder.'

Zimri shook his head. 'I am an exile just the same as you,' he said. 'There are no guarantees for me either – save what His Eminence and Uru Almighty will for me.' He devoutly made the sign of the Faith, raising his eyes to the gloomy heavens.

Anupe continued to sharpen her falchion unmoved. 'Perhaps,' she said. 'But you are exiled because of a foreign invader, one you hope to overcome one day. I was sent away by my own people, and that means for Anupe, there can be no returning.'

Zimri looked at her with pity in his eyes. 'Yours is a sorry tale, and I apologise if I have offended,' he said sincerely. 'But perhaps I can offer you some comfort. If by the Almighty's grace the hour I hope for comes, I offer you a place in my own kingdom, should it be in my gift to reclaim it.'

Anupe paused in her sharpening. That *did* surprise her – Zimri seemed more open-minded than most men, but she hadn't thought it would run quite this far.

'You'd offer me a place in your realm?'

Zimri opened his arms expansively. 'As a respected member of my honour guard in Kushia, why not?' He wagged a finger knowingly at her. 'It is not so strange an offer as you seem to think – in fact, our seventh king, Baraka, had a palace bodyguard comprised only of women to fight for him. Our *djalis* still sing of the Sable Lionesses and their puissance and loyalty.' A pained expression crossed his face. 'Alas, they were betrayed one by one, by the treacherous pretender, Kovi, who lured them into a trap – '

Anupe raised a calloused hand, cutting him off. 'Thank you, General Zimri, I think I like the first part of the story better,' she grinned. 'And should you be in a place to make good on this offer, I will most certainly consider it when the time comes.'

Zimri grinned and clapped her on the shoulder again. 'That is the spirit, Anupe of Hamazos! Never lose hope until you have breathed your last!'

Just then a Nazharyan *taziq* approached him, a perplexed look on his face. Zimri turned to address him in Sassanic.

'Our men on the palisades have just sent word back to us,' said Zimri, translating the brief exchange for Anupe's benefit. 'They've spotted an enemy host, approaching from the south.'

'How many?' asked Anupe.

'Not more than fifty, but all are heavily armed and mounted,' replied Zimri. 'And we've barely begun work on the palisades.'

Anupe tried not to grin as she rose, falchion in hand.

'Well, Anupe of Hamazos,' said Zimri, sensing her elation regardless. 'It seems His Eminence was right to be cautious. You will get the action you crave, and our dreams will just have to wait a little longer.'

Your dreams perhaps, thought Anupe cynically, her mind turning once more to bloodshed and plunder.

CHAPTER 12

IN THE ATTIC OF THE WORLD

He couldn't breathe. His body numbed by an awful cold that threatened to rob him of his last strength, Adelko tried to stay calm, the words of a psalm coming to him as he struggled to focus –

He felt the rope around him go taut and pull him upwards. He tried to help the effort, but all he could do was flail his arms around. Then he gasped as his head suddenly cleared the snowdrift. Hari was perched on a higher part of the ledge they had landed on, pulling for all he was worth.

'Stop thrashing around like a fish out of water!' yelled the rogue. 'Pull!'

Adelko realised what he meant and fastened his hands around the length of rope connecting him to Morcant, struggling to find purchase for his feet as he did.

It was agonisingly slow, but they managed to pull the mage free. But the rope connecting him to Azelin was severed...

With a great roar the knight erupted from the snow. Dirk in hand, he thrashed awkwardly towards the upper section of the ledge.

But where were Horskram and Elias?

'Azelin, pull!' Adelko repeated Hari's command, but then saw the futility of it: the knight had managed to cut the rope where it looped around his chest, freeing him entirely.

Just then a hand punched up through the snows, not far from where Azelin had emerged. In a flash Adelko's quarterstaff was off his back; holding it out gingerly, he touched Horskram's hand with it and the old monk grasped it desperately. Azelin was already reaching across, plunging his hands into the snow around the adept. With another roar he pulled the monk clear of the drift. As Horskram spluttered and coughed, the rest of them scoured the snow-shrouded ledge with anxious eyes.

'Elias!' cried Adelko. 'Where in Seven Princes is he?'

A growing patch of red that suddenly appeared next to Horskram gave the answer to that question.

But they had no time to dig their stricken companion out. Another roar, far louder, alerted them to the persistent danger above them. Looking up, Adelko felt his blood run colder than any snow as he saw the towering figure of the Gygant looming over the edge of the rock shelf, arm held high and clutching a boulder. No bigger than a child's ball in its hand, it would sweep them off the ledge if it made contact – if it didn't simply crush them outright.

'Azelin!' screamed Horskram. 'Your knife!'

Adelko's heart stopped as he registered the rope tied around Horskram's chest, disappearing beneath the snow towards where the bloody patch grew steadily bigger.

Azelin tossed Horskram the dirk and he began frantically sawing and hacking at the rope binding him to poor Elias. Just then the Gygant released its missile – the rest of them pressed themselves as far back towards the mountainside as they could.

The boulder hurtled past, missing the far edge of the ledge and crashing down into the ravine below it.

'I'm free!' cried Horskram, who had just cut through the rope with a frenzied strength. Reaching over, Azelin began pulling him from the drift. Hari was already scrabbling down the upper part of the ledge, which snaked back at an incline around the mountain. Adelko clumsily followed suit, Morcant hard on his heels.

Another roar. The giant had taken up a second boulder, and flung it downwards. This time it caught the edge, breaking off a great chunk and sending flurries of snow and shards of stone flying up in its wake as it hurtled down into the ravine.

The three of them rounded the bend of the incline, pausing to catch their breath. Morcant was last, and risked a look round the knuckle of rock now hiding them from the Gygant's view.

'Still there they are,' he said of their companions. 'But they can't follow us! Yon fiend's rock has smashed the ledge, too narrow it is now!'

Adelko grabbed the mage's reedy arm. 'Do something!' he yelled. 'We can't just abandon them!'

Morcant gazed at him desperately. 'Like what?'

'Another illusion, something to distract it, a bridge, I don't bloody know – just do something!'

He could see Morcant's energies were already sorely taxed by the morning's efforts, but he tightened his grip on the warlock's arm.

'I know your energies are weak, but you have to try,' he said, pushing his face up close to the wizard's. 'Just. Try.'

Morcant nodded and rolled his eyes up into his head

again, focusing as he conjured another spell. Hari had slipped agilely past them to take up point at the bend.

'Can't see our charming host, it's looking for another boulder I think,' he said. 'Probably won't be long till it finds one!'

'What are the others doing?' Adelko demanded.

'They're trying to navigate the broken ledge,' said Hari. 'Child's play for me, but not for them. At least yon brute has cleared the snows so they can see, but it's left them a perilous narrow crossing!'

Morcant was still muttering in the language of magick, his head inclined up towards the rock shelf that adjoined the cave exit. His spell done, he collapsed with a moan. Adelko had to catch him for fear of losing him to the ravine.

'They're halfway across!' cried Hari. 'Still no sign of that beastly colossus.'

'That's because... it's trying... to dislodge... a rock... that doesn't exist,' said Morcant in barely more than a whisper, a half-smile on his exhausted face.

Adelko hugged the mage as he held him. 'I knew you could do it! Well done, Morcant!'

'Can't hold it... for much longer...'

The mage suddenly went limp in Adelko's arms. He wasn't heavy, but his body weight caught the journeyman off-guard, and he would have slipped off the edge had Hari not caught him.

'Come, their fate is in Ashanti's hands now,' said the rogue, glancing over Adelko's shoulder with keen eyes. 'This part of the ledge widens out further down, let's get ourselves down there.'

Between them they managed to manhandle Morcant's limp form down the incline to where the ledge cut more deeply into the mountainside. They had just lowered him to the ground when Horskram and Azelin rounded the bend, moving towards them as the Gygant gave vent to a frustrated roar of anger.

The sound reverberated off the mountain tops, rocks and snow cascading downwards in its wake.

'There!' cried Hari, pointing to where a gnarled overhanging of rock overshadowed the back of the recess they now stood upon. 'It's our only chance against an avalanche!'

They would have had trouble dragging Morcant, but Azelin and Horskram wasted no time joining them, half sliding down the last of the incline, and together they hauled the unconscious mage to shelter.

The first rocks came crashing down around them as they reached the safety of the overhang.

Muttering the Psalm of Fortitude for the umpteenth time, Adelko registered the snows finally abating with grateful eyes.

None of them had dared move for the next hour or so. Fortunately the rockslide hadn't been as bad as Hari feared, but the keen blizzard kept up nonetheless, and it was then that they became fully aware of the next thing that would try to kill them: the shivering cold.

Now at least the skies were clearing somewhat, but they remained ill-prepared: they'd had the foresight to change into warmer undergarments back at the monastery, anticipating unpredictable climate in Varya. But high up in the mountains, with thinner air and starker skies... This they weren't prepared for.

At least Morcant had regained his senses – perhaps he could magick up a small fire to keep them warm. But one look at the mage's sunken eyes and wan complexion told Adelko there would be no magick to save them, not for now anyway.

For his part, Horskram stared out at the pewter skies with hard brittle eyes.

'Three good men we added to our quest,' he muttered. 'And three good men we lost. A thousand thank-yous, Reus Almighty.'

'Testing your faith is He?' sneered Azelin, his old sour humour emboldened by their circumstances. 'Don't worry, perhaps He'll conjure up a winged chariot for us in recognition of our efforts on His behalf.'

'No, he won't,' said Adelko, tugging at Horskram's sleeve. 'But He might just be giving us a sign – look there!'

All turned to see what the thinning snows had revealed to the journeyman's casual glance. Faint and far-off, yes, but unmistakeable. A mighty fortress: similar in positioning to Ortiz, it seemingly grew up out of the mountains. Its compact form, smooth regular symmetry and absence of ornamentation put it at odds with any castle Adelko had yet seen.

But Horskram recognised it immediately. 'Reus' teeth, that's one of the Seven Fortresses!' he exclaimed.

They turned to look at him questioningly.

'The mountain redoubts the Imperials built centuries ago, to guard the approaches to their realm. We're in the Great White Mountains, right on the border of the Urovian New Empire.'

Hari managed a wry smile. 'Well, that's one step closer to our ultimate destination, I suppose.'

'One step closer to succour is what it is,' said Horskram, growing excited. 'Morcant, are you fit enough to walk at least? We must get to that fortress – the Imperials might not let us through, but they're bound by their laws to offer food and shelter to any wayfarers who cross their path and aren't hostile.' He scoured the skyline. 'We've a whole day before nightfall to get there, or as close as we can. Once we're within sight of the fortress, maybe we can signal them.'

'It's as good a plan as any,' said Hari, helping Morcant to his feet.

With no further word spoken, they began their descent of the mountain.

The morning came and went. Their journey was a slow and painful one; for none of them had any knowledge of the Great White Mountains, leaving little choice but to take a meandering course while trying to keep the fortress in sight. The snows resentfully hindered their passage, and more than once Morcant, still fragile, nearly slipped and fell to his doom.

But they had to press on, for aside from the weather another unspoken problem lingered: with limited food and no guide, time was their newest enemy. At least the snows provided them with some alternative to water once their skins ran empty. Hard tack from the kitchens would just have to keep them going until then: salted and cured beef that had to be chewed relentlessly to be edible, and tough biscuit that put Adelko in mind of the horrible sea voyage to Ushalayim.

Abdel, we could use your winged chariot right now, never mind one from the heavens, thought Adelko as they paused to take their miserable afternoon meal. He was too far gone in despondency to care whether he was blaspheming now; if they didn't reach the fortress before nightfall Reus would soon get His chance to judge him for it in any case.

Once again he thought about contacting the sorcerer another time, but what could Sha'arza do for them? They were hundreds of miles away from his tower; a ride didn't seem a likely prospect.

'The clouds are breaking,' said Azelin, sullenly swallowing his last mouthful of food and pointing at the emerging blue patch in the skies with his waterskin. 'We must have descended a few hundred yards as well, at least we've a better chance of surviving the night if we don't reach yon fortress in time.'

'Which we aren't likely to,' put in Hari, gesturing towards where the thick edifice squatted on a mountainside some leagues away. More than six hours of travelling, and they'd hardly got any closer.

But Azelin was right: the cold was less biting now, and as the first rays of sun streaked across them Adelko felt his spirits rise somewhat. It was still cold, the air thin, but the dizzying ordeal of the morning was starting to feel like a thing of the past, to say nothing of the latest horror they had just escaped.

His limbs were sore and weary nonetheless. Once again he had to thank Edemus for his rigorous training of the previous summer; somehow he found the strength to continue when Horskram told them to get up and get going.

Not so Morcant. The poor mage groaned, slumping back down again as he feebly tried to rise. Azelin grunted non-committally and hauled the slight Islander over his shoulders, barely seeming to pause in his stride. Once again Adelko had to marvel at the man's strength, stamina, and sure-footedness, which rivalled his old comrade Sir Torgun's.

You put some potent tools our way, Reus Almighty, that much I'll grant you.

But as ever, he had to wonder if even the best of tools would be enough to finish the work that same deity had ordained for them.

～

The afternoon wore on, and every step brought relief to Adelko's gasping lungs – and pain to his ailing legs. By the time Horskram called another rest, they were cramping badly. His companions were faring little better – all except Hari, that is, who seemed as spry and sprightly as he had done at the beginning of the day. Adelko could only wonder at the rigorous training the Old Master of Time's Arrow had put him to before he went for a rogue.

Hari was shading his eyes now, as he squinted towards the fortress. 'It's definitely closer,' he said triumphantly. 'And the sun is right welcome too! The snows are thinning, we must have descended another couple of hundred yards as well.'

The dispersing clouds were indeed welcome, though the hardening sun they revealed was not entirely their ally: Adelko shifted uncomfortably at the layer of sweat that had permeated his undergarments. Somehow you always seemed to notice that kind of thing on a trek more when you stopped to rest.

'How much more daylight do you think we have?' he asked, keen to direct his thoughts away from his body.

Hari squinted some more as he tilted his head slightly towards where the sun was slowly scudding across the skies on its diurnal journey.

'Probably three or four hours.' He looked back towards the fortress, whose vast but seamless brickwork was now just about visible in the clear light. 'I think we should try to get closer, they might not see us from that far away if we light a fire signal now.'

'And we wouldn't be close enough for them to get a rescue party out before the sun sets in any case,' put in Azelin.

'I never said anything about a rescue party,' interjected Horskram. 'The Imperials are bound by their hospitable code to offer us succour if we reach the fortress. That doesn't mean expending valuable resources to help stray wayfarers get there.'

The party's spirits sank noticeably. A further gruelling trek followed by the prospect of a night in the open didn't appeal.

'At least our chances of survival are much improved,' added the old monk, trying to lighten the mood. 'As Hari says, we've made good progress – we should be less vulnerable to exposure now.'

Glancing at Morcant, who lay on his side exhausted and unmoving by the side of the rocky trail they were following, Adelko silently wondered if that applied to the mage. He seemed more fragile than ever.

'We'd better get moving then,' he told his mentor. 'The more time we spend walking the closer we'll hopefully get.'

Horskram glanced at him approvingly. 'Adelko has the right of it,' he said. 'Hardihood and dogged persistence will see us through this, by the Almighty's will. Come along, let's tarry not!'

The trail meandered fretfully for the next hour or so, eventually snaking back around the mountain. For a while they feared they would be stuck and lose their way entirely, but sometime before sunset Hari found a sloping bank of scree that broke off at an incline and down through a steep-sided gully before emerging onto another belt of peaks. The going was hard, especially for Azelin, who had to carry Morcant on his back all the way, but as the sun was disappearing behind the pinnacled skyline, the companions had cause to rejoice.

The gully had brought them out into the bottom of a ravine that passed between two more peaks, dipping down at an acute angle before climbing up again towards a third mountain, on which rested the fortress. It appeared to have been built out of the very side of the rocky slope; Adelko could only marvel at the stonemasonry that had gone into such a feat, but this was no time for sightseeing.

The other side of the ravine joined a path that wound up around the mountain; from their elevated position they could see it joined a much bigger road stretching from the west that terminated at a large platform of rock abutting on to a vast gatehouse guarding the fortress.

But to get there would be a matter of many hours, perhaps even days, for the descent and climb back up through the ravine looked punishing beyond belief.

Hari's tone was subdued as he said what they had all realised. 'Our way is clear enough, but there's no way we can reach it by tonight. If the Imperials won't come to our aid, we're probably better off resting here and now.'

He wasn't wrong; already the light was beginning to weaken. Scanning the ravine, Hari soon found what he was looking for with his keen eyes: he pointed upwards so they could all see it, a cave set back in the side of the ravine about halfway up its eastern side.

'All well and good,' muttered Azelin, 'but how are we going to get up there? The sides are almost sheer, and you had to leave your climbing gear behind when we fled that monstrosity.'

'And all the more bitterly do I regret it!' exclaimed the rogue, biting his lip fretfully as he considered the problem.

He didn't have long to ponder, for just then a piercing shriek turned their attention to the skies. Looking up to see what had made the sound, the companions let out a collective gasp. Winging its way high over the ravine with the westering sun at its back was the strangest, though hardly the most horrible, creature Adelko had yet seen: at first he took it to be a giant eagle, but then he saw its swishing tail and quadrupedal body.

'Palom's wounds, that's a Gryphon!' Horskram cried. 'Get back under cover, it'll have us for supper if it sees us!'

They ducked back into the gully. All except for Sir Azelin, that was, who unceremoniously dumped Morcant on the rock-strewn ground before drawing his greatsword in one fluid motion. He'd been forced to abandon the short sword and shield he'd taken off a Pangonian soldier at the monastery during the trek, but managed to keep hold of his primary weapon. Now he looked intent on using it.

'I've faced down a Wyrm and just survived a Gygant,' he snarled. 'This creature of fable scares me not.'

'Don't be so bloody foolish,' spat Horskram. 'You're too tired to fight!'

'I'll be the judge of that,' replied the warrior-monk, tilting his blade so its keen edge caught a last ray of dying sunlight. 'You four just stay back and leave this to me.'

Horskram cursed him using language that would have made his fellow adepts blush if they could have heard him. But it was too late for recriminations; the glint of light had caught the hybrid creature's eye, and with another shriek it wheeled around towards the gully, its huge feathered wings beating powerfully.

Sir Azelin held his ground, merely adjusting his stance on the uneven scree. His balance was superb, but even so he was clearly at a disadvantage. At least the gully mouth would restrict the Gryphon's movement somewhat as it swooped down to attack...

Morcant got up and dusted himself down. Carried all day, he appeared to have recovered slightly since the afternoon. Stepping gingerly to one side of Azelin, he began making arcane gestures as he muttered something in the language of magick. The knight was so busy focusing on his newest foe that he barely seemed to notice.

As the creature closed on them Adelko could see the description he'd read of such creatures in Jedrec's *Summation of the Elder Wizards' Fabulous Menagerie* was accurate: the Gryphon sported the head, wings and forelegs of a gigantic avian, its rear quarters being those of one of the huge cats of the Far South. Bred by the priest-kings of Varya for sport, few of the beasts survived – yet another stroke of ill luck, meeting one here.

But as it closed on them, Morcant finished his spell. The creature suddenly veered upwards, hovering some distance above Azelin, who remained clutching his sword, a puzzled expression on his face. Again the Islander spoke in the language of magick, but he did not appear to be reciting now; rather to be speaking.

The Gryphon bowed its head deferentially, before easing itself down onto the floor of the ravine, well out of range of Azelin's questing sword.

'You can put up your blade, sir knight,' Morcant told him. 'Quite safe it is! Morcant has... made a new friend.'

Azelin gaped. 'You... you can control such creatures? By the Hallowed Bethel...'

'Befriend, not control,' the mage corrected. 'Though 'tis true, it's the school of Enchantment that taught me such!' Turning to the others, he said: 'Nothing to fear now. Morcant's new friend will take us to its home.' He nodded in the direction of the high cave Hari had spotted. 'Stay there we can tonight, then tomorrow take us it will, to yonder fortress.'

Horskram's lip curled in distaste. 'Ride on the back of that blasphemous hybrid? I should think not – methinks I'll climb, thank you.'

Adelko could not resist rolling his eyes. 'Master

Horskram, we've made common cause with more than one warlock, and ridden in a flying ship commanded by one. Now you're complaining about riding a flying, um, lion?'

The crotchety adept folded his arms stubbornly. 'There are limits,' he said with a tone of finality.

Morcant smiled superciliously. 'Suit yourself.' Turning to the Gryphon, which waited patiently for them, he addressed it again in the alien tongue of wizards, before skipping lightly over the rocks and mounting its back.

'He certainly seems to have recovered his energy while I was carrying him down the bloody mountain,' muttered Azelin.

'Room for one more behind me there is,' said Morcant, still sounding tired but definitely more cheerful now. 'Two more it will carry in its claws. That leaves Horskram, who will climb up and join us.'

The mage shrugged wearily as the four of them stood staring. 'What are you waiting for? The day is waning, and Morcant is so very very tired. Coming or not?'

Hari lost no time. 'If a Gryphon it is to be, I for one will not be carried in its claws!' Darting nimbly across the rocky floor, he hopped up lightly behind Morcant.

Azelin exchanged glances with the companions and frowned. 'If it's all the same to you, I'll keep Horskram company,' he said. 'I agree our quest has brought us to strange passes, but as yon monk says there are limits.'

That just left Adelko. For a moment or two he pictured being carried aloft in the Gryphon's claws, the wind rushing through his hair as he enjoyed the exhilaration of yet another airborne journey...

Then he felt his gut tighten.

'Perhaps you're right, Master Horskram,' he said sheepishly, his eyes suddenly finding the rocky ground. 'Climbing it is, then.'

Dusk was yielding to true night by the time the three of them joined Hari and Morcant in the Gryphon's cave. Just to be safe, the mage had bade the strange creature hover above them in case one of them should fall, and a weak light spell helped them to see better in the gathering gloom.

None of that assuaged the physical torment of the climb, and Adelko collapsed gratefully on the floor of the cave just inside the entrance directly his trembling limbs had hauled him over the edge and into it. Hari grinned at him from the other side of the small fire he'd built while waiting for them, tossing him some smoked meat, dried biscuit and a waterskin.

'Feast, Adelko!' he said cheerily. 'You look as though you could use it!'

'You look as though you could rest that tongue of yours,' the journeyman managed to gasp, though he quaffed gratefully from the skin, emptying it in no time.

Before long the five of them were settled in the cave, which offered a magnificent view of the western peaks, starkly silhouetted against a deep blue sky. But soon that vision was lost to them, as the archangel Morphonus took up his sceptre for another night, when the world slept and perchance dreamed.

Glancing back into the cave, Adelko started as he was rewarded with an altogether less appealing spectacle. A hecatomb of bones picked clean greeted his tired eyes; though most of them were animals, he fancied he saw one or two ribcages that looked all-too human among the morass of remains piled up behind them.

'Krwoa'ark is rather untidy,' said Morcant, chuckling as he caught the look of discomfort in the journeyman's eyes. 'He apologises for not cleaning his lair, but after all he was not expecting guests!'

'This thing has a name?' said Azelin, glaring suspiciously at where the Gryphon sat proudly atop the pile of bones, its avian eyes inscrutable in the firelight. He'd sheathed his sword to make the climb, but had kept it right beside him since entering the cave.

'In point of fact many,' said Morcant. 'For hunted in these mountains he did when the Empire was young, aye and long before that. But he says he likes Krwoa'ark best of all. It was the name given to him by the the sorcerer Ashokainan, when that great wizard did dwell in these ranges in the Tower of the Elder Ones.'

Horskram's eyes lit up at mention of the legendary warlock who was distantly connected with their quest.

'It has known wizards?' he asked. 'Could it carry us to Varya?'

Adelko practically glared at his mentor now. 'After we almost broke ourselves climbing up here? Now you want to ride on the Gryphon after all?'

Horskram waved his understudy's protests away irritably. 'I had time to think during the climb is all,' he said. 'And you're probably right – any agency the Almighty puts our way must be used to His benefit, if it be His will.'

Adelko was shaking his head in disbelief, but Morcant forestalled further discussion.

'Asked him already I have,' he said. 'But Krwoa'ark will not venture there. Enslaved he was in Varya, he and many others like him. He will never return, for cursed his birthplace has become since the world's breaking. In fact he will not even speak of it.'

'So he – *it* – can't even tell us what to expect?' said Horskram sourly. 'Pah, I should know better than to place any kind of faith in a creature of the Elder Wizards in any case. Can it at least get us to yonder fortress?'

Morcant was nodding enthusiastically now. 'It must

remain out of range of its ballistae, but close enough yes,' he replied.

'That will have to do,' said Horskram, suddenly sounding very tired himself. 'I suggest we all get some rest, it's been a long day.'

No one disagreed. They wrapped themselves up as best as they could in their travelling cloaks, the cave and fire offering welcome respite from the shivering winds without.

Just before Adelko fell into Morphonus' arms, he caught the Gryphon, watching over them like a sentinel. Was it his tired imagination, or was there a hint of ages-old sorrow in its shining black eyes?

CHAPTER 13

SERPENTS FROM THE SEA

At least they didn't breathe fire, like their bigger cousins of legend. That was about the only crumb of comfort Vaskrian had to chew on, as he and Braxus and the other Thraxian knights huddled under the darkling branches.

The trees of the copse they'd sought for succour might protect them against the dread Wyverns, but the coming of night would not: terrified cries that punctuated the silence told that the airborne predators saw just as well in darkness as they did in daylight.

He'd been in this kind of situation before, of course. Cowering in the woods and hiding from a winged supernatural horror that chased him across the wilderness... That was how his great adventure had begun, after all.

But back then, in the Laegawood, they'd been pursued by just a single fiend, and one that couldn't attack them by day at least. Now they faced a host of horrors dozens strong that seemed to know neither rest nor respite. When they'd fled the Strang Ranges for their lives, scattering to the Four Winds, he'd managed to catch enough glimpses of them to fathom their size: they weren't nearly as big as the Wyrms were said to have been, but moved with a speed and ferocity that had devastated Thraxians and Northlendings alike. For their part, when the Northland reavers defending Strongholm had realised the awful things were on their side, they'd ditched crossbows in favour of flagons and jeeringly watched the show, as their enemies abruptly broke formation and fled in search of cover.

There would be no siege to retake Strongholm any time soon.

'What's the hour?' barked Braxus, his gruff tone doing little to hide his obvious terror. Though as bold as any knight, he'd nearly gone to pieces at the sight of a Gygant at the Warlock's Crown, although he'd held his nerve well enough against the Golem they'd fought during that adventure. And now this... It was an encounter to test the mettle of the bravest warrior.

'Hard to tell beneath these trees,' muttered the scarred veteran addressed by Braxus. He had the look of a common man recently rewarded with the spurs – a man of Vaskrian's sort, in other words. 'I'd say it has to be not more than two hours before Wytching Time.'

'We need to try to meet up with Sir Torgun and the others,' faltered Vaskrian, unsure of what he was saying. 'You know of our early adventures, before we met you, Lord Braxus. We were pursued by a winged... thing. But together we managed to fight it off, Torgun and I and the White Valravyn garrison at Staerkvit. If we can get together our toughest knights, we might stand a chance.'

Braxus's face could barely be seen in the gloom, but even so Vaskrian could tell he scarcely looked convinced.

'Aye, Sir Vaskrian, but that was one foe you faced. One thing it is to coordinate a single group of twenty against a dread enemy – quite another to do the same thing a hundredfold.'

Vaskrian's heart sank as a lizardine screech abruptly cut off all-too-human cries nearby. His old comrade was right: this time their enemies had conjured up a foe that seemed impossible to beat. They might not breathe inflammable venom like the Wyrms of old, but their teeth and claws and wings and barbed tails meant one alone would be a mighty opponent.

Hustle and bustle from the other side of the copse alerted the dozen or so knights to new arrivals. Swords went up in a flash, but there was no need to be afraid – not of this anyway. Vaskrian's face cracked a grin as he recognised Sir Dantos by his heraldic device: a gules ox on a diagonally partitioned black-and-white field. They'd been mortal enemies last time they'd met, but now of course Abrexta's magicks were dead along with her, and the heroic knight was a welcome sight.

Braxus clearly thought much the same, for jumping forwards he embraced the burly warrior.

'Sir Dantos! You escaped!' His face darkened immediately as he saw two other knights in his wake, leading their panicky chargers along behind them like Dantos.

'Sir Arianrod and Sir Diarmuid,' he said flatly. Vaskrian was puzzled. They'd been members of Abrexta's Wytchguard too – but surely they could be counted on as allies too now the Enchantment ensorcelling them had been lifted? Then he recalled the dispute he'd witnessed on the ridges.

Sir Dantos' eyes found the gnarled root of an old oak tree as he mumbled: 'I obviously couldn't keep them detained after... what happened.'

For the first time Braxus caught the ashen faces of the brothers.

'And what of your father?' he asked them. Now they were nearby and a single glimmer of moonlight penetrated through the branches overhead, Vaskrian could see both men had been crying.

Diarmuid found the courage to speak. 'Sir Dantos set us free. We were being detained in our pavilion, so our horses were nearby. The three of us had just taken the saddle when one of those... creatures swooped down at us. It missed Arianrod's head by a whisker with its snapping jaws, but that tail...' His voice trailed off as his eyes glazed over.

'It hit our father in the throat,' said Arianrod, taking up the story. 'He went down, there was... there was nothing we could do for him. Everything was – well, you saw for yourselves. Even if we'd had the courage to stay, our horses would not. In truth it was a miracle we were even able to stay ahorse and ride to safety. To safety...' He shuddered as guilty sobs wracked him.

'Peace, Arianrod,' said Dantos, laying a huge but gentle hand on the knight's shoulder. 'Every chivalrous knight was undone today – for who could have expected such as this to descend upon us?' Turning to look at Braxus, he added: 'Truly it is as the First Man of Clan Fitzrow told us in Ongist – darker forces than we could ever have fathomed are set against us.'

Everyone present lapsed into grim silence at that. Not even the Wyverns or their victims could be heard to break it: for now at least, the horrid creatures had run out of easy prey.

Vaskrian stared through the trees, where their own steeds stood numbly; their earlier panicked whickering had subsided, and they seemed almost docile now.

Fat lot of good our trusty steeds will do us now anyway, he thought disconsolately.

And that was when he had one of his bright ideas.

The blood was caked over the gouge in his thigh where a Wyvern's stinging tail had punctured past his hauberk, but that wasn't why Sir Torgun was crying. His heroic constitution had saved him from a ghastly death, and he had destroyed the creature that sought to end him, only to know a bitter sorrow that was worse to him than all the poisons of the world.

Hilmir, his beloved horse... He'd watched the Farovian steed fight valiantly against two of the winged beasts; endowed with an almost supernatural intelligence and courage, the destrier had fought hoof and tooth where lesser mounts could barely be ridden. But it had been futile: the creatures had mercilessly ripped him apart, carrying his carcass high up in the skies to feast upon.

Torgun had felled two of the monstrosities, Søren's blade hacking through their wings and necks like a knife through butter. The others, clearly possessed of a queer intelligence of their own, had thought better of harassing him after that and sought easier prey, but his horse was gone forever.

His cohort had scattered in a panicked rout as the Wyverns rose up out of the sea and descended on them. Some of the braver knights had tried to make a stand, but few had fared as well as Torgun. Was it his imagination, or had he spotted Toric carried far above the ground, the High Commander's helm falling from his head to reveal a bald pate splashed with blood?

Perhaps he'd never know. All that Torgun could remember of the past few hours was a red haze, as a wood fury had come upon him: dashing hither and yon, he'd dared the creatures to come at him again. One had obliged, its stinging tail wounding him before he'd lopped it off, following up with its head shortly after.

When night had fallen, he'd found himself crouching exhausted beneath an overhanging of rock high up in the Strang Ranges. From where he was, he could see the lights of Strongholm down below. Sounds of carousing drifted up to him from the walls. The Northland usurpers, celebrating a victory they'd done nothing to earn. Silently Torgun clenched his fists around the hilt of his two-handed sword, swearing it would taste reaver's blood before he was done.

It was only then that he noticed a faint pain in his shoulder too. Another barb wound... probably from his first encounter, in the heat of the engagement he hadn't even noticed it until now. The Wyverns did not dare come near his silvery blade, so they would use their tails to whiplash and sting him into oblivion.

Well, let them. The Kingdom was surely lost now; his own fate written in the heavens he hoped to see before long, by the grace of Virtus and Stygnos. His brother Toros had at least had the presence of mind to sound another retreat, but that had quickly turned into a rout as the Wyverns pursued them across the open fields surrounding the city. He had to hope as many knights as possible had managed to gain the safety of woodland or homestead, but though darkness had fallen Torgun knew the sloping ground between him and Strongholm would be carpeted with corpses.

Our King a captive and a fool for barbarians, our royal city taken, our people persecuted, our armies smashed by supernatural fiends... Ach, Horskram, not with all your cleverness could you have foreseen this, not with all your determination could you have forestalled it.

Thinking on that Torgun felt an uncharacteristic bitterness welling up in him. For months he'd followed the Argolian, taking up his quest and journeying across countless leagues to the end of the world – and for what?

To make an end of it here, that's what, he told himself, rallying his failing courage with some effort. *Yon apparition on the Island Realms told you as much.*

Yes, the archangels had chosen a curious agent to do it, but given him fair warning they had. Yet still he could not quash the bitterness. For the apparition had led him to believe that at least his death would not be in vain.

~

'Are you mad?' Braxus' eyes bulged in the flickering light. They'd decided to risk lighting a single dimmed lantern taken from his saddle bags: the Wyverns wouldn't be able to reach them through the trees.

But fire wasn't the element Vaskrian had in mind.

'I'm sure they'll help us,' he persisted. 'They did it once before.'

The other knights were peering at him curiously. They only spoke Thrax, leaving the young knight and his erstwhile guvnor to hold the exchange in Northlending. Something perhaps to be grateful for – if Braxus didn't like the sound of his plan, the other more worldly knights would positively revile it.

'You want us to travel – let me see if I have this correctly – *underwater*, all the way to Narborg, so we can attack the Sea Wizard in his lair? And how, pray tell, do we accomplish this without drowning? From what you say, it's that talisman of yours the Earth Witch gave you that protected you from the waters.'

'It was,' Vaskrian had to admit. 'But the Seakindred have a mermaid, she's kind of like a sorceress herself – I'm sure she could conjure up something similar to help us.'

Braxus shook his head in disbelief. 'Oh, a Mermaid? You know how many tales there are of sailors and coastal wayfarers succumbing to the Merrow's Kiss?' He waved an arm towards his nonplussed knights. 'Even if you could persuade me to go along with this madcap venture, I seriously doubt they will!'

'Well what else do you suggest?' Vaskrian demanded,

almost yelling now and eliciting numerous shushes from the timorous knights, who even now glanced furtively up through the canopy for signs of their tormentors.

'What do you suggest we do instead?' He repeated the question in a sibilant hiss, fixing his eyes pointedly on Braxus.

The Thraxian passed a mufflered hand over his brow. 'I don't bloody well know,' he conceded.

'Look,' persisted Vaskrian. 'You obviously came here with some good men to help us out, because you know better than anyone how much is at stake if we lose this war. Well, doing this now would be helping us not to lose! And speaking of losing, what do *you* have to lose? We're not going to win against these things by force of arms alone – even I can see that!'

Braxus averted his gaze, chewing his lip fretfully. He suddenly looked a lot older than Vaskrian remembered him. Clearly the cares of rulership already weighed heavily upon his old companion, probably now more than ever.

At last the First Man of Clan Fitzrow drew himself up. Heaving a great sigh, he said: 'Very well, Sir Vaskrian, I suppose you have a point.' Nodding towards his compatriots, he added: 'But you're going to have a deal of a time convincing them. And even if you do, for this plan of yours to work we're going to have to get to the Strang Estuary. That's nigh on a league of hilly countryside to navigate, with those dread things prowling the skies. Now, do you have a plan for *that*?'

Now it was Vaskrian's turn to look fretful. Because, truth to tell, he didn't.

Then something else occurred to him. 'We're still on the other side of the Strang Ranges from Strongholm,' he said. 'Though it's hard to be sure with all the panic...' He paused, shamed even now at the recollection of their frantic scramble for safety, unbefitting of any true knight. Pushing the thought away, he continued: 'The copse we're in, I think it sits in a dell at the foot of the ridges.'

Sir Dantos, who knew some rudiments of his language, pitched in at that point. 'Bottom of hills, yes,' he confirmed. 'Just now we came.'

Sir Vaskrian nodded at the older knight gratefully, secretly hoping he hadn't understood too much else of what had been said – judging by his perplexed expression he hadn't.

'So what of it?' snapped Lord Braxus impatiently.

Vaskrian chewed his lip thoughtfully. 'My guess is those creatures were summoned by the Sea Wizard – can't see who else was behind it. And if that's so then he'll probably intend them to stay around the basin of lands contained by the Strangs. Don't forget we had him on the back foot until now – those Wyverns are devastating, but I'll bet his purpose is to hold Strongholm, for now at least.'

Braxus was peering at him quizzically, but his eyes suddenly widened as he grasped Vaskrian's meaning.

'You think we might have a chance if we circle back? Try to approach the coastline from another direction?'

Vaskrian nodded, his enthusiasm growing as he warmed to his own plan.

'Look, I don't know these lands half as well as Efrilund, but I do know that the hills hereabouts will be dotted with copses just like this one, all the way to the shore. If we can skirt the ranges using the trees for cover, we might just make it.'

Braxus' face creased as he spotted the one flaw in Vaskrian's plan. 'Yes, but to get to the shore and contact your "friends" we'll have to break cover at the coastline. And how do you propose to contact them, indeed? It's not like you can just conjure them up, like our Sea Wizard antagonist.'

'No, I can't,' Vaskrian admitted. 'But just before we parted company, Logrim told me that if I uttered his name thrice by the coastline, the "sea would answer".'

Braxus offered Vaskrian a wry smile. 'You might have mentioned that part earlier,' he deadpanned.

Vaskrian grinned back at him. 'You don't think I learned a trick about storytelling after months on the road with you and old Master Horskram?'

Braxus was positively chuckling now, earning him startled looks from Dantos and the other knights.

'You know what this sounds like?' he said. 'Like old times together, that's what! All right, Sir Vaskrian of the seas, it's probably no more hare-brained than any of our other ideas were... I'd better tell this lot what we're up to though – and I should warn you many of them may choose not to join us. I can't really compel them in this matter – such fey undertakings surpass all bonds of feudal obligation.'

Vaskrian nodded in acceptance. What Braxus was saying was hardly unreasonable, in the circumstances.

'We'll need a few of them at least for my plan to work though – I seriously doubt the Sea Wizard will be unprotected.' Glancing surreptitiously at the two brothers Diarmuid and Arianrod, he added: 'If I were you, Lord Braxus, I'd play on their desire for filial vengeance.'

Braxus winked back at him.

'Oh, don't you worry,' he told Vaskrian. 'I've every intention of doing so.'

CHAPTER 14
A JOURNEY STALLED

Adelko feverishly clutched the Gryphon's neck as the morning winds whistled raw about him. He could barely make out the fortress – not because it wasn't a clear day, it was, but the giddy experience of flying on a winged creature's back was as dizzy as it was terrifying. Funny how flying on a winged ship had seemed a much smoother affair – he could almost believe ordinary mortals could accustom themselves to such an experience. But this? For the umpteenth time he felt his gut meet his gorge as the Gryphon banked eastwards, taking a circuitous route so as to avoid the ballistae that sat astride the gatehouse's four mighty square turrets.

Behind him, Hari was tensed, also clinging on for dear life: nothing in the former Shadowman's training had evidently prepared him for this either, though at least it wasn't his first time on the creature's back. But mercifully the giddy journey was over almost as quickly as it had begun: the Gryphon alighted on a broad outcropping of rock that jutted from the mountainside at right angles to the fortress, where the others were waiting for them.

Both Azelin and Horskram looked pale and near vomiting; only Morcant seemed unperturbed by their spectacular valley crossing. Rather an expression of joyous childish delight suffused his broken features, his hazel eyes catching the dawn light and sparkling. Hari lost no time sliding down off the flank of the Gryphon. Adelko followed him; resisting the urge to be sick over the side of the rock shelf, he drew once again on the psalms, this time simply to avoid embarrassing himself.

'Pleasant trip?' Horskram managed to force the spare humour from lips that curled with distaste.

Leaning over and placing his hands on his knees, Adelko gasped a response: 'It's not exactly the *Chariot of the Skies*, but it certainly got us here.'

Horskram's lip curled further. 'Yes, well, the less we have to do with demonolators such as Sha'arza the better I shall like it. Reus knows, we'll have enough to contend with once we reach our final destination.'

Adelko was feeling too ill to pay heed to residual feelings of guilt, but the talisman he wore concealed beneath his habit suddenly felt heavier about his neck.

Morcant had approached the Gryphon and was petting it affectionately, conversing with it in the sorcerer's tongue. Drawing himself upright, Adelko could have sworn he saw the creature nod at the mage, before it abruptly took to the skies again, winging its way back to its cave.

Turning to face his companions, Morcant clapped his hands in a satisfied manner. 'Take care of that, that does!' he beamed. 'Now master monk, sir knight, 'tis in your hands I believe – to see us received at yonder fortress.'

Azelin shrugged sourly. 'Don't look at me,' he said. 'I've never had anything to do with the Imperials. They refused to join us on crusade, and we've been sundered in matters of the

Creed ever since the Great Schism. From what little I know of them, they don't even have knights themselves.'

'No,' Horskram clarified. 'They have something much more dangerous – the Imperial Cataphracts are said to be the deadliest mounted fighting force in the Known World. So you might have a mind to treat them with respect and civility when you meet them.'

The erstwhile warrior-monk shrugged his shoulders dismissively. 'I don't even speak their language,' he told Horskram curtly. 'So it will be down to you to do the talking anyway.'

That reminded Adelko of something. 'He's got a point, Master Horskram – do you know any of their languages? Won't be much use if we have to converse with them in sign language...'

Horskram rolled his eyes. 'Don't worry, we won't. I sojourned here for a few months during my friarship as a journeyman when I was seconded to a diplomatic mission... one that sought to overcome the dogmatic differences our pious friend here referred to just now.'

Now it was Azelin's turn to roll his eyes.

'That came to naught, as you might well imagine, but it did give me a chance to pick up the Imperial tongue – it's a mishmash of the seven languages spoken by the diverse inhabitants of the Empire, for it was once seven separate kingdoms, before the Hundred Years Conquest unified them under the banner of the ruling house of Usharok.'

Horskram was already walking over towards a rough trail that led from the rock shelf up towards the road they had spotted the previous evening. Adelko fell into line beside his mentor, his nausea quickly forgotten as the old thirst for knowledge of the wide world reawakened within him. The other three followed on behind, at a somewhat more leisurely pace.

'I've read that the Empire was a continuation of the Old Thalamian civilisation,' hedged Adelko, whose more recent studies had in truth led him far closer to home. Now his Wyrd had unexpectedly brought him to the fringes of eastern Urovia, he was anxious to find out more about it.

'It is in a sense,' Horskram conceded, obviously pleased to resume his old role as tutor. 'But not quite as directly as you seem to think. As you'll know, the Thalamian Empire's final ruin was wrought by Wulfric of Gothia, who sacked Tyrannos nine hundred years ago. After that the Empire west of the mountains in which we now stand disintegrated back into fragmented states, for Wulfric could not hope to hold the barbarian alliance he had forged together for long, and the new confederation he inaugurated did not outlast his death shortly after. By then the Sassanian armies of the Faith had annexed the southern provinces, which left the imperial flame burning in Nacia, Grice and the age-old city-state of Aratheny on the far side of the Little Sea, many leagues east of here.

'That was where the surviving Thalamians chose to base their new capital, and so the old regime lived on in a sense, as the New Arathenian Empire. That lasted about three hundred years, and loremasters say it endured as a still glorious though somewhat dimmed reflection of the Ancient Thalamian civilisation, and the original Arathenian civilisation which that had absorbed centuries before. But even they couldn't hold together forever, and when the three constituent states finally separated and Aratheny chose splendid isolation, the era of the Seven Old Kingdoms began.'

'Nacia, Grice, Chalcedony, Sarcia, Hylund, Xanador and Algary...' Adelko listed them off. This much he did know at least.

His mentor favoured him with a sidelong nod of approval as he continued: 'Seven kingdoms, seven different tongues, seven different peoples, stretching from the coastal seas that abut our homeland in the north to the Sundering Sea we but lately crossed.'

Adelko found himself looking around. 'Which part are we in, I wonder?'

Horskram shrugged. 'Hard to say, given the unorthodox means by which we arrived here. I can't even tell from yonder castle, for the Seven Fortresses were designed in perfect likeness of one another – yet further testament to the engineering expertise cultivated by the Imperials.'

'So please continue with the historical tutelage – I'm dying to know what the mighty House of Usharok did next.' This from Sir Azelin, who had drawn level with the monks and lost no opportunity to pepper the conversation with his usual sarcasm.

'No doubt you are,' breezed Horskram, choosing deliberately to ignore the knight's caustic humour. 'Well, the seven kingdoms coexisted like that for another couple of centuries, during which time they were greatly influenced by one another through war and trade.'

'Of course,' cut in Azelin. 'They're both equally profitable, if done rightly.'

This time Horskram glared at him, and even Adelko felt compelled to shush him to silence.

'You might feel that you know everything there is to know about mortalkind, Sir Azelin,' he said, 'but I don't. Pray let Master Horskram continue.'

Azelin glared hatefully at him then, and Adelko suppressed a shudder as he recalled his calm dismantling of the tortured warrior's psyche back in the monastery.

He'll be one to bear a grudge, thought the journeyman, *or I'm an Imperial. I'll have to keep a close eye on this one – Reus, your tools are effective but dangerous to the user as well.*

Oblivious, Horskram continued his instruction as they

drew near the road that would take them up to where the main highway from the west met the fortress.

'Foremost among them was Chalcedony, which founded its splendid capital Illyrium during this time, drawing much on the learning and lore that had been preserved from the Golden Age by its civilised southern neighbours Nacia and Grice. But where those two kingdoms had fallen into sloth and indolence, brooding moodily on better days just as Thalamy did to the west, Chalcedony was growing vibrant and prosperous, with a sound administration and vigorous military caste. The other four kingdoms of central Urovia shared some of this vigour but were notably less sophisticated. The time was ripe for Chalcedony and its potentates in Illyrium – six neighbouring kingdoms, four of them rude and backwards and two civilised but grown hopelessly decadent. The seeds for the founding of a new Urovian empire, one to crown the Silver Age as Thalamy's had the Golden Age, were being sown.

'About five hundred years ago, the King of Chalcedony, Usharok I, began a series of expansionary wars that would last more than a century. This is known in Imperial history as the Hundred Years Conquest, and its end would see the foundation of the Urovian New Empire, as the seven old kingdoms were consolidated into a centrally ruled land empire. That ushered in the Great Period of Ascendancy, as the Illyrian regime reached heights of prosperity and sophistication not seen in Urovia since the decline of the Thalamians. Thus did the Silver Age begin, and the Imperials even mark their calendar thus, beginning their reckoning of years with the end of the Conquest. But it would be a mistake to think of them merely as a throw-over from Thalamy of old – they've developed many things new and strange, though they guard their secrets jealously. One or two of them have slipped out, however – if you've ever seen a mariner using a spyglass at sea, or been on the wrong end of a crossbow bolt, you've the Imperials to thank for it.'

That set Azelin musing. 'Useful weapon, the crossbow. I'd never countenance using one myself, but it helped us enormously when the Supreme Perfect sanctioned its use against the Sassanians.'

Horskram's face soured again as they stepped from the mountain trail onto the road. Though smaller than the main highway it approached, it was well kept, its paving stones broad and neatly placed.

'Yes, Sir Azelin, I would have thought that part of their genius might endear them to you a bit more,' said Horskram. 'But look lively now! We aren't far off, and we're in view of the fortress now – proceed cautiously, we don't want to aggravate them. Honourable the Imperials might be, but a haughty and suspicious bunch they are too.'

Sure enough, no sooner had they stepped onto the rocky plateau on which the fortress was built than a clarion blared from the gatehouse. A smaller postern door – still large enough to admit two riders abreast – opened at the foot of the gate, and half a dozen knights in gleaming lamellar armour rode forth to meet them.

No, not knights, Adelko mentally corrected himself: cataphracts. Truly they were a formidable sight to behold. Their piebald destriers were easily as large as any Farovian, a full eighteen hands high; their scaled barding fashioned in pleasing symmetry to the armour worn by their riders. Horses and riders were garbed in white-and-red diagonally patterned caparisons and surcoats, emblazoned with a pair of golden scales in perfect balance topped by a displayed eagle of likewise colour: the centuries-old coat of arms of the mighty house whose extraordinary fortunes Horskram had just sketched.

The cataphracts each bore a lance, but these remained

holstered behind them within easy reach: another curiosity of Imperial fashion unknown to their ruder western cousins. A great sword was sheathed at each one's back, a shorter stabbing blade girt at their sides for closer-quarters combat. Besides such myrmidons, even the Knights of the White Valravyn or the Holy Bethel seemed little better than mounted serjeants.

Adelko didn't need his sixth sense to detect Sir Azelin's envy as he laid eyes on them.

The six cataphracts ambled towards them, fanning outwards with an effortless discipline; before the companions could collect themselves they were being sized up by a horseshoe arrangement of half a dozen of the best fighters in the world, their eyes flat and emotionless behind the slits of their visors.

Then one of them spoke, in a strange lilting tongue that he supposed must be the patois used by the subjects of the Imperator.

Clearing his throat, Horskram did his best to respond in kind, though Adelko could tell by his faltering speech patterns that it was not a tongue he had ever mastered.

Their captain seemed satisfied, however: lifting his visor to reveal a tanned face decorated only with a pair of finely trimmed moustachios, he switched to flawless Decorlangue.

'Good morn to you, wayfarers from the west. Though you come by our bourne in circuitous fashion, the Empire welcomes you. Rest and succour thou seekest, and that thou shalt have, provided you consent to be bound by our immutable laws. If such be your wont and will, let disquiet depart from your hearts, as bitter chill flees the land at sun's touch!'

Adelko felt himself groaning inwardly. 'Do they always speak like this, Master Horskram?' he was courageous enough to whisper.

'He's drawing on protocol,' the adept muttered back. 'But I'm afraid it doesn't get much better than this, no.'

The journeyman kept his misgivings to himself as Horskram replied loudly in Decorlangue: 'Such is indeed our will and our wont. To be bound by the Imperial Law we do consent, so long as it brings us respite from the road, and no unjust harm or dishonour befall us by so doing!'

The leader nodded. 'It is well,' he said. 'Then let me have the honour of introducing myself, that words may ever be broken betwixt us by broad light of day – I am Justorian, son of Justorix, of the Presiding Patrician Clan of Nacia, Captain in His Imperial Eminence's Third Cavalry, at your service.'

So saying, the cataphract slammed a gauntleted fist to his breastplate, a move synchronised to perfection by the five others.

'Come now,' he added, as his cohort deftly parted to reveal similarly garbed footsoldiers accompanied by auxiliaries bearing satchels. 'Our men-at-arms shall take thy weapons, our healers shall see to any injuries or other afflictions the unkindness of the road may have placed upon thee. Follow them, and be not afraid – be as the treasured steed that consents to be groomed and shuttered, the better to rest and so speed another day!'

Azelin's face had turned a royal purple not unlike the words being levelled in his direction. 'Can I challenge him to a death duel?' he groused. 'Do their precious Imperial laws forbid that?'

Horskram favoured the knight with a sly smirk. 'Surely an erstwhile paladin of the Bethel finds much to admire and relate to here?' he demanded with mock innocence.

'Don't push your luck,' growled Azelin. But, to Adelko's surprise and relief, he relinquished his bastard blade to the soldier that approached him.

No, not soldier, the journeyman corrected himself again:

legionary. Just as the cataphracts were the finest mounted force in the Known World, so too their regular legionaries enjoyed a similar reputation for fighting on foot. Taking in their banded armour, which would put a rich knight's harness to shame, and sturdy maces and swords, Adelko found no reason to disbelieve the tales.

One of them had his hand outstretched, his dark eyes watching him intently from beneath a finely wrought open-faced helm. His other hand was a finger's breadth away from the hilt of a weapon, yet somehow he managed to appear almost casual at the same time, unthreatening.

Adelko relinquished his quarterstaff without hesitation.

Inside the gatehouse it was dark, though that darkness was punctuated in pleasing fashion by ingeniously placed window slits high up in the walls that allowed beams of sunlight to penetrate and air to circulate, making for an interior that was cool without being chilly. Two huge tapestries ran the length of a broad, richly carpeted through-way, simply repeating the heraldic motif borne by the fortress's guardians: one thing Adelko had heard about the Empire was that for all its evident glory it could also be surprisingly muted. No frescos depicting mighty battles won during the Hundred Years' Conquest, no lurid celebrations of its greatest heroes. Oddly enough, he began to feel homesick.

The cataphracts dismounted as the postern gate was shut behind them, giving their horses to servants to take to the capacious stables that adjoined the through-way; a haughty-looking official in charge of the auxiliaries motioned impatiently for the companions to follow him towards a side chamber just beyond the stabling area.

There they were motioned to sit at long mahogany

benches and tables, polished to perfection. The auxiliaries began inspecting them for ailments and injuries, naturally lingering on Morcant the longest, while servants clad in livery brought ceramic trenchers and copper ewers holding plain but nourishing food and drink.

While Morcant subjected himself timorously to the unguents and poultices applied to his injuries, Adelko fell ravenously on the provender gifted him. Azelin, Hari and Horskram followed in somewhat more perfunctory fashion, while the official beckoned to another servant to bring him a ledger, parchment and ink pot from an adjoining smaller desk.

No, it wasn't parchment, Adelko noted between mouthfuls. It looked similar, but it was smoother, neater; where a scroll had to be furled, unfurled and tied together or weighted down, this lay flat on the wooden ledger, in seamless neat oblongs.

'They call it *paper*,' Horskram supplied, catching his curious glance. 'It's a more refined version of parchment, allowing for convenient usage and mass production of tomes and pamphlets and the like. Above all else, the Imperials prize knowledge and learning.'

Adelko sensed his mentor's admiration was grudging.

'Impressive, surely?' he hedged, swallowing another mouthful of water. It was pure as the driven snow it had doubtless been distilled from.

Horskram wrinkled his nose slightly. 'If only their interpretation of the Creed was the same as ours,' he said sententiously, answering Adelko's unspoken question.

The journeyman had to smile. Though more open-minded than most, even Horskram would never completely let go of his prejudices. The smile abruptly faded as he recalled Sha'arza's difficulty with his mentor. Perhaps there was nothing funny about it.

The official had reached into the folds of his garment and produced a quill, as the servant opened the brass pot, whose contents were secured in place by a small but ingenious hinged lid. Dipping it in perfunctorily, he began to scrawl something in the bizarre script of the Imperials.

'I am required by the Fourteenth Protocol of the Imperial Codex Governing Border Arrivals to note the time and provenance of your arrival,' he said in flat emotionless Decorlangue without looking up from his ledger. 'As none of you holds a Deed of Port Passage, this is necessary.' Glancing up and peering down at them over his aquiline nose, which put Horskram's hawkish features to shame, he added: 'The manner of your arrival, and your several conditions, must also be recorded.'

'Do you need to record the manner of our pissing and passing following this fine repast too?' growled Azelin, still chewing on some bread and smoked pork loin.

'That will not be necessary to our investigation,' said the official. Did he deliberately choose to ignore Azelin's coarse sarcasm, or was he simply incapable of understanding it? Adelko wondered.

Hari's knowledge of the High Speech of Western Urovia was patchy, but he'd caught the last word.

'Investigation?' he asked nervously. 'Surely we are accused of no crime.'

The official made a casual gesture with his free hand as he continued to scrawl in impossibly neat and tiny handwriting. Still without looking up from his ledger, he added: 'The Empire extends charity and succour to all wayfarers, but it guards its secrets closely. Under the Second Protocol of the Imperial Code Governing Border Arrivals, all such arrivals are to be detained to assess that they are not a threat, before being sent on their way.'

Adelko felt his sixth sense tinkle faintly, but Horskram appeared unsurprised.

'Your records will indicate that I sojourned once before in your lands, many years ago. All we seek is safety, rest, and the freedom to travel on to the nearest port city, under guard as per your regulations, thence to exit the Empire – might I inquire which of the Seven Fortresses we are in? We were travelling from Thalamy, but became perilous lost, as you have doubtless fathomed.'

Horskram's bluff was a good one. The cataphract Justorian had referred to himself as belonging to the ruling caste of Nacia, which probably placed them in the Empire's southern portion, adjacent to the realm that had foreshadowed its civilisation long ago.

Unfortunately, the official was also good at his job. Peering again down his nose at Horskram, he said in the same flat voice: 'As to the particulars of your journey, I do not believe I have fathomed half of those. Yet.'

Justorian had approached and stood casually to one side. Politely beckoning him as an apparent equal, the official muttered something in the cataphract's ear as he bent to listen.

Adelko's sixth sense jolted up a notch. Glancing sidelong, he caught Azelin's hand slowly inching towards the single carving knife laid down beside the pork loin. Reaching over deftly while the two Imperials were busy conferring, he tapped the knight once on the wrist and surreptitiously but emphatically shook his head.

Azelin shot him a look of pure hatred, but Hari had spotted it too, and catching the warrior-monk's attention he also flashed him a warning glance. Morcant was still being attended to by the auxiliary healers, while Horskram was staring intently at the official and Justorian, trying to fathom what they were about.

Justorian nodded once curtly before drawing himself up to his full height. He wasn't the tallest fighter Adelko had seen, but his robust carriage spoke of a man well trained to arms.

The official had turned to speak to Horskram again. 'Your precise location will not be revealed to you at this time. As I said, the Empire guards its secrets closely.' A hardening look stifled Horskram's one of exasperation as the official went on: 'However, we find it as strange as a sun that sets in the east that you would have fallen so far out of your way as to beg such broad question of your location.' The official raised a hand to forestall Horskram's protestation; Adelko could see it was barely tainted with ink, though he had filled half a page with his cramped handwriting.

Just then one of the auxiliaries examining Morcant also beckoned to Justorian, though much more deferentially. The cataphract marched over to attend, while subtly flicking his wrist. Two of the footsoldiers who had disarmed them suddenly appeared in his place at the official's side, hands settling on mace and sword.

'They know!' hissed Morcant suddenly, speaking in Thrax.

'Know what?' Adelko replied, thankfully remembering to address the warlock in his own language.

The sorcerer gestured helplessly, then caught himself, immediately putting his hands down flat on the table where everyone could see them. He was glancing fearfully around him, looking for all the world like his old fox familiar Scratcher.

Adelko's heart rose in his mouth, just as Hari and Azelin rose from their seats. A split second later, both legionaries had drawn sword and mace – four weapons menaced them, expertly handled by myrmidons trained to ambidextrous fighting from early youth. Horskram was rising up too, hands raised in a placatory gesture and trying to forestall a confrontation.

Justorian and the auxiliary were conferring, but at the sound of steel leaving scabbard, the cataphract whirled on his sabatoned heel and produced his short sword in a flash.

'Our auxiliary suspects sorcery,' he declared. 'Not as sure as snows falling in first month of winter, but wayfarer Morcant bears hallmarks of psychic taxation caused by use of magic.'

Adelko gaped. 'How could they know that?' he could not help asking out loud.

Next to him Horskram muttered sullenly. 'Why do you think the Argolians went on a mission to treat with them in the first place? The Imperials have their own ways of divining sorcery, and we sought to pool methods.'

'You might have told us that, Master Horskram!' Their exchange was in Northlending, and bordering on heated.

'What was I suppose to do, abandon him to the mountains and Gryphons?' Horskram shot back. 'Besides, they don't punish sorcery in the same fashion as we do – this is a gamble we have to take, I'm afraid.'

Adelko stared at his mentor aghast. 'This is part of your plan?'

Even now, Horskram could not resist a wry half-smile. 'Plan is putting it rather generously,' he admitted.

'You're telling me,' breathed Adelko, as the official and auxiliary backed away, allowing their three armed compatriots to surround the five outlanders. Regular as clockwork, another four legionaries had arrived, weapons also drawn.

'Have no fear if your purpose be true,' said Justorian, though there was no smile in his voice nor on his lips as he spoke. 'Detained you shall be, by the Nineteenth Protocol of the Imperial Code on Border Arrivals, until we have had time to interrogate and examine you fully. Submit meekly to the gentle but persistent light of our search, and see all fears banished to the Four Winds.' His tone visibly darkened. 'But should you be found wanting or bearing ill will to the Imperial House of Usharok, expect to fear our wrath, as the miscreant blenches at noose's touch!'

'Horskram, this fellow is starting to remind me of Grand Master Tobin,' whispered Adelko. Though he had to admit, his sixth sense wasn't flaring quite as badly as it could have been. Justorian was clearly a devoted servant of his people who would carry out their laws to the last letter, but he probably wasn't of the same stamp as the fanatical Bethler who'd nearly had them executed. Probably.

'Trust in your sixth sense, lad,' said Horskram, trying to sound soothing as the five of them were led away back to the thoroughfare and up a broad flight of stairs running flush to the wall. 'We've found ourselves in worse scrapes ere now.'

Risking a quick look at his other companions, Adelko realised they must feel the same. Azelin looked galled at being a captive once again, but hardly fearful after all the danger they had just survived. Hari had the insouciant look of resignation and cool determination typical of a street-hardened criminal. Morcant still looked terrified, but considering his recent shameful treatment in captivity he could hardly be blamed for that.

As they made their way up the stairs, with their captors' armour clinking in time to their regimented movements, Adelko forced himself to focus on his surroundings, taking in every detail he could, however slight.

Being detained in the Empire... It wasn't the best outcome in the world, but perhaps it wasn't the worst after all. And certainly it was less dangerous than the place they had been trying to get to.

CHAPTER 15

A MYRIAD OF CONFLICTS

The First Woman of Clan McCullogh broke off from pacing her solar to scan the parchment on her desk once again. The message had arrived at Liathnoc castle several weeks ago. At first Lady Rowena, ruler of Tul Aeren, had scarce been able to credit it: they'd just fought a civil war to get rid of a meddlesome witch, and now Lord Braxus was at it again, mustering men and babbling to all and sundry of some great wizards' plot – one that the accursed Abrexta had been but small part of.

She'd been minded to dismiss it at first. The Crimson League she had somehow managed to retain control over had its hands full demanding justly due concessions from the fickle Kingsfolders in the north. A second civil war might well be in the offing: who needed a campaign down south, in Vorstlund of all places, and thoughts of warlocks plotting to take over the Known World to worry about? Lord Braxus had clearly lost his wits.

That's what she'd thought – until the ghostly shades that cavorted nightly around the haunted precinct of Anarlion had abruptly coalesced into corporeal form and started attacking her people.

At least Abrexta hadn't succeeded in suppressing the Argolian Order – because they'd been needed in pretty short order. She'd sent word to Kilucan monastery – or rather the remains of such that were being rebuilt after Abrexta's purge – and fortunately the Abbot there had not been slow to respond. The entire chapter of monks had arrived a week later, setting up a defensive ring to contain the fell shades coming out of Anarlion, chanting psalms day and night. Several brave monks had died in the attempt, but last night had finally seen a breakthrough and turning of the tide: the ghastly attack on Tul Aeren had just, and only just, been repelled and contained.

Of course, if Abrexta had lived and had her way, there would have been no Argolians left to help. Braxus, looks like you weren't so wrong after all. Now all I have to do is persuade the other lords of the Crimson League of that. Once again I must win them over to a common cause.

A knock at the door broke her reverie.

'Enter,' she said, rather more shrilly than she would have liked. Her nerves were on edge and no mistake.

Her marshal Cathsach entered her solar. He had a few more grey hairs to add to his growing collection, but that was hardly a surprise given what they'd all borne witness to these past few weeks. Rowena fancied she had a few that hadn't been there before herself.

'What news?' she barked, the shrillness not leaving her voice.

'We've just received a messenger from Lord Fannoch – his bannermen in Garro are mustering and will join us within a tenday,' said Cathsach. 'But there's been a delay in Penllyn…' He hesitated, his pale face a touch paler than usual.

Rowena arched an eyebrow. This sounded all too much like her nemesis and rival the First Man of Clan Pellyw. 'Penllyn lies on our route south in any case, surely Lord Penric can't be thinking of demurring yet again?'

Lord Penric was an uncertain ally at best: he'd tried to intrigue his way to overall command of the Crimson League forces that comprised the three southerly wards of Thraxia – Penllyn where he ruled, Tul Aeren that she presided over, and Garro where Lord Fannoch held sway. He'd even been willing to use base calumny to do it, pitting his formidable champion Sir Leathan against any who dared gainsay him after he'd accused her, falsely, of murdering her late husband to assume the wardship of Tul Aeren. None had... until the unknown outlander Vaskrian had stepped forwards to take up the gauntlet in her name. For that she'd rewarded him with a knighthood, and taken him into her household. Not long after, she'd taken him into her bedchamber. You'd think that would have been enough to keep a valiant young knight by her side, but he'd left just the same... vanished into thin air.

Bloody Northlendings, it was so typical. Even when you owed them your life and they owed you their livelihood, you still couldn't count on them, not really. And now here was Braxus talking about riding to help them against yet another invasion force...

She was so wrapped up in her own thoughts that she barely realised Sir Cathsach had stopped speaking.

'Out with it, for Stygnos' sake,' said Rowena, mastering the pitch in her voice with some difficulty. 'What's keeping Penric from joining his forces to ours when we march south? Does he require evidence that Braxus' conspiracy of wizards is real? He should ride north to meet us in that case – we'll show him Anarlion, aye and what its denizens did to the lands thereabout!'

Cathsach's face remained ashen as he stammered: 'I

hardly think he needs to travel for proof, Lady Rowena. His messenger bears ill tidings... The barrows of Dûn Ator in the east of Penllyn, they've opened... wights, they say. Twyleth Tûgannon and the other lords of the Middle Time... they've emerged from their burial mounds...' His voice trailed off.

Rowena swallowed hard. Twyleth Tûgannon had fought the Westerling invasion force led by Ifwyn Gold-Blind to his last breath during the Forty Years Kin Strife a thousand years ago. Some legends told that he and his warlords merely slept in their barrows, awaiting the Final Hour when they should rise and wreak havoc on the lands they lost so cruelly. But other, darker, tales said they had been buried on a much older grave site, where ancient servitors of Them had been laid to rest... The library in Liathnoc held one tome that treated of such: Rowena had been far more interested in wordly works written by the likes of Thalamian master-general Alcius, so she only remembered fragments: something about warlords in service to the Varyans who'd once ruled all of the Known World from their island stronghold far to the south being buried there; the loremaster she'd read had claimed that the eldritch magick of the Elder Wizards had infected or polluted the burial mounds of Twyleth and his ilk.

'Go on,' she told Cathsach, trying to keep the tremor from her voice. She'd proven more than capable of fighting earthly foes, but this was something altogether different: she very much doubted Alcius could help her win a war against the walking dead.

'Lord Penric has solicited help from his local Argolian chapter too, but he's hard put to stall a general panic among his people,' said the marshal. 'Says after everything he's witnessed these past couple of weeks he's prepared to believe what Braxus has been saying though. He'll try to contribute what he can to the Vorstlund relief force, though he can't promise more than a couple of hundred swords. The wars to the south may well be connected to what we're seeing, but he won't leave his lands on the brink of anarchy.' Cathsach shook his head, scarcely able to believe his own words. 'Things are bad, Rowena, worse than any of us could have expected. Wars are one thing, but everything that's happening now, it's straight out of witch's prophecy.'

Rowena took a shaky breath. Glancing back at the parchment missive on her desk, she added: 'Straight out of witch's prophecy... and straight out of the message the King sent, citing Braxus' tales of dark kingdoms to come. Hard to believe it is indeed.'

'Right now, I believe I could use a drink,' said Cathsach, eyeing the silver pitcher and matching goblets next to the unfurled scroll.

'By Euphrosakritos, I believe you're right,' said Rowena, before promptly pouring for them both. It wasn't the best wine, she couldn't even remember its provenance, but it was stronger than mead and would serve nicely.

Both felt better after draining their goblets.

'Are you sure we should be going ourselves?' Cathsach ventured. 'I like the man no more than you, my lady, but Lord Penric has a point. Fine well for Lord Braxus to say it's all connected – wizards and warlords and walking dead, but what does it avail us marching off to help others if we leave our own realms in jeopardy?'

Rowena pursed her lips. She had of course considered this, torturously and tortuously, tossing and turning through more sleepless nights than she cared to remember as her thoughts bent and twisted back on themselves agonisingly. At such times she'd missed having the feckless young knight she'd made and lost by her side to comfort her too, but she wasn't going to admit that, not to anyone but herself.

She shrugged. 'The Abbot assures me he and his brethren have our problem contained – and what good could we do with earthly troops against such foes in any case? The Argolian presence seems to have forestalled a general panic among our own populace. Better to fight a foe we can actually kill, it should calm the people somewhat if we're seen to be doing something at least.'

Cathsach's face betrayed his doubt. 'Lady Rowena, you know I'd follow you into the jaws of death,' he said. 'But can we be so sure that Lord Braxus is right? I realise these are far from ordinary times, but the First Man of Clan Fitzrow's tale... even with what we've witnessed, it all just seems so far-fetched!'

Rowena nodded. 'Aye, that it does, Sir Cathsach,' she agreed. 'But the King believes it, for one thing. And if anyone knows what happens when you turn a blind eye to witchery, it's Cadwy. No, it's too much happening all at once just to be a coincidence... First Northalde is embroiled in civil war, just as we are infiltrated by Abrexta. Then Braxus gets embroiled in some Argolian secret mission to foil a sorcerous plot. Ends up in the Warlock's Crown, of all places, and nearly loses his mind by the sounds of it. Then Thalamy and Pangonia attack Vorstlund, just as the Pilgrim Wars fire up again across the sea... Then Northalde is invaded by its barbarous neighbours, who also had a hand in this uprising of Thule's last year, and now we have undead stalking our countryside just a few months after we defeat a witch who conveniently almost expunged the Argolian Order.' She held Cathsach's gaze intently. 'Don't you see, Cathsach? This has been planned by someone for a very long time and as wood as he sounds, Braxus has the right of it methinks. And if he *is* right, then I'll be thrice-damned if I sit back and do nothing. We just fought a war on two fronts to get rid of Abrexta. Now it looks as though we must fight one on many more to get rid of the cabal or whatever in Gehenna it is she was serving.' She shook her head firmly, her mind made up. 'I don't see an alternative. Our suit with King Cadwy and the Kingsfolders will have to wait. Our route lies south.'

Cathsach sighed heavily. Still not entirely convinced, he knew better than to argue with his mistress.

'As I said, I'd follow you into the jaws of death,' he repeated earnestly, though his downcast eyes found his cup as he spoke the words. 'I just pray that isn't where you're leading us – and I sincerely hope there's a Tul Aeren to come back to when we return!' He returned his grey gaze to hers.

Rowena managed a wan half-smile. 'As do I, Sir Cathsach, as do I.'

Turning, she emptied the rest of the pitcher into their goblets. Night was fast drawing in. She almost fancied then she could hear the voices of the monks rising in a crescendo, as they kept the awful denizens of Anarlion fenced in – for now. She had half a mind to call a servant and order a second pitcher of wine, then thought better of it.

'You'll see to your own board this e'en?' she asked Cathsach. 'I'd fain dine with thee, but I've other fare to feast on.'

'Oh?' Cathsach inquired.

'I'm away to the library, it's time I caught up with my reading.'

Cathsach managed to return her half smile. 'More Alcius, ahead of our campaign?' he asked, brightening visibly at the thought of winning another war, one that could be won with men, steel and cleverness.

But the First Woman of Clan McCullogh shook her head. 'No need for that, I've got everything old Alcius wrote down right here where I need it.' She tapped her temple knowingly before downing her drink. 'No, I've got something else in mind, something rather more... numinous.'

Puzzled by a word that wasn't in his vocabulary, Cathsach showed it.

'Never you mind,' said Rowena, setting her goblet back

down on the table with a decisive *thunk*. 'Let's just say I need to learn as much as I can about how to fight an altogether different foe.'

Her marshal nodded silently, replacing his own goblet. His face appeared to have turned a shade paler.

INTERLUDE: HANNEQUIN'S LOG

Ah, what changes the weeks have wrought! But I would be a fool not to confess to these pages that they have not all been anticipated... The Great Old One-Eye sleeps no more: seven times seven nights it took to conjure him and his lieutenants, to release them from the binding that the Archangels placed upon them five millennia ago.

The greatest of the Draug Lords are freed at last, yet they do not entirely do my bidding.

No fool I am, did I write just now? Yet a fool I was, to reckon even my Necromancy could unconditionally control the greatest general ever to make war and command armies. Oh, he will obtain the final Headstone fragment for me, of that I am sure – our interests align too closely for it not to be so. But he insists on awakening his sleeping vassals before the appointed time... ah, my earthly minions, I fear you shall not find your new neighbours to be discerning allies!

But so be it: the Draug Lords must be appeased, and given their due. And what use in any case are the armies of mortal kings to one who has the half-dead fighting for his cause? Ivon, Tobin, Ragnar, surely you must understand that every game has its pawns and sacrifices, and this is surely the Greatest Game of all... Only the strongest and luckiest can hope to survive to see the Second Coming, and share in the rewards the Master has promised. I can only pray to Him that He sees fit to spare some of you at least!

As for my other allies, Beyond the Wall... without Scrying I have no way of knowing how they speed, but am confident that the Urovian Empire will be assailed before long. Imperator Justorix, try standing in my way with a horde of Easterners at your back!

And meantime, the Draug Army prepares for its final assault... Old Master of Time's Arrow, time herself has her bow trained on thee. Thou hast cheated death for many a decade, and the Hour of Reckoning is fast approaching.

And when the Headstone is reunited, then shall the True Summoning be at hand, and all the hosts of Gehenna at the Returned One's beck and call will make the Draug armies seem as trifling as the mortal hosts they now harass. The King of this World shall return to claim His rightful inheritance, and His foremost servants shall be first to share in His glory.

Though a lifetime of learning lies behind me, I cannot easily express in mere words the feelings this anticipation arouses within me.

PART III

CHAPTER 1

BAITING THE BEAR

By the time dawn broke there were just ten of them left. The Wyverns had sought to pick them off as they scrambled around the ridges, darting from copse to copse. Four of their number they'd carried off to an awful fate; Vaskrian's joy at seeing so many brave knights volunteer for his mission had quickly turned to sorrow.

As the first glimmers of sunshine dotted the swirling waves of the Strang Estuary, the survivors hunkered down beneath the trees lining the shore. In the past hour or so the aerial attacks had dwindled off; presumably even the serpents of the sea had to sleep sometimes.

Something to be grateful for, along with the narrow stretch of soil that lay between them and the rocks that tumbled down to meet a thin strand washed by the sea: they didn't have much farther to go.

'Well, we're here,' said Braxus, face set grim beneath his gilded helm. 'Now it's up to you to put your plan into action.' The faces of the other knights – Dantos, Diarmuid, Arianrod, Madogan, and four others who'd survived the night – looked no different. Vaskrian had expected a furore at his plan, but

435

there had been none. Tritons and Wyverns, witches who could enthral the waves and warriors alike… the past two years had shown all of them what kind of world they really lived in. Peasant superstitions would never be peasant superstitions again; tales of knights errant and grey friars were no longer just tales any more.

Pushing his expansive thoughts into the background, Vaskrian cast nervous eyes up at the strengthening skies, the hardening blue offering some comfort from betwixt the branches.

'No sign of them coming back just yet,' he breathed. 'I suppose now is as good a time as any.'

He forced himself to stand on legs that were cramping and weary. Their horses they'd had to leave behind; small use to them they'd be where they were going in any case.

Stretching out his legs and adjusting his hauberk and girdle, Vaskrian kept his shield raised then thought better of it. His heraldic device, designed to look resplendent and catch the eye, didn't seem like such a good idea all of a sudden. Timorously he lowered it.

One more sweep of the skies to check the coast, quite literally, was clear. Turning to where the others crouched behind him, he nodded once.

'Wish me luck.'

Swiftly he exited the trees, heading for the rocks leading down to the shore at a crouching run. He reached them and was just beginning his precarious descent when a shadow fell upon him. Turning, he saw a Wyvern emerge from above the treetops; the cunning creature had lain in wait for them to break cover.

His heart in his mouth, he wedged himself down between two of the biggest rocks, drew his sword and raised his shield to cover his head and shoulders – no more chance of subterfuge, and he'd need its protection. He was well defended by the rocks, but his ability to attack would be severely hampered; the best he could hope for were upwards thrusts.

The sea serpent descended towards him on cracking wings. It didn't roar or scream like such things were supposed to in the lays: just a silent predator, if a supernatural one at that.

As he felt the first lash of its stinging tail strike his heater with a pitiless force, Vaskrian was dimly aware of the cries of fear and dismay from his comrades. He tried to get in a counter attack, but the wyvern hovered well out of reach on its tenebrous wings – if he overextended himself by a dagger's length, he was dead meat.

His only hope was that Braxus and the others would find their courage and come to his aid...

'It's got him cornered,' said Sir Dantos. 'We can't just leave him there!'

'I know, Ezekiel dammit!' snapped Braxus. 'Let me think...' He turned back and looked up, scouring the canopy above them. No sign that the fiend had any hunting partners, that was good.

Turning to face the men again, he said: 'All right, all of you except Sir Madogan here have hunted in the woods with your knightly masters when you were squires, and some of you have lands of your own where you've done just the same. We need to bait this thing – Vaskrian can't hold out forever, but right now he presents a frustrating quarry. So we need to get out there, offer it easier prey. That should give him a chance to get to the shoreline and summon the Seakindred to help us.'

'How?' the question came from Sir Getrix. One of the

less valorous knights in their company, he'd been last to volunteer, probably only doing so to avoid being shamed by the rest.

'I don't know, Sir Getrix!' Braxus snapped again. 'We have to have faith that they can – they share the same waters, after all. In any case, if we all work together we've a chance of beating this thing. Sir Dantos, I doubt your warhammers will avail you much in this fight, so you'll have to be the bait, I'm afraid.'

To his credit, Dantos took that in his stride, simply nodding and giving Braxus his most determined look. Turning to the brothers, he added: 'Arianrod, Diarmuid, you're the fastest swords here alongside Sir Madogan and myself. We'll be the attackers. The rest of you – you're to move in and surround Dantos as soon he draws the creature's attention. Keep your shields high and be ready with swords, but not too ready! Let it come at you, as soon as it does the four of us will break cover and strike at it. If we don't bring it down at the first sally, that means we'll have to trade places – the brothers, Madogan and I become the bait while you four go on the offensive. We repeat that until it gives up and goes off in search of better prey – even if it doesn't, our efforts should give Sir Vaskrian the time he needs to reach the shore unmolested.'

The ashen faces told Braxus that the other knights thought his plan as desperate as he did, but they didn't have a better one. They swiftly arranged themselves, then Braxus gave the signal. Dantos broke cover of the trees, stepping out into the open as the Wyvern continued to batter remorselessly at Vaskrian.

'FIEND!' bellowed Sir Dantos, waving his hammers around almost comically. 'OVER HERE!'

The winged reptilian paused in its aerial assault, hovering just above Vaskrian and glancing over at Dantos evilly.

Some residual intelligence by the looks of things, Braxus thought. *That's good – something clever can be something fooled.*

Dantos continued to bellow in his stentorian voice, which almost appeared to shake the rocks. 'METHINKS YON KNIGHT CONSTITUTES SLIM PICKINGS. COME OVER HERE AND TASTE SOME REAL MEAT!'

If the situation hadn't been so deadly, Braxus would have laughed aloud. Next to him Madogan and Gwydion's sons were almost smiling.

The creature paused for an agonising second. Then it took the bait. Lurching towards Dantos on wings that flapped with an almost elegant languor, it careened towards its new prey.

It would be on the burly knight in a few heartbeats. Braxus gave the hunting signal, and the other four knights broke cover from their position, surrounding Dantos just as the thing drew level and snapped at him. Dantos ducked out of the way as it brought its stinging tail around, catching one of the men in the thigh just below the hauberk. He went down with a scream and began convulsing horribly.

Braxus gave no thought to that as he gave the order to charge. As one the four of them broke cover, dashing over to the Wyvern and lunging at it with their blades. Both brothers missed, but to his credit, Madogan's sword found its mark, puncturing past the creature's thick scales to elicit a spurt of black ichor from its slender flank. Braxus aimed a powerful downwards swipe at a wing, slashing through the membrane and damaging it, though it was too big to lop off with a single blow from an arming sword.

But the Wyvern wasn't done by a long way. Possessed of an awful speed and strength, it swivelled in mid air, simultaneously snapping at Madogan while it lashed Braxus with its deadly envenomed tail. The First Man of Clan Fitzrow instinctively dropped on one knee, taking the barb meant for his leg on his shield, while Madogan's combat instincts, honed on a hundred battlefields, narrowly saved him from losing his head.

Only two of the men guarding Dantos came in for the follow-up attack: one lay dying horribly, the other had dropped sword and shield to flee up the coastline, wailing in panic.

Getrix, curse you for a coward.

Again the Wyvern attacked, this time choosing the brothers for its target. Arianrod and Diarmuid fought with a steely determination, turning aside stinging tail and raking claw as though they were fighting mortal men armed with blades. The two had done their share of knight errantry; more than once had they fought the preternatural denizens of the world and lived to tell tale of it at the firepit. Besides that, they had their dead father to avenge.

The other two knights supposed to be menacing it could not say the same. Their furtive, timid blows did not even distract the Wyvern, and in the blinking of an eye Braxus' plan was in tatters.

Not quite. As the creature pressed them back towards the treeline, he caught a glimpse of Vaskrian pulling himself up from between the rocks and disappearing down towards the shoreline.

Good lad. I just hope there are some of us left to take with you by the time your friends arrive.

❧

Fretfully, Vaskrian scrabbled down the rocks towards the lashing surf of the Strang. In his haste and fear he'd abandoned his sword and shield, but they'd only slow him down now anyway.

The rocks became smaller as the slope levelled out, and

soon he was picking his way through squelching sands. He stopped when he was ankle-deep in the morning tide; his spurs anchored him in the wet sand, a good thing as his limbs were trembling. Already a strong breeze was blowing. Pulling back his cloak where it had threatened to wrap itself around his face and shoulders, he forced himself to concentrate, focusing on the salty skin of the wide seas that seemed to beckon him ever onward.

Raising his arms, he clenched his gauntleted fists and opened his throat.

'LOGRIM!'

Once he called the merman's name, praying to the un-angel of the waters Sjórkunan that he would be heard. If the perfects thought that impious, they could go and swyve themselves.

'LOGRIM!'

Again he called, in a voice that suddenly sounded much older in his ears than his nineteen summers. Still the seas lapped back and forth, placidly counting down the hours of the world.

'LOGRIM!'

Another shadow fell upon him. Only his superior reflexes saved him; throwing himself into the sea, he narrowly escaped the creature's snapping jaws as it swooped and passed above him, before circling back for another try.

Surely not... No, a quick glance back towards the trees told him the other sea serpent was still engaged by his brave comrades.

Desperately, he scrambled deeper into the waves, but that was a crucial mistake – for he was in the Wyvern's own element now. The thing descended on him: no tail, it had him right where it wanted. Vaskrian's last instinct could have been that of a child's – raising his forearms as he lay floundering in the surf, he crossed them before his face. The creature's jaws closed around him, even with his mail and gambeson he would probably lose his hands before he lost his life...

A three-pronged trident embedded itself in the creature's head, forcing it to release its bite just as its teeth began to pierce his armour. Recoiling, the Wyvern hissed sibilantly. It sounded like the sound a red-hot sword makes when it has been cooled at the forge.

More tridents flew over Vaskrian's head, each one finding a mark. The creature hissed again, but it was a weaker sound, like that made by a disgruntled fishwife unhappy with the morning's market prices. A sound of futile resentment.

The Wyvern flopped to the shore, shuddering as it expired. Half a dozen tridents were buried in it, thrown with a strength and accuracy that, even now, made Vaskrian marvel. Turning to look at the sea, he saw them: Logrim and a dozen other mermen in the deeper waters, their upper torsos exposed, half of them still clutching tridents.

'Greetings again, landwalker!' cried Logrim in his fluting voice, which sounded harsh and shrill above water. Yet the sound could not have been more mellifluous to Vaskrian's ears had it come from Braxus' harp.

'I see the sea serpents are giving you some trouble,' continued Logrim. 'They have been bringing us strife also, for they come from places deep below the ground underwater, and we have not seen them in such numbers since the seas were young. Yet we at least know how to fight them.'

'Good for you,' Vaskrian yelled back, recovering his wits. 'But my companions don't – help them!'

Logrim gestured helplessly at his lower parts. 'We do have our limits too,' he pointed out.

Cursing, the young knight realised he was right. The Wyvern up on the rocks was well out of range for a trident throw. His friends would just have to help themselves...

Another knight went down screaming as the Wyvern's tail lashed past his guard, catching him in the eye. All thoughts of hunting formation and guile were gone; now it was a straight-forward contest of brute ferocity.

One they weren't winning. Lightning fast, the creature brought its tail back around in a sidewise swipe, knocking another knight off his feet and sending him flying, while it kept the rest of them at bay with its teeth and claws. Braxus had damaged its wing sufficiently that it couldn't carry any of them off as prey; but as any hunter knew, an animal cornered and wounded is all the more dangerous.

The creature was just about to whip its tail back over its head to strike forwards when Sir Dantos pounced: timing his grapple perfectly, he caught the creature's tail just below the lethal sting in a mighty bear hug, throwing his entire body weight on top of it as he struggled to pin it to the ground.

He was as big and strong as an ox, but even he'd only be able to hold a monster like that for a second or two.

'NOW!' shrieked Braxus, and the four of them lurched forwards. Normally that would have cost at least one more of them his life, but the Wyvern was momentarily distracted by Dantos' audacious move, wrenching its tail free in a heartbeat as it snapped at Madogan. The veteran thrust his shield up, which groaned as it took the fearful pressure of the creature's jaws; he hacked frenziedly at its reptilian snout with his sword, while the brothers Arianrod and Diarmuid slashed at the creature's forelegs. Foul ichor spattered over Braxus' surcoat as he opened up its neck; again the stinging tail rose high before lashing down at him, but this time the strike was ill timed and Braxus caught it on his shield, though the force was still enough to knock him to the ground. Another strike from Madogan, a thrust this time, put the creature's eye out, and it flopped to the ground hissing horribly.

Standing over it, the four of them hacked the creature to shreds remorselessly. When it was done they stopped, covered in black ichor and gasping for breath. The thing was the size of a warhorse, yet somehow they had triumphed.

Then came the grisly task of assessing the casualties. The last knight to go down had suffered nothing worse than a couple of fractured ribs, but the other two had been caught by the venomous tail and already succumbed to Azrael's touch.

With shame Braxus realised one of them was Sir Getrix. Of the other knight who had fled in panic nothing was to be seen.

My humble apologies, Sir Getrix, thought Braxus as he gently closed the dead knight's eyes. *I misjudged thee.*

Excited yelling from the rocks alerted them to Vaskrian.

'They've come!' he said. 'Come down quickly, we need to speak with my friend Logrim. It's all right, he speaks Northlending, though his voice sounds strange enough.'

'Give us a moment,' muttered Braxus, still struggling to regain his breath.

The ashen faces of the surviving knights were scarcely less pale than the blanched ones of their dead comrades, faces locked in horrid grimaces. Their deaths had been neither honourable nor painless. How many more like that before this was all over, Braxus silently wondered.

Vaskrian, irrepressible as ever, was motioning to all of them with alacrity, keen as ever for the quest.

He's the greenest of us all, but at this rate he'll outdo everyone here for errantry and deeds of bard's song.

'All right, Sir Vaskrian of Hroghar,' he said, defaulting to the younger knight's place-of-origin honorific. 'Lay on! Now is the time to meet these peculiar friends of yours, before more of those wretched things come at us.'

Given his recent adventures, holding a parlay of war waist-deep in the sea didn't seem all that strange to Vaskrian, but he could see it discomfited the other knights. Their wounded comrade they'd bade return to the cover of trees to find safety: he was in no fit state for what lay ahead.

That left just half a dozen of them, but a finer pick of knights he couldn't have asked for, save of course for Sir Torgun.

'We can take you to Narborg, the place of the Great Disturber's command,' confirmed Logrim. 'But as you correctly surmised, Nereia's Thaumaturgy you'll need to breathe and move underwater. I've sent for her, but in the meantime you must stay out of danger. Return now to yonder trees, and await our signal!'

'What will that be?' asked Braxus, his face dour and suspicious. Despite his own adventures, he clearly did not relish dealing with the Seakindred, feared throughout the northerly realms of mortalkind. Judging by the looks on their faces, neither did Arianrod and Diarmuid, and as for Madogan, he simply stared stunned, unable to fathom the pass his spurs had brought him to. Only Dantos, the giant who could be both gentle and terrible by turns, seemed to display any kind of equanimity. Was that quiet courage in the big man or merely resignation to the force of his Wyrd, Vaskrian wondered.

But Logrim appeared unperturbed by the knights' mistrust. 'You will know our signal when you see it,' was all he said, his blue skin creasing as he smiled. Without another word, he and his fellow kindred disappeared beneath the waves.

The companions made all due haste to return to the safety of the trees. Of their wounded comrade there was no sign; doubtless he had decided enough was enough and gone his own way. Vaskrian could hardly fault him for that, though he didn't rate his chances.

~

The day wore on, but only a few strands of cloud arrived; of the ghastly Wyverns the skies showed no further sign. Once or twice they heard far-off screams: clearly Ragnar had his unwholesome allies plaguing the hinterlands surrounding Strongholm.

That's good, Vaskrian consoled himself. *The Sea Wizard isn't wise to us, not yet at least.*

It was around the fourth hour past noon when the signal came. True to Logrim's word, it wasn't hard to spot: a myriad water spouts that broke the surface of the waves not much deeper than where they had stood. He felt the periapt the Earth Witch had given him tingling in response: the elemental spirits trapped within, responding to their brethren.

'Now is the time,' he said in a low voice. 'Everyone has their kit packed? Then let's go!'

As one, the six knights dashed back down towards the surf, praying that no more winged horrors would arrive. They'd been forced to doff their shields and much of their armour, stripping down to their gambesons and taking only a single weapon. Scrambling down the rocks, they traversed the strand at a loping run before plunging into the icy waters, still chilly despite the afternoon sun.

It was a curiosity of knights that part of their core training covered swimming: even Vaskrian had been allowed to take a weekly dip in the Warryn, for pitting one's body against the rigours of the water was long known to develop bodily strength. Even so, he was hardly the strongest of swimmers, though the five older men moved through the sea well enough.

By the time they reached the water spouts, the waves were just past chest height. The spouts abruptly vanished, to be replaced by the glistening forms of Logrim and his colleagues. Vaskrian heard the sharp intakes of breath from his comrades as they registered the new arrival among them: bare-breasted and ravishingly beautiful, Nereia was at Logrim's side, surveying the knights with her trademark winsome smirk.

'Well, I must say, it usually takes more effort than this to seduce landwalkers to my bourne,' she said in a high fluting voice that sounded impossibly mellifluous above the waves. 'But fear ye not, brave knights! Stand firm while I lay my Transformation upon thee – and learn that there is naught to be feared from the salty realms besides the creatures we go to fight!'

Her lambent eyes rolled back, as she tilted her head and began her spell. Even the hateful syllables of the language of magick somehow sounded beautiful on her tongue; as though she had found a way to take the words of the archangels and make them palatable to mortal ears.

Vaskrian's periapt shimmered brightly in response, activating and coating him with its protective aura, but his companions were destined to travel the seas by a different means. Madogan was the first to notice what Nereia had done to them, clapping his hands to his neck in horror.

'Reus' teeth, what's this, you witch!' he exclaimed. Glancing at Dantos, who simply stood stupefied, Vaskrian gaped as he saw for himself.

'Gills, you've given them gills!' he exclaimed.

Nereia laughed her high musical laugh, while the mermen exchanged knowing glances and grinned.

'Turned them into dolphins I would have if I could,' she said. 'But no sorcerer save one could ever transform a living being into another form against their will, for such did the one you call Sjórkunan and the other gods decree at the beginning. But come! We haven't time before the creatures of the One Who Must Not Be Disturbed return and come upon us! Logrim and the others will carry you beneath the waves – do not fear, for you are quite safe.'

The other knights were defiantly shaking their heads now; the twins' hands had already moved beneath the waves towards their sword hilts as they realised the change Nereia's magic had wrought in them.

Catching them in the act, the sorceress mouthed a few more words in the language of magick that sounded distinctly syrupy. The knights suddenly stopped what they were doing, becoming glazed of eye and docile.

'You really might want to just do as we say,' said Nereia, switching back to her heavily accented Northlending and smiling sweetly. 'It'll be much easier this way.'

As one, the knights she'd enthralled nodded obediently.

Nereia flashed Vaskrian an apologetic glance. 'There was no easier way than Enchantment to get them to come,' she said.

'They won't forgive you for that easily,' countered Vaskrian. 'Three of the men you've just bewitched spent more than a year being enthralled by an enchantress.'

Nereia appeared unruffled by that remark. 'Perhaps they'll learn to forgive me when they're standing over the corpses of the Great Disturber and his henchmen,' she replied, before suddenly pointing to the skies behind them. 'In any case, there's no time to argue – look!'

Turning, he saw it was true. Four winged shapes, dark

against the cloud-riven firmament, were coming towards them from the direction of Strongholm.

'She's right,' said Vaskrian, throwing himself deeper into the sea. 'Let's away while we still can!'

The enthralled knights stood staring blankly; Nereia repeated the command and they obeyed without hesitation. Logrim whistled an order to his mermen, and two grabbed hold of each of them by the arms.

Before Vaskrian knew it, he was deep beneath the waves again, his breathing perfectly at ease as the Earth Witch's talisman protected him. Down and deeper they went, the travails of land a receding memory as Sjórkunan's domain took them swiftly into its watery embrace.

As he thought of the Sea Wizard and all the trouble he had caused his homeland, the young knight felt hot hatred bubbling up in him. It was too bad not to have his hero Sir Torgun at his side, because now was the time for a reckoning. They hurtled down towards the seabed at an astonishing speed, passing schools of startled fish that flitted to and fro in their wake.

Vaskrian felt his lips curl in a tight, grim, smile.

So you thought to conjure the seas against us, did you Ragnar? Well, two can play at that game.

The dark swirling waters rather mirrored Vaskrian's cast of mind as he went to face the warlock who had done so much harm to his people.

CHAPTER 2

TO THE BRINK OF
APOCALYPSE

Sieges. Long and dull, and no fit work for mounted knights. Wrackwulf supposed he should feel grateful – at least he was doing something, even if it was rather demeaning. But lately a sworn sword to King Carolus, he hadn't been judged fit to lead a sortie in the surrounding countryside by that worthy oppressor. Prince Franz had continued his strategy, sending out parties of Vorstlendings in hit-and-run attacks on the Pangonians; Hugon had responded by ordering groups of knights to patrol the areas where soldiers were foraging for food to feed the army.

No tourney prizes for guessing which detail Wrackwulf had landed.

At least I don't have to spill my compatriots' blood – not yet. His pledge of fealty had been one of pure expediency; his loyalty to Carolus would only stretch as far as it had to, his honour be damned. Unfortunately, Sir Hugon knew that too even if his pompous King didn't.

So here he was, leading half a dozen lightly armoured mounted serjeants, on a 'foraging' mission. *Pillaging* was a more accurate term: the hapless peasantry hereabouts had long since abandoned their clustered hovels and well-tilled fields, taking whatever grain and livestock they could with them.

That left slim pickings for Wrackwulf and his trusty foragers, but pillage they would anyway. One of the grim realities of war was that a large army needed to live off the land to sustain itself during a protracted campaign, and for an invading force that meant the enemy's land.

Or more precisely, the enemy's commoners' land.

Once again Wrackwulf sighed as he watched his serjeants comb a deserted village: their haul so far amounted to few loaves of mouldy bread, a bushel of overripe apples, and one scraggly chicken.

Ah, the glories of war. Wrackwulf old boy, you've really justified your spurs today.

Turning his eyes from the dismal spectacle, he glanced across the fields towards where a rise of hillocks cut the firmament. The skies were a mixture of blue and grey, the clouds having thickened in the past hour or so.

Looks like we'll be having a stint of summer showers in a while too. Yes, and that'll cheer me up no e-

His train of thought was abruptly overturned as his gaze caught it. At this distance it was a faint etching in the side of the nearest hill, but to his sharp eyes it was unmistakable. Three oblong stones, arranged in the shape of a doorway.

Wrackwulf felt the hairs on the back of his neck go stalky as his hackles rose, spurred upwards by a memory he would for all the world have left forgotten. His vision suddenly darkened, as he recalled a thick black fog, one he'd almost been lost in forever just a few seasons ago. Argolian power had saved him that time, pulling him back from the brink, but there were no Argolians to be seen now.

Shaking his head to clear it and blinking fretfully, he wasted no time barking an order in Panglian to his men.

'Finish up your business, lads, we return to camp now.'

The lead serjeant, a grizzled commoner of some fifty winters, looked up at him askance.

'But, sire, you said yourself there are other villages in the area. Our orders were – '

'Your orders are the orders I give you,' said Wrackwulf, cutting him off in a voice that was suddenly steely. 'I may not be Pangonian, but I still outrank you as a belted knight. Now do as you're told – pack up whatever you've managed to filch from this dung-hole, and retake the saddle, all of you. We've business back at camp.'

Involuntarily he flicked his gaze back towards the rise of hillocks. It wasn't just the foremost that sported the menhirs: at least two others lying beyond had the same. He glanced back at the men, but they were too busy muttering amongst themselves as they obeyed his order to follow his gaze. That was good, he supposed: the fewer questions they asked the better. He was going to have enough trouble explaining this to the Pangonian bigwigs as it was.

From her place of concealment in the trees, Ariadha watched her prey with feverish eyes. The heirloom weapon she cradled night and day was talking to her more than ever; an alien crooning only she could hear, did not understand, yet somehow had to heed echoed down the corridors of her febrile mind.

The footsoldiers would make poor pickings, she knew. Her spear demanded blood and souls, yet scorned the scraps she now offered up to it. Brigandines and pot helms, well-kept but simple spears and short swords – these weren't like the two rich knights she'd slaughtered yesterday. How joyously the spear had sung, as she leapt from her place of hiding to impale the first through the throat as he searched for a place to relieve himself. The other had fought bravely, but even in his fancy metal coat he'd been no match for her frenzied assault, not even when the squires had stepped in to lend a hand. That had been the last act of loyalty the poor boys had ever carried out, the last thing in fact they'd done before she'd fed them and their superior to the spear.

It's glyph-embossed shaft quivered in her hands, so much so she could barely control it. *Just a little closer, friends...* She tensed as she crouched, ready to spring. Four of them, foraging for food if she was any judge. Little knowing that today they *were* the food – albeit a poor second course after the rich knights who were supposed to be protecting them.

A happenstance glance. The foremost soldier's eyes alighted on her spot, widening as they registered the glaucous glare of her eldritch blade. In a flash she was out of hiding, closing the gap between them with half a dozen athletic bounds. His sword was barely halfway out of its scabbard before her spear point rammed between his eyes, feeding on his brains as it sucked the life from him.

Screams of fear and surprise as his three comrades took up arms. Three spears to her one. No contest. Her ancient weapon moved with a life of its own, guiding and augmenting her agile movements, pushing them up to a superhuman pitch. Sidestepping the first thrust, she half-circled in and rammed the howling spear into the soldier's side, pulling the blade free and whirling it around in an arc to disarm a second with the butt, before reversing her grip in the blinking of an eye to pierce his heart through his brigandine.

The final soldier dropped his own spear and turned to flee. With scarcely a pause, she hefted hers and threw it at his retreating back. It caught him square between the shoulder blades and he went down with a cry.

Stepping up to him and gripping the shaft, she felt the

delicious elan pouring into her wiry frame as the dying soldier quivered his last. Pulling the blade from his still form, she gazed abstractedly down at the four corpses she'd made in less time than it took a heart to beat a dozen times.

Casually, she ran her tongue across her top lip as she took in her handiwork – *its* handiwork – with a dull satisfaction.

There would be plenty more of this to come, before the Final Hour was out.

All the senior nobility were there, gathered into Carolus' splendid pavilion for the latest council of war as the last of the sun disappeared behind beleaguered Westerburg. The capital city of Westenlund had taken a hell of a pounding – but so far it had held firm. The castle that guarded it was high up and as yet unassailed; Prince Franz continued his sorties, and skirmishes had claimed the lives of several more doughty knights in the past week.

No, not just the sorties, Wrackwulf corrected himself mentally, though he'd been chary of sharing his insight with his new liege. The two knights from Gallia whose corpses had been discovered yesterday evening along with the bodies of their squires bore distinctive puncture wounds. At first some idiot had put it down to an unchivalrous lance attack by way of ambush, before realising that the trees that furnished ambushers cover would have precluded a lance charge in the first place. That had left the Pangonians puzzled, and set Wrackwulf thinking.

His hypothesis had been confirmed by the faint discolouration around the wounds: a putrefaction that had set in far too early for such fresh corpses. He'd managed to get a good look at the bodies brought back to camp before the perfects took them for burial – no Argolians, the useless priests hadn't even noticed. Too busy with their ineffectual prayers.

And to think the one useful Order the Creed gave mortalkind is now outlawed in so-called greater Pangonia. Horskram, wherever you are, tread carefully.

Dismounting and handing his horse's reins to an attending squire Wrackwulf scoured the surrounding trees as his mind returned to Ariadha. She was out there somewhere. And he'd be a coxcomb if the same eldritch forces he'd been so abruptly reminded of during his pillaging detail weren't to be found residing in that dread weapon she carried.

He supposed this was what came of keeping company with Argolians and taking up their quests: out there, on the Westerling Isles, such a fearful heirloom had seemed almost mundane, to be expected in a far-flung land where sorcerer-priests held sway.

Not for the first time, he shook his head ruefully as he made the short walk to Carolus' pavilion, guarded by two soldiers clad in mail and clutching halberds. He should have seen it sooner. No good could come of owning such a weapon – especially not now, when the world stood on the brink of some godawful Second Coming that would see such artefacts come to the full fruition of their power and –

He hesitated in his last thought, not wanting to finish it.

And the dead rise from their graves.

The chill returned to his spine as he halted before the guards. The Pangonian soldiers squinted at him suspiciously; naturally he wasn't yet trusted in the King's camp.

Pushing his icy thoughts away, Wrackwulf did his best to sound calm as he said: 'Sir Wrackwulf of Bringenheim, but lately sworn to King Carolus. I've returned from a pilla-foraging mission, and I bear news that His Majesty should hear at once.'

His Panglian, honed across seasons of freelance campaigning, was decent enough despite his thick accent. The soldiers exchanged a cursory glance before parting halberds to permit him entry. Wrackwulf passed between them with a curt nod, once again having occasion to thank the unwritten but immutable feudal code that gave him leave to pass common folk without explaining his business.

But he was going to have to explain that business to royalty and nobility, and that wasn't going to be easy.

Inside, the capacious tent was well lit by braziers, incense burners banishing the stink of the crowded camp. Tapestries and rugs completed the aura of opulent splendour befitting the vainest, most powerful and ambitious of monarchs, but Wrackwulf had little time to spare for such fine detail. Rather his attention was focused on the pavilion's occupants – oh, they were all here right enough.

He took them in at a sweeping glance. Sir Aremis Hare-Lip, by far the closest the Pangonians got nowadays to producing a decent chivalrous knight. Next to him was Sir Hugon, a stalwart and competent commander in his own right, though Wrackwulf sensed that living in the shadow of his older more famous brother Sir Azelin still rankled. Then there was brute-faced Lord Clovis – not yet out of his teens and a disgrace to the spurs, if half the stories Wrackwulf had heard held true. Then Morvaine, as haughty a lord as any that ever stalked a camp or castle – Wrackwulf had quickly made a mental note to steer clear of that one whenever he could, only now wasn't one of those happy times.

The Occidental Margraves were there too, of course – the barons who held sway over the western fiefdoms of Pangonia and soon hoped to say the same of his native country – but it was Kaye and Aravin who unnerved him most. Wrackwulf couldn't say why – at first glance they were little more than just another couple of pampered lords, exalted far above their natural prowess by the fortunate circumstances of their birth.

But there was something – *something* – about the pair that had him on edge. Was it the sly smirking way they had of exchanging glances when they thought no one was looking, as if privy to some private jest that only they knew about?

Wrackwulf honestly wasn't sure – but as he approached the assembled worthies gathered around an expansive oak table before which Carolus sat perched atop his ludicrous portable throne, he had a growing feeling that they were somehow connected to Ariadha's cursed weapon and the barrows he'd spotted on the heath that afternoon. He knew it wasn't an absurd notion either – during their association, Horskram had hinted at a conspiracy that stretched far and wide. Who was to say these two weren't in on it?

He could scarcely know how accurate his guess was at that time, but he was destined soon to find out.

'Ah, Sir Wrackwulf,' drawled the King as he drew level with the table, complete with all the accoutrements of a battle plan – castle, ships, troops and terrain all lovingly mocked up in miniature. 'So glad you could join us. You are the last to report back today – I do hope the wait proves worth it.'

A few sycophantic snickers showed the King his humour was appreciated, though it wasn't by the butt of it.

Suppressing his ire, Wrackwulf responded deferentially. 'I rather fear you shall find it all too worth the wait, my liege.' The last two words were forced between teeth that almost gritted, though Wrackwulf knew better than to make his disdain so obvious.

The King blinked mildly. 'Oh really? Surely you can't have anything that interesting to report from a routine forage. Or did you manage to locate a particularly succulent pig for us to dine on?'

This time the laughter was more genuine, the King having said something that almost approached a witticism.

Quelling his irritation again, with more difficulty this time, Wrackwulf responded: 'No, the villages yielded up their typically meagre haul, the yeomanry having long fled with whatever they could. It's what I espied just outside the last hamlet we ransacked that I thought you should know about, sire.'

Carolus arched an eyebrow. He'd been about to take a swig from the decorated golden goblet at his elbow, but deferred the motion as what Wrackwulf said caught his attention.

'And what would that be, pray tell?'

Wrackwulf took a deep breath, his mail hauberk jingling as he shifted awkwardly.

'This will sound passing strange,' he began uncertainly. 'But I glimpsed some ancient barrow mounds, and... previous engagements give me cause to think they might be dangerous.'

King Carolus simply looked bemused, while the gathered nobles laughed. No, not all of them. Catching Kaye and Aravin in the corner of his eye, Wrackwulf saw they were exchanging glances. Only this time there was no smirking between them.

'I see,' said the King flatly. 'You have a... superstitious fear of the long dead?' Carolus was putting in an effort at a straight face, but Morvaine and Hugon and the others were openly mocking him now. Even Aremis could not resist a grin that made his disfigured face even more ugly.

Wrackwulf didn't feel incensed now, he was too busy groaning inwardly for that. What in Virtus' name had he been thinking? But it was too late to back out now.

'I fear them with good reason,' he persisted. 'I was a knight errant as well as a mercenary. Barrow wights, also named Draugar by some, are real, Your Majesty, they are no superstition.'

Now the nobles were guffawing. Except Aravin and Kaye, who were staring at him fixedly.

'I see,' said the King, still struggling to control his mirth. 'You think the barrow men are coming to join us in our war? But, stay, Wrackwulf, why so glum? After all, they could end up siding with us!'

More guffaws. Wrackwulf clenched and unclenched his mufflered hands. He could feel his face flushing as mockery transmuted, as it so often does, into outright scorn. He felt like the court jester he currently appeared to be. What could he have expected from such a fool's errand? Not one of the high-born men present had even considered taking up knight errantry in their purpled careers, they could hardly be expected to believe –

Shouts and cries from outside the tent cut through the laughter. Instinctively, the occupants turned to face the pavilion entrance. A commotion was running through the camp, a great tumult that could not be lost on any martial ear.

'We're under attack!' cried Morvaine.

Saved by the bugle, thought Wrackwulf as he moved swiftly towards the tent porch. Many a time at tourney melees he'd narrowly avoided being unhorsed and forfeiting his harness by the clarion sounding the close of the day's fighting. Now it looked as though an evening of the same had spared him further embarrassment.

He was the first to exit the pavilion. In the dusky gloaming he could see knights and footsoldiers scrambling for horses and armour. A low rumble heralded the unmistakable sound of hooves; Franz had dispensed with the niceties of chivalry once again, this time to launch a treacherous assault on the army camp itself. Wrackwulf had to admire the audacity of it.

Dashing over to where his horse was hobbled, he set

about freeing the beast. He had no squire now Ariadha had disappeared, and the young man in attendance was busy obeying orders being barked at him by several other knights. Meanwhile, shouts had turned to screams: Franz's sortie had reached the outskirts of the camp. Hugon had sentries posted at regular intervals around the perimeter, but unmounted soldiers would be quick fodder for knights hell-bent on mayhem.

Wrackwulf kept his mind cool as he deftly undid the last knot binding his charger, which whickered nervously. Rising from his task he patted the creature gently, before mounting up in an easy fluid motion that belied his considerable girth.

'There, there, now lad,' he soothed. 'Nothing to worry about. We'll have you in thick of the action soon enough.'

No time or space for a lance charge; nudging his horse with his outside leg and keeping the reins in hand, he turned it towards the direction of the fighting and unslung an axe from his saddle. He could see them clearly: dozens of fully armoured knights rampaging through the camp towards the centre where he was.

You're brave and bold, Franz. Foolhardy and you don't know when you're beaten. But you're brave and –

'Just where do you think you're going?'

He whirled in the saddle. Kaye and Aravin sat mounted on their warhorses just behind him. They'd been on duty that day too, so they were still clad in harness as well, though their swords remained sheathed at their sides.

It was Kaye who had spoken. Wrackwulf had him down as the smarter of the two, though he only really had instinct to go by at this stage of their acquaintance.

'To defend my liege from a night-time ambush.' Best to play this one straightly.

Kaye was having none of it, however. 'Yes, I'm sure you

were,' he sneered. 'Of course, the oath of a Vorstlending freesword is always worth writing down in gold lettering.'

Wrackwulf smiled easily, though the rising sounds of conflict were dinning in his ears as the King's men began a confused fightback at the edge of the camp. Some of the attacking knights had already broken past their defences and were getting closer.

'Gold letters eh?' he breezed. 'Literacy is it, Lord Kaye? Your accomplishments are impressive.'

Kaye favoured that jibe with a nasty smirk, though Aravin glowered as though offended on his friend's behalf. *Oh yes, definitely the less clever of the two.*

What Kaye said next only confirmed how right Wrackwulf was, though not in any way he savoured.

'Oh yes, I can read, sir knight, in languages your superstition can barely begin to fathom.'

The hackles were back, pressing icy needles down the length of his spine. In a voice that was suddenly both guttural and sibilant, Kaye pronounced several syllables that sounded immediately hateful to the ear. Their effect was no less so to the rest of the body: Wrackwulf felt himself tense involuntarily as every muscle in his body seemed suddenly to cramp and spasm without reason. His charger, sensing a profound change in its master, began moving skittishly, anxious to be rid of the alien presence that burdened it.

As Wrackwulf sloughed helplessly off his horse, landing paralysed in the dirt, Aravin nudged his destrier slowly forwards. The bigger and stronger of the two margraves, his sword was out of its scabbard now, blade glinting dully in the light of camp fires and lanterns.

'It seems this jumped-up freesword learned rather too much of our ways on his errant journeys, don't you think Lord Kaye?' he said in a voice that was dangerously casual.

'Indeed, Lord Aravin,' said Kaye behind him. 'After all our

plans, we can't afford to have a superstitious freesword spoil things now can we?'

Aravin dismounted with a single athletic motion, keeping sword in hand. Wrackwulf was lying on his side, still in a sitting position. His muscles were screaming, but he couldn't budge an inch. Kaye's sorcery had robbed him of all motion but for the eyes.

Damn it, it's a trick, just a sorcerous trick. Fight it Wrackwulf, old boy, fight it!

Aravin drew level with him. With his sabatoned foot he pushed Wrackwulf's frozen shoulder, turning him over on to his back. He remained in that ridiculous sitting position, the axe clutched uselessly in his stiff fingers. With slow deliberation the margrave placed the tip of his sword under Wrackwulf's chin, just above the ventail, angling the blade so it would slide neatly beneath it into his throat.

Wrackwulf gazed into the margrave's pitiless grey eyes, and saw no mercy in them. Not that he could even beg for it if he'd wanted to.

The sword point was cold as it pressed at the top of his larynx. Wrackwulf closed his eyes, not wanting the Margrave's cold chiselled features to be the last thing he ever saw.

'WHAT IN STYGNOS' NAME ARE YOU DOING?'

Wrackwulf's eyes flicked open again as he felt the pressure released from his throat. He recognised the voice, but it was hard to be sure above the din of combat. A shouted exchange, Kaye and Aravin's voices mingling angrily with a third man's... Yes, it was him, it had to be.

Sir Aremis.

Sir Aremis almost flinched under the withering scrutiny of the two margraves. Technically they outranked him as lords of men, and he considered himself a humble knight averse to intrigue, but even he knew the Purple Garter served as a useful counterpoise to the old feudal hierarchy. And he hadn't sworn an oath to the most exclusive knightly order in the realm to watch while a sworn and belted comrade was summarily executed without so much as a trial.

Kaye was of a different mind.

'Stay out of this, garter knight,' he snarled from the saddle. 'This Vorstlending mercenary is a traitor and a recreant. Now his compatriots are among us, he's shown his true colours.'

Aremis was clad in plate and armed, though he hadn't taken the saddle yet. He'd been just about to, when he'd caught the bizarre exchange out of the corner of his eye. Good thing he hadn't lowered his visor – peripheral vision in these newfangled helmets was definitely something of a casualty.

'So you say,' replied the young knight evenly, glancing dubiously at Wrackwulf's prostrated form, his limbs bizarrely twisted as if gripped by some strange sickness. 'He looks rather too ill to be plotting any treachery to me.'

Kaye muttered something to himself under his breath. The evening air seemed to shimmer momentarily and unnaturally before Aremis's vision... He blinked, and when his eyes opened again, Wrackwulf was sitting up, rubbing his limbs and grimacing.

'He doesn't seem so terribly ill to me,' said Kaye in a voice that was rather too sure of itself for Aremis's liking. Aravin had resumed menacing Wrackwulf with his blade, though the Vorstlending looked to be out of immediate danger – for now.

'Whatever personal grievance you have against this knight can surely wait,' said Aremis, nodding his head meaningfully in the direction of the encroaching fray. He knew the haughty lords well enough to safely assume they were pursuing a personal vendetta. Now, of all times, when they were under attack by the real enemy: the margraves' pride reached the height of folly. Frankly, he'd had enough of cruel and capricious nobles on this campaign to last a lifetime.

Their stand-off was interrupted by the approach of half a dozen Vorstlending knights, who'd taken advantage of their surprise attack to cut a swathe through the camp. Without another word, Aremis launched himself into his saddle – in accordance with custom, he'd cleared "the leap" directly after being knighted, taking to the stirrups in full harness using only his feet and legs was second nature to him.

If the others marvelled at his skill, they had little time to show it. Aravin and Wrackwulf regained their saddles not a moment too soon, arming themselves just in time before the enemy engaged. The camp had disintegrated into skirmishing clusters; the footsoldiers had taken severe casualties, but they were beginning to rally. Pangonian knights and serjeants who'd managed to saddle up were fighting too, but others were in a parlous situation, either bereft of armour and mounted or partly armoured and bereft of horses.

Without a second thought Aremis engaged his first assailant, knocking aside his thirsting blade with an almost casual flick of the wrist before riposting at his exposed armpit. The blow was just slightly off-kilter; it failed to find the enemy's heart but was good enough sever muscle, ligaments and tendons. The Vorstlending knight gave vent to a pitiful shriek, his sword arm hanging uselessly at his side as he spurted blood from the wound. In an instant Aremis finished him, crumpling him from the saddle with a pulverising overhead strike to the helm. With a little luck, he might even live: Sir Aremis didn't see the point in killing good brave knights if you could incapacitate them instead and perhaps hold them for ransom.

Quick as a flash another knight was on him. Burly and

thickset and wielding a mace, this fellow was made of sterner stuff than his comrade. Aremis traded blows with him, before a deft upwards cut smashed the haft of his assailant's weapon.

Never bring a pole-arm to a swordfight, he had time to wryly reflect as the enemy knight put spurs to flanks and wheeled his horse clumsily around. Aremis went to strike his discomfited foe's exposed back... But held the blow slightly, so it merely glanced off his mailed shoulder.

Too soft, Stygnos dammit, I'm always too soft. This is a full-blooded skirmish you fool, not a chivalrous tourney melee.

But it was too late for self-recriminations: the Vorstlending had kicked his horse into a gallop and was fleeing the field. Glancing about him, Aremis saw all his compatriots that could were doing likewise: clearly Franz's aim had been merely to harass and perturb the invading army, which he'd done right well by the looks of things.

Hugon over to his right, bellowing commands to follow the retreating knights: level the scoreboard, by Stygnos. He'd hope in vain: Franz's knights were all mounted on swift coursers that easily outpaced the slower destriers of the Pangonian heavy cavalry. Not anticipating a lance charge, the Crown Prince had equipped his sortie perfectly for the kind of hit-and-run tactics that had just served him so well.

Suddenly remembering the stand-off, Aremis turned to look for the others. One of the Vorstlending knights that had assailed them lay groaning next to his courser, trying to staunch the flow of blood from his thigh just below the slit in his hauberk. But of Aravin and Kaye there was no sign. Nor Wrackwulf, for that matter.

From her latest hiding spot in the trees, Ariadha watched the bloodshed taking place in the camp with glee. The spear was crooning again, urging her to join the fray, and she had some difficulty resisting it.

No, not these ones, she mentally urged, as the Vorstlending sortie began a swift but orderly retreat from the camp they'd just rampaged through. *These ones are on our side.*

But she knew already that the cursed heirloom she called a weapon took no side but its own. Since claiming human lives with it, she had awoken something in its metallic form that had long slept dormant – for how long, she wondered? She could not recall if her father Madrix had ever used it in battle to kill anyone himself. If so he'd certainly never mentioned the unwelcome side effects that came with using such a dread weapon.

But casting it aside was already out of the question. Not only did it palpably augment her fighting abilities; she was dependent on it now, as though it were a bad bedfellow she could not bear to leave.

And what's more, she sensed it *knew* that. It knew that right well.

Patience, my love, she thought with only a trace of irony, *you'll have your blood and souls to feed on soon enough.*

She felt the spear almost purr with delight as she stood up and began stalking towards the camp, shielded by the thickening cover of darkness.

The two margraves were hot on his trail. Wrackwulf had made for the treeline as soon as he'd had the opportunity; he'd spent enough time with Argolians to know that sorcerers had their limits too – put enough distance between himself and Kaye and Aravin, and they wouldn't be able to enthral him again.

At least, that's what he hoped.

Digging his spurs into the flanks of the courser he'd

stolen, he directed it towards the thin hunting trail that disappeared beneath the boughs. As he passed under the eaves he half expected something dramatic – a bolt of lightning or a ball of fire. But no: clearly the margraves hadn't remained this close to the centre of earthly power by being so obvious.

He also hoped their need to maintain secrecy would be something he could turn to his advantage.

Ariadha was halfway towards the camp when she caught the horseman riding swiftly away from it towards the trees she'd just exited. The rider was making for the belt of woodlands to her left; not far behind were two others, pursuers by the looks of things. She felt the spear shiver excitedly – this was ideal, prey separated from the rest of the herd. Too busy fighting each other to spot the real threat... a vulpine grin split Ariadha's face as she turned about and moved back towards the trees at a crouching lope.

Tonight she would hunt.

Aremis hastily traded in his charger for a courser. He'd been noted for his prowess as a huntsman from early youth – his duties with the Purple Garter precluded him from enjoying the chase as often as he liked, but his old tracking skills served him well now. Three sets of hoof prints leading away from the camp and city towards the north-eastern edge of the wide clearing: it had to be the margraves and Wrackwulf.

By Virtus and Stygnos but I'll get to the bottom of this yet, he thought as he spurred his roan on. He'd never liked the smarmy margraves, but even for them this was suspect behaviour. Something was afoot, but he had no idea what. Abruptly reining in his horse he leaned down from the saddle and squinted at the tracks. The fading light was not his friend. But no; it was clear enough where they'd gone: straight towards the game trail he'd reconnoitred when Hugon had first given the order to settle the army here.

Putting spurs to flanks again he resumed riding, pounding across the gloom-shrouded sward towards whatever adventure the Unseen had in store for him.

It was fully dark by the time Wrackwulf reached a clearing. Hastily he dismounted; rummaging frantically through the saddle bags of the horse, he found what he'd hoped would be there – a pair of tallow candles. Grimacing, he pared off a chunk from the base of each and rolled them into little balls, which he then shoved into his ears. He'd have preferred wax of course – but wax was a luxury even rich knights could scarcely afford. Putting rendered animal fat into his lug holes was hardly the most appealing thing he'd ever done – but he had to hope not hearing the hated words of the language of magick would provide some defence against it. Then he retook the saddle and nudged his whickering steed off to the side. There wasn't enough room to conceal himself and his mount perfectly, but he wouldn't stand a chance against two mounted knights on foot. His sword was in one hand and his axe was in the other: he had to hope the element of surprise would allow him to get two quick strikes in before they had time to react.

Hope, hope, hope... that was all he seemed to do these days.

Presently a glimmering of unnatural light dashed said hopes. Peering through tangled boughs made ebon with night's touch he saw a strange apparition, what appeared to be a lucent ball of light like a miniature moon, hovering above the silhouetted forms of the two margraves as they ambled towards him, swords drawn.

Of course... they'd hardly be shy of using their black arts now there was no one else around to see.

Guess this is it, Wrackwulf old boy, he thought, tightening his grip on hilt and haft. *Stygnos willing, you'll at least have a chance to go down fighting like a proper knight ought to.*

He felt the first beams of the margraves' light spell fall on him like ghostly fingers. Aravin and Kaye grinned as they approached; one of them muttered something and Wrackwulf felt himself tensing as the same paralysis as before started to creep over his limbs. But wait... its power was muted this time. His ploy was working!

The margraves evidently sensed the same, because their swords were ready as they drew level with him. At least he'd get his brave last stand.

But if his stratagem had helped reduce the spell's effect, it hadn't completely erased its power; his limbs felt sluggish as he engaged his foemen. He'd watched the two lords sparring, and knew them for what they were: journeymen fighters exalted by birth high above their true status. In a fair fight he could have confidently bested them, odds be damned.

But this was no fair fight.

He barely managed to parry Kaye's predictable thrust, while locking Aravin's blade in the crook of his axe. Normally a riposte from his own sword would have sent Kaye tumbling from the saddle, but his movements were slow, hesitant. He saw rather than heard the margraves laughing as Kaye knocked aside his clumsy riposte before lashing out with a counter-strike of his own; at the same time Aravin disengaged his sword from Wrackwulf's axe before bringing it down onto his helm.

Wrackwulf saw stars as the two blows simultaneously took him, Kaye's blade catching him square in the chest. His helm and hauberk saved his life, but it was only a fleeting reprieve; the double impact of the blows threw him from the saddle, and Wrackwulf landed heavily in the soil. Even now, he wasn't quite beaten; lurching up he tried to stand, but the nagging slowness would not leave him; Kaye struck him again on the helm as Aravin slid neatly from the saddle and prepared to finish him off.

Ariadha closed towards the sound of clashing steel. The spear had almost completely taken over her will; she was anxious to arrive at the scene of combat soon enough to prevent any of the combatants dying before she – *they* – could feed.

Bursting through the trees into a small clearing, she saw her prey: three knights, only one of them still mounted. The second was stood over where the third lay prone, sword held high and point downwards, ready to deal the death blow.

Screaming defiance in Gnathtéanga, she launched herself across the clearing towards the second knight.

He barely had time to react as she cleared the distance between them, loping like a boar in high heat and bellowing more loudly still. Stunned by the spectacle of the wildling apparition, the knight scarcely had time to defend himself; Ariadha's spear curled unnaturally in mid-strike, circling around the Pangonian's hasty parry and dragging Ariadha's limbs with it. It crooned with delight as it plunged into his chest, puncturing pitilessly past the gilded breastplate and piercing his sternum just above the heart. She half expected his comrade to strike down at her from the saddle, but the strange knight had other ideas in mind: syllables that she recognised all too well escaped his mouth, and Ariadha felt her limbs grow leaden.

But if Kaye's spell was effective against the warrior woman, it had no power over the eldritch spear she bore. Ariadha felt like a wooden manikin as the weapon wielded its wielder, dragging its point from the unmounted knight's spurting body to plunge deep into the flanks of the warhorse ridden by the other. The agonized beast joined its screams to those of the dying knight, rearing frantically and hurling his companion from the saddle.

Just then a fourth rider burst on to the scene; this one was a tall well-made knight who sat his horse well. A true test of her mettle. Even now the other two knights who yet breathed were picking themselves up, groping through the darkness for weapons as the one she'd stabbed stopped screaming, his eyes freezing over. Whatever spell his comrade had been working had been broken by his fall; Ariadha felt herself able to move freely again. Bounding over to the fallen lord, she raised the spear high.

Aremis could barely register what his senses were telling him. The clearing was lit by a preternatural globe of light that seemed to hover in the air; Aravin lay dead while the rene-gade Wrackwulf clambered stiffly to his feet. A strange apparition clutching a spear of an odd metallic hue stalked over to where Kaye was lying prone, clearly intent on killing him.

Aremis's combat instincts took over. Spurring his horse forwards and unsheathing his sword in one fluid motion, he interposed the blade between the spear point and Kaye. A horrid shrieking sound set his teeth on edge as the blueish spear-point carved a second fuller down the length of his blade, almost forcing him to loosen his grip on the sword.

But Aremis was quicker and stronger than the best of knights; swiftly disengaging, he brought the blade round in an improvised lunge at the apparition's head, which appeared to be only half covered with a scraggly mane of wild hair. The creature reacted quickly, ducking back out of range, giving Kaye the chance to sit up and crawl backwards to safety. Meanwhile, Wrackwulf had rearmed and regained his feet.

'AREMIS!' he called, rather more loudly than necessary the young knight thought. 'DON'T KILL HER! THIS ISN'T WHAT IT LOOKS LIKE!'

Aremis peered at the apparition. It appeared to be struggling with something − with the *spear*? And that luminous ball of infernal light... The young knight's hackles rose as he realised sorcery was afoot. He'd been too busy with his duties to engage much in errantry, but he'd heard the tales from one or two of the older knights who'd given it a go in their youth.

'Lord Kaye,' he said, addressing the Margrave, who was only just beginning to compose himself enough to rise. 'What in Virtus' name is going on here?' The Margrave did not reply, but gazed ashen-faced at his stricken comrade, whose upturned face had turned waxy in the ghostly light.

'HE'S A' − Wrackwulf suddenly realised he was shouting and lowered his voice, pointing accusingly at Kaye with his blade − 'He's a *warlock*, Sir Aremis. Lord Kaye and his erstwhile chum here have been practising grammarye. Yon wild woman is an old adventuring comrade of mine − a savage from the Westerling Isles, but loyal and true. Please, Sir Aremis, I know you've little reason to trust me, but this isn't what it loo−'

Aremis was dimly aware of Lord Kaye muttering to himself. The Margrave had retreated back out of range of the wild woman and her spear, partially placing Aremis and his steed betwixt them. The words he couldn't quite catch, they sounded awfully jarring at first but then suddenly... quite appealing.

Kaye was addressing him directly now, in Panglian. Of course it was Panglian, what else would a true lord of men like Kaye speak in?

'You don't want to listen to this traitor,' he was saying, in words of honey. 'He slew the most honourable Lord of Varangia, First Scion of the House of Chorlangue, and yon barbarian is his accomplice. Justice must be done by thee, knight of the Purple Garter!'

Aremis inhaled sharply as the words suddenly hardened in his mind, striking at his psyche like a warhammer against a breastplate.

'Justice, of course,' said Aremis, tightening his grip on his sword hilt. 'Sir Wrackwulf of Bringenheim, I attaint thee of high treason – throw down your arms!'

Wrackwulf mouthed a curse and lunged at Lord Kaye. The wild woman shifted tack and came straight for Aremis – or rather his steed. Aremis was a superb horseman, but the outlander moved with a speed that wasn't natural. His manoeuvre quickly turned to a desperate effort to quit the saddle and land on his own two feet as the baying spear pierced his courser's flank.

Yes, *baying* – he was sure of it, the accursed weapon had a voice of its own.

He landed awkwardly just as his horse collapsed with a neighing shriek. He would have found his balance, but he was yet to get used to the extra weight of his new armour, and sat down hard with an ungainly clinking sound. Aremis only had time to raise his sword in a crosswise parry, clutching the blade in his lobstered gauntlets and pushing the flat up to intercept the spear point. He only just succeeded. The Westerling took the force of his parry, using it to spin around like a whirlwind before striking at him again. Quick as a flash he interposed his blade a second time, almost with enough force to knock the spear from her hands. Tightening her grip on the shaft she lunged again; but the precious second that move had cost her was enough, just enough, for the young knight to regain his feet. They traded blows and blocks and jabs, as she tried to use the spear's superior range to her advantage.

Aremis felt the sweat begin to pour off of him, though it was a mild summer night. Bad enough his opponent was a tidy match for him, but she was a woman to boot – in any case, he'd never seen anyone, man, woman or beast, fight like this. Over to his right and behind him, he was dimly aware of the clash of arms and a shout of triumph.

Wrackwulf struggled to keep his assailant at bay. Kaye was up to his tricks, mouthing some spell or other, but it seemed to lack power and he still could not hear the hated words. Even so, it had enough of an effect to slow him just a fraction.

Which meant that his fight with the arrogant Margrave was now a real contest.

Kaye grinned evilly as he lunged again at Wrackwulf. An obvious feint, the man's face gave it away, and the freelancer easily intercepted it with the axe before striking at the Margrave's face with his sword. But Kaye was well able for the task of stepping back and deflecting his counter strike, before stepping in again and assailing him with a methodical but precise series of cuts and thrusts. Wrackwulf gave ground on feet that seemed to cling to the sodden earth beneath them.

Can't beat him in a straight fight while he's got me ensorcelled, he thought desperately. *I'll have to outsmart him.*

Luckily, the spell Kaye had used on him hadn't dulled his

wits, unlike the one he'd used on Sir Hapless Hare-Lip but moments ago.

Giving ground a little more and goading Kaye to come after him, Wrackwulf saw what he was looking for. He was pressed close to the clearing's edge now, where the trees loomed resentfully over ground that human travail had reclaimed from their arboreous realm. One of these had a low overhanging branch under which Wrackwulf had just passed; edging back a little further, he waited for Kaye to follow.

When the Margrave did, Wrackwulf was ready: reaching back over his shoulder, he hurled the axe with all his might. His aim was true and strong: the axe sheared through the branch, causing it to land on Kaye's head. In his arrogance, the Margrave hadn't bothered to put on a helm, and though his mailed coif took the worst of it, the blow was enough to stun him. As the tree branch fell to the ground beside the tottering Margrave, Wrackwulf was already barrelling towards him. Kaye tried to recover his guard, but it was too late: with a roar of triumph Wrackwulf thundered into him, his sword clashing with his opponent's as he applied all his body weight to the charge. The Pangonian was tall but slight of build; Wrackwulf's stocky body was solid sinew and bone. The Margrave went down, swords pinned between them as the Vorstlending landed on top of him. With his free hand, Wrackwulf clawed up a sod from the earth and shoved it unceremoniously into Kaye's mouth.

'I think,' he said, in words he could barely hear through the animal fat clogging his ears, 'we'll have less of your cant, sirrah.' Wrackwulf shoved the sod further into the Margrave's mouth, almost choking him. Kaye thrashed desperately like a caught fish, trying to free his sword, but Wrackwulf had him pinned: sorcery or no sorcery, the Pangonian was no match for him in a straight contest of brute strength.

Just then he faintly heard a piercing cry. Looking up he

saw Sir Aremis had somehow managed to disarm Ariadha, who now nursed a cut to her wrist. The sheening spear lay buried in the soil next to her; Wrackwulf could swear it was quivering, trying to free itself from the unsatisfying turf.

~

Aremis gazed at the alien spear with loathing and horror. It had taken every ounce of swordmastery at his disposal to disarm his opponent – the last thing he wanted to do was kill a woman, even one such as this.

And come to think of it, he wasn't sure he could have, even if he had wanted to. The outlander had fought him with the puissance of three veteran knights; only by Ezekiel's will had he managed to get the best of her. She glowered at him as she clutched her bleeding wrist, but he'd moved in quickly after disarming her: if she wanted her weapon back, she'd have to go through his first.

'AREMI- Aremis!' cried Wrackwulf. 'Don't kill her! I swear by Virtus and Stygnos and the Redeemer's own wounds that this isn't what Kaye says it is.'

Aremis suddenly felt very confused. Kaye. Yes, Kaye... He'd never liked the Margrave, but hadn't he been willing to fight and die for him just now? The First Scion of the House of Guye was struggling beneath Wrackwulf's bulk, trying to free himself and sputtering incoherently. Was that *grass* he was spitting from his mouth?

Aremis shook his head in bewilderment. This evening only got stranger and stranger.

'You need to help me,' persisted Wrackwulf. 'Get some bandages from yon saddle bags – we need to bind up the outlander's wound and I need to gag this poltroon.' He favoured the struggling lord with a sour glance. 'I'll not have him bound only to ensorcel us with that poisoned tongue of his.'

Aremis narrowed his eyes and did not lower his sword. 'That's quite an accusation to make against the Margrave of Quillon,' he said. 'Why should I believe a Vorstlending who but lately turned cloak?'

Wrackwulf only shook his head. 'I CAN'T HE- I can't hear you!'

The Pangonian knight's confusion went up a notch. 'Why on earth not?'

Still holding the margrave down with his sword arm, the freelancer reached up to pluck something from his ear.

'Repeat your question, please.'

Patiently, Aremis did so.

'Your gracious King didn't exactly offer me a wealth of choices,' replied Wrackwulf. 'And you forget I was always a freelancer – I fight for those that pay. And Carolus's terms, they were reasonable enough though the alternatives he offered were paltry. But what I didn't sign on for was this' – he jammed the sod back down into Kaye's gullet as he almost spat it free – 'heathen witchery in our very midst!'

Aremis was having none of it, however.

'Oh no, Sir Wrackwulf – everyone at court thinks me a dolt, good only for the lists and terrible at intrigue. And there may be some truth in that – but even I can see you're hiding something! You don't seem half as surprised as you ought to be, given the accusations you're making!'

Wrackwulf sighed. 'Ah, you had to find your wits now of all times didn't you?' He sounded suddenly very weary. 'All right, Sir Aremis, I'll tell you what I know and how I know it – but I should warn you it's a very long tale, and I'll be damned if I'm going to tell it while sitting on top of this jumped-up popinjay and hedge wizard, while my boon companion over there bleeds to death! Now, please, just trust me a little longer and do as I ask.'

Aremis flicked his glance over to the warrior-woman. She had subsided to a crouching position, still clutching her bloody wrist. Though she glared at the young knight reproachfully, her eyes never strayed from the spear for too long. The strange eldritch weapon had subsided to a soft metallic moaning.

'Does the outlander speak your tongue?' he asked. 'Tell her to get it.'

'She might bleed out if she lets go of her wrist,' Wrack-wulf pointed out.

'Ezekiel's wounds,' cried Aremis, 'where's a good squire when you need one?'

The casual remark, so mundane and at odds with the situation, helped to lighten the mood somewhat. Wrackwulf chuckled, and Aremis could not help joining in. The warrior-woman just continued to stare at them reproachfully, before her eyes returned hungrily to the spear.

'Tell her to back well away,' said Aremis, his tone serious again. 'Right over there to the edge of the clearing, and sit down with her back to us – and that dread shaft she calls weapon.'

Wrackwulf repeated the command in Vorstlending. Slowly and sullenly, the outlander obeyed with a resentful hiss.

Feeling safer, Aremis crossed the clearing and swiftly rummaged through the bags to find what was needed. He tossed one length of bandage to the outlander and proffered another to Wrackwulf.

Just as Wrackwulf was about to take it, Aremis drew his hand back. What was he doing? He was allowing a landless renegade knight to hold a lord of men from his own country captive... True, Sir Wrackwulf could legally claim ransom rights from a bested foe, but he'd just broken his oath of fealty to the King they both served.

Wrackwulf had just reached up to take the bandage and in doing so relaxed his weight slightly. The margrave took swift advantage of their hesitation. Ripping his arm free, he clawed the sod from his mouth, suddenly spitting words in the same eerie tongue Aremis had heard before. The young knight felt his mind go foggy.

Then the sweet honey words, tinged with venom, again: 'Sir Aremis, this man is a traitor and recreant – kill him now!'

Powerless to resist, Aremis dropped the bandage and tightened the grip on his sword. Wrackwulf lurched backwards as the young knight came for him, regaining his feet and brandishing his own blade. The Margrave rolled to one side and stood up just as the outlander turned and bounded towards the spear, which was keening loudly again in the middle of the clearing.

Ariadha knew she was living on borrowed time. Aremis's cut wasn't deep enough to sever tendons, but it had opened up several veins in her wrist. Reaching the spear, she pulled it out of the ground and felt energy coursing through her again; her own lifeblood spilled on the glyphs covering the shaft, which pulsed as it absorbed her vital energy and fed it back to her again. Whirling to face Kaye, she saw the Margrave was back at his spell-casting; she felt an unseen force tugging at the spear, trying to pull it from her hands. Digging her feet into the soil she tried to resist... before realising the foolishness of the decision and changing tack.

You want my spear? Have it.

Dashing forwards, she let the conjoined power of the

spear and the Margrave's spell pull her along. Her feet barely touched ground as she hurtled towards the warlock: realising his error, he mouthed a different intonation of the same incantation, and Ariadha felt an unseen force like an invisible brick wall suddenly condense in front of her. As she was brought up short with a painful jolt, she was dimly aware of the two knights clashing towards the edge of the clearing.

Wrackwulf struggled to fend off Aremis's furious assault. Neither one of them was physically affected by Kaye's magick any more – but that didn't spell an end to the freelancer's problems.

Good as he was, Wrackwulf knew, Aremis was better: and he was younger than him by a good ten summers. There could be no doubting the murderous glint in the elite knight's eyes: fully ensorcelled by Kaye, he meant to kill him.

Wrackwulf old boy, he's younger than you, and he's better than you – so what are you going to do about it?

No convenient overhanging branches this time, and Aremis was too good a swordsman to fall for that kind of trick.

That kind of trick, yes, but perhaps another might fool him...

Giving ground, Wrackwulf slipped and fell over backwards. The young knight almost didn't take the bait. even under Kaye's spell, his chivalrous instincts were to let a fallen foe rise and fight him fairly.

But if Aremis was chivalrous, his bewitcher certainly wasn't: Wrackwulf had no idea how Enchantment worked, but clearly the enthralled was compelled to do a warlock's bidding. A moment's hesitation in which he appeared to struggle with himself, then Aremis stepped in with a downwards thrust.

Wrackwulf knew he'd have to time his next move to perfection. Bringing his own blade up to parry, he caught Aremis' sword, just above the hilt. Twisting his own, he locked both weapons together.

Aremis *was* good: swiftly disengaging his blade with a countering flick of the wrist, he brought it round again in the blinking of an eye, aiming another deadly downwards thrust at Wrackwulf's exposed throat. But this Wrackwulf had anticipated: it was the right move, the expert's move. Rolling to one side, he let Aremis' blade sink into the earth where he'd been lying a split-second ago. Wrackwulf was stocky, but thanks to his powerful frame he moved quickly despite his weight: rising from the ground, he counter-attacked Aremis from the side, aiming a high blow at his head. Unfazed, the young knight whirled to face him, bringing his sword up and across, deflecting the blow easily.

But it wasn't Wrackwulf's sword hand he needed to be wary of.

Bringing his left up, he flung the handful of soil he'd grabbed when he was lying prone: the last thing Aremis was expecting, it caught him full in the face. It took him but a moment to wipe it from his eyes, but that was the moment Wrackwulf needed.

Throwing caution to the wind, he ducked beneath Aremis's sword and threw himself into his opponent.

The unorthodox move took the straight-laced Aremis completely by surprise. Letting go of his sword, Wrackwulf clamped his arms around the young knight's waist in a desperate bear-hug, lifting him clean off the ground and hurling him over his shoulder. Strong as he was, the effort nearly snapped Wrackwulf's sinews: tall and lean, Aremis's body was solid muscle, and on top of it he was covered head to toe in that newfangled plate armour. But the extra weight told against him as he landed sprawled in a heap behind Wrackwulf.

The temptation now was to turn, to pin his enemy while he lay prone, but Wrackwulf knew better. He was now directly facing the Margrave, who stood a few paces away from him and appeared to be menacing Ariadha with some kind of holding or blocking spell. Bounding forwards with a cry he lunged at Kaye, who turned to meet him. Wrackwulf felt his knees go soggy as the margrave enspelled him again: but in doing so he'd relaxed his sorcerous hold on Ariadha.

The warrior-woman needed no second invitation. Clutching her spear in both hands, she leapt forwards, driving it into Kaye's side with a lethal thrust. The rune-etched blade emerged from his hip on the other side of his body as Kaye gave vent to a horrible scream. Immediately Wrackwulf felt the spell's effect ebb and fade. Whirling to face Aremis, he saw the young knight had regained his feet and was picking up his sword, a look of sorry confusion writ across his disfigured face.

Wrackwulf carefully raised a mufflered hand. 'Sir Aremis, stay your hand, I pray you,' he said. 'Just give me a chance to explain, and all this will hopefully start to make more sense.'

The Pangonian champion shook his head and blinked, like a man awaking from a deep sleep. Behind him, he heard the margrave breathe his last with a choking sob. A light crumping sound: risking a glance backwards, Wrackwulf saw Ariadha had fainted.

Returning his gaze to the bewildered Aremis, he said: 'My companion's wound needs binding.' Backing off quickly, he drew level with the unconscious Westerling and quickly scrabbled around for the bandage. The sorcerous globe had winked out of existence, leaving only the natural light of dusk to see by, but it was just enough.

Hurriedly Wrackwulf bound up Ariadha's wound, glancing fearfully at the spear by her side as he did. It had stopped its hideous crooning: shifting his eyes to the still forms of the margraves, Wrackwulf guessed it had fed enough for the time being. Something he was profoundly grateful for.

The wound had severed veins but shouldn't be mortal: a good field dressing and some bed rest and the wild woman would be fine. Judging by the pallor to her cheeks, she'd lost a fair bit of blood though: the spear's awful power had kept her fighting well past the point of her natural endurance.

A clinking of armour alerted the freelancer to Sir Aremis, who had wandered over to stand in the centre of the clearing. He was leaning on his sword now, looking down at the corpses Ariadha had made. The expression on his face was troubled, distant; like that of a man only just beginning to realise his Wyrd has thrown him without warning into events much larger than himself.

You'll get used to it, old boy, Wrackwulf thought, not without sympathy.

Sighing deeply, the freelancer sat back from Ariadha and rolled his mailed shoulders, which had begun to ache somewhat.

'Well, Sir Aremis, I said I owed you an explanation, and an explanation you shall have,' he began. 'Then I'll leave it in your gift to decide whether or not I'm telling the tru-'

His words were interrupted by a sudden commotion. It came from the direction of the Pangonian army camp, the raised voices of many men. Another sortie from the castle? But no: those weren't shouts of alarm, they were cries of terror.

Immediately Wrackwulf's eyes ghosted over as he recalled

spectral figures wreathed in eldritch black fog emerging from barrow mounds.

Aremis had heard them too of course; his hare-lip looked all the more frightful as he stood transfixed, his mouth agape.

Getting to his feet, Wrackwulf took up his weapon again in a hand that was suddenly clammy with sweat.

'Sir Aremis,' he said in a voice that had become small and dry. 'I have a feeling you're going to believe me.'

CHAPTER 3

A JOURNEY OF HEROES

His veins thick with venom, Sir Torgun barely knew where he was. Night had come and gone, and the poison had slowly done its work; he was dying, he knew with a dull certainty. Not even his iron constitution could hope to hold out forever against poison that killed most mortal men in less than a minute.

Time enough, he thought as he gripped his silvered blade feverishly. Time enough to destroy more of the creatures, and take some reavers too into the bargain. From his vantage point in the Strang ranges, he spotted what he was looking for. A foraging party of Northlanders timorously exited the gate of Strongholm and cautiously picked their way around the palisades. A dozen strong and well armed – Torgun didn't think it too many.

Silently he offered up a prayer to Virtus and Stygnos, that the archangels would send the pillagers up his way, as a last gift from the world he was soon to leave. He'd chosen his spot well enough: it was difficult to think clearly, but he'd picked an outcropping of rock that overlooked an abandoned hamlet at the foot of the hills.

Yes, you rug rats, plenty of fresh pickings here for you. Grain and corn and livestock, diligently tended by honest yeomen you so unjustly despoiled.

Crouching down so he would not be seen by the Northlanders, he swept the dawning skies with eyes that were starting to blur. No sign of the creatures yet – his plan was going to perfection. Even the Wyverns had to rest, and they seemed as nocturnal as many a beast he'd chased. Let them come for him afterwards – his blade would taste human blood one last time before they both rested.

Had he been disappointed to learn of his true fate, up there in that blasted wilderness at the edge of the world? No great triumph, no worthy sacrifice – just a brave last stand, a little more bloodshed purchased with his own final breath.

Smiling grimly to himself, Torgun thought how fitting a lesson in humility it was. He'd always striven to cultivate the modesty befitting a chivalrous knight – what could be more humbling than to know your brave last stand would ultimately avail nothing? His life's deeds had redounded through the halls of fame, but in the end he would be just one more soldier dying for his country.

Blinking feverishly to clear his vision, he returned his gaze to the Northlanders, who had sighted the deserted hamlet and begun to approach the belt of ridges leading up to it.

They hadn't been underwater for long when another flotilla of mermen joined them, falling into a flanking guard on either side of them. Their arrival came not a moment too soon: shortly afterwards, a school of Tritons sought to ambush them from a riotously coloured bank of sea plants. For a moment Vaskrian feared: his talisman allowed him some degree of mobility beneath the waves, but his companions were all but helpless.

He needn't have worried: the Seakindred were equal to the task, the flanking groups breaking off to engage their chitinous assailants while Nereia and Logrim sped them ever onwards towards their destination.

They moved at breathtaking speed, far faster than even a courser at full tilt could have managed above ground, but even so the journey to Narborg was a long one, and the hours seemed to drop away and melt into the inky depths of the deepest part of the sea as they sped on their bubbling course eastwards. Once only they stopped, in a grotto of underwater caves, to eat. How Seakindred ate was not something he'd ever stopped to think about, but it wasn't a pleasant sight watching them feast on raw fish.

Luckily it wasn't a repast they'd have to share: Nereia proffered them a peculiar sticky green paste wrapped in seaweed, bitter to the taste but somehow strangely nourishing. The amulet's protective aura seemed to relax just enough to allow the substance to pass through into Vaskrian's mouth, and though he wished for a while it hadn't, he couldn't deny its invigorating effects.

Catching his grimace, Nereia winked at him. 'My Alchemy is not the fine feasting you are used to above water, sir knight,' she giggled. 'But I assure you it will keep you strong of limb for the coming challenge!'

'When will we get our strong limbs back above water where they belong, that's what I'd like to know,' Vaskrian replied glumly.

The sorceress flicked a gaze upwards. She seemed able to tell the time of day from down here, though to the young knight it could have been night or day and he would not have known.

'Not long now,' she assured him. 'Soon we'll be

approaching the resting place of He Who Must Not Be Disturbed.'

'What is that exactly?'

For the first time since Vaskrian had met her, Nereia looked genuinely afraid.

'You will know it when you see it,' was all she said to that.

Torgun had a clear view of them as they came up the hill trail that entered the hamlet. The leader of the party was obviously what the Northlanders called a 'made man', the closest his barbarous cousins got to a knight. Dressed in a brightly polished hauberk and carrying a great axe slung casually over his shoulder, he looked every inch the proud northman warrior. The rest were shieldmen, standard fighters clad in boiled leather cuirasses and carrying stout swords and hand axes.

On their guard and ready for trouble: that suited Torgun perfectly, because trouble was what they were about to get.

Standing up as they drew level with his hiding place, he jumped down lightly from the outcropping of rock, landing half a dozen paces below on feet that had found their firmness again: by sheer effort of will he'd pushed the poison's effects back. It would kill him in the end, but it would have to wait.

The twelve men gaped at the apparition that had suddenly appeared in their midst. Deliriously, Torgun spoke in a voice that was strangely sepulchral and not his own: 'Greetings, depredators. I am Sir Torgun of the White Valravyn, a most noble and chivalrous knightly order founded by the warrior-saint Sir Ulred with the purpose of rooting out wrongdoers who oppress the weak and poor. And just as Ulred showed such no mercy, so will it be for you this day –

prepare to breathe your last, and painful futile gasps those breaths shall be, for know that the blood of the un-angel you call god flows through these veins!'

He stepped forwards then, beheading the two nearest warriors before they'd had a chance to react. The two heads had scarcely hit the ground before Torgun had cut down a third; a fourth managed to raise his sword to parry, but the knight's blade sheared clean through it, cleaving the man's skull in twain.

As one the rest rushed him, led by their chieftain, who bellowed a war cry and swung his huge axe.

What did those hapless reavers see in their last moments? Torgun fancied he knew all too well – they saw what the evil-doers had seen in St Ulred more than a century before. They saw a terrible white knight, with a pale face and merciless eyes, a gaunt parody of the man he had once been. A butcher, come calmly to settle a reckoning, and nothing more.

Torgun made sure the chieftain was the last one to live. Clutching the spurting stump where his right hand had been, he kneeled in the dust and begged mercy of the merciless.

Torgun looked him straight in the eyes.

'Do you believe in Sjórkunan?' he asked, his voice deathly calm.

Through pain and fading consciousness, the chieftain barely managed to nod.

'My great-father welcomes you to his hall,' said Torgun, and struck the Northlander's head from his shoulders.

The thing done, the white knight leaned heavily on his sword. The battle choler, which had never before suffused his being with such sublime coldness, slowly leached out of him, leaving the Wyverns' venom to fill its place. His mighty frame began to shiver, and he felt an altogether different coldness creep over him.

A shadow on the firmament alerted him to the presence

of new enemies. Summoning the last of his strength, Sir Torgun prepared to face his final foe.

Was it just his fancy, or the shimmering of the waters, or did the whorled rock move before his very eyes, undulating serpent-like as it shaped itself into dread forms? From a distance the shaft that men above water called the Cauldron, and which merfolk below it swore led to the heart of the world, looked mundane enough barring its sheer incongruousness: a straight pillar that seemed to bisect the sea, stretching up towards the surface and the island of Narborg far above, and down, down, to the inky blackness of deep waters not even the Seakindred dared venture into. This was surrounded by eight smaller columns that also went as far down as the eye could fathom; far above they supported the sea city that was now home to the man they were going to kill, Reus willing.

Wrenching his eyes away from the uncomfortable spectacle, Vaskrian saw that his guides were similarly discomfited. As for the other knights he'd dragged into his Wyrd, they seemed stunned: incapable of comprehending what their fate had brought them to, they simply floated limply. The young knight secretly hoped Nereia's enthralment was still in effect: traumatised fighters would be no use to him once they emerged above the waves.

The mermaid approached him with a flick of her tail. 'We mustn't delay,' she said, bubbles frantically escaping her mouth. 'To be in the presence of the Cauldron over long is to lose your very soul! We'll convey you up to Narborg now – I've counter-scried as best as I could while we were in motion, but you'll have to act quickly if you're to retain the element of surprise.'

'What about good old-fashioned Scrying?' asked Vaskrian,

shocked at how familiar his adventures had rendered him with sorcery. 'Any idea what kind of a bodyguard the Sea Wizard has up there?'

Nereia smiled sweetly at him. 'You're a clever boy, aren't you – always asking the right questions. You needn't fear the Wyverns, he has them busy attacking your homeland – the last thing he's expecting is to be attacked himself. He's cloaked himself well, so I can't be too sure of numbers, but he'll have Tritons guarding him though not in great numbers – their kind can't abide to be out of the water for too long. As for landwalkers, I know not... Doubtless he's had Northlanders bringing back slaves, but we can only hope they won't have stayed any longer than they had to – most mortals would shun that place just as we do, for fear of losing their minds, aye not to mention their very souls.'

Vaskrian sighed inwardly. This kind of sketchy intelligence was typical of the adventuring life, but it would have to do. He did have one final question though.

'What about my companions?' he asked, nodding towards the four passive knights, still supported by their mermen guides. 'I'll need them fighting fit if we're to have a chance.'

Nereia caressed his cheek then, and Vaskrian felt momentarily more aroused than he had ever done – with Rowena or any other mortal woman he'd been lucky enough to bed.

'You are brave *and* clever,' she told him sincerely. 'Your example will inspire them. The time has come for you to be a leader, Sir Vaskrian.' She didn't give him a chance to respond, but swam swiftly away towards Logrim, addressing the merman in their strange tongue. The Seakindred swam powerfully upwards, taking the knights with them, and Vaskrian hurried to catch up, the Aethi bound to his periapt obeying his will.

~

When the first of the four Wyverns reached him he was ready. Bringing itself up short, it reversed tack, lashing him with its tail. A clever feint from a cunning creature: but Torgun had fought these things and was expecting the move. His sword singing in his hands, he hacked off the tail just below the hateful barb. The maimed creature gave a resentful hissing shriek and fled, trailing spurts of black ichor in its wake.

Like lightning the second was on him. It knew better than to try a tail strike, gouging at him with its claws instead. Torgun sidestepped and took a wing off, bringing the creature crashing down onto the human corpses he'd already made.

He was about to administer the death stroke, but the third Wyvern came at him, snapping ferociously. Changing his grip he thrust his blade into the creature's maw, tearing it free and taking the thing's lower jaw with it. The fiend expired in a crumpled heap as its stricken companion moved with still-frightening speed to attack him on foot.

A pain shot through Torgun's back as he felt the fourth Wyvern's sting pierce past his hauberk and into his back. Coughing up a gout of blood, he realised his lung was pierced. His chest began to burn with fire as fresh venom entered the wound. Spinning around, he tried to strike down the winged serpent, but his blow was slow and weak and the creature easily darted out of range. Meanwhile the Wyvern he'd crippled had pounced, clamping its jaws around his thigh as it raked his torso with its claws.

Torgun was past the point of feeling pain now. He dimly recalled a chirurgeon had once told him pain was the body's way of telling the mind that you were hurt and needed treatment – but there was no earthly treatment for him now, so what use pain?

Abandoning the blade that had served him so well since Ereth reforged it for him, Torgun reached down and grabbed the creature's lizardine head. His strength had been near-superhuman in life; now it was augmented with that of a dying man. The Wyvern's grip tightened on his thigh, crunching mail and bone alike and shredding muscle, but Torgun paid that no mind: huge hands clamped to either side of the creature's reptilian skull, he pushed his gauntleted thumbs into its soulless black eyes. They popped like ripe fruits, just as another stinging lash, to the back of the neck this time, told him the fourth Wyvern had found its mark again.

The serpent menacing him let go of his leg, and he slumped to the ground as the blinded creature began thrashing about, trying desperately to fly away on one wing, but only succeeding in tumbling itself down the hilltop on which they'd fought.

Lying back on the bodies of dead men, Torgun stared up at the last Wyvern, which hovered above him, its tail flicking from side to side behind it as it seemed to savour the moment. He was dimly aware of his blade glinting at his side; a scrabbling hand, and he felt his fingers close reassuringly around its hilt.

Shagreen binding, nothing fancy. He recalled the words of the plain honest smith who'd unwittingly played a small but crucial part in his Wyrd.

Ereth, I hope I made you proud, Torgun found time to think. Black spots dappled his vision, and beyond that a greater darkness, reaching up, around, and down, closing in on him from every direction. He would die unshriven of course, but by now he wasn't even sure if the Heavenly Halls existed, or not in the way the perfects had told anyway.

He struggled to lift the blade, one last show of defiance, but the strength that had served him so well in his five-and-twenty years was fast fading now: a lifetime of prodigality brought to a sudden and brutal end. He sensed rather than felt his eyes blinking spasmodically as the spots grew bigger and darkness encroached further across his vision.

Still the creature had not dealt the final blow. What was it waiting for? It must realise he was powerless now to stop it; it would bear him off and devour him at leisure, if such was its wont.

With his other hand he reached up under his ventail and pulled free the other artefact he had: the rood of St Alysius seemed to catch the light of Søren's blade, and together they radiated in conjoined refulgence, as pagan and Palomedian artefacts mutually acknowledged one another's power.

From far off, Torgun fancied he could hear the perennial thrumming of the waves, as the Strang Estuary went about its diurnal gestation, reclaiming and releasing the land that so many had bled and died over.

And still the Wyvern did not budge, but remained suspended above him on diaphanous wings, staring down at him with inscrutable black eyes. Perhaps he really was descended from an ocean god, and not even his worst creations were willing to feast on the flesh of his kin. He would never know, not in this life at any rate.

At last, the young knight felt his eyelids close. His whole body seemed to relax, the piercing pain to ebb away and be replaced by a not unpleasant floating sensation. The sound of the crashing waves – surely only in his febrile imagination, for the sea lay a good league away – grew louder in his ears, and he fancied it was carrying him away now, far further than he'd ever been, even when he'd journeyed to the Island Realms.

Slowly, ever so distantly, he felt his grip on the sword at his side loosen. The crashing of waves became a tidal roar, the darkness of sight became one of mind, and Torgun's soul slipped lightly from its broken vessel.

A RECKONING FROM THE DEEPS

It was dusk by the time they arose from the waves. Shimmying up the massive pillars underpinning the conjoined platforms of the strange trading entrepôt of Narborg, the six assassins clambered onto the sea-sodden boards and paused in the shadows.

Braxus did not concern himself with what ancient craftsmanship had wrought the trading outpost; what warped architect had fashioned the hideous bas reliefs on the eldritch columns that they had just scaled. He'd encountered enough of the Elder Wizards' ancient craft in his time to understand that such things were best not dwelled upon: Nereia had warned them all before Logrim and the others bore them to the surface that time would be against them. Remain too long on cursed Narborg, and they would surely lose their minds, just as had the men they had come to kill. Sounding a more optimistic note, the mermaid had assured the landwalkers that the Seakindred would wait for them − as long as they could without losing their own sanity − to spirit them away to the mainland once the thing was done.

Once the thing was done. It was no easy mission, Braxus

knew that right well. Loosening his sword in its scabbard, he glanced at the others to make sure they had their wits about them. Their strange journey here, like so many of his other ghastly adventures, was already a blurry smudge at the edge of his recollection, and he was happy to keep it that way.

It was Vaskrian who spoke first. 'Doesn't look like the Sea Wizard's posted any sentries – strange, for he must know we've allies in the sea too by now.'

Madogan pointed to their left. Braxus had chosen his man well – he had the senses of a night owl, something that had proven all too useful when dealing with highland ambushers back in Thraxia. Now they paid their dues again: following the veteran's outstretched finger they saw them, silhouetted against the wine-dark firmament. The hateful multijointed forms of the Tritons were impossible to miss, patrolling Narborg's southern wharf. Logrim had thought to take them around to the eastern side of the platform-city, which faced away from Northalde and towards the Frozen Principalities; hopefully the direction Ragnar would least be expecting an attack from, although that depended on whether Nereia had managed to confound his Scrying sufficiently. Braxus shook his head, shaking salty droplets of seawater from his hair: even now, he found the ways of wizards hard to fathom.

But the Triton sentries apparently hadn't noticed them yet. The south-facing wharf could be reached from the one they stood on by a series of jetty-like structures that connected them obliquely: on the other hand, they could simply advance and enter Narborg proper, where the wooden platforms quickly gave way to the rocky tableau that was supported by the ring of pillars they'd just climbed. At that point, he could already see, the mundane log cabins of the Northlanders quickly gave way to much older structures of stone, fashioned in the same aggressive queer architecture of friezes and angles that affronted the eye and hurt the mind.

'Lord Braxus!' Vaskrian startled him out of his unpleasant scrutiny. Turning, he saw the young knight looking at him earnestly. Unlike the rest of them he was dry as bone, thanks to that fancy periapt he wore, though Nereia's sorcery had shielded them from the water's worst effects.

'Remember what she told us,' he said, keeping his voice barely above a whisper. 'Don't look at anything for too long.'

'I seem to recall being with you at the Warlock's Crown,' he replied, more irritably than he'd intended. Quickly changing tack, he added: 'What do we do about those sentries? Shall we bypass them or get rid of them?'

Vaskrian made a slicing motion across his neck. 'Better to deal with them now than have to do it later,' he replied. 'There's only four – we can take them.'

Once again, Braxus had to marvel at how quickly the lad had grown into his belt – the brash overconfidence of youth had been displaced by a steely determination married to a clear head.

'Fair enough, but we'd best be quick and quiet about it!'

Assuming single file, they loped along the interconnecting boardwalks, taking care not to tread too heavily for fear of making any unnecessary sound. But years of training in heavy armour paid off: bereft of shield and hauberk, the knights moved with a stealth and ease that a footpad might have envied. Braxus found time to wonder briefly if birth was all that separated the thief from the knight: he knew both were capable of taking wantonly when the opportunity presented itself.

As they drew towards the end of the platform directly connecting to the south wharf, he quelled such thoughts. The Tritons stood stock still, gazing out to sea and clutching short spears of serrated coral. Braxus was willing to wager the things could see well enough in the dark – but somehow they didn't strike him as the canniest of creatures. Prone to thinking and acting collectively, they lacked the nous to forestall being tricked.

As one the six of them exchanged grim nods, then moved swiftly on to the wharf. Speed and silence were essential. The chitinous humanoids remained in the same position until they were a few paces away. Then suddenly one of them turned. It opened a frog-like maw to scream a warning, but Braxus' blade sheared through its spindly neck before it got a chance to make a sound. Vaskrian and Madogan brought another low with pitiless sword thrusts, the brothers Arianrod and Diarmuid doing likewise, while Dantos didn't even bother to use his warhammer on the fourth – grasping it around the chest in a one-handed bear-hug, he wrung its neck like a chicken.

'Original,' Braxus deadpanned as the huge knight dropped the head into the waters below with a dull *plop*.

'Quieter than smashing it,' answered Dantos with a grin, gently lowering the headless corpse to the boards.

'Less of the banter!' cautioned Madogan, looking about him furtively. 'They might have posted sentries elsewhere...' The veteran continued to scan the buildings facing the south side with gimlet eyes, the deepening darkness giving his hard angular face an almost cadaverous aspect.

They did as he bade and held their peace. Silence slid by.

'No, we're in the clear – for now,' he said finally. It was eerily silent, but for the lapping of the waves. That, and a low-pitching whining sound just on the penumbra of their hearing. They all heard it, Braxus knew: the preternatural sorcery of one more creation of the Elder Wizards making its age-old presence known.

Best not to dwell on it.

'Then let's away now,' said Braxus, nodding towards where a short rickety wooden staircase ascended to the city proper, if such a place as this could really be called a city.

The whining gradually increased in intensity as they moved towards the centre of Narborg. It set the teeth on edge and the nerves jangling: but Vaskrian knew what to expect from the great old ones of Varya by now. What he didn't know was what kind of defences Ragnar would have set around himself: surely the blackguard priest didn't intend to make it this easy for them.

Presently they reached their destination: a hideous serpentine effigy that none of them dared look at for too long crowned the middle of a small plaza, if such an asymmetrical space could be called that. Off to their right, another group of Tritons stood guard, outside a building that looked as though it had partially melted before solidifying again.

Blinking feverishly, Vaskrian returned his attention to the pair of Tritons. Easy prey for half a dozen seasoned killers, but how to reach them before they could sound the alarm and summon more of the creatures? Between them lay only open space, and no one rightly fancied getting any closer to the cursed buildings to use them as cover.

The knights exchanged perplexed looks, undecided. By now it was fully dark: but the platform-city had a queer light of its own, one that seemed to radiate from the eldritch stones of its bizarre architecture.

Sizing up Dantos in the glowering light, Vaskrian hastily sketched a plan. Bearded and burly, the Thraxian might pass for a Northlander...

Hurriedly, he outlined his thoughts to the others.

'So I get to be the bait yet again?' said Dantos, but he was grinning as he spoke.

'And I get to be your captive,' said Vaskrian, smiling back. 'So quit complaining.'

Vaskrian disarmed and handed his weapon to Braxus.

Dantos hefted his warhammer and assumed a fierce demeanour, pushing Vaskrian out before him. The young knight kept his hands behind his back; hopefully the Tritons would assume they were bound. Slowly, with measured tread, the two of them approached the creatures. Their faces were impossible to read of course; but they were already halfway across the plaza and neither one had raised the alarm.

As they drew level, the creatures lowered their coral spears. Both knights stopped a few paces away, and Dantos recited his hastily rehearsed line.

'Another slave for the Cauldron.' Best to keep a lie simple; besides that, his command of the Norric tongue was for the hounds.

The sentries stared at them with nacreous eyes that were soulless and therefore inscrutable. Then, as one, they parted, allowing the knights to pass between them into the building's lopsided entrance.

They must be guarding the real slaves, Vaskrian thought, elated that he'd guessed rightly and his plan was working.

Just as he passed between the sentries, he saw the pearline eyes of the one nearest him fall on his untethered wrists.

'Now!' he hissed, suddenly whirling and lunging at the creature. But Dantos needed no instruction: with a speed that belied his bulky frame, he turned and swung his hammer without warning, striking down his Triton with a shattering blow. Unarmed, Vaskrian had more difficulty: grappling the creature, he felt its hard horny body struggle against his own with a wiry strength that surprised him. It threw him off and began screaming, a horrible high-pitched sound, like the noise a frog he'd killed in the Warryn as a boy years ago had made in its death throes: he'd never forgotten that sound and was sure he wouldn't forget this one either.

Mercifully, Dantos stepped in and struck the second Triton down, bringing it low and silencing it forever.

'We don't have much time!' said Vaskrian, beckoning frantically to the others and hastily rearming. 'They'll have reinforcements on the way – time we got some of our own!'

The entranceway led into what passed for a vestibule covered in more bas reliefs of sea creatures, but they did not pause to admire the hideous decorations, heading along a zigzagging corridor before finding what they were looking for: another chamber, much larger than the first, only visible through the black bars of the grille barring the entrance. Beyond it Vaskrian could make out dozens of his compatriots sprawled on the ground, some moaning pitifully at their fate.

His fruitless struggling with the grille was interrupted by Braxus, who tapped him on the shoulder and held up a single black key on a ring with his other hand.

'Didn't I teach you anything when you were squiring for me?' he asked sardonically. 'Always search a slain enemy – you never know what interesting things they might be carrying.'

With a wry grin, Vaskrian snatched the key from Braxus and put it in the lock. The grille swung open without a sound. The captives nearest to the entrance flinched back, clearly terrified.

Raising his hands, Vaskrian said in Northlending: 'Don't be afraid – we're here to rescue you.'

It was like something out of the lays, saying that. Even now, the young knight couldn't help but be thrilled: his Wyrd had roughed him up rightly on more than one occasion and no mistake, but sometimes, just sometimes, it threw him a bone.

The prisoners were a motley assortment of men, women and children, some old, many young: by the time they'd separated out the ones capable of fighting they were some twenty strong.

Not before time. 'We've got visitors!' yelled Sir Arianrod from a bend in the passageway where he was standing guard.

Seconds later, the knight disappeared around the corner and sounds of fighting could be heard. The zigzagging corridor was too narrow for more than one man to fight in, but the Tritons with their angular bodies and linear style of fighting were able to manage two: not exactly fair odds. Arianrod managed to put down half a dozen of the creatures before taking a gouge to the upper arm that forced him to drop his sword; his brother Diarmuid stepped in and took over, striking down more Tritons vengefully.

They continued like that for a while, taking turns to fight and dropping out when they began to tire. By the time they re-emerged into the plaza surrounding the Cauldron, they'd left a chitinous blanket of some two dozen of the creatures behind them – not without cost, for all of them now bled from light injuries. Another squadron of Tritons had assembled in the plaza directly before the serpentine shrine: behind them stood a dozen Northlanders, dressed in glaucous robes and clutching staves. And behind those, tall and imperious, brandishing a trident and clad in a voluminous mantle that seemed to shift before the eye like the eddying waves, stood Ragnar, the White Eye, Tamer of Oceans, Sea Wizard, the Great Disturber.

The man they had come to kill.

No order needed to be given. Freed and given a chance to avenge themselves on their tormentors, the tough yeomen they'd picked out and armed with Triton spears launched themselves howling at their former captors. Perhaps it was vengeance that stoked their rage; or perhaps exposure to their cursed prison had simply driven them mad. Whatever the reason, the hapless Northlendings gave no thought to their own safety as they threw themselves upon the Tritons: many went down to the enemy's spears, and the six knights were forced to step in and stiffen up the odds before the thing turned into a bloodbath and a rout.

Covered in blood from their own wounds and the inky substance that passed for Triton gore, the assassins broke through the smashed ranks of the creatures and advanced towards Ragnar's synod.

As one, the priests raised their staves and incanted a spell. The Elder Wizards' architecture seemed to amplify the words, or perhaps it was the other way around: whatever the truth of that, Vaskrian felt his sanity slipping away from him, the urge to drop his weapon and babble inanely washing over him like a cold, wet tide. The roaring of a thousand waves crashed through his mind, deafening his inner ear and drowning his wits.

His companions were similarly affected: the brothers Arianrod and Diarmuid dropped to their knees trembling, while Madogan let go of his sword and clamped hands to ears in a vain effort to shut out the spell's words. Braxus and Dantos remained upright and clutching their weapons, but like Vaskrian they were stopped in their tracks by the awful incantation as they struggled to retain possession of themselves.

The young knight was dimly aware of a faint pulsing at his breast. The periapt the Earth Witch had given him began to glow brightly, and more brightly still; he felt the conjoined Elementi bound within it suffuse his spirit pleasantly, as the susurrant whisperings of the spirits drowned out the awful atonal chanting of the White Eye's synod.

Thus emboldened, he gripped his sword more tightly and forced himself to approach the foremost priest, a dark-haired man with deep-set eyes that betrayed not an ounce of human sympathy. But fear told in them as he realised at least one of the men who had come to kill his master could not be so easily ensorcelled: abruptly changing tack, he began to mouth the words of a different spell, but Vaskrian was on him. It felt almost as though the amulet he wore drove his arm upwards, in an automated thrust that ended in the priest's belly. The priest gave a dull belching groan as Vaskrian's sword pierced his entrails; the fear in his black eyes quickly turned to one of pain as the young knight wrenched the blade free; the priest slumped to his knees, letting go of his staff as he tried to stop his guts spilling from the wound.

Bereft of its leader, the synod weakened just enough to allow Braxus to summon up an effort of will, advancing and cutting down another priest. Dantos was not slow to follow, his mighty warhammer braining a third; panicking, the rest broke off their chanting and scattered, as the other knights regained their weapons and their feet and bore down on them.

Before them alone stood Ragnar, the elemental warlock who had caused them so much trouble over the past two years. No, not quite alone: behind his undulating robes a loathsome figure cowered, mean of disposition and low of stature... some kind of apprentice perhaps.

Vaskrian gave that little thought as he sized up his foe. Ragnar was still clutching his trident, fashioned of a strange metal whose hue was redolent of a dark winter sea; he was tall after the manner of his people, and though ageing there could be no doubting the wiry strength in his body. Unperturbed, Madogan advanced on him, a steely glint in his eye. Levelling the trident, the Sea Wizard mouthed a quick, sharp, incantation: an icy torrent shot from it, swiftly encasing the hapless knight and turning him into a frozen statue.

But there was no time to mourn poor Madogan's awful fate: circling quickly around, the five survivors flanked the warlock, closing on him from all sides. This was to be a sacrificial fight: before Ragnar lay dead and defeated, others would doubtless share in Madogan's demise.

At least Ragnar's next spell was defensive: a blizzard seemed to spiral from his shifting robes, encasing him in a protective whirlwind and obscuring him from sight. His forgotten understudy cried out and lurched back towards Vaskrian; the young knight shoved him aside roughly and crouched, prepared to dodge any more deadly ice blasts that came his way.

None were forthcoming, but the whirling tornado of ice and sleet that now confronted them was a perplexing foe to say the least. Tightening his grip on his sword, Vaskrian remained tensed, his companions doing likewise as they waited for the warlock to make his next move.

It came swiftly enough. Five icy bolts shot from the tornado in quick succession; all of them were ready and nimble enough to dodge aside at the last moment. All except hulking Dantos that is, who simply remained where he was, feet planted firmly, and used his warhammer to smack the bolt aside dismissively. Deflected, it hurtled towards Ragnar's hapless understudy, who was struck and frozen on the spot. But the sorcerer remained encased in his protective vortex, unassailable.

Or was he? Vaskrian fingered his talisman as Braxus tried parlaying. 'Five of the best knights of the realms of men surround thee, Ragnar,' he declaimed. 'Not even you can hope to triumph. Your game is up, but you can still live. You fled us once before, at Salmor castle – I counsel you to do likewise now, and never return. Your depredations are over.'

From inside the icy whirlwind, a hollow sepulchral mocking laugh was the Sea Wizard's response to that.

All the while Vaskrian continued to hold the periapt, bending his will to the Elementi trapped inside. *You helped me survive those ice spirits in Thraxia – the Sea Wizard's magick doesn't seem so different. Do something!*

He sensed the Aethi and Lymphi – he was pretty sure that was the proper name given to air and water spirits by his

Argolian friends – responding uneasily, as though reluctant to cross the dangerous warlock.

I know he's powerful, dammit! I wouldn't be asking for your help if he wasn't, would I, I'd have just stuck him with my sword like I usually do. Do something... A moment of inspiration struck. *I'll set you free if you help me. I've no idea how, just give me a sign or whatever and I'll do it!*

Clutching at straws. The amulet remained sullenly unresponsive as spectral icy figures began emanating from the whirlwind, ghosting towards them on winds that had suddenly become deathly chill. Only now did Vaskrian's amulet pulse into life, protecting him from the flitting figures as it had done in Thraxia the previous winter. But his friends enjoyed no such comforts: the ice sprites tormented the five knights, who lashed out in vain as they leached their energy. Not half as deadly as Ragnar's ice bolts, but they'd do the trick given enough time.

Vaskrian was determined not to give the warlock that time. Throwing caution to the winds as he had done so many times before, he threw himself at the vortex, trusting to the amulet's power to protect him.

A mistake. The vortex was far bigger than it appeared to be from the outside; of the Sea Wizard there was no sign, just a howling blizzard that now enveloped Vaskrian. At least his talisman prevented his freezing to death, but now he was virtually blinded, lashing about helplessly with his sword.

And then he heard it, cutting through the keening: a low soft voice, cold to the ear.

'You are foolish to pit your powers against me. So young, yet so bold... put aside your reckless struggle, I would not see such a promising career brought to so sudden an end, so early in your journey.'

The voice could only be the Sea Wizard's, yet it seemed to come from many places at once, as the howling storm does from outside when one shelters from it within a mean hovel. The words were full of contempt, yet somehow he desired to listen to them, to obey... The warlock spoke in his own tongue, but behind the Northlending words were the hated symbols of the forbidden language of magick.

'I'll never surrender, not to the likes of you!' he yelled defiantly into the blizzardine vortex, slashing his sword through it for emphasis. But it was no use; his enemy was nowhere to be seen. Desperately, Vaskrian took faltering steps forward, hoping to move beyond the spell's compass: but the more he advanced, it seemed, the deeper in he went.

'I could raise you up higher than you could possibly imagine.' Again Ragnar's voice, seductive, luring. 'For too long have you been left to linger in the shadows of men who only believe themselves greater than thou... Join my cause, turn against thy companions, win me the victory this day, and you shall share in my conquest of the mainland! A host of men at your command, and lands and gold for thee!'

Vaskrian managed a sickly grin. 'You're howling up the wrong tree, you demonic white wolf!' he cried into the blizzard. 'I've already won the thing that mattered to me most in life, and I'll be damned if I throw away my spurs throwing my lot in with the likes of you – enough of your sorcerous tricks, come out and face me like a man!'

The preternatural blizzard seemed to grow thicker about him, the winds to intensify; he fancied he saw the surreal snowflakes whirling about him sport tiny but malevolent human faces.

And then suddenly everything dropped away. Vaskrian stood on a barren icy plain, akin to the surface of a vast frozen lake; above him the skies were night-black and bereft of stars, yet somehow there was light to see by.

He was not alone. Before him stood the Sea Wizard, and before his very eyes the image multiplied sixfold. Half a dozen identical Ragnars stood before him, each one clad in the same voluminous sea-coloured robes and clutching a trident.

'Where have you brought us?' He should know better than to trust a mage to tell him the truth, but Ragnar – or rather, *Ragnars* – stood above a dozen paces away, well out of sword range. Better to play for time.

'You are in the space between worlds,' replied the White Eye, smiling almost cordially now. 'Neither on the Other Side nor within the mortal vale.' All six pairs of lips moved as the conjoined apparition spoke; six sets of bright white teeth flashed menacingly in the unearthly light. 'It seems your resourcefulness is of greater stock even than I had fathomed – your mind has grown strong enough to resist suggestion, and yon talisman shields you from the power of my Elementi. Speaking of which...'

The six apparitions raised their left hands without warning, as six mouths let fall harsh commanding words in the forbidden tongue. Vaskrian felt the periapt jerk on its chain around his neck as Ragnar attempted to divest him of it; reacting swiftly he managed to prevent the warlock using his telekinetic power to lift it from him, but in doing so he let go of his sword. It made a dull clunking sound as it fell to the icy ground at his feet.

The six Ragnars laughed, the sound all the more harsh and horrible for being multiplied.

'I hardly think you are in a position to resist me,' they said in unison. 'My powers are far greater than you seem to realise. Here, let me show you...' Another syllable and a somatic gesture, and the amulet chain suddenly twisted back on itself, breaking free of the young knight's grip and constricting around his throat. Vaskrian's knees slumped to the hard hoar-frosted ground as it began choking the life out of him.

Of course... he'd seen a similar kind of magic at work,

many moons ago, when the last of the Northland mercenaries to pursue them between Kaupstad and Strongholm had perished, killed by a stone he wore about his neck.

'Are you sure you still want to keep your bauble?' the wizard's voice was coldly cruel as he intensified the spell. 'This is your last chance to relent! Give yourself over to me, now, or by Logi's tail you shall not breathe again!'

The silver chain was biting into the flesh of his neck. Breathing was indeed impossible; still clutching feverishly at the periapt attached to it, he could see the Elementi swirling about within it.

I already promised you your freedom if you help me! Do it now, or I'm dead and you're in the Sea Wizard's thrall forever!

More tightly the chain contracted, harder still he willed. Stars began to burst before Vaskrian's eyes as he felt his strength ebbing beneath Ragnar's pitiless magic, consciousness slipping away from him...

Then suddenly it appeared: a crack across the crystal surface of the amulet. Harder he willed, as the chain began to draw blood from his neck and he slumped over onto the icy ground.

The crack grew longer and then widened abruptly. The periapt shattered, releasing the Elementi bound within. The shock of the explosion was enough to break the chain, but it also sent crystalline shards flying into Vaskrian's face. One of them narrowly missed putting out his eye, but he didn't have time to concern himself with that.

The amulet's power broken, he was no longer protected: a deathly chill suddenly sank into him from all sides, freezing his bones to the marrow. He gasped aloud, appalled by the harsh fate the Unseen had reserved for him.

But his pain was not in vain. The swirling spirits of air and water shot towards Ragnar, who was immediately forced to defend himself. If his illusion magic worked on mortals, it didn't seem to on supernatural creatures gifted with senses beyond sight. The furious Elementi flitted about him: hurriedly, Ragnar bent his will to commanding them. His skill as a Thaumaturgist was great – even a layman like Vaskrian could see that – but the Aethi and Lymphi appeared enraged. It took all of Ragnar's sorcery to subdue them to his will – and in doing so he lost his grip on his other spells.

The surreal scene broke up before Vaskrian's eyes, shattering like so many pieces of ice. A final stultifying blast of freezing air that left him numb and almost paralysed, and the pieces blew away: he was back in the courtyard, in the midst of the platform-city of Narborg in the shadow of the temple. His five companions looked scarcely any better than he felt, but the conjoined Elementi menacing them had vanished. Likewise too his own Elementi had disappeared: unable fully to control them, Ragnar had settled for banishing them.

The Sea Wizard himself stood where he had been before. But if his Thaumaturgy had been cancelled out by his efforts to subdue the periapt's unleashed powers, his Enchantment still held strong: half a dozen Ragnars stood before them, tridents at the ready.

Cautiously the five knights advanced, wary of any more lethal ice blasts and unsure which was the real Ragnar. The Sea Wizard's next incantation caught them all off-guard: an icy glissade appeared beneath him, spreading out rapidly to cover a wide area around him. Dantos was the first to lose his footing, falling over backwards and landing heavily. The brothers Arianrod and Diarmuid managed to keep their footing, but the distraction proved fatal: levelling the trident again, the Sea Wizard shot three ice streams from its tripartite prongs at the three knights. Dantos somehow managed to roll aside, but the two brothers were caught full force, petrifying on the spot.

The illusion spell had vanished: upon attacking, Ragnar

had revealed his true self, but his glamour had cost the men who came to kill him dearly.

Nimble as he was, Vaskrian managed to skid across the icy sheen, turning Ragnar's spell against him and using the slippery surface to amplify his momentum, crashing into the wizard before the latter could react. Braxus closed on him at just that moment, but his sword was lost in the warlock's voluminous robe, which seemed to swallow the blade as the churning seas devour ships caught in a storm. For his part, Dantos still struggled to regain his footing, his burly form rendered cumbersome and awkward by Ragnar's conjuration.

Still clutching his sword, Vaskrian wrapped his arms around the Sea Wizard, pinning the warlock's own. His antagonist was almost a head taller than he was, but that suited him well enough as he head-butted the priest in the mouth. The effort cost him another cut to the forehead, but he was rewarded with a satisfying crunch as he felt Ragnar's front teeth loosen.

Try another spell while you're busy choking on your own chops, he found time to think as the pair of them tumbled over, crashing to the icy floor.

Vaskrian was on top of the warlock; abandoning his sword yet again, he grappled the warlock's throat and began to choke the life from him.

'See how you like it, you sorcerous bastard!' His voice sounded distant and faintly unreal in his ears.

But Ragnar wasn't done yet. An enormous strength was contained in those wiry limbs, which seemed to have refused the awful touch of age; with a gasping cry he threw the young knight off him. Braxus had lost both his footing and his sword, and scarcely recovered them when Ragnar mouthed another incantation: his form began to shift and undulate before them, the robes sloughing off of him as his limbs disappeared back into their folds, the trident falling to the ice with a hollow sound like the tolling of a death knell.

The apparition that burst up out of the robes was a sight that Vaskrian felt sure he would remember to the end of his days. In Ragnar's place was a glaucous leviathan: in grotesque mockery of the Great World Serpent the Sea Wizard had sought to appease with dark worship, its carapaced coils rose and stretched, looming high above the three surviving knights. Its serpentine face was crowned with two malevolent eyes, one the colour of the deepest sea, the other nacreous and cloudy. Behind him Vaskrian was dimly aware of friend and foe alike screaming in terror as their sanity left them; Braxus slumped back down to the ground, gibbering in horror, his sword clutched feebly in limp nerveless fingers, while Dantos covered his eyes and crouched on the ground moaning pitifully.

But Vaskrian had faced such denizens before, long ago now it seemed, in another age, when Andragorix's demonic servitor had hurtled across the waters of the Sördegil and his life had changed forever. He hadn't survived all the perils of this world and the next to quail now.

Regaining his feet and his blade, he hacked at a weak spot between two segments of the monstrous creature Ragnar had become. His blade passed cleanly between, and an off-white ichor bubbled freely from the wound. The serpent screamed, a sound that nearly burst his eardrums and set his teeth on edge, but Vaskrian would not be stayed. Again he struck, this time piercing deep into the creature's underbelly; it responded in kind, flicking him dismissively with its tail and sending him skittering across the conjured glissade to crash into the temple wall.

Ignoring his broken ribs (he'd suffered those too before), Vaskrian picked himself up. He had not let go of his sword. The creature's maw opened and an icy torrent shot from it;

Vaskrian hurled himself aside, barely aware of the jarring pain the effort caused him. The icy cascade hissed as it melted on contact with the temple wall, steam rising as the eldritch sorcery of the cursed precinct nullified it. Acting on instinct, Vaskrian ducked and ran through the entrance into the temple's dark spiny interior.

Dessicated corpses hanging from the spines made for grisly décor, but he barely paid them heed as his eyes locked on the whorled cauldron that had caused his homeland so much pain and suffering in recent months; the place practically reeked of – was it evil, or something else that lay beyond the ken of mortalkind? Forcing himself to dismiss his confounding thoughts, Vaskrian muttered the only prayer he knew and waited in the gloom. The stars glimmered faintly in the night skies above, visible through the temple's serrated apex. He could well believe he had fled one serpent only to be swallowed up by the greatest serpent of them all. Feverishly he summoned up the last of his courage, and called out a challenge to his foe.

'You're too big to follow me in here as you are,' he cried, his voice sounding tinny in the temple's ghastly interior. 'Why don't you come inside and face me man to man?'

A dreadful pause ensued, broken only by the wailing of the terrified men without. Nothing. Then an ugly clicking sound, repeated and repeated, multiplying. Vaskrian assumed a combat stance just by the entrance as the first of the chitinous Tritons came at him. At least the creatures could only come at him in pairs, but unarmoured and wounded as he was, it took all his worldly strength and skill to triumph.

When twelve lay dead, their corpses piled around him, Sir Vaskrian stood victorious and alone, breathing heavily. No more Tritons came. His forearms bled where a couple had managed to slash him with their coral spears, but he was still alive, still standing, still ready for the fight.

'IS THAT THE BEST YOU CAN DO?'

Again the tinny cadence to his shouting voice; as though the Mouth of the Serpent had turned him into a ghastly shade that did not know pain or fear. Right now that suited him well enough. 'I know all wizards are cowards, Ragnar, but still you disappoint me – no more minions, come inside and face me yourself!'

The White Eye obliged. A flicker of movement above him alerted Vaskrian just in time: down through the fanged oculus it flew, a winged creature not much different to the Wyverns, but its nacreous eye was a sure giveaway.

No more ice blasts: the thing that Ragnar had become snapped down at him powerfully, nearly taking his sword arm off at the elbow with its fanged jaws. Only Vaskrian's reflexes saved him, but he could not get in a counter strike as the creature hovered above him out of range, only darting down again to renew the attack.

Again Ragnar dived, again Vaskrian dodged, and again he struck back only to cleave thin air. He was suddenly aware of the pulsing pain in his ribcage, the fatigue stealing through his limbs.

He's going to win, Ezekiel dammit, he's going to win. Fighting to stall the rising panic, Vaskrian backed away towards the barbed circular wall of the temple's inner sanctum.

He felt the first barb pierce through the back of his tunic, drawing a drop of blood through a single tiny wound that seemed to burn with a cold fire. Vaskrian froze as Ragnar hovered above him on flapping wings, tail swishing menacingly as the transformed warlock prepared to deliver the death stroke. Words of prayer were back on the young knight's lips as he prepared to meet his maker.

A flickering of movement from the corner of his eye. Braxus thundered in, his courage regained if not his sanity: the Thraxian screamed a shrill, primaeval war-cry as he lunged at the winged serpent. In his contumely Ragnar had lowered himself just within striking distance to savour his victory: Braxus' sword sheared through the creature's wing as it spun in the air and impaled the Thraxian lord with its barbed tail, which passed clean through his midriff in a shower of blood. With the last of his strength, Braxus hacked it off just above where it protruded from his abdomen.

Two things happened at once. Braxus slumped to the floor, his gut transfixed by the severed tail; and the maimed serpent seemed to shimmer and dissolve, fading away to be replaced by the naked form of the Sea Wizard, bereft an arm and a leg.

Seizing his opportunity, Vaskrian propelled himself towards the warlock, who was struggling to rise despite the blood pumping from his severed limbs. Dropping his sword for the last time, the young knight hauled the maimed sorcerer up and over to the rim of the Cauldron. The bright blood washed sickly over him as he raised the screaming sorcerer, but Vaskrian did not concern himself with that.

Leaning over the lightless rim of the well, he yelled down into the stygian darkness that beckoned from the depths of the earth: 'HERE IS YOUR LAST SACRIFICE!'

Vaskrian heaved the sorcerer over the rim of the cauldron; Ragnar's echoing scream continued for a long time, reverberating off the walls of the inner sanctum before fading into chthonian silence.

Exhausted, Vaskrian slumped down by the edge of the well, its whorled surface cold and unpleasant against his back. Crawling over to where Braxus lay, he tried to revive the knight he had once called master, but it was no good: Ragnar's final wound was mortal. Braxus lay in a widening pool of his own blood, eyes blinking feverishly as he struggled to focus on the stars in the night sky high above. Instead of a Wyvern's barbed tail, a severed arm belonging to an old man was plunged into his bleeding torso; with disgust, Vaskrian pulled it free and tossed the limb as far away as he could.

Through blood-caked lips, Braxus managed to gasp out a few words. 'Not here... n-not here.'

Understanding at once, Vaskrian forced himself to rise, though his ribs felt as though they were on fire. With an agonized yell he began dragging his comrade's stricken form towards the temple entrance, but no one without dared venture in and help him.

After what seemed an age, he managed to drag Lord Braxus back outside. Most of the remaining men had fled; a few including poor Dantos, completely robbed of their minds, simply sat where they had once stood, babbling to themselves like loons. The stars seemed to stare down at them all with a cold, crystalline indifference.

Overcome by his exertions, Vaskrian collapsed again at Braxus' side. Turning to look at him, he saw the bright green eyes freeze over in the perennial sightlessness of death, as the First Man of Clan Fitzrow left the mortal vale forever.

Resting his bleeding head on Braxus's still chest, Vaskrian wept freely.

CHAPTER 5

A TWO-EDGED SWORD

'You seriously expect me to believe all of that?' Aremis's eyes bulged with incredulity in the moonlight. Mindful of the screams and sounds of conflict from beyond the copse, Wrackwulf had done his best to give the young knight 'the troubadour's version' – as when a bard auditioning before a lord offers a truncated rendition of a popular lay.

Only this was no age-old song, well-known to all – this was a new tale being written to dark strains even as they spoke.

The freelancer shook his head. 'It's time we were away,' he said. 'If what I think is out there waiting for us, you'll believe me soon enough! But first I need your help – let's get Ariadha onto that horse. We're going to need her – and that damned enchanted spear of hers.'

His eyes fell reluctantly on the weapon, which remained buried in the soil, quiescent for now.

The Westerling was somewhat heavier than her slight frame implied, but she was light enough work for two strong knights. They put her onto Wrackwulf's horse, then came the spear: though his hands were protected by mail gauntlets, he wrapped bandages around them before handling it. Wrack-wulf half expected it to turn in his hands and strike him when he did, but it remained dormant. Gingerly he lashed it to the courser's saddle beside its mistress.

Aremis had mounted Aravin's horse, and now beckoned to Wrackwulf impatiently.

'Let's tarry not,' he said sternly. 'My countrymen need me.'

Wrackwulf complied, making sure the Westerling woman was secured to the cantle of his saddle before retaking it, but as he mounted up he replied: 'Sir Aremis, men of *all* countries stand in need – you'll see that for yourself soon enough.'

They made their way back up the hunting trail and emerged from the trees. They sensed the palpable aura of evil before they did: the Pangonian camp had been transformed into a scene of pandaemonium that made Franz's night-time sortie look like a tournament bohort fought between squires.

Wrackwulf clutched the reins feverishly as he saw the roiling black clouds wafting through the tents; he could just about make out dark eldritch forms, impossibly tall, stalking among them, cutting down helpless men with great two-handed swords and impaling them with gigantic spears.

'Ye Almighty,' breathed Aremis, a tear rolling unbidden down his cheek. 'You spoke Virtus' truth.' Wrackwulf only nodded grimly as his younger companion made the sign of the Wheel.

'We can't fight them,' he said. 'That poisonous shroud of black fog you see is the Draugbreath – it knocked me and two of the best knights of the Free Kingdoms out for weeks. And we only survived thanks to the prayers of the Argolians.'

'The very same Argolians our King has suppressed,' said Aremis, his voice leaden.

'Now perhaps you realise what I meant when I told you of a conspiracy to confound kings,' said Wrackwulf. 'The likes of Kaye and Aravin have been playing men of power for fools, and the sorcerers we've managed to stop have been but foot-soldiers.'

Even now, the young knight was anxious for the struggle. Wrackwulf saw his plated legs tensing in the stirrups and moved quickly to stop him, laying a restraining hand on his forearm.

'No, Sir Aremis, not like this,' he urged. 'We can do nothing for your King or comrades now – they'll have to fend for themselves as best they can.'

Aremis flashed him an angry look. 'But I swore an oath, Sir Wrackwulf –'

The freelancer cut him off, his own eyes blazing. 'Your oath be damned, Sir Aremis!' he snarled. 'Can't you see what we're up against? Kaye and Aravin we've dealt with – but how many more are part of this? For all we know, the King himself might be!'

Aremis's look hardened, and Wrackwulf quickly relented. 'All right – he probably isn't, but even you can see that to charge in now would just add our corpses to the tally!'

Aremis's anger subsided into despair. 'Then what do you suggest?' he asked. Clearly the young man had little experience of errantry: this was no foe he knew how to fight, but at least that meant Wrackwulf could manipulate him. For his own good.

'We need to get back into the woods,' he said. 'Find somewhere to treat Ariadha – that weapon she bears is clearly cursed, but sometimes one must fight fire with fire. And I don't know about you, but I certainly don't fancy taking it up myself!'

Aremis's pained expression showed he could only agree with that.

'We have to forget the wars of mortal men for a while,' Wrackwulf persisted. 'I know your knightly honour means a lot to you, but it can't take precedence – this is a new kind of conflict we're fighting. Franz will have seen something of what has passed here – I already told him and his mother Utha what's afoot, so they'll quickly put two and two together. We need to play for time, and find a way to reconnoitre with them.'

'And then what?' demanded Aremis. 'If as you say the Argolians are the one Order capable of fighting such fiends, and the Argolians are being destroyed...'

'In your country, yes,' Wrackwulf corrected. 'But not here in mine – not yet, anyway.' He paused as he suddenly remembered something useful. 'There's an Argolian monastery not far from here. We need to get there as quickly as possible, warn them of what's happened. They'll take it seriously, believe you me. Sir Aremis, I honestly don't know what else to suggest, but we have to find a way to join forces with Franz and help him against the Draugar – it's curtains for us all if we don't band together and defeat them!'

The young knight lowered his eyes. The screams from the camp had subsided into still deathly silence: the tents and pavilions could barely be seen now for the shroud of black fog that enveloped them.

Aremis glanced sidelong at Ariadha slumped across the courser's saddle.

'I doubt a Pangonian will be a welcome guest at an Argolian monastery nowadays,' he said. 'A pagan outlander bearing a sorcerous weapon even less so, I should imagine.'

Wrackwulf shook his head. 'The Argolians are more open-minded than you think,' he said, before recalling Joram and his mysterious disappearance with the Headstone fragment. Perhaps, he reflected, Argolians were a little *too* open-minded.

Not for the first time, the freelancer wondered just how far this conspiracy really stretched.

In her mind's eye, Adhelina gazed down on the two tiny figures on horseback, watching them watch the ghastly revenants as they cut a hellish swathe through the camp. She knew she was seeing a far-flung vision of her homeland as she slept in her hammock: the Second Sight had amplified in power with every day that brought their ship closer to Westerburg, and now her dream-visions had become fully lucid.

It was a lucidity she could well have wished away. Somehow she was able to perceive that the pavilions and tents engulfed by roiling black fog belonged to the invaders, yet still it chilled her soul to see the wight lords walking abroad: she knew only too well what the deathly touch of the Draugbreath could do. And that wasn't the only threat they posed. The dark figures, impossibly tall, wielded spears and swords forged from Ebonite, the legendary unbreakable metal of the Elder Wizards' craft. Many Pangonians had managed to flee, scattering to the four winds to avoid sharing in the fate of their hapless comrades. Forcing herself to ignore the spectacle, she pushed her psyche beyond it, moving swiftly in her dream towards her ultimate destination.

Westerburg Point stood proudly guarding the city it was named for; untouched as yet by the Pangonian invasion, it looked much the same as she remembered it the previous year. Except that far more soldiers dotted the walls of its triangular bailey: zoning in on the foremost, she saw her future husband. Of middling height and blond hair, there was little to distinguish Franz from any of his countrymen: but for the fine armour and cloak he wore, he might have been any ordinary knight of Vorstlund.

A man next to him, a captain of the guards Adhelina presumed, was pointing towards the enemy camp, a perplexed expression on his face. Franz squinted, struggling to make out the scene in the gathering darkness, one that now seemed but amplified by the terrible aura of the Draug lords.

The captain said something, and Franz shook his head quickly, barking an order she could not hear before moving off hurriedly to the stairs that led down into the courtyard below. Adhelina began to feel the strain of her effort: her powers might have grown, but they weren't inexhaustible. She almost felt disappointed as she drifted back into consciousness, gradually aware of the swinging of her hammock as the ship braved yet another summer squall. Below decks it was impossible to tell the time of day. Making her way clumsily down the ladder, she narrowly avoided splintering herself again before dressing hastily. Of Hettie there was no sign – what time was it, Reus dammit?

Making her way above decks, she soon had the answer to that question: the storm was just beginning to abate, but it had to be well past noon judging by the positioning of the shadows – Adso, the sea captain, had told her yesterday they were travelling in a northerly direction after tacking into the Sargossian Straits that separated Mercadia and Murad. The two realms had once been part of the same empire, Adhelina knew: despite the hostilities engendered by that old piece of history and the Pilgrim Wars, the two had managed to maintain an uneasy but profitable trading relationship.

But history wasn't foremost in her mind right now. Climbing up another ladder leading to the forecastle, she found Adso sharing it with Sir Ulfstan and Sir Aescwine.

'What's the hour?' she demanded. 'How long was I out for and why did nobody think to wake me?'

Ulfstan turned to her, smiling his easy smile. 'So many

questions for someone who has but lately woken,' he breezed. 'Lady Hettie said she tried to wake you, but you were fast asleep and would not be stirred.' He gestured expansively at the retreating storm. 'You hardly missed anything, we've but lately emerged above deck ourselves.' The young banneret had begun to acquire his sea legs, but still did not relish being at the mercy of the wide waters.

'I see,' replied Adhelina tersely. 'And where is said Hettie, pray tell?'

Ulfstan and Aescwine exchanged knowing smirks. 'She's below decks in our quarters, playing Sir Wulfraed at cards. Beating him quite handsomely too, I believe – I do hope she leaves him with something, can't have a belted knight putting his gear in hock to pay off a gambling debt!'

The captain, a hearty Vorstlending slow to anger and quick to laughter, chuckled appreciatively, but Aescwine just deepened his smirk. Adhelina had long decided she did not like the man.

'Well, I hope that's all she's playing at,' she told Ulfstan bluntly. 'If he wants to win her most prized possession, he can bloody well court her and wed her in the proper fashion.'

That wiped the grins off the three men's faces. They weren't accustomed to her growing frankness – but if they really wanted her for a Queen, they'd best get used to it.

'Captain Adso, how far from Westerburg are we?' she asked, ignoring their reaction. 'How many days' sailing do you estimate we'll need to reach our destination?'

'We've been strangely fortunate with the storm,' he replied, pointing to the retreating squall. 'It came at us from the south, and we managed to ride its wings. By my reckoning we're halfway through the straits, and we'll be able to call in at the island of Akrytos tomorrow or the day after, for fresh provisioning. In peacetime of course I would have taken us to Montrevellyn for victualling, but we're a

Vorstlending cog and it won't be doing to stop in a Pangonian port with a war on.'

Adhelina nodded, scanning the salty horizon as the ship chased it. She'd read a little of Akrytos. Its people were ancient and strange, having developed what the loremasters called a high civilisation a thousand years before the Thalamian city states grew and prospered. But on the journey to Ushalayim, the old monk Horskram had told her how they had become tainted by the proximity of the accursed Dragon's Teeth, falling into devil-worship and taking a higher-tier demon for a deity; sacrificing to it by throwing slaves taken from the mainland into a labyrinthine pit whose entrances all led to its lair. Like the blasted fortresses of the Dragon's Teeth, the maze-like pit was thought to be just another throw-over from the Elder Wizards' time; yet another temple that had fallen into ruin but not been wholly destroyed by the Breaking of the World.

Given her recent vision, not to mention her ghastly adventures, it wasn't a place she had any desire to linger in.

'See that the victualling is done as promptly as possible,' she commanded. 'And no shore leave for the crew beyond what is necessary for that purpose. Our homeland is in dire need and we haven't a moment to lose.'

The jovial smile dropped from Adso's whiskered cheeks. 'The men won't like that,' he put in. 'We've been at sea for more than four weeks.'

'That's right,' replied Adhelina implacably. 'And you still haven't told me how many more of those we can expect before we reach home.'

The captain sighed, not wanting to meet her imperious stare. 'At least another four,' he admitted.

'No shore leave beyond what is necessary,' she repeated. 'At this rate, I don't even know if we'll have a homeland to return to.'

Ulfstan finally found his voice again. 'Your Majesty, you grossly underestimate the defences of Westerburg Point – '

'And you grossly underestimate how much I know,' Adhelina cut him off. 'And please don't call me "your majesty" until I'm actually wearing a Queen's crown, I've already told you this. If you want to show me your devotion, just try obeying my orders unhesitatingly. Try that.'

In no mood to brook further discussion, she turned on her heel and navigated the stairs back down to the main deck. Time to go and find Hettie, before she did something stupid and got herself dishonoured.

Above her she could just about make out Sir Aescwine muttering something, and was sure it wasn't complimentary.

Utha knew something unexpected had happened the moment Franz barged into her room unannounced. It wasn't that which told the story: it was the look she had never seen before on her brave son's face. A look that told of perplexity, horror and disbelief all rolled into one pained expression.

'Surely the night-time sortie didn't go that badly?' she asked, rising painfully from where she'd been taking her physick (her old malady, quite naturally, wasn't about to let up now at the worst of times).

'The sally-forth was an unmitigated success,' said her son, walking over to the pitcher of wine where it stood next to matching silver goblets on her walnut table. Pouring himself a brimful, he unceremoniously gulped it all down.

'Then why the face?' she faltered, her own pain soon forgotten as she saw her son the Crown Prince was well and truly rattled.

'Freeswords' tales might just be true, and we quite possibly needn't have bothered with our efforts tonight,' said

Franz, still refusing to meet her eye as he poured himself another goblet.

Utha stepped forwards and laid a gentle hand on his arm as he moved to down that one as well.

'In Siona's name, explain yourself!' she cried, with just the right hint of severity. He'd been a wilful enough child, and this wasn't the first time she'd had to wheedle the truth out of him, though she'd never seen him look this perturbed.

It was only then that he turned haunted eyes on her. That unsettled her far more than the flecks of blood that stained his vambraces and breastplate, both deliberately tarnished to offer better subterfuge in a night-time assault.

'Franz? For Stygnos' sake – '

'Sir Wrackwulf spoke truly,' he blurted out. 'The dead rising from their graves, demonic forces, otherworldly things... The Pangonian army, it's been scattered. It was already in disarray thanks to us, but we managed to surprise and harass them, nothing more. What's going on down there now...' He broke off, pulling his arm free and half-emptying his second goblet. 'I don't rightly know what we're even looking at, but sure as St Argo himself it looks a lot like the apparitions Sir Wrackwulf described. And here I was thinking the old sworder was just spinning his tales again.'

Utha frowned. She had been more prepared to believe Wrackwulf than her son at the time – when a man who usually jests suddenly speaks with sincerity and conviction, you tend to believe him. But she had to see for herself.

'Finish your drink, I'll don cloak and hood,' she said. 'I don't want to rouse a general panic by being seen on the walls without good cause, but I must see this for myself.'

Franz paused at his wine. 'Mother, I'm not sure that's a good idea. We're far enough away, but the very sight of it – '

'Oh, this isn't a conversation,' she said, resuming the affable manner with which she had chided so many high-born men including her ailing husband to better ways. She reached for her ermine cloak before thinking better of it, discarding it in favour of a plain black mantle of beaver fur. Less noticeable.

Wrapping it about her and fastening it at the shoulder, she said: 'Done with the wine? Excellent, now show me these apparitions...'

It was bad. The thousands-strong army had indeed dispersed, fleeing into the surrounding woodlands and leaving behind empty pavilions and untended fires in its wake. That, and dozens of corpses: the fires continued to shed light on the awful spectacle: the bodies of knights, soldiers and auxiliaries who had fallen to the new enemy.

But of that new enemy, there was no further sign: timorous sentries reported how the roiling black clouds had intensified, bringing a great blotting shadow down on the once-proud Pangonian war camp. It had cleared without warning, leaving naught but a few stragglers who had survived the Draugar only to be left bereft of sanity: like mewling babes they sat or crawled, the pitiful sound of their wailing brought to the Vorstlendings on winds that reeked of brimstone.

Not even Pangonians deserve this, Utha found it in her heart to think. Yet she could not deny a certain creeping elation behind the numbing horror of her thoughts: for now at least, the siege of Westerburg was raised.

But that thought brought her cold comfort at best. For she knew as surely as her son Franz that whatever would come in the siege's place would most likely be worse.

A lot worse.

CHAPTER 6

HOSPITALITY ENFORCED

'It's no use,' sighed Hari. 'I've never seen a lock this sophisticated, it's beyond my skill to pick.' Muttering to himself disconsolately, he packed his lockpick kit away, secreting it again in the hidden pocket on the inside of his boot.

Adelko looked about the expansive chamber. As prisons went, it could hardly be faulted: the great glass windows overlooked the mountains and valleys from high up in one of the fortress towers. It was night-time, so he couldn't enjoy that vista, but the room itself was amply furnished with a simple but elegant walnut suite that was artfully arranged in a fashion pleasing to the eye. A great carpet, itself a rarity where he was from, covered the stone floor, and a fireplace and chimney ensured they never got cold: the black rocks that burned for a long time were called *coal*, he had learned, and the embers kept them warm long after they had retired to their beds in the adjoining room.

There was even a small library. The single shelf of neatly bound tomes offered little of factual value relating to the present − the Empire did indeed guard its secrets closely −

but at least it was something by way of diversion. Most of the books were written in the Imperial Alphabet but a couple were in Decorlangue. Treatises on ancient laws of the Thalamian Empire, they were replicated in another compendium dating back to the time of Chalcedony and written in Cedonian, the old precursor to the Imperial alphabet. That helped Adelko to pick up the rudiments of their captors' language and script, and he was quick to get Horskram to teach him more.

Azelin, having some learning, had gone along with the lessons out of sheer boredom. It was of little consolation, for they were truly stuck: not even Hari's skills could get them out, the glass windows would make too much noise if shattered and besides, the sheer smooth walls of the fortress would have confounded the rogue, never mind the rest of them. As for using magic to escape, that was out of the question too: Morcant was sequestered and being held somewhere else. Adelko had to pity the hapless warlock, and hope that at least the Imperials were treating him better than his own Order had.

'The Imperials do not punish magic as we do.' Let's hope so, Master Horskram, for his sake.

'We must be patient,' Horskram told Hari. 'The Imperials can't hold us forever. Once they've determined we're no real threat, they'll let us go.'

'You can't still be clinging to that hope,' sneered Azelin. 'They've had two weeks, if they were so convinced we were no harm they'd have surely let us go by now. Besides,' he flexed his iron muscles, 'I can't honestly say I wouldn't harm them if I could.'

Horskram favoured the warrior-monk with a dark stare before returning his eyes to the book on his lap. But he was soon interrupted by the sound of an auxiliary approaching down the long corridor leading to the iron-bound oak door that kept them fast. Hari looked jealously through the wood as they heard the sound of a key rattling on a chain and being inserted into the lock.

The same auxiliary who had brought them their meals opened the door and walked in, preceded as always by two heavily armed legionaries; sure as the sun rose, another two stood behind in the passage, alert and waiting.

'Bathing time,' said the auxiliary in his stilted Decor-langue. Hari's tense expression relaxed, while Azelin shrugged resignedly. Only Horskram seemed decidedly put out: he stuck stubbornly to his counsel that bathing too frequently was bad for the constitution, but Adelko had to admit that the more he indulged in the leisure the more he wondered how he'd ever lived without it.

Besides that, the bathing room was magnificent. Located at the other end of the long passage lined with doors to other holding chambers, it was the closest Adelko had come to seeing the sights in the fortress so far. As their guard ushered the four companions into it, he took in the mosaicked chamber once again. The artist had indulged in more frivolity than Adelko had seen elsewhere in the fortress, with Seakin-dred and dolphins and other creatures of the deeps displayed in a manner somehow redolent of liveliness and motion. A large oblong pool filled to the brim with heated water steamed softly in the light of serried lanterns hanging from the walls at regular intervals, and mahogany benches lay flush to these, on which lay neatly piled towels, sponges, ceramic jars of oils and scents, and blocks of a waxy substance helpful in cleaning that the Imperials called *soap*. The auxiliary had haughtily told Adelko on their second night that the water was heated by an ingenious system of pipes that ran directly beneath the bottom of the pool.

'You're to take special care of your cleanliness this evening,' said the auxiliary, glancing meaningfully at Adelko's mentor. 'For you are to go before the Governor tonight. He has reviewed your case and is ready to grant you a hearing.'

That had Horskram striding over to the nearest bench to disrobe with alacrity.

'At long last,' said the crabby old adept, unfastening the cord binding his travel-soiled habit. 'Just for that, I'll even wash behind my ears.'

Adelko immersed himself in the water and thought it heavenly. What it wasn't, though, was freedom: the journeyman knew that depended on what transpired tonight.

They seem like a reasonable people, he told himself as he clambered out of the pool and began drying his body. He noted with some satisfaction that beneath the last receding layers of boy fat it was stockier and more muscular than it had been, even directly after completing Edemus' rigorous training earlier that year: clearly his months of travelling had toughened him up further. He had half a mind to avail himself of the scented oils provided by their captors, but thought better of it: he was a Northlending monk, after all, not an Imperial senator.

Hari for his part was applying it liberally to his tanned skin, which gleamed like burnished copper. But then the Sassanians had long held cleanliness close to godliness. Even Azelin seemed at ease with the custom: the Bethlers were known to have adopted those of the people they had conquered.

As for Horskram...

'You never caught the habit of bathing when you were crusading?' he finally had the courage to ask his mentor.

The adept scowled. Their clothes had been taken away, for cleaning the auxiliary had insisted. Horskram had let it be known he wanted their habits returned, or there would be hell to pay: the auxiliary had not demurred, but glowered at the adept, while the four guardsmen had fixed him with steely looks of their own.

'I tried it on occasion,' the adept muttered, dressing perfunctorily in the samite gown and sandals provided. 'I see no great need for it.'

Azelin laughed next to him. 'We were far too busy bathing in heathen blood to care much for aught else,' he said. 'But a good bathe does wonders, I'm told, for the constitution.'

'And I find the opposite to be true,' insisted the adept stubbornly.

'Oh come, Master Horskram!' said Hari, joining in the fun. 'Just a little scent, go ahead and try some.' He waved a pungent smelling jar of perfume at Horskram.

The adept fixed the rogue with his sapphire stare. 'Try that,' he said, 'and I'll ram it down your blasted throat!'

They couldn't help laughing at that. Apparently displeased with their levity, the auxiliary stepped forwards and declared: 'I would urge you break fewer words and hasten yourselves – the Governor's time is as precious as the rain that falls upon a parched desert, and he cannot abide to be kept waiting.'

'Tell him to wait on this,' replied Azelin, raising his middle finger and presenting it towards the outraged auxiliary. That had been the highlight of one of their recent lessons: according to *Common Mannerisms and Customs of the Thalamian City States*, presenting one's finger in such a way was an insult akin to inviting the object to, as Wrackwulf might have put it, go and swyve himself.

'As you can see, we've been hard at work learning your customs,' said Azelin, keeping a straight face as the auxiliary purpled. 'We thank you cordially for the opportunity to do so.'

A deep intake of breath and the auxiliary mastered his

anger. The four legionaries remained staring at the outlanders, but Adelko didn't need his sixth sense to know they were struggling to conceal their mirth. He guessed the haughty auxiliary, who had not even deigned to give them his name, was not well liked among the garrison.

'Peace!' said Horskram, freshly washed and dressed if not perfumed. 'There is no need to antagonise one another – pray take us to this Governor you speak so highly of, it's high time we broke words with *him*.'

Adelko did not like the faint smile that crossed the auxiliary's face as he acquiesced and beckoned them to follow him from the chamber, nor the faint jangling of his sixth sense as they did so.

A small man in a big room. That was Horskram's first impression of the Governor. To be fair to its chief tenant, the chamber was vast: King Carolus sitting on the Charred Throne might have envied its size. Dressed in an elaborate purple wig and a brocade frock coat that made him look even smaller, he was every inch the Imperial aristocrat – Illyrium might claim its wondrous Empire was run on egalitarian lines, but Horskram knew all too well that the patrician clans called the tune in the corridors of power.

The Governor motioned to the four ornate chairs that had been drawn up before his expansive desk, before relaxing back into his throne-like seat and steepling bejewelled fingers underneath a round chin. The penetrating hazel eyes and lightly tanned skin marked him out as a native of the central regions of the Empire: most likely he was from Illyrium itself or one of the lesser cities of Chalcedony, sent to the Fortress on a prestigious but somewhat undesirable posting on the fringes.

Feeling strangely self-conscious dressed in the white kirtle his captors had provided, Horskram nonetheless chose to break the silence: his sixth sense told him this was what the Governor was expecting, and for now he'd play along. Behind him stood two legionaries, hands never far from mace and sword.

'Your hospitality has proved passing fine,' he began in his halting Imperial. 'For which boon we are rightly grateful. Now I hope you are satisfied we pose no threat, and have brought us here to discuss our release.'

Best to get straight to the point: the Imperials could smell a stratagem a country mile away.

The Governor merely tapped his fingertips together, before motioning for the auxiliary and his guards to leave. This they did, bowing curtly and withdrawing up the rich russet carpet. The chamber, rectangular like the bath house only much larger, was festooned with elaborate gilded frames etched with dates that held oil paintings of previous Governors – another peculiarity of the Imperials was their art, which Horskram had never much cared for.

'As to the threat you pose, we are satisfied that the four of you are harmless enough – subject to continual supervision.' Horskram didn't like the way the official emphasised the last couple of words. He liked what he said next even less.

'But as for your... travelling companion, he is a mage. Of the benign Right-Hand Path, we have ascertained that much. But of course as a previous sojourner within our borders and a respected member of the Argolian Order, you will know that unlicensed use of any sorcery is illegal in the Empire subject to the Second Protocol of the Imperial Code on the Practice of High Sorcery.' The Governor's pert lips puckered in what Horskram supposed passed for a smile. 'And under the Third Protocol of said code, no outlander can legally hold such a licence.'

Horskram nodded deferentially. 'I am indeed aware that this is the situation,' he allowed. 'But the circumstances in which we arrived – '

' – are quite unusual,' the Governor finished for him. 'Yes, I am aware. Quite unusual indeed – in fact, one might say, suspiciously so.' He had pointedly switched to Decorlangue now, so Azelin and Adelko could understand; and though Hari still struggled to comprehend what was said, Horskram sensed the worldly rogue's instincts wouldn't let him down.

The official went on: 'Our investigations uncovered a strong psychic residue on your companion – he has evidently been using some uncommonly powerful magicks of late, magicks which our experts have determined would normally be quite beyond the compass of his natural talents. How interesting.' The Governor remained sitting in relaxed fashion, his fingers steepled, his calm gaze never leaving Horskram's. 'Clearly there is even more to you than meets the eye – and believe me, when a pair of Argolians turn up with a sorcerer not in chains and a pair of... sworders, there is already plenty to meet said eye. I am sure you follow what I am saying.'

Horskram cleared his throat hurriedly. 'Of course, Governor, and I may I say – '

'You may not,' the Governor interrupted with a tight smile. 'Just as this is not your first visit to the Empire, you are not the first of your Order to have crossed my path. I know full well how persuasive the Argolians can be when one allows them free rein to speak.' The tight smile did not leave his face nor his eyes move from Horskram's as he reached deftly across the desk and tinkled a small silver bell. 'And such efforts would be wasted, I am afraid,' the Governor continued. 'For my duty is clear, as cold water from a virgin lake in high mountains – under the Seventh Protocol of the Imperial Code on Suspect Arrivals, I am obligated to conduct you –

and your sorcerous companion – to a higher authority than mine, under close guard, pending further interrogation. You see, I cannot simply let you go now that you are on Imperial territory – you have become, to all intents and purposes, our responsibility. This means expulsion back to where you came from is out of the question – your road lies deeper within our bourne, to the Imperial Consul of Nacia at his seat in Khronos. It is for him to decide what to do with you.'

Any protest Horskram might have had was interrupted by the arrival of Justorian, the cataphract commander who had first welcomed them.

'Captain,' declaimed the Governor, falling back into the Imperial speech. 'These men and their warlock associate are to be conducted to Khronos under full guard including a presiding Guildsman, there to receive His Most Exalted Excellency's judgment and verdict. You are assigned to this expedition, under the Ninth Protocol of the Imperial Code on Suspect Arrivals. You will assemble your cataphracts and leave at first light tomorrow.'

The cataphract, still dressed in his lamellar armour, clicked his spurs together and slapped a lobstered hand to his scaled breast.

'What does he mean by Guildsman?' Adelko found time to hiss in Horskram's ear.

'A licensed sorcerer,' replied Horskram, his lip involuntarily curling. 'Anyone with legal permission to use grammarye in the Empire must join the Sorcerer's Guild.'

Adelko barely had time to mouth an 'oh' before they were being ushered from the Governor's presence.

Though his companions looked perturbed, Horskram was anything but. He couldn't have reasonably hoped for better, and this was indeed the best possible outcome he could have expected.

'So we've been held in Logos Acra – the most southerly of

the Seven Fortresses, as I suspected,' he muttered to Adelko as they walked back up the long carpet to the brass-bound double doors they had entered by. 'Ideally I would have preferred Calcaginapole, the provincial capital of Grice, from where we could have taken ship across the Little Sea to Aratheny. But Khronos is the closest capital to Logos Acra, so it makes sense to send us there. Looks like we'll be going back to the Sundering Sea coast, for a while at least.'

But the Sundering Sea wasn't the location Horskram had just mentioned to have caught Adelko's attention.

'Why do you want to go to Aratheny?' he quizzed as they reached the doors and two legionaries parted halberds to let them through.

'I've had plenty of time to ponder our route,' Horskram replied, keeping his voice low. 'Aratheny was never part of the Empire, and tends to be far less fussy about foreign visitors. If we can get there, we'll have reached the northern fringes of the Great Inland Sea. It's just possible we might be able to charter a ship to take us to Varya – freebooters and adventurers have been trying their luck stealing its riches for centuries, though few of the fools ever returned.'

'That doesn't sound too encouraging, Master Horskram,' whispered Adelko as Justorian was joined by half a dozen cataphracts outside the Governor's audience chamber. Moving around them, they steered the four captives towards a broad marble staircase leading down to the lower levels of Logos Acra.

'It doesn't,' Horskram admitted. 'But I see little other choice. First things first though! We have to go before His Most Exalted Excellency in Khronos and persuade him our cause is both just and essential. I wasn't going to reveal all our business to a border official, no matter how highly ranked he may be – and he knew that full well himself. My guess is he's happy to have us off his hands.'

Adelko mulled his mentor's words as they were returned to their quarters. More than ever, he wished he had the talisman Abdel Sha'arza had gifted him – though it was a blasphemous thing to desire for an Argolian, he'd have favoured the *Chariot of the Skies* over any ordinary vessel to reach their ultimate destination. But the periapt had been impounded along with his other belongings – and something told him it wouldn't be returned as readily as his monastic habit.

They retired to their beds after a brief conference. Hari and Azelin seemed content enough with Horskram's plan for now at least – getting out of the mountains and partway across the Empire was better than being held in the Fortress indefinitely, while being turned back would have availed them nothing.

But lying awake on his bed – an expansive affair that a nobleman might have envied – Adelko found his thoughts returning again to the pendant Sha'arza had given him, and the controversial treatise he had read at the monastery months before that.

Mages and monks, but two halves of a whole... Arnulf of Balzac, you weren't wrong were you?

CHAPTER 7

A PYRRHIC VICTORY

Of the men and women he'd freed, scarcely more than a dozen had retained their minds or bodies intact. Vaskrian went about it with a leaden heart: the corpses of the slain including Braxus had to be loaded onto the Northland longships he'd found moored at Narborg's western dock; after that came the poor souls including Dantos who'd lost their sanity, followed by the remainder who were able enough to man the ships.

At least they wouldn't have to struggle with the boats alone, for Nereia and Logrim were waiting for them in the churning waves. Vaskrian did what he could to allay the survivors' fears as the Seakindred drew near: just this once, the denizens of the waters were on their side. His allies registered the tally of the dead with grim countenance: even the bubbly enchantress was visibly subdued as the merfolk took their vessels out to sea.

The journey back across the waves passed in a blur for the young knight: it wasn't just because of the extra speed the Seakindred added to the fast-sailing ships. His companions were all dead, or driven hopelessly mad. He alone had survived, and not without extra scars to add to his tally. He'd caught his reflection in a pail of rainwater lying at the stern of the longship he now sat slumped in: the shattered talisman had conveniently struck the previously unruined side of his face, and now he had two defeated warlocks to thank for permanent disfigurement. He didn't even have a good side any more: whichever cheek he turned at court, he would never be handsome again.

He supposed that was hardly cause for complaint, given the dreadful fate his brothers-in-arms had suffered. At least his old adventuring chum Sir Torgun hadn't been on the mission, but he couldn't help regretting that too: surely his hero would have averted this tragedy had he been present.

Vaskrian could have no idea of it just then, but his sorrows were set to pile up, just as the gathering winds on the horizon presaged another storm.

At least some cheer was to be had in the spectacle that greeted them when they drew in sight of the coastline, though it was another fearful sight at first: dozens of winged forms blotted the firmament, before pivoting downwards and plunging back into the rain-lashed surf. The cries of dismay in the longships quickly turned joyous as they realised the Wyverns were returning to the dark deeps, though the faces of the Seakindred told a different story.

'With the Great Disturber died his wicked sorceries,' said Nereia, her winsome face a paler shade of blue than usual. 'Now they are returning to their natural bourne, which means they are our problem. Thus all victories are bittersweet.'

'Then why did you help us?' Vaskrian had to ask through the pounding rain and churning waves.

The enchantress managed a wan smile. 'You are not the

only one caught up in the great tale that the Farseers of Norn predicted,' she said. 'This day was anticipated, many tides ago... The serpents we will deal with, for we know how to fight them. It's what comes after that I fear the most.'

Vaskrian squinted at her through a sheen of water. Bereft of his amulet, he had been reminded of just how punishing the element could be; he felt enervated and thoroughly bedraggled.

'What do you mean?'

She smiled sadly. 'The evil you are facing will not be destroyed without cost. Even if you and those you hold dear should triumph, many things will change in our world and yours.'

She gave him no time to ponder that riddle, but darting up out of the waters one last time gave him a kiss on the cheek before splashing back down into the sea. Her fellow Seakindred were doing likewise, casting off the longships with one final shove and propelling them towards the shore.

'Farewell,' Nereia called above the pelting rain. 'For our paths are done crossing, and now must part forever – think kindly of us, Vaskrian, when you sit in draughty halls above water!'

Logrim gave a final salute to complement the mermaid's words, which was also a signal to his own people: as one, they turned upwards, vanishing from sight with a flashing of tails.

Vaskrian felt a pang strafe his breast as the longships, the winds at their back, sped on towards the coast of Northalde. Though glad to be in sight of home, he felt some vital part of him had disappeared beneath the Wyvern Sea forever.

Perhaps some final magic of Nereia's helped them, for they beached their ships with uncommon speed and ease. The rain and wind had abated somewhat: staring up the coastline, Vaskrian did his best to ascertain where precisely they were. Of Strongholm's white walls there was no sign; for whatever reason, the merfolk had steered them shy of the Strang Estuary.

Fortunately one of the survivors appeared to know the lie of the land.

'Beggin' yer pardon, sire,' said the grizzled yeoman. 'But I believe we must be in Stromlund.' Pointing inland to where the ground sloped upwards, he added: 'Beyond yon ridges lies Lake Strom – I spent a season workin' as a cottar there and I believes I recognises it.'

Stout of heart and limb, he'd managed to survive where others had not, though why the archangels had chosen to preserve his sanity over a belted champion like Sir Dantos, Vaskrian would never understand.

But he was grateful enough for the man's presence. Clapping him on the shoulder, he allowed just a hint of his own common accent to slip into his voice as he said: 'My thanks to you, I wouldn't have known – for I only passed the lake from the west, when we marched to war at Linden last year.'

The yeoman nodded, somewhat less deferentially than he might have done otherwise, and managed a half smile.

'Some of the others and I just wanted to thank you, sire – for what you did. Without your sacrifice and help... well, we don't like to think what might have happened to us.'

What would have happened, Vaskrian mentally corrected, his gloom returning. Saving a handful of captives was one thing, he knew; saving the realm quite another. A thousands-strong occupying force of bloodthirsty reavers still stood between them and victory – and they had possession of the capital.

'We'd best get to it before the dark sets in,' he said, banishing his troubled thoughts and raising his voice so all could hear him. The common touch was gone; now was a time to command and be obeyed without question.

'We'll need to bury the bodies,' he continued. 'And we don't have time to make it pretty – two mass graves will have to do it, one for my fallen comrades and one for the others. By my reckoning, we've about six hours before it gets dark – the soil here is soft enough thanks to the sea and wet weather, but you'll have to dig with your hands! A shallow grave is all we need, we'll mark them both so the corpses can be found and properly interred later.'

To their credit, the erstwhile slaves did not demur, though one or two of the tougher-looking yeomen dared to flash him a surly look. Vaskrian was too tired to make anything of it – besides that, the last thing he needed right now was a mutiny. Striding over to a nearby rock, he sat down wearily upon it and watched them go about the grim task with tired eyes.

He did not have the heart to look upon Braxus's corpse again.

It was close to sunset by the time they had finished. But that wasn't what was taking up Vaskrian's attention: rather it was the column of troops approaching from the south. A chance glance away from the macabre spectacle of mass burial and he'd caught it: a ray of westering sunlight as it broke free of the thinning clouds in the aftermath of the storm, reflecting off a polished helm. Long strides had taken him to the top of the nearest hill, from where he'd been able to spy the new arrivals better.

Some five hundred strong, the approaching army sported pennocels and standards he recognised from the last war. Casting his mind back to the newly minted Jarl of Thule's arrival at Strongholm, he realised this must be the last of the Southrons.

What was more, he recognised the coat of arms on the foremost standard. As the knights, footsoldiers, archers and squires in service to the Jarl of Salmorlund drew closer, he drew his sword and held it aloft, letting the sun catch its burnished blade. Another bone thrown to him by his capricious Wyrd, who was he to refuse it?

Stepping down lightly from the hill, he advanced to meet the host.

The knights and officers gathered about him and his ragtag band looked rightly sceptical at first, but his tale was no more outlandish than the horrors the southrons had but lately witnessed first hand.

'We thought something must have happened when the Tritons suddenly turned tail and fled back into the sea,' said Lord Kelmor of Salmorlund. Imprisoned by the Young Pretender, he knew all too well that wizardly plots to overturn realms were very real. He stroked his bearded chin reflectively. 'They seemed *confused* rather than afeared, as if they no longer knew why they were fighting. We made light enough work of them after that, though their numbers were dreadful!'

Taking in the dints in their torn surcoats and blood-flecked harness, Vaskrian didn't doubt it. Nor did he doubt that they had left many a wounded and dead comrade on stretchers behind them: they'd been left behind to fight a rearguard action against the coastal invaders while the rest of the southron army under Thule marched north to help retake Strongholm. The effort had clearly cost them dearly: he'd initially overestimated their numbers, which he could now see were closer to four hundred.

And Ezekiel knows how many of us northerners will be left, after what we had to endure.

He quickly quashed the cowardly thought. Torgun and Toros and Toric would see to it that the men rallied, and now at least they only had the Northlanders to fight – less their navy too, which they'd rightly smashed already.

Or had they?

'What about the coastal raids?' Vaskrian asked the Jarl of Salmorlund. 'We decimated the Northland fleet at the Battle of the Strang, how did you speed down south?'

The tall lord shook his head. 'Last we heard, Sealord Aesgir was sailing south to engage them – but that was before the Wyvern Sea itself rose up against us.' The gathered lords and officers exchanged chilly looks.

'The Wyverns you won't have to worry about any more,' said Vaskrian. 'So we have to hope Aesgir has engaged the rest of the Northland fleet – surely that explains why you haven't encountered any more raiders, or human ones anyway.'

'Not lately,' Kelmor conceded, hope kindling in his eyes as he nodded in agreement. 'We haven't a moment to lose,' he added, squinting up at the fading sunlight. 'We'll march on for another hour before making camp. If we move swiftly, we should get to Strongholm by dusk tomorrow.' Motioning to the men and women Vaskrian had led from captivity, he added: 'Draft the able-bodied men into the levies, we should be able to spare them some rudimentary weapons. Those who've lost their minds to fear we'll have to leave behind.'

'One of them is a belted knight, and fought bravely with me against the Sea Wizard before he lost his wits,' Vaskrian had to point out.

Kelmor frowned. 'This has been an ill-won victory,' he

sighed. 'Very well, your boon sword companion we'll take with us – but he's your responsibility.'

Poor Dantos, mewling like a loon and gibbering to himself, wasn't likely to cause anyone trouble. Vaskrian nodded his assent, remembering to thank the Jarl for his clemency.

Lord Kelmor curtly nodded his acknowledgement, then said: 'As for the women, have the young and able ones join the hangers-on – they'll serve as washerwomen, or whores if they so choose.'

No one batted an eyelid, as this was customary practice in wartime, but Vaskrian couldn't help but wonder what some of the women he'd met on his travels would think if they could have been there to hear Kelmor's last order. He suddenly wondered how Lady Rowena was faring: his last lover, and the person who had given him his spurs. But he had no time to indulge any pangs of sudden longing, for they were on the move again.

It was only then that he realised with a start he was still bereft of harness: just his breeches, boots, gambeson, belt and sword, he looked no better than a common freesword. No wonder Kelmor had looked at him askance before finally recognising his ravaged face.

Why on earth had the merfolk not sent them back to where they'd met? Surely there was a fair chance their arms and armour would still be where they had left them.

He was soon to learn the answer to that question.

A tumultuous sight greeted them as they crested the southern ridges of the Strang a day later. Corpses of slain Northlend-ings dotted the open countryside that lay between the hills and the city; but it was the naval battle that really caught the eye. The rest of the Northland fleet had apparently changed tack, sailing north to engage Aesgir: longships and war galleys could be seen up and down the coast as far the eye went, fighting hard.

No wonder Logrim didn't take us back to where we were before – that stretch of sea has turned into another battle zone while we were away.

He did briefly wonder why the Seakindred weren't coming to help them again, then realised the answer – their efforts would be bent towards dealing with the Wyverns and Tritons now they'd returned beneath the waves. Nereia had spoken truly. Her folk's part in the wars above water was done.

At least Aesgir and his flotilla looked to be holding their own – though outnumbered once again by the remainder of the Northland fleet, the odds were at least somewhat less ghastly. Clearly Ragnar had ordered the Wyverns to concentrate on pinning down their land armies, forcing them to disperse into hiding beneath the trees. It had been a close call though – if Aesgir's ships had been around when the sea serpents emerged, they might not have a navy left.

As it stood, they did, leaving them free to concentrate on besieging Strongholm, which looked to be still strongly guarded by Northlanders. When they'd realised the show was over, they'd put away the flagons and taken up their weapons again – from where he was Vaskrian could just about make out what looked like a tall berserker, striding up and down the walls and haranguing other strong men that looked like children next to him.

Vaskrian's hand instinctively dropped to his sword hilt. He had a feeling his Wyrd would furnish him with a much closer meeting with this barbarian, whoever he was. Good, let it be so: he yearned to avenge the deaths of his countrymen and comrades.

'What of the rest of the Northlending land forces?' asked

Kelmor, the one question Vaskrian knew remained unanswered.

Pointing grimly at the corpses, he said: 'Bad as that looks, it's not so many as we'd feared, so we have to hope most of the men got under cover, as I did.' He paused on that thought... Hadn't someone remarked that the gruesome creatures carried off their victims when they could? In that case there was no telling how high the casualties really were.

Soon it would be too dark to spot even the bodies that lay out in the open in any case: a forced march had served them well, but the sun was touching the horizon, and Kelmor's men were rightly tired.

'We make camp here,' the Jarl commanded. 'I want sentries posted along all the rises hereabouts, I'll have no nasty surprises if we can avoid it! Only such fires as are absolutely necessary, we must make subterfuge our friend until we know more.'

His marshal nodded curtly and hurried to relay the order.

'What do you think became of them?' Kelmor asked in a low voice once he and the young knight were alone. Ignoring the flush of pride that came with the realisation that a high lord now looked to him for counsel, Vaskrian shook his head.

'Impossible to tell for sure, my lord,' he replied, still scouring the darkening landscape for any more clues. None were forthcoming. 'We just have to hope that most of the army survived intact,' he finished lamely.

Kelmor nodded broodingly. 'If they had scouts posted on the fringes of yonder woodlands they should have seen us by now,' he said, as much to himself as to the young knight. 'But so far no signal... I like this not, Sir Vaskrian, it bodes ill.'

Vaskrian chewed his lip fretfully as the shadows lengthened across the land. To the east, the ships fought on.

CHAPTER 8

THE WHEEL AND THE SERPENT

The House of Coeurforte's standard vanished from sight beneath a horde of mounted *amluqs* as they slew the last of its defenders. Along with the other Princes of the Sand, the Palomedians had fought bravely, but a smaller host could not hope to stand against the vastly superior numbers Muqmurlish had gathered to his sceptre. The sable wheel bordered with gold spikes that signified the Coeurforte coat of arms disappeared abruptly beneath a tide of steel as the Sultan's forces gave vent to a bloodthirsty yowl of triumph.

The enemy's flanking battalions had fared little better than the centre. To the right, the crusading armies from Troye and Tristia had been similarly bested, their standards also captured and their remnant armies put to flight. Glancing to the left, Anupe could make out the Margraves of Thringia, Vania and Aquitania retreating, doubtless keen to avoid suffering the same fate. The crusading forces who had taken the Wheel and journeyed across the Sundering Sea had failed to tip the balance, and those that still could were now falling back towards Ushalayim.

Anupe could not resist joining her voice to the

triumphant groundswell of cheering: after seeing off the rear-guard engagement sent by the House of Agramonde several weeks ago, Zimri's garrison had apparently gained the attention of the Sultan, and before long the Southron general had received an order to leave footsoldiers behind to man the fort and deploy all mounted troops to the main muster.

That had seen them swept up in the most startling series of conquests Anupe had ever had the pleasure to be on the right side of: her plunder and prisoners could not easily be counted, and she felt confident that her dreams of retirement would soon become reality.

A week ago, Muqmurlish had sent a tranche of his army west, to complete a pincer movement with the Sultana of Kallandhar against the Kerakans. As was their wont, the Three High Houses and the lesser clans of Keraka had fought fiercely to a man, giving and asking no quarter, but faced with two armies and vastly outnumbered, they had been forced to flee the field and hole themselves up in their castles. As for Ranishmend, the most westerly of the Pilgrim Kingdoms that had elected to stay out of the Fourth Pilgrim War, word had come of further developments there to Muqmurlish's advantage: the people of its coastal capital Argon had risen up against their despised and bigoted ruler Athelhard III and his detested aunt, Alya. Recently arrived from Pangonia, she had brought with her a considerable amount of influence over her weak nephew – and all the prejudices of her native Troye. Both now enjoyed the Long Sleep thanks to their high-handed treatment of the Sassanian populace, who had put them to the cruellest death possible before opening the gates for the Kallandhari army. There would be no relief for Keraka from its rivalrous neighbour, which clearly saw the wisdom in submitting to the hurricane that now blew against it.

Mounted astride his sleek courser, General Zimri

approached Anupe, his face calm and a little sad, as it always was after the slaughter.

'The Princes of the Sand are broken, and must now put their faith in siegecraft,' he said. 'The Court Council in Ushalayim will doubtless convene when the crusader lords arrive to report their defeat – many in the city will urge its ruler Rexus to sue for peace.'

'Perhaps, but what of the Bethlers?' Anupe asked, her mood darkening somewhat as she felt her doubts surfacing. 'Grand Master Tobin will never concede victory and give up his precious sacred city. And I've heard rumours spoken that the King in Ushalayim suffers an illness of the mind... there will be a power struggle for sure.'

Zimri wiped a fleck of crusader blood from his mahogany cheek, shaking it from his hand in disgust.

'You are not mistaken, Anupe of Hamazos,' he conceded, returning his gaze to her. 'The Court of Barons and Holy Synod will be wrangling over the matter with the Bethlers in the Court Council before long. But let them quarrel! The more time it gives us, to cross the Taurans yonder and encircle Ushalayim. Once they see the host arrayed against them with their own eyes, they will become more pliant, I am sure.'

Anupe cocked her head slightly. She felt that Zimri said that to try to convince himself more than anything: his peculiarly pacifist nature made the warrior's trade odious to him, and the Harijan knew he would fain see the war brought to a swift close with an unconditional surrender.

But from what she had seen of the *jhufa'ar* warlords, such a peaceable conclusion to the Fourth Pilgrim War was unlikely. Oblivious to her thoughts, Zimri rode off, ordering his *taziqs* to reassemble when they were done plundering and executing the prisoners too badly injured to be treated. The Sultan had already given the order: there was to be no tarry-ing, the army would march north-east to cross the Tauran heights tonight.

~

Anupe could not resist a sharp intake of breath as she caught sight of Ushalayim the following day. It still looked as beauteous as it had done when she'd first glimpsed it from the deck of a crusader ship: a thing of coloured stones and trapped light, jewels and graceful curves, it could not fail to move even the most hardened freebooter such as she was.

All the more the pity then, that they were about to bring rain and fire on it. But so it must prove: Muqmurlish had sent emissaries ahead, to treat with the crusader warlords that had not yet fallen to his host, which now clustered balefully around the Tauran heights, perched directly above the city that was cradled by its lower slopes, but that had gone much as Anupe had suspected it would. The hapless messengers were sent back less their tongues, the wounds cruelly cauterised with iron and fire that they might live to 'tell' the tale.

Small wonder, then, that she and Zimri and his lieutenants Kufa and Batu found Muqmurlish in an ill humour when they went before him in his pavilion later that evening, his usual serenity challenged by the unreasoned and pointless barbarism of the enemy.

'These are not chivalrous men we treat with,' he was saying to his other generals and satraps, as the delegation from the Southron contingent joined the council. 'Ever the Princes of Palom speak of valour and their faith in the Almighty, yet where is Ashanti's mercy to be found in them?'

'They do not deserve Ashanti's mercy,' said Baraq tek Baraqa. Big and burly and bearded, the warlord from the southern deserts of Nazharya commanded five hundred *sarakim*, and had killed more than his share of the *jhufa'ar*. 'I say we kill them all when the walls of Ushalayim fall. They showed our people no clemency when first they took the Holy City a century ago – let us wreak the archangel of storms Hadad's divine justice on them, and redress the balance!'

Many of the gathered Sassanian nobles agreed with him, and were not slow to voice their opinions.

'No!' said Muqmurlish, evenly but firmly. Even now his charisma was palpable: a single raised finger, and the entire tent fell silent.

'We must not fall into that trap,' the Sultan continued. 'For surely it is set by the archdemon of anger Zolthoth himself, just as his dark brother Azathol laid a similar trap generations ago for the Ill-Guided Sultan, causing him to fall foul of his own hubris and give the *jhufa'ar* lords the excuse they so craved to visit wreckage and ruin upon our blessed lands.'

Many other lords were nodding the wisdom of that: Muqmurlish had made no secret of his avowed belief that the First Pilgrim War had been the work of archdemons posing as senior prelates and viziers on either side of the Sundering Sea. Recalling her own adventures with Horskram, Anupe privately had to admit that the Sultan was more right about that than even he could possibly know.

'Besides that, which ones would we kill?' Muqmurlish went on, speaking now in that low quiet voice of his that carried more power, more presence, than any other she had heard. 'For many of Ushalayim's residents are *al'Hajin* – crossbreeds of Urovian and Sassanian. Did they ask to be born such?' Looking around at the almost reverent faces, he went on: 'Did they, in fact, ask to be born at all? For such is the will of Ashanti, that we are placed in a time and place of His choosing, not ours. To us, this heavenly host I have by His grace assembled, it falls to ensure that He has not acted in vain – the Princes of the Sand shall taste their own blood if they refuse to surrender, but I shall not have the Holy City whence the Prophet ascended put to the sword for the sake of vengeance!' He finished by fixing Baraq with a look that somehow managed to be both mild and stern at the same time. The big warlord, towering more than a head above his liege, bowed his own in abject submission.

If ever I doubted the bloodline of the Seven Enlightened Sultans, I cannot now, Anupe found herself thinking – and meaning it.

His edict proclaimed, the Sultan relaxed his hands into his lap, letting his whole body go still. Anyone happening to glance at him for the first time might think he was at meditational devotions, not a war counsel on the eve of the greatest victory his people had seen in generations. He had disarmed too, and was now dressed in simple maroon garb with nary a trace of jewellery or ornamentation. She'd seen him in full harness on campaign of course, and once even fought close enough to the Sultan in the melee to see how he held himself. It had been as though he did not even need to fight: the pair of Pangonian crusaders menacing him, fired up by bloodlust and warped faith, had bludgeoned their way past his bodyguard with a reckless attack at the Battle of Tarsis, clearly relishing the chance to gain worldly glory and speed their souls on the way to the Heavenly Halls for their service to the Creed.

As things had transpired, the crusading knights had gone to the Long Sleep quickly enough, though not in the manner of their choosing. The Sultan had seemed to bend and shimmer before their blades, weaving casually between their twinned attacks... two deft flicks of his flashing scimitar, and the crusaders had sloughed from the saddle, their throats delicately opened.

Back in his pavilion, Muqmurlish tek Nazar closed his

eyes gently, indicating that the council of war was finished. His gathered dignitaries filed out, making the sign of the Faith with heads bowed as they did. Anupe followed suit, more out of instinct than habit, and joined Zimri and his lieutenants on an outcropping of rock that directly overlooked the city below.

The sun had disappeared, and stars were winking into life in the velvet canopy of evening skies rendered beautiful by its afterglow. Down on the coastline, Ushalayim showed itself no less ravishing a sight by night, as a thousand lanterns lit up the city.

Ravishing indeed... but the city itself would be ravished, if the Sultan's order did not prevail. Anupe did not doubt Muqmurlish's sincerity, nor the devotion his generals had for him, but she had been in enough wars to know what could happen when cities finally fell after a prolonged siege, as feelings ran high among ordinary soldiers.

And, gazing down upon the darkling cityscape, she guessed that the Princes of the Sand would spare no effort to make the siege as long as possible. Ushalayim's founders had chosen their spot well: between the hills and the sea there was little room to mount a siege, and most of Muqmurlish's equipment and sappers had been deployed already on the campaign trail, used on the plains to pin castles and walled towns that refused to surrender. That also meant Ushalayim would be getting no further assistance from the hinterlands: but it was well poised to stand alone.

'Time can only play to their hand,' she told Zimri, giving voice to her thoughts. 'The crusaders will try to hold the walls as long as possible, in the hope of getting fresh reinforcements by sea. We won't be able to starve them out for the same reason.'

Kufa glowered at her. Stern and unyielding as ever, he did not appreciate women with minds of their own.

'Did my salt-brother ask for your counsel?' he demanded, his tone harsh.

But Batu, his more amiable compatriot, quickly defused the situation. 'Peace, Kufa! Our most exalted salt-brother appointed her lieutenant for good reason – you were there when Anupe of Hamazos cut down three scions of the House of Agramonde.' The Southron flashed his surly comrade a *ketel*-stained grin. 'I believe your tally the same day was but two of their knights.'

Kufa's scowl deepened, but he fell silent. 'We all fought like lions that day,' said Zimri, clearly anxious to forestall any dissent. 'But Batu has the right of this, Kufa! A Harijan is not as other women in other lands – Anupe fights, and thinks, as well as do we. She has proven that many times since Uru willed our paths intertwine.'

If I had my way, many women in other lands would learn to think and fight as I do, thought Anupe. But she kept that to herself as Zimri turned to her and said: 'You are also right – though it pains me to admit it, the *jhufa'ar* will not surrender the city without a fight. My last hope of that vanished along with those poor messengers' tongues! But we fought thousands of their outlanders today – surely there cannot be many more to come? I hear the lands that lie north of the sea are less vast, less populous than ours.'

'That is true,' said Anupe, mulling it over. 'Unless of course you strike east, towards the Urovian New Empire and the great expanse of lands that lie beyond that – but they have no truck with the crusade, so we need not worry on that account. However, I would not be surprised if more came – Thalamy has ever been enthusiastic in its uptake of the Pilgrim Wars, and Mercadia can be counted on to provide shipping, supplies and mercenaries for the right price. Plus, we still have the Bethlers themselves and their reinforcements from Valacia to contend with – that is a Pangonian province given over entirely to their Order's usage, since Sir Azelin donated the margravate to their cause.'

Zimri frowned. 'And yet he has forsworn the crusade – I saw that for myself when first I met you.'

'He has – but that doesn't mean he gets his lands back. The Valacians will have joined themselves to the Knights Bethler, and while we may have crushed the crusaders from Troye and Tristia today, you saw the other Pangonians from Thringia, Vania and Aquitania retreating in good order – they conceded the field, but have lived to fight another day. On top of that we have the rest of the Sand Princes to think of too – the House of Coeurforte we smashed, but still we have Arjean and Jeandarme to deal with, not to mention all the minor lordlings they can command.'

Returning her gaze to where the city continued to twinkle by the sea with deceptive innocence, Anupe shook her head.

'No, General Zimri, this pilgrim war is not done,' she said. 'In fact, it has only just begun.'

The four of them fell silent at that, and stood still, watching the city over which so much blood had been spilled. More would be, a lot more, before the thing was done.

CHAPTER 9
INTO THE EMPIRE

Broad and well-kept, their road took them far from Logos Acra: in less than two days they had left the Great White Mountains behind for the sunlit plains of the Empire's western reaches. Having wound through the descending slopes with an easy languor, it became straight and true; great stones marking off the distance to Khronos at regular intervals.

'Milestones, they call them,' Horskram supplied, as they rode pillion together on a sturdy rouncy. Azelin and Hari shared another like beast, while Morcant found himself riding in a palanquin with the Guildsman, a stern patrician man in middling years who looked nothing like the wizard he was supposed to be: taking in his brilliant cobalt cotte and surcoat and sturdy leather boots and girdle, Adelko almost fancied the broad-shouldered warlock could have been a woad merchant. Morcant wouldn't be trying any tricks: his hands and legs were bound with links of cold iron; in that respect at least, the Imperials' treatment of captive sorcerers was not much different from their own.

The rest of them were free to move, though they wouldn't

get far two man to a horse, and none of their weapons had been returned. Adelko couldn't know for sure what they had done with the talisman Sha'arza had gifted him, but his sixth sense suggested the Guildsman had it in his possession.

As for Justorian and his five fellow cataphracts, little more could be said about them: as stoical and stolid as ever, they rode in formation down the Thalamian highway, ever maintaining their disposition of casual alertness. At least their leader was more talkative; in fact, Justorian seemed anxious to make them as comfortable as possible, continually pointing out landmarks and boasting of his beloved Empire's history.

The landmarks mostly consisted of towns and villages, very well-kept, with fields divided up neatly. All seemed prosperous. To his surprise, the villas and houses in every town they passed through had glass windows.

'One of our greatest inventions,' said Justorian proudly when Adelko pointed this out. 'Our loremasters and wizards say that its development has greatly enhanced their studies of Alchemy and chemistry, allowing them to observe liquids and compounds and the like. Thus does the Empire continually advance the cause of humankind!'

Humankind. It was an odd word in Adelko's ears – where he was from, people didn't refer to themselves as human, only mortal.

Justorian only smiled when he pointed this out. 'Yes, ever are you reminded of your frailty when placed next to the denizens of the Other Side,' he said. 'But thanks to the Sorcerer's Guild, we have kept such monstrosities in check. Oh, we have our haunted forests and eldritch ruins too, Master Adelko, but our people know better than to venture into them!'

'There is another theory as to why you experience fewer troubles with the Rent Between Worlds,' Horskram interjected. 'Brother Aldritch of Westerburg wrote a treatise some two centuries ago in which he suggested that the Empire's pursuit of knowledge would come at a price... The presence of magic would be diminished yes, but miracles and the like would also fade. That is to say, the Empire has become a less magical and less godly place. I believe Aldritch even believed this would leave you in perdition.'

Justorian frowned. 'I've read Aldritch and find him to be a zealot. Besides, he misses the point – surely a world with fewer supernatural horrors is a better one? As an Argolian you of all people would have to agree... Or is it also true that with no spirits to fight, your reason to exist would also cease?'

The retort, pointed as it was, had Horskram on the verge of a counter riposte. Anxious to forestall a pointless bickering and hungry to learn more, Adelko quickly interrupted: 'You mentioned something else when we were talking about glass... of Alchemy we know all too well, but what was the other discipline you mentioned? I've not heard of that.'

Justorian looked puzzled for a moment, before remembering. 'Chemistry, you mean? Why, I'm no loremaster, but I believe it simply means the study of different compounds and elixirs and their properties, benefits and hazards – in a fashion that does not involve using any of the Elder Wizards' craft. It was discovered in the last century of our reckoning by Cyrus of Illyrium, who realised there was much to be learned from such studies, quite separate from the warlock's craft.' He favoured the two monks with a look that was half conspiratorial. 'There are some in the Red City who even believe that one day the power of such knowledge may surpass that of the Sorcerer's Guild.'

'You'll forgive me if I don't pray for such an eventuality,' said Horskram, stubborn as ever.

But something else had piqued Adelko's curiosity. 'You say you're no loremaster... but you seem to know an awful lot about many things, besides fighting and war that is. You've even read Argolian treatises... How is it that a man of the sword knows so much?'

Justorian laughed, his demeanour suddenly becoming humble. 'I thank thee, Adelko of Narvik, for your flattery is as heady as a pitcher of Grician wine! But no, you were correct in your first surmise — I am indeed no loremaster. Here in the Empire, all but the meanest citizens receive learning. Our collegia and gymnasia are too many to count, you'll find them in Khronos where we're going and all over the Empire besides. Though I was but a tradesman's son from southern Xanador, I was fortunate enough to be given a place at the Great School in Illyrium in my seventh year. It's our most prestigious collegium, usually only for the rich, but a hundred places are awarded by lot every year. I was one of the lucky ones.'

Adelko blinked rapidly as he tried to keep up with this sudden overturning of the world order he was familiar with. 'Wait, I understand how a man of humble origins can get an education — that's my story after all — but the Imperial Cataphracts are the most illustrious warrior caste in the Empire! Forgive me my impertinence, Justorian, but how does a tradesman's son get to join?'

The smile did not leave Justorian's voice as he answered. 'A grocer's son, to be precise. But you are not entirely mistaken, Adelko of Narvik — the cataphracti were once chosen exclusively from a warrior caste, as you put it, able scions of the ruling Patrician Clans. But in time it was recognised that our military could only benefit from the "career open to talent" as Senator Paralsus put it. Paralsus inaugurated the assisted scholarships scheme a few generations ago, and it's been common practice ever since.'

'It's not quite the egalitarian paradise he makes it out to be,' Horskram could not resist pointing out. 'Of course the sons of richest families have far easier access to the Great School and other colleges than most, and they still hold the lion's share of political power in the Senate.' The monk glanced sidelong at Justorian, as if daring the cataphract to gainsay him.

'What you say is true enough,' Justorian allowed, returning his gaze to the road.

'Tell me more about this Senate,' Adelko pressed. 'I've read that it went too far in Thalamy, nothing could ever get done because the elected officials kept arguing about matters of policy... They say it's what led to the Old Empire's decline. Surely the Imperials have learned from that piece of history?'

'Oh, they have,' replied Horskram, quite happy to pick up the slack from Justorian, who kept his brooding silence. 'The Illyrian Senate is anything but democratic – they can make suggestions and propose legal bills and suchlike, but it is His Most Exalted Excellency the Imperator who has final say on any decree. And, some say, he and his hundred senators can be influenced...' While Justorian remained turned away from them, Adelko's mentor mimed the rubbing of coins together.

The journeyman could not resist a smile. Same old Horskram – always had to have the last word, one way or another.

Towards the end of the day they reached a crossroads straddled by a small city – Justorian had said it was called Thales and referred to it as a 'large town', but as far as Adelko was concerned any place such as this with stone buildings and a population of ten thousand souls could not be called anything other than a city.

'Siona's grace, Master Horskram,' he muttered. 'How

many people does the Empire have? If Thales is a town and Illyrium has more than half a million inhabitants...'

But it was Justorian who answered. 'We take censuses of the populace once every ten years,' he supplied, swelling up with pride again. 'The last one was in 401SA – that's three years ago to you – and it found we have nigh on a hundred million souls lucky enough to call themselves Imperial citizens.'

'Oh yes, how very lucky for them indeed,' chimed Azelin, eager to throw his sarcasm into the ring. 'Answer me this, lord cataphract – do you and your boys get to do anything more exciting than boast about your bloody empire and escort the likes of us hither and yon? No errantry needed thanks to your wonderful law and order and your lovely Sorcerer's Guild – when was the last time you lot had a real fight?'

The warrior-monk was looking intently at Justorian now, as though sizing him up for the first time with those dark eyes of his. Adelko's sixth sense told him the Pangonian wasn't just trying to bait their captor – he really did want to get the measure of him.

Azelin, for Luviah's sake don't try anything stupid – not even you could hope to beat six cataphracts unarmed.

'We hold Games,' responded Justorian, rather stiffly Adelko thought. 'After the tradition of our Thalamian fore-bears, tests of skill, agility, strength, and mind. And our training regime, I assure you, is as constant and harsh as the wind that blows – '

' – yes, yes, spare me the flowery rhetoric, I've already heard enough of it to last a lifetime,' interrupted Azelin. 'You didn't answer my question, so let me repeat it – when was the last time you and your lot got into a good proper scrap? You know the kind I mean, with bloodshed, hewn limbs, cloven skulls, and pleas for mercy, that sort of thing.'

Horskram rolled his eyes, but Adelko sensed that his

mentor was not entirely displeased with Azelin's line of questioning. It made sense to know what the men detaining them were really made of, after all.

As such, Justorian's reply was something of a disappointment. 'I and every man present in harness have shed blood in service to Mother Empire,' he stated flatly, meeting Azelin's fierce eyes with a mild look. 'You may recall I mentioned that I was from the southern reaches of Xanador province... Well, it pains me to say that not all of our northern kindred in the wooded hills away from the plains see the benefits of being aligned to Chalcedony. Twice in my lifetime we've had to go to war to suppress them. But suppress them we did.'

'The Xanadorian Uprising was in full swing the last time I was here,' Horskram put in. 'I'd hardly call it a war, Justorian – it was more a series of hit-and-ride skirmishes.'

The cataphract merely shrugged his shoulders, the segments on his elaborate armour clinking. 'Call it what you will, master monk – your companion asked if we had seen real action, and I answered him.'

Adelko had to tip his hat mentally to the stoical captain for not taking Azelin's bait. All but the most chivalrous knights like Sir Torgun would have allowed themselves to be inveigled into a boasting contest, a war of words that ultimately proved nothing. But the journeyman sensed that for Justorian, war was merely a matter of duty, not glory: the honour to be had from fighting was derived from service to the state, not any personal attainments in the field.

He silently wondered what Horskram made of that, then realised he was being naive – as his mentor had told him since the beginning of their adventures, men of the sword all shared the same blackguardly principle when it came down to it.

'We shall not stop at Thales long,' said Justorian, changing the subject. 'We take the south road yonder to Khronos.'

'How many more days?' asked Azelin. 'I'm sick of sharing the saddle with this half-breed scoundrel.' If Hari, sat behind him, understood the insult in Decorlangue, he gave no indication of it. The rogue seemed to have retreated inwardly during the journey, staring out at the flat plains and dotted copses with eyes that gave away nothing.

'We will arrive at Khronos at sunset in three days,' replied the captain, precise as ever. 'The road we have been following has taken us free of the southernmost belt of the Great White Mountains – our next will take us past it to the Bay of Barophas where Khronos sits in splendour, as she has done since time out of mind.'

Azelin shook his head. 'You folk really are in love with your Empire, aren't you?' he said, more wonderingly than anything else now. But he held his peace after, turning his gaze south to where the next leg of their journey would take them. Following suit, Adelko saw that Justorian had not been wrong: the mountains bent back in an easterly direction at their southernmost point, but had by now petered out: by craning his neck backwards he could just about make out the last peaks to the west, their gargantuan forms wreathed in an ephemeral canopy of mist. Thinking back to their deadly encounter with the Gygant, he could not suppress an involuntary shudder.

But such times were far behind them, and for the time being at least their immediate surroundings were comfortably mundane: riding through Thales, Adelko found it to be just as aggressively normal as all the other towns they had passed through. Glass windows twinkled merrily in shopfront windows, with every place sporting a painted wooden sign denoting the nature of its business. A single etched glyph crowned each of these: Horskram and Justorian explained this was known as a *mark of trade*, meaning the craftsman or tradesman belonged to the appropriate clan or guild.

'What happens if I learn a trade but don't want to join a guild or don't belong to the right clan?' he asked Justorian.

The cataphract simply pointed to the countryside beyond Thales. 'Then that is where you must go to ply your trade, as best you can,' he explained. 'The guilds and clans only really hold sway in urban areas. Anyone can legally set up as an artisan away from towns and cities, as stipulated in the Fourteenth and Fifteenth Protocols of the Imperial Codex on the Practice of Trades & Crafts – '

'Fascinating,' interrupted Azelin. 'Do you think we could maybe stop at a hostelry? You know what I'm talking about Justorian, I'm sure – it'll be one of those places that offer bread and board and have been licensed by the Four Hundred And Seventieth Imperial Law On Making Life Bloody Awkward. We haven't eaten since daybreak, and being bored to death makes a man hungry.'

Justorian frowned, but did not demur. The hostelry he took them to was on a side street that looked bigger than most roads Adelko had travelled on in Northalde, and a good deal better kept: taking in the broad tables arranged outside the establishment, itself a neat, well-constructed building with nary a lopsided corner, he could not help marvelling. The food they had eaten at Logos Acra had been simple but nourishing, and he found the hostelry's plain fare much the same. The owner, a matronly lady of about fifty winters, fussed fastidiously over her illustrious guests, but pointedly ignored the outlanders in their charge.

When they had eaten, Horskram resumed the offensive. 'What will His Excellency do with us, Justorian?' he asked. 'You know enough of our Order to know we cherish our secrets – but I can assure you our mission is by no means against the Empire's interests. In fact, quite the reverse.' Adelko sensed him wanting to say more, but his mentor held back.

Justorian stared back at him impassively. 'I am but a servant of His *Exalted* Excellency,' he replied, pointedly emphasising the part of the honorific Horskram had left out. 'Nothing more, nothing less. It is not for me to presume to say what the Imperator's trusted official will decide.'

Horskram frowned, having no choice but to accept what Justorian said. At a table behind them the Guildsman and Morcant ate in sullen silence. Adelko guessed the two sorcerers hadn't cultivated a kindred spirit.

Shortly after they rose to leave. A few locals had turned up to enjoy a pitcher of wine in the afternoon son – dressed after the fashion of the Imperials, in long frock coats and strange bright wigs, they were staring at the exotic foreigners and exchanging amused remarks with one another.

'Why the wigs?' Adelko could not resist asking.

'You have Imperator Justorix the Elder, father of the present emperor, to thank for those,' said Horskram, just the hint of a wry smile creasing his weatherbeaten face. 'He suffered from a malady that led to his going bald early. His vanity insisted he wear a wig, and the fashion caught on. It's been tradition ever since.'

Justorian returned the smile, nodding and quickly passing a gauntleted hand over his shaven pate. 'Hence we have a saying,' he added. 'When we wish to express a desire to go to court and enjoy time out of harness, we say "I shall put my wig on".' The cataphract's eyes twinkled merrily, as if he'd just said the funniest of jests.

'I see,' Adelko managed. 'That's, um, fascinating.'

Fortunately, Justorian was too preoccupied with his duty to notice Adelko's lack of real interest. Pulling up his coif, he took his helmet from the bench beside him, fixing it to the ventail as his five fellows did likewise.

'Our time grows short as winter day,' he said curtly. 'Let us be off.'

'We haven't paid,' Adelko observed.

Justorian dismissed that with a wave of the hand. 'Our hostess will enter a record of transaction into her accounts. The next time the local Praetor passes through, she will bill him, in accordance with the Thirty-Second Protocol –'

'We are sufficiently informed,' Azelin cut him off, also rising. 'Let's get back into the saddle. I can't wait to share it again with this *al'Hajin* rascal while I see more of your wondrous Empire's sights.'

Justorian pointedly ignored the warrior-monk, ushering his charges from the courtyard and back to the stables.

Horskram did not, however. Drawing closer to Azelin, he said in Panglian: 'It might be favourable to our cause if you let pass the urge to make jibes at his country's expense every five minutes.'

Azelin shrugged. 'Maybe so,' he allowed. 'But it won't be favourable to my mood.'

He turned away from Horskram, who followed him with a dagger-like stare.

'Trouble brewing, that one,' the adept said to Adelko in Northlending.

'Tell me something I don't know,' replied Adelko glumly.

The south road out of Thales took them in that direction for another day's journey before reaching a second crossroads: an elaborately carved signpost indicated that the western highway led to Khronos. A couple more hours in the saddle, and Adelko began to smell the familiar tang of the sea. He offered up a silent prayer of gratitude to St Ionus: once again the avatar of voyages had brought him safely to another historic part of the world he was fighting to save. Though parts of it had been left to fall into ruin since its heyday millennia ago, Khronos managed to boast a crumbling splendour: its high walls and barbican had been diligently preserved by the latter-day Imperials, mindful of the proximity of the Colossean Shelves along the Malhabra coastline and the more worldly threat posed by pirates.

As they approached the city, Horskram quizzed Adelko on his knowledge again, asking if he had chanced to read Brother Cedrian's treatise on the Urovian New Empire. Rather more favourable to Imperial civilisation than Aldritch's firebrand writings, Cedrian's prose was evocative if a tad on the purple side. Adelko rather smugly recited a passage verbatim from memory: 'And the capital of Nacia nestles in a bay located at the furthest corner of the Sundering Sea, and it is called Khronos; and from this Nacian jewel of a city the conquering Thalamians learned much of seacraft, building the ships that would enable it to expand its empire to the south.'

He went on, pointedly ignoring Azelin's look of obvious irritation: 'And though today Khronos has dwindled to a fraction of its erstwhile size, it still boasts its splendid waterfront buildings and harbour and barbican of old, and close on seventy thousand souls call it home. And around the entire circumference of that city is a great wall that meets the barbican, sealing its defences; and this was constructed in the time of the Conquest to defend the Empire's south-western tip. Flanked as it is by the Great White Mountains to the north –
'

'I should have known better than to ask,' Horskram interrupted, to Azelin's obvious relief. 'All right Adelko, you've made your point – I was wrong to treat you as though you were still but a novice. Your companions humbly thank you for your tutelage.'

Adelko held his peace, but refused to wipe the smug grin off his face.

Future events did that for him, however. Reaching the mighty gatehouse in the city's eastern wall, Adelko barely had time to admire the ancient friezes on the vast lintel stone depicting the hero mariner Antaeus fighting the Sea Serpents sent to trouble him on his third voyage by the un-angel Aqualcus; no sooner had Justorian given his name and rank than the garrison of legionaries parted to allow them entrance.

As things transpired, a missed opportunity to study Khronos at leisure was the least of his woes. Emerging into a small quadrangle enclosed on all sides by high walls, the companions saw another smaller gateway, presumably leading into the city proper. That wasn't their immediate destination: Justorian steered them towards a large low building that took up the entire southern side of the quadrangle, and motioned for them to dismount.

His manner had suddenly become curt and formal again; gone was the stiff but unfailingly polite host of their journey to Khronos. Adelko didn't need the jangling of his sixth sense, but jangle it did.

'How now?' asked Horskram, dismounting. 'What ails thee, Justorian?' The adept was staring at the cataphract captain, who had remained mounted. Out of the corner of his eye, Adelko caught Hari's hand instinctively reaching towards a scimitar that was no longer belted at his side. Azelin had refused pointedly to dismount, and was glowering suspiciously at Justorian. As for Morcant, he and the Guildsman had not exited the palanquin, which the servants had placed down next to the building's entrance.

'It is my regret to inform you that you are to be detained pending further interrogation, pursuant to the – '

'Spare us the legal jargon,' growled Horskram. 'And tell us why we are being kept here.' He motioned towards the building, which Adelko now realised was obviously some sort of prison. 'I had been given the impression that we would be treated as guests and taken to the Consul's palace for a proper hearing.'

Justorian refused to meet Horskram's eye. Adelko sensed the captain was conflicted, but his voice was stern enough as he replied: 'You will recall our investigation determined that your mage companion was a practitioner of the Right-Hand Path – unfortunately, the same cannot be said entirely of the articles we found in your possession.'

Horskram appeared thoroughly baffled, but Adelko felt his heart sinking.

'What are you talking about?' demanded the adept, still glaring up at Justorian. 'Come, man, no riddles – break words cleanly!'

Justorian cleared his throat. He actually looked nervous. 'One of the items our Guildsman examined... Well, it does not bear any traces of Demonology or Necromancy in itself, but appears to have been constructed by a sorcerer who trades in such. Forgive me, Master Horskram, for as you know I am not well-versed in such matters.' He barked a command in Imperial and the Guildsman, stern and unyielding as ever, emerged from the palanquin. He and Justorian spoke briefly in their tongue, and though he couldn't follow the exchange Adelko gathered it was far from cordial.

Turning reluctantly to address the outlanders he so clearly looked down upon, the Guildsman said in stilted but precise Decorlangue: 'The Guild is satisfied that none of you are Left-Hand warlocks. Unfortunately it would appear that one of you has had truck with such, for the article in question bears traces of having been handled by a practitioner of the Two Forbidden Schools.'

Horskram's face purpled as he turned towards the palanquin. 'MORCANT!' he thundered. 'BY REUS' TEETH, I'LL HAVE YOUR HEAD FOR THIS –'

'Horskram.'

The adept turned quizzically to look at Adelko.

'Heavens, Adelko, what now?'

There was no point in concealing what their captors surely already knew. 'The talisman they're talking about, they didn't find it on Morcant.' He let the words hang in the air. Horskram looked puzzled a moment longer, then his eyes bulged as he understood.

'I had meant to tell you about it,' the journeyman said with an awkward shrug. 'There just never seemed to be a good time to do it.'

Horskram's jaw went slack. 'But how...?' Then he slapped a hand to his forehead as he realised. 'Sha'arza. He gave you something – Adelko, do you have any idea of the gravity of what you've done? Our Order might not have as many rules as our Imperial friends here, but you've broken one of the cardinal ones!'

Adelko hung his head. He could not help but feel ashamed. 'These are hardly ordinary times,' he managed to mumble.

But whatever scolding Horskram had for him would have to wait. Justorian nodded to the legionary commander, and a dozen footmen advanced to take them into custody. It was too much for Azelin. With a roar giving vent to weeks of pent-up frustration, he spurred his rouncy towards Justorian, aiming to grapple his throat. Caught off-guard by the alacrity of his sudden attack, the cataphract was powerless to stop him – but two of his men drew swords and closed on him.

'Take your hands from off my throat,' Justorian managed to gasp. 'Or my men will cut yours.' With a pair of blades flush to his unarmoured neck and another three cataphracts bringing up the rear, even Sir Azelin, greatest knight of the

Free Kingdoms, had no choice but to admit defeat. With an angry snarl he released the captain and submitted.

'No chastisement,' Justorian had the decency to command as he rubbed his sore neck. 'A barbarian outlander he might be, but a true and valiant warrior he is too.' Adelko sensed the cataphract was deeply pained, and not because of the near-throttling he'd just received.

My fault, all my fault, he thought disconsolately as the Imperials prodded them into the prison building's cool, dark interior. Behind him he could sense Horskram boring holes in his back with his eyes.

But it was too late for regrets now.

CHAPTER 10

DEBRIS FROM OCEAN

Stormy weather returned to trouble them when they were two days out of Akrytos. The captain strode the boards, bellowing orders, and his harried crew struggled to obey. Adhelina and Hettie and their knightly escort cowered below decks, of little to no use; more than once the would-be queen of Vorstlund cursed her gift – why had her precious Second Sight not warned of this? She could hardly unite her home country if they kept sailing into one storm after another on the journey there.

On the third day of the storm her worst fears were realised. A hideous snapping sound that could be heard from where they huddled over buckets of their own vomit (sea legs be damned) told of a broken mast; the first mate, Saexwulf, briefly found time to come below and yell at them to stay put. Another day and night the winds raged, as Sjórkunan's domain vengefully battered the vessel that had dared intrude upon it. Adhelina did not need the Second Sight or a sailor's acumen to know that all sense of direction was hopelessly lost: to and fro the ship lurched, yet some of the archangels must have intervened with their unruly brother, for the ship did not go under.

What it did do was be flung ashore with a grinding crunch. The first mate was back below decks, with a rather different order this time: abandon ship, post-haste, taking only what was necessary. Water was already pouring through a breach in the hull as they clambered to the deck.

The ship, or what remained of it, was a ruin. The main-mast had indeed snapped, a third of the way up its length; its sails were lost, quite useless and abandoned to the deeps. Half the crew were gone, the remainder looked a bedraggled and sorry sight. The ship itself had been driven up onto an outcropping that jutted into the sea from a barren and rocky shoreline; that had at least served as a crude kind of jetty, albeit at cost of the ship.

The sailors lashed ropes to what was left of the inwale and motioned for the passengers to climb down onto the surface of the rock, which had punctured clean through the ship's prow. Proudly refusing all help, the damosels timorously descended.

Hard rock though it was, it felt heavenly beneath the feet. Adhelina gave vent to a great sigh of pleasure, before collapsing exhausted. Hettie wasn't far behind; the three knights were next, followed by Captain Adso and his eight surviving crew.

The rest of the afternoon was spent salvaging what they could from the ship before the waters claimed it altogether. The captain bewailed the loss of his precious cargo; Sir Ulfstan and the other knights bemoaned the loss of their even more precious warhorses. Adhelina could scarcely have cared less: at least they were free of the horrid sea, for a while anyway, and back on dry land.

But, where *were* they?

Looking up and down the shoreline the un-angel of the waters had brought them to, Adhelina saw few clues: the rocks were a dark ochre colour, and receded into flatter terrain a little further inland. She thought she could make out a line of cypress trees in the distance, but there was little else. The winds were still blowing fiercely, though the rain had abated to a light drizzle: clearly done with them, the storm was beginning to die.

'We'd best get further inland,' yelled the captain, mirroring her thoughts. Sir Ulfstan and his knights, glad to be of some use at last, had managed to erect a tent they'd salvaged away from the rocks where the ground was a little softer. They had no squires: the three knights had resolved to travel without them so as to attract less attention.

Damned secrecy and its consequences: Adhelina felt sure a squire or two would have been right handy now. Judging by the wearied looks on the knights' faces, she guessed they felt the same.

The three struck their makeshift camp and together with the crew they made their way further inland, towards the belt of cypresses lining the shore. The skies were just beginning to darken.

'Where in the Known World are we?' Adhelina asked the captain.

The burly Vorstlending paused, scratching his stomach idly. 'If I had to guess – which I don't normally like to do – I'd say we're on the Muradi coastline somewhere. Probably its eastern side, going by our position before the storm hit, but it's hard to be sure.'

Adhelina paused to mull that, chewing her lower lip. 'Murad... they aren't particularly active in the Pilgrim Wars, are they? I mean, they provide supplies to the crusaders for a price... Maybe they might help us.'

The captain shot her a sidelong glance that was brimful of

scepticism. 'Or maybe they might not,' he said, resuming his trudge towards the treeline.

Reaching the shelter of the cypresses, they found a hunting trail and followed it to a clearing.

Hunting trails mean hunters, Adhelina found time to think. *I just hope we don't become prey.*

By the time they had set up camp, night had drawn in. Back away from the ravaging tides under shelter of trees, the air was mild and balmy: something to be grateful for at least. Adso's crew soon had a fire burning, and the castaways huddled around it, drying out their clothes and chewing forlornly on salt beef from a keg the first mate had managed to salvage from the shipwreck.

It was a meal that was destined to be rudely interrupted.

The locals did not bother with subterfuge: a dozen lightly armoured men with swart skins dressed in turbans, they carried bows and scimitars. One of them, apparently the leader, barked something at the outlanders in a staccato tongue.

Adso had risen slowly, hands raised and well away from his cutlass, but the three knights had already drawn swords and formed a protective semi-circle around the damosels.

Adso replied to the leader in the same tongue, which sounded similar to Sassanic, yet somehow different. Adhelina guessed it was one of the many dialects spoken throughout the Sultanates.

'My guess wasn't awry,' said the captain a minute later. 'We've landed on the north-east tip of Murad, in the satrapy of Urshad. These men are in service to Zangid, the local ruler. We're to come with them and not cause trouble – His Eminence is a hospitable man well accustomed to taking in castaways.' Adso's voice sounded more hopeful than certain this was the truth.

Adhelina wished she had the Argolian sixth sense instead

of her second sight, an unwieldy tool at best. Knowing whether a lie was being spoken would have been right handy now. Taking in the stoical expressions on the Muradis' faces, it was impossible to gauge what they were really thinking.

Sir Aescwine had clearly made up his mind all by himself. 'Submit to these infidel fiends?' he snarled in Vorstlending. 'Let us chastise them, and show these foreign dogs how Palomedians wield steel!'

'We're the foreigners, you idiot,' Ulfstan shot back. 'Hospitality to wayfarers is held sacrosanct throughout the Sassanian Sultanates, or did you learn nothing on this mission? Lower your blade, dammit – there'll be no unnecessary bloodshed.'

Aescwine glowered at him, but did as he was told.

Turning to the captain, Ulfstan added: 'Tell this man we will gladly accept his offer, but we must have guarantees that our charges, these women, will not be harmed or dishonoured in any way.'

Nodding, Adso nervously repeated in the Muradi dialect.

Their leader nodded curtly and said a few more words.

'He says he swears it in sight of Ashanti Almighty upon the lives of his children and the departed souls of his ancestors,' said the captain. 'That's his bond given, sirrahs, I suggest we take him at his word.' His glance fell meaningfully on the scimitar blades and arrow heads that still glinted menacingly in the firelight.

Ulfstan nodded. 'It is well. Please introduce us formally – I would have our hosts know they are treating with folk of noble birth.'

The captain hastily translated, and the Muradi captain's demeanour seemed to soften. He even favoured them with a half bow, before motioning for his men to take their weapons.

Only now did the Muradis get a good look at Adhelina.

She felt herself flush as the swarthy men looked on her fair complexion with undisguised admiration.

'This isn't the Pilgrim Kingdoms,' Adso reminded her. 'But for the odd castaway like us, they don't see Urovians every day. I think your, ahem, appearance has made quite the impression on them, my lady.'

Quickly recovering, Adhelina straightened up and assumed her best regal pose. This was an old weapon that she knew well how to use, though she scorned the reasons for its effectiveness. She'd not been blind to the surreptitious but lustful looks many of the Vorstlending sailors had given her during the voyage – put next to that, and the Muradis seemed respectful, almost reverential, in their appreciation.

'Let us strike camp and be off,' said the damosel, once again in command. 'I would gladly meet our new host and benefactor.'

She glanced sidelong at Hettie, hoping her oldest friend wasn't jealous of the attention she was getting, but of course she was too busy making eyes at Sir Wulfraed.

Fool that you are, Adhelina. Hettie has nothing to be jealous of – by the looks of things, she's closer to getting married than you are right now.

Little did she know then how wrong she was.

CHAPTER 11

A PROPHECY FULFILLED

From his high place in Ortiz, the Old Master of Time's Arrow watched and waited. He had foreseen this hour, and tried to avert it. Then he'd realised his folly. There was no averting what Ashanti had ordained; his part in the Great Tale had been all but played out, and now it was time to let the veil fall, gently and without complaint.

Without complaint; but not without a fight.

'Are the Shadowmen ready?' he asked in a voice that was at once subdued and susurrant, like the hissing of a serpent that spies an intruder into its lair.

'Always, Old Master,' whispered his lieutenant.

The Old Master kept his gaze fixed on the darkening desertscape below him. A light wind blew through the vast open window that formed one side of his solar; he fancied he could already smell the taint of death upon it.

'It is well,' he replied. 'All that remains is to resist, to the final breath of the very last of us. The Kardin bloodline has been restored thanks to Muqmurlish tek Nazar, though his views on reconciliation between the Alamites and apostates are in error.'

The Old Master knew his right-hand man's question before he spoke it.

'Then why do we not oppose him, Old Master?'

'Ashanti's will,' he replied. 'I have seen it in the dream-visions bequeathed me by Sha'abat himself.' Both men made the sign of the Faith reverently. 'The One-Eyed Sultan who bears the same Kardin blood as I do shall keep the crusaders occupied, while the true Great Old One-Eye foretold comes for us. We shall fight him and lose, and in so doing earn our place in paradise. Then he shall take what we have guarded, and so the war to end all wars shall commence.'

'But why then did we aid the infidel monks, who seek to oppose the One-Eye, and the master he serves?'

'Masters,' corrected the assassin lord gently. 'Ashanti's will is thus: to save the mortal world, we must allow the very thing that threatens to destroy it to be made whole again. Only when the two poles are brought together, in ultimate conflict, can the great clash come about. And only through that can the world emerge, renewed – made whole again, but changed forever.'

'So why must we resist him when he comes?'

The Old Master allowed himself a slight smile. He did not turn from watching the desert as he answered: 'Because we must fight the servitors of Shai'itan always – even when they go about Ashanti's work unknowingly. That is why. Surely you are not afraid to die, my most esteemed apostle?'

The response was sincere: 'In your service and that of Ashanti's, never, Old Master.'

But he sensed his chief understudy's consternation, and was not entirely immune to it himself: Ashanti and His True Prophet had revealed to him the skein of the Great Tale's mighty tapestry but haphazardly, and he was not so foolish nor so vain as to pretend it was in his gift to understand it all.

But this he did understand: duty to the will of the

Almighty was all. It fell to him to play his allotted role without question; nothing more, nothing less.

From his vantage point at the summit of Ortiz, he could see where the Abydos and Cerulean ranges met to cradle the Ghorabi desert's south-eastern portion. From beyond the former swathe of peaks the Great Old One-Eye would come, sweeping from the Inland Sea across the coastal plains of Halepo; everything in his way would be destroyed by his deathly host, for not even the magicks of that realm's ruler the Warlock-Sultan would avail against such an enemy. But, the Old Master also knew, the host the One-Eye led would seem but a mere company when set beside the demonic horde the thing they were coming for would unleash, once reunited with its fellows at the appointed hour.

For the first time in many years, the Old Master knew something approaching fear. It was a strange and awful tool the Almighty had chosen to deploy, to perfect the world He had imperfectly fashioned at the Dawn of Time. And who could say whether the Fallen One was really the rebellious archangel who had defied Ashanti's will long millennia ago, or just another tool at His disposal?

It was the most maddening refrain, employed by holy men bereft of reasonable answer to the Almighty's seeming indifference to a world fraught with pain and peril: but truly it could be said He moved in mysterious ways.

The days passed, quickly. The high heat of Al'Nurë wore on, but at this altitude the Order of the Silver Shadow was immune to the parching heat that lay on the Ghorabi far below. Ortiz, long prepared for its great last stand, went about its final devotions in serenity: a thousand men and boys, weapons ready, minds honed, spirits bolstered for the final deed. The hidden gates of Ortiz would not confound the Great Old One-Eye; his eldritch cyclopean scrutiny would perceive all, and the battle when it came would be swift and brutal.

On the eve of his arrival, the Old Master assumed the meditative Wind Trance, carrying his soul far upon the ethereal currents that swept through the Rent Between Worlds; it did not take his old friend Abdel Sha'arza long to divine him.

- You are quite prepared to go through with it then? The warlock's spirit-voice, talking to him via the discipline his kind called Scrying.

- Quite prepared, yes. As I told you at the last full moon.

- I hope you will not take it amiss if I observe: rather you than me.

The Old Master felt sure that if he had been communicating in person, the sorcerer would have given one of his characteristic little giggles. Such strange bedfellows the Great Tale put one's way.

- My soul is prepared for death. As well you know.

- Indeed, pray forgive me. These mountains shall be emptier without you, Old Master.

- Never mind that. What of your own part? You said you persuaded the younger monk to take your talisman. Has he used it yet? I only know what the Unseen permit me to know at Ashanti's behest, but I would be surprised if He did not have something in mind for you as well.

- Hopefully with a different ending to yours, Old Master! But no, I have heard nothing from the monks or their companions since I left them near Shazra'am several moons ago.

The Old Master paused. If he had not been sundered from all feelings of desire, he would have relished the feeling of drifting weightless in a limitless void. And yet no: for he could not have felt anything in his present abstracted state, even had he desired to feel desire. Truly the sages spoke of

Enlightenment's being an imponderable; one either was or wasn't – there was no space for reflection once one surrendered to the ineffable, eternal, moment.

With an inward sigh, he realised there was nothing more to be communed.

- *We must trust to the Unseen and Ashanti and the True Prophet then – the monk will call upon you in due time, when your aid is needed.*

- *I shall not be slow to respond when he does. Fare thee well, Old Master, I wish you good speed on your final journey.*

- *Fare thee well, Sha'arza. May the crooked path you walk lead to the palace of enlightenment.*

An internal dissolution, as of recollections sliding from memory, and the Old Master was alone again in his solar, squatting on his reed mat. He focused on his breathing, gentle but so very deep, enjoying its circularity as he returned to the world of thought and sensation once more.

And then he sensed it, like the briefest of shadows darkening an otherwise well-lit room. Opening his eyes, he stood in one fluid motion. Without speaking a word, he commanded for his weapons to be brought to him.

The Final Hour had come.

A HERO'S FUNERAL

The skirling pipes cut the air as the Highlanders played their dirge. Tears rolled down Vaskrian's scarred cheeks, and he was not ashamed to shed them.

What did shame him was that he hadn't been there when his hero, his friend, his comrade, had needed him most. As the senior perfect of Vandheim intoned the words in Decorlangue to the Psalm of Spirit's Speeding, six attendant squires hefted the stone lid of Sir Torgun's tomb. The final strains spiralled up to the gabled ceiling of the temple as the lid was lowered in place with an echoing boom, scattering motes of stone dust and obscuring Northalde's greatest knight from mortal eyes forever. A few of the assembled ladies coughed, and one or two of the older knights. Quite a few more wept openly, for Vaskrian was not alone in his grief.

Of the younger knights, there were few besides Sir Vaskrian and Sir Torgun's older brother Toros. The Jarl of Vandheim was dressed in a sable cotte of mourning, which threw his ashen face into sharp relief. The priest finished his prayer and made the sign reverentially, as the thurifer beside him swung the censer: the smell of pungent incense filled the air, causing a few more ladies and greybeards to cough and splutter.

With barely more than a few dozen nobles in attendance, it was hardly the ceremony a knight like Sir Torgun deserved. The temple should have been packed, and in ordinary times it would have been. But of course, these were no ordinary times. In point of fact, they were lucky even to have the luxury of a funeral at all: several of the surviving lords had demurred at the idea, but Lord Toros had been adamant, and Vaskrian, but lately a hero of the realm himself, had not been slow to back him up. If it meant a few days away from the field, so be it: the siege of Strongholm would manage well enough without them.

That was one thing to be grateful for. The desolation wreaked by the Wyverns had been a fearful thing to behold, but the casualties had numbered in the low hundreds: no greater loss had the sea serpents inflicted than that of Sir Torgun. Sir Vaskrian and Lord Kelmor and the southrons had eventually reconnoitred with the scattered northerners and their highland allies: the young knight had been heartened to see that at least Whaelin, the clan chief who'd led the high-landers in the last war, was among the latter. When he'd offered his skalds to play at Torgun's service, few had demurred: again, these were not ordinary times.

The consolidated Northlending army had now regrouped around the capital, plotting bloody vengeance on Magnhilda, the Shield Queen, once the walls were breached. No quarter would be given: the regicides could expect a torturous death at the hands of their mainland cousins if they surrendered. Vaskrian had heard many of the common soldiers and even one or two knights discussing in lurid detail their plans for captives, and found that he did not disapprove. Not in the slightest. There was even talk of a reprisal raid, when the realm was retaken: of fire and steel being brought to the

Frozen Principalities to teach them a lesson they should have learned generations ago.

Wishful thinking. Vaskrian was by now wise enough to know that the retaking of Strongholm was far from accomplished, and that future wars lay to the south and not the east. But he would broach that subject in time.

'Sir Vaskrian, pray walk with me.' Toros was similar in manner if not stature to his heroic younger brother; the same mildness of tone married to firmness of resolve. But where Torgun had been a great knight, Toros was a wily lord; Vaskrian knew enough to realise there were as many differences between the siblings as there were commonalities. Not least the fact that Toros was still alive.

Wiping the tears from his ravaged cheeks, the young knight nodded curtly but deferentially and left the temple at Toros's side.

Outside it was a clear summer's day. Ripanmonath was more than a week away: but the only reaping to be done was that of the more bloodthirsty variety. Not that Vaskrian was complaining. The desire for vengeance burned in him, and though the Jarl of Vandheim must perforce keep his outward emotions in check, the young knight knew he felt the same.

Toros turned to Vaskrian, interrupting his thoughts: 'You have proven yourself a hero of the realm, and perhaps even a worthy successor to my dearly cherished brother, whom we have just given to the earth.' He held up a hand to forestall Vaskrian's protests. 'No chivalrous modesty, I'll have none of it. Without you, we'd probably all be dead just like my poor brother.'

Vaskrian lowered his eyes. 'I wish I could have been there to help him. There is nothing false in my humility, my lord. I don't deserve your praise.'

He felt Toros's grey-blue eyes staring hard at him, though

the noble's tone did not change as he said: 'Yes, you do. And what is more, the time has come to make it serve you.'

Vaskrian returned his gaze to the Jarl. 'What do you mean, my lord?'

Toros gestured casually at the nobles and knights and ladies retaking the saddle in Vandheim's central square, outside the sombre-looking temple. Up above on its hilly perch, the castle Torgun had once called home brooded silently.

'People here now regard you, quite rightly, as the saviour of the realm,' Toros went on. 'That is power, Sir Vaskrian – and it is power you must learn to wield, right soon, if you are to be of further service to that realm.'

Vaskrian frowned, painfully aware of his scars as he did. Hero or no, he was no comely romantic knight.

'I still don't quite follow.'

Toros inhaled slightly, betraying just a hint of impatience. 'We are a land without a king,' he went on, lowering his voice just slightly. 'Our entire royal house has been slaughtered, save the man who was supposed to be our ruler – and he by all accounts has gone completely insane, may Siona comfort him! On top of that we have lost many of our leading figures – not only my brother, our greatest warrior, but Lord Toric, the man who led our most prestigious order, the White Valravyn. The realm needs a figurehead, Sir Vaskrian – in the absence of a legitimate king, it needs a hero it can place its faith in. You are the obvious candidate.'

The words were delivered in Toros' trademark calm baritone, but they stunned Vaskrian nonetheless. Not more than a year ago, he'd despaired of ever becoming a belted knight... Now here was one of the most powerful men in the kingdom, albeit a broken kingdom, telling him he was not only a hero, but *the* hero of the realm.

As much as he relished the idea in his dreams of fancy, he simply could not compass it in his reality.

'But, Lord Toros,' he stammered. 'I'm of common stock, no blueblood. Why, it was just by blind luck that I won my spurs...'

Vaskrian's voice trailed off uncertainly as Toros' stoical features betrayed a hint of a smile and he laid a firm hand on his shoulder.

'Your modesty becomes you and only strengthens my suit,' he said. 'For it shows you to be the exemplar of chivalry that men now reckon you. Blind luck, you say? The tale I heard was that you had to slay a killer knight twice your size to win said spurs – when no belted man had the courage to face him! Granted, they were Thraxians, but still I think this bespeaks well of you. And as for your other adventures... do you know that the camp troubadours are fighting over you? They each want to be the one who gets to sit down – alone – with Sir Vaskrian of Hroghar to hear his tales of errantry. You, my young friend, are about to become the stuff of lays.'

Vaskrian let his jaw go slack as that sank in. The stuff of lays. That would not have even occurred to him, and yet... Well, it *did* make sense. His adventures with Horskram and Adelko, and those he'd been on since, quite simply *were* the stuff of lays.

'All right,' he said, after pausing to take a deep breath of his own. 'You may have a point, my lord. My adventures have been... quite something. But I've also run into a lot of trouble – you heard how Sir – your brother had to spring me out of gaol.' Even now he struggled to mention his hero, so freshly given to the earth, by name.

'All great men have done questionable deeds,' Toros said, the half-smile not leaving his face. 'Show me a man who has never done the world harm, and I'll show thee a commoner. Heroes are not innocents, Sir Vaskrian – I would have thought your erstwhile Argolian companions might have taken pains to tell you that.'

Vaskrian was shocked by the insight, perceptive as it was. He did recall Adelko mentioning Horskram and his lectures on morals and bloodshed, back in the day... His respect for Torgun's older brother redoubled. Toros would never be the mighty hero he had been, but he had great capacity, in his own way.

'I see the wisdom in what you say, sire,' Vaskrian hedged. 'But how do you propose to, erm, use my reputation? We're but a couple of weeks into what looks to be a lengthy siege, and that's hardly work for knights, great or otherwise.'

What Toros said next caught him off-guard. 'Are you familiar with the *Lay of the Fall of King Vasirius?*'

Vaskrian blinked his surprise. It was an old favourite, dwelling as it did on the last days of the legendary Pangonian king and his great knights – men in whose footsteps he and Torgun and so many others had striven to follow.

'Of course,' he answered simply. 'What good knight doesn't cherish such tales?'

Keeping his hand on Vaskrian's shoulder, the Jarl steered him towards where their coursers and squires were ready for them in the square. 'Then you'll recall the tale of the stalemate siege of Valacia – how every day for more than three months, Sir Balian of the High Castle, Vasirius' greatest knight after Sir Lancelyn of the Pale Mountain, rode up to the gates of his fortress stronghold and challenged him to single combat to settle the matter?'

This tale was well known. 'Sir Lancelyn refused him ninety-nine times,' Vaskrian replied, picking up the thread. 'Because he said the cause of their grievance was a false one, stirred up by the Traitor Prince Ancelet and the White Blood Witch... it would have been tragedy for the realm's two greatest knights to fall to blows over such.'

Toros fixed him with shrewd eyes as they drew near their horses. 'That's right – but do you remember what happened next?'

Vaskrian mulled it over as they stopped beside their whickering mounts.

'It's a while since I had the luxury of listening to bard's song, but I believe on the hundredth time, Sir Lancelyn finally agreed to Sir Balian's demands. He said as a true knight, he could not risk his knightly honour being impugned over cowardice... even though it meant falling into Ancelet's trap, he was left with no choice but to answer the challenge.' Vaskrian paused again, meeting Toros' shrewd stare, wondering where this was going. 'So they met in single combat outside the walls of Valacia, and Lancelyn slew him after fighting him for half a day.'

Toros nodded. 'Yes, that is the essence of the tale. But do you understand the point of it?'

The young knight shrugged helplessly. 'Never trust a lord allied to a warlock? I could tell anyone that from my own adventures, never mind the great tales of old.' He sighed exasperatedly as Toros continued to favour him with his intent look and half smile.

'My lord, you have me at a loss. What precisely is your point?'

'My point, young Vaskrian, is that a warrior can be persuaded to do things against his best interests – if you play upon his honour and reputation. That is what you must do, with the defenders at Strongholm. We will return forthwith to the siege, which as you rightly say looks set to be a lengthy one – well into the winter and probably far beyond, if we fight it out the conventional way. Or' – here the lord's face became cunning – 'we play upon our barbarian cousins' twisted sense of honour, or rather the honour they believe they have. Oh, they may be a barbarous and slaughterous people, but one trait they do prize is valour.'

Vaskrian reflected. He could see where Lord Toros was going with this, but he still wasn't entirely convinced.

The young hero said: 'The knights of King Vasirius were the – what's the word? – epitome of chivalry, its founding fathers, if you will. Of course they abided by their pledge – once Sir Balian was struck down, King Vasirius marched his army off... He was able to come to a reconciliation with Sir Lancelyn and his followers after that, just in time to join forces against Ancelet for the last great battle at Avalongne. But these Northlanders, my lord, even if I do fight their champion and win – they aren't likely to keep to their word and leave the city without a fight. And I seriously doubt we'd keep to ours, after what they've done to us and the House of Ingwin – they know it would be suicide!'

But Toros shook his head. 'Oh, I'm not saying we pledge them free passage if their champion wins – I'm suggesting we offer to let them keep what they have conquered. Our pledge will be to raise the siege and return to our homes if you lose.'

For the second time during their conversation, Vaskrian's jaw dropped. 'What you're proposing is madness!' he exclaimed, quite forgetting his place.

Toros only smiled more broadly. 'Perhaps, but there is a method to it... We need something convincing to entice the barbarians. They know enough of our knightly code of honour, while being sufficiently baffled by it, that we might just persuade them we are in earnest. Of course, we would return in spring – possibly the duel could be an ongoing arrangement, fought every half year or so to decide the matter.'

'I'm sorry, sire, but it still smacks of folly to me,' Vaskrian had to tell him. 'And what if I win? You really think they will simply hand over the city and consent to be slaughtered?'

Toros spread his arms wide. 'What choice do they really have? Their gambit has failed – they threw their lot in with a sorcerer whom you have defeated. All their resources they staked on this venture – they won't be getting any reinforcements or supplies by sea, Lord Aesgir will see to that. Essentially, they are already doomed. And from what I know of the Northlanders and their fatalistic beliefs, they will realise that all too well.' He changed tack slightly. 'Sir Balian had to issue his challenge daily for several months before Sir Lancelyn finally relented. I don't doubt you would need to be just as persistent. But eventually, and maybe sooner than you think, they will have no choice but to comply.'

Vaskrian remained unconvinced. 'Begging your pardon, Lord Toros, but it still doesn't make sense – if they send a champion against me and he loses, I think they will most likely renege and continue the siege. Fighting and dying to a man – and a woman – sounds far more in keeping with their fatalistic viewpoint, not to mention their twisted warrior code, to me. And believe me, I've fought enough of them to know what I'm talking about.'

Toros broke his gaze then, staring absently at the unfinished concentric rings of his castle while he rubbed his chin thoughtfully.

'Perhaps you are right,' he said at last. 'But what if we were *prepared* for them to renege, as you put it? We anticipate their going back on their word.'

Vaskrian shook his head, more confused than ever. 'I still don't see what you mean – then what's the point in my fighting the duel of chivalry at all?' *And risking my neck again*, might have been something to add to that, though his spirit yearned for mortal combat. His refusal to speak the words he was thinking demonstrated the wily lord's point though: anything but be seen to be afraid, even if the plan suggested sounded crazy.

The cunning expression had not left Toros's face as he returned his gaze to Vaskrian.

'I have something else in mind,' he said. 'Ride with me now! We must away back south to Strongholm, I'll do my best to explain as we travel.'

Resignedly, Vaskrian complied. It was already obvious to him that Torgun's older brother had received very different gifts from the hand of the Almighty, and he wasn't sure he liked them all.

He was only slightly surer once Toros had explained himself. The coastal road they took provided fresh air aplenty, and Vaskrian needed everything he could to keep his wits about him. Evidently he was becoming a pawn – no, technically a *knight* – in the Jedrez game played by high lords such as Toros.

'So let me see if I've understood this correctly,' he hedged as they ambled along the rutted highway overlooking sheer cliffs. 'We fool the Northlanders into thinking they have *us* fooled – that we're desperate enough to trust them not to go back on their word if I win, and honourable enough to keep it if I don't?'

'Correct.'

'And in the meantime, you're going to try to arrange for a spy or two to get into the city – while the Northlanders are busy watching me fighting for my life against whatever champion they send against me.'

'Correct.'

'You're staking your ploy on the distraction afforded by our clash, because we all know how the barbarians love to watch a good fight – they won't be paying as much attention as they would under normal siege conditions, which might just afford us a chance to get someone in to start stirring up trouble.'

'Correct.'

'So if I win and they renege, which is likely, it shouldn't matter because we'll hopefully have succeeded in getting our man into Strongholm. They will then try to find someone to bribe or otherwise, erm, persuade to open the gates for us at night, or incite an insurrection from within?'

'Correct.'

'And if I lose, I'm dead of course, because Northlanders have no concept of chivalrous mercy or taking prisoners for ransom – but that won't matter to anyone except me because by then you'll have at least one spy inside Strongholm, and naturally you don't see anything wrong in breaking troth with barbarian regicides who'd only do the same in our position?'

A slight pause this time.

'Correct.'

Vaskrian leaned back against the cantle of his saddle, sucking in a deep lungful of briny air and exhaling it in one go.

'So, what think you of my plan?' asked Lord Toros, keeping a watchful eye on their squires to make sure they weren't too close to hear anything.

'What do I think?' asked Vaskrian in response, turning to look at the lord with a wry grin. 'I think it's so madcap, so audacious, it might actually work. Frankly, my lord, I couldn't have come up with anything better myself! In fact, I think even my old adventuring chum Master Horskram would be impressed – you can count me in.'

'That's the spirit!' Toros leaned over in the saddle and clapped him on the back. 'Now all we have to do is broach it with the other lords, and the new head of the White Valravyn!' he added, his eyes twinkling mischievously.

That pulled Vaskrian's returning high spirits back down

with a jolt. Sir Redrun was as dour a man as any who could have been appointed High Commander of the Order. When he and Horskram and Adelko had first encountered the White Valravyn, Redrun had sided with the vindictive knight Sir Wolmar, who had been for having them 'chastised' in the dungeons. Their crime? Being pursued by demonspawn sent by Andragorix to eliminate them.

Vaskrian was sure the new High Commander would be quite happy to pour cold water all over Toros's plan.

Unfortunately, he could also see why.

'There is one flaw – what if your spies can't get someone in charge of the gatehouse to open the gates, or curry enough support from our people and theirs to foment an uprising?'

The merriment left Toros's face, which became set grim against the rising wind as he stared ahead up the highway.

'Then we're back to siegecraft, and a very long winter,' he replied glumly.

CHAPTER 13
UNLIKELY ALLIES

Sir Hugon wiped cold sweat off his forehead. Though the night was mild and the monastery well heated, he couldn't banish the chill from his bones. Days after the siege of Westerburg had been so abruptly terminated, he could still scarcely fathom it: fifteen thousand trained men put to flight by a few dozen attackers.

And yet that was precisely what had happened.

The first wave of brave knights to attack the ghastly apparitions had been cut down, their own blows turned aside contemptuously as though they were children; the second had choked on reeking black breath that emanated from tenebrous maws and been cut down like corn stalks; a third had met a similar fate, perishing on blades of the same hue as the black fog that enveloped them. That had only been the beginning. The same cloud of eldritch darkness had spread out, engulfing the entire camp: hundreds had perished as the dark lords stalked about at will, hewing down knights, soldiers, serjeants, crossbowmen, washerwomen, squires, prostitutes and other auxiliaries. Anything mortal that came their way in fact; not even horses had been spared.

He'd rallied what remained of the Purple Garter, sorely missing Sir Aremis, after half their number perished in the first disastrous assault. Their courage broken, the elite knights had fled just like the others, taking what horses and supplies they could and scattering to the Four Winds.

Sir Hugon was still too horrified by the experience to feel any real shame. What could be done against enemies that appeared to have already been long dead?

The erstwhile freelancer Sir Wrackwulf seemed to think he had the answer – and it lay in the small Argolian monastery whose precinct they were now crammed into. What's more, Sir Aremis stood with him, and seemed to have been won over to his plan. Hugon eyed the disfigured young knight askance: fleeing the field against an impossible adversary was one thing, being absent without explanation in the first place was another. He'd have words with his fellow crescent knight when he got the chance.

But that would have to wait. For now, they didn't even know the whereabouts of half the senior commanders: most of the Margraves including Kaye, Aravin, and Morvaine, not to mention King Carolus himself, were unaccounted for. Clovis he'd bumped into, in the middle of the forest several hours after fleeing the camp, with what was left of his retinue. Had the circumstances been otherwise, Sir Hugon would have been delighted to see the smug cruel lord so thoroughly cowed, but as things stood it just lent an extra veneer of surreal horror to their plight.

For some reason, his mind kept going back to his lover, the Queen, and her friend Ivon. Hugon couldn't shake the feeling that they were related to this somehow, but if anyone could answer that it was his crony lords Kaye and Aravin... and they hadn't been seen or heard of since the dread things attacked.

Wrackwulf raised his hands for silence among the gaggle of knights, squires and serjeants that had assembled at the monastery. Located deep in one of the woodlands that dotted the hinterlands of Westenlund, it was but an Argolian outpost: no more than a score of adepts and journeymen, with a handful of novices. Its Abbot, an unimpressive-looking greybeard of about sixty winters, cleared his throat and spoke: 'The apparitions you have but lately encountered are Draugar – wights or revenants of servitors of the Elder Wizards. Elite soldiers of that ancient empire, if you will – I shall not trouble you laymen with talk of scripture or prophecy, but suffice to say that the foe we now face cannot be overcome by swords alone.'

'I think we already worked that out for ourselves,' snarled Lord Clovis, his brutish face scowling in the torchlight. Sheltered within the walls of the monastery, he seemed to have recovered some of his febrile courage.

You're not so brave now you aren't just torturing helpless captives, Sir Hugon found time to think. Glancing over at Sir Aremis, he could tell from his twisted hare-lip that he thought much the same of the Margrave of Narbo.

'Be silent!' snapped the young knight, shocking many present. Scarcely more than a hundred Pangonians were crammed into the refectory, which had struggled to feed the unwelcome and sudden guests.

Pointedly ignoring Clovis's outraged glare, Sir Aremis went on: 'Our survival depends upon what Prior Cedric here has to tell us – I know that where we come from, his Order is held apostate, but here in Vorstlund things are different. We must listen to him if we are to have a chance of defeating these things!'

'How different?' shot back one stubborn Pangonian knight. 'Vorstlund is part of Greater Pangonia, what goes in our country goes here!'

Wrackwulf rolled his eyes. Aremis looked perplexed. If the old prior was offended, he hid it well enough.

'Please,' persisted Aremis. 'You have to put that aside for now – the wars of mortal men must wait! Prior Cedric says this country is dotted with barrows – Sir Wrackwulf here has experienced them twice now. That means that even as we speak, hundreds of Draug Lords as powerful as the ones we met have relinquished the grave and stalk the Free Kingdoms.'

'But why?' asked one grizzled serjeant. 'Why now, all of a sudden? We've known well enough to steer clear of barrow mounds and suchlike all our lives – leave well alone and be left alone, that's what my grandam always told me. What's causing this... this uprising?'

Though he was but a common soldier, knights and squires were not slow to add their questioning voices to his. Aremis suddenly looked like he'd come over with a bout of the Drinking Sickness, and Hugon almost felt pity for the young knight.

You might be the finest fighter amongst us, Sir Aremis, but you'll never make a leader of men.

Fortunately, he had Wrackwulf at his side. 'HOLD!' the veteran bellowed, silencing the gaggle again. 'Maybe if you let Prior Cedric finish a sentence, you'd learn the answer to that.'

Something in the freelancer's eyes told Hugon that he knew the answer better than any man present, the Argolian Abbot included. He'd be having words with the renegade too, when he got a chance.

Prior Cedric was shrugging his shoulders helplessly. 'If I explained to you all the lore and theories we have on Draugar, we'd be here all night and many more besides,' he said in a voice that quavered slightly. 'Most likely it is a powerful Necromancer, but we have not detected traces of such in the vicinity, so it most likely isn't a Left-Hander practising nearby.' His voice suddenly became firm as the throng teetered on the brink of dissent. 'But the what or the why aren't as important to us right now as the how... How we are to defeat these things.' He turned to look at his adepts and journeymen, gathered in an orderly ring behind him on the dais from where he addressed the refectory. 'Together, my brethren and I should be able to muster sufficient elan – think of it as spiritual power through combined prayer – to weaken the Draugar. We hope that will curtail the power of their breath somewhat, and render them more vulnerable themselves... when next you contend with them.'

'Are you mad?' One of the younger knights found the courage to speak. 'We lost dozens of knights and soldiers when we tried to fight them before – what you're proposing is tantamount to self-murder!'

'SILENCE!' roared Sir Hugon, cutting across the rising din as he finally lost his temper. Rounding on the knight who had spoken, he said in steely tones: 'Sir Guillarme, you shame yourself with such craven speech. There are but a hundred of us here, but need I remind you that we remain fifteen thousand strong – though I'll grant you, our battle formation has looked tidier ere now.'

That earned him a few grudging chuckles. Hugon knew the men respected him as much as they feared him – he'd never be the legend his older brother was, but he had enough glory to his name to put to use right now.

'Aye, they caught us unawares with their hellish tricks and sent us packing. That's beyond dispute. But, Stygnos dammit, they didn't wipe us out! A few hundred we lost, so what? We managed to inflict more casualties on the Vorstlendings than that – and that didn't stop them rallying to their standards and fighting on.'

He paused to let the significance of his words sink in. Judging by the slowly nodding heads, they had done. Out of the corner of his eye, Hugon caught Aremis and Wrackwulf favouring him with grateful looks.

Don't think this means either of you are off the hook, he thought as he went on: 'These Argolians have vouched to bolster us with the power of prayer – a generous offer considering the fate their Order has met in our homeland. But that wrangle for another day! Right now, it falls to us to venture back out there' – he pointed at the refectory walls for emphasis – 'and reconnoitre with as many of our countrymen as we can find. We needs must reunite, and seek out the King and other high lords as quickly as possible. Once that's done, we reassemble and take the fight back to these Gehenna-cursed things!'

'That's assuming they'll just wait around and let us reform,' Clovis interjected. Evidently the lord had recovered his wits somewhat too, for the point was a good one. What kind of tactics did undead soldiers employ?

Fortunately, Prior Cedric seemed to have a ready answer. 'The Draug lords crave destruction of all the mortals they see as encroaching on their rightful territory. If your account of your encounter with them is accurate – and the divination we but lately held in haste suggests it was – then we can safely assume their next target will be Westerburg.'

One of the Pangonian knights started laughing. 'Well that settles it! Let them do our work for us against yon Vorstlendings, while we regroup.' Many approving throats told of the popularity of such a view.

'NO!' Now it was Aremis's voice that cut across the hubbub. 'That is precisely what we must not do! Our aim must be to help the Vorstlendings – who knows how many more of these things are out there? To stand any chance of surviving, we must unite against the common foe!'

Prior Cedric was nodding sagely, while Wrackwulf pursed his lips in approval, but Sir Hugon wasn't entirely convinced.

'And say we unite and triumph, and send these things back

to hell where they belong,' he cut in. 'What then, Sir Aremis? We just go back to fighting each other?'

Aremis surprised him with the shrewdness of his response. 'And why not? It wouldn't be the first time allies have ceased to be friends once the mutual enemy has been despatched.'

The young myrmidon favoured him with a crooked smile, and suddenly Sir Hugon wasn't so sure how witless his subaltern was in matters politic. Approving nods and shrugs showed that the cogency of his argument had told.

The leader of the Purple Garter paused a moment longer, then made up his mind. 'Very well – there is some sense in what you say. But we'll have to divide forces from the outset, to have the best chance of finding the others. Four groups of twenty each! Knights, squires and serjeants divided equally – likewise the remainder of the Purple Garter. Sir Wrackwulf and Sir Aremis, you will be in my cohort – you can choose whomever you like according to my instructions.'

'Two adepts per cohort you shall have as well,' said Cedric. 'You'll be needing them if you run into any Draugar! Likely the fiends will concentrate on Westerburg, but they are the revenants of ancient soldiers themselves, after all, so who knows but they might send some of their own to harry the countryside thereabouts. The rest of the chapter will stay here and begin praying.'

Quick to reassert his authority, Clovis began barking orders of his own; before long, they were organised and armed. Most of the assembled men had managed to salvage at least one horse; in less than an hour they were drawn up in the courtyard, ready to leave.

'I will send a journeyman with a message to Princess Utha,' said Cedric. 'She is a wise ruler and will see the wisdom in our counsel. Expect to see the Vorstlendings muster to your side.'

'How will said messengers get into the castle?' asked Hugon.

The old Abbot's answering smile was rather too devilishly cunning for a man of the deity, Hugon thought.

'The same way the Crown Prince's men have been getting out of it to cause you trouble,' he replied smoothly.

Oh Aremis, you weren't wrong. These might be sometime allies, but they are no friends – hardly surprising given we but lately invaded their country.

Keeping his thoughts to himself, Sir Hugon nodded tightly. He still could scarcely believe the pass they had come to.

Clovis barked another command, and journeymen scurried to open the gates. Two by two they filed out on horseback, glancing timorously about as if half-expecting Draugar to lurch out of the night at them there and then. Which they might very well do, given everything that had transpired.

A flicker of movement from the undergrowth to his right had Sir Hugon reaching for his sword, but Wrackwulf stayed him.

'Have no fear, it's just my, ahem, squire.'

Staring at the scarecrow figure that had appeared from beneath the branches, Sir Hugon's astonishment was complete. He didn't know which appalled him most: the amazonian sight of the unkempt wiry woman herself, or the glyph-embossed spear she bore that caught the moonlight with unnatural lustre.

'You call... this, your squire?' he managed to ask.

Wrackwulf flashed him a broken-toothed grin as he motioned for the strange wild warrior to mount up behind him.

'You have no idea how hard it is to get proper help these days, what with there being a war on and everything,' he chuckled. 'My apologies if she startled you, Sir Hugon – we thought Ariadha ap Madrix of the Island Realms might be even less welcome in an Argolian monastery than Pangonian sworders.'

Sir Hugon shook his head and nudged his destrier back into a trot. 'Just keep her far from me,' he said curtly over his shoulder.

'Trust me, you'll be thanking her before this campaign is done,' breezed Wrackwulf, not bothering to catch up with him.

I seriously doubt that, thought Hugon disconsolately as they pressed on into the darkened woods.

CHAPTER 14

A RIVAL SUITOR

Something of a cross between a fortress and a palace, the Satrap's residence was both well positioned and well appointed. Built atop an islet reached by an isthmus from the mainland, it cut a splendid sight in the late afternoon sun; by now Adhelina was well used to the elaborate yet elegant architecture of the Sassanians, the gold-leafed onion domes and bejewelled minarets did not impress her.

Or not much, anyway.

What did impress her was the sophistication of the seaside town it guarded: swart men and women dressed in bright, rich garb lounged at ease outside coffee parlours and wine shops, taking their favoured drinks with a bedazzling variety of sweets, craftsmen in adjoining streets could be heard hammering and sawing, while hawkers and other merchants dressed in voluminous pantaloons and turbans plied a brisk trade from their shaded stalls.

Their escort took them through the teeming mass of prosperous humanity without so much as a sideways glance, though many locals paused at their leisure and trade to gawk at the strange rough foreigners; passing through the town, they reached a large mosaicked horseshoe arch that gave onto the isthmus: a road paved with bright green stones that reflected the sunlight with an emerald sheen cut across it, leading to the Satrap's palatial seat and broad enough to take three riders abreast. Drawing nearer they saw two concentric walls guarded the palace proper, which was almost as large as the King's in Rima.

'Tales of Muradi prosperity were not exaggerated it seems,' Adhelina murmured. Hettie and Ulfstan rode to either side of her on amblers requisitioned at a large village they had stopped in the previous day. Their escort had split in two as they rode onto the isthmus, half a dozen riding up front towards the gatehouse and another six guarding their rear – or making sure they didn't try to escape, depending on how you chose to look at it.

'If this is to be our guest-prison for a while, I can think of worse places we've been,' said Hettie, divining her friend's thoughts.

'I can't disagree with you there,' Adhelina replied with a half smile, though she noted that Sir Ulfstan's face remained downcast and serious. As the banneret assigned to escort her safely home, he felt rightly galled at having been stymied. A knight's reputation might well hinge on the outcome of such an important mission, but Adhelina had little words of comfort for her compatriot. The ocean deeps had spoken, and there hadn't been much any of them could do to gainsay Aqualcus in his domain – they were lucky even to be alive.

The leader of their group exchanged words in the high singsong staccato of Muradi Sassanic, before a duty sergeant dressed in curiously fashioned splinted armour ordered the teak gates swung open. Entering the outer courtyard, they were surprised to see a group of female dancers clad in brightly coloured silks. That was odd enough in itself, Adhelina supposed – but on top of that there was no music.

'What on earth do you make of that?' she asked Ulfstan, but the knight just shrugged sullenly.

'If you don't know, I certainly don't.'

The second gatehouse was open – clearly the Satrap did not anticipate attack any time soon, though during the crossing Adhelina had thought she could espy what looked to be warships beached further up the coast – and they passed through into the inner courtyard, filled with more traders and craftsmen.

At least now it's starting to look more like the sort of castles I'm used to, Adhelina thought, still mindful of the strange dancers they had just passed.

Again, richly clad townsfolk could be seen browsing and haggling. So far, not a beggar or cutpurse to be seen – even the peasants tending the fields on the way to the palace had seem well-fed and healthy.

Whatever the Satrap of Urshad province was doing, it appeared to be working.

The master of the house came as no surprise to her, but that didn't mean he wasn't striking. When she met the Satrap he was standing on a jade-and-garnet-studded stone terrace that jutted from the summit of the highest tower in the palace; directly above them an onion dome gleamed golden, as if in silent triumph over the slowly retreating sun. One of the Satrap's hands was encased in a hawker's leathern gauntlet; upon it perched a splendid eagle. The rest of him was swathed in bejewelled silks: the effect somehow managed to be simultaneously garish and stylish, though after the manner of her people Adhelina could not approve of such ostentation.

The Satrap flashed her a dazzling smile, displaying ivory

teeth in a handsome face. He was rather paler than most of his countrymen, she thought, though he looked to be the picture of glowing health, a young lord in the prime of life.

'Welcome wayfarers!' he exclaimed, in flawless Decorlangue. 'May I presume you speak the High Speech of the Imperators of Old?'

Adhelina managed a half smile, though she decided to forego the curtsey. She had no real idea of the customs of this place.

'You may presume it in my case,' she said, glancing sidelong at her companions. The common sailors were no longer with them, having been hived off to a side-chamber adjoining the palace vestibule for refreshments. That just left Adhelina, Hettie, the knights, and Captain Adso and his first mate Saexwulf.

Our escort barely spoke to us during the trip, but they worked out who was important easily enough – Adso, I'm not so sure that these people don't often deal with outlanders.

She kept her thoughts concealed as the Satrap strode over to a gilded cage, which was obediently opened by what she supposed passed for a squire or page in these parts. Putting the creature back in its luxurious prison with what could only be described as loving care, the Satrap turned abruptly and clapped be-ringed hands together sharply. In an instant scurrying servants appeared, bearing a low mahogany table laden with silver trays of sweetmeats and filigreed rhytons and ewers.

'You must be hungry and thirsty after your journey,' said the Satrap. 'Please allow me the honour to introduce myself – I am Zangid tek Zangid, Satrap of Urshad, and it is my pleasure and duty to be at your service.' More servants had appeared to lay sequinned cushions alongside the table – but so too had a fully armed guard of half a dozen *taziqs* or *amluqs*, whose eyes never left the outlanders.

'Come!' said the Satrap. 'Please sit, relax and drink and enjoy the pleasures of my home, while you tell me your tale. It is some moons since we had a shipwreck.'

'You have many?' asked Adhelina, raising an eyebrow as they sat down gingerly on the cushions, which were undeniably comfortable.

It was Adso who answered that question, in his halting Decorlangue. 'The Dragon's Teeth have long made for bad waters in these parts, my lady.'

Zangid nodded sincerely, while the servants poured them rhytons of dark Muradi wine.

'It is true that these stretches are dangerous, but oft frequented by virtue of their location,' said the Satrap. 'As such, I am rarely short of visitors.' He raised his rhyton, the only solid gold one in the set, by way of a toast.

Returning it, Adhelina sipped the wine, which was delicious and refreshing: Murad was rightly famed for its vineyards.

'I must say, you don't carry yourself as other rich men of power do,' she dared to observe. 'Your soldiers barely spoke of you on the journey here, and normally such a wealthy ruler would be introduced formally, before his courtiers. Are the customs so very different here?'

Zangid laughed, a genuine and open sound full of the joy of life and its unexpected pleasures. It wasn't an attitude that endeared him to everyone: she caught Sir Ulfstan snarling into his rhyton.

'How correctly you observe!' exclaimed the Satrap, his brown eyes twinkling. 'I am what you might call a merchant prince.' He paused and turned, gesturing across the expanse of sun-dappled sea that the terrace overlooked. 'For generations my ancestors plied their trade up and down these stretches – Dragon's Teeth be damned.' He paused to favour her with a sardonic wink. 'In time, the risks that entailed proved worthwhile – one ship became two, two became four, and by my father's time – may the Prophet's blessing be on him, always! – Urshad could boast a fleet of fifty well-armed galleys. But only for our defence, you understand, against pirates and freebooters and the like. Trade, not war, has ever been the Muradi way – we prefer to supply our more warlike neighbours with the things they need, and let them fight it out between themselves over land to their heart's content!'

'And what if your warlike neighbours decided to make war on you and take *your* lands?' Ulfstan asked pointedly.

The Satrap barely glanced his way as he replied: 'And in so doing, they would act as did the Avaricious King in the *Tale of the Cockatrice and the Golden Egg*, killing the very thing that helps them grow rich. War, you say, sir knight? War costs money, and there is plenty of it to be had through commerce, let me assure you!' His voice became earnest as he favoured them with a stare that was suddenly imperious. 'Mark this, and mark it well – for now the warrior-kings may hold sway, but in time it shall be merchants not swordsmen who rule the world.'

No one knew quite what to say to that. Sir Ulfstan frowned into his rhyton, clearly at a loss for words. Sir Aescwine and Adso looked at the Satrap, suspicion writ plain upon their faces, while Saexwulf simply looked awkward. As for Hettie and Sir Wulfraed, they only had eyes for each other.

Quickly changing the subject, Adhelina asked their host about the strange dancers in the courtyard.

'One would not usually expect to hear silence when presented with such skilful dancers,' she pointed out diplo-matically.

The Satrap smiled again, his demeanour affable once more. 'They dance the Dance of the Sea,' he explained. 'Every

Al'Nurë, or what you Urovians would call high summer, hand-picked Temple maidens dance to the rhythm of the waves.'

Ulfstan snorted, while Aescwine actually sneered. 'What a ridiculous idea,' he said, and Adhelina could have slapped him.

'Be silent!' she commanded. 'Where is your sense of hospitality – we are guests in the Satrap's palace, so act accordingly.'

Aescwine fixed her with a hateful glare, but Zangid raised his hands in a placatory gesture. 'No no, it is well – I understand this must seem a bizarre custom at first sight. The Dance of the Sea is an old practice among northern Muradi people – our *ulamas* believe if virgins dance to the waves, the elemental avatar you call Aqualcus will be entertained – and thus less likely to grow angry and send storms our way. Quite a delightful custom, I'm sure you agree!'

He raised his rhyton again, but Adhelina was too busy glaring furiously at the two knights to join his second toast: Aescwine and Ulfstan were barely troubling to conceal their obvious mirth.

We really must seem a barbarous folk at times, she could not help thinking. And then another thought hard on its heels, quite unbidden: did she really want to go back to a land where such behaviour was commonplace?

As if reading her mind, the Satrap said: 'But enough of my country and its peculiar ways! Tell me your story – how came you to be at sea, so far from home... and where precisely *is* home, pray tell?'

The Satrap was looking at her intently now. She had marked herself out as the leader of the group by her own actions, now it fell to her to speak for the party. Adso and Saexwulf kept their peace, while the two knights had fallen into sullen silence; even the typically suave Ulfstan had little to say. Hettie and Wulfraed could have been anywhere in the Known World, of course.

She proceeded cautiously, omitting all mention of Horskram and Adelko and their sacred quest – but she did tell the Satrap about the betrayal of her father by the Lanraks and his subsequent shocking death. She surprised herself at the flood of emotion recalling the event roused in her, even now more than a year later, and by the time she finished she was close to tears.

So too, by the looks of things, was the Satrap. 'Your tale is sadder than that of *Shahazardre and the Ninety-Nine Outlaws*,' he said sincerely. 'Such a monstrous betrayal! This Hengist deserves a swift and painful death, as do his viziers! Would that I could avenge thee, for know that Zangid tek Zangid commands a thousand *taziqs* well trained to arms!'

Adhelina managed a half smile through her incipient tears. 'I thought the Satrap of Urshad frowns upon war?' she asked.

The Satrap showed little sign of sharing her humour. 'Only unjust wars fought for land-greed,' he clarified. 'But this is a righteous cause – would that your homeland lay not so far away!'

'And yet it does,' Sir Ulfstan interjected, finally finding his voice again. Adhelina sensed he was probably grateful to her for not mentioning the last salient details of her voyage – namely why she was going home. 'And we must return there as quickly as possible, for I represent men loyal to the rightful Orla of Dulsinor.' Hearing her original presumptive title was a strange experience to Adhelina.

'And yet you yourself are not a native of eastern Vorstlund,' observed the Satrap, 'itself a country well known for lacking a king. So how comes a lord of Westenlund to support the cause of Dulsinor?'

If Zangid enjoyed watching Ulfstan's jaw drop, he at least had the good grace to hide it.

'How... how did you know that?' Ulfstan barely managed to gasp, astounded at being found out.

The Satrap smiled and casually pointed to a gold signet ring the knight wore on his left hand. 'Only nobles of Westenlund are in the habit of wearing their family crests on their fingers,' he said. 'I did tell you we have many visitors – and not only through the tragedy of shipwrecks. Trade brings many to our shores too. Also, I accompanied my father – may the Prophet smile on him, always! – on many of his voyages of commerce as a youth. It is true we never sailed as far as your country, but by the time I had seen sixteen summers I had sailed to every port from here to Ushalayim, including Montrevellyn. You would be surprised at how many people one meets in the great trading ports of the Sundering Sea.'

If Adhelina had been intrigued by the Satrap before, now she was downright impressed. This was no effete popinjay, good only for charm and hospitality: the affable facade hid a keen and observant mind.

You'd best tread carefully, Sir Ulfstan.

'You have me at a disadvantage,' said the knight, recovering his skills as an envoy. 'In truth, the concerns of Dulsinor have become, ah, intertwined with the concerns of Vorstlund as a whole... and indeed the rest of the Free Kingdoms. Somebody as obviously well informed as you will have doubtless learned that our nations are at war.'

The Satrap smiled, as if to say *now at last we speak plainly*. 'Indeed, I had heard such... Not content with waging yet another religious war on our Nazharyan and Kallandhari cousins, the Pangonians and their Thalamian allies have decided to invade Vorstlund as well.' Zangid shook his head, a rare frown creasing his lips. 'Such folly. If only more peoples would follow the Muradi way, there might be less conflict in this world.'

'And yet if they did just that,' countered Adhelina, 'you would have fewer markets to sell to. As you yourself said just now, trading with warriors makes for profitable business.'

The Satrap nodded deferentially. 'Just so – now it is I who am at a disadvantage.'

'Your eminence, this is all well and good and politic,' cut in Ulfstan bluntly. 'But I believe we are skirting around the salient issue. You now know our purpose of travel – we are returning home with the rightful heiress of Dulsinor to try to broker an alliance against the invaders. You currently hold us here, with host rights as per the custom in the known realms of civilisation. Will you lend us one of your ships so we can complete our journey? Westenlund, the most prosperous of the Vorstlending baronies, would of course compensate you handsomely for such service – over and above any loss to trade or other risks you might incur.'

'Would it indeed?' replied the Satrap, leaning back on his cushion. Adhelina was not fooled by his relaxed demeanour. 'And that leads me to think that there is more at stake here than simply returning Dulsinor's rightful ruler – though as I said, the circumstances of your deposition, Lady Adhelina, were egregious in the extreme! But no, it is clear to me that something else is afoot... The last news I heard from Vorstlund, Sir Ulfstan, said your ruler the Princess Consort had already succeeded in brokering an alliance of the Nine Lords against the common foe. Beyond that, I knew little of the details, but now...' His gaze fell meaningfully on Adhelina as his voiced trailed off. '... it seems to me that one of said details has been washed ashore on my bourne – and I find it hard to believe that the part she is to play stops at Dulsinor, for all the trouble you have evidently gone to recover her.'

Too shrewd by half – there's no fooling him.

Unfortunately, Sir Aescwine chose that moment to butt in. 'You have no right to hold us here!' he snarled. The strong Muradi wine, which the Satrap had only sipped, appeared to have gone straight to the young knight's head. 'By order of the Prince of Westenlund, we command you to set us at liberty! If you won't help us, we'll make our own way home!'

Ulfstan shushed him frantically, but it was too late: Adhelina saw now all too clearly the true purpose of the Satrap's hospitality. An old maxim from the Thalamian loremaster Senestheses sprang to mind: *if you would have your rivals off guard, disarm them with generosity and flattery*.

'In point of fact,' replied the Satrap, completely unfazed by the outburst, 'your compatriot Sir Ulfstan is right where you are in error – I have every right to detain you if such is my wish. But hold! Do not be alarmed, for I wish none of you any harm. On the contrary, I am very concerned for your welfare, Lady Adhelina – so concerned that I am not sure allowing you to travel on in such company is at all the best course of action for you.'

Ulfstan stood, all pretence of diplomacy gone. Reaching instinctively for a sword hilt that wasn't there, he thundered: 'That is an unmannerly remark to make, from one who was at such pains to persuade us of his hospitable disposition!'

The Satrap did not rise or even sit up. 'As I recall, you and your companion were less than polite yourselves a minute ago.' He flicked a jewelled hand languidly. The fingers she noticed were thin but not feeble; clever and strong and calloused in a way that no manicure could hide.

'In truth, the company of your exalted charge pleases me greatly – more than you can possibly imagine,' the Satrap continued, his eyes straying to the where the *taziqs* still stood to attention behind them. 'But as for you... your company grows wearisome.' Suddenly switching to his native tongue, he barked a command. Adhelina needed no translation to comprehend: in an instant half a dozen swordsmen stood around them, hands upon hilts that were very much there.

'The time has come for you to leave my presence for a while,' the Satrap continued. 'These good men and my servants will convey you to the baths, where you will be cleaned and rendered presentable for my court. After that we shall see you for dinner – a feast I shall hold, in honour of our guests! Oh no, not you, my lady,' he added as Adhelina started to rise. 'I would fain spend a while longer in your presence, without the distraction of your entourage.' Only now did he lean forward, his eyes twinkling again. 'I have a feeling you will be far more revealing alone.'

'What do you mean by that?' demanded Adhelina, appalled.

The Satrap looked momentarily baffled, then slightly disgusted. 'Clearly not what you thought I did,' he said. 'What kind of barbarous clime cultivated you, I wonder, so fair and vibrant a flower? I look forward to learning more about you, Lady Adhelina of Dulsinor... and the peculiar country that gifted you to the world.'

The Satrap motioned again, and the *taziqs* closed ranks around the others. Hettie was gawping at Adhelina helplessly, while her amour simply looked baffled: doubtless they weren't too pleased at being so rudely awoken from their lovesick daze.

But rudely awoken they had been. 'Just do as he says,' Adhelina told them both. 'I will be fine, don't worry.' She glanced awkwardly at Zangid, who had relaxed back into his cushion and was sipping again from his golden rhyton. 'The Satrap of Urshad seems... an honourable man.'

'My lady, are you sure this is wise?' asked Sir Ulfstan in Vorstlending, laying a restraining hand on Sir Aescwine, who looked ready to attack their captors bare-handed.

'What choice do we really have?' replied Adhelina. 'If it

makes you feel any better, this isn't the first time I've been held by powerful men against my will.'

In fact, that's been happening to me for nearly my entire lifetime. Tipu, a pox on you and your damned prophesying – I was free, Luviah dammit.

But the recondite Sufieli mystic was far away, somewhere in the Hot South, leaving her with nothing but the cold present. Watching her retinue being ushered off the terrace, she felt an inner darkness shroud her, almost mirrored by the waning sun. More servants arrived just after they had gone and began lighting braziers against the encroaching evening chill.

Taking another sip of wine, the Satrap beamed at her and said: 'Now, where were we?'

CHAPTER 15

A THREAT FROM THE EAST

Their new prison was less commodious than the last, but at least they were not destined to be held there long: two days after arriving at Khronos, the five captives were ushered from their cold stone cells and into the building's atrium: a stolid-looking official whom Adelko took to be the chief gaoler received them there, flanked by half a dozen legionaries.

At his side was the Guildsman who had travelled with them, but of Justorian and his cataphracts there was no sign: Adelko presumed him returned to active duties on the borderlands. Morcant stood beside them, still shackled: a sidelong glance at the warlock's pasty face revealed nothing of his thoughts, though at least the shameful marks of his Argolian captivity had begun to fade.

'You are to be taken into Guild custody,' explained the official, 'under the Twelfth Protocol of the Imperial Code on the Transfer of Witchcraft Suspects – sanctioned Right-Hand wizards shall know best what to do with you. Guildsman Avotus, please sign here.' The gaoler presented a sheet of paper on a ledger while an underling proffered an ink-pot and quill. The patrician-looking mage scrawled his signature cursorily before handing back the ledger.

The legionaries moved around the captives, ushering them from the atrium behind the warlock named Avotus, already striding towards the exit without a backwards glance.

Outside it was a bright late summer's morning: the sun hurt Adelko's eyes, but he was grateful for the light.

This beats a cell with one barred window hands down, he thought as they re-entered the quadrangle and headed towards the gatehouse leading into the city. His sixth sense was oddly quiescent, which gave him a faint hope, until another thought occurred to him: perhaps the sorcerous Guild which now held sway over them had found a way to dull it?

The bustling main thoroughfare of Khronos did little to allay his resurgent fears.

Of a size with Rima, the city was not quickly traversed. Already the street teemed with the usual denizens of urban life, and not even the Imperials had found a way to get rid of the stink, though close proximity to the sea helped. The buildings were a hotch-potch mixture of older Thalamian obelisks and colonnades and newer villas and manses: as with Rima, poor and rich seemed content to live cheek by jowl, with meaner hovels leering across side streets at their grander neighbours. The clamour was deafening, but Adelko was somewhat used to the din of big cities by now. The city was built on two levels: descending a broad flight of stairs onto the lower area that overlooked the barbican, Adelko saw that Cedrian had not lied, for it was a mighty structure indeed: similar to that he'd witnessed in Panya, dating back to the halcyon days of the Golden Age, when the Sundering Sea had been the theatre for a diverse host of rival powers. War galleys clustered among the merchant cogs, and even the odd trireme could be seen: the Imperials had made a point of relearning the shipcraft of their forebears.

No sooner had they descended the steps than their escort veered sharply right down a side street that was broader than any in Strongholm: this took them to a large but curiously nondescript sandstone building that abutted onto the harbour.

It makes sense, I suppose – even here the warlocks wouldn't want to draw too much attention to themselves. He glanced sidelong at Horskram, half expecting some nugget of lore to be tossed his way, but his erstwhile mentor had not spoken a word to him since their release.

Adelko felt a mixture of emotions – guilt certainly, but also indignation. How many times had their mission obliged them to fall in with sorcerers? That seemed acceptable, just, but take one trinket from a mage and you were bound for perdition.

The journeyman could see his superior's point of view, but the injustice of it burned within him all the same.

There were no guards. Double doors of pine inlaid with ebony patterns stood open, inviting them to step into the Guild's draughty interior. Passing through these Adelko realised the pattern was a simple motif of a raised right hand, repeated in myriad across the smooth varnished surface of the doors; as they entered the main chamber, which was even bigger than the Governor's office in Logos Acra, he spotted the same sigil, running all along the wainscotting of the high ceiling. The room was colonnaded to either side, in a manner that unsettlingly reminded him of the cloisters at Ulfang and Rima – beyond the partition that the pillars formed he could spot men in robes hunched over tomes in carrels, just as the monks would have been at either of the monasteries he had called home.

The far end of the oblong chamber ended in a dais, upon which thirteen men and women sat behind a row of neatly arranged trestle tables. In the far wall behind them a row of high-set windows whose lintels repeated the hand motif with hypnotic persistence allowed beams of sunlight to penetrate: no sorcerous lamps, clearly the Guild were not at pains to show off their craft.

Their escort marched them up a long carpet of leopard skins – Adelko only recognised these from an illuminated manuscript he'd looked at in Rima – towards the steps ascending the dais. Directly at their end was yet another large hand motif, painted in gold on a flagstone set before the centremost table. Avotus knelt upon this and lowered his head, stretching his arms to either side of him in what Adelko took to be some kind of traditional supplicatory gesture.

'My mission is complete, Guildmaster of Khronos,' he intoned in Imperial, Horskram hastily translating for the benefit of his companions. 'I have delivered the five outland witchcraft suspects, as per the rules of our association.'

The Guildsman sat in the middle – at some four score winters, by far the oldest mage there – nodded curtly.

'The Guild thanks you for your service, Journeyman Avotus,' he said in a whispery voice. 'You may rise.'

'At least they don't bother with pox-swyved protocols,' muttered Azelin, but Adelko wasn't focused on that.

Journeyman... assuming Horskram's translation was accurate, they grade themselves as we do. Arnulf, you truly had the right of it – mage and monk, how different are we really?

The Guild Master took two articles from his table. One was a ledger bearing a sheet of paper on it, the other was a strange contraption fashioned of glass and silver that he perched on his long nose. As he scanned the missive, Adelko deduced it was some clever invention to help the old man read: ageing adepts at the monastery had had to settle for being read to by younger monks as their eyesight began to fail them.

So clever and ingenious... If only we could get them on our side.

After reading the paper, the Guild Master cleared his throat and looked up at his five charges, who had been arranged by their guards on the step just below Avotus. The legionaries themselves stood just behind them – if Hari or Azelin were thinking about trying anything bold and daring, they could think again.

'This missive says one of you is a confirmed Right-Hand practitioner,' said the Guild Master, switching to fluent Decorlangue. Taking the contraption off his nose he used it to indicate Morcant, who was still chained. 'But it also makes mention of an article found upon.... Ah, the younger Argolian friar, so that would be you, methinks.' The man's manner was homely enough, and Adelko's sixth sense remained cool as the Guild Master gestured towards him briefly, favouring him with a brief glance from under the brim of his flat-topped skullcap. The other dozen mages – four of which were women – stared coldly at the captives. If their leader was homely, they most certainly were not.

'And said article, while in itself appearing to be a benign enough talisman with the powers of Scrying imbued into it, appears to bear traces of having been constructed by a sorcerer also trafficking in the Two Forbidden Schools. Do I have that correctly, Journeyman Avotus?'

While the Guild Master was speaking Avotus had risen and taken a seat next to one of the furthest trestle tables, from where he could survey his charges and superiors alike.

'Demonology was the trace we detected, Guild Master,' he clarified from his perch. 'Necromancy did not show up in any of our investigations. Also, all five of them appear to have recently been subjected to some kind of ensorcellment – we presumed Enchantment initially, but our investigations indicate that Transportation appears to be the more likely.'

The Guild Master cleared his throat again, setting the contraption and ledger down, before folding his long fingers on the table and staring at the five outlanders.

'Quite a strange tale appears to come with you to our door,' he said. 'And I'm certain it will prove stranger yet in the full telling.' He nodded at Horskram before glancing down at the missive again. 'May I assume that you, uhm... Master Horskram of Vilno, of the country of the Northlendings, are the leader?'

Horskram's face remained a virtual mask as he replied: 'May I first have the honour of knowing the name of he who asks me?'

A couple of the wizards sat nearest betrayed their irritation at the adept's impertinence, but the Guild Master managed a half smile. 'It is a fair question,' he acknowledged. 'And you may – I am Pyrrhus Quarn, First Practitioner of the Sorcerer's Guild of Khronos. These men and women you see before you are the Twelve Masters of our Guild. I trust this satisfies your curiosity, sirrah.'

Now it was Horskram's turn to register a half smile, as he responded: 'It does, for now. And, yes, you may address me as leader, although' – Adelko winced inwardly as the adept's hard blue eyes flicked his way momentarily – 'my orders are not always obeyed as I would like them to be.'

'Indeed no,' said Quarn mildly. 'Rarely enough are we blessed with a visit from the Order of St Argo, more rarely still do we find one of their number in possession of a periapt.' He drummed his fingertips on the ledger. 'What strange times we are living through.'

He knows more than he's letting on. Adelko's sixth sense rarely steered him awry, and he wasn't about to start doubting it now. Silently he hoped Horskram had sensed it too.

Clearly he had. 'Don't play the innocent with me, Pyrrhus Quarn,' Horskram spat back, underscoring the chief warlock's name with contempt. 'I didn't have the displeasure of making your Guild's acquaintance the last time I was here, but I know enough about it to know you'll have been Scrying to your hearts' content. That missive you keep referring to is just a formality, I've spent long enough fighting your kind to know a warlock's stratagem when I see one – so why don't we dispense with the games?'

Adelko managed to hide his shock, while Azelin and Hari grinned openly. Morcant looked momentarily awkward, then resumed his impassive demeanour.

As for the guild wizards, they scarcely looked impressed. An imperious-looking middle-aged sorceress sat near Quarn cut in sharply: 'You will show due respect to our Order! Yours holds no sway here, or had you forgotten?'

Quarn only smiled again. 'In point of fact, it holds increasingly little sway in the so-called Free Kingdoms, as we've managed to divine while we were, as Master Horskram put it, Scrying to our hearts' content.'

The female magus relaxed somewhat, while a couple of the younger Guildsmen snickered.

Quarn went on, addressing Horskram. 'But you raise a fair point – this is no time for games. I did say myself we were living in strange times. Strange enough for Argolian witch-hunters to hold truck with the very sorceries they were founded to oppose, and strange enough for my Guild to consider making allies of them as well.'

That had Horskram slightly on the back foot. 'What mean you by that?' The adept seemed about to say more, then held his peace. Thoroughly attuned to him despite their recent differences, Adelko sensed the older monk was stalling, hoping to draw more information out of Quarn before committing himself to anything.

Luckily, Quarn seemed of a mood to oblige, albeit in roundabout fashion.

'As it happens, we have been rather busying Scrying of late,' he said. 'Busier than usual. We note the growing wars to the west and south with some alarm – for not even your backwards kind are usually this fractious.'

This was an obvious slight against their culture, but Horskram let it pass, motioning Azelin to silence before he could rise to the bait. But the former Bethler was too busy translating for the benefit of Hari to find time for a retort in any case.

'Pray go on,' said Horskram.

'We have also been watching you for some time, for you have ever been nearby when powerful sorceries have been at work,' said Quarn. 'We picked up on your spoor when you entered the Warlock's Crown last year – naturally we are always at pains to keep tabs on the remnants of the Elder Wizards who pioneered our craft, as the devout priest will pay due homage to the birthplace of his saviour.'

'Blasphemy and sacrilege rolled into one,' interjected Horskram sourly. 'But I'd expect nothing less from an apostate who thinks the Creed and the craft can be married.'

If Pyrrhus Quarn was offended by that remark, he hid it better than his cronies. 'Our theological debate will have to wait for another time,' he said in the same mild tone. 'The point is, we have been following your... progress since that point. And we must say, we are rather alarmed. Your trail went cold as you approached your Order's headquarters in Rima – of course we put that down to Argolian psychic defences and nothing more. But when suddenly you reappeared, right here on our doorstep...' He spread his gnarled hands in a gesture that was almost supplicatory. 'Well, you'll understand why we found that most perplexing. And prior to that, your association with the noted Left-Hand sorcerer Abdel Sha'arza – '

Adelko couldn't resist butting in. 'With respect, Guild Master, he usually favours the Right-Hand Way, and he had to go through a lot as a child. His father – '

This time Horskram did not even bother to try and silence him, but Quarn instead it was who waved his objections away. 'Yes, yes,' he said. 'We are well aware of Abdel Sha'arza's background. We are also well aware that the talisman we took from you was crafted by his own hand – and that this is far from the first time he has put his grammaryes at your disposal.'

Adelko flashed Horskram a glance of his own, as if to say: *now do you see my point? I wasn't guilty of doing anything we hadn't already done.*

Quarn went on, oblivious to their unspoken dispute. 'I must say, it took us a while to put the pieces together – for as you'll know, our skills allow us to see things from afar but not to hear them. Eventually one of our number recognised you, from your last visit here. We were then able to determine your provenance – the Argolian monastery called Ulfang in Northalde. You stopped in Graukolos not long after your adventures in the Warlock's Crown, shortly before Dulsinor was engulfed by the Vorstlending civil war. Then on to Rima... which, mysteriously enough, has suddenly become easier to penetrate in recent weeks than it was before. That in turn would suggest it has lost a considerable portion of its psychic protection – and we wondered, in time, could that be due to the sudden absence of key members of the Order, who were no longer present to provide the Argolian headquarters with defence through the power of prayer... or magick?'

The Guild Master let the last word hang meaningfully in the air, which had suddenly become rather too thick for

Adelko's liking. Horskram could not hide the gape that suddenly slackened his jaw, and Quarn only smiled the more broadly, his victory complete.

'Oh, we didn't work it out right away,' he said, almost kindly. 'For days and nights we conferred and argued. Little is known of the Headstone, and what is known is regarded by those that have such knowledge as lying somewhere between legend and myth. The blackguard warlock you slew, Andragorix, we had been aware of for some time... we knew he'd had something to do with sending demonic servitors to trouble both your home monastery in Northalde, and the castle in Dulsinor. He wasn't the only mage we'd been observing – we had also been aware of unusually and increasingly high traces of Scrying in recent years. Ours is not a precise craft, but we do our best at the Guild to try to keep tabs on all our, ah, professional rivals, their comings and goings. To cap it all off, we registered a great disturbance in the Forbidden Isle just a few months ago – something out of the ordinary even for that dreaded bourne. Scrying is near impossible in that area, as you'll probably know – the chaotic energies that the Breaking of the World unleashed when the Almighty saw fit to destroy Varya five millennia ago render it so, and naturally we were both concerned and puzzled. And so, as I said, we debated and argued, casting our minds back over our findings and those reported by our Guild brothers in Illyrium and other cities here in recent years. And then... we began to ask if those findings and this latest occurrence might not be somehow connected – unusually high Scrying traces from warlocks scattered about the Sundering Sea, in both Urovia and Sassania, not to mention another one, far to the east of here.'

That last remark pricked up both monks' ears.

'To the east?' asked Horskram, intrigued enough to

momentarily forget that Quarn and his ilk appeared to have stumbled onto Hannequin's plot.

'Oh yes,' returned the Guild Master. 'For you would be naive to think that we in the Empire do not face threats of our own. For some years now, we have scried upon a growing power in the Uttermost East – a mighty warlord there has subdued dozens of realms, subsuming them into an Empire, larger than ours, perhaps even larger than that of the Great Wizards of old.'

'I know little of the Uttermost East,' Horskram admitted. 'And I don't doubt that your concerns are legitimate – but what does this have to do with us?'

Quarn leaned forward, folding his hands again. He suddenly looked every inch his eighty winters. 'What it has to do with it is this – this eastern emperor has a key adviser, a vizier if you like, who is often at his side. This vizier appears to have attained some rudiments of the craft and it is our working theory that he has been communicating with whomever it was that wielded such powerful magicks at your monastic headquarters. Whomever it was that used said magicks not only to hide from mages and monks alike, but also to transport themselves to Varya, the Forbidden Isle – the very same magicks your companion here apparently misused for the same purpose, bringing you here instead of there.'

The old wizard seemed suddenly to slough off the fatigue of years, his bright blue eyes becoming intense as he scruti- nised his charges.

Can he really know for certain about the Headstone of Ma'amun, or is he just bluffing? Adelko wondered. *And does it really even matter by now if he does?*

The chief wizard relaxed again, assuming a milder tone once more. 'I know the disregard you hold our Guild in, Master Horskram,' he said. 'But believe me, it follows rules that are just as strict as your Order's – and just as you do, we sometimes see fit to break with said rules. We are, after all, hardly Imperial Cataphracti.'

The old magus looked around to see if his fellows appreciated his little in-joke. Clearly they did, if the wry chuckles were anything to go by.

Returning his gaze to the captives, he added: 'So you can imagine how it pained us to breach protocol and reach out to a Left-Hand warlock with our beloved Scrying – oh, no, no! Nothing like that – we knew better than to try to contact the traitor in your ranks. But Sha'arza evidently had played a part in your mission, so we decided it would be best to question him, if possible. We debated that fiercely too – but when Journeyman Avotus here contacted me to say the five of you had been apprehended and were carrying an amulet most likely fashioned by him, our way was clear.'

Horskram tried to interject, but Quarn was having none of it. Raising a hand to forestall him, he continued: 'Fortunately, Sha'arza was in, shall we say, a receptive mood. He has been quite concerned about you all – he didn't seem to think going back into the lion's den, as it were, very wise at all, but said that you were bent on it. We presented our working theory and probed him, and eventually he confessed all – only confirming our darkest forebodings. The Headstone of the Accursed One – reunited by an Argolian Grand Master, of all people! Oh, we know about that too, no use in denying it – Abdel Sha'arza told me the time for secrecy between wizards had long passed, and on this specific point I am inclined to agree with him.'

The Guild Master sat back in his creaky chair, finally at an end.

Horskram held his peace briefly, then gave vent to a deep sigh. 'Secrecy has bedevilled us since this whole wretched business began,' he admitted, sounding old and tired himself.

'Very well, Guild Master – I can see no use in denying what you have obviously taken great pains to learn. Why it has fallen to us to work with the very kind we were set up to oppose, against a mastermind who was supposed to lead us against the dark and not betray us to it, I can never hope to fathom. Truly, the Almighty goes about His work in curious ways.' As Horskram made the sign of the Wheel, Adelko was stunned to see many of the assembled wizards following suit.

They really do believe they can wield magick in service to the Almighty... Arnulf of Balzac, I'm surprised you didn't turn renegade and defect to the Empire.

Pyrrhus Quarn nodded sagely. 'Indeed, Master Horskram, this state of affairs is as peculiar for us as it is for you. And now let me formally apologise on behalf of the Guild for having detained you in such a fashion – in truth the secular Imperial authorities would most likely have held you for much longer, we had to follow due protocol and get you transferred to our custody before we could act.'

'Oh, we know all about Imperials and their protocols,' Azelin couldn't resist putting in.

'Thank you,' Quarn managed with a flat smile. 'As I was saying, now we have you in our care, we can act more freely. No one will question us now you have become our problem. Our intention is to hold you here for a little while longer while we requisition supplies, then let you go.'

Adelko tamped down his elation as he asked: 'Supplies? Supplies for what?'

Quarn frowned as though he'd just been asked a stupid question. 'For your journey, of course,' he said. 'You must leave the Empire as quickly as possible, and get to Aratheny. From there you should be able to find a ship.'

'That was the original plan,' said Horskram. 'It will do nicely.'

But Quarn shook his head. 'Oh no, not quite,' he said.

'Journeyman Avotus is to return you the talisman that Sha'arza gifted you. I suggest you use it reconnoitre with him once you are far enough into the Great Inland Sea so as not to make it difficult for him.'

'Difficult for him how?' asked Horskram suspiciously.

'To come and collect you in that glorious flying contraption of his,' said Quarn, betraying more than just a hint of envy. 'Not even our authorities would take too kindly to a winged ship turning up in our skies – and once you get to Aratheny, you'll understand why they would take it even less so. Ever have they guarded themselves well – the League of City-States of Ancient Thalamy failed to conquer their walls after a generation of fighting. The proximity of the Great Inland Sea has taught the Arathenians to protect themselves as fiercely as the mother lion defends her cubs.'

'He's talking about the ballistae,' Horskram said, for the benefit of the others. 'They anticipate attacks by sea and land, but air also – devilish fiends have been known to rise up out of those accursed waters.'

'All the more reason for you to travel far above them rather than through them,' said Quarn.

Horskram was nodding thoughtfully. 'Much as it pains me to admit it, I had been wondering how we would manage the voyage. Few earthly ships have ever reached Varya and returned to tell the tale.'

Quarn nodded back, almost deferential now. 'Just so. My advice would be to charter a ship to take you to one of the archipelagoes that dot the fringes of the Great Inland Sea – scattered relics of the land kingdoms that once lay there before the Breaking of the World. Ruins of the Elder Wizards are still clustered about them, and many a freebooter has gone seeking them as an easier source of plunder than the Forbidden Isle itself.'

'Yes, that might work as a pretext,' mused Horskram. 'It

also helps that one of our number actually worked as a tomb robber.' He indicated Hari, who reacted with mock indignation as Azelin translated.

'I've moved up greatly in the world since then!' exclaimed the rogue, but no one paid heed to him.

'So that's it then?' Horskram asked. 'You'll not only let us go but you're helping us too?'

Again the old wizard stretched out his hands. 'What other sensible choice do we have? The Great Eastern Wall, built by the Elder Wizards themselves and restored by us with the best craft we could muster, guards our flanks, but our Scrying indicates this emperor has tens of thousands of men at his beck and call. It's enough to worry about as it is without having some renegade maniac from your Order on the loose trying to reconstruct Ma'amun's anti-relic and use it for his own ends. The sooner you destroy him, the sooner the Empire will have one less problem to deal with.'

Horskram wasn't quite done with his questions though. 'And speaking of the Empire, what will you tell the Imperator? How much does his Imperial Eminence know?'

Quarn shook his head. 'Only what the Guild deems he needs to – we have our penchant for secrecy too.' The merry twinkle had returned to his eyes. 'Of course the military threat from the Uttermost East he has been apprised of. As to the rest... I've already despatched the officer who brought you here, Captain Justorian, with a sealed and confidential missive explaining our decision and the reasons behind it.'

Horskram winced. 'So that means Imperator Justorix will know everything before long.'

'Not quite everything,' the magus corrected. 'I said His Imperial Eminence knows what he needs to – I didn't mention the Headstone, or go into the specifics of the Argolian betrayal. Justorix – may the gilded heavens shine on him always! – is a busy man in any case, he won't have time for such details. Suffice to say, he is being informed that a very powerful Left-Hand practitioner from the Free Kingdoms is on the loose and meddling with things in Varya that should not be meddled with, not to mention helping the Eastlanders against us.'

Horskram pursed his lips. 'From what I recall of Justorix, he is as shrewd as he is busy... I doubt he'll be fooled for long. Certainly he'll want to know what kind of plans a maniac wizard could have that extend to the Forbidden Isle and forging alliances with outland powers that lie thousands of leagues away.'

'Certainly he will,' allowed Quarn, the twinkle not leaving his eye. 'And in due course I shall inform him privately as to all said details – once the five of you are safely out of the Empire.'

A sudden thought occurred to Adelko. 'If you can use Scrying lawfully, why not just tell the Imperator that way instead of making poor Justorian ride all the way to Illyrium? I imagine that Justorix has a, erm, court wizard or something.'

The old magus favoured him with an approving nod. 'Clearly your tutors taught you well,' he said. 'But it wouldn't do, I'm afraid – for all we know Hannequin may have intercepted our communications already, or had one of his lieutenants do so – for of course not all of them will have gone with him to Varya. And I think we've just agreed it's better if the Imperator learn the news of this later rather than sooner. Enhanced security will be an adequate cover story when His Imperial Eminence asks why I deployed more conventional means of keeping him informed – I trust you will agree that is to the betterment of your situation.'

Adelko didn't need his sixth sense to perceive that many of the Guild Masters did not approve of their headman's chosen course of action, but it suited him well enough.

'And now,' said the Guild Master, 'I think that brings us to the conclusion of our business.' Motioning towards the legionaries, he dismissed them with a wave of the hand.

'And don't worry about them overhearing anything,' he added. 'I made sure the guards selected for your escort only speak Imperial.'

'I thought you imperials were well-educated folk,' snarked Azelin, still using Decorlangue.

'We are,' said Quarn crisply. 'Every single one of those legionaries can read and write – in the Imperial script. Most citizens of the Empire do not anticipate having to have dealings with outlanders. But enough of this badinage – it taxes us pointlessly. Journeyman Avotus, please see these gentlemen discharged to the care of our good chamberlain.' For the first time, he appeared to notice Morcant. 'I'm afraid we must keep you in chains a while longer, my foreign friend – we cannot have unlicensed practising warlocks under our roof. However, I can assure you that you will be well looked after, and I shall have written orders sent with you instructing for your shackles to be struck off upon your conveyance to Calcaginapole in Grice on the eve of your departure for Aratheny – and not before. I trust this decision pleases you.'

It wasn't a question. Picking up a small silver bell, the Guild Master rang it. 'Hearing of the Wizards' Council is hereby dismissed,' he declaimed.

The legionaries were already retiring. Getting up from his seat, Avotus strode over and motioned curtly for them to follow him from the room, through a mosaicked archway on one side of it just beyond the colonnades.

The Guildsmen resumed speaking among themselves in their own language. As he left the dais, Adelko could see and sense that several were still unhappy with the decision their leader had taken, but the old warlock was shaking his head firmly. Adelko felt a newfound respect for the profession it was his own to hunt down and oppose: magician though he was, Pyrrhus Quarn had conducted himself in a statesmanlike manner befitting a great king or prelate.

'See?' he said to Horskram as they followed Avotus under the archway into a broad corridor lined with life-sized statues of past Guildsmen. 'Everything turned out all right in the end – it's clearly Reus' will that mages and monks join forces.'

Horskram glared at him sourly. 'Were this any other time, Journeyman Adelko, I would have stripped you of your habit.' His demeanour softened. 'But it isn't. I honestly don't know which is worse – the thought of not succeeding in our mission, or the thought that even if we do nothing will ever be the same again.'

Their footfalls echoing along the chilly corridor, they continued to follow Avotus. Horskram had a point, as usual: once again, Argolian monks found themselves forced to join forces with warlocks to avert a greater peril.

Our proverbial deal with the devil, the journeyman mused. *What if it turns out to be no different from Hannequin's?*

THE ASSASSIN'S LAST STAND

The Old Master of Time's Arrow stood in the diamond-shaped courtyard of Ortiz, surrounded by corpses. His Shadowmen had sold their lives dearly: destroying things that had defied death for millennia wasn't easy, but at least a few dozen of the undead *amluqs* had been sent to a grave from which there'd be no returning.

Now it was his turn.

The Great Old One-Eye stalked across the flagstones towards him, a halberd of ebonite clutched in his lobstered fingers. Jet-black like the weapon he carried, his carapaced armour covered his entire body except for the face, which was like no other the Old Master had ever seen. The features resembled those of a man from the Arid Kingdoms, but the skin was ivory white, devoid of living hues. In the centre of his bare brows a single cyclopean eye blazed, its red iris a fitting match for the gore that dripped off the halberd's serrated blade.

In a sepulchral voice that seemed to echo across centuries, the Great Old One-Eye intoned: 'Your Shadowmen have all fallen, not one remains on this side of the Rent

Between Worlds. Your fortress is ransacked, and it is only a matter of time before my Immortals find what we came for – not even your mystical gateways could confound me, be assured I shall not leave empty-handed.'

There was leaden truth in the undead warlord's words. Behind the Old Master, the keep of Ortiz had begun to burn – contrary to some of the legends he'd heard, the Draug lords did not appear to fear fire. The last screams of the dying servants and pleasure girls in the adjoining buildings had been cut off: at least the women hadn't been dishonoured, the Old Master found time to reflect, for the half dead felt no such earthly desires.

Behind the One-Eye stood half a dozen other Draugar, his most formidable lieutenants, clad in similar harness, though none could match the baleful scrutiny of their leader's single eye. The Old Master wondered if he had belonged to a forgotten offshoot of the Gygant race before the Elder Wizards subjected him and his kind to their Necromancy long ago: certainly his stature, almost twice that of an ordinary man, suggested as much.

But the Old Master was done with idle speculation. Hefting both his scimitars and ignoring the pain from his many bleeding wounds, he issued his challenge.

'By the grace of the Unseen, to whose service I have dedicated my long life, grant me my final wish – you and I, in single combat. If I triumph, your dread kindred shall depart bereft of spoil. If not, then do as Ashanti wills.'

The Old One-Eye grinned a death's head grin. 'Your god has nothing to do with this,' he said in the same emotionless voice. 'You know you cannot triumph against me, I who conquered the grave aeons ago.'

The Old Master flicked a meaningful glance towards where a couple of Draugar lay hacked to pieces, their armour pierced and bodies dismembered at last after hundreds of frenzied blows.

'I am sure they thought themselves impervious too.'

'You presume too much,' replied the revenant warlord, his tone remaining flat and expressionless. 'I am the Great Old One-Eye of legend, now the time has come for you to taste the scythe.' Hefting his halberd, he stalked towards the Old Master, the flagstones cracking and tilting beneath his armoured feet. The six lieutenants remained where they were, leaning on their night-black greatswords and watching the spectacle with cobalt eyes that never blinked.

The Old Master caught the stench of him as he drew near: a thousand graves suddenly opened all at once could not have yielded such a noisome stink. But his mind was far too well trained to succumb to simple nausea: just as the Old One-Eye drew within striking range, he leapt high, somer-saulting over the mighty warlord and slashing at his unpro-tected head with both blades as he cartwheeled through the air.

Long decades of intense physical and psychic training had given the Old Master near superhuman strength and agility; yet even this was not enough. The One-Eye barely altered his stance as he swept his halberd up and around, swatting aside the deadly twin blows as though they were flies. The impact of his improvised parry nearly knocked the scimitars from the Old Master's grasp, disrupting the fluidity of his motion: he came down hard, landing on one leg and almost losing his balance.

Almost. Righting himself in the blink of an eye, he charged and leapt again, determined to keep up the offensive. But this time the One-Eye was better prepared: stepping back with a speed that belied his gargantuan frame, he thrust the halberd upwards in a stabbing movement. Fresh pain erupted up the Old

Master's leg as the black blade tore open his calf, but he ignored that too as he entered the Whirlwind of Steel trance: at that point he became something truly more than human, spinning through the air with a velocity that defied mortal compass, his blades releasing sparks as they slashed at the One Eye's armour.

All to no avail. The ebonite showed not so much as a dent, and the Old Master landed, hobbled on the shattered flagstones where his enemy had trodden but a moment ago.

He tried to re-enter the trance, but his elan was faltering, seeping from his spirit just as the lifeblood pumped from his severed veins. Ducking under the halberd, he tried one last desperate move, lunging upwards at the One-Eye's groin.

But a thing that ceased to live thousands of years ago has no such weaknesses. Casting aside the halberd, the One-Eye reached down and grasped both the Old Master's wrists. He could not suppress the cry of pain that erupted from him as the undead warlord squeezed and twisted mercilessly, crushing and breaking bones as though they had been twigs. The scimitars fell to the ground with a dull clatter.

This close the damp stench of the Great Old One-Eye was almost as unbearable as the pain of his shattered wrists. His antagonist hauled him up to leer in his face. The Old Master tried one last gambit, lashing out at the One-Eye's unprotected throat with a Scorpion's Tail kick. It would have pole-axed an ordinary mortal, sending his spirit to the judgment of Azrael; but the Old One-Eye and his ilk had spurned Azrael's Judgment long ago.

Staring into the pitiless crimson eye, the Old Master resigned himself to the inevitable and raised his eyes to the darkening heavens: a storm was brewing farther up in the Cerulean Mountains, and the late afternoon skies had turned an ugly deep grey. At last thunder broke, rolling with deep timbre down the peaks; he felt the first touch of rain fall upon his bloodied cheek. Behind him a preternatural screech, which he took to be a howl of triumph: the Old One-Eye's eternal *amluqs* had found what they were looking for.

Shutting his eyes, the Old Master focused on the sensation of rain spattering against his face.

'It is over,' he murmured.

That was the last thing he ever said.

EPILOGUE: HANNEQUIN'S LOG

Sweet success... The Great Old One-Eye has returned with the final fragment. I am told his Immortals ploughed a furrow through the Sultanate of Halepo en route to the mountain fastness of Ortiz, leaving scorched earth, razed towns and smashed armies in its wake – that should serve as due warning to the petty realms of mortal kings, and the fewer that choose in their contumely to oppose us, the sooner they shall know the bliss of eternal bondage.

For the peoples of the Known World shall learn to love the One True King, or they shall perish in perdition.

But I digress. Now we have our defences secured against Varya's inhabitants, and the four pieces in our possession, the work of reconstruction must begin. As I reckon it in mortal time – increasingly difficult to compass here in the Forbidden City, where the hours move strangely – we have but three to four lunar months to reassemble Ma'amun's Legacy. But the Grimoire I went to so many pains to obtain is quite specific on the point: Midwinter's Eve, in earthly reckoning, is the allotted hour, and we shall know it when the Seven Stars from whence the Seven Maligned Princes fell aeons ago are in conjunction. Already I have learned to use the instruments of the Priest Kings of old; nightly will I scour the skies, for we must not err in our judgement by a hair's breadth!

Abaddon Almighty, Thy humble servant dedicates these words to Thee, that Thou mightest see them and know Thy long captivity in Gehenna has not been in vain! The work begun by Thy first disciple Ma'amun is close to completion, and this time the Father shall not stand in our way. The celestial tyrant's time has come at long last – when once again he sees the way open for his True Son to resume His rightful throne upon the world He architected, not even Reus will be so reckless as to intervene a second time.

What should have been done millennia ago shall be done and that right soon, and the Diamond Age of mortalkind be ushered in!

It is our birthright. It is our destiny. And not all the false angels of the Unseen shall prevent it.

GLOSSARY OF NAMES

Here follows an overview of some of the more common names relating to legends, geography, history, religion, magic and supernatural entities that feature in this book. It is not intended to be exhaustive but may be used as a reference to guide the reader.

Abaddon: Foremost among demonkind; led the revolt against **Reus** and the loyal angels and **archangels** during the Battle for Heaven and Earth at the Dawn of Time. Was condemned to languish in the Kingdom of **Gehenna** on the **Other Side**, but has been influential in the affairs of mortalkind ever since. Corrupted **Ma'amun**, foremost among the **Elder Wizards** of **Varya**, by teaching him the **Left Hand Path** of sorcery. Also known as the Fallen One, the Dark Angel, the Author of Evil, and the King of Gehenna in mainland **Urovia**; known as Sha'itan, Loth, **Logi** and the Cloven-Hoofed God in other cultures.

Abelard of Montrevellyn: Firebrand preacher who whipped up support for the **Purge** against the **Argolian Order**, later discovered to be a secret disciple of **Xamiel of Avalongne**, a demonic sub-avatar responsible for starting the **Pilgrim Wars**. Abelard was subsequently executed in sight of all in Rima, his dastardly tomes on magick burned along with him on the orders of Hannequin, later to become Grand Master of the persecuted Order of St Argo.

Acolytes: **Palomedes'** seven closest advisers and disciples who afterwards were instrumental in spreading the **Creed** – a religion based on his teachings and life examples – throughout **Urovia**. Generally heralded as bringing spiritual salvation to benighted peoples, though dissenters argue that their teachings were flawed interpretations of the **Redeemer**'s beliefs and practices.

Alric: Most holy of the knights of the **Purple Garter**; saved King **Vasirius** from the curse of the White Blood Witch using a drop of the Redeemer's blood.

Alysius: One of the Seven **Acolytes** of **Palomedes** the **Redeemer**; brought a phial containing His blood to the shores of **Northalde** shortly after the prophet's execution in Tyrannos.

Ambelin: Ruling royal house of the Kingdom of **Pangonia**. Its present incumbent is Carolus III, a scheming and self-serving monarch who has alienated many of his barons with high taxes since ascending the Charred Throne. Ambelin has held power for more than a hundred years since it emerged victorious from the Fourth War of the Royal Succession, fought after the reign of King **Vasirius** was brought to an end at the Battle of **Avalongne**.

Amluqs: Nominally considered a slave caste in **Sassania**, these elite warriors are trained from birth and in reality wield far more political and military power as a group than many a freeman.

Ancient Thalamy: Also known as the Thalamian Empire, a **Golden Age** hegemony that straddled the Sundering Sea and incorporated the modern kingdoms of Thalamy, **Pangonia**, Mercadia, the southern reaches of the

Urovian New Empire and northern **Sassania**, lasting for several centuries until its destruction by Wulfric of Gothia. It most notable potentates include Vaxus, who first unified the warring city-states of Thalamy, and Tycius, the gifted general and warlord who sacked **Shamaria**.

Antaeus: Legendary mariner and adventurer belonging to the **Golden Age**, said by some to have been the son of the **archangel** Aqualcus, worshipped as a god in pagan times before the coming of the Faith and the **Creed**. Hailed from **Ancient Thalamy** in the Era of Warring City-States before the empire was consolidated. His exploits against **Gygants**, Ifriti, **Seakindred**, **Wyrms**, **Wadwos**, warlocks and other supernatural foes are celebrated in song and poetry throughout **Urovia**.

Anti-angels: Demonkind or evil spirits; angels who sided with **Abaddon** in the Battle for Heaven and Earth at the Dawn of Time. Known by different names in various cultures, for instance Ifriti in the **Sassanian Sultanates** and Juju in some parts of the **Arid Kingdoms**.

Aquitania: Most powerful of the southern margravates of **Pangonia** and foremost participant in the **Pilgrim Wars**. The scions of the Kingdom of Keraka in the **Blessed Realm** are descended from its ruling house.

Archangels: Most powerful of the angels who stayed loyal to **Reus**; foremost among them are the **Seven Seraphim**.

Archdemons: Most powerful of demonkind along with **Abaddon** himself; foremost among them are the seven **Princes of Perfidy**.

Argolian Order: Founded by Saint Argo five hundred years ago, this learned order of monks and friars is tasked with fighting evil spirits and hunting down witches and warlocks throughout the **Free Kingdoms** and **Pilgrim Kingdoms**. It is also celebrated for its learning.

Ashokainan: A legendary left-hand wizard who reputedly lived for hundreds of years until **Søren** slew him seven centuries ago. One of the most powerful warlocks to walk the Known World since the demise of the Priest-Kings of **Varya**. Believed to have been understudy to Cleops, another Golden Age sorcerer of immense power, before becoming his rival.

Avatar: A collective name intended to summarise a complex terminology that covers all supernatural entities regarded as a manifestation of **Reus Almighty** (i.e. a direct extension of His being). This includes **archangels**, angels and their demonic opposites; the word is also commonly used to describe such entities sent to earth in mortal form to guide mankind for good or ill. The term can also be used to describe a saint who is rewarded for a virtuous life by being exalted to the ranks of the **Unseen** upon death. Most religious scholars across the Faith and **Creed** agree that the **Two Prophets** fall into the former category of avatar (i.e. that they were angels or archangels sent to earth to help mortalkind), though some cleave to the second interpretation (that they were mortals rewarded in the Afterlife for their service to mankind).

Azrael: The Angel of Death, tasked by **Reus** with judging the souls of the dead, determining whether they go to **Gehenna** or the **Heavenly Halls**. Known by many different names across cultures throughout history, including Orcus, Osirian, Mortis, Mahatsu and Imraan.

Battle of Avalongne: Decisive battle fought a century and a half ago that brought about the end of King **Vasirius** and his reign. Even though his forces were victorious, it ultimately proved a pyrrhic victory as most of the Knights of the **Purple Garter** and his loyal nobles were slain; this created a power vacuum that prompted the Fourth War of the Royal Succession. For this reason the Battle of Avalongne is still mourned by loremasters and troubadours alike as heralding the end of the halcyon era of Vasirius' just rule.

Battle of Corne Hill: Decisive battle of the northerly **Border Wars** that saw **Thraxia** and its Vorstlending mercenary allies crushed by the **Northlendings** half a century ago; this cemented the young King Freidheim II's reputation as the greatest ruler of **Northalde** since the Hero King Thorsvald, and paved the way for an era of peace and prosperity in the kingdom.

Battle of Kurushan Heights: This battle finally brought to end the era of the **Seven Enlightened Sultans**, when their last scion Abu tek Jahib was slain by Muhmet Iron Breaker, a rival warlord. However, many of the Unorthodox **Faith** believe the Kardin bloodline did in fact survive, when Abu's grandson Alamuz was spirited out of **Ushalayim** before Muhmet's forces seized the city.

Blessed Realm: Common name given to the **Pilgrim Kingdoms**.

Border Wars: Series of internecine conflicts between **Thraxia** and **Northalde** that lasted for a couple of centuries and culminated in the **Battle of Corne Hill**.

Breaking of the World: Cataclysm visited on the Known World by **Reus** and the **Archangels** five thousand years ago as punishment for **Ma'amun**'s attempt to open the gates of **Gehenna** at the behest of his master **Abaddon**. Resulted in the destruction of the **Varyan** civilisation and substantially altered the geography of the **Urovian** and **Sassanian** continents. Ushered in the **First Age of Darkness**, during which nearly all the vast learning of the Varyan Empire was lost.

Cael: A learned youth from the **Island Realms** tasked with taking the fourth fragment of the **Headstone of Ma'amun** to **Sassania** after it was broken by **Søren**. Disappeared with the fragment centuries ago, though since rumoured to have become one of the undead, wandering the Ghorabi desert in southern **Nazharya**.

Cierny: Ruling royal clan that holds the throne in **Thraxia**. Current incumbent is Cadwy, whose ensorcelment by the witch Abrexta the Prescient was recently lifted after she was slain by a group of adventurers.

Creed: Monotheistic religion founded by the **acolytes** of **Palomedes**, one of the **Two Prophets**, who opposed the tyranny of the **Thalamian Empire**. It falls into two mainstream churches: the Orthodox Temple in the **Urovian New Empire** and the **True Temple** in Western **Urovia** and the **Pilgrim Kingdoms**.

Draugar: Undead race of warlock kings who are believed to have served the **Elder Wizards** as vassals. It is not known if they were themselves **Varyans**, subject peoples who were rewarded with great power by the Elder Wizards for their service, or a mixture of the two. Draugar are reputed to occupy certain remote areas, including the Draugmoors in central **Vorstlund** and the Valley of the Barrow Kings in the **Westerling Isles**, and have numerous powers including shapeshifting and draugbreath, a curse that afflicts victims with the preternatural Rotting Sickness.

Dulsinor: Lands in northern **Vorstlund** ruled by the House of Markward, until Eorl Wilhelm Stonefist was treacherously murdered by the rival Lanraks. The Eorldom is one of nine principal states that compose the Vorstlending realm.

Efrilund: Stretch of the kingdom of **Northalde** comprising lands lying between the **King's Dominions** in the south and the **Wold** and **Highlands** to the north. Ruled over by three jarls: Lord Vymar of Harrang, Lord Fenrig of Hroghar, and Lord Aesgir of Sjórvard. These are loyal provinces and though not directly ruled by the King generally apply most of his laws.

Elder Wizards: Ancient race of warlocks who ruled over the Known World from their island homeland of **Varya** for a thousand years until the **Breaking of the World**. Foremost among them was **Ma'amun**, who became corrupted by **Abaddon** after he learned the **Left-Hand Path** of black magic at his feet. Known by various other names throughout the Known World including the Priest-Kings of Varya and the Magi.

Elementi: Race of spirits belonging to the **Other Side** corresponding to the four elements: Terrus (earth), Aethi (air), Saraphi (fire) and Lymphi (water).

Faith: Principal and monotheistic religion of **Sassania** based on the teachings of the Prophet **Sha'abat**, who preceded the coming of **Palomedes** by several generations. Unlike Palomedes, Sha'abat was never a warrior and always counselled peaceful resolution of conflict wherever possible. However, this has not prevented adherents of the Faith from making war in his name. The Faith is divided into two principal camps: the Orthodox adhered to in the Sultanates of **Nazharya** and Kallandhar; and the Unorthodox branch cleaved to in **Halepo** and **Murad**. The Unorthodox branch still believes in the bloodline of the **Seven Enlightened Sultans**, and is more tolerant of mysticism and sorcery as such.

Firedrake Wars: Series of conflicts between the **Westerling Isles** and the **Wyrms**, foremost of whom was Erebon, which straddled the **Middle Time** between the **Wars of Kith & Kin** and the subsequent Latter Time. The **Northlanders** also suffered greatly due to Erebon's depredations, leading the two peoples to make common cause. The Firedrake Wars came to an end when the Northlandic hero **Søren** slew Erebon and his wife Antelywa, crippling their son Anglaurang. After this the Wyrms went into terminal decline; Anglaurang was slain by Sir **Lancelyn** of the Pale

Mountain centuries later, and when Sir Azelin of Valacia slew his son Baphomet, their race became extinct.

First Age of Darkness: A thousand-year period of backwardness and strife directly succeeding the **Breaking of the World**; few civilisations if any flourished during this bleak era.

First Clarion: Marked the Dawn of Time and the creation of the Universe by **Reus Almighty**, who set his angels to work creating the galaxies, solar systems and planets thereafter. Scholars dispute over what timeframe this occurred, with estimates varying between a few hundred years to aeons in mortal reckoning.

Free Kingdoms: Collective name given to the six principal realms of Western Urovia: **Northalde**, **Thraxia**, **Pangonia**, **Vorstlund**, Mercadia and Thalamy. The epithet 'free' comes from the fact that slavery was abolished throughout these realms with the coming of the **Creed** – although serfdom and other types of feudal bondage still persist.

Frozen Principalities: Name given to a string of petty kingdoms belonging to the Northlanders, barbarian tribes who still worship angels and demons as gods and cling to their age-old customs. Also known as the Frozen Wastes, these lands are ruled over by the Ice Thegns and their seacarls and housecarls – fierce warriors who pledge fealty to their liegelords. Recently the Ice Thegns have become united under one ruler – Magnhilda, **Shield Queen** and Magna of the Frozen Wastes.

Gaellentir: Stretch of lands in northern **Thraxia** ruled over by Clan Fitzrow, recently overrun by highland rebels. Its principle seat is Gaellen, a town and castle being rebuilt since its destruction by the highlanders.

Gehenna: The island prison on the **Other Side** to which **Abaddon** and his demonic followers were banished by

Reus after the Battle for Heaven and Earth was lost. At its heart lies the City of Burning Brass, divided into Five Tiers – the first and highest of these is reserved for **Abaddon** himself, the **Seven Princes of Perfidy** and other archdemons.

Golden Age: New era of civilisation that flourished after the end of the **First Age of Darkness** some four thousand years ago and lasted for three millennia. During this time the civilisations of Sendhé and Ancient Thalamy flourished; much lore was relearned or rediscovered, though the glory of mortalkind never attained that achieved during the apogee of the preceding **Platinum Age**.

Grand High Monastery: Informal name given to the headquarters of the **Argolian** Order just outside Rima in **Pangonia**. Its proper name is the Most Reverend Priory of St Argo, and it is the first chapter of the Order founded by the saint of that name five hundred years ago.

Great Old One-Eye: Term given to denote the **Elder Wizards**' most fearsome general, who lived on after the **Breaking Of The World** as one of the **Draugar** and is believed to haunt **Varya** to this day. Many prophecies speak of the 'one-eyed general's return' though this has been rein-terpreted down through the ages to mean just about any reputable army commander lacking an eye.

Great World Serpent: The first of **Reus Almighty**'s sentient creations along with Aurgelmir the Titan. Fathered the race of Wyrms with Hydrae the Many Headed (whom **Søren** slew on his Seventh and final Deed). According to legend, the Great World Serpent's body was used to create the world when Reus crushed him and Aurgelmir together to stop them destroying the Universe with their constant fight-ing. The same legend states that the World Serpent lies coiled at the centre of the earth, surrounded by the flesh of Aurgelmir; should he ever be woken from his slumber the

Known World will fall apart and be destroyed. As such, the Great World Serpent is also referred to as He Who Must Not Be Disturbed, particularly among the Northlanders of the **Frozen Principalities**.

Gygant: A race of giants, believed to be **Reus'** first attempts to fashion mortalkind from the rock and clay of the earth (itself created from Aurgelmir the Titan, who is thus also known as the Father of Giants). Many times larger than their human descendants, though extremely violent and stupid, Gygants terrorised early human settlements until the **Elder Wizards** slew most of them and enslaved the rest.

Halepo: Sassanian sultanate that lies along the western shore of the Great Inland Sea; of the Unorthodox branch of the Faith, its scions have long been more tolerant of sorcery than its neighbours. Once the centre of the Kishan Empire, ruled by a race of sorcerer-sultans in the **Golden Age**, the realm has a strong heritage of magick. More prosaically, it is also noted for its spicy stews.

Headstone of Ma'amun: Tablet of incalculable power wrought by **Ma'amun** five thousand years ago; inscribed with hieroglyphic writing said to represent additions he made to the Sorcerer's Script under the tutelage of **Abaddon.** It is said to contain the power to break the hold placed on the Fallen One by **Reus** and summon him and his followers back to the mortal vale. It is not clear whether Ma'amun sought to control Abaddon or serve him, and as such whether the Headstone will enable its user to bind him to his or her will.

Heavenly Halls: The Kingdom of **Reus**, where the **Seven Seraphim** sit at his side and the rest of the **archangels** and angels dwell. The most splendid of the island realms of the **Other Side**, where the souls of those judged fit by **Azrael** are sent to reside until the Hour of All's Ending and Judgment Day.

Hierophant: A member of the **Argolian** Order who has

attained exceptional psychic powers, outstripping those of even the most accomplished adepts. In this era there are thought to be three: Horskram of Vilno; Hannequin, current Grand Master of the Order; and Malthus of Montrevellyn, who left Rima years ago on a secret mission and is rumoured to have sought audience with the Fays of Tintagael before vanishing into the uttermost north. Adelko of Narvik, a journeyman who was seconded to Horskram for training, is also believed by him to be a potential fourth hierophant.

Imperial Cataphracts: Elite mounted cavalry of the **Urovian New Empire**, roughly synonymous with a knight of the **Free Kingdoms**. Cataphracts are distinguishable from their knightly cousins in that they take an oath to serve the Imperator above all and have no concept of feudal ties; also, thanks to the progressive 'career open to talent' measures introduced by Senator Paralsus, noble birth is no longer a prerequisite to joining.

Ingwin: Ruling royal house of the Kingdom of **Northalde**; current incumbent is Prince Wolfram, but he is said to have lost his mind since being deposed by the **Shield Queen** and her invading army of Northlanders. Coat of arms is two rearing white unicorns facing each other on a purple background.

Island Realms or Westerling Isles: Series of islands, the two principal ones being Kaluryn and Skulla, ruled over by the Marcher Lords and Druids, lying in the Great Western Ocean. The most westerly known civilisation, the Island Realms cling steadfastly to their ancient beliefs, having been visited by Kaia the Moon Goddess during the **First Age of Darkness** and taught the **Right Hand Path** of magick lost to man when the **Varyan** Empire was destroyed at the **Breaking of the World**. Also known as Druidsbourne and the Islands of World's Ending.

Kardin: Name given to both the ancient tribe and the

bloodline they founded when Abu'cuchaza'ar Kardin became the first of the **Seven Enlightened Sultans** by taking the teachings of the Prophet Sha'abat into his heart. The tribe still exists today, albeit in greatly diminished form; its leading figure is the Sultan of **Nazharya**, Muqmurlish tek Nazar, who is of Kardin ancestry on his mother's side.

Kallandhar: Ruled by the ambitious Sultana Nesrine, this Sassanian kingdom is poised to take the fight back to the crusading infidels of the **Blessed Realm**. Allied to **Nazharya**, its fellow Orthodoxer nation of the **Faith**.

Keraka: Most warlike of the **Pilgrim Kingdoms**, ruled by the House of Agramonde. Their coat of arms is an *argent* (white) gauntlet crushing a *vert* (green) serpent on a *sable* (black) field.

King's Dominions: Stretch of rich lands between Efrilund to the north and the Southern Provinces ruled directly by the **Northlending** King. Here royal law is strongest; consequently this is the wealthiest and most stable part of **Northalde**. Recently it was extended to include the Southern Provinces after a successful war against southron rebels.

King's Fold: Northern half of Umbria in **Thraxia**, ruled directly by the Royal Clan **Cierny**. The rest of the ward is parcelled about between several barons.

Knights Bethler: Elite military religious order of warrior-monks, charged with defending the **Pilgrim Kingdoms**. Said to be the most formidable warriors in the Known World, believed by many to be able to channel a sixth sense akin to that of the Argolians to fight better. Founded by the Seven Paladini, knights who took the Wheel and distinguished themselves during the First **Pilgrim War**.

Lancelyn: Greatest of the Knights of the **Purple Garter**, most renowned for slaying the Great Wyrm Anglaurang in the time of King **Vasirius**. The latter's skull he brought back to court at Rima, where it was used to fashion the Charred Throne where the Pangonian king sits to this day.

Laurelin: Ruling house of Vichy, a prosperous margravate close to the heart of **Pangonia**. Its present incumbent, Lord Ivon, is a wily politicker of notoriously dissolute appetites, often connected to intrigue at the court of King Carolus. The House of Laurelin is one of the oldest and most prestigious in the kingdom, and has ties to the Ruling House of Rius from the time of King **Vasirius**. Some of its elder scions are also rumoured to have practised sorcery.

Left Hand Path: Black magic, derived from the teachings of **Abaddon** to **Ma'amun** more than five thousand years ago. Comprises Necromancy and Demonology, the two **Schools of Magick** most closely aligned to the Left Hand Path. However, some sorcerers who practise left-hand magic claim it is not necessarily wholly evil of itself, for instance those who use it to ask the dead for advice.

Logi: Name given by **Northlanders** to **Abaddon**, reviled by them as a trickster god.

Lower Thulia: One of the nine major baronies in Vorstlund, the Dukedom is perhaps the most powerful in the realm along with the Principality of Westenlund and the Dukedom of Stornelund. It is ruled by the House of Alt-Ürl.

Lower Vallia: Old name given to the southern margravates of **Pangonia**, of which **Aquitania** is the most powerful. Its inhabitants have a distinctive identity and are on the whole more zealous in the **Creed**. As such they have a proud tradition of crusading and have contributed many knights and soldiers to the **Pilgrim Wars**.

Ma'amun: Most powerful of the **Elder Wizards**, became corrupted by **Abaddon**, who taught him the **Left Hand Path** and encouraged him to extend his powers. Ma'amun was slain along with all the other Magi at the

Breaking of the World, when the **Unseen** punished him for perverting the Gift of Magick and daring to challenge the Laws of Reus. His shade is believed to be trapped in **Gehenna**, where he languishes in the City of Burning Brass ruled by his erstwhile teacher along with all the other souls of the damned.

Maegellin: Thraxian bard who lived three centuries ago; widely held to be the greatest poet and songsmith of the **Silver Age**, surpassing even the classical poets of the **Golden Age**. Most noted works include *The Tales of Antaeus the Mariner* and *The Seven Deeds of Søren*.

Mercadia: Most southerly of the **Free Kingdoms** and arguably the most wealthy; a former province of the short-lived Muradi Empire, its people have absorbed many customs of the **Sassanians** including a lively respect for trade. Less feudal than most of its **Urovian** neighbours, Mercadia has nevertheless thrived by providing shipping to crusaders in the **Pilgrim Kingdoms**.

Middle Time: In the Westerling reckoning, this is the era that spanned the ending of the Nine Pestilences (Kaia's punishment for the folly of the **Wars of Kith & Kin**) and the Forty Years' Kin Strife. Something of an 'electrum age' for the Islanders, it was marked by a renewal of contact between the **Island Realms** and the Four Old Kingdoms of **Thraxia**, that saw both sides enriched by trade in goods and ideas. During this era, which lasted around two centuries, magick revived somewhat and nearly approached that of the fabled **Old Time**. For this reason it is recalled fondly by many in the Island Realms and Thraxia, which greatly benefited from contact with its ancestral motherland.

Morwena: Beloved of **Søren**; a sorceress of fearsome repute who hailed from the **Island Realms**. Ensorcelled the great hero and sent him on his Seven Deeds, which were ultimately purposed to recover the **Headstone of Ma'amun**

from the Forbidden City on the Island of **Varya**. Slain by Søren after she spurned him on completion of his Final Deed, in which he brought the Headstone from Varya to the Island Realms.

Morwena's Doom: Name given by folk of the **Westerling Isles** to the **Headstone of Ma'amun**.

Murad: Most mercantile of the Sassanian Sultanates, has prospered during the era of the Pilgrim Wars by trading with either side. Famed for the quality of its wine, sweetmeats, dancing and other refined pleasures, Murad cleaves to the Unorthodox interpretation of the **Faith**, and is thus less strict in its practice of dogma and doctrine than its more zealous neighbour **Kallandhar**.

Narborg: Centring on the Cauldron, a shrine to the **Great World Serpent** leading all the way down to its lair at the heart of the earth beneath the waves, Narborg is a town built on a group of islets linked together by platforms and walkways. Currently controlled by the **Northlanders** of the Skjel Isles, it was built by the **Elder Wizards** and was once a mighty city; today its magicks still redound, and though it is a great trading entrepot in the Valhalla, few stay there long after transacting their business.

Nazharya: Greatest of the sultanates of **Sassania**, named after the house of Nazhar that founded it shortly after the **Battle of Kurushan Heights** that brought to an end the rule of the **Seven Enlightened Sultans**. Has suffered as a result of the **Pilgrim Wars**, losing territory to the encroaching **Pilgrim Kingdoms**, though it looks set to recoup some former glory under its new ruler, the Sultan Muqmurlish tek Nazar, who has reunited the realm.

Northalde: One of the **Free Kingdoms**, settled by Northland reavers from the **Frozen Principalities** seven hundred years ago. Comprises the lands north of the Argael and west of the Hyrkrainian mountains that divide the north-west peninsular of Western **Urovia** between it and the kingdom of **Thraxia**. **Northlendings** are famed for their skill in warfare, horsemanship, shipwrighting, armoury and castle-building.

Northlander: Inhabitant of the **Frozen Principalities**, whose ancestors founded the mainland colonies that would eventually become the Kingdom of **Northalde**. Northland raiders also settled the coasts further south and such many Vorstlendings can also trace their ancestry back to the Principalities.

Northlending: Inhabitant of the Kingdom of **Northalde** in north-western **Urovia**; not to be confused with **Northlander**, an inhabitant of the **Frozen Principalities**.

Occitania: Western peninsula of **Pangonia** comprising more than half a dozen margravates. Occitanians are fiercely independent and have historically caused the crown trouble. Its foremost powers are probably Gorleon, noted for its maritime tradition, and Vichy, which has access to vital trade routes with the northerly Free Kingdoms via the city of Broullion. Armandy province is also widely celebrated for the quality of its wine.

Old Time: In the reckoning of the Westerling calendar, this roughly corresponds with the early Golden Age, between the Coming of the Moon Goddess to the **Island Realms** at the end of the **First Age of Darkness** and the Wars of Kith & Kin two thousand years later. A halcyon era for the islanders, when the right-hand druiding way was at its peak and folk enjoyed greatly increased prosperity and longevity.

Other Side: Collective name given to all the dwelling places of spirits, **elementi**, **fays**, demons, angels and **Reus Almighty** Himself. Said to be an endless sea of vapour punctuated by islands, including the **Heavenly Halls**, **Gehenna**, and the Place of Judgment where **Azrael** dwells. All supernatural beings hail from the Other Side, and this is consequently where warlocks of all bents derive their powers using the Language of Magick and the Sorcerer's Script.

Palomedes: Second of the **Two Prophets**; inspired the **Creed**, the major religion of **Urovia**. Born to a soldier in Ushalayim about a thousand years ago in what is now the **Pilgrim Kingdoms**. Initially intended to follow his father into the Thalamian Legions but began hearing the Voice of **Reus** shortly after coming of age at fourteen. Resolved to use his martial skills to lead a revolution against the tyrannical Thalamian Empire and acquired a great following, but later forsook the sword and led his supporters in a campaign of passive resistance. Was finally apprehended by the Thalamians after being betrayed by his former lieutenant Antiochus the Red-Handed, taken to Tyrannos and broken on the **Wheel** at the Emperor's command. Also known by his abbreviated name, Palom (which becomes Palomat in the lands of the **Faith** by way of derivation), and his most common epithet, the **Redeemer**.

Pangonia: Most powerful of the **Free Kingdoms**, though its influence has waned somewhat since its apogee under the Chivalrous King Vasirius, who ruled some two centuries ago. Its capital Rima is also the headquarters of the **True Temple** and the **Argolian Order**. Currently ruled by King Carolus III of the House of Ambelin, a scheming, ambitious monarch known also as the 'wily' and the 'greedy' for heavy taxes imposed on his barons.

Pilgrim Kingdoms: Collective name given to northern **Sassanian** territories carved out by **Urovian** crusaders a century ago, consisting of the Kingdom of **Ushalayim**, named after its principal city, where **Palomedes** the **Redeemer** was born, the Kingdom of **Keraka** and the Kingdom of **Ranishmend**. Also known collectively as the **Blessed Realm**.

Pilgrim Wars: Series of crusades – holy wars against the heathen **Sassanians** sanctioned by the **True Temple** – begun more than a hundred years ago that recaptured the holy city of Ushalayim where **Palomedes** the **Redeemer** was born. Many factions besides the victorious crusading dynasties have profited from the Pilgrim Wars, most notably the merchant houses of Mercadia, most southerly of the **Free Kingdoms**. However, the Pilgrim Wars have not been endorsed by all Palomedians: the Orthodox Temple in the **Urovian New Empire** has openly voiced its disapproval, whilst the **Argolian Order** has refused to condemn or condone them. And few knights from the northerly Free Kingdoms of **Thraxia** and **Northalde** have taken the **Wheel**, with most crusaders originating from **Mercadia**, **Vorstlund**, **Pangonia** and Thalamy.

Platinum Age: A thousand-year epoch during which the **Elder Wizards** ruled all of the Known World from the Island of **Varya**; during this time mankind, though in bondage to the Priest-Kings, reputedly lived in a state of ease, comfort and luxury unparalleled in mortal history. According to some scholars the average lifespan exceeded a century and even the lowest of birth were well educated and literate. This era came to an abrupt end some five millennia ago when the **Unseen** punished **Ma'amun** for daring to challenge their authority by destroying Varya and much of the Known World, laying waste to the great civilisation it had built.

Princes of Perfidy: Collective name given to the seven most powerful **archdemons** who serve **Abaddon**: Sha'amiel (**avatar** of greed and bigotry); Azathol (vanity and hubris); Zolthoth (wrath); Ta'ussaswazelim (cruelty); Chreosoaneuryon (gluttony); Satyrus (lust and sexual depravity); and Invidia (envy). The Seven Princes are themselves dark emanations of the **Seven Seraphim** and thus have their celestial opposites among the **archangels**, whose virtues they seek to corrupt and subvert.

Princes of the Sand: Collective informal name given to the crusader warlords who rule the **Pilgrim Kingdoms**. Of Pangonian origin, the scions of these high houses have adopted **Sassanian** customs to varying degrees.

Purge: Calamitous event a generation ago that saw the **Argolian Order** falsely accused and tried for witchcraft by clerics of the mainstream **True Temple** in Rima. Many Argolians were tortured and made false confessions which they later retracted. The Order eventually succeeded in refuting the charges and even turned the tables on their accusers − a divination led by Hannequin, Grand Master of the Order, revealed many of their accusers including the Supreme Perfect to have been themselves acting under the influence of the **archdemon** Sha'amiel. The guilty perfects, led by **Abelard of Montrevellyn**, were burned alive in the main square at Rima. However, in another twist, since then the Temple has been held to be itself 'purged' of all wrongdoing, its traitors having been brought to justice, whilst much suspicion continues to fall on the Argolians, whose psychic and spiritual abilities are held by many to be akin to sorcery itself.

Purple Garter: Also known as the Crescent Table, this elite Order of thirty knights was founded by King **Vasirius** and is supposed to comprise the flower of Pangonia's chivalry. Nowadays it is more a political tool, used to keep more powerful nobles in check by appointing their younger brothers to key posts of state.

Ranishmend: Most peaceable of the three **Pilgrim Kingdoms**, said to prefer trading to crusading. Its current ruler is Athelhard III, sadly notable only for his bigotry and corruption. He is head of the ruling house of Or, aptly named for its wealth of gold and other desirable commodities. Or's coat of arms is a golden hippogriff *rampant* encircled by a stylised wheel, also in gold, on a fuschia field.

Redeemer: Common epithet by which **Palomedes** is referred to among believers of the **Creed**.

Rent Between Worlds: The name given to the gap between the mortal vale and the **Other Side** that wizards of all kinds use to draw upon the supernatural powers essential to sorcery, using the Language of Magick and the Sorcerer's Script. This gap was greatly widened during the **Platinum Age** when the **Elder Wizards** ruled the Known World, and is said to be responsible for all manifestations in the mortal vale, be it **elementi**, demonkind, **Fays**, **Gaunts** or other supernatural entities. The Rent widens in accordance with how much sorcery is being used; hence if a warlock is particularly active in one area, the Rent there will be widened, increasing the likelihood of possessions, hauntings and other apparitions.

Reus Almighty: God; responsible for the creation of the Universe and everything in it, including the Known World, the **Other Side**, **archangels**, angels, spirits, **elementi**, mortalkind and the animal kingdom. Sages differ on whether His power is truly infinite or simply incalculable according to the reckonings of mortalkind. The Almighty was unknown to pre-Faith mortals, who worshipped the archangels and **archdemons** as gods in their own right during the **Platinum** and **Golden Ages**.

Right Hand Path: More benign white magic originally taught to the **Varyans** by the **Archangels** to help them fashion their civilisation during the **Platinum Age**. Some thinkers, the **Argolians** among them, hold that all magic is a mistake, and that even the Right-Hand Path can be used to do evil in the wrong hands. Others such as the pagan followers of Kaia The Moon Goddess – who retaught aspects of white magic to the folk of the **Island Realms**

during the **First Age of Darkness** – disagree on this point.

Ryøskil: Treaty signed by the **Northlanders** several generations ago forcing them to stop officially raiding mainland **Northalde** (though clandestine raids have continued sporadically). The Northlanders were brought to the treaty after being defeated decisively in battle by the **Northlendings** under King Aelfric III.

Sarakim: Desert warriors of southern **Sassania** who specialise in horseback archery.

Sassania: Lands of the hot south lying beyond the Sundering Sea that comprise the Four Sultanates, the **Pilgrim Kingdoms** and various other petty principalities. Principal religion is the **Faith**, founded by the First Prophet **Sha'abat** several generations before the coming of **Palomedes**.

Sceptre: Term synonymous with 'the crown' used to denote state power wielded by a Sultan in **Sassania**.

Seakindred: Legendary hybrid race of merfolk, said to be created by **Sjórkunan** in playful mockery of the mortal race of men and women above waters. Like their un-angelic creator, they are intrinsically neither good nor evil – much like their human counterparts above water, in other words. Their sworn enemies are the **Tritons**, a similar though far more hideous aquatic hybrid.

Second Age of Darkness: Another period of decline marked in Western **Urovia** by the destruction of the Thalamian Empire after Tyrannos was sacked by Wulfric of Gothia more than nine hundred years ago. It is generally agreed to have ended with the consolidation of barbarian petty kingdoms into the six **Free Kingdoms** more than three centuries ago, ushering in the advent of the present **Silver Age**. Note that other cultures differ in their reckoning of the Second Age of Darkness; for instance the **Urovian New**

Empire dates its ending with the completion of the Hundred Years Conquest slightly earlier, while the **Sassanians** date it from the demise of the last of the **Seven Enlightened Sultans**, two generations after Wulfric sacked Tyrannos.

Second Sight: A mystic gift, conferred only on women, that allows them to experience visions of the future (both their own and that of others they may be connected to). Like the **sixth sense** cultivated by the **Argolian** friars, it is not a precise craft.

Seven Enlightened Sultans: Gifted bloodline of the first rulers of the Sha'abatian world, established when Abu'cuchaza'ar Kardin took the teachings of the First Prophet into his heart; believed by the Orthodox branch of the **Faith** to have been wiped out at the **Battle of Kurushan Heights**, when the last of the Seven Sultans, Abu tek Jahib, was slain. However, many Unorthodox sects, including the **Sufielis** and the Order of the **Silver Shadow**, believe the bloodline survived this calamitous defeat, which brought to an end the halcyon era of wisely guided sultans in Near **Sassania**.

Seven Fortresses: A remarkable feat of engineering, these seven identical castles were built from the very rock of the Great White Mountains to guard the **Urovian New Empire**'s western flank. They are each named after the **Seven Seraphim**: Stygnos Acra, Sionos Acra, Virtos Acra, Euphros Acra, Luvos Acra, Aeros Acra, and Logos Acra.

Seven Schools of Magick: The core disciplines of sorcery practised by warlocks and witches of varying bent and aptitude throughout the Known World. These are: Thaumaturgy, Transformation, Enchantment, Scrying, Alchemy, Necromancy and Demonology. The first five are broadly classified under the more benign **Right Hand Path**; the last two belong to the darker **Left Hand Path**. Many sub-divisions of the major schools also exist; for instance *artifice*, which is a sub discipline of Alchemy and involves the manufacture of various magical charms and other items.

Seven Seraphim: Foremost among the **Archangels**, those that sit at the right hand of **Reus Almighty**. They are: Logos (**avatar** of prosperity and tolerance); Siona (grace and dignity); Virtus (courage); Stygnos (stoicism and fortitude); Euphrosakritos (merriment); Luviah (love); and Aeriti (aspiration). The Seraphim are opposed by their dark emanations the **Princes of Perfidy**, who represent twisted or corrupted forms of the virtues they embody.

Sha'abat: First of the Two Prophets, an avatar of the Unseen who manifested somewhere in the Zhosa Desert region beyond the Hierocracy of Sendhé more than a century before the coming of **Palomedes**. Sha'abat preached in Sendhé but was exiled by the Priest-king Pankott, who felt threatened by his enlightened doctrine of peace, yet could not undo him with his sorcerous powers. Sha'abat was eventually taken on as vizier by Sultan Abu'cuchaza'ar of the Kardin tribe, who went on to found the line of the **Seven Enlightened Sultans.** Today adherents of the Faith across Near Sassania cleave to the teachings of Sha'abat, though since the Great Schism there has been a violent split within the **Faith**.

Shield Queen: Informal title given to Magnhilda, the former berserker who rose to become sole ruler of the **Frozen Principalities** – and a fair chunk of **Northalde** since invading the kingdom and taking its capital Strongholm.

Silver Age: The present age; regarded by most Western **Urovians** as beginning with the consolidation of the **Free Kingdoms** some 350 years ago. Distinct from the previous **Golden Age** in that it is an era in which **Reus Almighty** has made Himself known to mortalkind – yet civilisation in

Western Urovia is acknowledged by the learned to lag far behind that of the preceding epoch.

Silver Shadow: Elite order of adepts trained in both the psychic arts and assassination. Established by the Old Master of Time's Arrow more than a century ago, this Unorthodox sect of the **Faith** claims to derive its supernatural powers from the **Seven Enlightened Sultans**, of whom the Old Master claims to be a lineal descendant. Based at his fortress stronghold of Ortiz in the Cerulean Mountains, the Old Master and his sect have long been a thorn in the side of the Orthodox sultanates of Kallandhar and **Nazharya**, sometimes even allying with the crusaders (most notably the **Knights Bethler**) against their common enemy.

Sixth Sense: Special talent particular to the **Argolian Order**, honed by years of prayer and meditation. Its abilities are somewhat vague and thus difficult to define, but broadly speaking they allow a monk of the order to detect the following, with varying degrees of accuracy: when a person is lying or concealing something; when danger (particularly supernatural danger) is near; past pain or sorrow that continues to plague a victim; the presence of a warlock or witch and the type of magick being used; and a demon's psychic spoor. Other mystic orders including the **Knights Bethler**, the **Silver Shadow** and the **Sufielis** are thought to have cultivated similar powers of varying degrees of potency.

Sjórkunan: Foremost deity of the **Northlanders**, revered for his mastery of the waves and said to preside over the Halls of Feasting and Fighting below the Sea of Valhalla, the Northlandic equivalent of the **Heavenly Halls**. Known as Aqualcus, Baha'muhit and the Salt King in other periods and cultures. Believed by the Northlanders to have been the true father of Søren.

Søren: Legendary hero who hailed from the **Frozen Principalities** and came over with the First Reavers who began conquering and settling what is now **Northalde** seven centuries ago. Reputed to have been fathered on a mortal maiden by the archangel Sjórkunan, Lord of Oceans, whom the Northlanders worship as a god. Is most famed for his adventures thereafter, when seeking the westerly **Island Realms** in his magic ship Jürmengaard he stumbled upon the sorceress **Morwena**'s lair in the ruins of one of the **Watchtowers of the Magi**. She ensorcelled him into performing his Seven Deeds, the last of which saw the **Headstone of Ma'amun** recovered from the Forbidden City of **Varya**. Søren subsequently slew Morwena and broke the Headstone into four pieces, before taking his ship and sailing out across the Great Western Ocean, never to be seen again by mortal eyes. Has gone by various epithets during and after his lifetime, including the Doomed, Irongrip, Wavetamer and Wyrmslayer.

Sorcerers' Guild: Operating in the Urovian New Empire, this body of licensed Right-Hand warlocks can legally practice sorcery within the territories ruled from Illyrium. The Two Forbidden Schools, that is to say Necromancy and Demonology, are still strictly prohibited, and any Guildsman found practising either can expect to be expelled from the Guild, and most likely executed as well.

Sorcerer's Script: Hieratic script taught to the **Varyans** by the Archangels and used to express the Language of Magick. It is used to store and communicate spells and incantations of all kinds. Like the Language of Magick, its darker modes constitute the Left Hand path taught by **Abaddon** to **Ma'amun**.

Stornelund: One of the richest of the nine baronies that compose the realm of **Vorstlund**, neighboured by **Dulsinor** to the west and Ostveld to the south. Ruled over by the House of Lanrak; the current Herzog is Lord Hengist – a vain, inept and bibulous man unworthy of the title. Most believe his steward Albercelsus to be the true power in Stornelund.

Sub-Avatar: A secondary avatar or host body that allows a greater demon to bridge the gap between **Gehenna** on the **Other Side** and the mortal plane, inhabiting this human form (often at a powerful demonologist's behest). This enables a greater demon to operate on the mortal plane, albeit with limited powers. The most notorious examples of sub-avatars are **Xamiel of Avalongne** (the archdemon Azathol), and the Vizier Khartoun (the archdemon Sha'amiel), who are believed by some to have jointly provoked the **Pilgrim Wars**. It is not known whether archangels have ever made use of sub-avatars, though some theologians claim that the **Two Prophets** were in fact just such, hosting angels of unknown identity.

Sufieli: A sect loosely affiliated with the Unorthodox branch of the **Faith**, widely respected (despite their perceived heresy) throughout the Sha'abatian world for abilities to combat evil spirits and lift curses. In their learning and ascetic wisdom they of all sects in Sassania most closely parallel the **Argolian** Order, with whom they have had some contact since the **Pilgrim Wars**. Where Argolian friars rely on chanted psalmody to fight demonkind and the undead, the Sufielis tend to use sacred fluting and main force of will to accomplish the same effect. They take their name from the savant Suf, who founded their order several centuries ago.

Taziqs: Elite mounted cavalry of **Sassania**, closely approximating Urovian knights.

Tritons: This horrible species – said by sages to be a spiteful attempt by **Abaddon** to confound **Sjórkunan** after he created the **Seakindred** – dwells in the deepest stretches of the northern seas. Resembling double-jointed humanoids that share features with aquatic species such as toads and barnacles, they reputedly worship the **Great World**

Serpent, whose scales Abaddon is said to have used to fashion them when the world was young. If this theory is true, Tritons could be regarded as distant kin of **Wyrms** and **Wyverns**.

True Temple: The church of the **Creed** that holds sway in Western **Urovia**, with the Supreme Perfect headquartered in Rima, the capital of **Pangonia**. Its name differentiates it from the Orthodox Temple, which administers the Creed in the **Urovian New Empire** east of the Great White Mountains. The True Temple was created by a schism, known as the Sundering of the Temple, six hundred years ago.

Thraxia: One of the **Free Kingdoms** of Western **Urovia**, composing the lands west of the Hyrkrainian Mountains that divide it from **Northalde**. Originally settled by clans fleeing the **Island Realms** after the Wars of Kith and Kin two thousand years ago. The last of the kingdoms to embrace the **Creed**, Thraxia has somewhat more tolerance for right hand magic than the other western kingdoms, although the **Left Hand Path** is punished severely. Thraxians are famed far and wide for the excellence of their poetry and music, and their greatest bard **Maegellin** is celebrated throughout the Free Kingdoms and beyond. Their skill at hunting and their fine mead are also noteworthy.

Tyrnor: War god worshipped by the **Northlanders**. Reviled in Palomedian culture as Azazel, the archdemon embodying war.

Two Prophets: Collective name given to the **avatars**, **Sha'abat** and **Palomedes**, whose teachings inspired the **Faith** and **Creed** respectively and brought the knowledge of **Reus Almighty** to mortalkind. Due to religious conflict, particularly the **Pilgrim Wars**, adherents of both religions respectively call the prophets 'true' and 'false' – though some loremasters acknowledge both. Note that the term 'false prophet' is also used to describe those possessed or impersonated by **archdemons** in order to lead mortalkind astray.

Upper Thulia: Lands adjacent to Dulsinor ruled by the House of Ürl, long hostile to the House of Markward. Its ruling Eorl was crippled by Sir Balthor during the last war between the Ürls and Markwards, and has nursed a bitter grudge against them ever since.

Upper Vallia: Ancient name given to the northern and central margravates of **Pangonia**, including Rima where the royal seat is. Besides the capital its foremost provinces is Gorlivere, long rich in arable lands, vinyards and iron ore. Its smiths are renowned for their smelting skills, and the fineness of its wine is surpassed only by that of Armandy province in **Occitania** and Aquitania in **Lower Vallia**.

Un-angels: Collective name given to 'neutral' entities that are considered neither angels nor demons. Foremost among them are **Azrael**, judge of souls; Kaia, worshipped as a nature goddess throughout pagan communities in the **Island Realms**; and Nurë, the archangel of fire, prayed to by smiths of all kinds. The **Fay Folk** are also considered by many loremasters to be lesser un-angels, being far from good but not truly evil.

Unseen: Collective noun given to all inhabitants of the **Other Side** after the **Breaking of the World**, when angels and other supernatural entities ceased to walk openly among mortalkind. Throughout the **Golden Age** they are said to have reappeared occasionally, though with diminishing frequency, and by the advent of the **Silver Age** such manifestations had become virtually unknown. Note that demonkind will manifest in the form of possessions and in response to summonings by a demonologist meddling with the Other Side using the **Left Hand Path**.

Urovia: Name given to all the lands lying north of the Sundering Sea and the Great Inland Sea, as far the Steppes of

Koth that lie beyond the Mercenary Kingdoms to the east of the **Urovian New Empire**. Nowadays Urovian culture is usually associated with the **Creed**; but note that the Three Emirates lying directly south of the Mercenary Kingdoms and Koth are considered **Sassanian** by virtue of their religion and culture.

Urovian New Empire: The most powerful and technologically advanced country of the **Silver Age**, a land empire comprising seven former kingdoms that were consolidated four centuries ago by the House of Usharok during the Hundred Years' Conquest. Protected by a string of fortresses in the Great White Mountains to the west and the Great Wall to the east, the Empire guards its secrets jealously and trades selectively with its neighbours. It is said to have preserved or relearned much of the lore of **Ancient Thalamy**, and former outlying provinces of that fallen empire are now part of the New Empire. Its capital, Illyrium, is said to be the greatest **Urovian** city since Ancient Tyrannos, and is the seat of the Imperator, the Ruling Senate, and the Orthodox Temple.

Ushalayim: The Holy City, consecrated by virtue of being both the birthplace of **Palomedes** and the site where **Sha'abat** ascended to heaven when he was recalled by the Unseen after serving mortalkind. Nowadays it is the heart and soul of the **Pilgrim Kingdoms**, though the realities of politics and war mean it is also a colonised city, ruled by Pangonian occupiers often at the expense of the native Sha'abatians. The name is also given to the crusader kingdom ruled from that city, which is ruled by the House of Arjean that takes a *gules* (red) wheel intertwined with *argent* (white) roses intertwined about its spokes as its coat of arms.

Usharok: The ruling imperial house of the **Urovian New Empire**, boasting a dynasty that has lasted more than four centuries. The present incumbent is Justorix IX.

Varya: Name given to the civilisation and the island city that spawned it more than six thousand years ago in the midst of the Great Inland Sea. Inspired by the **Archangels**, who regularly visited them and taught them the Language of Magick among many other arts and crafts, the Varyans founded an empire that covered the Known World, from the **Island Realms** in the West to the Steppes of Koth in the East. They were ruled over by the Synod of **Elder Wizards**, said to number some five dozen warlocks of power unsurpassed before or since. This empire lasted about a thousand years until it was destroyed by the **Unseen** at the **Breaking of the World**, by which time it had fallen into demonolatry, decadence and corruption thanks to **Ma'amun**, foremost among the Elder Wizards, who was seduced by **Abaddon** during his astral wanderings through the **Other Side**. Varya is also frequently referred to in texts as Seneca, the name given to it in Decorlangue, the language of **Ancient Thalamy**.

Valley of the Barrow Kings: Site of the **Watchtower** of the same name, which was where the enchantress **Morwena** made her lair and her thrall the hero **Søren** brought back the **Headstone** from **Varya** and broke it, after slaying his fickle mistress. From this piece of history it takes its alternative name of the Vale of Shadow's Lingering. Its more common name derives from the hundreds of **Draugar** that lie in wait for the Second Coming, when the power of the **Elder Wizards** shall be unleashed again.

Vasirius: Also known as the Chivalrous King, lauded by poets and loremasters alike for his uncommonly just rule, he was the Scion of the House of Rius who ruled Pangonia more than a hundred years ago and instituted the Code of Chivalry, designed to reform knighthood and rein in its worst excesses. Since Vasirius' death at the hands of the Traitor Prince Ancelet at the Battle of **Avalongne**, the code has waned in influence, though it still attracts adherents among idealistic young knights across the **Free Kingdoms**.

Vorstlund: Formerly a kingdom until the Partition Crisis that sparked the War of the Four Kings some two centuries ago, Vorstlund is now a loose federation of nine baronies, although it is still classed as being one of the **Free Kingdoms**. Vorstlendings are known for their gluttony and generosity, but can also be quick to anger and are doughty fighters.

Wars of Kith & Kin: Tragic series of conflicts between Kaluryn and Skulla, the two principal isles of the **Island Realms**. It ended two thousand years ago with the defeat of Kaluryn, and saw the Exiled Tribes found the early kingdoms of **Thraxia** on the mainland. It also marked the beginning of a long and steady decline of Westerling civilisation, as magic began slowly to fade from the realm.

Watchtowers of the Magi: A series of huge towers built by the **Elder Wizards** to watch over their vast domains across the Known World. Many were destroyed during the **Breaking of the World**, but some survived partially intact, including the Watchtowers of the Leviathan in the Abydos mountain ranges, the **Valley of the Barrow Kings** in the **Island Realms**, and Mount Brazen in the Great White Mountains that divide the **Free Kingdoms** from the **Urovian New Empire**.

Westenlund: Richest of the nine major baronies of **Vorstlund**. Ruled over by the House of Drüler, which insisted on retaining the title of principality after the kingdom was broken up two centuries ago, on account of its scion Aelle being the last king of a united **Vorstlund**.

Westerling: Name given to an inhabitant of the **Island Realms**.

Wheel: Chief symbol of the **Creed**, derived from the execution of its prophet **Palomedes** on a torture wheel in

Tyrannos a thousand years ago. The sign of the Wheel is made by first touching the forehead and then splaying the fingers of the hand across one's chest, in representation of the spokes the **Redeemer**'s limbs were broken on.

White Valravyn: Chivalrous order founded by the Hero King Thorsvald of **Northalde** a hundred years ago, in memory of the warrior saint Ulred; charged with upholding Royal Law throughout the **King's Dominions** and bringing justice to all during peacetime, defending the realm in times of war, and the King's personal security.

With-Y-Passes: Ancient name given by **Westerling** settlers to the Hyrkrainian Mountains that divide **Thraxia** from **Northalde**. The name is still commonly used in the former kingdom.

Wyrm: Also known as dragons and wyverns; the ancient offspring of the **Great World Serpent** and Hydrae the Many-Headed. Now an extinct species, after the last of the great venom-spitting reptiles was slain by the Pangonian knight Sir Azelin of Valacia some years ago. A weaker but more numerous sub-species (known as wyverns) are believed by some loremasters to have once existed too, although this is disputed.

Wyvern: A smaller cousin of the **Wyrm**, said to dwell in the deepest fathoms of the sea of that name. Unlike their larger, more powerful brethren, Wyverns do not have any noxious breath – instead using their tail sting to poison prey. The last Wyvern uprising was millennia ago, for the **Seakindred** have largely kept them confined to their underwater caverns.

Xamiel of Avalongne: Firebrand preacher who whipped up support for the First Pilgrim War, launching the era of crusading that led to the establishment of the **Pilgrim Kingdoms** in northern **Sassania**. Rumoured by some to have been a **sub-avatar**, channelling the **archdemon** Azathol.

Zaruman: The so-called 'little prophet' who took the conjoined entity of Mithras into his heart and founded the Sect of Light and Fire. Mithras is believed by his cultists to have been a unique fusion of the archangel Solus (worshipped by pagans as the god of the sun) and the un-angel Nurë (fire). Originating before the time of the **Two Prophets** in Near **Sassania**, the sect still survives in the present day, practising in its secretive lair in the foothills of the Abydos ranges in the Sultanate of **Halepo**.

A WORD ABOUT THE WORDS...

This has been quite the labour of love. Oftentimes, I haven't had much more than my own education and instincts to guide me, and I'm well aware that one or two grammatical idiosyncracies may have been spotted by the more attentive reader. A few words, then, to clear things up.

I've done my best to be consistent across all volumes, and as such there are a few oddities I have stuck with – and one or two I haven't. The earlier 'stoop' – used to refer to a drink of wine or ale – I have since amended to the somewhat more favoured 'stoup'.

The spelling 'serjeant' may seem particularly barbarous to some readers, but it was an old medieval form I retained on purpose, as I thought it would better distinguish the unknighted light cavalryman it is supposed to denote from the obvious modern-day connotations of Uncle Sam or the police station.

'Parlay' as opposed to 'parley' was a peculiar one, that much I'll admit... Honestly, I'm not sure why I opted for the first spelling from *Devil's Night Dawning* onwards – both are accepted in my dictionary, but the second spelling is quite obviously the more commonly used. I hope the reader will forgive me.

At times I have deliberately dropped the 'ly' endings in adverbs – to start a fight uglily (as opposed to ugly) may be grammatically more correct, but it just seemed so... well, ugly on the page. Likewise, the term 'his face was set grim' would have been more accurate with the 'ly' suffix, but for some reason it just seemed more poetic to me without it. I don't pretend to make sense!

Similarly, the word 'inchoate' – used as an adjective to describe something in an unfinished or rudimentary state – I have taken some liberties with, creating a noun ('inchoacy') to replace the somewhat less poetic 'inchoation'. If I'm free to invent entire kingdoms that don't exist, where's the harm in one little word I dared to ask... I humbly ask the strict grammarian to pardon my self-indulgence.

I've been a journalist for long enough to realise how difficult a job editing can be, and I pretend to no expertise (well, OK, some maybe...). Self-editing – which, beta readers notwithstanding, I've had to do quite a bit of during this project – is by definition the most difficult of all. I hope readers will agree that I've managed to do a half-decent job of it, on the whole.

I have always loved language for its complexity and diversity, perhaps above all its malleability – I trust that some of this sentiment shines, or glimmers at least, through the text.

Damien Black
London, 2025

www.ingramcontent.com/pod-product-compliance
Lightning Source LLC
Chambersburg PA
CBHW020636120726
47906CB00001B/3